Gary Shearston is one of Australia's best-known singer-songwriters. Born and brought up in the bush, he has a knowledge of Australian history and a feeling for the land, its people and its wildlife, to rival that of the towering central character of this novel.

Michael Thomas is a highly successful film writer whose screenplays include *Countryman*, *Burke and Wills* and *Scandal*. He has written extensively for *Rolling Stone* and *The Sunday Times*, and divides his time between Sydney, Los Angeles and Wiltshire.

'*Balkenna* . . . rival[s] the best of Wilbur Smith, so there's another treat in print, this time set "down under" spanning wars, drought, personal tragedy and generations . . . As big a book as the country it's written about' *Woman's World*

'Keep an eye out for *Balkenna* . . . one of those sprawling, family-on-the-land sagas. It is very well done indeed – exciting, entertaining and logical. You won't be sorry you tried it.' *The Sun*, Brisbane.

# Balkenna

**Gary Shearston
and Michael Thomas**

**HEADLINE**

Typeset in 10/10¼ pt Plantin
by Colset Private Limited, Singapore

Printed and bound in Great Britain by
Collins, Glasgow

HEADLINE BOOK PUBLISHING PLC
Headline House
79 Great Titchfield Street
London W1P 7FN

for
Bonnie Keturah
with love

# Prologue

Having failed to take Port Moresby by sea, the Japanese invaded New Guinea at Lae on the north coast. Two battalions of Australians were already pushing forward along the Kokoda Trail to establish an airbase at Buna. But the Japanese landed another two thousand men there and the Australians were forced to retreat. By the end of July, the Japanese had taken Kokoda and were pushing the Australians back along the Trail. But they had problems. They had to cross the razor-back ridges of the Owen Stanley Mountains at a point over 8,000 feet high and their supply difficulties were rapidly compounded by Allied air attacks. They got to within thirty miles of Port Moresby before grinding to a halt.

The Australians fought them back along the Trail to retake Kokoda at the beginning of November. The Japanese resistance was fierce. They needed Port Moresby as a base to mount air attacks on Queensland where the United States already had two divisions and new Australian divisions were fast being formed. At Templeton's Crossing, at the top of the mountains, and then on the Kumusi River, the Japanese made stands which were only routed when fresh Australian and American troops were brought forward by air. The Japanese fell back to join forces with those at Buna for a last stand.

At Buna, Australians and Americans fought side by side in one of the cruellest campaigns of the Pacific war. The Japanese beachhead was strongly fortified and mercy was pretty thin on the ground. In stifling humidity, ravaged by malaria, dengue fever, jungle rot and dysentery, their bodies way beyond simple exhaustion, both sides hunted each other in a bright green hell where the falling of a leaf meant maybe a puff of breeze on the cheek or maybe a bullet in the head.

# PART ONE

# One

Jack Mackay had been in the thick of it all the way to the top of the mountains and down the other side. As a sergeant in the 2/16 Battalion, Australian Imperial Force, he'd had more than his own survival to think about. He'd pushed himself to the limit and beyond, and beyond that again, to keep those in his charge alive, only to see them shot to pieces in a hail of machine-gun fire, or fall to a single sniper's bullet round the next bend. By the time they reached Buna, Mackay's platoon had been chopped in half.

Now, gaunt and feverish, his bloodshot eyes sunk deep in his skull, he squatted in the exposed roots of an incense cedar tree, his back pressed so hard to the trunk he could feel congealed blobs of sap slowly spreading and melting from his body heat. And there, not ten feet away, this magnificent King of Saxony bird of paradise was looking him right in the eye, its brilliant plumes trailing beneath its wings.

Suddenly, the bird stretched its mannequin's neck, raised its beak and blinked. A quick, beating flurry of iridescent colour and it was gone. Jack gripped his Owen gun even tighter and held his breath, all antennae tuned to catch the merest hint of movement. It was deathly still. He could hear the moisture dripping, feel the mud oozing all around him. Slowly, every aching muscle begging for mercy, he slid his back up the trunk and braced himself to inch round and check the blind side.

A barely readable track emerged from the hostile jungle no more than fifty yards away. Jack froze, then whipped back out of sight. Someone had just crawled out of the jungle.

A thousand miles to the south of him, on the edge of a bone-dry gully near Longreach in central-western Queensland, his six-year-old son had just spotted something too. A western brown snake, sunbaking on the opposite bank.

* * *

5

Jack steeled himself for another look. He could see him now. A soldier from the 32nd US Division, inching forward on his elbows, dragging bloody legs.

Eye on the snake, young Jim picked up a gnarled old stick of dead gidgee, then inched his way back, closer and closer. Suddenly, the snake sensed him, lifted its head. Jim took aim and hurled the stick as hard as he could.

Budda-budda-budda-budda! The ground around the American erupted in a spray of decaying vegetation as a Japanese sniper nest opened up. In a frenzy, the American rolled off the track, dragging himself out of the line of fire. He propped himself behind a sandalwood tree, the panicles of red flowers matching the colour of his legs.

In a frenzy, the snake coiled itself in knots as the gidgee stick whacked the side of its head. Jim watched, fascinated. Suddenly, the snake uncoiled itself and slithered frantically for the gully, over the edge and down. Jim didn't wait to see if it came up on his side. He turned and ran like buggery for home.

Jack swivelled behind the cedar. He had to move further round this time to see the American's position. Just as he spotted him, two Japanese soldiers stepped out of the jungle and charged the wounded man for a bayonet kill.

Jack didn't hesitate. He rolled round the tree and his Owen gun cut them to pieces. But the snipers up there somewhere saw him and their bullets rained down. One smashed into his right shoulder, another shazzamed off his ribs, opening up his side in a scalpel flash of searing white-hot pain. The Owen gun fell from his useless right hand as he tumbled back to the cover of the cedar. A hail of machine-gun fire began to shred the tree all around him. Jack glanced down at his pulped shoulder and the jagged rip in his shirt, already drenched in blood.

Not now, he thought. Not now, when it's nearly bloody over. Like a wounded bull, blind rage flooded his senses. He snatched a look at the stranded American, pulling his head back just as another machine-gun burst slashed through the leaves. Then another, and another.

Bastards'll chop the bloody tree down in front of me, he thought.

6

The machine-gun spat again. In the split second it stopped, Jack went for his gun. In a scooping, agonising dive he got it back behind the cedar. Squatting on his haunches, he moved slowly back, keeping the tree in what he guessed was the line of fire. The Japanese opened up again and he spotted their nest almost directly above the fallen American. The pain from his wounds pounded through his head, but his rage had control of his senses. He stood up, stepped round the tree, and sprinted into the field of fire on a zig-zag run, his Owen gun in his left hand, his bloody right arm flopping against his side.

The machine-gun spat again, but Jack was too quick, too sudden. They couldn't get a line on him. Now it was too late as he hurled himself at the base of their tree. The foliage parted and a sniper appeared, pointing a pistol straight down at him. Jack held the Owen up at arm's length and yanked the trigger. The burst shook the Japanese like a rag doll, and he died upside down, hanging by his legs from the nest. Another appeared, leaning over his comrade to drop a grenade. The Owen gun ripped across him and he tumbled from the nest, landing on his own grenade. Jack dived for the American and scrambled on top of him, shielding him with his body. The grenade exploded and the dead soldier's body was sprayed across the clearing. The American clutched desperately at his saviour, gurgling a warning in his ear. In the nest above, another Japanese was frantically trying to drag the machine-gun round and point it down at them. Jack held his Owen gun up and pulled the trigger until there was nothing left, sending the enemy toppling to the ground below.

'Easy, mate. Easy,' he whispered.

Now he could see how badly the man's legs were shot up. Bits of bone jutted through the charred bullet holes in his trousers. Blood from his own wounds was dripping all over the American's shirt as he lent over him and the pain hit him like a hammer. For a moment, they just stared at each other, brothers in agony, stranded on the hairline between existence and extinction.

The American raised a bloody hand.

'Bob Coulter.'

Dropping the Owen gun, Jack seized his hand and gave it a fierce squeeze.

'Jack Mackay.'

Jack slid his good left arm round the American's shoulders to ease him away from the sandalwood and lay him on his back. Coulter's eyes clammed shut and his face knotted in agony. As Jack eased his head to the ground, Coulter's eyes flickered again, then flew open in horror. He clawed at Jack's shoulder.

'Look out!'

Jack lunged for the Owen, rolled into a somersault, leapt to his feet, rammed home a fresh clip and spun round to meet the threat.

'God almighty . . .'

The last Jap to fall wasn't quite dead. He was moving towards them on his knees, his guts hanging out through the rags of his shirt, blood pumping from a bullet wound in his cheek, one eye hanging blindly from its socket. His arms were out in supplication. He seemed to be begging Jack to take the bullets back, to undo what he'd done.

Jack's eyes filled with horror. He stood, stupefied, watching the man come on and on.

He half-heartedly extended the Owen gun, then let it drop. The man had something in his hand. As he dragged his dying body towards the Australian, frightful pleading noises gurgled through the blood in his mouth. Black bile rose in Jack's throat and he gagged. He felt like he'd been turned to stone.

The Jap got within ten feet of Jack before he stopped and sank slowly back on his ankles. His body quivered. He spread his arms like infant wings and died. Jack stood rooted to the spot before moving to clear the bloody fingers from their prize. It was a photograph. The Japanese soldier in uniform, posing with his wife. He was proudly cradling their tiny baby. Jack stared at it in disbelief. It had no right to be so ordinary. It had no right.

In that moment, six months in New Guinea caught up with him. The terror of the faceless jungle, the abattoir of the Kokoda Trail, the stench of charred and rotting corpses, the dying mates left behind to keep the enemy on the run, the smell of grease and cordite, the unholy din of percussive explosion, the sickening sound of bayonets ripping tissue and bone, the screaming drones of aircraft by day and mosquitoes by night, the endless days and nights shivering with fever in the malarial bilge, in the tropical rain, in the equitorial sun. Hot tears flooded his war-blasted eyes. No pride could hold them back.

Suddenly, the Japanese twitched. As the muscles spasmed, black blood belched from his mouth. Jack jumped out of the trance and back to the jungle in one beat of his heart. The bile tore up his throat again. He dropped the photograph and spun away to be violently sick. He squatted for a few seconds to get his breath, spitting away the last of the bile. His stomach felt a little better but the metronomic waves of pain coming off his shattered shoulder quickly made him stand again. Somehow, it was better on his feet.

The whole of his side was saturated, the warm and sticky blood already clotting and feeding a mob of flies. He knew that this moment would haunt him for the rest of his life. The American was mercifully unconscious. Kneeling, Jack put his ear to his chest. There was a heartbeat. It was faint but it was there. He hung the Owen on the nearest bush and used his good arm to haul Coulter into a sitting position against the tree. Then, inch by painful inch, he dragged him upright, pressing the American's body to the tree with his own to keep the weight off Coulter's mangled legs, hugging him like a lover. When he had him up far enough, he took a deep breath, gritted his teeth and allowed the American to flop forward over his shattered right shoulder. He nearly blacked out from the bolt of pain that shot through him. He had to lean against the sandalwood, waiting for the waves of giddiness to pass. Then he stood free and took the full weight.

It was a blind, headlong rush. A kind of madness took over. He tripped and stumbled, staggered and ran. He couldn't let this American die now. The image of the dead Jap kept flashing like a neon sign in his head. This American would be his absolution. The forest floor oozed and squelched around his boots. It was like running through glue. He couldn't let him die. The bright green jungle turned ghostly grey and deathly black. He'd lost too much blood. He was out on his feet but his legs wouldn't stop. On and on, he smashed his way to some unknown salvation, dragging a human cross. He heard a call. He threw himself against a tree, swung his gun round to face it. But he couldn't see. Everything was a blur. The grey and black exploded into white light, blinding his eyes, burning them in their sockets. A hand fell on his shoulder, a gentle voice in his ear.

'All right, mate. All right. Hang on.'

Then more voices. Lots of them. A babble of adenoids. More hands now easing him of his burden. It was gone. The weight was gone. He was falling, falling, falling. An image blinked into focus. A cross. A bloody cross. He wasn't falling, he was floating. Something was lifting him. Something stabbed his arm. Now he was falling again, but slowly, oh so slowly.

They laid him on the forest floor. Two medics dammed the blood with wads of gauze and bandage, dammed the pain with morphine. They worked with a speed and precision that defied their own chronic exhaustion. Gangrene was another enemy to be beaten back.

As the first shot of morphine receded, Jack felt another sting in his arm. He was floating again. The blinding light was disintegrating into shapes. As he stared up, anxious faces swam into focus. One of them loomed down, closer and closer. It was smiling. It spoke. It boomed in his head.

'Crack hardy, mate. You'll pull through. Here.'

Something was pushed between his lips. The smell of tobacco lunged up his nostrils. It was nauseating. He pushed it out with his tongue.

'Later,' said the voice.

The faces were spinning. Jack squeezed his eyes tight shut. The faces were spinning out of control, spiralling away from him, sucking him in. His eyes were closed. But he could still see something. What was it? No. No. No. The Jap was coming towards him on his knees, half his guts hanging out. The words found his throat and emerged in a volcanic scream.

# Two

The stitch in his side was pulling like mad by the time the house came in view, but only then did Jim break his run and flop down in the dry strands of Mitchell grass, roll on his back, cautiously massage his ribs and, with short, shallow breaths, wait for it to pass. Above him, an endless blue skyway, burnt white by the December sun. Not even a wisp of cloud. Just this burning blue from horizon to horizon. He remembered the conversation that morning between Tommy and his mother. Rain. It was a question that always guaranteed him an answer from even the most uncommunicative of childless grown-ups.

'Think it'll rain today?'

'Could do, Jim.' 'Better do, son.' 'Maybe we'll get lucky.' 'God knows.' God knows always seemed the best answer to Jim. The way it looked to him, this bloke 'God' was actually responsible for turning on the taps but sometimes he fell down on the job. For years. They'd had a few good showers in November, enough to keep the grass yellow. He smiled to himself, remembering the way one of last year's stockmen had taken his hat off at the yards, turned his face to the sky and yelled at the top of his lungs.

'You little beauty. Send 'er down, Hughie.'

It was the first time Jim had heard God's name. He thought of the snake at the gully and how Tommy always referred to everything from a centipede to a horse as 'one of God's creatures'. God sure had a lot to look after. He shouldn't forget to give them a drink. That reminded him to feed the chooks as soon as he got home. But not before he'd had a big glass of lemonade and, with a bit of luck, one of those rock cakes.

A wedge-tailed eagle sailed into the flanks of his vision and he turned his head to watch it gliding effortless spirals way, way above him. Jim loved these lords of the air. He would follow them for hours as they arced over the land, and sometimes he found a feather where they had killed. He had a secret store of them in an old shoebox in the barn. A sadness he could always taste overcame him when another one was shot and strung up on a fence as a warning to others: a knot of wire round its neck, wings stretched out as far as they would go on either side, seven sometimes eight feet across. It always knocked his sense of justice to see something so wonderfully free lifeless and rotting away, its great fans of feathers splayed and buffeted by the wind as if it was trying to lift the eagle back into the sky. It happened most in the lambing season. They only ran a small number of sheep on the place now. Mr Henderson had explained to him that the birds were a menace and would kill newborn lambs, even attack the ewes as they were giving birth. Jim had nodded, but he didn't really see it like that. There were thousands of sheep and only a few eagles. It didn't seem fair.

Streams of sweat were running off his forehead, stinging his eyes. The broken stalks of grass that he'd crushed with his body were pricking the back of his neck and bare legs. Time to go. He brought his dilapidated riding boots far back over his head, swung them down and barrelled forward onto his feet. One more glance at the eagle, now just a speck in the far distance, and he turned towards Balkenna, its iron roof rising above the plain like a giant silver sail.

No matter what adventures he'd had that day, even if he expected a few cross words from his mother for being late or neglecting some chore, this moment was always the same. In this vast, lonely landscape, the house was his friend and the woman inside his best friend of all. Always, when he still had a few hundred yards to go, a strange anticipation would well up and he would see himself already inside, feel the sense of home rushing through him. Just about everyone else on the place referred to it as 'the house'. But Jim always spoke its name to himself at these moments. The name people called it on their rare visits to Longreach or neighbouring properties. The name painted on the wooden flap of the mail drum perched beside their front gate on the Jundah road three miles away. The name his mother said came all the way from a place called Scotland on the other side of the world. Balkenna.

She said his father would tell him lots more about it when he came home from the war and Jim had added the promise to the list of things he and his father would do together that went under the general heading of 'something to look forward to'. He had only the vaguest recollection of his father and hoped he would hurry up so he wouldn't forget all the things they had to do and talk about. Balkenna. It was one of his magic words.

It was a fine house of white-washed stone. Four huge, fan-shaped stone steps led up to a wide, shady verandah that ran all the way along the front and halfway down the right-hand side, ending at the door that led into the little private room that was his father's office. There was a tiny cement-floored annexe on the far side that you could enter from the outside as well, with a shower-head the size of a dinner plate hooked up to the big water tank. The rule of thumb for showers had been impressed on Jim by his mother the first time he was allowed to stand under its downpour and wash himself.

'You must be quick, darling. It's more precious than gold and we mustn't waste a drop.'

In fact, run-off grooves in the floor carried the spill to a brick gutter that ran to a cement tank in the ground at the corner of the house. This water, the surface scum rich with drowned bugs and spiders, was used to water the vegetable patch at the back of the kitchen.

The front door led into a hall running the length of the main body of the house. Immediately inside were two large bedrooms, his parents' on the right, one for visitors on the left. Each had its own pair of half-glass French doors, with a fly-screen beyond, opening onto the verandah. On the far side of the spare bedroom, another door led into a narrow library, lined floor to ceiling with bookshelves, and containing the busily carved Chinese blackwood desk that was his mother's writing table.

Further down the hall on the left was a dining room, for special occasions only. It led in turn to the bathroom with its huge tub standing primly on shell-shaped legs by the window, a chip heater at one end, a washstand at the other. Across the hall, a small annexe housed their two-way radio and above that a staircase rose to the two attic rooms under the great vaulted roof. The first was Jim's room, the other doubled as another spare bedroom and playroom for him on the house-bound days of the wet season. They were big, light and airy rooms with gabled windows overlooking the front of the house.

They were Jim's special territory. The only drawback was a small door that led into a space between the rafters and the beams. Tongue-in-groove planks had been laid in here to create a dark storage space for old trunks, suitcases, boxes of books and papers, discarded coats and hats, a graveyard of broken chairs, an iron bedframe, stringless racquets, an old washstand with a shattered mirror and a job lot of unloved pictures and paintings, stacked against string-bound bundles of years of livestock and machinery journals.

It felt like something lived in there and Jim always double-checked that the bolt on the little door was well and truly home before his mother came to tuck him in at night and turn out the lamp. The creatures of the graveyard on the other side of the little door peopled his nightmares. He'd wake up bawling with fright, relieved to hear his mother's footsteps hurrying up the stairs. He could never bear to confess his fears to her, and it was years before she solved the puzzle of chronic stomachaches miraculously cured in time for a hearty breakfast. At least, that's what she claimed at the time. Jim suspected she had known all along and decided to add no more flesh to the bones of the creatures of the night by talking about them.

They had talked about one of his bad dreams though. His daddy came walking up to him in front of the house and announced that he had better get himself a new daddy because his old daddy had gone away and wouldn't be coming back. That was the first time she explained the way dreams worked. Afterwards, he had found her crying in the kitchen. When he asked what was wrong, she had quickly wiped away the tears saying it was nothing, just tiredness. But in the months following, and sometimes still, he would remember it and wonder about his father, if he was ever coming home.

When the house was built, the back door was at the end of the hall. A brick path led to a separate kitchen building: one enormous room with a walk-in fireplace and two pantries about ten feet square, covered by the same triangular iron roof as the house. The first thing Jim's great-grandfather did when he bought the property was change the name to Balkenna. The second was to close the space between the back of the house and the kitchen building. He laid a floor of hardwood timber slabs, made the side walls from timber slats, built another walk-in fireplace and covered the whole with a high-ridged iron roof that fell away in gentle slopes to overhang slightly the side walls. A panelled wooden ceiling a couple of years later had completed the job. Balkenna acquired a high and handsome lounge room of great charm and character, a serene and atmospheric haven in all weathers.

Jim loved walking through it in the early mornings. It some-how promised all the good things of the day ahead. Then up the steps to open the kitchen door and he'd be instantly dizzied by the delicious smells of porridge, eggs and homemade bread toasted in the fire.

He was nearly there now. He broke into a gentle lope that ended with a final sprint to the door of the laundry his father had built on to the back of the kitchen just before he went away to the war. Jim clumped down its ribbed wood floor and flung open the kitchen door.

'Hello, Jimbo,' said his mother. 'Would you like a glass of lemonade?'

It never ceased to amaze Jim how she always seemed to know what he was thinking.

'Guess what! I saw a snake. A huge big snake. I threw a stick and I hit it.'

Elizabeth disappeared into the pantry.

'Well, I hope you didn't get too close,' she called. 'What sort was it, do you know?'

'A brown one,' Jim yelled. 'With a black head and yellow underneath.'

Elizabeth reappeared with the lemonade and, to Jim's delight, one of her rock cakes on a plate. She ruffled his hair.

'Have this first, then you can tell me about it.'

Jim sank half the lemonade on the spot, took a mouthful of cake, jumped off the chair and stretched his arms as wide as he could, swallowing furiously to get going on the story. His arms weren't enough.

'It was this big, at least. Bigger.'

'Good Lord,' said his mother, suitably wide-eyed and shak-ing her head in mock astonishment. 'But what have we told you?'

Jim took another mouthful and dropped his head, chewing more slowly.

'What have you been told about snakes, Jim?'

'Don't go near them,' he answered, still looking at the floor. 'But it was on the other side of a gully, Mum. One of those explosion cracks down near the creek.'

'Erosion,' said Elizabeth gently. 'You mean erosion cracks.'

'Yeah, one of them. It couldn't have bit me from there.'

'Maybe not. But just remember what Tommy said. You never see the one that does.'

'I suppose so.'

'Promise me now. Never again. Promise?'

Jim thought about it for a moment.

'Promise me, Jim.'

He looked back into her pale blue eyes. There was no anger in them, just a plea for this agreement to be made and never broken.

'I promise,' he said.

She leaned over and ruffled his hair again. 'Good boy.'

She disappeared into the pantry, emerging with another cake and slid it onto his plate.

'Here. Bravery should still be rewarded, I suppose, even if you shouldn't have done it.'

Jim grinned and got stuck into it. It was all right. What was one stupid old snake? His mum made the best rock cakes in the whole wide world. He would keep his promise. He'd decided.

'Now that I'm six, will I have to do different lessons?'

Elizabeth laughed. 'You sure are in a hurry to be an old man. You won't be six for another two weeks yet. Let's get through Christmas first, then we'll see about your birthday.'

'I suppose so,' said Jim. Six seemed such a bigger number than five and he'd been anticipating this development for weeks. He was looking forward to Christmas, too, but not nearly as much as the sixth of January. He'd been reciting these figures in his head like a poem.

'Six on the sixth. Six on the sixth. Six on the sixth.'

Dougie was six already and he wanted to catch up.

'We'll just go on as we've been doing this year. Learning a little bit more each day from the books you've got. They're for up to when you're seven.'

Jim actually enjoyed these sessions and was terrifically proud that his mother conducted them. Twice a week, on Mondays and Thursdays, they would all gather round the long table in the lounge room with their books and pencils to learn about what his mother called 'the three Rs'. Weather permitting, Mr or Mrs Henderson, or one of the stationhands, would bring Guy and Anna from their place, twenty-five miles further on down the Jundah road.

Not long ago Mrs Henderson had arrived in tears. Jim overheard her tell his mother that someone had sent Mr Henderson an envelope full of white chook feathers. Something to do with the war. Afterwards, his mother told him it was because

16

Mr Henderson had once had a disease called TB and wasn't well enough to go overseas. Though he sometimes resented the fact that Guy and Anna had a father and he didn't, Jim thought it was a pretty funny present to send a sick person.

Guy and Anna were eight and seven and a bit hard to deal with, but lately Dougie came too, and that evened things up a bit. Patsy Douglas told his mother how grateful Tommy was that she included Dougie in the lessons. His mother just smiled and said that she was more than happy to do it. It would be years before Jim understood why there should be anything so unusual about it. After all, Dougie was his best mate and Tommy was looking after Balkenna.

Tommy Douglas never went to a white-fella school. He was a full-blood Yarandhali Aboriginal. He'd taught himself what he needed to know to get by in a white man's world. He'd been a stockman since he was sixteen. He worked all over central and southwestern Queensland and up north in the Gulf country before old Angus Mackay offered him a job. Tommy said yes because old Angus treated him with more respect than anyone else he'd ever worked for, and offered to build him a four-room, slab-timber hut on the Thomson River side. When Angus and Harriet Mackay retired to live out their remaining years in Rockhampton, Tommy stayed on. He married Patsy the same year Jack brought Elizabeth home as his wife. Dougie was born on a mattress on the Mackay's kitchen table after Jack made a frantic dash to get Barbara Henderson to assist Elizabeth with the delivery. Jim was born two months later in Longreach Hospital.

'Have you fed the chooks?'

'Not yet,' said Jim, washing the last mouthful of cake down with the rest of his lemonade.

'Let the dogs out for a run, too, will you? There's some rabbit on the chopping block in the barn.'

Through the pantry window, Elizabeth watched him run to the dogs' pen at the end of the barn, throw open the wire gate and, one by one, unclip their chains. Jim's own dog, Brud, leapt all over him in a delirium of anticipation, making negotiation of the clip even more difficult. Elizabeth chuckled to herself as, hand over paw, they wrestled with the problem. Finally he was free and, leaping and bounding with the other three, followed Jim in the direction of the chook yards where she knew he would sternly command them to 'sit' before opening the gate. She grabbed a tin of soup from the shelf above her head and returned to the kitchen.

Jack was never long out of her mind. There'd been no letter since his last from Port Moresby over six months ago, followed a few weeks later by the arrival of two parcels, one marked 'Christmas', the other marked 'Birthday'. She'd carefully hidden them away behind the blankets on the top shelf of the linen cupboard. Radio news had been scarce on the war with the Japanese. Elizabeth understood the military necessity for such limited information, but she longed for some detail.

Queensland was the most likely target for a Japanese invasion of the Australian mainland and, at the outbreak of the war, there was panic up north. The government closed all coastal belt schools and a steady exodus of women and children had streamed south, particularly to Brisbane. In March, the Japanese bombed Darwin for the third time and then, in July, dropped more bombs on the harbour area of Townsville. Vast herds of cattle had been mustered in the far north and driven over a thousand miles south to deprive the enemy of potential food. Then, late in the year, had come the rumours that New Guinea was simply a holding operation, allowing defences to be established to fight the Japanese on Australian soil. The whole of the country above the Tropic of Capricorn was to become a war zone. This conflicted with counter-rumours that the Allies were driving the Japanese out of New Guinea and had recaptured Kokoda. Longreach airport had been turned into a base for American Flying Fortresses carrying troops and supplies to and from New Guinea and some days they flew in low overhead to Jim's delight and her alarm. Figuring the crews of these colossal machines got closer to the truth than anyone else, she tended to believe the rumours of Allied advances in New Guinea. Tommy reckoned any Jap that did come in from the north would soon get lost and perish in its trackless wastes. But you couldn't be sure. If they did invade, the American base at Longreach would be among their primary targets. News of the school closing in Rockhampton brought the war even closer. It was her home town.

Elizabeth had been born there after her parents emigrated from Aberdeen. The lazy days growing up on her father's dairy farm, the beautiful old colonial buildings of the town perched on the Fitzroy River. Special treat holidays to luxuriate in the fine white sands of the spellbinding Pacific coastline and marvel at the wonderland of the Reef. The lilt of her parents' strong Scottish accents that refused to surrender to the great Australian monotone which was her native tongue. She remembered her first kiss holding hands with Jimmy Degotardi on the back seat of the bus taking them for a school trip to the Mount Morgan goldfields, the truck . . . Six months after she left college in Brisbane and was working as a teacher, her parents were crushed to death when their car met a meat truck hurtling round a blind corner on the wrong side of the road.

The headmaster and the school board had given her two months' leave of absence on full pay. In that brief time, Elizabeth had settled all her father's affairs. There had been just enough left over to pay her parents' funeral expenses, buy headstones for their graves and put a deposit on a tiny weatherboard cottage which she crammed full of family possessions she couldn't bear to sell or throw away. She had to send telegrams to Aberdeen and Edinburgh, and then deal with the flood of letters that began arriving just as she was gearing herself to go back to work.

Two weeks after she threw herself back into teaching, she took her class on an excursion to the Botanic Gardens. An elderly couple were walking along the path just ahead of them, shepherded by a young man. He kept turning to snatch a look at her across the tousled heads of her pupils. At first she thought he was amused by their tongue-twisted attempts to decipher the name plates on the tropical flowers. Then she realised he didn't seem to notice them at all. She was the sole object of his attention. He smiled a couple of times but she had not smiled back. She pinned him for an 'outback type' immediately. She steered the children off down a side path to avoid further embarrassment. There had been an eagerness in the way he smiled at her that reminded her of a few other raw young bushmen she'd met; she'd found them, in the main, to be dull as dishwater.

That afternoon, he was waiting at the school gates. By the time he'd walked her home, she knew she'd got him wrong.

For the remaining four days of his stay, he spent as much time in her company as he could. On the last night, he took her to dinner in a hotel dining room. When it was over, Jack leaned back in his chair to look her in the eye.

'Would you marry me?' he said.

'Quite possibly,' she was surprised to hear herself answer. He'd not even held her hand.

He hadn't pressed it.

'I'll be back to spend Christmas with my parents. We can talk about it then.'

For the next three months he wrote to her every week. He told her in strong, precise handwriting of the life she could look forward to in Longreach. He described the beauty and wonder of the country, the birds and animals of the distant black soil plains, the character and good-neighbourliness of its people. He also told her all about the hardships and struggles to be endured. He wanted her to have no illusions. After the first few months at Balkenna, with their child growing in her womb, she'd been reminded many times of the conscientious truthfulness of everything he'd told her, good and bad.

They were married on the morning of Christmas Eve 1935. Now, seven years later, the world had gone mad. Staring at the photograph of Jack on the kitchen dresser, she wondered if he was alive or dead.

Proud and handsome, if slightly self-conscious, the chin strap of his Digger's hat pinching a jawline set with fixed determination for the fight to come, a grim, hellish uncertainty tugging at the corners of his mouth, Jack Mackay was on his way to fight for his family, Balkenna, Queensland, Australia and King George VI, in that order. His eyes shone with love for those he must leave behind.

The photograph was one of three he sent from training camp and she'd had it enlarged and framed to look down on the daily hubbub of life that centred round Balkenna's kitchen. Many times she found Jim gazing at it, his thoughts an unknown world away, and she fought back the tears that sprang to her eyes as she heard herself say, for the umpteenth time, 'He'll be home soon, darling . . . Soon as the war's over . . . Won't be long now.'

Putting her finger to her lips, she reached out and touched a kiss to the glass over his cheek.

Two fuzzy wuzzy angels were setting out on the long haul back to Kokoda. On the stretcher between them, a war-torn Jack Mackay was on his way to the plane that would take him to the relative security of the hospital at Port Moresby. The Army doctor watching them leave shook his head. It wasn't the flesh wounds he was worried about.

Three weeks later, the Allies took Buna from the Japanese.

# Three

The day after his ninth birthday, Jim set out on his pony to check the mail drum at Balkenna's front gate. He was in no particular hurry and he allowed Robin to wind down to an easy canter, a trot, then a plod. Brud was panting at his heels, padding along with his tongue hanging out slobbering saliva all over the red-baked earth.

The land around him was dry as a sunstruck bone, beginning a great thirst that would last for two years, devastating Queensland's wool clip and leaving the landscape littered with the rotting carcasses of thousands of beef cattle. The wind had been blowing steadily from the south and southeast for weeks, holding back the monsoonal air that normally brought the steady, driving rain of the wet season in the first three months of the year. Tommy had been cursing it as a 'no-good bloody wind' that meant 'things'd be crook'.

But these were early days and Jim had other things on his mind. The long years of waiting for his father's return were over at last. His mother had wept for joy back in September, the day she carefully explained that the Japanese had lost the war and it was over. Next day, like families from hundreds of miles around, they piled into the Dodge and drove to Longreach to join in the victory celebrations. People danced all night on Eagle Street, hugging and kissing, yelling at the top of their lungs. It was the first time he'd been to Longreach since his mother took him and Dougie to watch the giant, lumbering Flying Fortresses taking off and landing at the airbase. Now they would no longer rumble through the sky over Balkenna, bound for the island jungle where his father was. He'd miss them. They had given him a strange kind of link with his father all these years.

He remembered the morning a few weeks after his sixth birthday when his mother got off the two-way radio, white as a sheet and unable to hold back the tears as she told him his father had been wounded in action. Then they had to wait in a terrible vacuum of uncertainty before receiving a letter from the Army to say he was all right.

Another two whole months passed before a letter arrived from his father saying the injury to his shoulder would prohibit his return to active duty. He'd been offered repatriation but declined, volunteering instead for a desk job at the Australian headquarters in Port Moresby. He apologised for the delay. He was three months in hospital before his arm was sufficiently healed for his hand to hold a pen again. In the months that followed, they took the slow return to his usual precise hand-writing as their grasp of his overall improvement. His corre-spondence, however, had been irregular and never once referred to what had actually happened to him, or why. The long periods of silence that followed in the intervening years had hurt. Elizabeth always put on a brave face for Jim's benefit, but there were days he found her staring at his father's photo-graph or leafing through his old letters, her eyes full of doubts she couldn't name.

The news demanded a new sense of responsibility. Her laughing reference to Jim on occasions as 'the man of the house' imposed a maturity beyond his years. At the expense of the thing he loved to do most, days spent ranging alone far across the property on his pony or on foot to discover yet another bird or animal and speculate on the cause of a thousand and one things, he found more and more tasks he could do to help his mother in the daily running of Balkenna. Jim and Dougie became Tommy's 'right-hand men'. Twice, because of money matters that try as he might he couldn't fathom, Elizabeth had sold off double quotas of cattle, prolonging the mustering, branding, cutting and dipping for weeks. He and Dougie worked harder than they'd ever done in their lives so that his mother could hire one less stockman. Mainly, they'd worked on the musters, driving the stock to the yards, shooing the cattle down the chute to the dip, wielding hefty sticks to prod and whack the wild-eyed bellowing beasts into the bath, to flounder through the dip, and scramble up the other side to shake them-selves in the dripping yard.

But he missed the wonderland of his private zoo. Pink and white galahs. Snowy corellas. Flocks of black-winged, wobbly-throated pelicans that somehow reminded him of the ungainly Flying Fortresses. Brown-feathered emus, speckled with black and grey. Quarrions with orange blotches the shape of a lipstick kiss on their white cheeks, crests raised in startled surprise. Swarms of chattering budgerigars, mobbing the horizon like a plague of locusts. Giant, copper-red kangaroos. Echidnas standing their black and yellow quills on end to turn themselves into a ball of needles. Sleepy old bearded dragons, so well camouflaged he sometimes nearly stepped on one before it raised its head, extended its frilly beard around its neck and hissed a lazy warning. Sky-diving hawks and the giant, endlessly soaring wedge-tailed eagles that were still, somehow, his totem. And, of course, those creatures he'd promised his mother to steer clear of and not make cranky. Particularly the king browns, with their salmon-coloured bellies covered in orange splotches. Six feet of sudden death. Collared and yellow-faced whip snakes. Red napes. Ringed browns. Eastern browns. You had to keep a crow's eye on the way ahead.

All these creatures lived out their lives on the limitless, black-soiled plains where the surface was baked by the sun's furnace to crack, erode and disintegrate into particles of fine, red-brown dust that swirled in great willy-willys through the thirsty branches of gidgee, corkwood, mulga and sandalwood trees, ghost and river gums. Except if there'd been some good, early summer rain in October or November; then the humidity brought a magical transmutation and carpeted the land with a shimmering palette of wild flowers as far as the eye could see. It was Jim's world, his horizon. It was all the world he knew.

Beauty! There were two letters. One addressed in his father's handwriting, the other in official looking typescript. He held his father's up to the sun, twisting it round to different angles, but he couldn't see a thing inside. He gave up, stuffed the letters down his shirt, jumped back into the saddle, flapped the knot of the reins across the pony's shoulders, gave him a heel in the ribs, yelled at Brud to catch up and galloped like the wind for home. The cattle dog had only just managed to settle himself comfortably in the meagre shade of one of the gateposts and looked decidedly underwhelmed. He let them get a good head start before leaping to the hot thirsty chase.

Elizabeth switched on the radio just in time to hear the news from ABC. Edward Hanlon was being tipped to succeed F.A. Cooper as Queensland's Labour premier in the March elections. The world wheat shortage was forcing Britain to ration bread, and restrictions on most other food staples were expected to follow. In other news from London, the United Nations had opened its first session and William Joyce, the infamous Lord Haw-Haw, had been hanged for treason. At home, the federal government in Canberra had announced that the Australian and British governments would establish a rocket range at Woomera in the central Australian desert, three hundred miles northwest of Adelaide. The first celebration of Australia Day would be held on 26 January.

She switched it off. It was an old habit. She always wanted to know what was going on but, somehow, the fruity old baritone of history always depressed her and she rarely heard it out. She had to make three trips with her arms piled high before all the ironing was safely stored in the linen cupboard under the stairs. She was wondering what she'd fix for lunch when she heard Jim gallop down the side of the house and come to a propping halt at the back of the laundry. She decided to use up the cold leg of lamb. Jim burst through the door brandishing the mail.

'It's from Dad. It's from Dad. Open it. Quick.' His excitement blew across the room like a force-ten gale.

'Patience, young man. Patience, for goodness sake. Sit down before you have apoplexy.'

'Aw, Mum. I don't even know what that is.'

'Brain seizure. Do you want some milk?'

'Yes, please.' Jim knew it was hopeless to push her at such moments. He lurched into a chair and began drumming his fingers on the table as Elizabeth poured herself some tea from the pot on the stove, got some milk from the pantry, poured a glass for him, got a peeling knife out of the drawer to slice open the letters and brought the lot to the table beside him. She took a sip of tea, and reached for the brown envelope.

'Aren't you gonna read Dad's first?' Jim asked, incredulous.

'I'll just quickly see what this is.'

Jim couldn't believe it. He took a few gulps of milk to keep his mouth shut as she unfolded the letter. She skipped through it. Then she leant forward to read it a second time. Jim thought he'd burst.

'Please hurry up, Mum. Please.'

Elizabeth glanced at him, then back to the letter in her hand.

'I've got something to tell you,' she said, very quietly, almost too quietly. 'Something very important. Something wonderful.'

She turned to him, a lovely, warm knowing smile dawning in her eyes.

24

'This letter is from the Army. It's to tell us your father did something very brave in the war. It involved saving another man's life, evidently. He's going to be decorated at his battalion's demobbing parade in Brisbane at the end of this month.'

'What's that mean? Decorated?'

'It means they're going to give him a medal.'

'You mean like a hero?'

Elizabeth leant across and ruffled his hair.

'Yes. That's what it means.' Her eyes brimmed at the look on her son's face. 'He's to be awarded the Distinguished Service Order. That's one of the highest awards there is . . .' She couldn't go on. Emotion clutched at her throat and the tears spilled down her cheeks.

Jim knotted his fingers on the table in front of him and stared at them. He felt like his eyes might pop right out of their sockets. He was numb and tingling all at once. All over. The years of longing for his father's return rose up to choke him. His dad. His dad. His dad was a hero. His dad was getting a medal. His dad had saved another man's life. The words and pictures flooded his mind in a torrent. He waited until his mother looked back to him, brushing at the corners of her eyes.

'What else does it say?' he asked, with as much calm as he could muster.

'It just invites us to attend if we want to. Just to let us know, that's all.'

'Can we? Can we go?' Jim pounced on the idea immediately.

Avoiding the question for a moment, Elizabeth leant across again and brushed her son's hair back out of his eyes.

'Can we?'

'It would be nice if we could. But you know how far it is to Brisbane. The end of the month's not that far away. Besides, who'd look after the place?'

'Tommy could.'

'Not without our help.'

She reached for Jack's letter and applied the knife.

Jim leant forward, concentrating on her fingers as they extracted a thin, single sheet of writing paper. In all the excitement, he'd momentarily forgotten there was a letter from his father himself. Elizabeth opened the page and scanned the lines. Jim couldn't help but notice her look of expectancy went a bit blank.

'Dear Elizabeth and Jim,' she read. 'I'm in Brisbane. Glad to be back. We're demobbing at the end of January. Will get there as soon as I can after that. Not quite sure when. I'll probably catch the train to Longreach and hitch a ride from there. Looking forward to getting home. Hope everything's all right. Love. Jack.'

'He didn't mention the medal,' Jim exclaimed, flabbergasted by the omission of something so important.

Elizabeth was puzzled too. After all, he would probably know the Army would send an invitation to his family. Strange, too, the empty economics of his letter.

'Your father's hardly the sort of man to boast about such a thing. I'm sure he'll tell us all about it when he gets home. It'll be something to look forward to.'

That phrase had long ago taken on a life of its own for Jim. It only, somehow, increased his sense of longing.

'Will he have the medal? Will I be able to see it?'

Elizabeth was doing her best to be matter-of-fact. But the note had set off alarm bells in her imagination like so many times before.

'I expect so,' she said.

She'd have been even more alarmed if she'd been on the dockside when the troopship disembarked its battle-weary cargo. Amid a shower of streamers, deafened by the ecstatic shouts swelling in a great roar above the band playing a victory march, watching the soldiers stream down the gangplanks, she'd have seen that her husband was one of a very few not smiling.

A mate slapped him on the back. 'We're home, mate. We've bloody well made it.'

Jack was forced to give him a half-hearted grin. 'Yes. Yes, we have.'

His mate gave him a funny look and pulled a face. 'Well, you could cheer up a bit, for Christ's sake.'

Later, at the end of the month, his name was called and he marched alone from the ranks up to the reviewing stand. Watched by the rest of his company and the huge civilian crowd on all sides of the parade ground, he snapped to attention to have a DSO pinned to his chest. The brass offered him hearty congratulations, their admiration for a job well done. He stuttered his quiet thanks, saluted, wheeled and marched back to his place. The commander lead the company in three cheers. From the heart. For one of their own. Louder and louder. It left

26

him feeling a terrible dizziness, rocking on his heels, fighting desperately to keep the pictures in his head from overwhelming him. He'd just received the next best thing to a Victoria Cross but you'd never know it.

'Are you sure we can't go?' Jim thought he'd try just one more time.

'No, darling. It's much too far. Besides, we'll have to work twice as hard now and make sure the place looks its very best when he arrives. We'll give him our own parade when he gets home. He'll be as proud of you as you are of him just now.'

Jim stared into her eyes a moment, reluctantly digesting the common sense of what she said.

'Will he look the same, Mum?'

'He'll look a bit older, I expect. He's been through a lot. He'll have aged a bit.'

'I can't really remember what he's like,' Jim muttered, staring at the picture on the dresser, struggling to. 'As a person, I mean. As my dad.'

'I know.' Elizabeth leant across and patted his arm. 'But that's not so surprising. You were only just two when he went away.'

Jim stared at his father's face a moment longer. Then he leapt to his feet, sending his milk flying and his chair tumbling on its side.

'Yaahhhoooo!'

# Four

Ten days had already passed since the end of January. Jim tied Robin to the fence, climbed up to perch on the gate and watched Brud rid himself of a few fleas by wriggling frantically on his back in the ridge of loose gravel and dust on the edge of the road. Although there'd been no further word and his mother thought it was still too soon, he had found time between schoolwork and chores to squeeze in a vigil at the gate for the past five days.

Brud rolled to his feet and shook himself from head to tail. Jim gazed off down the road in the direction of Longreach longing for a car, or the speck of someone on foot to melt out of the dusk. He wouldn't be able to stay for long. The sun was already at the lip of the horizon.

Hero. The word hung in his mind like a talisman. Yesterday, for the umpteenth time, he climbed on a chair to haul the big Bible down from the library shelves and study the family tree inside the front cover. He loved the crest above it: a hand holding a dagger pointing straight up inside a circle made by a buckled belt with the words '*manu forti*' on it. His mother had long ago explained that it came from Scotland and the Latin words meant 'with a strong hand'. Sometimes, these moments staring off down the road would make him think of how it led, beyond Longreach and Jundah, to all the other places in Queensland and the rest of Australia, even to the distant lands in his atlas. Like Scotland. Or Africa. Or America.

Suddenly, Robin and Brud pricked up their ears. As Jim swung round to look, Brud let go a few excited yaps and tore off to confront the approaching horse and rider. It was Dougie. Jim felt a quick pang of regret that his solitary watch was about to be broken but he let it pass as his mate rode up.

'Where've you been?'

'Down the road.'

'What's there?'

29

'Nothing much.'

'Why'd you go?'

'Just to see.' Dougie dismounted and joined Jim on the gate. 'Waiting for your dad, are you?'

'He'll be home any time now.'

'Yeah. I know. How long've you been here?'

' 'Bout half an hour. Have to go in a minute.'

'Yeah. Me too,' said Dougie.

The sun was a fireball, turning the western horizon into a blaze of golden yellow that fanned out shooting flames of a fiercer blood-orange through the few scraps of thin wispy cloud that had hung about all day without spilling a drop. In good times, even more so in bad, the effect was the same. A sense of overwhelming power as it gave way at last to a pale, nocturnal light. They watched in silence until the sun had gone.

Dougie jumped down and unhitched his pony. 'You comin' now?'

The two boys mounted up and turned their ponies' heads for home. Jim whistled up Brud then stood in the stirrups for one last look.

'Let's hit the toe,' said Dougie, heeling his pony. Brud tore after them and, with a sigh, Jim whacked Robin to race in pursuit.

They had just finished dinner that night when they heard footsteps. Jim was at the kitchen door in a flash and flung it open. It was Tommy Douglas, in his dusty stockman's rig, his high-crowned, wide-brimmed drover's hat in his hands.

'Hello, Tommy. How's it been?'

'Not too bad, missus.'

'Cup of tea?'

'No thanks. I'll be getting along home. Just wanted to check with you about the muster. Wouldn't mind a glass of water.'

Jim stared at the floor, unable to hide his disappointment. Tommy was quick to pick up on it.

'Your father come tomorrow, Jim. I betcha.'

'Hope so,' said Jim, finding a grin. He liked Tommy a lot.

He was a big man, six foot two, with bottomless, jet-black eyes, a permanent stubble and a pot belly that hung over his kangaroo hide belt. He'd told Jim his two missing front teeth had just decided to go walkabout one day. But Dougie told him they'd been punched out when some white drovers beat his father up in the back yard of a pub in Hughenden.

'Is there a problem about tomorrow?'

Tommy shook his head. 'No, missus. No worries. Just wondered if maybe we should wait a couple of days. See if Mr Mackay get back.'

'I'm sure he'd want you to get on with it. I heard on the radio the trains are absolutely jam-packed with servicemen trying to get home. God knows when he'll get here.'

Jim pulled a face.

'Okay. We'll get cracking first thing tomorrow. Just wanted to be sure. I'll push off then.'

'What about the boys?'

Tommy glanced at Jim, then back to Elizabeth. He knew what it would mean for Jim to be away from the house too long at the moment.

'They can have the day off, I reckon. Give us a hand later on at the yards.'

Elizabeth flashed him a quick smile. 'I've got plenty for him to do around here, don't worry.'

Tommy looked back at Jim and gave him a mock scowl. 'Work 'em hard, I reckon. Best thing for 'em.'

Jim crossed his eyes at him and Tommy cracked up as he went through the door.

'Was that true?' Jim asked immediately he'd gone. 'About the trains?'

Elizabeth gave him a gentle look. 'Yes. That's what they said. A lot of men are sleeping in the corridors to get home as quickly as they can.'

Jim looked down at the table in front of him, calculating the odds. Elizabeth moved round to the back of the chair, leaned over and kissed the top of his head.

'You'll pee your pants, if you don't calm down.'

There was a copy of *The Bulletin* and a big brown envelope from a machine company in the mail drum when Jim got to the gate. He sat on the gate to unroll *The Bulletin* from its wrapper and check out the cartoons. A couple of them made him smile. He shoved it back in the drum.

Two sand geckos scampered out of the way as he hit the ground and looked around for a rusty old jam tin he'd chucked there the other day. He clambered back to the road in a small landslide of sand and gravel that filled his boots. Then he set the tin atop a fence post and chose a good assortment of gidgee gibbers. When he had a pocketful, he stepped back and measured what he reckoned was a fair distance. He had a good eye which was great and a nuisance all at once: he had to keep setting the tin up again. He ran out of the wind-polished bits of wood and went looking for more. The old-man bearded dragon gave him a bit of a fright for a second. He stamped his foot on the baked earth and the lizard rose a little on its front legs, showed him its throat and hissed a warning. Jim managed to land a flat gibber on its back, but old beady-eye ignored it and lay down to continue his contemplation of things. Jim knocked the tin for six a few more times before he got bored. He sprawled on his back under the lone gidgee tree and stared up at the wide blue yonder to have a think about things too.

Chunk. Chunk. Chunk. Three darts at the bull's-eye. One went in. One hit the tyre. He retrieved them and stepped back to try again. Brud watched the darts fly by with a roll of his watery eyes.

It was twilight by the time Jim had finished feeding the chooks and checked the dogs' water on his way back to the kitchen. Dinner would be in about an hour.

Chunk. Chunk. Chunk. There was a queer hollow loneliness in the sound of them hitting the board. If he turned and looked out, he would see no other sign of man in any direction. Just a great sweeping panorama of empty, rolling plains that could make you rich or break your heart.

Chunk. Chunk. Chunk. Brud suddenly snapped to attention. He pricked up his ears and turned to stare off into the dusk. Then he began to bark. Probably a couple of rabbits at the far end of the garden. But Jim couldn't spot anything. He picked up his darts. Brud wouldn't quit. There was something there. In the murk of the middle distance Jim caught a flicker of movement. Way down the rutted track that led to their front gate, something was moving. Brud was going crazy.

'Sit down. Sit down,' Jim yelled at him, keeping his eye on the speck so as not to lose it. Bigger and bigger it got until, suddenly, the apparition defined itself and Brud tore off the verandah. Jim stared at it a moment longer to be absolutely sure he wasn't seeing things. No doubt about it. It was a man.

'Muuuuuum! Muuuuuum! Muuuuuum!'

His shriek echoed through the house, frightening her out of

her wits, giving her goose bumps all over. She took the peas off the boil and raced to see what on earth had happened.

Jim was off the verandah in one mighty leap and running. Running faster than he'd ever run in his life. He couldn't go fast enough. Brud circled back to run and leap at his side and Jim nearly tripped over him, stumbling for a few paces before regaining his headlong stride.

Jack Mackay saw him coming. He dropped his kitbag. He stood waiting for this boy he didn't know to come to a floppy, breathless halt in front of him.

Words wouldn't come. It was a long, exploratory moment before Jim finally found his tongue.

'Hello.'

Jack continued to stare at him a moment longer before, rather stiffly, offering his hand.

'Hello, son.'

Jim took his father's hand and gave it a shake. A few more awkward seconds passed between them. Neither of them knew quite what to do.

Jack withdrew his hand and passed it quickly, just once, through his boy's hair. Then he shouldered the kitbag and turned Jim towards the house.

Elizabeth was walking with full, measured steps. When they finally came together, she and Jack searched each other's eyes. Jim, sensing his duty, stepped back to watch, intrigued.

'Hello, love.' His father's voice was tired and husky.

Tears filled his mother's eyes as she threw her arms round him and buried her face in his shoulder.

'Jack, I almost thought you weren't coming . . .'

They stood like that for a long, long time, moulded together, until Elizabeth reached out and pulled Jim in to share their embrace. Shyly, awkwardly, Jack Mackay hugged his son to his side. The pulse of his father's body running through his own and the heady smell of the kitbag at their feet made Jim feel giddy. He thought maybe he should be crying as well. But he was too stunned, struck speechless by this sudden unknown man, the focus of all his longing, all his hopes and dreams.

At last, Elizabeth pulled away, put her arms round their waists and began to walk them towards the house. Halfway there, Jim suddenly remembered and broke away to race back for the forgotten kitbag. It was incredibly heavy. There was no way he could lift it. So he grabbed the rope and dragged it after him through the dirt. It was a hard pull but he didn't give a damn as he looked up to see his mother and, at last, his father enter the house with their arms round each other. The stars in the southern sky were appearing one by one overhead. They seemed to be brighter than he could ever remember. He looked up at them for a moment, and for the first time in his life he had a private word with the other, unknown father.

'Thanks, Hughie,' he said.

Late that night, tucked up in bed, his excitement banishing sleep, he listened with some puzzlement to the muffled sounds coming from his parents' room below. His mother moaning softly. His father's voice, deep and low, hushing her, followed by what sounded like his mother sobbing. Jim stared at the ceiling, wondering what they were talking about, until his eyelids flickered closed.

He slept like a log. It was already past nine when he woke next morning. He was out of bed and into his clothes and halfway down the stairs in thirty seconds flat. He raced through the lounge room and burst into the kitchen to find his mother at the table, a cup of cold tea in front of her, all the light drained from her eyes.

'Where's dad?' Breakfast was something he could do without today.

His mother kept smiling, but it was dying on her lips.

'Gone over to see Tommy. He wanted to catch him before he got away to the muster.'

She said it as casually as possible, knowing in her heart that nothing on earth could help the terrible disappointment spreading across Jim's face as he just fell into a chair.

'When did he go?'

'Just after sun-up. He didn't sleep very well, I'm afraid.'

Jim swallowed. He couldn't believe it. 'Why not?'

'Just the relief of being home, I expect.'

An awful silence descended. Elizabeth scrambled eggs. Jim just sat there staring into space until anger welled out of disappointment.

'Why didn't you wake me up?' he asked, brusquely.

'I told you. It was only just light. I didn't get up myself until long after he'd gone. He just wanted to catch up on everything with Tommy, that's all.'

She brought him the eggs and toast, giving him a quick kiss he never felt.

34

'Here. Eat up. Then you can ride over and meet him there. How's that?'

'Yeah. Okay,' Jim mumbled. But he was hurt, and it showed.

Elizabeth turned back to the stove, seeking the right words. But they wouldn't come. For the life of her she couldn't understand why Jack hadn't woken Jim to take him along as he'd said he would. She'd offered to get up and make them a cup of tea, but he'd said not to bother and she'd drifted off to sleep again. She got a shock when Jim burst into the kitchen. She'd imagined the two of them riding, side by side, through the crisp early morning light.

Their first evening together had started well enough. A long, drawn-out dinner, a bottle of wine from Jack's kitbag. Their conversation had lingered in the lounge room until way past Jim's bedtime. But as the initial euphoria had worn off, Elizabeth realised with a jolt that Jack was very different from the man who went to war. He had always been solid as a rock. Now he was nervous, restless, fidgeting with his hands one minute, massaging his shoulder the next. His conversation had occasionally tapered off in mid-air and she could see he'd not only forgotten what he was about to say, he'd forgotten how to say it. She managed a quick word with Jim while Jack was taking a shower and impressed on him not to ask questions about the war unless his father volunteered to talk about it. They both steered well clear of the subject. Elizabeth went to sleep that night feeling like she'd just made love to a total stranger.

Jim arrived at Tommy's place to find Jack and Tommy sitting on the front steps having a smoke. He trotted Robin up to stop in front of them and again the right words just failed them.

'Hello, Jim. Come to see Dougie?'

'No,' Jim answered. 'Come to see you.'

'Got things to talk over with Tommy.'

'That's okay,' said Jim. He led Robin away and tied him up beside his father's horse in the shade of Tommy's water tank. 'I'll wait.'

He took a seat on the steps beside them and did his best to follow their discussion of the current state of Balkenna, slanting swift, furtive glances at his father. This was not what he expected. Not at all. Once, his eyes caught Tommy's and the big black man read his mind.

35

'Dougie took off somewhere. Could be down by the creek.'

'It's okay. I'll see him later.'

They talked on and on into the heat of the day. Jim was nearly out of his skull with frustration by the time Jack finally stood up, dusted the seat of his pants and said he'd be getting back to the house.

They cantered in silence for ages before his father pulled back on the reins to bring his horse to a walk. Jim fell in beside him. It was the same matter-of-fact tone.

'How've you been gettin' along then?'

'Okay,' was all Jim could say. Another bawling silence threatened. 'Been looking forward to you getting home,' he finally said.

'Yeah. Me, too.'

His father was miles away. Jim's mind was racing to latch onto a topic of conversation, anything that would get them talking. He grabbed at half a dozen things, but rejected them all as silly or irrelevant beside the one he really wanted to hear about.

'Tell us about the man you saved. The one you got the medal for.'

It was frightening. His father's face went chalk white, his mouth bit into a thin, tight line and the veins above his temple seemed to swell up. He didn't say a word.

'How did it happen?'

Still his father said nothing.

'Did you have to kill people in the war?'

Jack gave a savage yank on his reins and stopped his horse in its tracks. He grabbed at Jim's bridle and brought Robin up short beside him. Jim found himself staring into his father's face, inches from his own. There was spittle at the corners of his mouth.

'Don't ever ask me, do you hear. Not now. Not ever. The war's over. Finished. Dead and buried. There's nothing to talk about.'

He said it too fiercely. Jim felt some of the spittle hit his face. His father dropped Robin's reins and kicked his horse on ahead, breaking back into a canter.

'Dad?' Jim just managed to blurt out the word before his father was out of earshot. But Jack didn't turn.

Jim just sat there, watching him ride away. He remembered his mother's advice and wished to hell he'd stuck to it. He should have talked about Balkenna, the stock, the school, any-thing. He should have remembered heroes never liked to boast about their exploits. He'd been stupid. Really stupid. Tears sprang to his eyes and tumbled down his cheeks, turning his father's receding figure into a blur. He quickly wiped them away and heeled Robin to follow after him. But some terrible dam had cracked inside him and, as the pony broke into a gallop, huge, salty tears spilled down onto the pommel of his saddle.

# Five

The drought ran on well into 1947. Scorching, restless winds brought endless dust storms, 'bedouries' as they were known locally, to fill every corner of the house with a fine, grey-brown powder and turn outdoor work into a daily battle with the stinging, choking, gritty dirt. Whirlwinds would come out of nowhere to rob the horizon and race in wild, roaring frenzy across the land, tossing topsoil, shrubs and grasses high in the sky. Tangles of roly-poly bushes would float back to earth looking for all the world like grass clouds. They lost a lot of stock.

Jim worried more about his mother than himself. There were stretches when his father would suddenly wake with a tremendous burst of vigour and his mother would respond. She would do her level best to keep them going. But again and again, Jack's enthusiasm dried up. As though he didn't care.

For months, Jim took the blame. When he couldn't take it any longer, he had a long talk with Elizabeth. She heard him out in silence. Then, as she usually did in moments like this, she ruffled his hair before replying.

'It's not your fault, Jimbo. You mustn't think that. It's just how things are at the moment and we have to make the best of them.'

He'd wanted more and, for a moment, he thought she was going to tell him something else. But she changed her mind.

'Just be as cheerful and helpful to your father as you can. I know it's hard for you to understand, but war is a terrible thing and it takes some men a long time to get over it. Not all the wounds show.'

He'd gone away wondering what it was she hadn't told him.

Elizabeth had asked Dr Hawker in Longreach to find out all he could from the Army about Jack's service record and medical condition. Weeks had rolled by before the report arrived.

It cited Jack's outstanding qualities of leadership, his

distinguished war record and his decoration for bravery above and beyond the call of duty. The medical report that followed was lengthy and specific. As Dr Hawker read it to her, breaking off occasionally to explain a particular term or phrase, all Elizabeth's worst fears were confirmed. In the opinion of the Army doctors, Jack had suffered a severe mental breakdown at the time of the action for which he was decorated. This had been the reason behind denial of further front-line duty. He'd been subjected to periodic check-ups, including several sessions with Army psychiatrists in Brisbane while waiting to be demobbed. In their opinion, Jack was suffering from a battle trauma that could possibly deepen and lead, at some stage, to psychosis. They had attempted to persuade Jack to remain at the repatriation hospital for extended treatment but he refused. If, however, his family could persuade him to return, every effort would be made to assist him.

Later, when the moment offered, Elizabeth told Jack what she'd done. It might not be such a bad thing to reconsider their offer of further help. Jack hit the roof. He left her in tears, his violent shouts ringing in her ears.

'It's all a load of bullshit. Doctors' clap-trap. Stupid bastards wouldn't know their arse from their elbow.' As far as he was concerned the subject was closed and that was that. But what was worse, his eyes had betrayed him. She could see he knew just what they meant. Deep inside, he was losing his grip and, try as he might, there didn't seem to be a damn thing he could do about it.

The funny thing was she didn't stop loving him. Not for a second. In his moments of wild enthusiasm and good humour he remained the man she had married. The man who'd brought her to share his life in this forgotten country that, despite its dangers and heartbreak, had cast its spell over her as well. The father of her son. Like the wedge-tailed eagles that Jim loved so much, she had mated for life, for better, for worse. It was not a matter of social or religious conviction, though Elizabeth did not deny their importance. It was as if the force that made her, call it God, call it Hughie, had manifested the man of her dreams. Dreams undreamt until he came along. She knew in these good moments that Jack still loved her as he'd done before the war came between them. Now that she knew he was ill, her love just grew to cure him.

\*     \*     \*

40

The drought finally broke with some good rain in early September 1947. The river gums shed their earth-brown bark to reveal a swirl of white, grey olive and red ochre underneath. At the rockfall pool on the creek, Jim and Dougie tucked into their sandwiches and cakes and murdered a big bottle of lemonade. The big gymkhana was on in Longreach next week and they both reckoned they'd have a go at the flag and bending races.

'My dad's going in the buckjumping,' said Dougie proudly. 'Might do the bull-dogging too.'

'My dad doesn't really want to go, I don't think. But he knows me and Mum do.'

A silence fell. Each went his separate way. Dougie was staring off into space and Jim glanced at him a few times. For the first time in his life, he suddenly found himself thinking about the difference between them. There was Dougie, black as could be, with his great mass of curly black hair and pale pink skin on the palms of his hands and the soles of his feet. Here he was, a white boy burnt brown as a berry, with straw hair and his mother's blue eyes. They were such good mates. But he knew then, and it came with a terrible jolt, that one day they would have to go their separate ways. He hoped Hughie would find the time to look after them both the same.

'Your dad's not himself,' Dougie said. 'That's what my dad says. Been different since the war. A lot of things aren't getting done that should be, he reckons.'

It was meant well, Jim knew that. But he resented it.

'My dad's sick,' he answered angrily. 'The war made him sick. He can't help it. I heard Mum talking about it to Mr Henderson. He said it was something called shellshock.'

'I didn't mean to get your back up. Just telling you what my dad said, that's all.'

Jim picked at some lichen on a rock beside him. Dougie and Tommy were great mates. Jim didn't begrudge it, but it sometimes made his own lonely days and nights that much harder to cope with.

'That's okay.'

Dougie stood up. He picked up a gibber and hurled it at nothing in particular.

'You comin' back in?' he asked, heading for the muddy water.

Jim went on slicing the lichen with his fingernail. 'In a minute.'

\*   \*   \*

41

Eagle Street was packed. Jim drifted from window to window. But he kept coming back to one window in particular. In C.T. Fry's hardware shop there was a shiny new Daisy air rifle, just like Dougie's.

He found his parents with a group of people in the ladies' lounge. His father was laughing too loud. He gave Jim a hearty thump on the back. He reckoned Jim was old enough for a shandy. His mother didn't look too happy about it, but it was Jack's shout and he was well on his way. He was weaving on his feet.

He came back with an armful of schooners and plonked the shandy down.

'Get that under your belt.'

His mother's eyes said it all – 'That's enough'. There were a few chuckles from the Hendersons. Jim had never had beer before. It was so cold it gave him hiccups. His father thumped him on the back again.

'Come on, Jim. Drink up.'

He did his best. He could feel it coming up but he couldn't stop it. He hiccuped with a mouthful, and it spilt down his chin, onto his shirt. His father pulled a face and Jim felt a scarlet flush of shame burn up his neck.

'I think I forgot something upstairs,' he stammered. He dumped the glass and headed for the door as fast as he could. In the hush that followed the din, Elizabeth glared at her husband. Jack just shrugged and downed half his schooner at a swig. The Hendersons stared at their glasses.

Elizabeth found Jim sitting on a stump in the back yard of the hotel. She put her arm round him and held him to her for a moment.

'You all right?'

'Yeah.' He wasn't, but it seemed the right thing to say. 'What's the matter with dad?' He guessed the answer, but he thought he should ask.

'He's a little bit tiddly, I'm afraid. Don't worry. He didn't mean anything by it. What would you like to do?'

'There's some sideshows down by the river.'

'That sounds like a good idea. You go and have a look. I'll have to go up to the room for my bag. You go on and have a look and I'll catch up with you. All right?'

Jim still couldn't look at her. He felt in some unaccountable way he'd let her down as well.

42

'Okay,' he muttered. He pushed himself to his feet and headed for the river.

Jack lurched out of the back door just as Elizabeth was about to enter. He stood glaring at her for a moment, swaying on his feet.

'Sorry, love. Got a bit carried away.'

'He's upset, Jack. If you want to make it up to him you better go and find him. He's gone to look at the sideshows down by the river.' She fought to keep her anger at bay. She didn't want to make things worse.

'Okay. Okay.' He gave her a lopsided grin and turned on his heel. As she followed him down the hall and watched him go out through the front doors she realised she might have made a mistake. Jack wasn't just tiddly. He was drunk as a skunk.

Jack realised the same thing as Eagle Street swam before his eyes. He gulped a few deep breaths to steady himself.

Buggered if I know what got into me, he thought. Never could drink at this time of day.

He found Jim staring at the spruiker outside the Buddy Williams tent show. He dropped a hand on his shoulder and asked him if he wanted to go in. Jim looked up in surprise. He felt a strange mixture of alarm and relief all at once.

'If you do.'

Jack bought two tickets and ushered Jim inside. It was pretty full already and they just managed to squeeze into a place as Buddy rolled on. He gave the mob a big grin, hooked his guitar over his shoulder and kicked off with 'The Overlander Trail'. Jim was clapping like mad. Buddy cracked a couple of jokes and then he got serious. His next song meant a lot. It was one for the Diggers in the audience today: 'Stockmen in Uniform'. Jim turned to his dad. But Jack was starting to sweat. As Buddy sang the song, the booze froze in his blood. The next one was another song about the war, 'The Dying Soldier's Prayer'. Jack clawed at his collar, shaken by a wave of suffocating panic. He staggered to his feet and pitched out of the door. For the second time that day, Jim blushed beetroot.

Jack was waiting for him outside, brandishing a toffee apple on a stick. 'Sorry, son. It got a bit hot in there. Let's have a go at the knock-a-dolly.' He paid for three wooden balls and shoved them into his son's hands. 'There you go.'

Jim passed him the toffee apple to hold. Three tins went flying.

'Whacko,' said his father. 'Can't do better than that, but I'll give it a go.'

Jim watched his dad throw the first ball as hard as he could. He skittled a tin. Not bad. But Jack was wincing in pain and rubbing his shoulder.

'You all right?'

'I'm afraid the old shoulder isn't quite up to it.' He handed Jim the remaining balls. 'Here. You finish them off.'

Jim threw them, but he missed.

'Better luck next time.' His father grabbed his arm. 'Come on. Let's see what else there is.'

They headed on down the row of tents and stalls until Jim spotted a shooting gallery. He ran up and grabbed a rifle. The owner held out his hand for a zac and Jim looked round for his father to pay, to be met with an icy stare as the rifle was torn out of his hands. It snapped the chain anchoring it to the counter.

'Hey. Look out,' the owner protested. 'Who do you bloody well think you are?'

'Mind your own business,' Jack challenged.

'What kind of bullant bit you?' Sulkily, wary of the look in Jack's eye, the owner retrieved the rifle and stuck it under the counter.

Jim was dumbfounded. 'Can't I have a go?'

'No guns.' His father spat the words at him. 'I told you before.'

'But Dad, even Dougie's got his own air rifle. Why can't I have a go?'

His father's eyes were molten silver. They withered him on the spot.

'I don't give a damn what Dougie's got,' he shouted. And he was gone.

Elizabeth got there in time to see him leave. She stared at his retreating figure then turned back to Jim. He tried to be brave and hold her look, but three embarrassments in a row was too much. The tears pricked, and spilled.

In their hotel room that night, Jack and Elizabeth undressed in silence. They climbed into bed and Jack immediately rolled on his side, leaving her to stare at the silent fan on the ceiling. She took a deep breath and tried again.

'Jack.'

Nothing.

'I really don't see why Jim can't have an air rifle if he wants one. Dougie's got one. It's very hard for him to understand your attitude.'

'No guns, and that's final.'

'How in God's name do you expect him to understand that when we have a closet full of shotguns and .22s at home?'

Jack continued staring at the wall.

'Well? What's the difference?'

Still, Jack said nothing. Another grim silence fell.

'Jack. Please. At least answer.'

Jack grudgingly rolled on his back to stare at the ceiling.

'You know the answer. It'd be a bit bloody obvious, wouldn't it?'

Elizabeth put her arm round him and lay her head on his shoulder.

'Obvious to you but not to Jim. All he sees is your anger. It's very hard for him to understand. He loves you. He'd do anything for you. He is just a boy. Our boy. With normal, everyday expectations. I don't particularly like the idea either, but he's got his heart set on an air gun. Like the one Dougie's got. He saw one in Fry's window today. He'd be the happiest boy on earth if you got it for him.'

Jack's mind was racing. He'd avoided the old broom closet in the tack room where his shotguns and .22s were stored under lock and key. Hadn't opened it once since his return. He'd gone to so much trouble to clean and oil them before he went away, wrapping them in oil-soaked strips of old sheets. The rare moments he'd given them a thought, he'd pictured their barrels a seething mass of nesting red-back spiders, their webs choking them for ever. The thought of seeing Jim, or anyone, with a gun, any gun, filled him with dread. He was frightened of what his reaction might be. Frightened he might be overtaken by an ungovernable impulse to lash out. To maim. To kill. Perhaps even his own flesh and blood. It was madness. He was sweating now. He knew it was madness. They'd told him all about it, but still it took him over. Elizabeth was right, of course. Jim was just a boy. Why should he understand? Why couldn't he just explain it to him, get it off his chest once and for all?

'Tell you what I'll do. I'll let him have one of the .22s when he's sixteen. How's that?'

Elizabeth was alarmed. She could feel the agitation pouring out of him. His face was like a mask, the skin taut and damp, his eyes focused on something far beyond the room. She quickly put her hand to his cheek, turned his head and kissed his lips. They were clammy, feverish.

'You tell him then. Sixteen's a long way off. I know he'd love an air gun now but maybe if you promise him that he'll be happy. But it must come from you. It'll mean so much more to him if it comes from you.'

She gazed into his face, then kissed him again, pulling back to study him some more. Jack gave her the merest whisper of a smile, the slightest nod of his head.

'Okay, love. I will.'

She kissed him again, whispered it against his lips. 'I love you.'

He clutched her to him then pinned her in a fierce embrace, ready to ease the burden of his thoughts in her willing arms. Slowly, tenderly, she enfolded him, caressed him, then rolled on her back to take him into her, drawing the full weight of his body down on her own till she felt the tension across his shoulders relax, till he unknotted himself . . . When he finally rolled off her to lie on his back, he reached out and held her hand. It gave her another flush of pleasure. It was an old habit from their early years, but he hadn't done it since he got back from the war. Not that they'd made love that many times, she reflected. But it made her feel very happy now, lying there in silence beside him. It was a long time before he released his grip and rolled on his side to settle for sleep.

Jim couldn't sleep. The excitement of being in town and his father's behaviour kept him wide-eyed and restless. He was on the balcony in his bare feet and pyjamas leaning on the rail watching the passing parade in the street below. It had been lively for a while, but it was late now and the street was just about deserted. He yawned and figured this time sleep would come. Just as he turned away to go back to his room, he spotted Tommy and Dougie. He knew Tommy had pitched his old gangers' tent down by the river and he guessed they were on their way to bed as well. They were playing some sort of game as they went along; Dougie was whacking Tommy on the bum then dodging away from his reply, swinging round the veran-dah uprights fronting the street. The pair of them were giggling like schoolkids. Tommy felt Jim's eyes on him. He glanced up, spotted him on the balcony and stopped in his

46

tracks to give him a wave. Dougie joined in, semaphore fashion. Jim waved back. That was easy. But he couldn't conjure up a smile. He watched until they'd disappeared, then he went back to his room. He left the door open for what little cooling breeze might stir in the night.

It wasn't that hot but Jack was sweating like a pig. Inch by inch the last Japanese soldier was dragging his dying body towards him. The frightful pleading noises gurgled through the blood in his mouth as he shook the photograph in his hand. Jack wanted to wake up. But the nightmare kept coming closer and closer. He couldn't move. It was going to suffocate him. This time, the Japanese didn't fall back on his ankles to die. He just kept coming, right up to him. Jack wanted to back away but his legs had turned to stone. The Japanese clawed at his legs, grabbed hold of his clothes, all the time pleading. Now the man's face was right in front of his own. He got his hands round Jack's neck, smiling through the awful open wound that was his mouth. He was incredibly strong. Jack put his hands up but couldn't make him let go. The man kept pulling his head closer and closer. He pulled Jack's face right into his own and kissed him on the lips.

Jack's scream woke the whole floor of the hotel.

Jim's eyes flew open. What the hell was that? He lay there for a moment, getting his bearings as the sounds of doors opening and a low hubbub of voices came to him from the corridor. He steeled himself to open his own door and see what was going on. Three people were standing outside his parents' room. Other doors were opening and more people came from their rooms, pulling on their dressing-gowns. A flood of panic shook him. He didn't know what to do. Then his mother appeared, white as a sheet, tears streaming down her face. She asked one of the people to fetch a doctor. There was a terrible urgency in her voice.

'Please . . . My husband's having an attack . . .'

A woman put an arm round her to steady her. One of the men scuttled off down the corridor. Jim let go his grip on the door-frame and ran towards his mother. She pushed the woman away, pulled the door shut behind her and grabbed him, all at once. She held him tight, pushing him away with her body. Her voice was cracked and broken.

'Not now, Jim . . . You mustn't go in just now . . .'

But he had to. He had to see what was wrong. He tore himself out of her grip, ducked round her, dodged to the door, pushed it open and stepped inside.

He never forgot what he saw. His father was lying on his back on the bed, naked and shaking from head to foot. The sheet underneath him was sopping wet and stained. There was a rank odour in the room and Jim realised with horror that his father had shit himself.

His mother was at his back now, desperately trying to pull him away. But he resisted, mesmerised by the sight. He wouldn't go.

His father's head suddenly came up off the pillow. He was looking across his quivering frame right at them. He made a hideous gasping noise, as if the sight of his wife and child absolutely terrified him. He dragged himself up to the head of the bed and drew his knees up to his chin. He was still staring at them. He raised one crippled arm. It was shaking so violently it looked like it might fly right off his body. He unpeeled a finger and pointed at them. Then he brought his other arm up and held his palms towards them, to push them away. Then he screamed at them. A blood-curdling scream in a voice that Jim had never heard before. The force of it blew across the room at them.

'Get away from me! Get away! Get away! Get away!'

# Six

Jim wasn't really hungry but his mother insisted he eat something. Pale and drawn, his eyes swollen and red-rimmed, he toyed with the food on his plate. Across the table, Elizabeth was doing the same. One hand supported her weary head.

'Mum?'

She stared into his eyes.

'How long will he be there? In the hospital?'

'Dr Hawker thought a couple of weeks at least. He needs a complete rest.'

'What's the matter with him? Really?'

Elizabeth looked down at her plate.

'I heard Mr Henderson talking to you that day. I heard him say dad had shellshock.'

'So we've been eavesdropping, have we?'

'Yes,' he admitted. 'That day I was.' But Jim refused to be sidetracked. He wanted an answer. 'What did he mean?'

'Nothing really. All soldiers get it a bit. Especially if they're fighting near big guns. Dr Hawker thinks your father had malaria. A very bad bout of malaria and he can only treat it properly by keeping him in hospital.' She never lied, especially to Jim, and she had to look away.

Jim was only half convinced. She was dodging the issue.

'Malaria's a sort of fever, isn't it?'

'Yes. Very bad fever.'

'You get it from mossies.'

'Those kind of mosquitoes live in tropical climates. Like New Guinea. He would have picked it up there.'

Jim stared at her, his eyes betraying his disbelief. 'Is that the truth?'

She was thrown again by the direct question. Relief came with a knock on the door.

It was Tommy Douglas. No sign of his usual grin.

'Hello, Tommy.'

'G'day, young Jim. Evenin', missus. Bad business for Mr Mackay.'

'Can we manage, do you think? Or should I see about getting someone out from town?'

'Might have to,' Tommy acknowledged. 'Bull's broken out again.'

'Oh, for God's sake. How did that happen?'

Tommy looked empty, as if she should know the answer.

'Well, you know . . . Boss forgot to order the new wire. Been patchin' her up best we could but that old bull, he's strong. Too clever. Anyway, he's gone. Have to go find him tomorrow.'

'Damn,' said Elizabeth, near to breaking point. 'I'm sorry, Tommy. I didn't know about the wire. I'll order it first thing in the morning.'

' 'Bout ten rolls'd do for now, I reckon. Boss said that'd have to do, anyway.'

Elizabeth nodded. Tommy turned to Jim.

'What about you, young fella? You come look for the bull with us tomorrow? Might take a couple of days to find him.'

Jim wasn't sure. But it was a good idea and Elizabeth said so. It might help to take his mind off what had happened in Longreach.

'Be a big help if you come along,' Tommy pushed.

'Yeah. Okay.' Jim stood up and headed for the door. 'Better go and get some sleep, I suppose. What time do you want to start?'

'You get to my place soon as you can. We'll wait for you.'

'Okay.' Jim nodded in agreement. ''Night, Mum. See you, Tommy.'

When the door was closed behind him, Tommy fixed Elizabeth with a look.

'Not to worry, missus. She'll be jake.'

Despite it all, she could still smile. But it cost her.


By the time Jim got there the next morning they were ready and waiting. Three Aboriginal and two white stockmen, Dougie, and Tommy himself. He divided them up into pairs.

After cantering a good mile through open country, Jim and Dougie dropped their ponies to a walk, good news for slavering Brud, who'd got himself in on the act. They rode on and on, keeping a crow's eye in every direction for a sign of their quarry. By mid-morning they were both pretty glad they'd worn their hats. The early morning clouds had disappeared, leaving them sweating under a great arc of burning blue. It made sense to head for the creek; if the bull wasn't there they could wag the hunt and go for a swim.

The bull wasn't there. They ditched their clothes and wandered naked along the bank, looking for the best spot to get in. It was nothing like their favourite rock pool here and the water was muddy and sluggish. They found a pool where the creek made a bit of a dog-leg turn, checked the far bank just above the waterline for snake holes, and waded in. The water might be dirty, but it was wet. It felt like heaven. They finished up having a bit of a water fight, sending thrilling sheets of spray flying at one another with their hands.

Jim didn't know this part of the creek at all, couldn't remember having been here before. But Dougie knew it well. He'd been this way with Tommy. They flopped down under a river gum and rolled on their backs for a breather. But not for long. Jim leapt to his feet and hurtled back into the sunlight.

'Pyyyyython!'

Dougie rolled his eyes and there it was, its lazy coils hanging off a triple fork directly overhead. Dougie didn't move. He just lay there looking at it. Then he hauled himself casually to his feet.

'What's the panic?' he asked, nonchalantly. 'It's a Children's. They sleep in the day. You know that.'

Jim looked a bit sheepish.

'Don't give a shit. I'm not lying underneath it.'

'Look out!'

Both Jim's feet left the ground as he spun in fright. But there was nothing there: just the hard crust of sun-baked earth. Dougie was howling with laughter. Jim hurled himself at him and they wrestled each other to the ground, tying themselves in knots and rolling all over each other before they called it quits.

'I'll get you for that,' said Jim.

Then because his self-esteem had taken a bit of a knock there, he grabbed a couple of sticks and chucked them at the sleepy python. It took no notice whatsoever.

'I guess we better get on with it.'

'Yeah, s'pose we should,' Dougie grinned. 'Let's go back on the other side. I can show you something if you like.'

'What?'

'It's a secret.' He said it seriously, rather formally, his voice dropped.

'Let's go.'

'There's one thing, though. You mustn't let my dad know I showed you, okay? It's his secret, too. He'd be real cranky. Okay?'

Jim's anticipation rose a notch and he took the oath: he crossed his heart and spat in the dust. 'Promise.'

The outcrop of red-brown sandstone and quartz boulders was bigger than it looked. Dougie led the way in, picking his way through the outer circle of stones to the biggest clump in the middle. Jim saw him squeeze sideways through a cleft and disappear from view.

He found him sitting in a small sandy enclosure overhung by a huge shell-shaped slab of stone. The stone was a revelation. It was completely covered in Aboriginal paintings. The central motif was a coiled snake.

'What is this place?' Jim sounded a bit nervous, even to himself.

'My dad says it's been here for ever.'

'What's it about? What does it mean?'

Dougie got up, stretched himself full length on tiptoes so he could just brush the rockface with his fingertips. He ran them round the painting of the snake.

'This is a Rainbow Serpent. And these,' pointing to seven white blobs inside the snake's coils, 'are the seven ages of creation.' He knew it all: the hunting scenes and fertility scenes, the technique used to stencil the dozens of handprints on the rock walls all around them.

'Sort of like signing the visitors' book at the church in Longreach,' he laughed, then waved his hand to indicate the whole show.

'They're all signs of our old tribe. Yirandhali people. Dad says they were here long before white people came. Thousands of years, he reckons.'

They lapsed into silence. They sat side by side soaking up the atmosphere of this ancient place. It was a first for Jim and he was spellbound. He reached up to touch the serpent for himself. He stretched and stretched. Just as he touched the rockface – crack! It came from outside. Both boys froze. Crack! There it was again.

Jim's voice was a whisper. 'What do you think it is?'

Dougie shook his head. He didn't have a clue.

'Maybe the rocks are falling down.'

Dougie's eyes flared. Maybe you're right, they said.

'Let's get out of here.'

Hanging onto one another, they edged over to the cleft. Shoulder to shoulder, they squeezed in. Jim held his breath as Dougie stuck his head out for a look-see.

'I can't see anything,' he reported.

'Have another look.'

There was only one thing to do: on the count of three, make a dash for the creek, dive in and swim like buggery for the ponies on the other side.

'You ready?'

Jim nodded and crossed his fingers.

One, two, three and they went for it. They got halfway to the water and stopped dead in their tracks. There, not more than a dozen yards down the creek, stood Barnaby Joker the Third, Balkenna's prize Hereford bull, laboriously working his missing bulk down the bank to the water's edge for a drink. He looked up at them, bellowed once, dug in his heels and plunged his nostrils into the muddy water. He lapped it up in huge, sucking draughts.

Jim and Dougie dropped to their knees in a fit of giggles as all their fear went up in smoke. Barnaby came up for air, eyed them a moment, and went back to his drinking. Each time they tried to look at each other, Jim or Dougie would burst out laughing again till they ran out of wind.

Barnaby suddenly lunged back up the bank, took one last look at them and went plodding off down the creek. Quick smart, the boys snapped into action. They ran in the opposite direction until they found a place to leap across the water and raced back for their ponies. They soon caught up with the water-logged bull and mustered in on either side of him. He turned to rake his horns in the air at the horses a couple of times and bellowed his annoyance, loud and clear.

'Come on, you old bastard,' yelled Jim. 'You know you'll get a feed at home.'

The bull seemed to like the idea. He bellowed once more, then he allowed himself to be pushed along until Brud came flying out of nowhere to dart in for a nip at his heels. The bull was furious. He scuttled forward and wheeled round and gave the dog a mean and beady eye.

'Come out of that.'

'Get behind! Get behind!'

Brud took his place sulkily behind the ponies as the boys turned the bull for home.

They got their reward that night. When supper was over, Elizabeth produced a big slab of dark chocolate, broke it in two and sent them upstairs with half each.

Tommy watched them go with a twinkle in his eye.

'You must be so proud of him.'

'You too, missus. Jim's a good bush fella.'

'It'll be some good news for Jack. He'll be pleased as punch, I expect.'

'He should be,' Tommy smiled. But there was a slight lack of conviction in his voice. 'We'll have to get the new calves branded next week. The shearers are booked for the week after unless you think Mr Mackay want to be home first.'

'No. That's fine. We better just get on with it. Dr Hawker didn't seem too sure how long he'd like Jack to stay in. He said two weeks, but it might be more. I ordered the wire, by the way. Mr Fry said they could have it here by Tuesday at the latest.'

'That's good, missus. I'll get Jim and Dougie to give me a hand while the shearing's on. I've wired an old gate where he broke through this time. That oughta hold him. That whole line of fence is pretty rusty. Best to rip the lot off, I reckon.'

'Whatever's best. I'll leave it to you. I'm going in to see Jack on Saturday, so I'll fill him in.'

They talked for half an hour, planning stock moves for the months ahead, planning an all-out blitz on an influx of Bathurst burr in the sheep paddocks, whose sharp spines and seeds covered in little barbed hooks were beginning to play havoc with the fleece. And, all the time, Elizabeth was bracing herself for the moment she was dreading but which she knew had to be brought out in the open with this big, friendly man who had been her ally and strength in Jack's absence. There came a lull and she could see Tommy thinking it was time to go.

'Tommy . . .' She glanced down at her lap, seeking the right words. Tommy waited, half-expecting it was just one more task she was reluctant to add to his work load. He certainly wasn't ready for it when it came. She gestured awkwardly with her hands and spoke in hesitant tones.

'It's just that . . . well, I thought it was only right that you

54

should know . . . Jack has mentioned the possibility of putting a manager on the place . . . if he feels the need to take a much longer time off to be really well again . . .' She had to look away as it sank in and humiliation spread across Tommy's face, followed by a scowl of annoyance.

'I'm sure it won't come to that . . .'

Tommy took the news in silence for a moment. All he knew was the truth. 'Not my fault things going badly. Things been bad a long time. I try to talk it over with Mr Mackay lots of times. He don't really listen to what I say. Different since before the war. We got along pretty good then. It's not my fault, missus.'

Elizabeth leant across to place a hand on his arm. 'I know that, Tommy. Please, please believe me. I do know that. Jack's just not well at the moment. It's only a possibility. I'm hoping he'll be able to come home soon and we'll go on the way we always have. He may not be able to work so hard, but we'll manage. We did before. It hasn't changed all that much since he's been back.'

But Tommy wasn't reassured. He was hurt and his hurt was slowly turning to anger. Old Angus Mackay had particularly asked him to stay on with Jack when he retired. As a special favour. The prospect of bringing in some strange white man to boss him around was a cruel slap in the face to reward years of hard struggle and loyal service.

'Not like before the war,' he repeated quickly. He couldn't blame this woman. He knew her heart was in the right place, how thankful she'd been to have him to fall back on. But Jack was the boss and she'd have to go along with whatever he decided, even though he could see how upset she was at this moment. He stood and retrieved his hat from the pegs near the door. 'I better be pushing along, missus. Patsy'll be wondering where we've got to. Will you give Dougie a shout. I'll wait in the truck.'

Elizabeth looked at him. She could read the hurt in his eyes. 'It's not easy . . .' She couldn't go on.

'It's okay, missus. No worries. She'll be jake.'

'I'll get Dougie.'

After they'd gone and Jim had gone to bed, she felt utterly, utterly weary. As she turned away from the table, she dropped a plate and it smashed to smithereens on the floor. She stared down at the splintered shards a moment before getting the dustpan and broom. She knelt to pick up the bigger pieces, but her timing was shot and one of them sliced her fingertip. She winced, put it to her mouth and sat back on her heels, sucking away the blood in abject despair.

'They were the heroes of the day,' Elizabeth told him, finishing the story of Barnaby Joker the Third. She smiled at Jim and he grinned back, but Jack just nodded his vague approval. There was a terrible distance in his eyes. He was obviously better than the last time they'd seen him, but far, far from cured. He didn't seem to care one way or the other.

When the bell rang, Elizabeth brushed the dampness from Jim's eyelashes, ruffled his hair and sent him to wait in the car while she had a quick word with Dr Hawker. Jim said it was too hot in the car and he'd wait on the verandah instead.

'I'll be as quick as I can,' she promised as he slouched off.

Dr Hawker offered her a glass of brandy. She took three hasty gulps as he returned to his desk to stare down and double-check his notes. Finally he shook his head. 'It's not good, Elizabeth.'

'No. I guessed as much.'

'You must realise this attack was serious. He was quite psychotic. It didn't really let go of him until Tuesday night.'

Elizabeth couldn't help it. Her eyes filled and she had to look down at her glass.

'Yes. I understand,' she whispered.

'He must be persuaded to go to Brisbane. Somehow we have to convince him it's for the best. What little I can do here is only going to hold up the symptoms for a while each time. But it's the root cause that needs the real attention and that's a specialist job. He has to go to Brisbane for that.'

Elizabeth pulled herself together and faced him again. 'I have tried, Michael. I've tried to get him to talk about it. He just won't hear of it . . .'

'These attacks will continue. They'll get worse. They'll be more frequent. He may go for months, possibly more, before something triggers off another one. But when they do occur they'll be more debilitating each time. What have you told Jim?'

'Oh, Lord,' Elizabeth sighed. 'I've been trying to pretend it's malaria. I'm not sure he's convinced . . .'

'Nevertheless,' Hawker interrupted. 'I suggest you stick to it for as long as you can.' He rose, came round his desk and perched on Elizabeth's chair. 'At this stage it's better he should suffer a little morbid curiosity than be forced to try and understand that his father is suffering a progressive loss of sanity.'

Elizabeth broke down completely then. All the anguish of the past few days doubled her over and she sobbed uncontrollably into her hands. Hawker let her get it out of her system.

'They told us he'd come home a hero,' she sniffled. 'I wish to God he'd just come home as Jack.'

Three weeks after they brought Jack Mackay home to Balkenna, Tommy Douglas was killed.

Jim and Dougie had managed to round up three brumbies that had got through the fence and were running wild on one of the main cattle paddocks on the Thomson River side. They brought them back to the holding yards at the house. Two of them were gone in the wind, they'd bring a few bob from the local knackers in Longreach. The third was an evil-looking nutmeg, much younger and stronger. Tommy decided he'd be worth breaking.

The shearers and other stockmen knocked off for a couple of hours to watch the show. Tommy had been working the brumby on a halter in the yard for the last couple of days. Now the moment had arrived. They got the saddle on it in the chute and put a sugar bag over its head. Tommy led it into the centre of the yard. It was pulling like mad, and pig-rooted a couple of times in fright. When he was in the middle of the yard, Tommy eased himself along the reins until he was its head, talking all the while in a low, soothing voice. He got the reins back over its neck and waited, quietening it all the time, until it splayed its front legs, shivering from head to tail. In one graceful movement born of a lifetime's experience, Tommy swung himself into the saddle and pulled the sugar bag away.

The brumby went berserk. With everybody cheering him on, Tommy dug his knees in and rode the storm as the nutmeg brumby corkscrewed, pawed the air and kicked at imaginary demons behind. It arched its back, bucking like a runaway train. It came down on all fours at once, jarring every bone in Tommy's body. It pig-rooted across the yard, it kicked at the railings as it turned. It tried every trick but Tommy knew them all. He'd done this a thousand times before. He stuck to its back like a sucker fish on a shark. The brumby sensed it was losing the contest and that only made it madder. It was bolting across the yard, slamming into the railings, time and time again. Then, its eyes wild with fright, it tried one last impossible move. It tore back across the yard and tried to jump the fence. Tommy came unstuck and went over first. He landed on his back, stunned and winded. The brumby thrashed through the two top railings, corkscrewed in mid-air and came crushing down on top of him, legs pedalling.

Jim just stood there paralysed. Dougie raced round the yard to join the others rushing to Tommy's side. The brumby kicked itself back on its feet and galloped away, the saddle hanging under its belly, the broken reins flying like ribbons from its mouth. Dougie dropped to his knees by his father's side, screaming.

'Dad! Dad! Dad . . .!'

They had to pull him away. The brumby's rump had crushed Tommy's chest to pulp and splintered rib bones jutted out of his shirt. There was nothing anyone could do.

When Jim heard the shrill pleading tones of Dougie calling his father back from the dead and saw the men dragging him away, kicking and struggling, he knew. He turned and ran with all his might for the house, a scream trapped in his throat.

They buried Tommy Douglas at the poor end of Longreach Cemetery. There weren't many there. Elizabeth could feel Jim's hand trembling in her own as they lowered Tommy into his grave. On the other side of her, Jack was staring stony-faced at the ground, his hands folded in front of him, shifting restlessly from one foot to the other.

When the straps were pulled away, the white mourners backed a little way off while Tommy's family and Aboriginal friends paid their last respects. Patsy Douglas turned and headed towards Jack and Elizabeth.

'Me and Dougie will be moving on now, Mr Mackay. In the morning.'

Jack just looked at her. He didn't seem to know what to say. Elizabeth came to his rescue.

'That's not necessary, Patsy. We wouldn't dream of it. You know we want you and Dougie to stay on at your place.'

But Patsy didn't respond. She had her eyes fixed on Jack.

'Please don't do anything hasty. We all know how terrible this is for you. You must take a little time to think about it.'

Elizabeth was desperate to get her message across. She reached forward and grabbed Patsy's arm. But she could do no good.

'I appreciate you're saying it, Mrs Mackay. But you know me and Dougie've got people up in the Gulf Country. We'll be going there now.'

Elizabeth released her grip. 'I wish you wouldn't . . .'

'Mind's made up, missus. Thanks all the same.' She turned back to Jack and her warm eyes turned to frost. 'I'll come by the house tonight to settle up, if that's good, Mr Mackay.'

Jack remained stony-faced, uncomprehending. 'All right.'

'I'll come along sundown.'

'Good.'

Patsy found a quick grateful smile for Elizabeth and turned away. Jack finally snapped out of it and made a grab for her arm that missed.

'Patsy . . . What Elizabeth just said, that goes for me too, you know.'

But her eyes froze over. 'That's okay, Mr Mackay. Like I said, we'll be moving on.'

Jim had been straining his ears. He'd just about got the gist of it. Now, he could only watch as Dougie came to meet her. They stopped and spoke for a second. Then Patsy took her son's hand, he fell in beside her and they walked away. They were quite a way off before Dougie suddenly remembered and turned to wave at Jim. As he raised his arm to wave back, sorrow gusted through him like a southerly buster. He waved until Dougie was out of sight.


'He was hurt by the thought of you putting him under someone else,' Elizabeth said, that night.

'Oh, I don't know,' Jack grunted. 'They don't think about things the same way we do.'

'That's a terrible thing to say.'

'Maybe,' Jack muttered. 'I think it's true enough though. He was a good worker. I won't quarrel with that. Great horseman. He did well enough with the place while I was away. But he'd have been just as happy doing it for someone else.'

'That's not true,' she snapped. 'You've lost a friend. A good friend. He loved Balkenna. He never flinched in his loyalty to the place or to us. He's been keeping things going since you came back too, don't forget.'

Jack rolled away in annoyance. 'For God's sake, let it drop

will you? He's gone and that's that. I'm not going to argue with you about it.'

'You're not being fair, Jack.'

Elizabeth never gave up hope. But she came close that night. They lay there side by side, staring at the ceiling beams. They lay in the trap they had made. The trap was Balkenna. Balkenna could give you everything. But it would make you pay.

'I saw Mackenzie,' Jack muttered. 'I'll have to sell off the top river block.'

'How much is that?'

'Three thousand acres. He says that'll do to keep the bank quiet. It's a bastard but it looks like I don't have any choice. If Ray Henderson wants to lease it, that might be a go. Whatever, I'll have to level the stock off and get rid of those two blokes Tommy hired.'

'We can't manage without some help.'

'We'll have to. No two ways about it. Jim'll have to chip in. Cut a few hours out of his lessons. I'll be buggered if I'm going to let the bank take the lot. If he wants to come into the place some day, he can start working for it now.'

Elizabeth was furious. She had to take a few deep breaths and swallow hard to check her anger.

'He's not big enough to have an air gun,' she began. 'Yet suddenly he's big enough to do the work of a grown man. Quite apart from the fact that he's hurt . . . confused . . . He doesn't know where he is with you half the time. For that matter, neither do I.'

'For Christ's sake, Elizabeth. The war was the bloody war. I'll be damned if I'm going to take the blame for it. You didn't expect I'd come back as if nothing had happened.'

'No,' she answered quietly. 'But I thought you'd still love us.'

It was the first time she'd said it out loud. There seemed no way he could tell her he could hardly believe the sound of his own words at times. The dead weight in his heart seemed to get heavier by the day. There was a voice in his head that told him over and over he was ill, he was getting worse, he must trust the woman he loved, face up to it and do something about it. But another voice said he was perfectly all right, hadn't changed at all, it was everyone else that was different. They just didn't understand – couldn't understand – what it had been like. He didn't want to think about it, let alone talk about it. Why couldn't everyone just let it be? But then, of course, how could they let it be when he'd acted like a madman in Longreach?

He pressed his palms to his ears, to dam the voices in his head. Silvery moonlight played on Elizabeth's profile on the pillow beside him. How beautiful she looked. How peaceful. How complete her dedication to this wild and lonely life. How lucky he was to have her there beside him. Jack reached out to place a rough and trembling hand on her shoulder and she turned to look at him. She looked so sad, her eyes full of confusion. But still he saw her love for him there.

'I do,' he whispered. 'Of course I still love you. And the boy.'

He leaned over and kissed her. He stroked her brow, her hair, wrapped his arms round her and pulled her into his embrace.

They lay there for ages before the muffled sounds of sobbing drifted down from Jim's attic room above.

'I better go up and see him for a moment.'

She went to get out of bed but Jack pulled her back. 'I'll go.'

He slipped out of bed and into his dressing-gown before padding round in his bare feet to lean down and kiss her again. She wrapped her arms round his neck.

'Be kind,' she whispered.

She lay back and listened to him climbing the stairs, opening the door and walking across the room above.

Jim was standing at the window.

Jack moved in beside him and hugged his son to his side. 'It's all right, mate.'

Jim hesitated a moment. Then he slipped his arm round his father and buried his face in his side.

'I loved Tommy,' he finally managed to sniffle.

'We all did,' Jack told him, hugging him even tighter. 'He was a good bloke.'

'Do you reckon he's in heaven yet?'

Jack smiled to himself. 'Sure. Sure. Would have galloped all the way.'

They stood together for a while in silent contemplation of the vast, shining skyway.

'I wish Dougie wasn't going away.'

Jack didn't know what to say to that. His fingers knotted in his boy's hair.

Below them, Elizabeth was on the edge of sleep. The sound of crying had stopped. New hope deceived her once again.

They'd get by. They'd manage. Things could be good. Jack could just as well get better as worse. Balkenna would grow again. She lay there thinking how happy they could be . . . If only . . . If only . . . The last image to float into her mind was the smiling face of the big man they'd buried that morning, smiling his ever-ready, gap-toothed grin.

'I'll miss you, Tommy,' she said.

'No worries, missus. She'll be jake.'

# Seven

In many ways, Elizabeth's dreams came true. Michael Hawker kept his promise and three months later talked to Jack about returning to Brisbane for treatment. He wouldn't hear of it. He refused even to consider it and begged them not to bother him with it ever again. Hawker raised his eyebrows to Elizabeth. They couldn't force him to go, so that was that. Jack assured them he'd be far too busy working and worrying about Balkenna's problems to allow himself the luxury of falling ill again. Despite their fears, they thought they saw a newborn sense of resolve to deal with his illness on his own terms and they let the matter drop.

Thereafter, Elizabeth simply kept the doctor informed of any sudden shift in Jack's mental or physical condition and she came to know a pattern of his seesawing moods that helped her identify telltale signs of impending trouble. He could be in a foul mood for days on end, barely acknowledging anyone's presence. This would be followed by weeks of shining optimism when the whole world was at their feet. Day after day he did the work of three men. Occasionally, if he were working on the Thomson River side of the property, he insisted on camping alone at the old Douglas place and they mightn't see him for a week or so. Sometimes without a word, he disappeared altogether.

They discovered he was driving all the way to Barcaldine or Blackall, booking into hotels and going on almighty benders. Returning from a lost weekend in Blackall, he rolled the car four times and walked away without a scratch. He complained bitterly afterwards that he and everyone else paid enough bloody taxes and it was about bloody time the bloody shire gave them some bloody value for money on the bloody roads. He blamed the whole thing on a drift of loose gravel. But the Longreach police found him sleeping it off in a sandstone hollow several hundred yards from the scene of the accident.

He suffered a couple of severe breakdowns like the one in Longreach. Just before Christmas 1949, Jim found him sweating, shivering and being violently sick in a corner of the tack room. The door to the old broom closet containing his guns was open, the key in the dirt beside him. They managed to get him to bed and summoned Dr Hawker. He had to make daily journeys to Balkenna for the two weeks Jack was ill because Jack refused, point blank, to go into hospital. Heavy sedation kept it under control until Jack was on his feet and back to work as if nothing had happened.

The second occasion was more serious. Jack was so debilitated by the time they found him, he'd been forced to accept a stay in hospital. In June 1950, they were listening to the evening news broadcast announcing the outbreak of the Korean war and the commitment of Australian troops. Jack snapped the radio off and went to bed without a word. Elizabeth was kept awake half the night by his tossing and turning and awoke in the morning to find him gone. The car was in the shed, his saddle still hanging in the tack room, and they realised he'd just wandered off on foot. They spent two whole days riding in circles all over the property and repeatedly checking the Douglas place without success. By lunchtime on the third day Elizabeth reluctantly informed the police and a two-way radio alert was sent out to neighbouring properties to be on the lookout. Nobody was at the Henderson house when the call was put through. That night they were frightened out of their wits by something knocking violently on their window as they sat down to dinner. It was Jack. Dishevelled and tormented, all he wanted was a glass of water. He didn't seem to know who they were or where he was.

For Jim and his mother, the bad times were more than offset by long stretches when Jack exhibited a healthy exuberance for life in general and Balkenna in particular. The shadow of his illness was always there. On these occasions, however, it disappeared in the sunshine of his smile. He seemed to be able to pull himself back from the brink if he was allowed to do so in his own time, without undue fuss. It was a delicate balancing act and they learned to judge it well as the seasons came and went.

To Jack's relief, Ray Henderson leased the three-thousand-acre river blocks and the bank accepted the income in lieu of a forced sale. Elizabeth was greatly relieved too. To cut off a piece of Balkenna would have been a bad knock for Jack with unpredictable results.

She found herself working harder than ever before in her life just to keep the household on an even keel. But they scraped through from one year to the next. She ran the house, kept the books and looked after Jim's education. She cooked for the shearers when they came to take the fleece and for the extra stockmen they took on for musters. On rare occasions she found time to look in a mirror and remind herself that the golden brown, hair-on-end, fiercely determined woman of the outback she saw was the same rather quiet and retiring Elizabeth Humphrey who used to teach school in Rockhampton.

Jim helped Jack as much as he could. Painfully at first, he came to grips with his father's black moods and bouts of illness. Theirs was a working relationship, built on the knowledge that Jack respected his son's abilities and seemed to enjoy teaching him the ways of the land. If there was a gulf a mile wide between them, it was not without love. Not what Jim had hoped for. Not like Tommy and Dougie. But it was there and his mother's love for them both never failed. He grew to like his father, to enjoy being with him, to learn from him. The golden rule was not to question Jack about himself in any way whatsoever. They could talk about the future but never the past. So Jim learned to live in the immediate present of the daily battle for existence and survival. It was a good training for the rest of his life.

Under his mother's careful guidance, his education continued until his fourteenth birthday in 1951 when Queensland state law allowed him to leave school and devote all his time to being Balkenna's right-hand man. The decision was an obvious one but Elizabeth was disappointed. Jim had been good at his books.

Guy and Anna Henderson came to fill the void left for Jim when Dougie went away to the north. They would come to stay at Balkenna for a few days or he would go to their place. Although they continued their correspondence schooling long after Jim stopped, there was still time for childhood.

At first he and Guy excluded Anna from their exploits or tolerated her presence as an unavoidable nuisance. But by the time he left school, that had all changed. Jim found himself wanting to spend more and more time in Anna's company to the exclusion of her brother. She was a year older than Jim. Until she was twelve, they all used to swim naked together whenever they got the chance. Now, she brought along a one-piece black cotton swimsuit and would disappear behind the rocks to put it on. Next thing they knew, Jim and Guy were provided with Speedos and told to do the same. This arrival of store-bought fig leaves in their paradise only increased Jim's curiousity about the budding female form now hidden from view but sharply defined under the wet, clinging cotton.

Gradually he came to realise that Anna had similar feelings about him. They found themselves tossed in the furnace of teenage passion. They kissed and cuddled in secret places in the outbuildings of Balkenna. They went for long rides together, holding hands as their horses plodded along side by side. They exchanged passionate notes pledging undying love until the end of time and keepsakes to remind them of each other in the long, sometimes unbearably long, periods between visits. Jim gave her his treasured first place ribbon, won at the first gymkhana he ever entered. Anna gave him a lace-bordered handkerchief and a blue and white hairclip, carved in the shape of a butterfly. Jim nicked some tissue paper from his mother's desk, wrapped the sacred objects in its fold and hid them under a corner of the lino. It never ceased to amaze him that the scent of Anna lingered on in the small square of cotton each time he gave in to dreams of her and took the package from its hiding place.

Dreams came true in January 1952, just after his fifteenth birthday. Guy should have been there too but he'd just had his appendix out and was recovering in Longreach Hospital. It meant he could have Anna all to himself.

On the last day of her visit, they rode off together for a swim at the old rock pool. Once in the water, after a bit of skylarking, Anna allowed him to peel her shoulder straps down and fondle her budding breasts in a fever-pitch of excitement. She slipped her hand down his trunks. They stayed locked together in a kiss that never ended, frantically treading water to stay afloat. Then they got rid of their costumes altogether and found a nesting place among the rocks to conduct the oldest experiment in the world. Afterwards, lying curled together in rapt exhaustion, Jim rather nervously expressed his concern about the possible consequences of their manoeuvres. He was greatly relieved by Anna's adamant assurance that it would be all right. Even so, it worried the hell out of him in the weeks following until she advised him her 'time' had come, just as she'd said it would.

As their romance continued, when time and place allowed,

Jim was extremely thankful that Anna seemed to know exactly when she could, or couldn't, and he left it up to her. He was still far from sure just how this 'period' business worked, though she explained it to him a dozen times. Many years later, he would tease his future wife about having been seduced by an older woman in his youth.

Later that year, he made a friend for life. The struggle to keep Balkenna had been rewarded by two really good seasons and Jack felt he could afford to increase their stock levels. The wool clip had been excellent, prices had almost trebled since 1947 and Elizabeth was able to announce the property had edged back into the black for the first time in five years. Jack bought a Holden. Then he roped Jim into giving him a hand to fix up the old Douglas house for the new permanent hand he'd hired.

Finding the right man for the job had proved hard work. Since the end of the war there had been a steady drift of the rural labour force to the cities and coastal towns where a man might find a job, in grim contrast to the drought of work on the land. Local word of mouth produced only two applicants for the job, both men in their forties and both worn out by years of back-breaking toil on other men's land. Jack wanted young blood that would seize the chance with both hands. He ended up placing ads in local stock and station agent bulletins. As a result, Tim Daley arrived.

Just nineteen years old, Tim was an orphan, raised by foster parents in Blackall. He'd been jackarooing on properties in the Blackall district since he was fifteen. Elizabeth was immediately impressed by the tone of his carefully penned application and they paid for him to make the long journey for an interview. He was shy, tall and gawky and he talked so softly you could hardly hear him. They all liked him at once.

Six weeks later the old Douglas place became known for ever more as 'Tim's place' when Tim returned to take up his position, walking all the way from the front gate carrying his life's possessions in a huge leather suitcase and his saddle on his shoulder.

'For goodness sake,' Elizabeth protested. 'Why on earth didn't you let us know. We'd have picked you up in Longreach.'

'I didn't want to put you to any trouble,' he replied.

In the following weeks Jack was pleased to find he'd been spot on. Tim Daley quickly showed himself to be an extremely conscientious, self-reliant and hard-working young man. Tim and Jim got on famously, discovering in each other a rich vein of love and respect for the land and its creatures. Elizabeth made him one of the family and insisted he take his evening meal with them whenever he felt like it.

Jim quickly filled him in about Jack. In time, he became as quick as Elizabeth and Jim themselves to judge when to leave Jack alone as they all knuckled down to the job in hand: the slow and painstaking resurrection of Balkenna.

Bush fire wiped them out in January 1953.

The summer's rainfall had been mean. There were some good falls in other parts of the district, but the swollen clouds rolled perversely across Balkenna's acres, pissing only useless drizzle. Bone dry roly-poly bushes had been snapping their stems at ground level for weeks. Caught by the wind, they blew across the empty acres to pile in mountains of fire hazard against the fences. As far as the eye could see, the treeless downs and plains were an undulating sea of dull, grey-brown grass, brittle, crumbling and waiting for the spark. The cattle and sheep mobbed at the bore holes and they kept them pumping flat out.

One livid lightning bolt was all it took. Jack and Tim had been watching a slow build-up of thunderheads from the south-west. They promised relief but it never came. They knew the flash had hit the ground.

'Oh, Christ,' was all Jack said.

'Down towards the creek,' said Tim.

With cruel precision the bolt struck a dead gum, exploding it in flaming shrapnel over a wide area. The wind seized on the flying sparks. The surrounding scrub was ablaze in minutes.

Grassland fire is a terrifying thing to see. It advances in every direction at once, a plaything for every malicious shift of the wind. On the great empty spaces of almost treeless plains it can lay waste thousands of acres in a few hours.

By noon the next day they were fighting to save the house. As always, great angry columns of smoke summoned neighbours from miles around to the rescue. Ray Henderson and three of his stockmen were first on the scene, getting there as dawn mingled its fiery light with the raging inferno that drove beasts, animals, birds and reptiles before it in blind panic. Three more men they'd never met arrived an hour later, having driven thirty-two miles down the Longreach road in record time.

Scurrying like ants between the water troughs and the lines of flame, they beat back the fire with wet sugar bags. Fighting for breath, ignoring the cries of aching muscles, bent double in fits of coughing, and blinded by the smoke, they beat and beat at the flames, charging from one new flare-up to the next.

Elizabeth came staggering out of the smoke and fell to her knees gagging for air, her face streaked with soot. Jim raced to her side, thumped her back, shot back to soak his bag in the trough and dumped it over her head, gently patting her face with the dripping hessian. Elizabeth came out from under and gave him a smile.

'Ahhh. That was good.' She squeezed his arm, jumped to her feet and charged back to the battle, pulling the bag from her shoulders as she ran.

'Muuum! For God's sake . . .'

But there was no point. She'd fight till she keeled over. Jim ran to get another bag and returned to the fray himself.

Two hours later they'd stopped it in its tracks. All they had to do now was keep a crow's eye for any rogue sparks buffeting about in the wind. One end of the big barn had caught but they'd managed to smother it and limit the damage. Apart from that, Balkenna stood unbloodied, alone in a sea of smoking ash.

The weary firefighters sprawled like zombies in the shade of the verandah, stupefied by the mindless destruction the fire had wrought. Jim helped his mother rustle up some tea; jam sandwiches and biscuits, eaten in silence. Nobody could bear to look at Jack for more than a quick glance. His eyes said it all. Breakdown on a tight leash.

Tim joined Jim on the steps and they gazed glumly at other lines of fire still sweeping across the land at jacknife angles in the distance.

'What a bastard.'

'Yeah,' Jim muttered. 'Sure is.' He felt like crying but there were no tears left. The heat had sucked them all out of him.

'Your dad looks crook.'

'I'm afraid to look,' Jim whispered. 'This'll break his heart. God knows what'll happen . . . I guess your place has gone up.'

'Don't worry about that. I can always doss in the barn.'

'Like hell. Mum wouldn't hear of that. You can have the room upstairs next to mine. It's empty. At least until we get this sorted out.'

Jim dried up. Tim wanted to say something but was completely at a loss for words. Better to act.

'We'll have to ride out first thing, Jim. See how many fences are buggered, get the survivors to water, get started on a tally . . .'

Jim raised his head and nodded. 'Yeah. We better.'

Next day they rode through the valleys of death. They only managed to cover a third of the property but it was obvious the survival rate was going to be fifty per cent if they were lucky. The sheep runs were the worst: gluey heaps where bunches of them had gathered in terrified shrinking circles until the flames danced in their greasy wool. Some of the Herefords had survived by wallowing in the mud in the dams, or hunching in gullies as the fire licked across their backs. It looked like the northwest corner of the place had escaped the worst of it. Tim decided to get started up there tomorrow. For most of the day, they rode in silence. Each new discovery told its own grim story. Miles and miles of fencing lay in blackened tangles of useless barbed wire. It would take months to clear away the debris and months more to rebuild them.

Jim was glad his father hadn't come. Long after the firefighters had taken their leave, Jack had remained on the verandah staring at some point in the distance. When Jim took him a cup of tea at dusk Jack nodded, put it beside him and never touched it. Elizabeth put in a call to Dr Hawker.

There was nothing left on the Thomson River side. Tim's place was a charcoal shell, just mounds of fluffy, grey-black ash. As the sun lipped the horizon, they picked their way through to see if any of his belongings had survived. The littlest things can hurt the most. Tim found himself swallowing hard and fighting back the tears when he came across a brass lock and buckle, all that remained of his suitcase. He'd carted it from pillar to post in the four years of jackarooing since leaving his foster parents' home. It had been their parting gift.

Elizabeth spent the day fighting a trembling lip, washing the grime off the windows and boiling all their fire-stained clothes in the copper. Jack mooched around the house, occasionally stepping outside to look about and shake his head. There was an old chest of drawers in the barn and Elizabeth got him to help her move it up to the attic room she was getting ready for Tim. Jack hung around as she made up the bed. He kept drifting to the window to stare from its higher vantage point at the world he'd lost. The last time, Elizabeth's lip gave way and the tears streamed down her face. He held her then. They clung to each other for dear life, staring out in silence at the failure of the light. It was a good ten minutes before Jack broke the spell.

'We've got a fight on our hands now, old girl.'

She looked up. The veils of abject despair had lifted from his eyes. She reached up and planted a kiss on his cheek. 'I'm for that, Mackay . . . All the way.'

Jack looked down at her a moment, gently brushing the tears from her cheeks.

'God love you. He's a fool if he doesn't. I love you enough for both of us.'

Queen Elizabeth and Prince Philip had arrived for the first Australian tour by a reigning monarch. Australia had signed the Seato Pact with the United States to contain communist expansion in Southeast Asia. France had appealed to America for help to relieve her beleaguered troops at Dien Bien Phu but President Eisenhower had declined. Promising deposits of uranium had been discovered at Mary Kathleen near Mount Isa. Queensland had imported fifteen hundred cane cutters from Italy for the northern sugar industry . . .

As they listened, Elizabeth busied herself repairing one of Jim's shirts with swift, experienced stitches. She had to do something with her hands.

Jack snapped the radio off and took charge. 'Right. Let's see what we've got.'

Not wishing to intrude, Tim immediately excused himself. 'If you don't mind, I think I'll hit the hay. I'm really done in.'

'Go for your life,' Jack responded, immediately. 'I'll sort through this lot with Jim and we can discuss it in the morning.'

'I'll show you up,' Elizabeth offered. 'You'll be needing a pair of pyjamas.'

Tim gave a shy smile and indicated his stockman's rig. 'I'm afraid so. This looks like all I've got left.'

As they got to the door, Jack called him back. 'Thanks, Tim. It's not exactly been the best twenty-four hours on record.'

'That's for sure.'

'Thanks for all your help,' Jack went on. 'Hope you'll be okay upstairs. I'm afraid it'll be a while before I can even think about rebuilding your place.'

'I'll be fine,' Tim cut him off, with a smile. 'Don't worry

about it. You've got enough on your plate. See you in the morning.'

'No need to be up too early,' Jack nodded. 'Get a good rest. We're all going to need it.'

When Elizabeth came down she found them side by side, studying the notes on Jim's lap. She went back to her stitching, glancing at them occasionally, thinking to herself how much a young man Jim was now, the living likeness of the man she had married . She was still marvelling at Jack's response. All day she feared the fire would trigger his shattered nerves and send him screaming over the edge. But there was a new fight on. Untapped reserves of strength and determination had come good.

'Good,' he said finally, slapping Jim on the knee. 'We'll start shifting them around tomorrow. We're damn lucky to have the sheds and gear intact. Damn lucky.'

As Jim shuffled his notes, Jack leaned back and read the ceiling, lost in thought. Abruptly, he stood up and strode out of the room without another word.

'Is he all right?' Jim asked, the minute the door was closed.

'I think so,' Elizabeth assured him. 'We can only hope and pray. I was quite stunned by the change that came over him late this afternoon. He seemed to have come to terms with it. All he wanted to talk about was what needed to be done.'

'He always manages to go on somehow, doesn't he,' said Jim.

'God knows how,' she sighed. 'But yes. He does.'

'Hardly seems to notice me most of the time,' Jim added, sadly. 'Except in a crisis like this.'

'It's been the same with me, darling,' she told him. 'You know that. We just have to keep loving him, no matter how much it hurts.' The day caught up with her as she spoke and she dropped her head to hide her eyes.

'I know, Mum. I know.'

It was a good half hour before Jack returned. He looked rather pleased with himself. He held something behind his back. He strode across the room and held it out at arm's length before Jim's astonished eyes. It was a .22. Its stock was shining from a good polish, the barrel gleaming, the breech block freshly cleaned and oiled.

'Here. I know I promised it for the sixth but I'm afraid I still had my doubts.'

Incredulous, Jim slowly took the rifle from his father's hand. Elizabeth watched in total amazement.

'You fought like a man yesterday,' Jack told him. 'You are a man now, I suppose. A young man though, so treat this bloody thing with the respect it deserves.'

'Of course,' Jim gulped.

'Never point it at anyone, even when it's empty,' Jack continued. 'You just never know when you've forgotten the one up the spout.'

'I won't.'

'Always put it through a fence before yourself. Okay?'

'I will, I will.' Jim rubbed his hand across the stock and slid the bolt to check the breech.

'And one more thing.'

Jim continued staring at the rifle but Jack wanted his full attention.

'Jim.'

He looked at his father, eyes dancing with thanks.

'Do me a favour. Don't fire it anywhere near the house. Okay? Is that a deal?'

'It's a deal,' Jim agreed. 'Thanks, Dad. Thanks a million.'

'Okay,' Jack nodded. Then with the stiff, self-conscious formality that had grown between them over the years, he offered his hand to seal the bargain. Jim stood as he shook it. But it wasn't enough. He let go and flung his arms round Jack's shoulders. Awkwardly, Jack patted his son's back.

'Fine. Fine. Look after it.' He pulled away and threw a look at Elizabeth. 'I'm for the sack.'

'Yes, me too. I'll just finish this.'

He was gone. She stared at the door for a moment as another wave of relief rushed through her. Relief and deep appreciation. She turned to look at Jim and their smiles lit up the room.

The next day Tim headed off with three dogs in tow to check the northwest corner. Jim and his father set off with Brud to round up the survivors straddled along the creek.

Jack's buoyant mood of the night before quickly dried up into grim, hardset lines as they crossed the trackless grasslands. They were reduced to blackened stubble, littered with the carcasses that spelt ruin and the bones of the helpless roos and emus, burnt alive as they ran. He'd been quite talkative as they set out. By the time they got to the creek he was mute with shock and throttled rage.

By late morning they'd managed to find over four hundred head and bring them together. The pitiful looking Herefords were too tired to resist except for an odd kick Brud's way. From yesterday's inspection with Tim, Jim knew the fences across the creek had stood up to the worst of it. He suggested they use the thousand-acre paddock for temporary holding. Jack agreed in theory, depending on the state of the bore. It was across on the other side and it took Jim three quarters of an hour to make the journey. But he was able to report it was still pumping. Support struts at the base had been damaged but the windmill was still turning.

They crossed the mob to the fold-back gate and herded the animals through. They drove them on to a wide sweep of grass Jim had spotted on the way back. A whim of the wind had saved it from the flames. They left the stock to graze; they would find their own way to the water.

Jack led the way to the top gate into the adjoining paddock at a point furthest from the creek. They could work their way across its two thousand, five hundred acres on a diagonal to the lower creek corner.

They checked it thoroughly, in long arcing figures of eight. The sharp, clawing stench of burnt rubble stung their noses and parched their throats. The noonday sun threatened to reignite anything left smouldering.

When they came through the bottom gate and into the open country around the creek again, Jack pointed out a clump of shade.

'Let's have lunch.'

The horses slurped great gulping draughts from the mud. Brud took a good long fill beside them. Jack grabbed the thermos and sandwiches from his saddlebag and they got comfortable in the shade themselves and tucked in. After a few mouthfuls and a swig of tea, Jim broke the rules. He took a step into enemy territory: the secrets of the past.

'You know the family tree in the Bible?'

Jack seemed to hesitate and stared at the dirt before replying. 'What about it?'

'The first name there, Arthur.'

'He's your great-great-grandfather. Came out here on a ship called *Artemisia*. Way back in 1848. It was the first ship to bring immigrants to Moreton Bay. He was just twenty-two when he got here.'

Jim was encouraged. Jack was opening up. It was only a crack. But he could see some light.

'Did he start Balkenna?'

'Good Lord, no. Never got anywhere near that far. He was a wheelwright to begin with. Worked hard and saved hard by all accounts. Ended up marrying the daughter of another immigrant who made a few bob off the squatters. Storekeeper.'

'I thought store people didn't make any money in those days.'

'Some did. They'd advance goods to the squatters for a season or so. Then, when they brought their crops in to sell, the storekeepers'd deduct the market price of the goods they'd had. Things were always going up. Just like now. Some of 'em made a killing.'

'Doesn't sound very fair.'

'Maybe not,' Jack mused. 'Seems everybody did it in those days. Things haven't changed all that much.' He stood up and Jim was meant to follow. 'Come and have a look at this. There's something down there I can show you.' He headed off towards a large expanse of flat, exposed rock. Jim leapt to his feet. Jack was pointing to a clearly visible imprint on the rock's surface.

'See that?'

'What is it?'

'A dinosaur's footprint,' Jack announced. 'Found it myself when I was about your age. Your grandfather wrote in about it and a bloke came all the way from Brisbane to have a look.'

'How come there's only one?'

'God knows. I know where there's a whole lot of them though. Not here on Balkenna. Southwest of Longreach. We could go and have a look some day, if you like.'

'That'd be great,' said Jim. And he meant it from the bottom of his heart.

On the long ride home Jim tried his father with more questions, and it all came spilling out. Jim wanted to know everything. He wanted his roots.

'What did he do after then? Arthur?'

'Tried cotton first. There was a boom in those days. Catherine – his wife – her father set them up near Rockhampton. They had about three hundred acres evidently. The boom went bust in three or four years and they sold up. He went back to working from place to place. Eventually they found their way out here and he took up droving. Worked for

Nat Buchanan on Bowen Downs and that's where he died. Drowned.'

'How?'

'Tried to cross a mob when the river was in flood. My grandfather was only twenty at the time. Always said his father was the hardest working man he'd ever known. Could turn his hand to anything.'

'Did they find his body?'

'No. Never did.'

'What happened to your grandfather?'

'Took over the droving job on Bowen. Catherine worked there too. As a cook. Then her father died and left her some money. They put that with what they'd saved and got the pastoral lease tenure for Balkenna. Riverside it was known as then.'

'How big was it then?'

'Same as now. If you had the blocks Ray Henderson's leased. Fifteen thousand acres.' Jack pulled himself up in the saddle and flapped his reins. 'Come on. Let's get home before it's dark.'

They cantered the rest of the way in silence. Jim was glowing with pride. He felt closer to his father than ever before in the long, troubled years of their relationship.

After dinner, they spent some time at the table comparing notes with Tim. He brought good news. The northwest corner had escaped most of the fire. His random count amounted to a good stock tally. But overall a fifty per cent loss still seemed probable and it didn't look good. The sound of Elizabeth playing the piano drifted up from the lounge, something she hadn't done for months. Jack suggested they relax and have a listen.

Jim went through the lounge and headed for the library to collect the Bible. He wanted to keep striking while the iron was hot. By the time he returned Elizabeth had finished her piece. Despite their requests, particularly from Tim, she could not be persuaded to continue. She wanted Tim to have a look at an assortment of Jack's old clothes she'd dug up to tide him over until their next visit to Longreach.

They disappeared and Jim lugged the Bible over to Jack on the couch. When he saw what it was, he responded by sitting up and patting Jim into a place beside him.

'Let's see what we've got here. It's been quite a while.' Jack ran his finger down the family tree. 'See . . . There's my grandfather married to Ruth Thompson. She was a school-teacher, too. Used to teach in Winton. They married in 1882. Here's me down here. Born in 1913. And there's you . . . January 6th 1937.'

Jim nodded and glanced at his father. 'I looked at this lots when you were away.'

'Make us a cup of tea, will you?'

Jim leapt to oblige, thrilled to bits.

# Eight

By year's end Balkenna's fortunes had sunk to an all-time low. Jack was forced to sell all the cattle and sheep that had survived the fire, including their stud rams and Barnaby Joker, their prize Hereford bull. All the proceeds from the sale went straight to the bank in Longreach against the overdraft. They were hanging on by a whisker.

Within weeks of the fire the place was drenched with rain. Soon, healthy young grass shoots appeared amidst a panorama of wildflowers. They did as much seeding as they could afford in the worst hit areas and Balkenna's grasslands slowly returned to their former glory. But they had no stock to graze on them.

The day came when Jack had to tell Tim he could no longer afford to keep him on. He offered to do all he could to find him another job. But Tim wouldn't hear of it. Balkenna's battle had become his, too. He told them he'd stay on for his board and keep if they'd have him, and they were happy to agree. Nobody wanted to lose him. He'd become one of the family. With that out of the way, Tim got stuck into disentangling the miles of barbed wire brought down by the fire, culling it carefully for lengths to use in rebuilding.

With little else to do, Jim joined in and together they salvaged roll after roll. They scoured the place for damaged trees to bring down and cut into posts to take the strain. Many posts left standing had suffered only surface damage; they chipped away the charcoal and used them again.

But Jack's initial steely resolve was gradually rusting away. Elizabeth did her best, but there were days she stood on the front steps and looked out and all she saw was hell on earth and she wished to God she'd never set foot on Balkenna. The humiliation of having to submit their bimonthly grocery orders for the bank's approval was hard to bear. Little luxuries were slowly whittled away. They were down to the barest essentials.

The final straw for Jack came in July with news of his father's death. Angus had suffered a massive heart attack at the wheel of his car and the crash put Harriet in hospital with a broken collarbone and a fractured pelvis. They couldn't all go, so Jack made the long journey alone to bury his father and be at his mother's side. Her bones would heal but her spirit was broken. Jack begged her to come back and live at Balkenna when she was fit to travel. In frail, dignified tones she told him it was too hard to imagine going on without Angus. She never left hospital. Harriet died in her sleep at the end of September. Jack returned to bury her beside his father and wind up their affairs.

It turned out that Angus had lost most of his savings in a Brisbane building development company that had gone bust owing millions. Jack assumed his father had been too proud or too ashamed to let them know what had happened. The sale of their house meant he could think about a partial restocking of Balkenna. But thinking about it was all he did.

He suffered a terrifying relapse on the train home. He was in a state of collapse when Elizabeth met him at the station. She rushed him to Dr Hawker's surgery to be heavily sedated for the drive home where they got him to bed. She and Jim then took it in turns to stay with him until he started to come out of it a week later. Once again, he lost himself in violent seesawing moods and long periods of total disinterest in all around him. Elizabeth, Jim and Tim handled him as best they could.

For Jim, the only bright spot in a black year came late in November when an old friend of his father's turned up out of the blue. He looked like he'd stepped straight out of 'Waltzing Matilda'. A great, lumbering bear of a man, with a wild beard and sulphurous anarchic eyes, Fred Paterson had spent a lifetime in the bush, looking for gold he never found. Jack had staked him many times in the years before he met Elizabeth. Jim had vague memories of other visits he'd made when he was very young. Fred had come by a few times to check on Elizabeth when Jack went into the Army. But Jim knew him best from his father's stories.

Elizabeth was startled out of her wits when Fred turned up without warning in the kitchen door with a pretty little ragamuffin of a girl balanced on his arm. He gave her a crushing hug, thrust the toddler in her arms and, before she could utter a word of warning, lurched through to the lounge looking for Jack. He soon found him.

'G'day, you old bastard. Christ! You look like death warmed up.'

She was hugely relieved to hear Jack burst out laughing.

Fred kept dragging Jack off to Longreach to sink a few schooners, and night after night he entertained them with endless tales of his adventures. Jim figured about half of them were probably true, but it didn't matter. He made Jack laugh a lot and he seemed to lift his spirits just by being there.

The little girl was called Annie. She had enormous, pale blue eyes. Her mother had immigrated from Germany and Fred found her working as a barmaid in Cairns. He married her on the spot and whisked her off to share his nomad's life in the bush. Late one night, in hollow tones, he told them how she died on a lonely track on Mount Mulligan. Annie had arrived five weeks premature, foiling his plan to get her mother to Cairns in time. She died giving birth in the cab of his truck.

Annie attached herself to Jim like a leach. She followed him everywhere, bombarding him with questions. She was just three and a half, but she needed to know the whys and wherefores of everything in sight. He put up with her at first and then became more and more engaged by her. She helped him feed the chooks, hurling handfuls of feed in all directions and shrieking with delight. One day, with ferocious concentration, she helped him polish his saddle, hanging onto the brush and the cloth, demanding to know the name and function of every bit of gear hanging from the tackroom walls. At night, Fred or Elizabeth gave her a bath and she'd yell and yell until Jim came. In the end, it made more sense for him to bath her and he took over the job. Afterwards he read her Little Golden Books. It made him realise how much he missed the brother or sister he never had. Occasionally he felt his mother's eyes on him and he knew she was thinking the same.

Things got a bit tricky when Anna turned up for a couple of days. Annie objected. Firstly their names sounded the same. She suggested Anna call herself Heather or something instead. Secondly, Anna took up all Jim's time. They couldn't get a moment's peace and no hiding place was secure. So they had to resort to long rides away from the house for their own breathless fun and games.

When Fred finally declared it was time to hit the wallaby, Annie burst into tears and said she didn't want to go. She would go only if Jim came too. Long after they'd gone, he found himself missing her impish grin and squeals of silvery laughter much more than he'd expected.

They tried everything they could think of to get Jack started restocking in November but he just couldn't face it. He kept saying he was expecting lower prices in the New Year. Christmas was a very glum affair.

Jim's seventeenth birthday came and went. By the end of January he found himself in daily discussion with his mother about what they should do. He was getting more and more worried about her health. The strain was starting to show. One bad night, he floated the possibility of seeking power of attorney so Elizabeth could negotiate directly with the bank herself and get something underway. She was shocked he'd even thought of such a thing.

'You do realise, don't you, your father would have to be declared mentally unfit for us to do something like that.'

Jim hadn't realised but he wasn't going to be put off. 'Well. That's the truth, isn't it? So maybe we should.'

His mother gave him the coldest look he could ever remember and walked out of the room. He apologised later. But it didn't help matters. Neither of them knew what the hell to do.

Then, just as suddenly, in February, Jack broke out like a blaze of sunshine on a frosty winter's day. His mood swung full circle again and he took charge as if he'd never been away. He got in touch with the stock and station agents in Longreach, Barcaldine and Blackall, asking for information on all the upcoming sales and expected prices. Firing on all cylinders, he went to see Will Mackenzie at the bank to argue his case and he came home that night well pleased with the outcome. He rode out alone to inspect the lines of fencing Jim and Tim had so painstakingly restored, and lavished praise on them afterwards for a job well done. He thought a few areas of over-patching should be replaced by new wire altogether.

'Nothing personal, mind you,' he added, with a grin.

He organised a massive clean-up of the barns, outbuildings, shearing and dipping yards, machinery and tack. They checked every windmill and bore on the place, repairing them where necessary. His reborn enthusiasm was so infectious it carried them through the autumn months to the first bite of winter in June.

Jack went off to inspect stock and made plans for a late winter buy-up that would have new stock grazing on Balkenna by mid-spring. He tracked down Barnaby Joker's buyer and arranged to lease the old bull back for a season with an option to buy if all went well. Barnaby Joker would have a long journey home. He'd been trucked all the way to Augathella to compete with two others for the cows' attention on a fifty thousand-acre stud.

None of it ever came to pass.

No rain fell at all that spring and forecasts were bad, raising the spectre of another drought. By mid-December the land was parched.

Jim poured himself another cup of tea. He carried it outside to stare at the unforgiving, cloudless sky. Jack had suffered another attack last night. Now, as Jim watched a willy-willy gathering dust in the distance, his young face was hard and troubled.

Elizabeth came out to join him. 'You all right?'

'What do you think?' he snapped, instantly regretting it. 'Sorry, didn't mean to bark.'

She rubbed his back a moment. 'I know. I know. It can't last for ever, you know. The weather, I mean.'

'How is he?'

'Much better. Doesn't seem as bad as last time.'

Jim turned to look at her, his eyes gently mocking. 'That's what you said last time. We've been saying it for years . . .'

'Please, Jim,' she cut him off. 'Not now. Not right this minute.'

'What did Mackenzie say?'

She was fighting for control but she was losing the battle. Tears spilled down her cheeks.

'Mum, please. I just need to know, that's all.'

Elizabeth wept on her son's shoulder for a moment. Then she brushed away the tears.

'We can keep the place and that's it. Everything else has to go. All the machinery. Everything.'

'Bastards,' Jim growled.

'No, they're not. They've got their job to do. Will Mackenzie's gone out on a limb for us time and again. They just can't go on, that's all. He doesn't want us to lose the place and I thank him for that.'

Jim turned away to stare into the distance. Elizabeth studied him a moment: he was still only seventeen but he looked twenty. She couldn't bear the sorrow that tugged at the corners of his mouth.

'Let's keep busy, darling. The more we stand about moping, the worse it'll be.'

'The tack room,' Jim mumbled. 'Will all that have to go too?'

'Everything. I was going to talk it over with you and Tim at lunch. We'll have to get everything ready. The valuers will be here on Monday.'

In the tack room, Jim stood for a while just looking around the walls at the saddles, bridles, collars, yokes, traces, old stirrups and horseshoes, leg ropes and whips hanging from their pegs. It was incomprehensible that in a few days this little room where he'd spent so many hours saddle-soaping, polishing, knotting and stitching would be completely bare. He'd grown up in there. He turned to go just as Elizabeth came rushing in.

'There's a huge brown after the eggs again. It's gone in the little roost in the yard.'

Jim got his .22 from the gun closet, grabbed some cartridges from the shelf and hurried back to the chook run. Gingerly he lifted the corrugated iron roof and peered inside. Elizabeth bent down beside him but he gently pushed her back a bit before lifting the iron away altogether. The snake was coiled in the corner. A full-grown king brown, cranky as hell. It lifted its head, tongue darting in and out. Jim slowly edged the .22's muzzle closer and closer until the snake gathered itself to strike. In the split second it was still he fired. The shot echoed round the yards. Bull's-eye. The bullet mashed the snake's head and it writhed over and over itself in a frenzy. Elizabeth stepped forward to watch its final convulsions.

'Well done.'

One last shudder and it was dead. Using the barrel of the rifle, Jim tried to lift it out but it kept sliding off.

'I'll get a rake.'

After several attempts he finally managed to hook the snake out and carried it across the yard. He hung it on the fence. It was a whopper. Six foot six, at least.

'God. What a brute.'

'Bloody things are all over the place. Looking for water . . .'

From behind them came a sudden splintering crash. They

both jumped with fright and spun round. When they saw him, they froze.

In his pyjamas and riding boots, Jack was smashing Jim's rifle to bits. The stock was already in splinters and he was smashing the breech end again and again against a stone boot-scraper by the feed shed. It was coming apart in his hands.

Elizabeth raced across the yard. 'Jack! For God's sake! What are you doing?'

Jim stayed rooted to the spot, struck dumb by his father's fury.

'I told him! I bloody well told him! Never near the house! Never! Never! Never!'

His voice rose with every bang of the rifle against the stone. He was frothing at the mouth.

Elizabeth leapt on him and tried to smother him in her arms. Jack pushed her off, violently, and she fell into the dirt. She grabbed his leg, trying desperately to break his murderous rhythm. Jack kicked out to free himself and his boot smashed into her face.

That was it. Jim snapped. He was across the yard in a flash. He wrenched the rifle from his father's hands, pushed him back against the wall of the shed and held him there with his forearm across his throat.

Jack gave in for a moment. Then all his old training and cunning came rushing back, and he had the strength of a madman. He tore the arm from his throat and, before Jim knew what had happened, he twisted it high and hard up behind his son's back and shoved Jim sprawling in the dirt.

Mother and son looked up in anguish at this madness towering over them. Jack stared down at them as if he was seeing something else. Then he seemed to recognise himself for a moment. But what came out was gibberish.

'Chooks . . . Must kill the chooks . . . I . . . I'm going out now . . . Listen to that . . . Sorry . . . No . . . I have to go out there now . . .'

'Jaaack!' Elizabeth's scream cut through the storm in his head. He blinked at her, his mouth hanging open, his eyes boiling.

'Jim shot a snake, Jack. That's all.' She raised a trembling hand to point. 'There. On the fence. He shot a snake.'

Jack looked at it, then back to her, once, twice, three times.

But nothing connected with anything. In horror, she saw his face suddenly sag into imbecility.

'I have to go now . . . I have to go out there, you know . . . I really have to go now . . . Out there . . . Listen to that . . . Listen to it . . .'

He ripped the snake off the fence and staggered away with it dangling from his hand, disappearing through the gate at the side of the shed.

Jim dragged himself over to his mother. Elizabeth sank her head in his lap and sobbed her heart out. There was a vicious red welt where Jack's boot had caught her cheekbone and the skin was broken. Blood mingled with her tears.

Jack staggered through the paddock on the far side of the holding yards. He was still clutching the dead snake. He ploughed on and on. The sun bore down, stoking the fire in his head. An ant heap loomed in his path and he lurched to a halt. He stood stock still, staring at it, as the ants scurried about their business at his feet. Then he knelt down and dropped the snake on the hill.

'Eat that you miserable bastards . . .'

In a split second the snake's carcass came alive as the ants swarmed over it from head to tail. Jack squatted back on his ankles to watch, splotches of sweat darkening the dirt beside him. He was too hot. It was too fucking hot. He tore the pyjama top open and ripped it from his back. No good. He was still too hot. The sun was burning him alive. He stood up and wrenched the pyjama pants from his legs, tearing them to rags. The sweat was flooding off him now, running down into his boots. He fell back in the dirt and pulled them off, hurling them away as far as he could. Still no good. He was too hot. Too hot. He was melting. He felt he was melting away. He had to keep moving. He stood up and looked back at the house. No. Not that way. Mustn't be that way. He turned and staggered off in the opposite direction. Stark naked, the earth scorching his feet, he pitched forward another quarter of a mile before he started to wander in aimless circles. He tried to stare straight into the sun. The fireball was mocking him, damning him.

'Mongrel bastard . . . Filthy rotten mongrel bastard . . . Go down you bastard . . . Go down . . . Go down . . .'

He thought he was screaming but it was barely a croak. His mouth was full of burning sand.

\* \* \*

Long after the Brisbane train carried Jack away the following Monday, Elizabeth and Jim sat on the bench at Longreach station watching the trails of smoke catch in the wind to fray and disappear in the distance. In the last days at his bedside, this morning as they kissed him goodbye, they had fought hard to deal with the total lack of recognition in his eyes. Once or twice at the hospital he had suddenly gripped their hands as if he remembered and Michael Hawker told Elizabeth he had woken one night and asked for her by name. It wasn't much. But it was something to hold onto until they saw him again.

That afternoon they went to see Will Mackenzie. He was shocked to the core by what had happened. He bore his share of guilt. Though she knew the bank's actions had certainly not helped matters, Elizabeth quietly put Mackenzie at his ease.

'I know how difficult it's been for you, Will. I do appreciate all you've tried to do. There had to be a limit. That goes without saying.'

Jim was far from convinced but he did his duty. 'Yes, Mr Mackenzie. We understand.'

Elizabeth wanted to outline their plans for his approval and Mackenzie heard her out in silence.

They wanted to close the house and leave Balkenna standing empty. She was going to Brisbane to be with Jack. Jim would look for work on the north coast. He couldn't bear the thought of working for someone else in the district while Balkenna stood idle. Ray Henderson had offered Tim Daley a position on his place and Tim had promised to keep an eye on the house in his spare time.

'Would that be all right?' she asked at the end. 'After the sale? Can we hang on like that for a year or so?'

Before he could answer, Jim spoke up.

'I might be away longer . . . I can send some of my wages back each month. When I get work. I just don't want us to lose the place, Mr Mackenzie.'

Mackenzie smiled and castled his banker's fingers. 'Under our arrangement with Jack we have first option to pick up the lease if he should be forced to sell.'

'Yes. I know that.'

'The sale of equipment will reduce the figure to just over nine thousand. I can live with that for a year . . .'

He turned back to Jim.

'. . . Longer, if we have to. I don't want to see Balkenna go under the hammer any more than you do. Your father served this country with high distinction. He's paid a terrible price and that has always been my yardstick. It will remain so in his absence. I want you to know that, young man.'

Jim felt a flush of relief. Mackenzie turned back to his mother.

'Should the occasion arise, would you have any objection to us using Balkenna to graze any stock we may have in transit? Liquidated stock, purchases for other districts – that sort of thing?'

Elizabeth hesitated a moment. 'Would you want to use the house as well?'

'No. Not at all. The keys can stay with Tim Daley. I have no worries on that score. Any stock would be trucked in, trucked out.'

Still Elizabeth hesitated. She wondered what Jack would do.

Mackenzie gave her a reassuring smile. 'The reason I'm asking is that we normally pay rent on such occasions. It could go directly against the debit if we were to use Balkenna now and then.'

Elizabeth checked with Jim and he gave her a nod.

'Certainly,' she agreed. 'Whatever will help.'

'Good. I'll draw up a simple letter of agreement.'

Elizabeth looked down at her hands. 'I'll be leaving as soon as I can. I have to organise the house . . . Tim's taking the dogs to the Hendersons with him. I'm not really sure. A couple of weeks, I suppose.'

'How long do you think you'll be away?'

'It's impossible to say at this stage. I just don't have any idea.'

'I'd appreciate it if you kept in touch from Brisbane. Not for the bank. For my sake. I'd like to know how he's getting on.'

'Of course,' Elizabeth whispered. 'It is good to know so many people from home are egging him on, wishing him well. Thank you, Will.'

Mackenzie then made an awkward attempt at looking on the bright side. 'Anyway, if the weather boys are correct we're in for another drought. So perhaps it won't be such a bad time to be away.'

'Perhaps not,' said Elizabeth, dropping her eyes. 'Nevertheless . . .'

'Of course, of course.' Mackenzie was momentarily embarrassed.

Jim stood up and took Mackenzie's hand. '*Manu forti*,' he said.

'What?'

He caught his mother's eye. 'With a strong hand.'

# Nine

'Slaughterer, boner or slicer?'

The question set Jim's mind racing. He was sitting in the tiny office of the Australian Meat Industry Employees' Union in Townsville.

'Doesn't matter.'

The Northern District Secretary eyed him with suspicion. 'It matters to me.'

Jim swallowed. He had to get the ticket. Should he try to bluff it or own up?

'Come on, mate. Haven't got all day. Which one are you?'

Jim took the plunge. 'Bit of everything, I suppose. I used to help my father butcher stock. On our place. At Longreach.'

The secretary sat back in his chair. He never smiled if he could help it. 'Is that a fact?'

'Yes. So I could do a bit of everything if you like.'

The secretary leant forward to make a note on the card before him. 'Washer.'

'What's that?'

'What you bloody well are, mate. If you want this ticket.' He passed it over. 'Ask for Norm Davidson when you get there.'

Jim took the card and had a quick look. There was his name all right. Jim Mackay. He was in.

'Thanks very much.'

'Come back and thank me in a month and I'll believe you.'

'It's a deal,' Jim grinned. 'Can't be that rough.'

The secretary cracked a smile. This one he couldn't help. He liked the look of this young bloke.

'It's not all that smooth, either.'

Jim emerged into the brutal glare of Flinders Street.

'Thanks, Hughie,' he said and set off to cross the bridge leading back to Townsville South where he'd managed to get himself a room in a boarding house.

Not a bad place, Townsville. Since his arrival ten days ago

he'd seen a lot of it in the course of looking for a job. He was struck by the beautiful old colonial architecture of Tattersall's Hotel with its arabesques of wrought-iron lacework. That's where Tony Halpin had shouted him a beer and given him the drum about the job at the meatworks. All he needed was a union card and now it was burning a nice big hole in his pocket. The meatworks were on the southern side, at Ross River. He would be able to walk to work and back. He'd checked it out already. He'd been to have a good look at the fleet of professional fishing boats down at the docks and listen in on the harbourside gossip about how the prawns and mackerel were running. The harbour itself never stopped. Ships collected bulk sugar, meat, livestock and the copper, zinc, lead and silver that came by rail from Mount Isa in faraway western Queensland. The waterfront hadn't changed much since the early gold rush days. Its higgledy-piggledy terrace of colonial buildings overlooked the modern-day hustle and bustle, their colonnaded verandahs still providing the same welcome relief from the noonday sun.

Jim lingered a while on the bridge, grateful for the breeze coming off the water, gazing up at the massive outcrop of Castle Hill to the north of the town. The fortress-like cliffs of pink granite, nearly a thousand feet high, frowned down with a primitive glare at the town sprawled at its feet. He decided to make the climb the following weekend. Tony reckoned the view was pretty spectacular. Perhaps he'd come along.

Jim let himself into his room and straightaway sat down with pen and paper to write to his mother. She would be relieved.

Just before they parted in Rockhampton after Christmas, Jim found work as a dairyman for a Dutch farmer. He was a widower. A dogged, unfriendly man and a hard taskmaster. Jim stuck it out for three months, then he wrote to tell his mother he was heading for Townsville where he'd heard lots of work was going. She suggested he come to Brisbane instead. But Jim wasn't ready for the big city. He was finding it hard enough to get along with new people as it was, still fresh from the shelter of Balkenna. After all, there were only about two and a half thousand people in the whole of Longreach district.

Their parting was a harrowing affair. They managed to keep busy until the moment came for Elizabeth to board the train. Then, eighteen years flashed between them and they clung desperately to one another in one last frantic rush of love. Long after the train disappeared from view, Jim stood staring down the thin parallel of silver steel snaking away in the moonlight.

Afterwards, he walked through the streets of Rockhampton to his grandparents' old house and peered over the gate, half expecting to see them. The lights were on, silhouetting the new residents against the curtains. The faces of his grandparents kept flashing into his mind as he watched. Then his mother. Brud. Robin. Tommy. His father. Anna. Tim Daley. Balkenna. Balkenna. Balkenna. The tumult of memories fought in his head and he had to check himself from crying out loud. At that moment of utter loss, Jim's resolution was born.

'I'll hang on to the place, Granddad. Don't you worry about that. For you. For gran. For mum and dad. For everyone. I'll work and work just like you all did. I'll hang on to Balkenna if it kills me . . .'

Jim spent his first week at the meatworks wondering what on earth had hit him. He had never worked so hard in his life. Luckily, Tony Halpin worked as a washer himself and they were able to team up most of the time which helped a bit. Now he saw for himself what happened to all the contented cattle raised for slaughter on places like Balkenna.

The cattle were prodded from one holding yard to the next, each one smaller than the last. Eventually they funnelled into a chute that led into the works, big liquid eyes bulging from their sockets, bawling in terror. Inside, the chute led them to the knocking box where, one at a time, they were stunned by a pneumatic gun that slammed a bolt through the curl on their foreheads. As they dropped to their knees the side of the box fell away to form a ramp that rolled them onto the killing floor where they were hung upside down for the slaughterman to cut their throats. Occasionally, the bolt didn't penetrate to the brain and a beast would roll from the box, stagger to its feet and charge through the building, sending workers flying in all directions.

Their throats blue-black and gaping, the overhead tramway ferried the dead animals down the line to be skinned and gutted. The skin was peeled down to the head and then the head was severed altogether and passed on to a guillotine machine that sliced them in half to get the brain, the tongue and other organs. The offal and tripe fell through a hole to be sorted on the floor below into meat for canning, sausage meat and casings, surgical gut, edible fats, technical greases, dog food, glue, fertilisers, glands for family medicines. The raw pink and white carcasses then trundled along the tramway to be sawn in half and then on to Jim and Tony to be hosed down. Graded and stamped by an inspector, they disappeared into the chilling room.

It was hell. Until he got used to it, Jim spent a lot of time fighting sudden rushes of nausea. Suspended on meathooks the size of anchors, the sickly-sweet-smelling carcasses never stopped coming. Stripped to their shorts, they had to work like mad to get one beast washed and on to the inspectors before the next one bashed into it. The impact set the carcasses swinging and knocked them off their feet in the swill of blood and guts.

Most days, when they finished work, they'd head for the pub to down a couple of beers then dive into Tony's battered Holden and race out to Pallarenda Beach for a swim. Weekends were spent perving on the underdressed girls around town, a few hours at the beach for an even better view, or exploring the Townsville area. Tony knew it well. Originally from Brisbane, he'd been at the works for a year before Jim showed up. He took him on long hikes through the spectacular eucalyptus and rainforest on the upper reaches of Alligator Creek. Sometimes they caught the boat out to Magnetic Island and spent a day exploring its rugged, secluded bays. Or they might spend a weekend between the beach and the common land on the northern tip of Cape Pallarenda that teemed with Pacific birdlife. Another bloke at work had a boat and a couple of times he took them snorkelling on John Brewer reef. There, Jim saw for himself the wonders his mother had so often told him about. Listening to her in the wilderness of the central west he'd found it hard to picture. Now, his lungs pounding, his heart booming in his ears, it took his breath away.

His correspondence with Anna had dwindled to a trickle. The passionate exchanges during the months at Rockhampton that had kept their relationship alive over the intimidating distance between gradually lost their heart. Finally he plucked up the courage to tell her she shouldn't feel bound as he was so far away and had no real idea when he'd be back. If she found someone else, he'd understand. She wrote back to say she already had. A young grazier from the Jundah district. They were thinking of getting engaged. So that was that. It stung a bit at first but it set him free to do more than just ogle the girl in the florist shop.

But Jim was getting nowhere. After six months of hard yakker, he'd only managed to save forty-two pounds. He left the two on deposit and forwarded the forty to Mr Mackenzie with his very best wishes and high hopes of increasing the amount next time. It was a drop in the bucket but it was something. It brought him face to face with his first real moments of doubt. He had a mountain to climb to save Balkenna and he still didn't know where to begin. He had toyed with the idea of racing down to Brisbane to see his father and spend Christmas with his mother. No way, he decided. He'd bank the money instead and knock Saturday nights at the pictures on the head as well. With renewed resolve, he knuckled down to his job and ploughed on until a week before Christmas when he lost it altogether.

For weeks, Tony had put up with Don Roper. For some unknown reason this bloke really had it in for him. Don Roper seemed to think Tony was a bit gutless and he took every chance he got to lay it on with a trowel. He jeered and sneered until Tony couldn't take it any longer and told him to get well and truly knotted. It was Jim's bad luck that Tony chose the middle of the afternoon shift to throw the first punch. Everyone downed tools to watch and the assembly line was thrown into chaos as carcass thumped into carcass until they had to throw the switch and stop the tramway altogether.

Roper was a mean and dirty fighter and Tony was getting the worst of it. A big left hook slammed into his face and he went down. Roper leapt on him, dragged him to his feet, shoved his head inside a half-gutted carcass and held him there, bringing his knee up between Tony's legs from behind and screaming every foul abuse under the sun. Tony came out gulping for air only to get another punch in the face and go down again. Roper started putting in the boot. Jim grabbed Roper's skinning knife off the floor, barrelled into him, shoved Tony out of the way and shook the knife in Roper's face. Roper just grinned and gave him a finger. Jim ditched the knife and beat Don Roper to a pulp. It was the first real serious fight of his life and he was amazed at the strength his fury gave him. He took a bit of hammer but Roper took more than he could stomach. They had to carry him out.

They appealed to the union rep but there was nothing he could do. They started it and they must take the punishment. It turned out the rep was a mate of Roper's. But there was nothing he could do to help big Don either. The three of them were out on their ear.

Jim and Tony retired to the pub to lick their wounds.

'What a bastard,' Tony grumbled. 'What a filthy rotten mother of a bastard.'

Jim couldn't agree more. He downed half his schooner at one gulp. He was smarting all over and his eyebrow was blowing up like a balloon.

'Jesus. You didn't half give it to him though. Where'd you learn to fight like that?'

'Dunno really. It just sort of came to me on the spur of the moment.'

'Well, you're a bloody bottler. Down that and have a dozen on me.'

After a couple more, things didn't look so bad.

'Have you ever been to Isa?' Jim asked.

'Yeah. Last year. Worked there for three months.'

'What's it like?'

'The money's good but it takes another three months to cough up all the dirt out of your lungs.'

'What do you reckon about going back?'

Tony shook his head. 'No way in the world.'

'Fancy a job in the fresh air?' The question came from the man at the bar beside them. His whisky eyes stared out from underneath an ancient tennis hat.

'What's that then?'

'Fishing. I need one crew.'

Tony threw up his hands in horror. 'Not me, mate. Not a bloody chance.'

The man shoved out his hand. 'Barry Baldman. And no jokes . . .' He lifted the hat to show off a full head of curly silver-grey hair. 'I've heard the bloody lot.'

Jim shook his hand. 'What's the pay?'

'Ten quid a week and found. Bunk and grub.'

'How long for?'

'Long as it takes. Three weeks. Six. Depends on the bloody fish, doesn't it?'

Jim did some quick calculations. He'd been on eleven at the meatworks. A good whack of that had gone on food and board and the girl in the florist's shop. Out of harm's way he could save a lot.

'What about the next time? Would I get to go again?'

'If you're any good.'

'I've never been to sea,' he admitted. No sense in trying to pull the wool. Might as well start with a clean slate.

'Don't know what you're missing, mate.'

Jim glanced at Tony but he just raised his eyes to heaven. Jim stuck out his hand. 'I reckon I'll give it a go, Mr Baldman.'

Baldman cracked a grin. 'Good on you. I'm at Ross River. Know where that is?'

'Yeah. I live out that way.'

'I'm on the far side of the pier. Third boat from the end.'

'What's she called?'

'Kingfisher.'

'Gee!' said Tony. 'That's original.'

Baldman glared at him. 'Called that when I bought it. Bad luck to change a boat's name. But then a man of your experience'd know a thing like that.'

'Don't know what you've let yourself in for,' Tony said when Baldman had gone. 'You're mad.'

'It's only three weeks. I can give it a go for that. Lucky to hit on him after today's effort.'

'Reckon I'll head back to Brizzie.' Tony rubbed his sore ribs. 'Had a bellyful of the north for a while. I can have a nice bludge at my parents' over Christmas.'

Jim felt a pang of regret. He wouldn't mind doing the same. It would be fun to hitch down with Tony. He'd have someone to show him around.

'That doesn't sound too bad . . .' But he didn't want to go on with it. He dug up a big, battered grin. 'I'll look you up if I ever get down there.'

'I should bloody well hope so.' Tony shoved the next schooner at Jim's elbow. 'Come on. Let's get full as googs and leak all the way home.'

Boxing Day was clear and bright. Jim found himself twenty miles out, trawling for mackerel on a gentle rolling swell. And he was beginning to discover, like many crewmen before him, that a reasonable, level-headed skipper on land can turn into a raging bull of a tyrant out at sea. As far as Baldman was concerned, Jim was useless as the day is long and he wasn't worth ten bob, let alone ten quid.

'You could give us a chance to get the hang of it,' he protested.

But Baldman had all the bland arrogance of a man who's

been doing something his whole life long and just can't understand why anyone else can't get it right first go.

By the end of the week he'd changed his tune, but Jim hadn't. The actual work wasn't so bad but his sea-legs never grew. The constant rolling motion, the claustrophobia of the little trawler, the smell of oil and petrol all had him feeling pretty filthy most of the time. Baldman insisted on frying up bacon and eggs every morning and Jim would have to make himself scarce until breakfast was over to keep from throwing up. His own diet consisted mainly of bread. Bread and honey. Bread and cheese. Bread and jam. Bread and Vegemite. Whichever seemed the best bet to stay in one place in his stomach, washed down by endless cups of tea.

The fishing was good. They were hauling them in hand over fist. *Kingfisher* trailed four lines, each with a silver spoon-shaped lure. When the mackerel were up, the lines were slightly leaded to trail just an inch or two under the surface, and the strikes were easy to spot. If the fish went deeper, they added lead. The lines were attached to the stern by double layers of rubber cut from old truck inner tubes. When they stretched you knew you had a strike down deep. The trick was to get the mackerel off the lure, scaled and gutted and into the ice boxes before you could say fish-and-chips. Jim's initial lack of speed in this department had been the main cause of Baldman's original griping. But he was getting the hang of it. The less time he spent down below, the better he liked it. He couldn't wait to get topside again into the fresh air. The fish went into boxes of crushed ice they got from big blocks in the main icebox and smashed to smithereens on the spot.

Baldman had a good supply of magazines and old newspapers on board and even though it was tempting fate to read for any length of time, Jim dipped into them to pass the early evening hours or when a rising swell made sleep impossible. One night, he came across a full-page article in the *Courier Mail* about the Queensland shearers' strike that had begun at the end of November. The Industrial Court had called for a ten per cent cut in their wages. The Australian Workers' Union defied the decision and found themselves at loggerheads with the United Graziers' Association. It was a bitter dispute that would drag on for nine months. Jim read the story from beginning to end. It brought back visions of Balkenna and the shearers he'd known there. It conjured up visions of another sea, with different horizons. Seas of rolling grasslands, horizons broken only by the stark silhouette of a solitary windmill. That night it was home-sickness that broke the banks of unconsciousness to haunt his restless and disjointed sleep as the ocean slapped *Kingfisher*'s side just inches from his head.

In two and a half weeks they were full up and Baldman turned the boat southwest for the run back to Townsville. He was in a good mood. Not only a good catch, they'd lost only two lines to the reef. Last time out he'd lost seven.

They arrived early the following morning and Jim waited until they'd finished unloading before he told Baldman one trip had convinced him he was a born-again landlubber. If he ever went to sea again, it would be on the *Queen Mary*. Baldman took it well.

'Suit yourself. Let's get up to the bank for your cash. I guess you were worth it after all.'

Money in his pocket, just as he was turning away, the old salt produced another quid and shoved it in his shirt pocket.

'Have one on me and mind how you go.'

Jim fished it out and tried to hand it back.

'It's a bonus, you half-wit. Don't bloody deserve it, mind you.'

Jim watched him thread his way through the crowd.

'Not such a bad old bastard after all,' he thought.

There were two letters from his mother and he read them quickly. The news of his father was the same. No significant change for better or worse. Elizabeth had written to Mr Mackenzie to advise him their absence would be longer than expected. The bank was finding plenty of use for Balkenna's grazing. The income, plus Ray Henderson's rent for the river blocks, meant they could persevere with the situation. Mackenzie added a p.s. thanking Jim for his forty quid.

Next day he was on his way. First he went to the station to check the schedules and deposit his suitcase. Then he went to the post office to post a long letter to Elizabeth. He closed his account with a flourish. He wanted them to know he would continue using the same bank where he was headed. They didn't seem to give two hoots and he wished he hadn't bothered. Then he went to the pub for a couple of sandwiches and a beer before heading for the florist's shop to meet Marjorie after work.

He took her to dinner at Theo the Greek's. They'd both known all along there was a clock running. They'd made no promises. But it was a bit sad all the same. They'd had fun together and they'd miss each other.

Marjorie offered to see if her parents would let him spend the night on their couch but Jim declined. He'd only met them once and he thought it was a bit inappropriate under the circumstances. The wine was like petrol. The streets were almost deserted by the time Jim walked her home. When the time came, she planted one last kiss on his cheek and hurried up the path.

Next day, as the train sped towards a longed-for view of the western plains, Jim found himself tapping the windowsill and humming a song under his breath. It took a while to place it. Then he remembered. It was an old one Fred Paterson had sung them during his last stay at Balkenna. They'd all joined in on the chorus. Bit by bit, the fragments came back until he was able to juggle them into the right order. He hunched down to watch the passing landscape and sang it over in his mind.

> So, blow you winds, heigh ho,
> It's digging I will go,
> I'll stay down south no more, my boys,
> So let the music play.
> In spite of all I'm told,
> I'm off in search of gold,
> And makin' a push for that new rush
> A thousand miles away.

He was on his way to Cloncurry. From there he would make the connection to the Isa.

# Ten

Deep in the bowels of the earth, an electric train trundled along a single trackway, towing a string of box trucks filled to overflowing with copper ore on its way to the jaw crusher. In its wake, a group of miners struggled along the tunnel.

They walked in silence, each lost in thought, buried alive in their weird underworld of clanging metal and harsh light. At the foot of the shaft they filed into the cage. As the hydraulics whinged and the multi-rope friction winders began the 3,500 foot pull to ground level, still nobody spoke. Heads back, eyes uplifted, the atmosphere was like you get on board a plane coming in to land after a long flight. So far, so good. Don't let anything go wrong now. It's nearly over. Except they would be back down here again tomorrow, and the day after that, and the day after that.

The cage came to a slow, grinding halt inside the headframe of the shaft and sprang its doors. The miners pushed forward now, eager to be on their way to the pubs, lodgings, homes. Safety helmets perched on the backs of their heads, set at rakish angles or already off, their boisterous humour returned in a babble of tongues as they left the shaft head.

Jim strode away in the company of a tall middle-aged man, built to last. His name was Jock Donnelly and Jim was more than happy to have him as his landlord. He'd spent nearly three months in one of the company hostels for single men before finding bed and board with the Donnellys. Although they had a room to spare, they'd not really intended to let it until Jock told his wife about this young bloke from Longreach who was new on the job and looked as if he could do with a bit of home life. When they offered him the room, Jim jumped at it. Now, seven months later, he was one of the family.

It had been Jock who'd solved a big problem that caught up with Jim a few days after he moved in. Something he'd given absolutely no thought to at all until a letter that had chased him through Balkenna, the bank, Rockhampton and Townsville finally caught up. It was his call-up for National Service training. On Jock's advice, he managed to get it deferred for two years on the strength of his father's illness. He had another fourteen months on good money to go, more than double he'd been getting at the meatworks in Townsville. He'd definitely made the right move and his AMIEU ticket had paved the way for union membership at the Mount Isa mines.

Jim and Jock joined the throng taking long, thirsty pulls from their schooners to wash the day's grit from dusty throats.

'So, Mackay. How was it?'

'Still bloody terrifying,' Jim admitted. 'I guess I'll get used to it some time.'

'Could still get you into the smelter,' Jock said. 'Or on a fork lift, maybe. Loading the wagons for Townsville.'

'I'll stick it out if I can. The money's better.'

'True,' Jock agreed, grinning back. 'Still not enough in my book. We earn every penny of it and then some . . .'

The bar was jammed full of them. From all over Australia and half the countries of the world. Jock told him there were sixty different nationalities in Isa. Raucous, clubby, matey, these were the worker ants who burrowed underground to gather, inch by inch, grain by grain, the silver, lead, zinc and copper payload from one of the richest and most highly mechanised mines in the world. The beer was doing its job, putting smiles on tired faces, creasing others with gales of laughter, adding furrows of concentration to the more serious business.

It had all begun in 1923 when a prospector by the name of John Campbell Miles found a huge outcrop of oxidised ore. He chipped away some samples and sent them to Cloncurry, where they were found to contain a high content of silver and lead. Miles immediately pegged out a couple of leases and named them Mount Isa. Jock reckoned he was thinking of the Mount Ida Goldmine in Western Australian when he chose the name. The news spread like wild fire and the gougers came in droves. They lived in shelters made from boughs, flattened fuel drums, hessian sacks and broken packing cases. By 1925, when Mount Isa Mines took over the lot, there were over five hundred leases. Jim took another swig of beer.

'Good on him,' he thought, in silent toast.

In the distance, the surrounding circle of ironstone hills

covered in sparse, stunted spinifex danced in the crimson sunset. Some chunks of lead-coloured clouds rolled away before the Selwyn Ranges to the south, a backdrop for the wheeling flocks of pink and grey galahs squawking their way home. Isa's industrial sprawl lay before him, the Leichhardt River meandering through the regimented lines of company houses, hostels, private homes, shops and the governing shapes of the mining complex.

'Not a bad old dump, eh?' said Jock as he joined Jim on the verandah.

'Some of the blokes were talking about Mary Kathleen,' said Jim. 'You were here when all that started, weren't you?'

'Yep. Been here since 'fifty. Two Finnish blokes found the first lot. Just twenty miles north of here. Town went bananas the day the news leaked out. Epidemic it was. Uranium fever. You couldn't buy a geiger counter for love or money. They reckoned the area actually lit up at night it was so charged. Glowing Hills, they called it. The roads were jammed with uranium hunters for months. Then these two other blokes found a whole mountain of it at Kathleen.'

'Didn't you want to get in on it yourself?'

'Not for a minute. Against my grain, that lot.'

'How come?'

'Just don't like the stuff. Do more harm than good in the long run. Anyway, the word's out already it'll be a short-lived boom.'

'They're spending a fortune on the town, they reckon. Hospitals, cinemas, the lot.'

'Yep. But there's a big difference. Here, we can cut the pie lots of different ways. There, it's uranium or bust. If the market goes, then it's 'bye 'bye Mary Kathleen.' Jock drained his glass. 'Stick to it here, Jim. They're playing with fire up there. Come on, down that and let's push on.' He stood and adopted a mock-lecturer's pose, making Jim laugh with its accompanying pronouncement.

'. . . And, so, we understand man to be an animal conditioned by reflex. Come off his work, he craves liquid refreshment. Come off the grog, he craves nourishment. Come off the feed, he craves a cuddle. Come off the job, he craves a sleep. Come off the snooze, he craves a lie-in . . . and so on and so on and so on. Right now I could eat a horse.'

Next day, back in the hole, Jim flattened himself against the

103

rockface as a monster diesel-powered loader rumbled past with a scoop full of jagged busted rock. Up at the tunnel head the drilling jumbo was smashing its way forward like a demented praying mantis. Jim joined the knot of men clearing the smaller rock falls from the path of the jumbo's caterpillar tracks as it attacked the rockface. In next to no time, Jim's face was covered in dust-stained sweat. Across the tunnel, a German he knew was tussling with a particularly large ugly rock. He just managed to get it to the side wall in time. He stood back and gave it a significant finger, to Jim's amusement. The German gave Jim a wink as he bent to heave on the next lot. Every day was like every other day.

In September that year, there was a lot of talk in the work canteen about the new wonder of the age. Australia had its first TV station in Sydney and the papers were full of photos of crowds in the street watching the black-and-white transmissions in shop windows. In the forgotten latitudes of north-western Queensland it all seemed a long way off. It would be another eighteen months before the state had its own stations broadcasting from Brisbane.

In November and December, Jim and the Donnellys spent every night huddled round the radio listening to the Olympic Games in faraway Melbourne, barracking like mad for swimmers Dawn Fraser, Lorraine Crapp, Murray Rose and the Henricks kids and, loudest of all, for the golden girl from Lithgow, Betty Cuthbert, who won the 100 and the 200 metres and then another gold in the last leg of the 4 x 100 relay. Every day the town was buzzing with the latest news and the off-course bookies were going hell for leather.

By June the following year Jim had managed to send £243.00 to the bank in Longreach. He was pleased with what he'd managed to save but he added a note to Will Mackenzie saying how dismayed he was not to be able to send more. He received a businesslike answer expressing the bank's appreciation of his contributions and hopes that he would find himself able to continue making them. There was a personal postscript: 'Keep up the good work. Every penny counts. Regards. W. Mackenzie.'

A steady flow of letters from his mother kept him up to date. According to her reports, Jack was making good ground though still a long way from being discharged. Elizabeth had found work as a private tutor to a number of families whose children were a bit backward with their schoolwork. She was happy to be doing something she enjoyed to occupy her time and glad of the extra income. She filled her letters with long, detailed descriptions of the plays and films she'd seen, and the new friends she'd made in the Bayside area where she was living. Try as she might, she couldn't always hide the pain and isolation which Jim read between the lines. Sometimes he would be almost overwhelmed by the desire to pack it in, head for Balkenna and call her up and tell her to come home. Irrespective of his father's condition, in these moments of longing he figured they'd manage somehow or other. He maintained a regular correspondence with Tim Daley who kept him informed about the state of the place, the bank's regular use of Balkenna's pastures despite spells of severe drought. He filled him in on bits and pieces of district gossip. Anna Henderson had married her young grazier from Jundah and they were expecting their first child.

A letter from Tim was waiting for him on his return from work one Friday evening. In the course of relaying the latest news, Tim inadvertently mentioned how lonely it felt sometimes when he went to check the place over, and approached the house knowing there was nobody inside. The image burst a dam in Jim and took him on a long, nostalgic journey of the mind through every nook and cranny of the place. That Friday night, sleep wouldn't come. For the first time in his life, he set out quite deliberately to get drunk. He got home so blotto Maureen and Jock had to carry him to his room to sleep it off.

Jim would sometimes babysit for Jock and Maureen when they went out for a night on the town. They had two kids. George was ten and Judy was five. Or five and a half, as she liked to say. One night when they were safely tucked up in bed, he settled down with the week's papers to catch up on the news. Albert Namitjira, Australia's most famous Aboriginal artist, had been gaoled for six months with hard labour for supplying liquor to Aboriginal friends in his camp. Controversy was raging over the sentence, highlighting not only the liquor laws but all the other anomalies in white Australia's attitude to the country's indigenous people. On the same page was a smaller related article noting the progress of the Federal Council for the Advancement of Aborigines and Torres Strait Islanders that had been formed the previous year. It listed various Queensland delegates who attended a recent conference in

Canberra. One name made Jim sit up in his chair. He double-checked. The age given was twenty. It must be him. Jim stared and stared at the page. Then he spoke the name out loud to himself.

'Dougie Douglas . . . How amazing.'

He quickly culled the other papers and found two more articles on Namitjira and the Aboriginal question. Jim spent the rest of the evening until Jock and Maureen returned thinking about his boyhood days with Tommy and Dougie. For the first time it dawned on him why Tommy had so revered his grandfather, and how Angus's attitude had been something a long way out of the ordinary. It gave him a deeper appreciation of Tommy's conscientious dedication to the job of running Balkenna in his father's absence during the war. It also made him realise he was developing a strong distaste for self-serving sectarian political argument, no matter which side of the fence. As far as he could see, Namitjira was in gaol simply for following an age-old custom of his own people, the communal sharing of food and possessions.

Jim got on well with the Donnelly kids and they made him realise he was quite good with children. It was a gift he figured he probably got from his mother. Sometimes they led him to imagine some distant day when he might have kids of his own. But that day would have to wait. Such thoughts always took second place to his immediate goal: the resurrection of Balkenna.

'Time for all the rest of it later,' he told himself. But he had to admit he quite liked the idea.

His months in Mount Isa produced no close romantic attachment. He went to a few of the local dances and whirled the night away with passing crumpet. Now and then he took a girl to the pictures, but that was where it ended. At least as far as he was concerned. He wryly admitted to himself that he'd become a bit of a tightwad. Girlfriends cost money and he wanted to save every penny he could in the time available to him in this boom town. Jock and Maureen used to tease him about it. But they understood his motives. They'd been battlers their whole lives long and they felt an instinctive respect for this nineteen-year-old who could impose his own financial restraints and self-discipline in order to achieve an ambitious goal.

On many weekend family excursions, the Donnellys always included Jim. They took him for swimming picnics to Lake

Moondarra, twelve miles north of Isa. Once they went on all the way to Camooweal so he could always say he'd been to Queensland's most westerly town, right on the Northern Territory line. Another time they visited the spot west of Cloncurry where Burke and Wills crossed the Corella River in January 1861, on their fateful attempt to cross the continent from south to north. Jim knew the story of the four-man party that made it to the Gulf of Carpentaria. Only a youngster named King survived the return journey that ended in one of the most tragic twists of fate in the history of exploration. After waiting an extra month for Burke and Wills' return, the base camp party at Cooper's Creek had packed up and headed south a mere nine and a half hours before Burke, Wills and King staggered in to discover they'd left that very same day. The fourth man, Gray, had already died. Burke and Wills died at Cooper's Creek; King was sheltered and kept alive by Aborigines until he was found. As Jim stood staring at the memorial marking the spot where they'd crossed the river, he reflected that this pitiless land that had taken their lives had not changed a skerrick. Without water, you could die of thirst in twenty-four hours while mirages of shimmering lakes mocked you from every horizon.

Another weekend was spent exploring the sandstone gorges in the Selwyn Ranges to see rock paintings left behind by the Kalkadoon tribe who inhabited the area for thousands of years before the arrival of European settlers. The Kalkadoons had probably been the most aggressive tribe in Australia and defined their territorial perimeters with the mark of an emu's foot. Jim and the Donnellys saw many of them that weekend. When their spears ran out in the final battle for their land, the Kalkadoons threw rocks and earth at the oncoming ranks of carbines. They fought to the last man. As he stood staring at the paintings they left behind, Jim smiled. He remembered the fright he and Dougie got that long-ago Balkenna day looking at paintings like this in Tommy's secret place.

Their weirdest and funniest time together came one Saturday night twelve miles east of a place called Boulia where they were taking it in turns to get some sleep bent double in the back of Jock's Ford. They'd parked on the site of the old Min Min Hotel. Before it burned down in 1918, the Min Min had been a depot for drovers on the local stock route. Now it was even more famous for the so-called Min Min Light. There was a graveyard in the nearby sandhills and the mysterious light made its first appearance there in 1926, scaring a local stockman half to death and following him all the way back to Boulia. Since then thousands of people had witnessed its spooky manifestation, shining as big and as bright as a headlight. Jock and Jim had no such luck. But they had a right old time of it frightening the wits out of one another, daring each other to walk up to the graveyard and back alone. Jim could never remember holding his breath for so long at a time in his life, especially when he nearly trod on a Woma python out on some starlit quest of its own.

Apart from the mining industry, Mount Isa also provided a vital cattle-trucking service for the surrounding pastoral districts. Maureen's brother was the manager of a local firm and, through him, Jim was able to keep his hand in working stock on the local holding paddocks. Maureen reckoned he should be getting a few quid on top but Jim was grateful for the chance to be doing what he loved best. When the annual rodeo rolled round in August he put his name down for the buckjumping.

The rodeo was the big day of the year in Isa, and the town buzzed with excitement as the world and his wife poured in from the outlying districts to take part. Jim spent the Saturday morning taking George and Judy through the whirligig of sideshows and stalls out at the showgrounds at Kalkadoon Park. George liked the look of the Wall of Death. As they approached, a very pretty girl in full motorcycle rig saw them coming.

'Come on, handsome. It's the greatest show in town. Bring your kids in.'

She was very pushy, very sexy and already she had her hand on Jim's arm, pulling him in the direction of the ticket box. He had always been half in love with these sideshow girls who followed what he could only imagine must be such a reckless, gypsy life. Her grip was making him tingle with pleasure and he found himself blushing beetroot.

'They're not mine, they're my friend's kids . . .'

She gave him a knowing pout and a saucy wink. 'I've heard that one before, lover.'

She held on until he'd paid up then gave him a pat on the back. Another punter hooked and landed.

'Enjoy the show, handsome,' she teased before launching her cleavage at a stringbean drover who was staring at her like he'd just had a glimpse of heaven.

'Your ears have gone all red,' said Judy as they climbed the steps to the viewing platform.

'I'm a bit hot.'

'Why did that girl wink at you like that?'

'She was flirting,' George declared flatly.

'What's that mean?' she asked.

'She wanted to kiss him,' George explained, pleased as punch.

'Tie a knot in it, you two. We'll miss the show if you don't stop talking.'

But he couldn't help glancing back down at the girl below. He wouldn't mind giving her a kiss or two, for a start.

That afternoon he drew a distinctly mad-looking brumby. He eased himself down onto its back in the chute with some trepidation.

'Number eleven,' boomed the PA system. 'Jim Mackay on the Brown Bomber.'

The horse was frantically banging him against the sides of the chute even before the gate opened. When it sprung, it bolted across the arena in a lightning series of humping pig-roots that had the base of his spine numb after the first two and his legs flaying the air like pistons to keep his balance. He gripped the surcingle for all he was worth and kept his eyes glued on the pivoting point at the base of the Bomber's neck. As the shrieks of delight and bellows of encouragement echoed around the ground, Jim stuck on for an eight-second count before the horse sent him flying through the air and screwballed away, snorting in fury. As the flank riders raced to gather it in, Jim hauled himself slowly to his feet, dusted off and limped gingerly back to the chutes, wincing a bit from the pummelling he'd taken. The PA announced his time. He was lying third with six riders still to come.

'What a coot!' roared Jock, grinning from ear to ear.

Jim pulled a face and rubbed his bum. 'Tick on the brain, for sure.'

'Not too many miners can ride like that,' Maureen chipped in. 'Well done.'

'Thanks,' said Jim. 'I had a good teacher, bloke called Tommy Douglas. Used to work for my father.'

At the end of the day no other rider had overtaken him and the Balkenna kitty was twenty-five pounds better off. That night, stiff as a board, he slept like a log.

On the morning of 3 January, 1958, Jim stood at the departure gate of Mount Isa airport, still feeling the aftereffects of the wildest New Year's Eve he'd ever had and finding it difficult to say goodbye. Passengers pushed past them heading for the DC-3 on the tarmac. Time was up. He had to go.

Jock suddenly pulled an envelope from his pocket. 'Here you go, mate. A few of the crew tossed this lot in the hat, in lieu of a long-service bonus.'

Five ten-pound notes. Jim swallowed, shook his head and attempted to hand it back. 'I can't take that, Jock. It's too much. Tell them thanks but . . .'

Jock quickly silenced any further argument by reaching out to tweak his nose, push the envelope in his pocket and shove him through the gate.

'Shut your trap and hurry up or you'll miss the bus.'

'Plane, Dad. It's a plane,' Judy corrected in her usual fashion.

Jock gave her a mock glare. 'I'm well aware of that, pint-size. It's a figure of speech.'

'Thank them for me,' Jim said to Jock. He quickly scanned their faces, one by one. 'Thanks. For everything.'

'It's been a pleasure, Jim,' Maureen assured him. 'Best of luck.'

He managed to catch one last fleeting glimpse of their upturned faces as the plane revved up and turned away. Jim had hardly slept a wink the night before, tossing in restless anticipation of this, his first plane ride. Now, as the pilot gave the engines full throttle, he gripped the arms of his seat. The plane shook from head to tail. When he felt the brakes give and it began to hurtle down the runway, Jim glued his eyes to the back of the seat in front of him, not daring to look out of the window until some time after it lifted its nose and climbed into the blistering heat of a clear blue day. When he finally did, he was enthralled by the limitless view of northwestern Queensland sweeping to the far horizons below.

His apprehension returned as they came into Winton. The ground seemed to be coming up a bit too quick. The plane bounced a couple of times, screamed down the runway, and came to a shuddering halt. Jim let go a sigh of relief and smiled at his fright. As one or two passengers disembarked and new arrivals filed on, he remained in his seat. He was so close. Longreach was a short hundred miles or so to the southeast. He suddenly realised they would probably fly right over it on the way to Charleville. He should have let Tim know. He could have got up on the roof and waved a sheet. The grin died on his face as he wondered how he'd feel if he did manage to catch a glimpse of the place.

His dreams of Balkenna were interrupted by the arrival of a tall man with salt and pepper hair checking numbers. Dressed in an expensive suit and clutching a wide-brimmed Akubra, he checked the number of the vacant seat beside Jim against the ticket in his hand. Jim uncrossed his legs and straightened.

'Sorry,' the man grinned.

'Not at all.'

The man removed his coat, plonked into the seat and immediately began loosening his tie.

'Brisbane here we come,' he muttered.

'Yeah. Me, too.' Jim turned to stare out of the window as the door banged shut and the engines revved again.

# Eleven

He had been a bit taken aback at first. Elizabeth seemed to have aged more than the two years that had passed since he'd put her on the train in Rockhampton. For her part, Elizabeth had been equally surprised by the mature young man who rushed through the arrivals gate to sweep her off her feet and crush her in his arms. No doubt about it. Her boy was a full-grown man. And, she noted with unreserved motherly pride, he was every bit as handsome as his father.

That night she took him out to a wonderful Italian restaurant she'd found in a quaint little weatherboard in the middle of a suburban street. It had a fixed menu on different nights that was always headed 'special'. 'Fantastic' would have been nearer the mark. They had *pollo in porchetta* and Jim had never tasted anything quite so delicious in his life. With Tuscan bean soup to start, Tuscan pudding to finish, helped along by a couple of carafes of white wine, mother and son caught up with each other again.

They were up until two in the morning. Jim had the uncomfortable feeling his mother was holding something back about his father, but he let it pass when she told him she'd arranged a visit on Jim's birthday in three days' time. By the time she made up his bed on the couch, Jim was aching with tiredness. Elizabeth had to tiptoe round the flat all the following morning. He hardly moved until noon.

They spent the next day sightseeing. It was school holidays, so Elizabeth was able to spend all her time showing Jim the city that had become her home for two years. They crammed in as much as they could. He didn't have much time. His National Service training began the day after his birthday.

Jim tried Tony Halpin's number, hoping they might be able to meet up for a yarn. But Mrs Halpin told him Tony was down in Byron Bay for a bit of a holiday. He had landed on his feet though. Starting from scratch, Tony sold sports goods door-to-door and he was now the proud owner of his own shop. Jim scribbled down the address and they managed to track it down. Big loud red and yellow letters on the window read: 'Good-On-You-Sport'. Smaller letters in the bottom right-hand corner pronounced Tony Halpin to be his own boss. Jim was pleased as punch for him and slid a note under the door to let him know he'd been there for a look-see.

Elizabeth produced a bottle of champagne for his twenty-first birthday breakfast. She stood by his chair as he opened his present. He unwrapped a beautiful pair of oval-shaped, twenty-one-carat gold cuff links engraved with his initials.

'Mum, you shouldn't have. They must have cost a fortune.'

'Nonsense,' she chuckled. 'You're only twenty-one once.' Then, as she always did, she ruffled his hair. 'It's a big day for me, too, you know. My boy's become a man.'

Jim leapt up and held her in a long, loving embrace, so tight she could hardly breathe. She managed to gently push him off and hold him at arm's length. She gazed into his face, her eyes dancing with pride.

'And a big hulking brute of a thing he is, too. Come on. Let's have some more of that champagne.'

Jim topped them up, planted a kiss on her cheek, and raised his glass.

'Thanks,' he grinned. 'And thanks for looking after me all these years.'

'It wasn't so hard,' she grinned back. 'You were always pretty good at looking after yourself.' She raised her glass. 'Happy birthday, Jimbo.'

Jim was proudly wearing the cuff links later that morning when they set off for the hospital.

Jack Mackay was sitting in a deck chair under an enormous Moreton Bay fig. Elizabeth leaned over to give him a kiss.

'Look who's here,' she said quietly.

'Hello, Dad.'

Jack stared up at him for an eternity. For one awful moment Jim thought he didn't know who he was. But Jack was just sizing him up, taking him in. Now his face creased with pleasure and he offered his hand.

'Hello, Jim. Grown a bit, haven't you?'

Jim grinned with relief. 'Just a bit.'

Despite his mother's vague warnings, he was shocked by his father's appearance. All the muscle tone seemed to have gone from his once-strong frame. His skin was pale and blotchy. His cheeks had caved in and they were covered in stubble from a vague attempt to shave. His eyes were hollow. He'd lost a lot of hair. What was left was shot with white.

Jim squatted and dropped his hands on his father's knees. 'How's it going?'

'Not too bad,' said Jack, throwing a mocking wave at the surrounding greenery. 'Living in the lap of luxury, you might say.'

Jim patted his knee. 'Good. I'm glad. It looks good.' His mind was racing for the right words.

'Bloody awful food,' Jack spluttered. He turned to look at Elizabeth. 'What's for lunch?'

She offered a gentle reminder. 'Don't forget what day it is.'

It took him a moment. Then he turned back to Jim and wished him a happy birthday.

They spread a rug and she unpacked a hamper of cold chicken with all the trimmings and a bottle of white wine, kept in the freezer until just before they left.

As they got stuck into it, Jim told him about the north and Jack listened attentively, sometimes asking for more detail about one thing or another. He seemed particularly taken by Jim's success at the Isa rodeo and they reminisced about Tommy Douglas's horse-breaking abilities. But now and then, Jack lost the thread and went off on his own. At these moments Jim felt utterly helpless and lost for words until Elizabeth quietly prompted his father back to the subject and gave Jim a guarded nod for him to pick up where he'd left off.

'I met a man from Winton on the way down,' Jim told him. 'On the plane. Athol Ferguson. Have you heard of him?'

Jack shook his head. 'Not that I can remember.'

'He's offered me a boundary-riding job on his property, if I want to take it on. After I've done my training . . .'

He could have bitten his tongue off. They'd agreed not to mention his call-up for National Service. Elizabeth shot him a frantic look but it was too late.

'What training's that?'

Elizabeth quickly took over. 'Jim's off to do his National Service tomorrow,' she told him, as evenly and matter-of-factly as she could.

Jack riveted his eyes on his son. They were so haunted, Jim had to look away.

115

'I should have told you the other day,' Elizabeth continued. 'Sorry. I clean forgot.'

Jack continued staring at Jim , as if he was seeing a ghost. Then he turned to gaze off across the lawns. Jim braced himself but when his father spoke there was a dreamy, faraway note in his voice.

'I drove a mob of sheep through Winton once. When I was about your age. Thirty-four or -five that would have been.'

Jim and Elizabeth snatched a look of relief and, again, she took over. 'I've had another letter from Will. He sends his regards . . .'

'What's he want now?'

'Nothing in particular. Just to let us know everything's all right at home. The country's very dry again, he says. They're only running five hundred head there at the moment, but we've still got some rent coming in.'

'They always want something,' Jack growled. Either he didn't understand the real news or wasn't all that interested.

But Jim had been very relieved when his mother told him about it the day he arrived. He gave her a sly wink. 'They won't even have to take it out of the safe.'

As the afternoon wore on, Jim had to fight hard to keep cheerful. Jack's digressions became more frequent and disjointed. It was like trying to talk to somebody who was talking to somebody else who wasn't there. Now he could see the awful strain his mother had been under, he could recall all the hints of pain and isolation he had read between the lines of her letters, he could understand the sudden ageing that had given him such a shock. As Jack harked back to some long-forgotten incident involving his own father, reliving it in the most minute and vivid detail, Jim excused himself and headed for the visitors' washroom. If there hadn't been two other men there already, he might have burst into tears. He splashed his face liberally with cold water and gathered his wits as well as he could.

Elizabeth was packing up. It was time for Jack to return to his room, time for them to go. Jim folded the rug, his mind racing again for the right words of farewell.

When the moment came, Jack hauled himself unsteadily to his feet and Jim offered his hand. His father took it, gave it a half-hearted shake, then abruptly reached out and wrapped his son in a fierce embrace.

'I'm sorry your number came up, son,' he said. 'I always hoped to God you'd never have to go in.'

'I'll be all right, Dad,' he whispered. 'Don't worry about it. It's only for a few months. I'll be all right, I promise.'

Jack abruptly pulled away, snatched a last look at his son, gave Elizabeth a peck on the cheek, and turned on his heel.

'Thanks for the grub,' he called over his shoulder.

A few yards away he stopped dead in his tracks. He wheeled about and headed back to them, pulling something from his pocket.

'Here, I almost forgot. For your birthday. I got it on my twenty-first.'

Before Jim could speak, Jack patted Elizabeth on the arm and headed off. The late afternoon sun danced of its burnished antique gold. It was the signet ring Jack had worn as long as Jim could remember. He didn't have to check the maroon onyx stone to know what was on it. The same crest as in their Bible at Balkenna. The same motto. *Manu forti.* With a strong hand.

They watched his retreating figure cross the lawns until he disappeared through a door. They studiously avoided looking at one another as Jim put his arm round his mother and steered her towards the front gate. Each knew the other was crying.

That night Elizabeth laid her cards on the table. It was painful, this was their last night together, but it had to be done. He'd seen for himself. It was only right that Jim should know the truth. The latest reports indicated there had been little progress in real terms. Jack was still suffering the aftermath of neurosis and breakdown, sometimes lapsing into deep psychotic traumas that could only be partially controlled by massive sedation which reduced him to a state of helplessness requiring constant attention. The writing was on the wall. They had to face the harsh fact that Jack might not be able to return home for a long, long time, if ever.

At that precise moment, two doctors were holding Jack down with all the force they would muster. A third colleague was desperately trying to get the syringe into his arm.

Ever since he returned to his room, Jack had felt very tired and confused. It had been a near thing. All morning he'd been reminding himself not to forget the ring. Then he damn well nearly forgot. Why were they leaving him in this place? Sometimes he thought he knew but he couldn't fathom it. He was all right most of the time. He knew that. Sometimes he just wanted to sleep and sleep, that was all. They'd make him go to sleep then they'd put him in a chair, make him open his eyes, make him eat. They talked to him like a baby. He hated that. They made him mess himself like a baby. He was tired now. So tired. His mind was a jigsaw. There was a picture. But there was a jagged hole in the middle. He must find the missing piece. He had to know what was in the centre. Where was it? Why couldn't he find it? He searched his memory but he couldn't remember where he'd put it. He was so tired. He turned on his side and closed his eyes.

When he awoke, there were two more people in the room. His father was standing by the door. He looked as if he were about to leave. He was saying something to somebody in the chair by the window. Who was it? He was dressed like a drover. He knew that face. Who was it? The figure leaned forward and light spilled across the face. Oh, yes. It was Jim. It was his son, Jim. He glanced back to the door. His father was crying. Why? What had happened? Tears were running down his body. He was standing in a pool of water. He raised his hand in salute. He was gone. He'd disappeared. Jack glanced back to the chair. Jim was smiling at him. But why did he look so strange? What had happened? The clothes. It was the clothes. Why was he in uniform? Where did he get it? Did I give it to him? Did I give him a uniform? He's all grown up. Why does he have a little boy's head? It doesn't match his body. Jim slid from the chair onto his knees. He was coming towards the bed. It didn't make sense. That little boy's head on a man's body. Perhaps he wasn't seeing it properly. Did I give him the uniform? Ah . . . that's better. The head's growing . . . changing. It's the right shape now. Getting closer and closer. Why was it taking such a long time? The head was much better. Yes. Much better. The face was changing . . . growing up. Jim. Jim. Come and talk to me. The face loomed up. It's not Jim at all. It's someone else. Who is that? Who? Who? His eye. There's something wrong with his eye. Why is his eye like that? I know . . . I know . . . I know who that is . . .

His screams had the medical staff there within minutes.

They were late getting to the station and Elizabeth just had time to buy a couple of magazines and thrust them in Jim's hands as he prepared to board. They'd almost run out of words. Their parting was confused, both putting on a brave face lest the other crack. The train shunted, the carriages did a bump and grind, the whistle blew and 'all aboard' echoed along the platform.

'Look after yourself.'

'And you.'

'I will. I will . . . Quick!'

The train was starting to move. Jim gave her one more kiss that missed, threw his case up and jumped on. He waved and waved until she was swallowed up by the crowd and disappeared.

He dropped a window, rested his arms on the sill and allowed the wind to whip his hair as the Brisbane suburbs flashed by. His father's face seemed to loom at him from every street corner. Try as he might, he couldn't stop seeing his face. He could feel the ring on his finger. He stared at it for a good couple of minutes before balling his fist in response to the legend that was written there.

# Twelve

It was a different train that pulled into Winton at the beginning of August. Jim had enjoyed the Army but he was glad it was over. Though he was required to remain on the Reserve for another five years, there was not much chance he'd have to go in again. Most of all, he'd enjoyed the couple of weeks he spent in Brisbane having a good holiday before getting on with his new job.

Jack's condition remained unchanged. Some days he was smiling, content and lucid. Other days he was like a blank wall. The message was clear: Balkenna was up to Jim. His mother would help, but it was up to him to find the way. He had mixed feelings starting work on a property just a hundred and twenty-five miles northwest as the crow flies of where he'd give everything to be. But he would make the most of it. At least he would be in familiar country and doing what he loved best. He figured he should be able to save a few quid from the generous terms Mr Ferguson had offered.

They'd told him to look out for a dark-green Holden utility vehicle, but it was nowhere in sight. Jim settled back on a station bench and watched the noisy reunions all around as other passengers were picked up and driven away. Twenty minutes later, the place was deserted. There was nothing to do but wait. He gazed out over the roofs of the famous old cattle-trucking town that had given birth to Australia's most famous song.

The words of 'Waltzing Matilda' were written by Banjo Paterson in 1895 while he was staying at Dagworth homestead in Winton district. They were based on a story he heard of events at a place called Combo Waterhole. Dagworth had been owned by a family called Macpherson at the time and their daughter had been playing an old tune called 'Craigielea' on the piano. Banjo wrote the words to fit the tune.

His grandfather told him the story long ago, during the war.

He wished he'd known his grandparents better. His grandfather had been a mine of information about the early outback days. Jim had learnt as much Queensland history from him as he ever did out of his schoolbooks, especially about the early explorers and pioneers. Alexander Kennedy had been a pioneer. In the Cloncurry district. He put up the money to get Qantas off the ground, on condition he could be its first passenger. The company opened its first office in Winton, in 1920: QANTAS stood for Queensland and Northern Territory Aerial Service. The office was moved to Longreach in 1922 and the airline began the first regular passenger and mail service between Cloncurry and Charleville in November that year with the 84-year-old Kennedy on board.

Jim's reverie was interrupted by a spray of gravel.

'Jim Mackay?'

Jim nodded, slung his case in the back of the Holden and climbed in.

'G'day. Bill Tulley. Have a good trip?'

'Not too bad.'

'Sorry I'm late. Cut it a bit fine,' Tulley apologised, slamming the ute into gear and roaring away.

'That's okay. How far we got to go?'

'Forty miles. I've got to pick up some stuff in town on the way out. Fancy a grog?'

'Wouldn't say no.'

An hour later, as they headed out of Winton, Jim was feeling right as rain. As the head stockman, Tulley was his immediate boss and he liked him a lot. He was a tough, direct, no-nonsense sort of bloke with a good sense of humour and a friendly disposition. He sized Jim up pretty smartly in the pub, probing his knowledge of horses and cattle, getting the gist of his background. He was glad to find Jim knew what he was talking about. Tulley was not the sort of man to suffer fools gladly.

'Your stretch'll be around a hundred miles,' Tulley told him now as the speedo nudged eighty-five. 'Reckon you can handle that?'

'Do my best.'

'Good enough for me,' said Tulley, and he banged the wheel with the flat of his hand. 'The best and nothing but the best.'

'How big is the place altogether?'

'Two hundred thousand acres.' Tulley adjusted his hat as the road swung east into the noonday glare. 'How was your Nasho?'

'Okay . . . Bit of a long haul. I'm glad it's over.'

'Any stripes?'

'Oh yeah,' Jim admitted with a wry grin. 'I'm down for sergeant in the Reserve.'

Tulley shot him a glance. 'You must've been good at it then.'

'Did a couple of specialist courses. Couldn't handle just doing drill all the time.'

'Yeah. Know what you mean. I was in Korea. Stupid bastards even made us drill there. In between killing people, of course.'

'Don't envy you that,' said Jim. 'My father was in New Guinea. He's never got over it.'

'That's too bad,' Tulley sympathised. 'Wars are a pain in the arse, no two ways about it. Any luck, you won't have the pleasure.'

In fact, Jim had been a bit modest about his training. Not only was he down for sergeant in the Reserve, he was one of only three trainees out of fifteen hundred selected as SAS potential.

'Two hundred thousand acres is a hell of a lot of country.'

'Sure is,' Tulley chuckled. 'He owns a couple of dairy farms in Victoria, too.'

'He must be pretty rich then,' said Jim, not without a twinge of envy.

'Got enough dough to sink a battleship. Hasn't gone to his head though. Top bloke to work for. Good as gold. Spends most of his time on his polo ponies, leaves the stock to us.'

'Polo?' Jim was surprised. 'Out here?'

'Well, out here it's mostly polocrosse. Polo for real at the shows. Brisbane, Quirindi, Sydney, you name it. Either way, he's mad about it. Built up one of the best studs in the state. Sells them all over.'

'Must cost a fortune, going all the way to Sydney just to play polo.'

'It's a whole way of life. Athol'd go to Timbuk-bloody-tu and back for the chance of another cup.'

'Do you play?'

'Have a whack now and again.'

'I've never tried anything like that. Just a bit of buckjumping. Not quite the same thing.'

Tulley adjusted his brim again and laughed. 'No, mate. Not quite. No doubt you'll get roped in for a game or two. Here we go . . .'

Tulley slowed and they left the hardtop. He swung onto a well-worn red-dirt road and gunned the motor. The ute fish-tailed a bit, straightened up and took off. Jim had just enough time to catch sight of the signpost that said Glenmore Station before it disappeared in a cloud of dust.

Six weeks later he was out along the fence and had never felt so lonely in his life. Already Jim and his horse and dog had endured just about everything the country could throw at them. Huge, magnetic, fire-cracking thunderstorms. Monster bedouries reducing visibility to thirty yards. Days so hot he could hardly touch the fence wire to carry out repairs. Nights of shivery cold, huddled in his blanket and hugging the dog for warmth. Sudden rain, so thick it surrounded him like a lead curtain.

He saw a lot of life. Bearded dragons, brolgas, emus, an echidna or two. A couple of days back he'd come across a Woma python at a waterhole with the hind legs of a baby wallaroo still hanging from its distended jaws. There were birds. Flocks of budgerigars would suddenly appear from nowhere mobbing the horizon like a swarm of bloated locusts. Wedge-tailed eagles hung on the wind. Kangaroos were everywhere. He couldn't remember ever seeing so many. He saw a lot of death, too. Dead dingoes, dead sheep, dead cattle. Seemed like he was constantly stumbling on half-rotten carcasses or lacework skeletons, already picked clean and ice-white in the sun's relentless glare.

He spent hours every day talking to the dog. Now, making camp for the night, he stuck his hat on a fence post and held an earnest conversation with it on the subject of fires. They were bastards to start when you were dying for a cup of tea and bastards to put out when you were in a hurry to get a move on.

'Thirty miles to go,' he thought. 'Then a bloody long ride home and off in the opposite direction. Hope to God I can stick it.'

Stick it he did. By mid-December, much to his satisfaction, he had barely touched a penny of his salary. Board and keep came with the job, and there was nothing to spend it on out on the wire. Now he was back at Glenmore for a few days before setting out again.

It was Sunday morning and most of the station hands were enjoying a day off. Jim spent the morning on his bunk reading a book called *Peyton Place* that one of the stockmen reckoned was a bit of all right. Bill Tulley stuck his head round the door.

'The boss'd like to see you up at the house when you've got a moment.'

'What about?'

'Search me,' Tulley replied. 'I'm sure it's nothing to worry about,' he added, when he saw Jim's sudden concern. 'There's no rush.'

Jim lay there a moment wondering what the hell it would be about. He decided to get it over with.

Athol Ferguson greeted him warmly out on the verandah.

'I was wondering if you'd be interested in a change,' he said as they sat down.

Jim immediately felt a hint of unease. 'Is something wrong?'

'Good Lord, no. Sorry. I wouldn't want you to think that. I've had nothing but good reports from Bill. No. It's not that. It's just that one of my hands on the stud side of things has had to give notice. Morphett. I'm damned sorry to be losing him. Excellent man with horses. First rate. Came up from Victoria a couple of years ago. Feels he has to go back. He's got some family there, some problems to sort out. Unfortunate, really, but it can't be helped I suppose.'

He paused a moment and fixed his wintry eyes on Jim.

'I was wondering if you'd like to take over his job with the polo ponies.'

Jim was startled. 'Do you mean like a groom?'

'Good Lord, no,' Ferguson chuckled. 'There's a bit more to it than that. A great deal more.'

'I don't know much about thoroughbreds. Stockhorses and buckjumpers are all I know.'

'You'd soon pick it up,' Ferguson prompted him. 'You probably haven't had a chance to meet Dud yet. Dud Brewley, my stud manager?'

Jim shook his head. 'No. I haven't. Been out on the wire all the time.'

'Yes. Of course.' Ferguson lit his pipe. 'Well, they don't come any better. He'll soon show you the ropes. Been with me for years, Dud.' He smiled broadly. 'Got me over a barrel, the old goat. Knows I wouldn't part with him for all the tea in China. There's been a few blokes tried to poach him. When it comes to raising polo ponies, he's the best there is.'

Jim glanced away, his mind racing. It was a challenge. It was certainly worth a try. He could learn. Learn about blood lines and breeding. But he didn't quite know how to put the all-important question.

Ferguson eyed him shrewdly. He had taken an instant liking to this young man on the plane to Brisbane. He liked the quiet, dignified way Jim had told him about his family's misfortunes. Jim had come across as a true son of the outback and he had no hesitation in offering him a job. He was pleased when Jim wrote from his National Service camp to say he'd like to accept, if it was still going. The Fergusons had no children of their own. It was the one big hole in a happy marriage. As he watched Jim sizing up his options, he thought to himself if any son of his had turned out like this young man he'd have been well pleased.

'I should say there's a small increase in salary,' he said, pre-empting Jim's question. 'Another fiver a week. It's skilled work.'

Jim's grin broke. 'I was wondering if I should ask.'

'Still with your keep, of course,' Ferguson added. 'Dud'll probably rope you in for a few games of polocrosse once you've got the hang of it. Nothing extra there, I'm afraid. That's written off as fun.'

Jim offered his hand. 'I'll give it a go, Mr Ferguson. Thanks very much. I appreciate it.'

Athol Ferguson watched him stride away.

'You've got a good one there,' he muttered to himself as he headed into the house. 'That young feller's got what it takes.'

Jim presented himself to Dud Brewley on Tuesday morning. The wizened, 56-year-old stud manager led him on a whirlwind tour of the stables, tack rooms, blacksmith's forge, and promptly set him to work. He kept up a running commentary the whole time as if he wanted Jim to know everything there was to know by lunchtime at the latest.

'We still call them ponies,' he said. 'In the old days the limit was fourteen, then fourteen-point-two hands but they chucked that rule after the first war. Now they can be any size, like these beauties here.'

Jim stroked a few noses, rubbed a few necks. The horses responded, tossed their heads against his chest and nuzzled him. Dud was pleased. He knew that horses, like dogs, sum up a man at first glance.

He tossed Jim a curry comb. 'Right. Let's get on with it. Comb, rub down and brush.'

They set to work in adjoining stalls. Dud kept up his running commentary as the horses side-stepped, snorted and stamped their feet.

'They reckon it all started in Persia, though I've read that Attila the Hun had a team.'

'I thought he rode an elephant.'

Dud raised his head over the stall. 'That was Hannibal, you git. What's the matter? Didn't you go to school?'

'Sort of,' Jim grinned. 'My mother taught me at home. Correspondence, you know.'

Still Dud stared at him as if he'd just bitten into a sour plum.

'Just joking,' said Jim.

Dud's head disappeared.

'The British brought it over here. Eighteen seventies, that was. They really rated our bush horses. Used to take them back to India. From New South Wales, mostly. Called 'em "Walers". The Poms wrote the rules. Place called the Hurlingham Club. Then the Yanks got into it. South America, Canada . . . the Kiwis. These little beauties cost a bomb, so we treat 'em right. Understand?'

'Understood.'

Athol Ferguson's judgement was vindicated when he joined Dud at the fence of the practice field a few weeks later. Jim was working one of his thoroughbreds. Racing at full stretch from one end to the other, windmilling the stick in his hands to strike the ball time after time, first go. The pony responded to his horsemanship instantly, instinctively. They were a nice combination.

'Not bad, eh?'

'Not too bad at all,' Ferguson agreed. 'Hope your bloody polocrosse doesn't bugger up his stick work.'

'Tell you something, Athol,' Dud muttered out of the side of his mouth, keeping his eyes on horse and rider.

'What's that?'

'You're a bloody fanatic.'

Ferguson chuckled. 'That's still a couple of rungs down from tyrant.'

Dud continued to watch the action as if he hadn't heard a word.

All the while Jim concentrated on the pony's work-out, changing its gait and direction with the slightest touch of his knee, a sharp tug on the rein. He loved his new job. It was all play and no work. Dud Brewley was a master of his trade and Athol Ferguson was right. Behind the laconic rough-as-guts exterior beat a heart of gold. Best of all, he didn't mind showing his respect for a job well done. But if things weren't up to scratch, look out.

Swish! Whack! He even liked the sound of the cane whistling through the air, the club head meeting the willow-root ball at the pony's feet with a rich, woody resonance.

# Thirteen

The monster horse float rolled through Winton early in March 1963, and headed out along the Longreach road. Dud craned his neck out of the window to check the one behind. They had a long way to go. It was just over thirteen hundred miles to Sydney. Athol Ferguson was heading the Queensland syndicate having a crack at polo's premier prize, the Australasian Gold Cup. Jim and Dud had been working like trojans the past couple of months, getting the ponies in tip-top condition. There was a thrill of anticipation in the air as they loaded up that morning. Ahead lay days of mesmeric highways. They might take the edge off a bit, but not much. Ponies and handlers were as keen as mustard.

Jim knew this road like the back of his hand. The first weekend of every month for the past two years he'd made the journey to Balkenna and back, a round trip of just over four hundred miles, four hours each way. He met up with Tim Daley on the Saturday morning and the two of them worked hammer and tongs every weekend to get the house and barns and outbuildings in good working order. They patched fences, built gates and water troughs, painted roofs and windmills, rooted out acres of noxious Noogoora and Bathurst burr, plugged leaking tanks and filled in hundreds of rabbit holes in warrens that had taken hold and spread. All so that, when the time came to give it a go, Balkenna would be ready. Now, he reflected, that time may not be so far off.

The overdraft over these years had been gradually whittled down to next to nothing. The place was within coo-ee of edging into the black. His own regular deposits, what little his mother made in Brisbane, Ray Henderson's rent and Will Mackenzie's astute management of income from the pastures had done the trick. A couple of months ago, Mackenzie had offered him a new overdraft with enough credit for Jim to make a modest start at establishing some stock on the place again. But Jim was determined not to get into a hole that might bury him before he even got going. There was still all the machinery, vehicles, stockhorses, tack, and the thousand and one little extras that were needed to make a fresh start. He was tempted by Mackenzie's offer. Anything to get back there. But the impulse was tempered by a hard unsentimental determination to have all their debts paid in full and enough funds of his own before he and Tim set on what he knew would be years of back-breaking slog.

It was taken for granted that Tim would join him when the time came. Best of all, Elizabeth had indicated her willingness to return when the time was ripe. She would go back to Brisbane as regularly as possible to visit his father. But she would be there where she belonged, at his side.

As Jack's condition deteriorated, the wretched impotence she felt watching the man she loved slowly wasting away to a shadow of the handsome, hard-working bushman who'd gone away to war, had become almost unbearable. With nagging guilt she realised that the times when Jack was morose and uncommunicative were easier to handle than when he was feeling cheerful, looking forward to the day he'd be out of hospital and they'd be able to go home.

She'd become so sought after as a private tutor, she often took weekend classes as well. Jim worried she was overdoing it, running herself into the ground. But, like her son, she found enormous satisfaction in sending off her own monthly deposits to Will Mackenzie to keep their grip on Balkenna. For Jim's future, certainly. But, above all, for Jack. He had courted her, married her and taken her home. War had snatched him away from her just as their love had been blessed by a son. Snatched him away from the joy and happiness of their love for each other. The fact that she could still sit and talk with him about Balkenna as theirs, as home, somehow helped keep alive her promise to love and honour him, in sickness and in health.

At the risk of 'buggering up his stick work' as Athol put it, Dud Brewley wasn't long in getting Jim involved in the local polocrosse. He'd taken to putting the thoroughbreds through their paces on Glenmore's practice field like a duck to water. It was only natural, Dud figured, to let him have a bash at the game. When Jim finally turned out with the home side for a game at Winton showgrounds, he came off half a dozen times and kept dropping the ball. Dud put it down to youthful exuberance and bashed Jim's ear for a week afterwards. By the end of 1959 his skill had matriculated to the point where hardly a game went by in the district without young Jim Mackay.

In polocrosse there are six players on each side. You carry an ordinary polo-cane shaft with a racquet-shaped net on top. Whereas in polo, the idea is to drive the ball along the ground, in polocrosse you carry the ball to the goal mouth and chuck it in. Its popularity in Australia's remote country areas was rooted in the fact that a player must use the same pony throughout and working stockhorses were tough enough and smart enough to run all day. Regular polo, where a change of horses is allowed, remained the preserve of those rich enough to support teams of horses and reserve riders.

Jim recognised the niceties of the gentleman's game but he enjoyed the physical combat of polocrosse just as much. Like Dud said, there was just as much skill in catching a rubber ball in mid-air at full gallop as bashing one along the ground.

He seemed to learn something new from Dud Brewley every day. His natural affinity with horses stood him in good stead, but he quickly came to realise there was a wealth of knowledge to be had from this wily little jockey of a man. His position as Brewley's assistant brought him into closer contact with the Fergusons and he often joined Dud for dinner in their house. And he appreciated the extra privacy of his room above the stables. In some ways he missed working with cattle but he made up for it at mustering times when all hands were called on to help. Sheep he could take or leave, but he did not under-estimate their potential in his ceaseless plans and calculations for Balkenna's resurrection. Wool spun wealth, no doubt about that.

He was a bit peeved when National Service was suddenly abolished in 1959. But, in a way, he was still glad to have done it for the experience. Last year there'd been a big hoo-ha when thirty Australian military advisers were sent to help train the South Vietnamese Army. These were the only times Jim gave a thought to his own few months of Army life. Already it seemed a lifetime away, as did his brief spells as a meatworker and a miner. But he hadn't forgotten the Donnellys and he wrote to them from time to time about this new working life at Winton and his steady progress towards returning to Balkenna. He had a few scrawled notes in return and they always sent him a Christmas card.

'Hey, Dud! Did you hear about that bloke at Opalton a couple of weeks back?'

'No. What was that about?'

'Some galah,' the driver went on. 'Rank amateur by all accounts. Rabbiting around in the mullock heaps at the old Quartpot mine. Stubbed his toe on a lump of ironstone some other galah had thrown away. Cracks the bastard open and bingo! Five and half thousand quids' worth!'

Dud raised his eyebrows. 'Takes all sorts,' he observed, dryly.

Jim made a mental note to ask Dud about opals when he got the chance.

A few minutes later they were approaching the outskirts of Longreach and he was lost in a welter of memories. They were still flooding through him miles out the other side on their way to Barcaldine.

# Fourteen

There were long queues at the turnstiles of the Sydney show-grounds. The weather was perfect for the last day of the Royal Easter Show and the thrill was on. In the ring, horses and riders trotted and cantered through the agonising configurations of the dressage, watched closely by the thousands packing the stands. All around the grounds, families trailed through the exhibition halls, inspecting displays of the nation's agricultural wealth, towing kids lumping as many sample bags as they could carry.

Down sideshow alley the spruikers were frothing at the mouth, pulling in the punters, imploring them not to miss their last chance to see the shows 'just starting on the inside now'. Jimmy Sharman's Boxing Troupe offered would-be pugilists the chance to swap punches with the washed-up pros on the catwalk. In their tatty satin and crumpled high-laced boots, they glared down into the upturned faces, challenged any upstart larrikin to settle it on the inside. The Slim Dusty Show offered dinkum country music, well-worn jokes, whip tricks, rope tricks and a sensational finale where a man caught a .22 bullet in his teeth. Another tent displayed hand-painted canvas banner pictures of the exotic human exhibits on the inside. The spruiker was going hammer and tongs, the microphone was covered in spit.

'She wears ten thousand pounds' worth of diamonds on her tiny fingers, ladies and gentlemen. The smallest Princess in the world! Only three feet high! Step right in and see for yourself! Definitely her last appearance in the Sydney Show! Pygmies from Africa, ladies and gentlemen! On the inside now . . .'

In the stalls of one of the horse pavilions, Athol Ferguson had a problem. Huddled in a worried group that included his wife, Dud Brewley and the other owners and riders of his syndicate, he could hardly credit such rotten flaming luck.

'How bad is it?'

133

'Double fracture. Above and below the knee. Car's a write-off.'

'Blast it,' Ferguson spat. 'That takes the cake. Was it his fault?'

'He'd had a few but the other bloke jumped the light, evidently. Atherton might ride for you, if he's available.'

'Atherton's a Pom!'

The group broke up, leaving Dud and Alison Ferguson to comfort her downcast husband. As soon as the others were out of earshot, Dud had a thought.

'Give it to Jim, Athol. Give Jim the ride.'

Ferguson shook his head. 'You've got to be joking. It's too big . . . too big an occasion. You can't expect me to tell the others we've battled all the way through to the final only to offer a stick to a kid who's only ever played practice sessions. It's not on.'

But his resistance petered out a bit as Dud eyeballed him with a look of absolute conviction.

Alison Ferguson touched her husband's arm. 'I'll go and see if the Athertons have arrived, shall I?'

'All right. I'll be along in a minute.'

She left him to Dud. And Dud wouldn't quit.

'It's my final, too, don't forget. I wouldn't be stupid enough to suggest it if I didn't think he could cut the mustard. He's helped train the bloody nags for three years, he's ridden in enough polocrosse to know what it feels like. I'm telling you, Athol, he works the ponies with a stick every day of his life. What've we got to lose?'

'The Cup,' Ferguson declared with emphasis.

'Two matches even,' Dud persisted. 'It's win or lose tonight anyway. Why give the ride to a Pom like Atherton when we've got a bloke on hand who knows the ponies inside out?'

'It's the game, Dud. You know that as well as I do. He's never actually played in a grown-up professional game . . .'

Dud's idea was getting to him, nonetheless. He could see a glimmer of blue sky.

'I'd just as soon have him up as anybody else, in the circumstances,' said Dud. 'If some bloke's got to have us by the short and curlies, better a bloke we know, don't you reckon?'

Ferguson flicked him an uncertain smile. 'I don't know, Dud. I honestly don't know.'

Dud flashed him a dead cert smile in return. 'I'll sound him out. See if he fancies the idea.'

'All right,' Ferguson gave in a notch. 'No harm in having a word with him I suppose. But just a word. No promises. You know this isn't just my decision. I'll have to talk to the others.'

'Use the art of gentle persuasion,' said Dud. 'Show 'em a shotgun.'

That did it. Ferguson allowed himself a smile and a slight sense of relief. He gave his manager a good-natured punch on the arm. 'You're a bloody old pirate, Brewley.'

'Anything you say,' Dud grinned. 'Just don't turn into Judge Jeffreys if it goes the other way.'

'If it goes the other way, I'll be too busy hanging myself.'

Late that afternoon the teams took the field for the final between Queensland and the team from New Zealand. There was standing room only in the grandstands and a roar went up as the riders appeared through the gates. In the members' stand, Alison Ferguson clutched her husband's arm. He was on the edge of his seat, sixty minutes short of a lifetime's ambition. He clasped his hand over hers and they both turned their eyes back to the ring. The air was charged with drama. It was almost too much to bear.

In the ring below, Jim was momentarily deafened by the roar of the crowd. He took a few quick, deep breaths to steady his jangling nerves. But he couldn't stop his hand shaking as he made some last-minute adjustments to the stirrups and threw a look at the opposition. They looked fit to kill. Dud caught his eye and tipped him a wink. The crowd burst into applause as the umpire cantered into the ring and Jim nearly lost his seat as his pony pivoted and pranced a few nervous sidesteps. He quickly gathered it in.

'Easy. Easy. I feel the same myself.'

They won the first half at a canter. At the interval, Queensland were four-one up and the Fergusons had grins from ear to ear. But Athol knew the game too well to start counting his winnings. More than anything, he was relieved that Jim had stayed the course reasonably well. He'd missed a few, nearly come a cropper a couple of times, but he was keeping his end up.

By the end of the first chukka of the second half, their grins had died on their lips. The Kiwis came storming back in a seemingly unstoppable surge, lifting the score to four-three with two goals in the space of a minute. Then, right on the bell, their captain hit a seventy-five-yard drive that ricocheted in off one of the goalposts and that was four-all. The Fergusons couldn't believe it and Dud felt sick.

The scores stayed level until the beginning of the fifth chukka when a New Zealand rider clipped one through to put them five-four up. The Queenslanders fought back desperately but the New Zealand defence shut them down. Dud noted with rising alarm that Jim seemed to get more and more hesitant as the chukka wore on, deferring to his more experienced team-mates when he should be taking up the cudgel himself. Then disaster struck. A New Zealand rider suddenly broke from the pack and whacked the ball into open space. Jim was the only Queensland rider in sight and they both raced for the ball. Jim got there first but he was forced to knock the ball away right across his own goal mouth. The Kiwi came thundering in and shouldered Jim's pony off the ball. Their sticks tangled. Before he knew what had happened, Jim's stick took a divot between his pony's front legs and cartwheeled him out of the saddle. He hit the ground with a sickening thud and a great gasp went up all around the arena. The Kiwi quickly took the gift and New Zealand were two goals up.

Athol Ferguson hung his head and wished to God he'd never listened to a word Dud Brewley said. For his part, Dud was just plain angry. Jim was back in the saddle in a flash. But it was too late. The bell had gone.

As the riders changed mounts for the sixth and deciding chukka, Dud Brewley gave Jim Mackay the biggest tongue-lashing of his life. It was ringing in his ears as he rode out into the floodlights.

'Stop fuckin' pussy-footing around, Mackay. Stop fuckin' pussy-footing around . . .'

The sixth chukka was a thriller. Jim chased everything and the Queenslanders bore down relentlessly on the New Zealand goal. The crowd went wild when they finally managed to chip one through and haul back to five-six with five minutes to go. The Kiwis were still blaming each other as the umpire dropped the ball to restart. The Queensland captain was presented with a golden opportunity and the Kiwis let him get away with it. He was several lengths in the clear before they set off in hot pursuit. He let go an almighty 120-yard drive that flew high through the air and through the New Zealand goal on the first bounce. The crowd went berserk. Six-all! Sudden death! A huge moan went up all around the ground when the bell rang to end the chukka with the scores tied. It changed to ecstatic applause when the PA announced extra time to decide the match.

The riders changed horses. Jim got up and asked Dud to tighten his saddle girth a notch. Dud's anger had cooled. This was not the time to be upsetting anyone. He dropped the flap and stirrup strap back in place and wedged Jim's boot into the iron, holding the pony back just long enough to look him in eye.

'Go for broke, Mackay,' he whispered, slapping the pony's rump to send Jim on his way.

With a minute to go, the New Zealanders forced their way into the Queensland goal mouth. The Queenslanders managed to keep them out but one of them got a lucky shot and banged the ball just short of the line. The Queensland captain got there first. He lunged in for the one shot on and belted it as hard as he could. The ball shot back through the ruck and streaked away to centre field. Everybody gave chase, one of the Kiwis had a big start, but Jim was gaining on him. The Kiwi got to the ball, galloped over it and connected with a perfect backward swing that sent it soaring back the way it had come. Jim was caught in no man's land. He'd expected it to be dribbled out of his way to one wing or the other. The ball was coming through the air like a cannon ball, straight at his head. All those afternoons playing polocrosse paid off. He wheeled his pony, swung his stick and clubbed the ball out of the air, dead at his pony's feet. The Kiwi realised his mistake and tried to correct it. But it was too late. He was going the wrong way. Jim dribbled it out of his path, walloped it forward, dug his heels in and whacked it again as the pony hit full gallop.

He could hear the seven other riders thundering up behind him, getting closer and closer. He slowed the pony a notch to be on the safe side, leaned down and clipped the ball again. The other riders were right on his tail. He could see one pony's flaring nostrils out of the corner of his eye. Friend or foe? He didn't know. All he knew was he had to keep his eye on the ball. The goal mouth still seemed a hell of a long way away. He knew people were yelling their heads off all around him but all he could hear was the sound of his own lungs and Dud Brewley whispering in his ear. As he came over the ball again, he went for broke. Whack! It was a perfect strike. The ball hurtled through the New Zealand goal, dead centre. The bell rang. It was over. Queensland won the Cup, seven-six.

The applause rang round the showground long after the exhausted teams had left the ring. In the members' stand, the Fergusons were on their feet, surrounded by smiling faces. It was a supreme moment to savour and the tears in Athol's eyes said it all.

As the riders dismounted in the tunnel, Dud stuck out his hand. 'Good on you, Jim. Not a bad hit . . . Under pressure,' he added with a wry grin.

'Thanks.' Jim was still reeling. He could hardly believe he hadn't mucked it up. Now he managed a grin. 'Didn't fancy the idea of walking back to Winton.'

Dud laughed. 'After you got out of hospital, you mean.'

The triumphant syndicate arrived just as the last pony was being led into its stall. Amid a welter of backslapping, Athol Ferguson simply stepped forward and took Jim by the hand. 'Well done, young feller.'

Alison Ferguson planted a kiss on his cheek. 'You've made his day . . . And mine.'

Jim felt a little embarrassed. He just stood there, grinning.

'What'd I tell you?' Dud leered at Ferguson.

Athol playfully pulled the old goat's hat down over his eyes and thumped his arm. 'The gospel . . . As always, you old bugger. Grog's on me for the rest of the show.'

'Have to have a word with the stewards then,' said Dud. 'See if I can get them to stay open another couple of months.'

The Trocadero was a sea of tulle and satin, a blur of flushed and ruddy faces. The band pumped out all the old favourites as the rich, the nearly-rich, the up-and-comers and their sons and daughters gathered for the Polo Ball. At the Queensland table, the Fergusons and their guests held court, winning streak glowing from the lot.

Jim arrived at the front door feeling a bit nervous. He'd never been to a do like this in his life. He gave the doorman a friendly smile, handed over his ticket and began pushing his way through the throng, craning to catch a glimpse of his employer's table. Heads turned as he passed. They may not have recognised him as the bloke who hit the winning goal, but the women certainly knew a handsome young man when they saw one. In his borrowed dinner jacket and black tie, Jim had never looked better. He wore his outback aura like a halo.

Athol Ferguson rose to greet the man who saved the day and

immediately began squiring him round the table like a proud father. Everyone wanted to congratulate him and Jim got more and more embarrassed by all the praise and dewy-eyed adulation. But he was in the pool now and he had to swim. Already there were more names than he could possibly remember. The next guest half-rose from his chair.

'David Leslie. David's a well-known player here in Sydney.'

He was all city-slicker charm. He shook Jim's hand with the practised arrogance of the very rich.

'How do you do,' he said abruptly and immediately resumed his seat.

'And David's fiancée, Rachel Barclay.'

She turned her head to look up at Jim over her shoulder. One look was all it took: Jim knew then that nothing would ever be the same again. Without any shadow of a doubt, Rachel was the most beautiful girl he'd ever seen.

'Hello,' she said, offering her hand. 'It was a wonderful game. Congratulations.'

Jim was stupefied. He took her hand and held it much too long.

'Hello,' he managed to murmur. 'Thanks . . . Thanks very much.'

She looked him right in the eye, gave him a lovely slow smile, then glanced down at her hand, still clasped in his. She returned her eyes to his, gave him a funny look and tilted her head a little. Jim came back to earth. He shook her hand a couple of times more and released it with the utmost reluctance.

The moment was not lost on David Leslie nor, for that matter, on Athol Ferguson. Jim just couldn't help glancing back. He caught her looking at him as she chatted to her fiancé. For his part, Leslie decided to keep an eye on this country bumpkin and put him in his place if he had to.

Jim couldn't keep his eyes off her all night. He was toying with a large brandy, doing his best to listen to a steady stream of chit-chat from a friendly but rather haughty old dowager sitting beside him. She had to admit she'd never been north of Coolangatta, but she still had plenty to say about Queensland and none of it was good. As she waffled on, Jim's eyes slid off again in Rachel's direction. They were met by the steely gaze of David Leslie. Jim held his look and offered a friendly smile. Leslie ignored it.

The dowager prattled on and Jim returned his attention to

her. But the old girl was a lot shrewder than she looked. She abruptly changed gear and gave him a ridiculous wink.

'Perhaps she'd like to dance. That rat David Leslie has only danced with her once all night.'

Caught off guard, Jim could only grin and shake his head. But she refused to be put off. She dug her elbow into his ribs.

'Go on, for God's sake,' she admonished. 'Don't be shy.'

Then, to Jim's horror, she took matters into her own hands. 'Rachel!'

Jim felt like crawling under the table. The dowager placed her hand firmly on his shoulder.

'This young man would like to dance.'

A few heads turned. Leslie shot Jim a look that was meant to cut him to the quick but it had exactly the opposite effect. Jim swallowed his own embarrassment and moved quickly to cover hers. He strode round to hold her chair as she rose.

'Do you mind?' she quietly enquired of Leslie.

Leslie humphed.

The song was 'In the Mood'. Jim held her further away than necessary, but appropriate to his own sense of decorum. But the Troc was jam-packed tonight and they were soon bumped and jostled closer together. Jim couldn't think of anything to say. He was absolutely tongue-tied. Just the scent of her was making him feel giddy. He couldn't even bring himself to look at her. Finally he gave her a nervous smile.

'It's a nice ball.' It was all he could manage. There was a catch in his throat and he had to turn his head away. She waited until he focused on her again.

'Lovely,' she agreed, and the smile she gave him lit up the night. Jim had to fight an irresistible urge to kiss her right there and then. The band highlighted the last few bars, and promptly went into a reprise. Jim breathed a sigh of relief and plucked up the courage to pull her a little closer.

The next song was 'Tuxedo Junction'. Jim twirled Rachel away through the crowd, his confidence catching up with every step. He found his tongue at last and they chatted about the game. He was thrilled to discover she visited Glenmore with her family when she was a little girl and knew the Fergusons well. But one word kept ringing in his ears. Fiancée. He forced it to the back of his mind and surrendered to his giddy senses. She was slim and graceful and her spine felt ridiculously supple under his hand. The more he gazed at her face, the more beautiful she looked, framed by rich waves of shoulder-length auburn hair. She had wise, slightly knowing, hazel eyes that glowed every time she smiled. It was the smile that kept doing him in. Warm and open, it also hinted at a wicked sense of mischief.

Life ends with a tap on the shoulder. It was David Leslie, cutting in.

Leslie swept her away before she could respond. But each time they turned, her eyes found his over Leslie's shoulder as Jim remained standing stock still, copping a few bumps and elbows from other couples swirling around him. He was in a trance and far too green to try to hide it.

All morning he'd been trying not to think about it. Trying not to dwell on it. What was the point? She was from another world. She was engaged to another man. A city girl through and through, living a heady, expensive, cosmopolitan life. But as the horse floats drove over the Bridge and through the sprawl of Sydney's northern suburbs, all he could see was her face.

Two days later, coming out of Armidale on the New England Highway, Dud and the driver were stuck well into yet another earnest discussion about bloodlines. 'I Left My Heart In San Francisco' was on the radio. Jim stuck his elbow out of the window, cupped his chin in his hand and gazed at the passing landscape, lost in daydreams. Now Nat King Cole was doing 'Rambling Rose'.

'What do you reckon, Jim?' Dud yelled.

'About what?'

'Sydney skirt,' Dud leered.

Jim was forced to give them a self-conscious grin.

'All right,' he said, turning back to look out of the window.

Dud and the driver swapped a look, raised their eyebrows and creased themselves.

'Lay off, will you?'

'Rambling Rose' was followed by the pips. Dud and the driver cut the teasing to listen to the news.

Considerable controversy had greeted Australia's agreement to the United States establishing a naval communications installation on the North-West Cape in Western Australia. There were fears it might attract a nuclear attack in the event of war. In London, Britain's War Minister, John Profumo, had denied any impropriety in his acquaintance with Christine

Keeler. In Canberra, the Liberal government had announced it was considering the commitment of Australian troops to Vietnam to augment a token force of thirty-two advisers already there. National Service was to be reintroduced at the beginning of 1964 with previous trainees eligible for call-up to the Reserve. Widespread opposition was expected from the Australian Labour Party and the trade union movement.

'Suppose we should give the Yanks a hand,' said Dud.

'One of their bloody bombs would do the trick,' said the driver. 'One of the big ones.'

But it was all lost on Jim. He was looking out of the window, seeing nothing, lost in his own sweet dreams. Herb Alpert was doing 'The Lonely Bull'.

# Fifteen

Back at Glenmore, Jim threw himself into his work with a vengeance. He took on more and more responsibility for the daily running of the stables and went on working like a beaver at Balkenna on his monthly runs to team up with Tim. He tried to leave as little free time as possible to reflect that he had fallen desperately in love with a woman he would never see again. Dud was quick to realise his jokes about 'Sydney skirt' actually hurt and he gave it away.

He took Jim off at weekends fossicking around the old Quartpot, Yellow Jimmy and Lyre bird mines at Opalton, eighty miles south of Winton. Jim had pumped him about the chance of making a few quid on the side when they got back from Sydney. They culled the old mullock heaps on the off-chance. They found an occasional chip or two, but nothing to write home about. They soon gave it away to go digging at random in the ironstone ridges surrounding the old town.

Australia produces the best opals in the world. The fields at Opalton were first discovered in 1888 and they were worked continually until the price of opals dropped at the turn of the century and the town became a deserted ruin, haunted by the echoes of gouging picks and the voices of hundreds of diggers who poured into the wilderness chasing dreams. Some of them did strike it very rich indeed. Many, many more went stark raving mad and lived on in bonecrushing poverty, trapped in a dream from which they never awoke. Their graves litter the barren hills.

Dud once spent a year at Lightning Ridge in New South Wales, hunting for black opals, the most precious of them all. He remembered a man buried alive in his shaft by angry diggers who thought he was trying to jump a neighbour's claim by digging a tunnel through to his shaft from his own. By the time the district police sergeant got up to the ridge, everyone had the story down pat. A most unfortunate accident. The shaft just collapsed on top of him and they couldn't get him out. They'd done their best. Everyone knew the fields were a law unto themselves. If they didn't, they found out pretty quick.

Dud made himself nearly two thousand pounds at Lightning Ridge, big money in those days. He blew the lot on a six-week holiday in Fiji. So he knew how to go about it. He had a nose for a likely looking spot. Trouble was, there was nothing left at Opalton to sniff out. They still made occasional forays, as much for the chance to camp out as anything else. Which was just as well. Much to Jim's disappointment, overnight fortune eluded them.

By the end of August 1963, the day came when the debt was paid. From now on, every pound in the bank was another stepping-stone on the long road home. When his mother forwarded the statement showing them three hundred pounds in the black, Jim took it up to Balkenna and nailed it up on the back of the kitchen door. It was always the last thing he saw when he locked up and no talisman ever offered a better charm. Elizabeth did some additional calculations based on their respective salaries and they figured they could give it a go in about eighteen months' time. Will Mackenzie made a special trip out to Balkenna one Sunday to talk things over with Jim and confirm his promise of the bank's support. He was willing to underwrite down payments on essential equipment and transport, and the outright purchase of two hundred and fifty Herefords and a pedigree bull. Ray Henderson offered Jim some of his sheep at bedrock price and the loan of a couple of rams. In his quiet, hesitant way, Tim Daley offered to put his own small savings in the kitty and he said he'd work for his keep until they got on their feet. Jim accepted the latter offer, but he insisted Tim hang onto his money in view of the struggle ahead. So much would depend on the weather – 1961 had been a particularly dry year and the long-range forecasts promised less for 1964. As it turned out, Jim's refusal to accept Tim's offer proved timely. They didn't know it then, but the years 1964–6 brought one of the most severe droughts ever recorded in Queensland and New South Wales. Strangely, it didn't affect their plans. By that time, Jim was in another country.

In the last weeks of November, Jim and Dud were hard at work in the stalls when Athol Ferguson appeared with the mail and grim news.

144

'Kennedy's been shot dead in America. Just came over the radio.'

Jim and Dud downed tools.

'Where?' Dud grunted.

'Dallas. In Texas. A sniper got him in his car. Had the top down, evidently. So the crowd could see him.'

Jim shook his head. 'Bloody hell. Do they know who did it?'

'Yes. They've got the bastard. Shot a copper trying to get away.'

'Wouldn't like to be in his shoes,' said Dud. 'Probably had the shit kicked out of him already.'

'Better not be a bloody commo,' said Athol. 'Or we'll all go up in smoke.'

Jim identified his mother's handwriting on one of his letters and absently opened the other, an official-looking brown envelope. He glanced down at its contents and sagged like a wet sack.

'Oh, shit,' he moaned. 'Of all the bloody things to happen now.' He read the letter over again. 'How do you like it, I'm bloody well called up again. Into the Reserve.'

Ferguson and Dud were both taken aback.

'When, for Christ's sake?' Dud demanded.

'January. In Brisbane,' Jim told them. He crumpled the letter and threw it away in disgust. 'Bugger it . . .'

Athol Ferguson retrieved the ball of paper and read it for himself.

'If you don't want to go, Jim, I may be able to get it deferred. I know there's some allowances made for country workers.'

Jim nodded. 'Thanks, Mr Ferguson . . . I don't know.'

Dud dropped a hand on his shoulder. 'Not your day, mate.' Keeping his hand on Jim he turned to Athol. 'I think we can say his job will be here . . . When it's over?'

'Absolutely,' said Athol, eyeballing Jim, putting him on a promise. 'That goes without saying.'

After supper that evening, Jim went up to the house. He decided to answer his call-up and get it over and done with. Ferguson reluctantly accepted his decision. He couldn't argue with Jim's sense of duty and had to respect it. He reminded him the job would always be there, if he needed it. But they both knew that, unlike his previous Army experience, this call-up was for an unspecified length of time. The future would have to wait.

It was as Jim was getting up to go that Athol Ferguson had his inspiration. It had probably been at the back of his mind for

145

some time. Jim was half out of his chair when his boss waved him back into it.

'Hang on a minute, Jim. About Balkenna. Now's as good a time as any. It's just an idea, mind you. I haven't had a chance to look at the nuts and bolts.'

Jim hung on. 'I'm constantly going over the nuts and bolts where Balkenna's concerned. Nuts, bolts, the lot.'

'I bet you are,' Ferguson chuckled.

Jim sat back in his chair and waited. His boss contemplated his fingernails a moment before he spoke.

'As I said, your job will be here on Glenmore for as long as you wish. It'll be here. But I'd like to suggest an alternative.'

Jim leaned forward in his chair again.

'I'd like to suggest a partnership, a pastoral company, if you like. Roughly what I have in mind is to finance you to get started on your own place again. Form a separate company, for a period of, say, five years. Until you're in a position to turn a reasonable profit, at which point I'd take a forty per cent share of annual turnover, after tax, until my investment is recouped with sufficient interest on top to cover inflation on the capital. As I said, I can only put it to you as a broad proposition at the moment. How would you feel about something like that?'

Jim was still feeling the same about it at half past three the following morning. It had been a hell of a day. But the mullygrubber of his Army call-up had been completely hit for six by Athol Ferguson's stunning proposal. Jim was dumbfounded. He knew Athol liked and respected him, but never in a million years had he anticipated such a move. It was everything he could wish for and more. No need to be under the bank's thumb, even if it was Will Mackenzie. They talked and talked and it began to sound better and better. Athol was full of suggestions. He was strong on Poll Shorthorns and the Hereford – Brahman cross stock he'd found so successful on Glenmore. He could provide some of his own stud rams to cover a suggested initial purchase of five hundred ewes. As the night wore on, the roles of employer and employee changed to something like uncle and nephew, perhaps even father and son. Partners in a new and exciting adventure. When Jim finally took his leave that night, it was impossible to find the words to thank someone who'd just offered him the chance of a lifetime, out of the clear blue sky. So he just said, 'Let's talk about it again as soon as possible.'

Ferguson smiled and suggested they wait until he had a chance to draw up some plans and put the whole thing down on paper. 'It's a good moment for Anthony Barclay to be paying us a visit. He's good at contracts and that sort of thing. Pity David Leslie can't make it up for Christmas as well. He's got a good head for business.'

Jim didn't mind. The only thing he minded was the lump in his throat the size of a soggy pear. He got no sleep that night. The next day was exercise day. Six o'clock on the dot. Dud'd tear strips off him if he was late.

Three weeks later he was at Winton airport. He got there much too early and had to wait ages for the plane to arrive. Rachel Barclay came down the steps with her parents and her ten-year-old brother. Jim fidgeted nervously, dreading the moment they cleared the terminal building. She spotted him right away. She gave him a friendly wave and a warm smile dawned in her eyes. As they waited for the luggage, she introduced him to her family.

'Can I go riding?' was all young Johnny wanted to know.

'You sure can,' said Jim. 'As much as you like.'

He took it easy on the long drive to Glenmore. He'd come in Alison's station wagon and all their gear was piled in the back. Jean Barclay sat like a duchess between her husband and son on the back seat. To Jim's everlasting delight, Rachel was up front beside him. The conversation drifted: the state of the country, the weather, Lee Harvey Oswald, polo, their previous visits to Glenmore. Through it all, it was impossible not to look at Rachel every time she spoke, every time she moved. It was a good thing he wasn't doing more than fifty, because a couple of times he nearly went off the road. She was wearing a simple, short-sleeved, powder-blue frock. She kicked off her canvas slip-ons and drew her legs up and hugged her knees in her arms. She was so near. And so far.

Anthony Barclay offered cigarettes. Rachel leaned across to light it for him, cupping her hand round the flame. In the moment their eyes locked he knew. Jim sensed that in some way his feelings were reciprocated by this beautiful girl who'd been on his mind ever since the moment they met. Rachel flushed a little and quickly straightened in her seat as Jim slewed off the blacktop into the roadside gravel. He swung the car back in line just in time and snatched a look in the rear-view mirror.

'Sorry.'

'You country drivers are all a bit wild.' Jean Barclay made light of it. But her eyes told Jim that the moment had not gone unnoticed.

The following afternoon, Jim thought it'd be a good idea if he accompanied Rachel and her brother for a ride to the creek.

'She knows the way, you know,' said Dud. 'Been here before.'

'Not for quite a while,' Jim argued. 'Better to be on the safe side.'

'No sheila's safe with your sort.'

'I was thinking more of her brother . . .'

'Yeah. Like hell you were. Go on, get out of here before I do my block. Just remember I'm not stalling the whole bloody lot on my own tonight, okay?'

'I'll be back,' Jim grinned.

'I won't count on it,' was Dud's parting crack.

Once they were out of sight of the house, Jim and Rachel dropped their horses to a walk, letting young John go cantering out and back on either wing. Rachel stood in her stirrups, closed her eyes and took a few deep grateful breaths.

'I'd forgotten what it felt like to be a dot in this landscape.'

'A lot of people find it quite lonely and monotonous, quite apart from the heat.'

'And these little so-and-sos,' Rachel added, brushing away the flies. 'You should see your back.'

She pulled a face and quickly waved her hand across his shoulders to dismiss a cloud of them.

Jim knew they'd be back in two ticks.

'How long have you been engaged?'

It fell out unbidden. He could've kicked himself. But she just smiled and shook her head.

'Ever since we were children, in a way. We grew up next door to each other. Officially since January this year. We probably would have got married last year, but David's father died and he had to take over. It was all a bit sudden. He always knew he'd take over but not until his father retired.'

Jim was stricken. It all sounded so wrapped up. So final.

'What sort of business are they in?'

'Brokerage, basically. Real estate, property development, that sort of thing. Plus the stud.'

'A polo stud?'

'No. Racing. David's family have a property at Scone.'

Jim swallowed hard and struggled to phrase the next question. 'When do you think you'll get married then?'

Rachel shrugged and tossed her hair. 'As soon as we can. David wants to sort it all out first. There's a lot to do. Dad's helping him with a lot of the reorganisation.'

Jim had heard enough.

'My family have a property. Near Longreach.'

'Yes. I know,' she said, turning to give him a sympathetic look. 'Alison told me. About your father and everything.'

Jim felt a shock of pleasure. She'd been asking about him. He glanced away. 'It'll work out. I know it will.'

He didn't see the look she gave him. If he had, he would have seen much more than idle curiosity there. Astonished by her own unbidden feelings, Rachel heeled her horse into an easy canter and called back over her shoulder. 'See you at the creek.'

Jim geed his horse to respond and quickly caught up. Rachel shot him a laughing challenge and their canter leapt into a gallop. Young John came racing in from the flank, kicking his pony like mad and yelling his head off.

'Hey . . .! Wait for me!'

At the creek, John was swinging in an arc out over the water on a handy river-gum branch. Full of ten-year-old enthusiasm, he did it again and again. Sprawled in the shade, Jim and Rachel checked him out now and then.

'How long will your call-up last?'

'Nobody seems to know for sure. I suppose it'll all depend on this thing in Vietnam.'

'They won't send National Servicemen there, will they?'

'Could do.'

Rachel had her eyes on her brother as she spoke. 'I hope not. I'd hate to think of you there . . .'

Something in her tone gave Jim his first real, solid clue. Slowly, she turned her face to him and held his look, unable to hide what was happening to her, the confusion in her heart. Suddenly, impulsively, Jim knew he had to tell her, had to let her know. He swallowed and summoned the courage.

'I . . . There's something I must say . . . It's something I've . . .'

Crack! Splash! The branch gave way and dumped young John in the creek. He came up spluttering and spitting, his arms thrashing before he went under again. Jim jumped straight in beside him. It was deep and he went under as well.

149

He couldn't find him. Then he blundered into his arms and dragged him to the surface. Holding John up as high as he could, Jim struggled towards the bank. He could only just touch the bottom and, when he hit a hole, they went under again. He came up, gulping, groping for Rachel's outstretched hand. She managed to get a grip on her brother's shirt and, with her pulling and Jim pushing, they got him clear and tussled him up the bank. He hunched down on his knees, coughing creek water. He gagged a couple of times and coughed up some more water before Rachel and Jim got him into a sitting position, his head down between his knees. He was wet through and shaking but otherwise he was all right. Except for the fat black leeches already lunching on his arm.

Jim quickly pinched them off and checked him over. There was another one on the back of his neck.

'Bloody things.' He quickly rolled up the boy's jeans and found a couple more at work on his calf. One was well dug in, already gorged with blood and it took several attempts to get it off.

'They don't waste any time,' he muttered as Rachel cradled her brother in her arms until he stopped shaking. He glanced up and Jim shot him a grin.

'Okay?'

'Yes,' John croaked, without any degree of certainty.

'Don't worry, mate,' Jim chuckled. 'Even Tarzan falls in now and then.'

John gave him a wan smile. Jim pulled off his own boots and rolled up his pants. There were four of the buggers. Three on his left leg, one on his right. He started pinching them off. Rachel brushed his hand away. Her face screwed up in disgust at touching the monsters. But Jim loved it. Her hair blew in his face and the scent of her wafted over him in waves. She got the last one off, tossed it aside and rolled down his trouserlegs. They eyed one another for a moment and they couldn't help it. They cracked up. They glanced over at young John and he cracked up as well, managing a rueful laugh at his own expense. Jim and Rachel looked at each other, still chuckling. As their eyes met, the laughter died. She leant forward and kissed him on the cheek. It was too quick, but she meant it. 'Thank you.'

There was a big crowd for Christmas Day at Glenmore. The Fergusons put on a magnificent spread that stretched the length of the verandah. Cold ham and chicken, huge bowls of salad, piles of asparagus, tomatoes, cucumbers, mangoes, pawpaws and all the trimmings – Christmas lunch, Australian style, dressed up with streamers and balloons all laid out under bead-edged gauze fly-cloths. At one end of the verandah, there was a 42-gallon drum filled with sawdust – full of lucky dip for the kids. Sprawled about the verandah in cane chairs or out on the blankets under shady trees on the front lawn were all the Fergusons' employees, several neighbouring grazing families and the Barclays.

Jim blushed as Jean Barclay entertained a couple of neighbours with a melodramatic account of young Johnny saved from drowning.

'It was all over in a flash,' said Jim with a grin, to cover his embarrassment. Jean Barclay threw up her hands in mock-horror and gave him a playful push.

'Nonsense! Don't be so modest! Thank God you were there, that's all. The thought of it gives me the willies.' She gave a theatrical shudder to emphasise her point.

Rachel was sitting beside Dud Brewley on the verandah steps, plates on their knees. Her eyes just got wider and wider. Dud got to the punchline and Rachel cracked up. Her silvery laughter drifted over the lawn and a few heads turned. Jim glanced over to her as well as her giggles redoubled. His face lit up. Rachel didn't see it, but her mother did. Jim excused himself and headed off round the house.

Rachel just managed to catch Jim's retreating figure before he disappeared.

He didn't want to be away any longer than was absolutely necessary. As soon as he was out of sight, he broke into a loping run towards the stables until he was out of breath. As he went down the line of stalls, the ponies whinnied and tossed their heads in recognition. Jim responded with a few words of greeting and a friendly pat here and there. He got to the end and shovelled a couple of buckets into the feed bin then worked his way back along the line, topping up each pony's feedbox. He didn't see Rachel in the doorway. After a moment, she drifted inside and stroked the nose of the first horse in line. It whinnied loudly at her touch.

Jim looked up and immediately dropped everything. The horse nuzzled her a couple of times. Then he bumped her backwards with a toss of its head.

'Hey! Easy does it,' she chuckled. 'Mind your manners.'

Jim strode quickly along the stalls to join her. 'You've won a heart there.'

She was still smiling. 'Can I help?'

'I'm just about done. Come along and watch.'

They headed back to the buckets and Rachel insisted on carrying one, handing it to him when his ran out. She ran an admiring eye over each horse as Jim introduced them to her in turn with playful formality. When he had finished, they strolled back down the line to return the buckets to the bin.

'When are you leaving?'

She sighed. 'The day after tomorrow. We have to be back in Sydney for New Year's Eve.'

'Couldn't you stay longer?' Jim pressed, with the emphasis on the 'you'.

Rachel quickly looked away. 'David's family always give a New Year's party. It's sort of a tradition. We've been going for as long as I can remember. I have to be there . . .'

Her voice trailed off, as if she didn't like the sound of herself. She tossed her hair and turned back to him. 'When do you have to leave for Brisbane?'

'The week after next, I'm afraid.'

She studied him a moment and Jim noticed a delicious nervous flutter teasing her lip. 'Will you come and see us? In Sydney? If you get sent there, I mean.'

'That might be a bit awkward . . .'

'Why?'

Jim gathered himself and took the plunge. 'I think you know why.'

She held his eye for a fraction for a second before she turned away. When she spoke, her voice was a whisper. 'David wouldn't mind . . .'

He had to tell her now. There was no going back. 'He would if he knew. If he knew how much I love you.'

Rachel stiffened. Hesitantly, oh-so-slowly, Jim reached out and placed his hand on her shoulder.

'Rachel . . .'

She pivoted back to face him and tried to bluff it out with a plucky little smile. But her eyes were misty. She tried to speak, but the words wouldn't come. The studied reserve between them came tumbling down as Rachel folded against him for a moment before turning her face up and offering her lips to receive his kiss.

All the way down the stalls, the horses craned their necks and pricked their ears to watch the show. A couple even whinnied their approval.

They returned to the party from different directions and tried as hard as they could to avoid each other's eyes. But it was impossible.

'What's the matter?' Anthony enquired, as his wife's eyes narrowed.

'We've got a problem,' she whispered dramatically.

'News to me . . .'

Jean nodded in Jim's direction. 'Him. What's his name . . . Jim Mackay.' She tucked her arm through her husband's and began pulling him towards the house. 'Come inside. I want to talk to you in private.'

Anthony was a bit put out. But he did what he was told.

By the time night fell, the last visitors had taken their leave and the Fergusons and the Barclays were busily engaged in tidying up, lugging trays of toppling crockery to the kitchen. Jim stayed behind to lend a hand and he and Rachel quickly found work on the same table. They piled the crockery onto the traymobile, lifted the large chequered tablecloth, gave it a good shake and began folding it. The folds got smaller and smaller until their hands touched. For a brief furtive moment their fingers interlaced and they made love with their eyes.

'This ready to go?' Dud demanded loudly, coming out of nowhere to grab the traymobile.

Their fingers parted in a flash.

'Wish you could fold horse rugs like that,' said Dud, eyes twinkling with mischief. He glanced approvingly at Rachel then back at his protégé. 'There again, I'm not such a pretty partner, am I?'

Jim wanted to top him but he couldn't think of a thing to say. They watched Dud go then glanced at each other. They'd been caught out. But it was all right. There was no threat there. Old Dud had just let them know he was wise, but he was definitely onside.

The kitchen was bedlam. Everyone pitched in to help with a mammoth wash-up, orchestrated by the Fergusons' housekeeper. The table was already piled high with clean crockery and utensils, but there were still mountains to go. Athol and

153

Anthony were on tea-towel duty. It was a while before Athol spoke.

'Damn nuisance, Tony. Today of all days.'

Barclay hesitated a moment. His lips were tight. 'Can't be helped, I'm afraid. Lucky your charter chap could come to the party.'

Jim and Rachel overheard and swapped a fleeting look.

'What's up?' Rachel asked.

Barclay looked uncomfortable. But he kept up the front, acting like it had completely slipped his mind. 'Oh . . . Sorry, darling. I should have told you. We'll have to cut it short, I'm afraid. I'm wanted back in Sydney. It's urgent and can't wait. Athol's arranged for the charter people in Winton to fly us to Brisbane tomorrow.'

Rachel knew at once. Someone had twigged what was going on between Jim and herself. She turned and fixed her mother with a stare, eyes blazing. Jean Barclay didn't even attempt to hold it. Her eyes fled and she turned away, praising Athol, yet again, for a wonderful, wonderful day.

Rachel turned back to her father and arched an eyebrow. 'I better get an early night then,' she said.

Later that night, as he waited in the dark by the corner of the house, Jim heard the muffled chimes of the Fergusons' grandfather clock strike ten and wondered if she'd come. Just as he was becoming resigned to the terrible possibility she might not, Rachel called his name in a whisper. Stepping quickly to her side, Jim slid an arm round her and they sneaked off across the lawns until they were out of sight behind a clump of hydrangeas. He reached for her at once, but Rachel held him gently away. Time was crucial. He had to press his case. Despite his best efforts to keep it under control, his voice broke as he pleaded for their future.

'Marry me, Rachel . . . Please . . .'

Rachel stood stock still, unable to answer.

'I have to say it,' said Jim. 'I can't let you go hundreds of miles south . . . I can't let you go out of my life again without asking you.'

There was a long pause before she gathered herself enough to reply.

'It's impossible.'

'Why?'

'You know as well as I do. I'm already engaged to be married. To David. It's arranged . . . Settled.'

The rest of her argument got trapped in her throat.

'Do you love him?' Jim asked quietly.

'Of course,' she responded, with a shade too much emphasis, as if she needed to remind herself. 'We've known each other all our lives . . . Grown up together.'

Jim's desperation was mounting but he kept his tone even.

'I love you, Rachel . . . I've loved you since the moment I saw you. You know that.'

Rachel was rapidly losing control. She'd come to meet him with a firm resolve to hold her emotions well in check. It was hopeless. It was falling to pieces.

'Yes,' she whispered. 'But . . .'

'It took me completely and utterly by surprise. Turned my whole world upside down and inside out before I knew what had hit me . . .'

He meant to make it sound as if it had all been hard to handle, but his voice was rich with wonder and delight. Rachel couldn't help smiling as she relived their introduction herself.

'It took me by surprise, too. I tried not to think about it afterwards . . .'

'Me, too . . .'

'I never fell in love before,' she admitted.

'Me, neither . . .'

'With David and me it just seemed to grow . . . From childhood, I suppose. Then when we were teenagers –'

Jim cut her off. 'What about us?'

Rachel was inwardly kicking herself. She hadn't wanted this, she hadn't wanted to admit to a thing. Whatever it was, it was driving her, compelling her to answer.

'You just came out of nowhere . . .'

'And you're telling me we should just pretend it never happened. Just let it go? How can we, for God's sake?'

Rachel took a few steps away from him, needing the extra distance to frame an answer. Jim held his breath and gave her time. Finally she turned and stepped back and reached for his hands.

'We must.' Her voice was held in check, the words barely audible. 'You must get on with your life and I must get on with mine. I . . . We . . .'

It was no good. The dam burst and flooded her defences. She

brought his hands up to her shoulders, folded herself against him and hugged him tighter than she'd ever hugged anything in her life. Tears filled her eyes. Jim enveloped her, stroked her back, kissed her brow and buried his face in her hair. They clung to each other like thieves in the night. They stood that way for a good ten minutes before they began to kiss.

'Rachel? Raaaaachel?' Jean Barclay's shrill voice shattered the night. 'Raaaaachel? Are you there?'

Rachel eased herself away. 'Just getting a breath of air. Coming.'

'Hurry up, dear. I need you to help me pack.'

'Okay.'

She tried to pull away but Jim clutched her fiercely back.

'I must go,' she whispered.

'Please . . . Please,' Jim begged her. 'We can't do this. Let me tell them.'

'I think my mother's guessed already. That's why we're leaving tomorrow.'

'Let me explain . . .'

'They wouldn't listen. Not for a minute.'

Jean Barclay called again, her voice rising. 'Rachel? Where are you?'

'All right. All right!' she snapped. 'I'm coming. Go and start. I'll be there in a minute.'

She pulled away again and Jim clutched her right back, like a drowning man in a raging sea.

'I must go . . .'

'I can't let you go.'

'Yes, you can. You must . . . For both of us.'

She held him at arm's length for one last, long look.

'I love you, Jim.'

She broke his hold. Jim reached for her again, but it was too late. She was gone. He was left stranded like a bird with a broken wing, silhouetted against the sea of diamonds in the night sky. A great, gushing sob came welling out of him and he bunched his fist and punched the heavens in utter despair.

At Athol's request, Jim drove them to the airport. Hardly a word was spoken until the station wagon left its cloud of dust behind and turned onto the hardtop. Jim's face was stony, like the crack of doom. Rachel was rigid beside him on the front seat. In the back, Jean Barclay kept a beady eye on their driver.

Her husband said Jim really must fix up a game of polo if he ever happened to be in Sydney.

'David's crowd play every other weekend,' he advised cheerily. 'At Windsor, mostly.'

'I'd like that,' said Jim, struggling to keep it polite. 'If I get down that way. The Army's got my time now.'

'Of course. Of course,' said Barclay. 'Just remember you'd always be welcome.'

'Yes. Thanks.'

Rachel held her breath and choked a cry. She couldn't bear to look at him. She fixed her unseeing eyes on the road ahead, her hands trembling in her lap.

It was a four-seater. As they got to the door of the terminal building, Jean Barclay gave her son a swift elbow in the ribs. John stuck out his hand.

'Thanks, Mr Mackay. For helping me at the creek and everything.'

Jim managed a smile and shook his hand. 'No worries. I'll see you again some time.'

Next in line, Jean Barclay offered an insipid smile. 'Goodbye,' she said, bland as you like. 'Thank you for all your chauffeuring.'

Jim couldn't help himself. He locked eyes with her and let her know. 'Goodbye, Mrs Barclay. I hope you have a comfortable trip.'

Anthony Barclay eased his wife aside. 'Cheerio, Jim. All the very best.'

Jim was fit to burst but he kept the lid on. For her sake. 'Thanks. Have to take it as it comes. I'm sorry your visit's been cut short.'

'Yes,' Barclay muttered. 'Still . . . Can't be helped.'

He shook Jim's hand warmly and followed his wife, then propped himself in the door and looked back, waiting for Rachel.

She offered her hand. Jim clutched it fiercely. He didn't give a damn who was watching.

'Goodbye,' she said simply, keeping control. 'Good luck.'

With equal simplicity, Jim spoke an absolute truth. 'I love you, Rachel . . .'

She slowly pulled her hand away. 'I'll be thinking of you.'

Anthony Barclay looked decidedly feeble. He gave Jim a slight nod and another feeble smile.

'Goodbye,' he said crisply and followed his daughter through the door.

Jim didn't wait to see them take off. He dived behind the wheel, gunned the motor and roared off, spitting gravel.

He flattened his foot to the floor the moment he was free of the city limits. A few miles on, waves of sorrow were coming at him like a force-ten gale. He hit the anchors, flung the car through a blistering, dove-tailing U-turn and headed back to Winton. He shuddered to a halt outside the first pub he came to. He knocked back the first schooner like he'd just crossed the Simpson desert on his hands and knees.

Two weeks later, he was back in the Army.

Two years later, he was in Vietnam.

# Sixteen

The 3rd Sabre Squadron of the Australian Special Air Services arrived at Nui Dat in the Vietnam province of Phuoc Tuy in July 1966. Within the area designated as Australian Task Force Headquarters, they conducted their intelligence-gathering missions from a well-secured compound that became known to one and all as 'SAS Hill'. One of their patrol units was led by Sergeant James Mackay, known affectionately by his four team members as the 'Longreach Larrikin'.

Jim spent the first eighteen months of his call-up in standard retraining programmes for National Servicemen. By mid-1965, he was bored out of his skull. His initial selection as SAS potential had not been forgotten, however. At the end of June that year, following a long and exhaustive interview, he volunteered to undertake a three-week selection course, designed to test the recruits to the absolute limit of physical and mental fitness. He had to run 2 miles in 16 minutes, 9 in 90 minutes and complete a forced march of 20 miles in 4 hours. For those who came out the other side, it was more a matter of sheer willpower than actual physical courage that got them there. Of the 150 volunteers on his course, only 3 officers and 30 men of other ranks came up to scratch and proceeded to the next round: six weeks of intensive, non-stop training in basic SAS skills. Unarmed combat, shooting, demolition, signals, patrol tactics and how to live off the land. At the end of that period they'd been allowed a short rest before going on a three-week parachute course, followed by further training in specialist skills. Jim didn't much like lugging the signals equipment around and he didn't rate his potential too highly as a medic either. He certainly didn't fancy the idea of someone being able to take pot shots at him with forty pounds of gelignite on his back. So he put himself down for scout/tracker as primary, medic as secondary and came through with flying colours. By January 1966 they were ready and put on stand-by.

159

History has confirmed that the results were not worth the costs of the Vietnam war. But to anyone that served there, to the families of the 424 Australian servicemen who died there, hindsight has a hollow ring. Beyond a shadow of a doubt, Australia's participation in Vietnam produced the greatest internal debate and the most bitter division of opinion among the population of any conflict in which the country had been engaged, with the possible exception of the First World War. Those who believed in dominoes fought those who believed in the lottery of peace at any price. Both lost the war. Australia's greatest SEATO ally, the United States, suffered the most humiliating defeat in its history and the victors gave the name of their leader to the shattered shell-pocked city that we used to call Saigon.

The debate was already raging by the time the 3rd Sabre flew away from the Australian mainland. There were those among them who could see both sides, even those who had reservations about going. Others looked on the mob on the streets of every capital city in Australia as vermin of the lowest order, lice in the golden fleece of the ANZAC tradition. But it didn't matter two hoots in hell once they were in the air. They were off to do a job, to play a game of chance with fatal odds. Kill or be killed. In his heart of hearts, Jim prayed he wouldn't have to kill anyone. But when it came right down to it, Jim knew the chances were pretty slim.

For Elizabeth Mackay, the day of her son's departure wasn't just a ghastly case of *déjà vu*. Beyond any shadow of a doubt it had happened before and she was still living with the nightmare of the result. All through his Reserve and SAS training she had steeled herself for the inevitable while praying some miracle would save him from being sent overseas. Each leave became harder and harder to bear as the day approached. Now he was gone. She would have to relive her life all over again, waiting on a knife-edge to learn if her son would come back dead or alive, in one piece or damaged in some incomprehensible way as his father was.

Jim's call-up had been a killing blow to their hopes of being back on Balkenna in the not too distant future. Her teaching had suffered as a result. Well known among the parents who employed her for her tolerance and patience with even the most difficult children, Elizabeth found herself losing her temper and bursting into tears.

160

The doctors agreed with Elizabeth and Jim's decision to withhold all information from his father regarding Jim's posting to Vietnam. It was thought better to keep it from him. As far as Jack was concerned, Jim was working in faraway Winton and came to Brisbane on holidays. Nobody could be sure whether or not he guessed the truth. It had proved impossible to keep him in the dark about the war itself and he often mentioned it in conversation with Elizabeth.

'So, you'll be going deep into enemy territory, well behind their forward positions . . .'

Jim followed the pointer across a map of Phuoc Tuy province, mounted on the blackboard of a lecture room in the SAS compound.

Jim's demolition expert raised his hand.

'What's their security like in base camp areas?'

'If they think they're safe, they tend to get a bit slack. But don't let it fool you. Always remember, this is their paddock.' Their commanding officer paused for a moment and unpeeled a grim little smile. 'There's an old saying that's well worth keeping in mind. In the jungle, the monkey is killed by the leopard. There are no real leopards in this jungle. But if you think of the VC as leopards, then, just possibly, you won't make monkeys out of yourselves.'

One or two of them chuckled at his little joke, but not for long.

'The man who moves silently has the edge. Remember that at all times. Avoid the ridge lines and keep off the tracks or anything that looks even vaguely like a path. It's hard going out there, I can promise you that. Our experience has been that for every ten minutes you're moving, you'll spend twenty just listening. Trust your ears as well as your eyes. Until you're back behind the wire. Then you can plug your ears and enjoy the sights. Right. Any more questions?'

Nobody said a word.

'Okay. Sector notification tomorrow morning and then you're in at the deep end. Good luck.'

The captain donned his cap and gathered his notes. The men stood as he left the room. The rehearsals were over. It was time to take the field.

Late in the day, Jim's patrol clambered into a Huey on the 'Kanga Pad' of the 9th Squadron, Royal Australia Airforce, clutching their M16s and 7.62 SLRs, eyeing the chopper's twin M60 machine-guns. They were five in number. Barring loss, they would be together as a team until the end of their tour of duty. Lead scout, medic, signaller, a corporal specialising in demolition, and Jim as patrol leader. In their olive-drab tiger stripes, stripped of all insignia, bush hats, and camouflage cream smeared all over their faces, it was hard to tell who was who. At dusk, their transport chopper, shepherded by two gunships, delivered them deep in enemy territory. They dropped from the winch, went to ground and zigzagged away from the drop area as quickly as their 50-pound backpacks would allow, communicating with one another in frantic hand signals. None of them had shaved for a week. In the bright green hell of the jungle a scratch could turn septic before your eyes and their eyes were needed elsewhere. This was a free-fire zone where what the boys said in the pub applied with interest: if it moves, shoot it.

An hour later, after a thorough recce, they shovelled some food into their stomachs and settled down to try and get some sleep.

By mid-afternoon the following day, they'd covered roughly one grid mile of their nine-mile sector. They'd seen some enemy movement, taken note of numbers and equipment and were feeling a couple of degrees more relaxed. This was an intelligence-gathering mission. There was no future in engaging the enemy unless he stood right up in front of you and barked.

Next morning, Jim decided it was safe to stash their packs and split up for individual sorties in direct lines away from the perimeter. Regroup at two, on the nose.

Within minutes, as he moved like a ghost through the eerie lightlessness, Jim felt an isolation many times more intense than anything he'd ever experienced in his brief spell riding boundary for Athol Ferguson. All those now so very far away kept flashing into his mind as his senses strained to the limit. His mother and father. The Fergusons. Tim Daley. The Donnellys. Dud Brewley. One after another they came and went and came back again a few steps further on. There was only one face he wouldn't allow. Each time he anticipated her, he shook his head, gripped his SLR and took another silent, invisible step into jeopardy.

He'd gone only a few hundred yards when he heard a sudden

babble of chatter. He went to ground and spent another fifteen minutes just listening before he dropped into a crouch and crept forward. When he was close up, he went back on his belly and inched forward, straining for a view. He tunnelled into a large bush and cautiously parted the foliage in front of him.

Washing was hanging from ropes strung up in the trees. In the middle of the compound, surrounded by a couple of make-shift shelters and tents, a huge pot was simmering over a low fire. Still as a mouse, hardly breathing, Jim watched his enemy at play. Dressed in nothing but baggy shorts, they lolled about, smoking, reading pamphlets and newspapers, yabbering away as if the war didn't exist. One side of the clearing, seven of them were practising a tumbling routine. They were pretty good. There were piles of weapons everywhere.

By the time he had finished noting the details in his book, the gymnasts had begun to form a pyramid. Three at the base, two on their shoulders, another man climbed up to take his position on top and braced himself for the last man to clamber up and stand on his shoulders. He jacknifed, stood on his hands and slowly drew himself up into a perfect handstand. He only managed to get up for a split second before the whole assembly began to sway and kelter. The base men frantically shuffled their feet looking for balance. But it was no go. They lost it. The whole thing came tumbling down and the little one with the Ho Chi Min moustache fell on his bum in the fire. He got a bad burn all the way down the back of his thigh. He rolled away screaming, leapt to his feet and had a fit, yelling his head off and hurling abuse at his grinning brothers-in-arms.

Jim couldn't help a sly grin himself.

'Serves you right, you little galah,' he whispered under his breath.

Five days later, with their first patrol behind them, Jim and his team were back in the relative security of their compound on SAS Hill. Any relief was tempered by the prospect of a great many more patrols before their tour of duty was up in February 1967.

Half a world away, Elizabeth sat down at the kitchen table of her Brisbane flat. She opened the writing pad and picked up her pen. But her mind was as blank as the page before her and the pen started to shake in her hand. As the events of the day before came crushing in on her, the page was covered in splotches from the tears that began pouring down her cheeks. A sudden bird-like cry of anguish escaped her throat and she pushed the pad aside. If she was to keep her resolution not to give the slightest hint, even between the lines, this letter would have to wait for a moment. She'd only known for twenty-four hours. The results of Jack's thorough physical check-up. The doctors had been kind. But there was nothing they could do. The disease was spreading like wildfire.

'How long?' she finally managed to ask.

'Eighteen months . . . Two years, possibly. With a little luck and some natural remission.'

# Seventeen

In January 1967 an American Army captain, in uniform bearing the insignia of the US 5th Division, climbed a flight of stone steps and rang the bell of an expensive residence in the Sydney suburb of Vaucluse. Jean Barclay answered the door.

'Yes?'

'Mrs Barclay? Jean Barclay?'

'Yes.'

The American stood there a moment, waiting for recognition to dawn, then he grinned and mimicked a little bow.

'Afternoon, ma'am,' he drawled. 'Dean Coulter.'

Jean Barclay looked puzzled. Then her eyes flew open wide as the penny dropped.

'So it is! I didn't recognise you.'

'It's been quite a while.'

She pushed the door back behind her and stepped aside. 'Come in . . . Come in for goodness sake.'

As Coulter stepped into the hall, Jean Barclay patted him on the back. 'How wonderful to see you. Just look at you! All grown up and a soldier.'

She steered him into the living room, instructed him to make himself comfortable and hurried off to the kitchen for some refreshments.

In her absence, Coulter wandered about the room, inspecting the various paintings on the walls and admiring bits and pieces of family knick-knackery until Jean returned bearing a tray.

'Now . . . Tell me all about yourself. What on earth are you doing here?'

Coulter grinned. 'Rest and recuperation, they call it. Had the choice of Brisbane or Sydney so, naturally, I thought I'd better seize the chance.'

'I should think so,' Jean beamed. 'Mind you, it's all changed so much I hardly recognise it myself half the time.'

'Doesn't seem to have changed all that much around here.

165

The streets got more and more familiar the closer I got.'

'I'm surprised you remember it at all. You couldn't have been more than six or seven.'

'Five, I think.'

Jean fluffed her hair and tried a little smile. 'Well, there you are. Now, tell me, dear . . . How are they?'

'Mom's fine. Still the same. Organising more committees than there are causes.'

'Now, now. Your mother was the best charity organiser I've ever known. She was sorely missed around here, I can tell you. Sorely missed. And your father. How's he? Such a wonderful looking man.'

'His legs are pretty bad these days. Still uses a stick.'

'All our very best colonial pieces were bought on your father's advice. For an absolute song at the time. Worth a packet these days, of course. Mind you, I wouldn't part with any of them.'

Jean dropped her head back on the couch, briefly lost in a host of memories. 'It would be so lovely to see them again. Any chance of them paying us a visit some time?'

'Mom could. She'd love to. But she'd never leave Pop behind. He'd never be able to handle the ride. Even a couple of miles in the car are pretty painful.'

'They could come on a boat. One of those lovely Pacific cruise things.'

'I'll see what I can do,' Coulter grinned. 'When I get home.'

Jean turned to study his face a moment, real concern banishing frivolity. 'When will that be?'

'I've got another twelve months in Vietnam. After this lay-off.'

Jean took his hand in hers and held it tight. 'How wretched for you. Thank God you Americans are there, that's all I can say. I'm sure we'd never manage on our own. It's just too horrible to think about. All our young men . . . and yours . . . in that dreadful place. Why on earth those wretched people can't settle their own differences is quite beyond me.'

There wasn't much future in following that particular tack and he was quick to change the subject.

'And Rachel? I guess she's all grown up.'

'She certainly is,' Jean declared, unable to keep the vexation out of her voice. 'Do you remember her at all?'

'I can remember all of us playing here. And at our house . . . Visiting the Leslies. I think I may have been guilty of pulling her braids more than I should have.'

Jean laughed, pulled herself up from the couch and disappeared into the dining room. She was back at once with a ten-by-eight photograph in a silver frame.

'You better not try any rough stuff now. She'd probably give you a black eye.' She handed the photograph to Coulter and he weighed it in his fingers.

'She was engaged to David Leslie for a couple of years. They had some ridiculous row and broke it off. Anthony was absolutely furious with her. She wouldn't even speak to David for months. But they've been seeing one another again recently, so we've all got our fingers crossed . . .'

As she spoke, Coulter stared at the photograph, bewitched. When he spoke it was a whisper.

'She's very beautiful.'

'It seems she is,' Jean sighed wearily. 'She's gone up to Windsor. There's a polo tournament there this weekend. Perhaps you would like to come up with us? On Friday? We'd love to have you and it would be such a surprise for them. You still play, don't you?'

'As much as I can.'

'Can you come?'

Coulter glanced down at the photograph on his lap then back to Jean and smiled. 'Wild horses wouldn't keep me away.'

The following Saturday afternoon, Dean Coulter and Rachel sat side by side as the game sashayed backwards and forwards across the dusty Windsor polo grounds. Rachel was doing most of the watching. Coulter could hardly take his eyes off her.

The game ended with a last-minute goal stolen by the opposition and a frustrated David Leslie rode over to the sidelines, his pony chomping at the bit and prancing nervously.

'Tough luck,' Coulter sympathised.

'Can't win them all, I suppose. Get our own back tomorrow.' He glanced quickly at Rachel, then fixed his eyes on Coulter. 'I meant to mention it to you, there's a knock-up in the morning. If you'd like a ride, I'm sure we can kit you out.'

'That'd be great,' said Coulter.

'Okay, I'll organise it.' Leslie nodded at this grinning American he could remember in name only. Then he pivoted his pony and rode off. With exaggerated chivalry, Dean Coulter offered Rachel his arm and they wandered off through the crowd, plunging back into each other's company.

Four nights later, a taxi pulled into the driveway of the Barclay's house in Vaucluse. Dean Coulter, dressed to kill, in a handmade, single-breasted, off-white suit was out of the door before it stopped. He took the front steps two at a time and rang the bell. He jiggled some loose change in his pocket and tapped his foot. At last, the door swung open and she was there. Behind her, Jean Barclay was smiling, a shade anxiously.

'Have a nice time, you two.'

'We sure will,' Coulter assured her and quickly hustled Rachel down the steps to the waiting taxi.

They had dinner by the harbour under the stars. Afterwards they strolled along the beach. They never stopped talking. Coulter told her about New York, his house at the beach on Long Island, his weekend playgrounds in Connecticut and Pennsylvania, the group of sales promotion and advertising companies that had already made him a dollar millionaire at the age of thirty before Uncle Sam requested his presence in Vietnam. He dropped a few names but quickly realised this stunning Australian girl was not in the least bit impressed and pulled his head in.

'Sorry,' he grinned. 'Getting a bit ahead of myself. There's not much time for us to get to know each other.'

'Oh, I don't know,' said Rachel. 'After all, we used to bath together, don't forget.'

Coulter laughed and tossed the pebble he'd been carrying far out over the water.

They went on to Romano's where Coulter promptly ordered champagne. When they'd exhausted themselves on the dance floor, Coulter ordered another bottle and they settled in their corner booth.

Rachel was enjoying herself. Very much. This smiling Yank was so easy to be with. He hadn't pressed her about David Leslie, though she knew he was curious. She hadn't spent an evening like this for a long, long time, with no sword hanging over her head. It was only when they'd exhausted the second bottle that Coulter broached the subject. For a moment she resented it. She found her relationship with David increasingly difficult to explain of late, even to herself.

'Something keeps drawing us back together. I'm not sure either of us knows exactly what it is. Habit, probably. The families. I just got fed up with one postponement after another. The funny thing was I'd come to think we were already married, just living under different roofs.'

'And now?'

'He wants to go through the whole thing all over again, formal engagement, all the right notices in the papers, keep up appearances, all that nonsense. At least, it's nonsense to me.'

'Is there anyone else?'

Caught off guard, Rachel looked away, finding a sudden interest in the bandstand. But she had to answer. She gathered herself and turned back to him.

'No,' she said. 'Not really.'

He didn't believe her. But he let it pass. 'If David ever gives up, will you marry me?'

Rachel threw back her head and laughed. 'My gosh. You Americans don't waste any time, do you?'

Coulter was smiling, too. But the look in his eye told her it wasn't a frivolous suggestion.

'That would set a few tongues wagging.'

'Seriously . . . I hope we can spend as much of my leave together as possible. Or as much as we can without David coming after me with a cricket bat.'

'Oh, he'd never do that. Very easy going, Mr Leslie, in his own way.'

'Excellent,' Coulter declared. 'Then for the next four days you're mine.'

Rachel picked up her glass, leaned over and clinked it against his.

'Done,' she announced.

True to her word, Rachel twisted her brother John's arm for the loan of his VJ and they had a wild time scudding in and out of Sydney harbour's southeastern shoreline, turning turtle time after time, bouncing side by side on the fin trying to drag the little boat's water-logged sails upright again. They rode the Big Dipper at Luna Park. They languished through a blazing hot afternoon at Taronga Park Zoo, marvelling at the creatures that had peered out at Coulter from the pages of his children's books in faraway Connecticut.

The third day, they set off early, took the long ferry ride to Manly and spent the day swimming, sunbathing, wandering the esplanade, sharing the best caramel malted milkshakes in the world. They managed to land a few shiny new 20 cent coins on the backs of the Grey Nurse sharks swimming in blind circles below the catwalk at the Aquarium and made their fervent wishes before the coins slid off.

As evening fell they caught the ferry back to the city. They sat outside on the top deck, watching the dance of harbourside lights as they came on in the homes and streets hugging the shoreline. The wind got up as they crossed the rolling swell coming in through the Heads. Coulter whipped off his jacket and wrapped it round her shoulders. Rachel grinned and snuggled into it.

'I'll make dinner at home tonight, if you like,' she suggested.

'Your folks came back today, didn't they?'

'No. They won't be back until tomorrow night.'

'Here,' Coulter held his arm in front of her face. 'Twist my arm.'

'That's extra,' Rachel replied, poker-faced.

'I'm rich.'

She snuggled against him for a moment. Then, taking him by surprise, grabbed his arm and started twisting like hell.

'Owww!' Coulter yelled, fighting back.

They stopped at a bottle shop on the way back to the house for more champagne. For weeks afterwards, Rachel blamed that stop for what followed. But she had to blame herself as well. She'd thrown it all away.

After the engagement to Leslie had ended, before they drifted back together, she made several attempts to write to the man who had her heart. Each time she'd given up in despair. It seemed a dirty trick to reject him in the first place only to do an about-face and offer him a chance to play second fiddle now. Their moment of parting at Winton airport tormented her. She knew then she'd broken his heart. Over and over again she told herself he'd welcome her back with open arms. But what if he didn't? What if her rejection had hardened Jim's heart, turned him against her, perhaps even turned his love to hate. It was the possibility that he might tell her to go to hell that caused her courage to fail as much as her inability to find the right words. The love she still felt for Jim, the strange fractured love she still felt at times for David Leslie were obliterated in one night of uninhibited passion with this reckless American who had appeared out of her distant past without a word of warning.

Rachel grilled steaks for their dinner and mixed up her own famous dressing for the salad. She lit candles in the dining room. When the moment came, one look was all it took. Coulter opened his mouth to speak, changed his mind and just reached for her hand. Rachel simply kept hold of it, slowly stood up on unsteady legs, pulled him to his feet and led him up the stairs to her room.

An hour later it was all over. They lay naked under the sheet, her head resting on his shoulder as he stroked her hair.

'You okay?'

Rachel bit her lip. She felt sick. Despite the booze, Coulter was a patient and generous lover. It was so different from her occasional lovemaking with David Leslie. Their times together were always brief, and to the point.

'Yes,' she whispered. 'A bit guilty.'

'Me, too,' he confessed.

'David would never forgive me . . .'

'Does it matter?'

'Yes. In a way.'

'I'll marry you tomorrow morning if you'll have me. David or no David.'

Rachel raised her head and pecked his cheek. 'These have been the nicest few days I've spent in ages. Let's not spoil them.'

Coulter didn't reply for a time. He just stared at the ceiling, rehearsing the right words.

'Tell you what, I've got another twelve months to go in 'Nam. Soon as it's over, I'll be back.'

'I think I'll be in a nunnery.'

'I'll come right in after you.'

'You'll have to get past mother superior first.'

'I'll bring a tank.'

Rachel chuckled, the joke easing her blues a notch. Coulter kissed the top of her head.

They lay in silence again for a while, simply absorbing each other's presence. Doubts flew like bats in the dark.

He was up before she woke. He made coffee, and it tasted good.

'Do you know Queensland at all?' he asked.

Rachel started. 'A little . . . Not very well. Why?'

'The man who pulled Pop out of the fat in New Guinea lives up there somewhere on a ranch.'

'We've got friends there. The Fergusons. A place called Winton. That's the only bit I know.'

'Pop wrote him a couple of times after the war, through some returned servicemen's organisation. Never got a word back. He was hoping I might look into it while I was here but I figured my time was short enough without going off on a wild goose chase. Especially as I'd decided to come to Sydney.' Their eyes met in the early morning light. 'Thank God I did.'

'What's his name?'

'Mackay. Jack Mackay. He was a sergeant . . .'

It hit Rachel like a sledgehammer. Coulter rambled on, a blow by blow description of his father's rescue but she wasn't listening. She was staring at him as if she was witnessing an execution. She just couldn't believe that fate could be so cruel. Coulter broke off when he saw her tears spill.

'Hey . . . hey . . .' he whispered, pushing her up and a little away from him to see her face. 'Hey, sweetheart. Don't feel bad. David will never know any of this from me. I swear to God.'

Rachel tried to hold his look. But it was hopeless. She had to turn away as a sob strangled in her throat.

Coulter held his tongue, waiting for it to pass. It took a couple of minutes. She snuffled a bit and wiped away the tears on the back of her hand. Even then, it took a moment longer before she could take a deep breath and face him. She gave a helpless little shrug and the ghost of a smile.

'Sorry . . . It's just a bit of a shock . . .'

Coulter took the pledge. 'I swear to God, Rachel. Nobody will know a thing about this . . .'

But even before he finished speaking, Rachel was shaking her head and he broke off.

'No, it's not that. It's just . . . Well . . . Jack Mackay. I know his son. He's in Vietnam now.'

Coulter was amazed. 'I'll be damned. Do you know where?'

'No. But I know he's there. He used to work for the Fergusons. I met him there when we went up for Christmas, three years ago. He'd just been called up.'

Another catch was clawing at her throat. She struggled to continue but failed and had to turn away again as more tears filled her eyes. Very gently, Coulter reached out and massaged the back of her neck. But it didn't make matters any better. Rachel struggled a moment before continuing, her voice just above a whisper.

'He's nice. He's had a terrible time . . . Sad, really. His father was destroyed by the war . . . I . . . We all felt sorry for him.'

Rachel continued looking away as she spoke. Coulter didn't

172

reply. He continued kneading the base of her neck and contemplated the ceiling until she finally managed to pull herself together, turned back to him, kissed his brow and forced a little laugh.

'Sorry, Dean. I'm being ridiculous. Bit on edge, I guess. Think I'll take a shower.'

She tried to keep her tone bright, make light of what had happened, but Coulter's curiousity had multiplied tenfold. As she threw back the sheet to leave the bed, he grabbed her with both hands and turned her back to face him, staring at her so intently she was forced to drop her eyes.

'What's his name?'

She was hanging on by the slimmest thread but she forced herself to look up again.

'Jim,' she answered, as simply as she possibly could.

Coulter kept his grip on her arms, kept looking her right in the eye until he felt a shudder run through her body.

'Lucky Jim, by the look of it,' he said. 'Go on. Go and have your shower.'

He released her and Rachel twisted off the bed, grabbed her robe and disappeared through the door. Coulter eased himself back on the pillows and stared at the ceiling, digesting all the vicious twists of fate. He filled his lungs all the way down, released a long hissing sigh and reached for a cigarette.

# Eighteen

The Australian canteen was jam-packed. All the boys were knocking back the booze as if it might be their last drop on earth. Half a dozen Vietnamese girls were struggling to keep it coming. A mess sergeant, with a belly that looked like it was in urgent need of independent suspension and a sordid towel hanging from his back pocket, kept a beady eye on proceedings.

Dean Coulter was in the door. Jim Mackay's SAS captain stood on tiptoe and strained to see over the heads of the crowd.

'Over there. At the end of the bar.'

'Thanks a million.'

Coulter pushed his way through the mob and finally managed to squeeze in beside Jim. He tapped him on the shoulder.

'Dave Reynolds tells me you're Jim Mackay.'

'That's right,' Jim nodded, taking Coulter's hand.

'Dean Coulter.'

The name rang a vague bell but he couldn't place it. 'What can I do for you?'

'No favours,' Coulter assured him. 'Just thought I'd look you up while I had the chance. We have mutual friends in Australia. Well, friends of friends. Winton, is it?'

'That's right,' Jim smiled, even more surprised.

'I play a bit of polo, a lot back home. We were talking about the Fergusons' stud.'

'Oh, I see,' Jim grinned, then nodded towards the bar. 'What'll you have?'

'What's that you're on?'

'Aussie brew.'

'That'll do just fine.'

Jim waved to one of the girls and got the order in.

'When were you out there?'

'Just got back. R & R. Could have stood a bit more, no trouble at all.' Coulter took a good swallow and smacked his lips. 'Christ, that's cold. How do they do it?'

175

Jim grinned and nodded towards the mess sergeant. 'It's an art. Rumour has it he nicked one of the freezers from the mortuary.'

'Does the trick,' Coulter laughed. 'How long have you been here?'

'July last year.'

'Must be about due for a break yourself.'

'End of February.'

'Three weeks. Lucky man!'

'Too right,' Jim grinned. 'Snag is I've been asked to sign on for another tour. Instructing the new mob.'

'No field?'

'No. All behind the wire.'

'Might be worth it.'

'That's what I was thinking,' Jim nodded. 'Get another one out of the way in comfort.'

'When do you have to make up your mind?'

Jim glanced at his watch and pulled a face. 'About twelve hours from now.'

Coulter drained his glass. 'Better have another one then. While you think it over.'

Just as he turned away, there was a sudden almighty *keruuuump!* that shook the entire building and dimmed the lights. Just for a second, you could have heard a pin drop. Everybody froze in mid-sentence. But, as the lights came up again, the hubbub renewed. Everybody was talking much too loud.

'That was close.'

'Crooked as a dog's hind leg, they are. Been trying to dump one on here for weeks.' Jim nodded at the mess sergeant. 'Makes old Wozza cranky as a cut snake. Reckons the shock makes the beer go flat.'

Coulter laughed. 'Probably the same friendly locals who do your laundry.'

'Wouldn't surprise me.'

They drank in silence for a while. Jim glanced round the bar. Coulter studied his profile and wondered if the time was ripe to play the next tricky hand.

'You married?' he asked casually.

Jim shook his head. 'No. You?'

'Not yet,' Coulter replied, with a lopsided grin. 'But I'm working on it.'

'Best of luck.' Jim raised his glass.

176

'Got someone waiting at home?' Coulter pressed.

'No. Wish I had.'

'Anyone in particular?'

Jim shied at the question and glanced down at his glass. He didn't really want to talk about it but the beer had loosened his tongue.

'There was someone, before I came away. It was a bit complicated . . . Difficult situation.'

'Aren't they all,' said Coulter. And repeated it later to himself with bitter conviction.

Jim managed a grin. 'I guess so.'

'Another man's wife?'

'No. Well . . . sort of. It's a bit hard to explain.'

The questions were having their effect. Jim was starting to look like a man who'd just lost everything on one throw of the dice. He pulled himself out of it, took a swig of beer and changed the subject.

'This girl you're working on, that's back in the States, is it?'

'Sure is.'

'What's her name?'

'Rachel.'

Coulter had never seen the colour drain from a man's face so fast in his life. The name had blown Jim Mackay away, frozen his lips to his teeth.

'You okay?'

Jim put his glass on the bar. 'Yeah . . . Fine. Beer's caught up a bit, I reckon.' He tried to smile. But it curled up and died on his face. 'A bit one over the eight. Think I might have to turn in.'

'I'll walk back with you.'

They emerged from the canteen and walked across the sick-lit quadrangle, weaving a bit on their feet. But drunk as he was, Coulter was well pleased: he'd found out what he wanted to know. When they got to the fence he stopped.

'I go this way. Been good talking to you, Jim. Come over to our place tomorrow night. I'll buy you a bourbon.'

Jim felt sick to his heart at that moment. His thoughts were miles away and he could hardly raise a smile as he shook hands. But he managed to accept with good grace. 'You're on.'

*Keruuump! Keruuump!* The words were hardly out of his mouth when two enormous explosions blew the canteen to bits behind them and the shock waves knocked them off their feet.

Stunned and shaken, they hauled themselves up as men came running across the quadrangle from all directions, heading for the flaming building. Sober as judges in an instant, Jim and Coulter joined the rush to the rescue, dusting themselves off as they ran.

The following evening, Jim kept his appointment in the American canteen. Coulter greeted him warmly and shoved a drink in his hand.

'All drinks are on me tonight.'

'What's the occasion?'

Coulter studied the bourbon in his glass. He looked a bit embarrassed.

'I should have told you last night. Sort of wanted to get acquainted first. Then the booze took over. Truth is I owe you, Jim. More to the point, I owe your father.'

'How's that?'

To Jim's astonishment, Coulter spelled it out: all the links in the chain that bonded them, that went right the way back to the jungles of New Guinea all those painful years ago.

'. . . And now, here we are,' he concluded. 'Doing the same thing all over again.'

Somewhere along the way the penny dropped for Jim.

'Funny thing, the name rang a bell but I couldn't place it. I haven't seen the thing for yonks. But that's the name on Dad's citation, isn't it, Robert D. Coulter?'

'You've got it.'

'Well, I'll be buggered,' Jim smiled. He stuck out his hand as if they'd only just met. 'How you doing?'

'So far so good,' said Coulter, clasping Jim's hand like a long lost brother.

Jim studied Coulter as he went to the bar. He'd liked the American from the start. He seemed like a good bloke, refreshingly free of the bravado and swagger of some of his countrymen. They could be friends. They could hardly not be now. When Coulter returned and slapped the next round on the table, Jim began quietly to explain the course of events that had overtaken his family following his father's return from the war and the slow, withering deterioration in his condition. Coulter heard him out with respect and shook his head in dismay when he finished.

'Pop will be real sad to hear it. You must let me have the address of the hospital so he can write to him. It beat the hell out of him he didn't make contact before.'

'He mightn't get a reply this time, either. Dad's pretty much in a world of his own these days.'

Coulter nodded. 'Maybe your mother's address. Pop could write to her, leave it up to her.'

'Yeah,' Jim agreed. 'That's probably the best way to do it.'

'I know for sure if there's anything, anything at all that Pop could do, he'd jump at the chance.'

'It's pretty much in the lap of the gods I'm afraid. Has been for a long time. He was showing some signs of improvement just before I came away. My mother says he's not too bad at the moment. She leaves a lot out. Doesn't want me to worry about it too much while I'm here, I guess.'

'Are you staying on?'

'Yeah. Told them I'd give it a go. Means another six months . . .'

'Behind the wire, that's the main thing.'

'Yeah. Maybe I can get out of here for good then.'

'There'll be nothing left to fight over soon,' said Coulter. 'Our fly-boys seem to have been told to wipe the place off the face of the earth.'

'It's the poor bastards caught in the middle that get my goat. I guess they're the ones we're really doing it for. But I don't think they give a damn who wins in the long run. Just want it to stop.'

'Don't we all,' Coulter sighed.

'That's for sure.'

Coulter headed to the bar again for refills. As he waited his turn, he attempted to put his own feelings in some perspective. Here was the son of the man his father owed his life to. Here was the man he believed stood much more squarely in the way of his love for Rachel Barclay than David Leslie, and he had to admit he could see why. He liked the guy. He was friendly, open and direct in the way of a lot of Ausssies, rock solid underneath. He came across as someone who'd seen more than his fair share of trouble yet managed to come through with his balance intact, unembittered, determined to make the best of a bad lot. His bushman's eyes betrayed a sagacity born of coming to terms with disappointment.

'Just my luck,' he said to himself as the drinks arrived and he dug for the money.

'Better make this my last,' Jim said when he returned. 'I'm off into the scrub tomorrow afternoon.' He raised his hand and crossed his fingers. 'With a little luck, it might turn out to be my last patrol this time round.'

'Here's to that.'

Coulter passed him his lighter. It was an expensive silver job, by du Pont.

'Christmas present,' he shrugged. 'Rachel's Dad.'

The same thing happened. His Aussie friend looked like a stunned mullet.

When Jim raised his eyes again their mellow bourbon glow had been replaced by a dull, haunting ache. He fished in his pocket for a notebook and pencil, and Coulter saw his hand was shaking as he scribbled the address.

'Here. That's mum's Brisbane address.'

Coulter carefully folded the paper, took out his wallet and stashed it safely away. 'I'll keep you posted,' he grinned. 'How long are you going out for?'

'Not sure. See how it goes. Ten days at the most, I hope.'

'Stick your head in here when you get back. Let's keep in touch.'

'You're on,' Jim laughed.

The laugh was a bit forced. The Australian obviously had something else on his mind at that moment. Someone, more likely. Coulter felt his own confusion mounting. Above all, he felt Rachel's presence between them. Who would she have her eyes on at that moment? If only he didn't love her himself, the question might be easier to answer. After all, hadn't she loved him too? Willingly spent days of her time in his company. Days that had drawn them closer and closer together? Taken him to bed?

As the Australian threaded his way to the door, Coulter watched his retreating back with tired eyes. He had to smile at the irony of the situation. At the same time he could taste the bitter juice of loss.

'You're in deep shit, now,' he muttered.

180

# Nineteen

It took Jim's letter nearly six weeks to reach Brisbane. Elizabeth was amazed by his chance meeting with Dean Coulter and decided right away to tell Jack.

After some skilful detective work and cross-questioning the doctors, Jack now knew his son was in Vietnam. He also knew that he was dying. It seemed to have brought him some peace at last. His interest in his surroundings revived, his memory churned with a string of forgotten details of history, his court-ship of Elizabeth, their broken life together. Of one thing he was certain. He told her to sell Balkenna and invest the money for the future. She assured him that was the furthest thing from their minds. Jim fully intended to take the property on when he returned and she told him about Athol Ferguson's offer. It didn't shift Jack. He insisted they should sell because the life was just too hard. The struggle too punishing. He had only one last wish. He wanted to die there. He wanted Elizabeth to take him home to Balkenna while he still had enough strength to get about, to drive over the land of his youth, the thankless acres of his manhood. He wanted a little time for the two of them to sit out on the verandah in the evenings. He wanted to taste the dust in his throat, smell the sweet promise of rain in the air, hear the laugh of the kookaburra rather than the chattering sparrows of the suburbs.

Elizabeth was shredded. She fought hard to keep a tight rein on her emotions until her visit was over, till she could retreat to a quiet corner of the grounds, watch the wind bend a line of stately poplars to its will and shed her sorrow in private. Next day, she returned to consult the doctors. There were no objections. For what there was left of it, Jack Mackay's life was his own. They would provide her with all the relevant medication and send his file on to Michael Hawker in Longreach. When she told Jack, he simply nodded, reached for her and held her to him for several minutes before he whispered his thanks in her ear.

The other news in Jim's letter presented unexpected complications in her carefully laid plans. She had been preparing for his imminent arrival on home leave and had prepared herself for the task of telling him the bad news. Time and again, she justified her injunction by telling herself it would be far better face to face. Vietnam was enough on its own. Now he had signed on for another tour of duty. His two paragraphs assuring her he would be more or less out of harm's way and possibly not have to return once it was over did nothing to address her dilemma. Now there was no choice. Jim would have to be told. She would have to ask him to see if he could get compassionate leave while there was still a little time. Time to keep the promise she made Jack. To see his son before he died.

Before, the letter would have been so difficult to phrase. Now, the sudden urgency allowed her to set it all down fluently, with all the love and compassion she could muster. She only wished she could accompany the letter, to be there and hold him at the moment they needed each other most.

At the end of April, five hundred miles to the south, Rachel Barclay also received a letter from Vietnam. She made herself comfortable on the swing couch on the verandah, unfolded the sheets of paper and smiled at the opening lines.

'My dearest Rachel,

How's my Sydney sweetheart? I trust this should not have been addressed Mrs Leslie. Your last letter implied no change in the weather but you were a bit vague to say the least.

Eight months to go and I'll be free of this hell hole. Still a long way off but it's hard to think of anything else. Hard not to think of getting back to Sydney to drive a tank through your mother superior! Please know that I love you and long to see you.

What follows will be some of the toughest words I have ever attempted to put on paper, so please bear with me if they get a bit jumbled or confused.

As you know, I returned here with the long-range objective of getting back Sydneyside as fast as I could. I hoped I'd fall right in at your side and we might pick up where we left off if you found your way clear as far as David was concerned. A simple mission. Easily accomplished because you would want it too. Sweetheart, my heart is starting to ache as I write this. Martyrdom is not my strong suit. On the other hand I'm not blind or stupid (I hope!). Not too stupid anyway.'

She was already starting to fear the worst as she turned the page.

You gave the game away that night in Sydney. I know how hard you tried to hide it. I know too that what we share can never be forgotten. It will always be there. I hope you feel that too. But it doesn't take away from the fact that a little black cloud appears overhead whenever I try and picture us together. I won't try to pretend I haven't kidded myself it wasn't there. But it won't work. I knew that night – I knew at that moment – that even if David was out of the picture, you would still not be free. There would always be a ghost in the corner.

Well, I've seen your ghost, sweetheart. I managed to track him down. I don't know what I had in mind. But we've gotten to know each other pretty well. It hurts to admit it but I like him a lot.

Rachel. This is hard. I just hope and pray it makes sense.

Jim knows nothing – absolutely nothing – about us. He never will as far as I'm concerned. He believes I tracked him down because of the connection between our fathers. The man is a walking heartache. He's got a ghost too. Unfortunately, I know her name. I've seen your presence pass right through him, just as I saw his pass through you. I didn't want to see it. I suppose I hoped there'd be little or no memory there at all. But I dropped the name Rachel and I thought I'd have to call the medics. Never seen a guy so pole-axed by one little word before.

I'm not completely stupid. I know enough to know when I'm beaten. If he makes it out of here, don't waste any more time. To hell with David. To hell with the family and all the rest of it. Otherwise your life will be one long regret. Mine, too, for that matter. I would hate to think I stepped aside for nothing. I would regret it even more if you were unhappy. I love you, Rachel. I want to make you happy. If this is the way, then so be it.

Jim Mackay loves you. There's no doubt in my mind about that. Loves you as much as I know you love him. If he makes it home, don't blow it! Don't throw it all away. Reach out and grab it with both hands, that's all I can say. Just remember, I'll always be around if you need me. No matter what happens. Even if I end up married with ten kids! I'll be there. What we share, we share for life. God bless you, sweetheart, and keep you safe.

I better quit while I'm ahead. Whoever said 'all's fair in love and war' never knew much about either one.

Love,

Dean xxx

Rachel stared at the letter in her hands for a long, long time. Her eyes were damp as she gazed across the garden at the harbour waters shimmering in the distance. She held the American in her mind's eye and thanked him for the generosity of his spirit. She felt an overwhelming sense of release. He had read her heart and accepted what he saw written there. Now he demanded she act upon it. The only thing he couldn't know was that her relationship with David Leslie was over for good. They had both come to face that fact over the past few weeks. Whatever had pulled them back together again had not been strong enough to last. At least, this time, there was no bitterness.

In turn, there was something she couldn't know about Dean Coulter, though she would come to realise it later on. He had confessed the difficulty he found in putting his thoughts on paper with considerable understatement. In fact, he had agonised over his decision, found umpteen ways to avoid the issue. If it had been any other man under the sun, he wouldn't have given a damn. But this man's father had saved his father's life. There was no getting away from that. Until now, there had been no way to repay the debt. He knew Rachel Barclay had been strongly attracted to him, loved him for a brief moment. But he also knew she loved Jim Mackay. More than himself, David Leslie or anyone else. When he finally came to put pen to paper, it seemed to him that in making their match, he could honour the debt on his father's behalf, make Rachel happy for her own sake, favour the friendship he felt for the man she loved. Even so, when the moment came to drop the letter in the post bag, he hesitated. He ran the whole thing over in his mind again before releasing his grip on the envelope. Then he retired to the bar to build a formidable defence against a crippling attack of the blues.

Jean Barclay appeared round the side of the house, decked out in her favourite gardening gear, a pair of pruning shears firmly in hand.

'How is he?'

'Fine. Counting the days, I think.'

'Is that all?'

'Just about.'

'No news is good news, I suppose,' Jean announced airily, a bit flummoxed by Rachel's paltry revelation of the letter's contents. She turned away and headed for the rose bushes, working the shears in her hand even before she got there.

Rachel watched her for a moment, then retreated into the house. She climbed the stairs to her room and hauled a large, overstuffed scrapbook down from her bookshelves. Taking it to a chair by the window, she balanced it on her lap and began leafing through the pages until she found what she was looking for. It was a clipping from the sports pages of the *Sydney Morning Herald*. There was a large photograph beneath a noisy headline: 'Best Match Seen for Years'. The photo itself was captioned 'Jim Mackay from Winton, Queensland, who hit the winning goal'. Rachel stared long and hard at his image, drinking it in, before running her finger over his outline, returning the clipping to the book and closing it. She held it on her lap and gazed out of the window into the distant haze. Below her, on her knees, her mother was still happily clipping away at the roses.

# Twenty

As it turned out, Jim was refused home leave, compassionate or any other kind. Captain Reynolds had done everything he could. But the higher powers refused to play ball. They insisted Jim's frontline experience was invaluable to the war effort and it was he himself who had volunteered to stay on. After the third attempt, Reynolds reluctantly informed him there was nothing more he could do. Jim would have to count the days.

A flurry of correspondence with his mother only confirmed his father's tenuous grip on life was growing weaker by the day, and every day in Vietnam was another day lost in the race with time he could never win. Then at the end of July he was suddenly summoned to Reynolds' office.

'I've managed to swing it,' his captain told him. 'Sorry it couldn't have been longer. But four weeks is better than nothing in the circumstances.'

Relief rolled over Jim in waves.

'That's for sure. Thanks, Dave. I really appreciate it.'

'No worries. You've more than earned it as far as I'm concerned. I've also taken the liberty of putting you up for a post in Brisbane after your leave's over. Same job – instructor. With any luck, you should be able to swing a discharge before another year's out, given your family situation.'

'That's very good of you, sir,' Jim acknowledged. Then he couldn't help it, he broke rank altogether. 'In fact, it's bloody fantastic! Do you think you can swing it?'

'You know me, Jim. Not exactly a betting man. Only ever fancy a dead set sure thing. But, yeah, I'm pretty sure it'll work out. With a little more luck, I'll be back there myself before too long. Here, I need you to sign these.'

He pushed the papers across the desk and Jim got busy with the pen.

'What's the news from home?' Reynolds asked quietly.

'Not too good,' Jim admitted. 'This four-week let off could just make all the difference.'

'Hope you make it in time.'

'Thanks.'

'Our mob have got a transport flying out of Bien Hoa on Thursday. You can hop on a chopper ride with the Yanks. Better get over there on Wednesday, to be on the safe side. Nobody seems to have a clue what time they're leaving.'

Jim returned his pen. As he stood, Reynolds offered his hand.

'Good luck, Mackay. We'll miss your ugly mug around here.'

'Thanks,' Jim grinned. 'I'll miss you blokes, too. Can't say the same for this joint, I'm afraid.'

'That makes two of us.'

Jim donned his hat, came to attention and gave a crisp salute. Reynolds gave him the thumbs up. 'Go for your life.'

A corporal marched in as soon as he'd gone. 'All set?'

'Yes,' Reynolds replied, handing over the papers. 'He's on his way. Here, you can file this lot. Is that the list?'

'Yes, sir. Whittled down to six.'

'He's going to be a hard act to follow,' Reynolds mumbled as he began going through the names. 'Game as they come, sharp as a tack . . . Let's see who we've got here . . .'

That night, Jim went looking for his American friend, only to discover Coulter had been called to Saigon for a week. So he went back to his bunk and scribbled a long note to leave at 5th Division headquarters the following morning. After explaining his sudden departure, Jim volunteered the hope that Coulter might be able to pay him a visit at Balkenna some day. And he asked him to pass along his own thanks to his father. Bob Coulter had written Jack a deeply moving letter. Elizabeth had quoted the closing lines.

'Obviously, I deeply regret that circumstances now prohibit us from meeting again. I just want you to know how strongly I can still feel the grip of your hand in mine that day at Buna. Across the ocean that lies between us, please know that I grip your hand in the same spirit at this time. There is no need for me to tell you to take heart and summon courage for what lies ahead. Those qualities I know you to possess in abundance. I owe my life to them and I am for ever in your debt . . .'

Jim finished his letter to Coulter on a jaunty note: 'Queensland – best place on earth! The Outback – an unforgettable experience – not to be missed! Mackay Tours guarantee a good time! See you there!'

It was late by the time he finished, but he felt like celebrating his good fortune and headed for the American canteen for a few shots of bourbon in his friend's honour. The place was half-empty and he settled down in a quiet corner to drink a silent toast to fortune. He was going home. Unless some VC rocket managed to bounce off his transport on the way out, he was also going home in one piece. With a little more luck, he wouldn't have to come back.

He now understood all too well the damage done to his father. He'd seen enough death, in enough grotesque and bloody postures, to last for ever. Like so many others before him, he'd steeled himself to the carnage. You had to, or someone else would be looking down on your own mangled corpse. He'd seen children burning to death on the run. Against all his hopes, he'd been forced to kill, time and time again. He knew what it felt like, the flashpoint when you imagined the man already dead as you brought your sights to bear, the reality when your bullets tore his life to bits.

He had to instil his first-hand knowledge in those he instructed. The unblooded virgins fresh from home. He had to make them believe that the enemy was fierce, and unstoppable, passionately convinced of the justness of his cause, formidably artful in the ill-equipped, undernourished guerrilla techniques that mocked the might of the US war machine. He had to instil in them what it meant to kill. What it meant to find the courage to move forward on command a second after your best mate had been chopped to death beside you. He taught them tricks of the trade for not going stark raving mad on the spot. How not to present a target for all the world to see by suddenly standing up in the middle of a paddy field and screaming at the top of your lungs, 'Why are we doing this?'. If you had a shred of decency left. A flicker of humanity.

Jim had seen an awful lot of men who'd forgotten. Robots of violence, in love with it for its own sake. Pigs in shit. He thanked whatever it was up there time and again that the men in his patrol group shared his own contempt for those who went mad with hate. To survive intact, mentally and physically, it was essential to maintain not only the healthiest respect for those who were out to kill you, but a sense of compassion for those you killed.

One night he never forgot, Jim plunged his knife into the heart of a North Vietnamese soldier. If there was one image above all else that he would carry away from this foreign land, one image he would have to live with, it was the look of utter disbelief in the eyes of the man who quivered to death underneath him, his lips silently begging to know why Jim had done such a terrible thing. He couldn't have been more than eighteen years old, if that.

He certainly didn't want to be thinking about it now. He swallowed the last of his bourbon in one gulp to burn the image into black.

Two weeks later Jim was sitting by his father's bedside at Balkenna. He'd made it in the nick of time. Michael Hawker confirmed it. Jack was down for the count this time. He was still on his feet the day Jim got back and they managed to talk for a good part of the evening before a terrible fit of vomiting had forced his father back to bed. Since then, for the past three days, Jim had waited patiently at his side for those moments when Jack came out of it long enough to say a few words before exhaustion dragged him back to sleep.

His father had insisted, over and over, that they should sell Balkenna after he'd gone. Each time, Jim told him not to worry about it and avoided committing himself one way or the other. It was only now, in the brief exchanges of these last fading hours, that it dawned on him that his father was using what strength he had left to sound him out, to see if his son had the stomach for the fight.

As he gazed down at the strained and wasted face on the pillow, his father's eyes flickered open again and stared up at him with a terrible urgency. He tried to say something, then gave up. Jim leaned over and offered a few words of comfort. Jack nodded, ever so slightly, and closed his eyes again as his face knotted in agony.

The doctor was sitting with his mother by the fireplace in the lounge room, comforting her as best he could.

'Can you give him another shot? He's pretty bad.'

'Of course.'

Jim perched himself on the arm of his mother's chair, slipped his arm round her shoulders and rested his cheek on the top of her head, rocking her a little. Elizabeth simply patted his hand.

She'd run out of words. They both had. Dr Hawker was only gone a few minutes.

'He's awake. He's asking for you again, Jim.'

As Jim returned to his chair by the bed, Jack turned his head to stare at him for a moment. Then he reached out his hand. Jim took it and held it on the bedcover. His father's voice was a croak, barely above a whisper.

'Things . . . Things didn't work out like I planned, Jim.'

'It's all right, Dad. You just take it easy . . .'

Jack shook his head and gripped Jim's hand with surprising strength. 'I just want you to know, boy . . . Things didn't work out like I planned. You know I always hoped you'd take over the place some day . . . As I did from your grandfather and on back down the line . . .'

He had to pause as another bolt of pain shot through him and it took him a few moments to get his voice back. When he did, it was a lot more urgent. Time was running out fast. He was desperate to make amends, to be sure his son understood that things had just got out of control through no fault of his own, only because of the rotten deal fate had saddled him with. The harder he tried, the more rambling and incoherent he became. Jim had to lean closer and closer to decipher the words.

'Wanted it to be a going concern . . . Like it was for me . . . Not empty . . . Broken down . . . I couldn't keep a strong hand . . .'

He crushed Jim's hand in a vice-like grip that belied his words. His fingers were twisting the ring on Jim's finger.

'You've got a strong hand, Jim . . . You could do it, couldn't you? With a strong hand . . . With a strong hand . . . You know what I mean, don't you, boy?'

Fighting back the tears streaming from his eyes, Jim leaned even closer, his lips at his father's ear.

'I know what you mean, Dad. Believe me, I know what you mean. It's always been my dream. Ever since I was a little boy, I dreamed of us working the place, together. It's not your fault, what happened. I'll work the place for both of us, if you want . . .'

He thought his father might actually break a bone in his hand. His grip got tighter and tighter with every word. Jack's breathing had whittled down to short, sharp stabs now, his eyes open one second, closed the next. But still the words formed in his throat.

'Could you stay on, boy? Look after your mother? . . .'

'Of course, Dad. Of course. That's all we ever wanted, to be here with you.'

'Balkenna,' Jack whispered. 'Balkenna.' The word tumbled from his lips with heartbreaking wistfulness. Balkenna was lost to him for ever. 'Hold on . . . You must hold on . . . Build it up again . . . Strong hand, Jim . . . Strong hand . . . Balkenna . . . Build it up again . . . You can do it . . . You can do it . . . Strong hand, boy . . . Strong hand . . . Look after your mother . . .'

The words were fracturing, disintegrating before they could properly form.

'I will, Dad. Easy, easy. I will. Do you hear me? I will . . . I promise. It's all I ever wanted . . . Do you understand?'

His father nodded, quite firmly, several times, and released his grip. His eyes flickered open and focused on Jim's for a few seconds. They suddenly seemed ridiculously alert, filled with laughter.

'Good on you, son.'

His head dropped back and he closed his eyes again. He seemed to relax. Jim eased himself back onto his chair and resumed stroking his father's hand. It was a good fifteen minutes before Jack's breathing suddenly faded to a hiss, rattling at the back of his throat. Jim was out of the door in a flash.

As Dr Hawker followed them into the room, Jim and Elizabeth sat on either side of the bed holding Jack's hands. His eyes flickered open again, still surprisingly clear and bright. They shone with love as he focused on Elizabeth. It was unmistakable. His hand moved slightly in hers as his eyelids flickered and then closed for good. He was gone. Michael Hawker placed his hand gently on Elizabeth's shoulder, brave face no longer needed. Jim gave his father a farewell kiss on the brow.

'I will, Dad . . . Don't worry,' he repeated, in a whisper.

Jim and his mother remained in the room for a long time, holding Jack's hands, wishing him God speed for his ride with the ferryman.


The Longreach Returned Services League saw to it that Jack Mackay was buried with full military honours. They sent a large delegation of their own. The Army sent a man up from Brisbane. The Fergusons and Dud Brewley drove down from Winton.

Jim and Tim Daley carried the coffin to the graveside. It was draped with the Queensland flag, his DSO presentation box open on top displaying his medal. They placed the coffin carefully across the planks over the grave and stepped back. The Reverend Kendon said all the right things.

When the words were over, the Army captain from Brisbane came to attention beside the coffin and gave a long, farewell salute. The RSL men followed suit. The captain retrieved the DSO and folded the flag with studied solemnity. Then he wheeled about, marched over to Elizabeth Mackay, stamped to a halt in front of her, saluted again and presented her with the flag and the medal. She found him a gentle, tearful smile.

The local RSL bugler stepped forward to the foot of the coffin and blew the first, long, mournful notes of the Last Post. He took his time. He played it well. When it was over he stepped back for Jim and Tim Daley to take the weight on the straps as the undertakers slid the planks away. They lowered Jack Mackay into his grave. The Reverend Kendon scattered a handful of earth down onto the lid. When he had finished, the RSL president stepped up and recited the final vow to a fallen comrade-in-arms. After the first few words, his voice was joined by dozens more.

'They shall not grow old, as we that are left grow old. Age shall not weary them, nor the years condemn. At the going down of the sun, and in the morning, we will remember them.'

Forty minutes later, the last carload of mourners set off on the long drive to Balkenna. The cemetery was deserted, except for the solitary figure of the grave digger, sweating buckets as he swung his shovel in the scorching heat of a merciless outback sun.

The gathering at Balkenna went on all afternoon as people came and went to pay their respects to the family. There were only a few people left by the time Michael Hawker managed to get there from the hospital. He brought a telegram that had arrived at the post office a couple of hours after Jack's burial. It was postmarked Charters Towers and addressed to 'Jack Mackay, Balkenna, Longreach'. They smiled when they read the simple message.

'So long, old mate – Fred Paterson.'

Last to arrive, Dr Hawker was also last to leave. He placed his hand on Elizabeth's shoulder and studied her a moment.

'You all right?' he asked.

'I'll be fine. Bless you for coming . . . Thanks for everything you've done. He may not have let on, but I know how much Jack appreciated all you did for him.'

'That goes for me, too,' Jim added quietly.

'I'll look in tomorrow, if I can.'

Jim accompanied the doctor out to his car. Once behind the wheel, he slipped Jim a small phial.

'Give her one of these. It'll help her sleep. Just one. I know how she hates taking pills, but she must get some rest. Let her sleep on in the morning if she's still out to it.'

Jim slipped the phial in his shirt pocket and tapped the windowsill. 'Thanks, Michael. Don't bother making another trip all the way out tomorrow. I'll call you. I'm sure she'll be fine.'

'Okay. But don't hesitate if you need me.'

'I won't. Thanks. Take it easy.'

He watched until the doctor's car was a mere speck on the track to the far horizon.

Later that night, after a bit of a tussle, Jim persuaded his mother to take one of the sleeping pills. He sat by her bed, talking a bit before it finally took effect. As her eyelids began to droop, she gave her son a drowsy smile and snuggled down for sleep to take over. Jim leant down to kiss her goodnight. 'Sleep well.'

Elizabeth's eyes were closed, but she nodded another little smile.

He wandered through to the lounge room. He poured himself a stiff brandy, swallowed it in a couple of gulps, poured another one and carried it on up to the kitchen.

For a long time, he just stood looking at the photograph of his father that had been on the shelf there ever since he was a boy. He took it down, held it in his hands a while before returning it to the shelf, adjusting it to the right position. He went to his coat which was draped over the back of a chair and retrieved the DSO presentation box. He took it back to the shelf, snapped it open, studied it a moment, closed it again and placed it alongside his father's image.

'God speed, Dad.'

There were a couple of leftover plates of sandwiches on the kitchen table. A 'Blot on the Gold Coast' said the headline of the *Courier Mail*. Jim couldn't help a wry grin as he read the report. It was a quote from the acting police minister, Mr Joh

Bjelke-Petersen, part of an attack on female impersonators who, he claimed, were 'patronising local hairdressing establishments'. Joh promised the voters 'to rid the Gold Coast of this sore'. He'd been forced to admit, however, that it was not actually an offence under the law for a man to appear in a public place dressed in women's attire. There didn't seem to be much else going on. Jim pushed the paper aside, reached for another sandwich and went outside.

It was a bright, moonlit night. The stars were so big he could just about reach up and pluck one down. The air around him hummed, clicked, buzzed and croaked with the anthems of nocturnal insects. Jim ran his eye over the silhouette of the house as he took a last drag from his cigarette, ditched it and heeled it with his boot. As he turned, something caught his eye. It was just a blink. But it soon turned into the twin headlights of an approaching car, still way down the track. Jim headed back to the front steps to await its arrival, wondering who it could be, hoping its motor would not disturb his mother's sleep. Whoever it was stopped a good fifty yards from the house and Jim headed towards the approaching figure, doing a bit of a double-take when he realised it was the man he'd just been thinking about.

'Hello. What's up? Did you forget something?'

Athol Ferguson smiled and shook his head. 'No. Well, not that I can remember, anyhow. How's your mother?'

'Fast asleep. Doc Hawker left some sleeping pills.'

'That's good. Pretty exhausting business, one way or another.'

He took Jim's arm and ushered him in the direction of the car. 'There's someone to see you. Wasn't sure if you'd still be up. It's a bit urgent, I'm afraid. Hope you don't mind.'

'Not at all,' said Jim as another figure emerged from the car. He stopped dead in his tracks.

He was thunderstruck. He just stared at her. Athol stepped quickly round them, hauled out a couple of suitcases.

'I'll be off then,' he called. 'See you the day after tomorrow.'

Rachel turned and waved. 'Thanks, Athol.'

If Jim had heard, it didn't show. He still had his eyes riveted on this impossible gift from God. Ferguson slid behind the wheel, turned the car and headed off down the track for the long drive back to Longreach. Rachel watched the receding tail lights for a moment.

'Sorry I wasn't here in time. The plane was held up at

Charleville for hours. Engine trouble, or something.' She gave him a quizzical look and tilted her head a little. 'You could say hello . . .'

But he couldn't. Couldn't say a word. Wondered if he'd passed out on the verandah and was dreaming all this. Only one way to find out. He reached out and drew her into his arms. Tighter and tighter and tighter. Rachel's fingernails dug deep into his back. Now at last words escaped Jim's throat as he buried his face in her hair. Words of deliverance.

'Oh, God . . . Oh, God . . .'

As they had the night they parted seemingly for ever, they clung to each other in the moonlight, rocking slightly, locked in silent communion.

Eventually Jim eased her back so he could see her face.

'God, it's good to see you . . . And today of all days.'

Rachel cupped her hand round his neck and pulled him back. It was a long and loving kiss. Simple, direct, worth a thousand words. When they came up for air, Jim eased himself back to hold her at arm's length and gaze at her again. Her face was radiant in the moonlight, as beautiful as his most precious memory of her.

'I'm not dreaming, am I?'

'Not unless I am too,' she said, her eyes dancing in the starlight.

'How long can you stay?'

Rachel gazed into his eyes for a long time before she spoke. When she did, all Jim Mackay's dreams came true at once.

'The rest of my life,' she said.

# PART TWO

# Twenty-One

Around one hundred million years ago, there was a stampede in central-western Queensland. A mob of one-foot-high coelurosaurs and two-foot-high ornithopods fled in panic along the muddy banks of a vast inland lake. They were chased by nine-foot-high flesh-eating carnosaurs and the evidence suggests they didn't go hungry.

As the world turned and they became extinct, their tracks were filled by sand and silt which eventually compressed to form solid rock. Climates changed, the oceans rose and fell, continents merged and transformed landscapes. Where the lake had been, a low mountain range thrust its humps at the sky. For thousands and thousands of years, erosion whittled away at its western edge until only the isolated hills of the Tully Range remained.

The dinosaurs' tracks were officially discovered in the early 1960s and the first footprints were excavated in the early 1970s. Today, the site is known as Lark Quarry Environmental Park and, from an elevated walkway, evidence of the stampede is there for all to see. The surrounding flat-topped ironstone hills are covered in gaunt spinifex. The ground around the site is littered with hard ironstone rocks. It is a lonely, waterless, inhospitable place.

As Rachel Mackay leant on the railing and stared down at the tracks, she felt at least a million years old, fossilised in a way of life she had come to find unbearable. All that she had refused to admit for so long, kept at bay because of the love she felt for the man she had married, came welling up and she felt as desolate as the surroundings.

That man was squatting on his haunches a couple of hundred yards away, picking through the pebbles at his feet, holding the odd one up for a closer look.

Rachel turned towards him. There was her hero, her lover, her partner for twenty long years, father of her four children.

The gifted bushman who, true to his word to her and the deathbed promise he made his father, had transformed Balkenna into one of the most flourishing and successful properties in the Longreach district. How in God's name, she wondered, could she ever find the courage to tell him she had loathed the life for years, had borne it in stoic silence for his sake, for the way of life that fed his soul and ran with the blood in his veins? Did he know already? Had he guessed long ago and, like herself, been unable to utter a word? Would bringing it out in the open force him to deal with the consequences? As the thoughts tumbled through her mind, their life together came crashing in on her, like unruly waves on some forgotten beach.

For the first fifteen years, she'd been far too busy raising her brood to give much thought to herself. The battle to make a life in the outback had quickly stripped her of any city pretensions, though she had applied her sophisticated tastes to the interior designs and furnishings of the house and its later extensions.

If there was one person who may have guessed when things began to get out of kilter for her, it was the woman who had stayed on with them to take her share of the load. If she had, Elizabeth Mackay never let on. It was her mother-in-law who'd found the way to heal the only terrible rupture that had ever threatened to sink her marriage to Jim. To this day, Rachel didn't know what possessed her at the time. It just came up one evening in conversation on the verandah as she and Jim were having a drink before dinner. She took it for granted their life together was so full and secure that it wouldn't matter a fig. But Jim was devastated by the confession of her brief liaison with Dean Coulter. It had taken all her guile, all her cunning and loving affection to heal the rift that opened up between them. Only when she took Elizabeth's advice and bore him another child was she able to persuade him that it didn't matter, that he should appreciate the generosity of Coulter's gesture all those years ago. But she knew, even now, it still niggled away at him.

The gift of another child had smoothed the troubled waters. Young Jack emerged as the real heir apparent, the one who loved Balkenna as intensely as his father, cared nothing for the world beyond its boundary line.

His elder brother, Tony, proved just the opposite. Tony had more or less been at war with his father ever since he was old enough to make a point. Jim always managed to find some humour in the situation and joke with her about it. He blamed it all on the time, at the tender age of nine, when Tony was bitten by a red-back spider while helping his dad root out an old fence post. It was a female of the species and they had to race him to the hospital in Longreach for antivenin. He'd been a very sick little boy. It was a close shave that scared the living daylights out of everyone. But, underneath, she knew that Jim despaired of his son's rejection of Balkenna. As her own feelings had grown more mixed and confused, she found it impossible not to side with Tony's ambitions for a different way of life, more in keeping with the sharp intellect that had emerged in his early teenage years and grown steadily as he got older.

'Hey! Come and see what I've found.'

Jim's voice cut through the shimmering heat.

'I can't move,' she called. 'It's too damn hot to breathe.'

Jim joined her on the walkway. He'd found a fossil bearing the skeleton image of a tiny fish.

'Billy says they became extinct when comets hit the earth,' said Rachel. 'Happens every seventy-four million years, evidently.'

'Not due this year, I hope.'

'No. Not for another million, according to Billy.'

'Thank God for that.'

Jim was fifty-one years old. Bronzed, rugged, broad-shouldered and tough as old redgum. A Queensland bushman to his boot heels. The still beautiful woman at his side was forty-five, but she didn't look a day over forty. Despite twenty years in the outback and bearing four children, she still retained her exotic, willowy figure. Her skin, baked brown by years of sun, was still supple, unblemished, mysterious. Her face, especially the eyes, spoke of a loving earthy wisdom that belied the troubled mind behind. If you didn't look too hard, that is. If you did, there was something else. Just a hint, but it was there. If Jim ever saw it, he never let on.

'My father was going to bring me here once . . . we never got around to it.'

'It seems such a long time ago,' Rachel sighed. 'Your father . . .'

Jim put his arm round her.

'Half our lifetime.' He turned her head to give her a kiss on the mouth. 'I couldn't have asked for better.'

Rachel grinned and pushed him away. 'Get off, you old rogue.'

Jim smacked her bum. 'Don't call me old.'

Quick as a flash, Rachel responded by giving him a critical thumb-punch on his bicep. 'Cop that then, callow youth.'

'Owwww,' Jim yelped. 'Christ, you pack a wallop when you want to.'

'Oh, my poor darling. Bruise easily these days, do we?'

Jim grabbed her in a fierce bear hug and lifted her off the ground. 'Maybe I should tie you up and leave you here for a dinosaur's dinner.'

'They're all dead,' she gasped. 'I will be, too, if you don't let me breathe.'

Jim eased her down. But he didn't let go.

'My God,' she protested. 'How can you be randy in this heat?'

'How can you not?' Jim enquired, grinning cheekily from ear to ear.

'Come on,' she said, tugging at his arm. 'Let's get back to the creek before I melt.'

'And then?'

'And then we'll see,' she grinned.

'Promise?'

Rachel threw her arms up in mock despair. 'You know what's wrong with you, lover boy?'

'No. What?'

'You've spent too much of your life watching bulls at work.'

With that, Rachel jumped off the walkway and headed back towards the Land Rover, relishing the thought of getting her lips round the nozzle of the water-bag. Halfway there, she heard a clatter and turned to discover Jim chasing her, bent at the waist, his fingers sprouting from his forehead. Giggling like a schoolgirl she ran like the dickens from the maniac bellowing like a bull behind her.

Rachel had committed herself to this strange holiday a long time ago. Normally they spent a couple of weeks on the Gold Coast. They'd been to Tahiti, Fiji and New Zealand. Once they went to New Guinea and visited the site of Jack Mackay's last stand. But Jim had always wanted to take her off on a tour of the country behind Balkenna. At the risk of hurting his feelings, she wriggled out of it time and again. But this year, she'd kept her promise and now, here they were, on the banks of Vergemont Creek, one hundred and twenty kilometres west of Longreach. Kilometre. How she detested the word. Australia's metrification had been completed by 1976. Gone for ever was the friendly old 'mile' with all its poetic connotations spanning the centuries. In its place, a word that implied you killed distance with every step you took, every yard you galloped, every mile you drove. The whole thing caused unending confusion for everybody except Jack and Billy. 'Mile' was past history to them. Now, twelve years later, it was still impossible to know whether half the signposts in the district meant what they said.

At sundown, Rachel was squatting by the fire, tilting the frying pan to and fro as the oil began to hiss. She eased it away from the flames and turned to call to Jim at the water's edge.

'Where's the fish?'

He gave her a hopeless shrug. 'Nothing doing here. Better open a couple of cans.'

As he said it, the float went under and the reel ratcheted a few spins before hitting the lock.

'Hang on!'

The salty-blue catfish made a few runs, but it was well and truly hooked and soon gave up. Jim reeled it in, dumped it on the bank, brained it with a hunk of wood and had it skinned and gutted in two minutes flat.

'Not the tastiest fish in the world,' he qualified. 'But beggars can't be choosers.'

As the fish fried, Rachel produced tomatoes, cucumber and lettuce from the Esky. It was a beautiful, tranquil evening with a light, cooling breeze, the calm broken only by the sputtering of the fire.

'The service here isn't too good,' Rachel announced, with a pained expression.

'Bugger,' said Jim, downing his plate, 'I forgot.'

He went back to the creek and hauled out a bottle of white wine on a string. He filled Rachel's glass and handed it to her with a low bow.

'Madam . . .'

'Thank you.'

'Where's my tip?'

'I'll give it to you later.'

Above, and as far as they could see to the west, an unending sea of rolling cloudbanks were shot with bolts of purple and crimson. The sky was the colour of fine burnished gold. As the sun finally dropped out of sight, filling the western horizon with a fan-shaped riot of pinks and copper reds, a majestic pale-white full moon came sailing into view in the cloudless eastern sky. Standing together at the creek's edge, Rachel slipped her arm round his waist and rested her head against his shoulder.

'Beautiful.'

It was, too. Like being, for one brief moment, the last two people left on earth.

Later, that same moon bathed the after-glow of their love-making as they lay naked side by side, gazing through the fine mesh of the tent's fly-screen. Outside, it was clear and bright, the countryside lit by the gigantic orb overhead, the starry southern sky dancing in the waters of the creek.

'Jilba should be leaving New York about now.' She ran her fingers through her damp and tangled hair.

'Yeah,' said Jim. 'I suppose so.'

'I do worry about her,' Rachel sighed. 'I just can't help it.'

'I'm sure she's all right. Got her mates there. She's a big girl now. Have to let her do what she wants.'

'God! Listen to you! Threw a blue fit the first time it was mentioned, wouldn't hear of it.' She dropped her tone way down and did a passable imitation of his voice. 'I'm not having my daughter go off to the wilds of New York on her own, career or no career . . .'

'Yeah, I know,' Jim admitted, a bit sheepish. 'Taken by surprise, that's all. It all seemed a bit quick. Hard to let go when the time comes.' He paused for a while and gave her time to simmer down. 'Anyway, don't worry so much. I'm sure she's fine.'

'I suppose so.'

Jim kissed her cheek and they gazed out in silence for a time before he spoke again.

'How do you feel about Jack tossing school at the end of the year?'

'I knew that was coming,' she replied. 'I told you, I wish he'd stay on and do his leaving certificate . . .' Her voice petered out. 'But he seems to love Balkenna more than you do, so I suppose there's not much point. It's all he seems to want to do. Sometimes I think it was a mistake to call him Jack. Sealed his fate, in a way.'

Jim was tickled pink at this sudden shift, but he didn't want to gloat. 'We called him John, remember?'

'You've never called him John in his life, except at the christening. Even then, you had to struggle.'

'Well, he is the spitting image of dad,' Jim chuckled. 'You know that. Everybody says so. He does love the place. Knows what he's doing. I don't mind him leaving . . .'

'Don't mind! You're thrilled to bits.'

Jim gave her another moment to simmer down again.

'Yeah,' he finally agreed. 'I am. Must admit.'

'Maybe you'll ease up on Tony a bit from now on then. You're too hard on him.'

'And you're too damned soft,' Jim shot back. 'Wouldn't mind so much if he didn't keep having a go all the time.'

'That's just it. He knows you don't approve. You think he owes everything to Balkenna, just like the rest of us.'

'What the hell's wrong with that?'

'Stop cursing.'

'Who's cursing, for God's sake?'

'You are, every time we talk about it.'

'Give us a break, will you?'

'I'll break your bloody neck in a minute, you cranky old coot.'

Jim grabbed her leg just above the knee and started squeezing. Rachel shrieked and started writhing, laughing and yelling all at once.

'You'll what?' Jim demanded, using his other hand to tickle her under the arm.

'Nothing! Nothing! Stop! Stop! You'll have the tent down in a minute . . .'

Jim eased her down and they searched each other's eyes in the deceitful light. Rachel grinned. Then she threw her arms round his neck and pulled him down on top of her.

Long after Rachel had fallen asleep, Jim groped for his tobacco and matches, unzipped the fly-screen and eased himself out of the tent. There was a chill in the air now and he wished he'd had the sense to slip his shirt on. But, by the time he'd rolled his smoke and lit up, his skin had accepted the drop in temperature and he wandered down to the creek to stand naked at the water's edge. He had a momentary sense of strange, primitive isolation.

What kept him awake was what she'd said about Jack. What he'd told her was true. He was thrilled to bits. It confirmed Jack's commitment to Balkenna, confirmed the family's lineage on the place, a lineage he hoped might yet include their youngest son. Billy seemed to be taking an interest in the running of the property, but his fourteen-year-old enthusiasms were still easily distracted, especially when his elder brother made a fleeting appearance on the six o'clock news.

Secretly, Jim admired Tony and always felt a little rush of pride whenever he appeared on the screen. He just wished there was a closer bond between them, wished their views on politics and a host of other subjects didn't always produce such head-on collisions. Tony had always had the gift of the gab and he often managed to reduce his father to frustrated anger as a last resort. Perhaps Rachel was right. Now that Jack's inheritance of Balkenna was confirmed, the tension between them would cool down a notch or two. He knew well enough it must have been difficult for his son to live with the disappointment his rejection of the land had brought his father. Perhaps as difficult as it had been for him. On the other hand, he was only eighteen, he might yet tire of his life in Brisbane, want to come home . . . No. Wishful thinking. Jack was the one.

Jim flicked the butt of his cigarette into the water and glanced up at the moon.

'Poor old thing,' he muttered to himself, without quite knowing why.

After a long and leisurely breakfast, followed by an early morning swim in the only decent pool the creek had to offer, it was time to break camp, and head for home.

The Land Rover was parked way at the top of the slope and the swim wore off fast. As they dismantled the tent and stashed bits and pieces in various bags and boxes, Rachel's effort seemed half-hearted at best. He let it pass. But now, as he crested the top and looked back to see her still only a little way up and moving slow, he couldn't help geeing her up.

'Come on, darling. It's a long haul home.'

Rachel just pulled a face and handed over the Esky.

'What's the matter?' In his heart of hearts, he knew, in a way. But it was better to ask.

'It's been too quick,' she muttered.

Jim put the Esky down and wrapped his arms round her. 'We've had two weeks, all on our own. It's been fun, hasn't it? Time to get home, that's all.'

'I could do with two months,' Rachel declared. And she meant every word of it.

Later, as they bumped and ground their way out of the trackless country, looking for the minor road that would take them on a long roundabout journey back to Balkenna, Rachel's mood was unchanged. She stared out of her side window, lost in her own thoughts.

'Cheer up.'

Summoned back to the present, she brightened. 'I'm fine . . . Look out!'

There was a small gully right in front of them.

'I'm fine,' Rachel repeated, with a chuckle. 'Just watch where you're going.'

Jim pulled a face. 'Sorry . . .'

Within minutes, Rachel was back in her trough, her face turned away again, staring out of the window. Jim kept glancing at her whenever there was space in front of him. She had him rattled, but he held his peace.

# Twenty-Two

At Balkenna's landing strip, sixteen-year-old Jack Mackay had his bum propped against the fender of a Ford station wagon, watching a Cessna four-seater come swooping out of the heat haze. The plane turned at the end of the strip and taxied back to park alongside. The cab door opened and Athol Ferguson's feet hit the dirt.

He was seventy-three, but he wore it well. The merest hint of a paunch, salt and pepper hair turned a distinguished silvery grey, dapper and elegant as always, he was the living image of a Queensland cattle baron. Behind him, Dud Brewley picked his way down the steps. Eighty-five if he was a day, Dud was as skinny as a rake and had a face like a startled cockatoo. He was all sinew, all wrinkled and weathered, his too-big pants bunched round his waist by a traditional bushman's plaited kangaroo-hide belt. As soon as he was clear of the plane, he pulled a ready-rolled smoke from behind his ear, shoved it in his mouth and lit up. Behind him, dressed in expensive casuals, Anthony Barclay turned to help his wife. She'd put on weight, but it suited her. Manicured and lacquered, all the evidence of a lifetime of expensive salons, hairdressers and running battles with the bulge, Jean Barclay still retained indelible traces of the beauty she had passed on to her daughter. Fluffing herself up and twittering with excitement, she rushed to embrace her grandson.

'Hello, darling. My, how you've grown.'

Jack greeted her warmly and accepted her welter of kisses with good grace.

'G'day, Gran. Good to see you. G'day, Granddad.'

Twenty years on, Balkenna had grown. Matching wings had been added to both sides and the old verandah extended to run the full length of the front, looking down on immaculate gardens and a pond full of water lilies. The red oxide, high-vaulted iron roof plunged to curl gracefully over the stretch of the verandah, making Balkenna a homestead of elegance and distinction.

As the station wagon pulled up, Elizabeth emerged from the front door and hurried down the steps to greet her visitors. Grand matriarch of all she surveyed, she had carried her husband's torch for two decades, helping their son keep his promise to hold on to Balkenna and build it up again. You could rely on Elizabeth Mackay. You always could.

At the front door, Betsey was beaming. Athol and Dud greeted her like a long-lost cousin, but Jean Barclay was a little more stand-offish. Try as she might, she couldn't bring herself to be familiar with a servant. Still smiling, Betsey Johnson greeted her with a withering Aboriginal eye. 'Come in, Mrs B. Plenty cool inside.'

Halfway up the steps, Elizabeth stopped. 'Tim, Billy's train gets in at five. Jim's not back yet. Do you mind another trip?'

Tim Daley had worked on Balkenna for thirty-six years. Step by step, season by season, he'd helped Jim bring the property back from the point of no return, and he was a confirmed member of the family.

'No worries,' he waved. 'I'll get going.'

'Don't you want a cup of tea or something first?'

'No, that's okay. I'll grab a beer in town.'

Balkenna's old lounge had also been extended on both sides to create a main living room full of charm and country character. Sprawling couches and chairs invited rest and relaxation. An immense cedar sideboard was covered with photographs and trophies. A Steinway grand piano, Elizabeth's pride and joy, stood in the corner. The walls were hung with original prints of early Queensland life and paintings by Drysdale and Nolan. Over the piano was a large, framed, colour photograph of Jim Mackay, on a thoroughbred polo pony.

It was Rachel's room. She'd poured her energy into it, shifted it around repeatedly until the proportions clicked to create an elegant room her husband could walk into straight from the cab of his truck without feeling like a bull in a china shop.

It had been years before they'd been able to think about buying another chair, let alone anything else. Jim had gone to Brisbane to complete his stint in the Army, managing his discharge papers by the end of 1967. With Tim Daley as best man, they were married on Jim's birthday in 1968.

210

That way, Rachel said, he'd never have an excuse for forgetting their wedding anniversary. Her father splashed out, filling St Andrew's Church in Longreach with flowers and putting on a slap-up reception at the Rotary Club. And Anthony insisted on paying for their three-week honeymoon on Hamilton Island and taking shares in the Balkenna Pastoral Company.

They came home to discover Elizabeth had moved herself, lock stock and barrel, up to Jim's old attic room and converted the adjoining room into her own private sitting room, insisting that would be her domain from then on and they should use the rest of the house as they wished. Rachel had been deeply touched. Balkenna had a new mistress and Elizabeth respected that. Elizabeth had also managed to sort through all Jack's papers, box them and store them away in the barn before getting Tim to help her convert the office into a bedroom for himself, till the day finances might allow his own place to be rebuilt. It had been a heady and exhilarating time that propelled them all into the first, grinding stages of bringing Balkenna's pastures back to life.

Betsey appeared with tea. Dud Brewley arched an eyebrow.

'Any chance of a beer?'

'Bit early, isn't it?'

'Only got a few years left. Don't want to waste them.'

Betsey eyed him a moment, then she whipped a napkin off an ice-cold can of 4X on the bottom shelf of the traymobile. 'No glass, right?'

'You're a marvel,' Dud declared, with unreserved admiration as everyone had a good chuckle at his expense.

Betsey made the rounds.

'Funny sort of holiday, if you ask me,' Jean scoffed.

'It's just what they wanted,' said Elizabeth. 'On their own to do as they pleased.'

'I suppose so.' But Jean wasn't convinced.

'I'm afraid they're in for a disappointment,' Elizabeth continued, immediately getting everyone's attention. 'Jilba rang up this morning, from New York. She can't make it.'

'Why not?'

'She's been offered some enormous new contract. A new brand of cosmetics or something. Said she couldn't possibly turn it down.' Elizabeth paused and smiled, remembering the lingo. 'A positive career move, she called it. It means she'll make an awful lot of money.'

'She hardly needs it,' Anthony huffed. He adored his grand-daughter and was really miffed she'd cancelled out.

'You know what it means to her to make her own way.'

'Yes, I know,' Anthony admitted. 'She's got a head on her shoulders. Pity though. You're right. They'll be very disappointed.'

'What about me?' said Jean. 'Don't I come into this?'

Elizabeth patted her arm, went to the sideboard, took a bundle of clippings from a drawer and placed them in Jean's lap.

'She's the toast of New York,' she announced proudly. 'These came last weekend.'

They were all from high fashion magazines, the last a front-page cover from *American Vogue*. A band across the corner announced: 'Jilba Mackay – Dream Girl From The Outback.' She certainly looked it, no worries about that.

With her honey blond hair, sea-green eyes, a hint of freckles across a delectable nose and high cheekbones, her face lit up by a beguiling smile, Jilba was a stunner by anybody's standards.

'Wonderful,' Anthony declared. 'Absolutely wonderful.'

'I'll say,' Athol seconded.

'No make-up,' Jean muttered, perplexed. 'Just a touch around the eyes.'

Dud joined the group. 'It should say from Queensland.'

'Taught to ride by Dud Brewley, I suppose,' Jack said.

'Yeah,' Dud nodded slowly. 'Now that you mention it.'


Jilba's parents had just cracked the minor road that would lead them back to the Lansborough Highway at Cramsie for the short drive into Longreach. As the wheels hit the smoother surface, Rachel turned to face the road ahead, much to Jim's relief.

'You okay?'

'Fine,' she nodded. 'Feeling a bit drowsy.'

'Put your head down.'

'I might, in a minute.'

'I better stop off at the Commercial Hotel on the way through. Make sure they haven't forgotten the grog for the weekend.'

'Not much chance of that.'

'No, guess not. Still . . . Just to be on the safe side.' He turned and shot her a grin. 'Not every day a bloke celebrates his twentieth wedding anniversary, you know.'

Rachel smiled. But it dried on her lips. Jim adjusted his hat over his eyes, struggling for the words that wouldn't betray his fear of asking.

'Not getting sick of me after all these years, are you?'

She brightened. She snaked her arm round his neck and kissed his cheek. 'Never. It's just the time of year. Heat, dust, flies. You know what I'm like.' She kissed him again and straightened in her seat. Jim reached for a cushion.

'Here. Roll your window up and have a snooze.'

She did as she was told, shifting the cushion a few times to get her head comfy before closing her eyes.

'Dream about the South Pole. They don't have any flies there.'

Rachel couldn't help a little smile. Without opening her eyes, she swung her arm and thumped him on the shoulder. Then she plumped the cushion again, kicked her sandals off, drew her legs up onto the seat and snuggled down. Five minutes later, she was out to it. Jim glanced at her a few more times to make sure, then concentrated on the road.

It was true. He was looking forward to the gathering of family and close friends to celebrate their twenty years together. Sometimes, he felt he had absolutely no idea where the time had gone. He could remember the day of his father's funeral and Rachel's unexpected arrival at Balkenna as vividly as if it were yesterday.

Their first five years had been a hell of a struggle, but tremendously exciting. To witness the arrival of the first stock and then turn them loose to graze had been a triumphant moment for him and his mother. Knowing what it meant, Rachel baked an enormous celebration cake and insisted on feeding a fat slice to the grumpy Hereford bull. To everybody's surprise, he downed it in one gulp and licked his lips.

After a lot of discussion, Jim and Athol had gone for parallel herds of pure Herefords and Brafords, a breed which had been developed in Queensland between 1946 and 1952. A fifty per cent Hereford, fifty per cent Brahman cross, they exhibited many Brahman characteristics like a small hump above the front shoulders, loose skin and a short coat. But their colour markings were the same as Herefords, deep red with a creamy white face, chest, flanks and leg points. They performed well in the hot, harsh conditions of the outback, producing good yearling and steer carcasses that bore a minimum of waste.

At the beginning, Jim insisted he and Tim draw a stockman's wage only from the company funds and Rachel and his mother stuck to the lowest possible budget to keep the household ticking over. Every other dollar went into stock and equipment. Athol Ferguson had always been willing to advance more capital whenever they hit a crisis and Rachel's father had invested quite heavily in the rebuilding programme. But Jim lent over backwards to keep a tight rein on the mounting debt in order to put the property in the black at the earliest opportunity. That came at the end of their fifth season in 1973 and the profits allowed Tim's place to be rebuilt by the middle of 1974. They did most of the work themselves, Rachel and Elizabeth scouring the district for good second-hand bits and pieces to furnish it with once it was done.

The long droughts of the mid-sixties did not finally break with any conviction until 1971 and, for their first three years, Jim kept the cattle herds at a steady level and tripled the number of his Merino flock. The wisdom of this policy came good in the years 1973–5 when beef prices plummeted while wool went on going up through to the end of the seventies.

The late seventies proved a good time to buy land, and, through tragic circumstances, occasioned Balkenna's first major expansion. Jim's boyhood playmate, Guy Henderson, was killed in a plane crash within weeks of taking over his family's property when his father retired. Ray Henderson lost his will to continue and he offered Jim first refusal on Bindra's twenty thousand acres. Athol and Anthony leapt at it and they bought the Henderson place outright, including the stock, for half a million dollars.

Bindra homestead itself was pretty old and in need of a lot of repair. Instead, Jim had it dismantled and trucked to Balkenna to be stored away under tarpaulins for future use. Everyone thought he was a bit mad at the time, but when the first plans were drawn up to extend the house, prices had skyrocketed and the good timber, stone and iron saved from Bindra proved invaluable. The outbuildings at Bindra were left intact and, as the properties were adjoining, the name Balkenna stretched to the whole thirty-five thousand acres.

In 1981, a beef substitution scandal rocked the industry. A consignment of Australian beef to the United States was found to contain horse, donkey and kangaroo meat. As Queensland produced nearly fifty per cent of the nation's beef exports, disaster stared them in the face. However, the first companies implicated all proved to be operators from the southern states. Premier Joh Bjelke-Petersen immediately disassociated Queensland from any involvement and headed off any long-term effect on the state's cattle industry. It was a classic act of separatism for which the leader of the National Party had become notorious.

'If we took back Qantas, Waltzing Matilda and the lamington,' said Joh, 'they'd only have the meat pie left, and even that's filled with Queensland beef.'

It was the politics of the state that generated the most friction between Jim and Tony. Like the majority of graziers, Jack Snr had been a lifelong supporter of the Country Party. After his father's death, Jim followed suit and, when the Country Party became the National Party in 1974, he transferred his vote accordingly. Apart from anything else, he admired many of Bjelke-Petersen's qualities. Any man who, from the age of thirteen, had lived his next fifteen years in a cow bail, using teams of horses and chains to clear the land on his father's farm, was worthy of some respect. But he deplored the man's attitudes to Aboriginal people and the continual failure of his government to better their lot.

Tony, on the other hand, reckoned Joh was a joke. A short-sighted, hard-line reactionary who, for years, had presided over and profited from the wholesale plunder of the state's wealth by overseas, multinational interests. In his usual way, Tony was always able to come up with a welter of facts and figures to back up his argument and, more often than not, Jim would have to retreat to the position of being just a traditional country man, voting for those he felt would best look after Balkenna.

As prices plummeted during the beef scandal, Jim was able to purchase a further ten thousand acres adjoining Balkenna's southeastern boundary to make the property one of the largest holdings in the district. They nick-named the new acres 'Big Jack's Whack'.

In 1983, Jim's job was done, and they had one hell of a shindig to celebrate. The long process of extending and refurbishing the house had been completed and the bank loan repaid in full. He repaid all loans from Athol and his father-in-law, and bought out their shares. The Balkenna Pastoral Company was dissolved and full ownership of the property reverted to the family that bore his father's name. It had been a moment to savour. Alone in the privacy of his office, Jim took the crest ring from his finger, placed it on top of the new deeds, thanked his lucky stars and sat a while with the ghost of Jack Mackay, DSO.

Jim glanced at the sleeping form beside him and offered up his silent thanks to Hughie for the years of their life together. But, as his eyes returned to the road and he spotted a couple of emus up ahead, running with ungainly, high-stepping strides away from the approaching vehicle, his gratitude was tempered by his concern for Rachel's unsettling moods of late.

# Twenty-Three

Lillian Tompkins sat behind her huge, half-moon desk, piled high with paperwork, in-trays, out-trays and enough phones to run a small town all of her own. The 'Guilder' to her friends, Lillian was a frumpy, chain-smoking, gang boss who never missed a dog fight and whose dogs generally won. She stubbed her cigarette, flapped at the smoke and unpeeled her dental-work.

'Well? How's our overnight sensation?'

'A bit glazed,' Jilba grinned. 'Still can't quite believe it.'

'You'd better believe it. That nit-picking agent of yours has made you the deal.'

'Max looks after his girls,' Jilba reminded her, still grinning.

'He sure does, honey. He sure does. I told him I'm gonna call him *clause* célèbre from now on.'

Jilba rabbited in her bag for a pen. No luck., 'Have you got a pen?'

Lillian raised her eyes to heaven. 'Paying the girl the moon and now she wants a pen thrown in. There . . . Please note the engraving. Return to sender.'

Jilba began sifting through the pages of the contract, initialling as her agent had done. It was a long haul and five minutes passed before she hit the last page. In the space reserved for Jilba Mackay, she signed her name with an excited flourish. With the exception of her agent's familiar scrawl, she hardly noticed the other names on the page. She never read the bottom line, which said: Dean Coulter, President.

On her way to the top floor, Jilba made a few quick adjustments and checked her hair in the brass button plate of the lift. Lillian said it was unusual, something like a royal command. Normally, the president was happy to leave the day-to-day running of the company's various accounts to his subordinates. The doors opened and she stepped into a large, open-plan reception area. From a desk by the windows, a woman rose to greet her.

'Hi, I'm Gina. Mr Coulter says for you to go right in.' She knocked once and stood aside. The man Jilba had come to see was standing at his office window, looking out over a spectacular view of Manhattan's skyline. He waited until he heard the door close again before turning to face her.

Dean Coulter still carried an aura of engaging, almost boyish charm. Years of squash and polo and sailing had served him well. He was a very handsome man. She figured he was probably in his mid-forties. In fact, he was the same age as her father. He gave her a long, exploratory look that immediately unsettled her.

'Lillian said you wanted to see me.'

The man continued staring at her for several more seconds before gesturing to the armchair. Even then, he just continued staring at her and Jilba, now definitely unsettled, had to look away and glance around the luxuriously appointed office before returning her eyes to his face, giving him her best smile to break the ice.

'Will I do?' she asked.

To her relief, Coulter returned her smile. 'Welcome aboard.'

There was still something disconcerting about the way he was looking at her as he spoke. Jilba couldn't know that Coulter was actually far, far away from this moment between them. Half a world away and twenty years . . .

Jilba's call came through just as they were sitting down to the anniversary dinner. Betsey returned the soup to the kitchen and Jim and Rachel hurried to the phone.

An hour and a half later, the dining room's superb oval cedar table was littered with the debris of a feast. As Anthony Barclay sat down, Athol Ferguson rose, glass in hand.

'Another toast,' he announced, raising his glass to Rachel and Jim in turn. 'To you both . . . From all of us. Here's to another twenty years of good health, great happiness and prosperity.'

Amid cries of hear! hear! and much scraping of chairs, everyone rose to toast them. Jim and Rachel remained seated, grinning at one another like Cheshire cats. Jim was positively glowing. Rachel was happy, too. Happy for him, at least.

That moment by the dinosaur trackways had knocked her for a loop. She was still head over heels in love with the man at the other end of the table. But she knew, finally, she was head over heels out of love with Balkenna. It seemed wherever they went together, away from Balkenna, Jim's heart and mind stayed home. Their annual pilgrimages to Sydney to spend a week or ten days with her parents had become more and more difficult to handle. She would indulge in a heady mix of theatre, concerts, films and galleries and feel starved for months when they got home, until Balkenna regained its claustrophbic stranglehold on her senses. She often harked back to her mother's casual warning of the difficulties she would face coming to terms with life on the land. Land imprisoned by distance.

For long years she kept all her doubts in check. But in that single instant, in the God-awful desolation of the Tully Ranges, staring down at three-toed footprints of eternity, she knew she had to get away. For a time, at least. She had no idea just how. Jim would have to try and understand, release his hold for a time to let her go off and find her bearings again. One month? Two? Six? A year? She didn't have a clue. How, how, how could she open these secret pages of her heart without breaking his?

As everyone plonked down into their chairs again, cries of 'Speech! Speech!' bounced around the room, mostly from Billy, but quickly taken up round the table. Jim's smile faded. But he rose to his feet, anxious to round things off as best he could. He topped up his mother-in-law's glass and passed the brandy on to Dud. He looked around the assembly for a moment, swallowed a couple of times and cleared his throat.

'Well, now . . . I'm not too good at this . . .'

'Rubbish!'

'Oh yeah!'

'Tell us another one!'

'No,' Jim grinned, holding up his hand. 'It's true, I'm not. But on this occasion I would like to offer a few toasts of my own. Quite a few, in fact . . .' He gestured to the decanter. 'So I suggest you get stuck into the good stuff and I'll kiss you goodnight.'

He had them now and they quickly simmered down. Jim looked the length of the table at his wife and sought her eyes. Everyone turned. There's an old song that says when you're laughing on the outside, you're crying on the inside, and you could've sung it for Rachel at that moment. She gave him her most beautiful smile as Jim raised his glass.

'To the beautiful Rachel Barclay, who has given me, in

twenty years of marriage, more happiness than any man is legally entitled to.'

Elizabeth leaned over and patted Rachel's arm. 'Hear! Hear!' she whispered.

Jim turned to his mother. 'To you, Mum. I know Rachel feels the same as I do. Balkenna would not be what it is today without your support and wisdom and, above all, your love and care for us all. I hope you know how much we love you in return . . .'

'Hear! Hear!' said Athol, a little too loudly, grinning down the table at her. A special bond of affection had grown between these two since his wife had died ten years ago. They went on the occasional holiday together and enjoyed each other's company without any consequences to worry about. 'That's my girl,' he added, with a bit of a leer.

'You old lecher,' Elizabeth chuckled. She was moved by Jim's words and gave him a special nod. 'Thank you, son.'

'To you, Jean,' Jim went on. 'I know you didn't really approve of me in the beginning . . .'

'Oh, go on with you,' she protested, with a stagy wave.

'No,' Jim corrected, wagging a finger. 'It's true. I well remember that day at your house when you took me out to show me the rose bushes and told me you'd changed your mind about me after all.'

'Not true,' cried Jean, for everyone's benefit. 'Don't believe a word of it.' But they all knew it was and had a bit of a giggle at her expense.

'Anyway,' Jim continued. 'There'll be no tired old mother-in-law jokes this evening . . .'

'Thank God for that.'

'You have given us endless support, through good times and bad. Your thoughtfulness, particularly in your role of grand-mother . . .'

'Heaven forbid,' Jean gasped. 'That word makes me shudder.'

The others laughed with her and Jim waited it out before he went on.

'Nevertheless, grandmother you are, and a wonderful one.'

'Good on yer, Gran,' bellowed Billy.

Jean beamed at him. 'Quieten down, you little larrikin.'

'You gonna make me?'

'Later,' Jean promised, returning her eyes to Jim as he picked up the thread.

'Above all, I thank you for being the mother of the most

beautiful girl in the world and your acceptance of me as her husband.'

'I didn't have much say in the matter.'

Her response released more chuckles as Jim turned to her husband.

'Anthony. It goes without saying, mate, we couldn't have done it without you.'

'Too true,' his father-in-law quipped, reviving the laughter.

'Only too true,' Jim chuckled. 'Not only for the resources you contributed to our job here, but most especially for the fact that you've managed to wrangle us out of every legal shenanigan and roadblock along the way.'

'All except one,' Anthony corrected and the whole table cracked up.

'I tell you . . .' Jim did his best to hold the floor but it was a losing battle. 'I tell you . . .' Still no good. The joke was on him and they intended getting full mileage. Finally, he managed to get a hearing. 'I tell you that barn was *not* there before the plane hit it . . .'

That did it. The table erupted.

'Rubbish!'

'Bush pilot!'

'Flying blind!'

'Don't know which end's up!'

There was no way in the world he was ever going to live it down. Up in their very first plane, a second-hand, single-engined Piper, spraying fertiliser on the acres newly acquired from Ray Henderson, Jim badly misjudged the landing and demolished Bindra's old barn. He walked away from the wreck with a dislocated shoulder and some glass in his right hand. But Anthony was unable to persuade the insurance company to pay up. They failed to understand how a willy-willy could totally obscure an entire barn on an otherwise perfectly clear day. More importantly, they pointed out that Jim had not actually gained his pilot's licence until seven weeks after the accident.

When they finally quietened down, he gave Anthony a rueful grin. 'Seriously, Balkenna is for ever in your debt. The kids could not have asked for a better grandfather . . .'

Tony, Jack and Billy broke into spontaneous applause. They all adored Grandfather Barclay.

'You three . . .' Jim proposed, looking to each of his sons in turn. 'And our absent Jilba . . . What can I say?'

'Only good,' said Tony.

'Not always,' said Jim. 'But tonight I'll do my best.' Jim's expression sobered as he addressed his eldest son. 'Tony, there's no use in pretending, especially tonight . . . We both know I was disappointed you didn't want to stay on Balkenna. You stuck to your guns and I just want you to know that, despite everything, I admire your determination. I hope your ugly mug gets to be the most famous TV journalist's face in Queensland . . .'

'In the world,' Tony quipped.

'Okay,' Jim conceded. 'In the world.' Then, with a nice piece of timing, 'I thought Queensland was the world.'

Athol and Dud chiacked yahoos of agreement.

'There's more to the world than meets the eye,' Tony grinned down the table at them.

'Not out here,' Jim shot back. 'Anyway, whatever you do, I know you'll do it well and give it all you've got. You may think it's a bit late coming, but tonight I wish you good luck . . . With no regrets. If there's ever anything I can do, all you've got to do is ask.'

Tony couldn't miss the opportunity. 'Vote Labour.'

'Hear! Hear!' chipped in the girl at his side.

Susan Young was making her first visit to her boyfriend's ancestral home. Tony grimaced, put out for a moment by her ill-timed entry into the family banter. But Jim was in no mood to be put out by anything. He simply raised his hands in supplication to whatever benevolent gods lay beyond the ceiling. 'There he goes again!'

Rachel grinned and intervened. 'Don't interrupt your father.'

'Yes, ma'am,' Tony complied, with a mock salute. But his tone was sincere as he turned back to Jim. 'Thanks, Dad. I appreciate it.'

Jim gave him a thumbs up and took the chance to address his son's girlfriend.

'It's very nice for us to have you here on this occasion, Susan. Rachel and I both feel we know you pretty well already from Tony's letters. We hope you'll enjoy your first stay with us here on Balkenna and trust we can all look forward to more visits in the future.'

Tony stole a glance at her. He knew she was feeling a little ill-at-ease in the wealthy surroundings. But she was smiling warmly in response to Jim's words.

'Tony tells me you'd like to learn to ride, so . . .' Jim reached past Jean and patted Dud Brewley on the head. 'We'll pass you into the capable hands of this old rogue.'

'Mind your language.'

'This long streak of stringybark and greenhide.'

'Strewth!' Dud barked, putting on his best hurt look.

'Who knows more about horses than any man alive.'

'We'll see you right, love. Show you which end's which, at least.'

'While I've got your attention, Dud . . . Thanks, mate. Thanks for your friendship and all I've learnt from you over the years. Most of all, thanks for that day in Sydney all those years ago.'

'How's that then?'

'No kidding, you old galah. You know exactly what I mean.'

Dud fixed him with his special Chinese look. 'Do I, now?'

'You know exactly what I mean,' Jim grinned. 'You talked Athol into giving me the ride that got me invited to the ball.'

'Yeah,' said Dud. 'And then you went and turned into a bloody pumpkin again.'

Waiting for the hoots to die down, Jim kept his eyes on Dud, filled with affection for the wily old bird who had been his teacher, friend and collaborator for so long. He opened his mouth to continue, but Dud jumped in.

'It was all his doing!' He was pointing at Athol.

'So much has been his doing,' Jim agreed, turning to his former boss, saluting him with his glass. 'Athol, from all the family, our everlasting thanks.'

Athol looked from mother to son. 'It's all been repaid, many times over. Best of all in friendship and . . .' Athol's eyes passed from Tony to Jack to Billy in turn. 'Watching you lot all arrive and grow up. If I was taking a bit of a punt, I've been more than amply rewarded.'

'You know our thanks include Alison, God bless her,' said Elizabeth.

Athol dropped his eyes.

'She's very much with us here tonight. In spirit and happy memories.'

Around the table, everyone quietly, respectfully added their agreement. Wordless at that moment, Athol simply gave Jim a nod.

Their old bank manager was next in line. Will Mackenzie

had been retired for five years or more. His wife had died eighteen months ago and the Mackays had seen to it that he was well looked after and never at a loss for a bit of company. He was a regular visitor to Balkenna, particularly at mustering times when he loved to lend a hand.

'Will, neither mum nor myself have ever forgotten, or ever will forget, your kindness and generosity to us when dad was ill. You promised us we'd keep the place and you were true to your word.'

'I was taking a bit of a punt, too,' Mackenzie smiled, with a wink for Athol Ferguson. 'Like Athol, I've not been disappointed. It's nice to have a few successes to look back on.'

'You've had your fair share of those,' Jim reminded everybody. 'There's more than a few in this district who owe their start to you.'

'All part of the job,' Mackenzie accepted, matter-of-fact.

'Wish my bank manager had the same attitude,' said Susan Young. 'I asked him for a loan to buy a car and he told me my collateral wasn't up to scratch.'

This time, for just a beat, Jim looked a bit peeved at the interruption. But he let it go and left it to Mackenzie to reply.

'Out here, we really get to know people. It's a bit different. But I've had to refuse a loan or two in my time, don't worry.' He quickly turned to Elizabeth and changed the subject. 'Let me just say how happy I am to be here tonight. Very happy, indeed.'

'This is a celebration of Balkenna as well as Jim and Rachel's twenty years,' she told him. 'Without you . . .' She broke off and glanced round the table. 'Without you all, there'd be no Balkenna to celebrate.'

'Jack,' Jim called. 'There's some special news for you tonight.'

Jack immediately sensed what it might be and glanced at his mother. Rachel just shook her head in mock resignation. He twisted back to his father and jumped the gun. 'I can leave?'

'Your mum's agreed. You can leave at the end of the year.'

'Faaaaaantastic!' Jack was up in a flash. He hurtled round to his mother to give her a big slobbering kiss.

'Thanks, Mum. That's really fantastic.'

'Well, it's what you really want, isn't it?' Rachel asked, knowing the answer.

'You bet it is,' Jack confirmed and kissed her again.

'On one condition!' Jim reminded him in the midst of it all.

'You've got to do what you promised. Correspondence courses in animal husbandry and agricultural sciences, or put yourself down to do them a couple of days a week at the Pastoral College in town. Okay?'

Jack stood up and took the oath. 'I promise. Thanks, Dad.'

Rachel smacked his bum and sent him back to his seat. 'I'll be holding you to that.'

'Tim,' Jim announced. 'Your turn, mate.'

'What about me?' Billy demanded.

'You're already the apple of your mother's eye, and I'm quite fond of you. What more could you want?'

'I want to leave school, too.'

'Not a chance. Two more years, at least. And that's that.'

'Can I have a new saddle instead?'

'Keep an eye out around Christmas.'

'We've only just had Christmas,' Billy protested. 'Anyway, I was gonna ask for an air rifle next time.'

Jim blanched and took an extra couple of beats to reply. 'Don't push your luck, okay?'

'Okay.'

Billy feigned further misery as Elizabeth and Jim shared a quick look before snapping back to the present.

'Come on, Billy boy,' she commanded. 'Cheer up.'

Jean immediately backed her up. 'Yes. Pipe down.'

'You gonna make me?'

'Later, later,' Jean promised, sticking to the time-worn formula of this long-running game with her youngest grandson. 'Go on, Jim.'

Jim paused a moment to focus the table's attention back on Tim Daley.

'Tim, old son, you've been on Balkenna almost as long as I have. I well remember the difficulties dad had in trying to find the right bloke at the right time. The choice he made has helped us hold things together ever since. Even the years when things were at their worst. Dad once told me his great-grandfather was the hardest working man in Queensland. With what you've put in alongside us here, I think it's fair to say you took that title a long, long time ago.'

'God bless you, Tim,' Elizabeth called, and Tony, Athol and Anthony backed her up.

'Laziest bugger I ever met in my life,' Dud declared, with a big wink.

'At least I don't sleep in the afternoons,' said Tim.

'Wait till you get to be my age.'

'Will you shut up a minute?' Jim pleaded. 'This is important.'

'Well, get on with it, then,' said Dud.

'I'm trying to, for God's sake . . .'

'Don't let me stop you . . .'

'I'll ring your bloody neck in a minute.'

Dud's grin turned to serious concern. 'Should I wait in the laundry?'

The laughter took a while to subside.

'I better make this quick, Tim. Before he gets his breath back. I want you to know this was mum's idea in the first place and Rachel and I wholeheartedly agree.'

Tim looked puzzled, wondering what on earth was coming.

'As you know, I don't exactly get on like a house on fire with our new bank manager.' Jim turned a moment and tipped a wink to Will Mackenzie. 'A very different kettle of fish to the old school, Will, if I may say so . . .'

Mackenzie refrained from comment. He simply raised his eyebrows.

'Nevertheless, he's given me the go-ahead. When we first got hold of Ray Henderson's place, you said no to the house there because you wanted to stay on with us here. We're going back . . . ten years, is it? Eleven?'

'Eleven.'

'Eleven. Anyway, Ralph Kidd has agreed to finance a brand new bungalow on the old Bindra homestead site. Not much point putting it anywhere else when the water's already there. Old Bryant Grogan reckons he can have it up in six months. The family would like it to be your new home.'

Wide-eyed, Tim glanced quickly at Elizabeth and Rachel, then back to Jim.

'We thought you might like to bring your brother and his family down from Cloncurry to help you run things over there, on the spot . . . For a twenty-five per cent share of what those acres produce. On top of salary, of course.'

All eyes were on Tim who was stunned, to say the least, and struggling for words.

'I don't quite know what to say . . .'

'Yes'll do,' Jim grinned.

'Can't refuse an offer like that,' prompted Athol.

'Oh, I don't know,' said Dud. 'Bloody hard yakker . . .'

Tim had a grin a mile wide now. 'That's for sure.'

His grin turned to heartfelt thanks as he looked from Elizabeth to Rachel again before turning back to Jim.

'Thanks, Jim. It's a wonderful offer. I'll be a bit sad to leave my old place . . . But, of course, I'll do it. The very best I can. Thank you all, very much indeed.'

'Bravo,' Anthony called, leading another round of applause.

Elizabeth stood up, walked round, leaned over his chair and gave Tim a big motherly hug. 'It's not too far away. It's still Balkenna and you're one of the family. You know that.'

Tim tipped his head back to look up at her. All he could do was gulp. Elizabeth squeezed his shoulder and headed back to her seat, eyes damp with tears. For years, Tim had been like a second son to her and she felt she had finally honoured the special bond between them. She'd worked hard on Jim to get him to agree. He'd been reluctant to raise a new mortgage on Balkenna for the funds needed to build. She could sympathise with his feelings. Years of doing the book-keeping had taught her all too well that each year Balkenna had to make more and more just to hold on to what they had. Jim had only just paid off the last mortgage they'd raised to put Jack and Billy through school. But, as she sat down and glanced back at the expression on Tim's face, she knew they'd done the right thing.

Tim got up himself and moved round to offer Jim his hand. Jim shook it warmly, then grabbed him in a big brotherly bearhug and slapped his back.

'Good on you. That's settled then.'

'I'll give it all I've got . . .'

As he headed back to his seat, Tony grabbed his arm in passing. 'An excellent move,' he said.

'Right,' said Jim, taking a deep breath. 'Not to forget our wayward daughter, way off there in the land of the free.' He was looking directly at Rachel now. 'We wish she could have been here tonight, but it can't be helped, I guess. At least we spoke to her. She's doing all right, by the sound of it . . .' He raised his glass. 'So here's to Jilba and we hope to see her in the not too distant future.'

A hush descended as Jim dropped his head and stared at the table in front of him for a moment, gathering himself before raising his eyes to them again, lifting the glass and fixing his gaze on Elizabeth.

'Finally, here's to the memory of Jack Mackay, DSO. It was

his wish that Balkenna might rise again . . . Build it up again were the words he used. If he's looking down on us tonight, he'll know that, with the help of you all, his wish has been our command. It is in that sense, perhaps more than any other, that I thank you, for all you've done, for all your comfort and support. And for being here tonight. Balkenna welcomes you, as always.' He lowered the glass and saluted each of them in turn round the table. 'Good luck, good health and great blessings.'

He drained his glass in one long gulp and sat down to sustained applause. Grinning now, he waved his empty glass for a refill.

Rachel immediately stood and waited for the hubbub to diminish. Elizabeth helped to bring the table to order.

'Shsssh! Shsssh!'

Rachel raised her own glass. 'I'd like to propose a toast.' Eyes shining, she was looking the length of the table, straight at Jim. 'To a sentimental bloke.'

They rose as one.

Swallowing hard, Jim dropped his eyes to the table again.

# Twenty-Four

Off Montauk Point, Long Island, a fully rigged forty-foot yawl with Dean Coulter at the helm skimmed through a moderate swell, giving thirty degrees to a good breeze. In a skimpy bikini, Jilba lay face down on the cockpit bench, putting the finishing touches to a seamless suntan. On the foredeck, her boyfriend, Danny Serrano, was deep in conversation with Dean Coulter's teenage son, David.

'Everything all right?'

Jilba turned her head to give Coulter a sleepy smile. 'Good as gold.'

'Great,' Coulter grinned. He winched the jib's leading edge a little tighter.

'You didn't mind me bringing Danny, did you?'

'Not in the least,' Coulter reassured her. 'This old girl's a bit of a handful. The more the merrier.'

He made another adjustment to the jib as Jilba sat up, propped on her elbow, shaded her eyes and peered up at the sails.

'What's his line of business exactly?'

'I'm never quite sure,' Jilba chuckled. 'The sand seems to shift from one week to the next, rock bands, that sort of thing. Bit hard to keep track. I met him in Max's office.'

Coulter's fifteen-year-old daughter, Joanna, appeared from below with a tray.

'Like to take her for a while, Danny?' Coulter called.

'Sure,' Danny replied, slipping his wiry frame into harness.

'Keep her around the seventy-one mark.'

Danny took the wheel and quickly corrected a couple of loose degrees. Coulter gave him a nod of approval and pointed to the top of the mast.

'Trick is, try and keep the pennant flying to the leading edge of the mainsail. Okay?'

'Okay.'

The boat jibbed slightly a couple more times as he found his touch on the wheel, but he soon had it under control. Danny Serrano's features suggested a long line of Italian-American ancestry with a pint or two of Jewish blood along the way. It was a strong face. Not handsome in the best sense, but arresting, with piercing, coal-black eyes and a don't-mess-with-me line to his mouth. Stripped to his shorts, he had the suntan stakes won. His long piano-player's fingers toying with a chain of fine antique gold round his neck, he checked backwards and forwards between the compass and the pennant. Coulter tossed him a can of beer.

'Better keep the skipper happy.'

Danny caught Jilba eyeing him. He gave her a saucy sailor's wink and she blew him a little kiss in return.

Half a world away, her brother Jack was at the controls of Balkenna's new Piper, concentrating hard as his father scanned the ground below.

'We're going to have to book you in for proper lessons when you leave school. You'll have to clock up your hours officially, just like I did.'

'What about mum?'

Jim thought a moment before replying. 'She understands. Can't stop the clock. Planes in the air, motorbikes on the ground, five days' work in two. Can't really argue with that . . . There they are. I'll take her now.'

They'd come up on the mob. A thousand head of prime beef, strung out in a long line with six stockmen in a wide arc behind and cattle dogs out on the flanks. Tim Daley was in charge. As Jim cut his speed to circle round them, Tim waved his hat. Jim waggled the wings in reply.

'Always remember, son, never, never fly directly over their backs if you can avoid it. Really spooks them.'

They made two more circuits for Jim to assure himself all was well, then they headed away, rolling the wings again in farewell. Jack took over.

'Don't muck about. I promised to take your mum into town. Running a bit late already, I'm afraid. Straight home, James.'

That afternoon, Rachel and Jean returned to the station wagon, squeezed under the scant shade of the trees on Eagle Street.

Outside the bank, Jim was deep in conversation with the

past. Fred Paterson reckoned he was on to the find of his life and he was looking for funds again. Jim was a bit shy this time. In memory of his father, he'd gone on backing various Fred Paterson schemes over the years, none of which had ever lived up to expectations. But he couldn't help liking the old gouger. Fred was one of a vanishing breed of die-hard loners who carried an encyclopaedic knowledge of Queensland in his head, hanging on by his fingernails to a lifetime's golden dream. If there was one thing you could put your money on, Fred Paterson would never give up. He'd find his dream, or die trying. Jim had been listening to Fred for no more than five minutes before he knew he'd give in again and kiss goodbye to another pile of dollars.

In the car, mother and daughter picked up the thread of a conversation that had been going on in whispers from shop to shop all afternoon. Rachel had sworn her mother to secrecy and taken her into her confidence. She had to. She couldn't contain it any longer. But already she was feeling guilty.

'We've never been apart for more than two weeks in twenty years,' Rachel reminded her, wishing she could tuck the problem back under lock and key.

'That's not the point,' Jean scolded, relishing this moment of complicity, enjoying the opportunity to exercise a little authority over her daughter.

'One thing I know, Jim's never been a fool, to my knowledge. If you go on trying to hide it, it will only come out as resentment and then he'll get to realise in the worst possible way. You should discuss it, openly and frankly –'

'Shsssh!' Rachel hissed. 'Here he comes.'

Jim was still chuckling at Fred's parting shot as he slid in behind the wheel.

'All set?'

'All set,' said Rachel, calming herself. 'I think we've got everything.'

'Looks like it,' Jim cracked, and he grinned at Jean. 'Fancy a short snort before we head home?'

'Who was that?'

'Fred Paterson.'

'Looked like a swaggie,' Jean frowned.

'In a way,' Jim chuckled. 'He's a gold prospector. Dad used to stake him occasionally before the war.'

'Jim's carrying on the tradition, I'm afraid.'

Rachel's tone was only slightly mocking. They both knew she thought he was a bit foolish to go on throwing good money after bad. Jim pulled a face as he dropped into first and inched out of their parking spot.

As they headed down Eagle Street for the short drive to the Commercial Hotel, Rachel steeled herself. Her mother was right. The time had come. At the first quiet moment, she would have to open her heart to the man now tipping his hat over his eyes against the dazzling glare of the late afternoon sun that reflected from every surface in sight. As it turned out, she never got the chance.

Jim and Tim had been out in the Piper, running their monthly check over the whole of Balkenna's fifty thousand acres. As they returned to the strip and banked for a landing, Tim noticed someone jumping up and down in the Land Rover.

'That looks like Betsey down there.'

Jim didn't bother parking properly, he just cut the engine on the spot. As they jumped out, Betsey rushed at them, her eyes full of wild fright. She grabbed Jim's arm and tugged him towards the Land Rover.

'You've got to come quick. Mrs M. had terrible fall . . . Doctor Hawker come quick as he could . . .'

'Is she all right?' Jim demanded of the breathless woman beside him. They were still yards short of the vehicle, but Betsey stopped in her tracks and spun Jim round as sobs wracked her body.

'Oh, boss . . . Oh, boss . . .'

Jim rocked back on his heels and looked like he might topple had Tim not instinctively shot out an arm to brace his shoulders.

There was a party going on in the East 50s. Jilba's apartment was full of expensive faces, leggy models and languid young men about town, all sipping champagne and laughing at Nancy Reagan on TV. Danny Serrano broke away from a conversation to check the room: where was Jilba?

He found her in the bedroom, slumped across her bed, the phone clutched in her hand between her knees, crying her heart out. He prised the phone from her, checked to see if there was anyone on the other end, got rid of it, put his arm round her and gently pulled her upright.

'Hey, what's going on?'

She couldn't answer. She could only sob.

'Hey, hey. What is it?'

There was still no answer and Danny had the good sense to just hold her for a while until her shakes diminished a bit.

'Come on. What's it all about?'

'That was my mother . . .' But the words trapped in her throat. Danny gave her time.

'My grandmother's died . . . She fell down the stairs . . .' It was enough. Danny cradled her head on his shoulder and stroked her hair.

'We've all got our time,' he whispered, as gently as he could.

Jilba clenched her fists, slammed them on her knees and wailed. 'But I should have gone . . . You don't understand . . . I should have been there . . .' She tried and condemned herself on the spot. As her grief took over again, she buried her head and cried like a baby.

# Twenty-Five

St Andrew's Church was full. Every seat was taken, every standing space; the overflow gathered at the doors, straining to hear. Elizabeth Mackay's coffin stood at the head of the aisle, barely visible under a mountain of flowers that spilled to the floor.

The Mackay family were seated in the front pew. Behind them, their dearest and closest friends listened with numb incomprehension to Reverend Kendon's eulogy. Tim Daley, Athol Ferguson, the Barclays, Will Mackenzie, Michael Hawker and Betsey Johnson. They sat, huddled side by side, trying to come to terms with where they were and why. At the end of the row, Dud Brewley was parked in a wheelchair. Despite his years, he'd climbed into the holding yards at Glenmore to give a cranky bull a kick in the ribs to get him into the chute. Instead, the bull went for him, slammed him into the railings and broke his pelvis. There was little chance he'd ever walk again. Few, except Athol, thought he'd survive the operation. Now, only forty-eight hours out of hospital, he'd insisted on being flown to Longreach to pay his respects to his old protégé's mother. He gingerly eased himself into a slightly less painful position as the Reverend Kendon moved towards his close.

'And so, as we have come from far and wide today to fill our church to overflowing, so our thoughts come from far and wide, to remind us of her loyalty, her determination, her devotion to her husband through years of illness and thereafter . . .' He paused to run his eye along the Mackays' pew. 'And to you, her family.' He kept his gaze on them as he continued. 'Use these loving memories to harrow the field of sorrow and plant seeds of rejoicing for a life well lived. For a life lived in the firm belief of the fundamental goodness of the human spirit. For a life of conviction and great character. Her love and wisdom were given with grace. In grace she most assuredly rests.' He gave a small nod in the Mackays' direction, shuffled his papers and closed the book. 'And now, let us sing together hymn number 197, The King of Love My Shepherd Is.'

As the opening chords thundered from the pipes, the congregation rose to sing the farewell hymn. By the end of the second verse, Jilba, Rachel and Billy were sobbing uncontrollably. Jim was next to break and Rachel hugged him to her side as they struggled to sing the words. Their own tears not quite falling, Tony and Jack held their heads high and sang their hearts out.

Elizabeth Mackay was laid to rest beside her husband. Athol took his leave of the family at the graveside to fly Dud straight back to Glenmore. The old-timer was in a lot of pain and needed to be put to bed as soon as possible. Jim squatted by the wheelchair to say thanks. Old Dud gripped his hand till it hurt and dismissed Jim's thanks with a toss of his ancient head.

'They don't make fillies like her any more, Jim. She was a thoroughbred, through and through.'

That night, after the last visitors had taken their leave, Jim and Tim got stuck into the whisky in no uncertain fashion, brothers in grief. Tim had been shocked to the core by Elizabeth's sudden death and now, as they hunched together over their drinks, he was trying to put it into words, but the words weren't there.

'She knew, Tim . . . Believe me,' said Jim. 'She loved you as one of the family, without question.'

The lump in Tim's throat nearly choked him as he twisted the glass in his hands. 'I know. It's just . . . Well . . . I never actually came out and said it . . . Told her what it meant to me . . . Right from the beginning . . .'

Jim patted his knee and grabbed his empty glass.

At the sideboard, Jack and Billy came to say goodnight. Jim threw his arms round the pair of them and hugged them together in a long, tight hold.

'Been a long day, you blokes. Try and get some sleep.'

He gave each of them a brusque kiss on the brow and they headed for their beds.

Jilba sprawled across her parents' bed as Rachel made busy, sorting out a few of Jim's shirts for the laundry.

'If only I'd come for the party,' she said, for the umpteenth time.

'There's absolutely no point in torturing yourself about it,' said Rachel. 'Dad was a bit disappointed, we all were. Naturally. But he understood and so did she. She was just thrilled to bits for you, that's all. Pleased as punch . . .'

A sob stopped her and she turned from the wardrobe to discover Jilba in floods of tears again. Wearily, Rachel sat on the edge of the bed and cradled her daughter in her arms.

'Come on, darling, please. Of course she would have loved to see you. But certainly not at the expense of such an opportunity. She was tremendously proud of you, proud of your achievement.'

Jilba managed to pull herself together again. 'Dad's taking it awful hard.'

'He'll be all right. He's got her strength. It's going to be hard for us all. I'm going to miss her terribly . . .'

Jilba sat up, wiped away the last of her tears and gave her mother a sympathetic kiss. 'I know you will . . .'

'You two still at it?' Jim interrupted, coming through the door, tugging at his tie and eyeing Rachel.

'I wanted to tidy up a bit first, Jilba was just telling me about New York.'

'Anyone in particular?'

To her parents' surprise Jilba blushed and dropped her eyes. Jim glanced at Rachel and they both raised an eyebrow.

'There is, as a matter of fact,' Jilba confessed. 'I'll tell you about him tomorrow.' She kissed her mother goodnight, then turned to Jim and hugged him. As she turned away, he grabbed her arm, and walked round to eye her with amused inquisitiveness.

'Is he a nice bloke?'

'He makes me laugh a lot. Yes . . . He's nice. Very nice.'

Jim's smile vanished as quickly as it came and Jilba gave him another hug before heading for the door. As she was about to go out, her father stopped her again.

'Jilba . . .'

She turned back and felt another wrench on her heartstrings, he looked so sad.

'You know what it would have meant to her, your being here . . .'

Jilba nodded and opened the door. 'Yes, I know. Get some sleep. You look exhausted.'

Just before lunch the following day, Jilba found herself standing with her maternal grandmother by the pond in the front lawn, deep in conversation. Jean had decided to take her granddaughter into her confidence.

'Why hasn't someone said something to dad?'

'Your mother would skin us alive, that's why. Now, you promised me, Jilba, not a word.'

'But he must have a clue, surely?'

'He doesn't let on, if he has. Not to us, anyway. Maybe to Elizabeth . . .' She paused and stared down at her old friend's waterlilies. 'That's her secret now, if he did. Your father's a man in love, bless him. Has been ever since the moment he saw her. I'll never hear a word spoken against him on that score. But love can be blind to things, sometimes. He's so wrapped up in Balkenna, so wrapped up in all the detail day after day. I don't think it would ever cross his mind that your mother doesn't love every minute of it, too.'

'But she does,' Jilba insisted. 'She's always said she's never regretted it for a minute.'

'Of course she loves it,' Jean corrected. 'For him, for his sake, because he loves it so much. Grandpa and I just think it's a golden opportunity, that's all. Your dad can hardly mind her going off to spend some time with you. Just a little holiday on her own, a few weeks to herself to get her bearings. It will be as hard for her as for Jim. But it will be twice as hard on everybody else if she doesn't get a break. Wouldn't you like to have her? You can't be all career and no family . . .'

'That's not fair,' Jilba flared. 'Of course I'd like her to come, if she wants to. I just don't think she will, that's all. Not unless they came together.'

'All we're asking is that you suggest it to her,' Jean prompted. 'Write her a sweet little letter in a few weeks and plant the idea. If she says no, then that's it. At least we will have tried.'

Jilba eyed the waterlilies herself and wrestled with her loyalties. Her initial reaction on seeing her mother again after so many months had been puzzling. She'd quickly dismissed it, putting it down to the loss of Elizabeth. But, that morning, after breakfast, Rachel seemed more and more restless and preoccupied. So distracted, in fact, Jilba decided against mentioning that, as well as the nice bloke who made her laugh a lot, she'd also developed a bit of a crush on a man her father's age. It just hadn't seemed a prudent moment, even though her mother obviously wanted to talk about anything except Balkenna.

She couldn't have known that the more she told her about her heady, round-the-clock life in New York, the more her mother had been struggling against a rising tide of something approaching jealousy. Now, her grandmother's revelations shed light on her mother's strange mood. It seemed inconceivable that anything could be seriously amiss in her parents' marriage. The strength and depth of their love for one another had been the rock all the children had anchored themselves to. That her mother should feel disillusioned with Balkenna was not a thought she relished carrying away the next day on her long journey back to New York. Troubled, she turned back to her grandmother.

'Okay, but I'll feel a bit of a traitor to dad.'

Jean put her arm round Jilba's shoulders and gave her a quick squeeze.

'It's in his interest, too, don't forget. She can have a good rest, you can show her the sights and, hopefully, she'll come back feeling like a new woman.'

'He'll be as miserable as a bandicoot.'

The few remaining hours she had to spend with her family just evaporated. At nine o'clock the next morning, she climbed the steps of the plane that would take her from Longreach to Cairns for her Qantas flight to San Francisco.

Sitting between her parents on the drive in from Balkenna, she felt wretched. She'd never been too good at secrets and this one compromised her, forced her to be too bright, too talkative, rushed her into tight-reined, eye-avoiding farewells.

Now, as she turned on the top step to wave to them, she couldn't help feeling relieved that, in a moment, the aircraft would gobble her up and whisk her away. But, as her parents waved and blew kisses in return, she longed to run back down the steps and across the tarmac and sweep them into her arms and bind them together for ever in a fierce, desperate hug. As the last couple of straggling passengers pushed past her, Jilba waved one last time and pivoted through the door.

Jim and Rachel remained on the fence, watching the plane taxi to the end of the runway. They waved like mad as it thundered back past them, lifted its nose and carried their daughter into the blue. They went on watching until it was little more than a speck.

Neither of them uttered a word until they were clear of town and out along the Jundah road.

'She'll be a tired girl by the time she gets there . . .'

'She's got two days to recover before she starts work,' said Rachel. 'She'll be all right.'

'Ridiculous amount of money she's getting, I must say. She'll have more dough than the whole family put together, if it keeps up.'

'She'll earn it,' Rachel smiled. 'It might be glamorous, but it's damned hard work, by the sound of it. Like being a sportswoman. Got to be in top form all the time.'

'Good on her for making the effort, anyway. It's a long haul.'

Rachel put her hand on the back of his neck and began to knead away some of his tension. It felt good.

'It's the Hall of Fame the week after next.'

'I don't think we have to bother, do we? In the circumstances.' Even before Elizabeth's death, Rachel hadn't particularly relished the idea, but she knew she'd end up going for his sake.

'I'm sure mum wouldn't have wanted it any other way, especially after all the committee work she put in. Anyway, it'll do us good.'

'If you like . . .'

'The new sheep'll be in next week. Should be just enough time to get 'em sorted out beforehand. Tim flew out to take a look yesterday. They're doing well.'

'I thought you were going to cut back on the wool for a while.'

'Yes, I know. But at the price they're coming at, it just seemed stupid to turn them down. We can handle it. It's going to be a bugger not having mum to do the books, though. Will Mackenzie always said it was a pleasure to read our books, she was so thorough.'

'What about Will? Couldn't he do it for us?'

'No. I've already put it to him. He reckons it wouldn't be quite right, in the circumstances. Stepping on the new man's toes, or something. I think he couldn't care less if he never saw another column of figures in his life. That's fair enough.'

'She tried to teach me, once,' Rachel reminded him. 'Remember?'

Jim shot her a grin and adjusted his brim against the glare. 'I remember what she said.'

'Hopeless.'

'Not just hopeless.'

He was teasing her now and Rachel took the bait.

'What? What did she say?'

Jim shot her another grin and played mute. Rachel thumped him on the arm. 'Come on, you big lump. What did she say?'

Jim adjusted his hat again and laughed at the memory. 'She reckoned you were the kind of person who'd work out the total of a mob of sheep by counting their legs and dividing by four . . .'

Rachel giggled as a lovely, smiling image of Elizabeth floated into her mind.

'Oh, she did, did she?'

' 'Fraid so,' Jim laughed. 'But don't hold it against her.'

He glanced at her again and their smiles quickly faded. Elizabeth Mackay would not be there to welcome them home.

# Twenty-Six

Two days after Jilba's return to New York, Tim met up with Jim in his study at Balkenna to go over the plans of the bungalow. Jim unrolled the architect's drawings his mother had commissioned and spread them across the desk.

'We thought if it was laid out something like that, you could have this part as a self-contained unit. This hallway here would connect into your brother's bit – there's a door at each end. Run the verandah in an L down this side, like that . . . You'd have your own entrance through this doorway here.'

'Looks fine to me, Jim. It looks much bigger than I expected.'

Jim raised his eyes to reassure him. 'She wanted you to have the best we could afford. So do I. I think we'll need to make a few suggestions, change a few things. It would probably be best if you took these away with you. Check them over on your own. Bryant reckons he could make a start fairly soon after the Hall of Fame shindig. About three to four weeks, I guess.'

Tim stared down at the drawings for a while, nodding his head. 'I wish she could have seen it finished,' he muttered.

Jim patted him on the back. 'A good result will be the best reward we can offer her, mate. As long as the rain holds over the next eighteen months, we should be in like Flynn, I reckon. All we need is a good start.'

Tim looked up from the plans and nodded. 'Yeah. Forecasts aren't too bad, anyway. Look, Jim, I just want to say . . . Well, if you'd prefer to put Ted on salary, too, I don't want you to feel tied down by the quarter share offer. Especially until we see how things go over the next couple of years. If you'd rather hold off . . .'

'I knew you'd get around to something like that, you old bastard,' Jim grinned. 'If it's there, it's yours, and that's final. This is family, remember?'

The phone by Jim's hand suddenly came to life, startling them both. Jim pulled a face.

'Blast. Hang on. Hello? Speaking. I'm a bit tied up at the moment . . .' He rolled his eyes and listened to the explanation coming down the line. 'How long will you be staying in Longreach? Oh . . . I see . . . No. I'm sorry, it's impossible at the moment . . . What?' He paused again to consider the implications as the voice on the other end went up an octave. 'Yes . . . All right . . . If you like. It's quite a drive. Okay . . . Fine . . . If you can do that. Fine. Yes. The earlier the better for me. Yes . . . Okay. I'll see you then.' Jim dropped the phone back in place and stared at it a moment. 'Never rains but it pours,' he muttered.

'Trouble?'

Jim shrugged. 'Some bloke from Brisbane. Coalmec, whoever they are. Something about mineral surveys.'

Tim's worried expression didn't fade.

'Don't worry, old son,' Jim chuckled. 'None of that mob are getting on here.'

'They've already been,' Tim confessed, awkwardly, much to Jim's alarm.

'The hell they have. What do you mean?'

'The day after your mother died,' Tim owned up. 'I didn't tell you about it. Didn't want you to be worrying about anything else on top.'

'What happened?'

'Two blokes in a ute. Caught them sniffing about on that claypan by the north dam.'

'At Bindra?'

'Yeah. Had some weird gear in the back. Tried to pretend they were doggers, of all things. I shooed them off. They gave me a bit of yak at the start, but they went quietly enough in the end.'

'Good on you.' Jim paused a moment to give it some thought. 'They've got a bloody hide, some of these people. I'm glad you told me. Give me something to whip this bloke's ears with tomorrow, if they're connected.'

'I've got a feeling they might be.'

'Soon find out,' Jim shrugged, slowly rolling up the architect's drawings. 'Sort the bloke out well and truly, if so.'

As Tim slapped his hat on the back of his head and stepped out onto the verandah, Jim returned to his desk. He arranged the mounting paperwork in sequence and spread it out in separate piles, meaning to get on with it. But thoughts of his mother, Rachel, the phone call from Coalmec, all fought for his concentration. He ended up just staring out of the window.

In Brisbane, Tony read the sign on Ben Molloy's desk: 'The Buck Doesn't Stop Here. I Take It To The Bank.'

'We need to update the whole sheebang,' said Molloy, slapping a fat file on the desk. 'The outstation movement, liquor-related homicide statistics, that sort of thing.'

'But no film?'

'Bang off some stills, if you want. But, for Christ's sake, be clever about it.'

'Do you want me to rewrite the whole file?' Tony asked, eyeing the size of it and not particularly relishing the idea.

'No, no need for that. Just make sure the percentages are up to date. Get the figures right, that's the main thing. I'll organise the permits. You'll want to go to Weipa, Aurukun and New Mapoon, I should think.'

'What about the powers that be?'

'Between you and me, for now,' Molloy confided. 'If anyone asks, you're researching road-trains.'

'How long?'

'Two weeks.'

'When should I start?'

'How's yesterday?'

Tony grinned at his editor and jumped to his feet. 'What was it like?'

'What?'

'On the galleys? When you used to whip the poor bastards on the oars?'

Tony was halfway to the door but he still didn't manage to duck the pencil that came flying through the air after him. Out in the corridor, he decided to chance the canteen for a quick cup of tea and a sandwich.

To his relief, it was practically empty and he settled down to make a few notes. He liked Molloy a lot and valued his trust. Budget and station policy aside, he knew his editor shared his opinions on a lot of subjects, even though he was still, technically, only a junior reporter.

He opened the file and leafed through the first dozen pages, immediately realising he'd probably rewrite some of it anyway, just for his own satisfaction. For Tony Mackay, the shocking treatment handed out to the Aboriginal people of Queensland could never be rewritten enough. He was glad to have this opportunity to see Weipa at first hand.

Weipa lay on the western coast of the very tip of Cape York Peninsula. The area had been an Aboriginal reserve of over 1,600,000 acres, administered by the Presbyterian Church. In 1957, the world's largest known deposit of bauxite was discovered there. In the subsequent exploitation, a port was built at Weipa and, under act of parliament, nearly 1,500,000 acres of the Aborigines' land was taken away for the allocation of mining leases. After a running outcry and demands for compensation, the mining companies did the honourable thing: they set aside 2,500 acres of badland for the original occupants. Even then, with no security of tenure, this had been whittled down to just over 400 acres.

Supported by the state government and its Department of Native Affairs, the companies would have actually preferred to evacuate all the Aborigines to the Aurukun Reserve, eighty kilometres south of Weipa. They changed their minds and allowed them to remain only after the Presbyterian Church agreed to drop all demands for compensation and royalty payments to the traditional owners of the land. It was the tip of an iceberg, a forerunner of similar events that would occur over vast areas of Cape York as subsequent mineral deposits were discovered and any Aborigines who happened to be there given short shrift. Blindness was the operative principle. The blind refusal of white authorities to recognise that Aboriginal people had a different view of the world, that they were entitled to those views, that they were entitled to their own way of life. It had taken over a quarter of a century before any noticeable shift in white attitude occurred. Even then, it was too little too late. The fight continued and Tony looked forward to this chance of seeing one of the old battlegrounds, perhaps finding some small way to see about setting the record straight.

The following evening, on the verandah at Balkenna, Jim and Rachel relaxed over a couple of after-dinner brandies.

'What did he want?' Rachel asked.

'Permission to survey,' Jim replied. 'Bit of a hard case. Wasn't too pleased to be knocked back.'

'What did he say?'

'Not a lot after that. They could force our hand, of course, apply for government licence. Just have to wait and see. We're all right for now, at any rate.'

'What is titanium? What do they use it for?'

'High-speed aircraft, rockets, that sort of thing.'

'Could there be some here?'

Jim pondered a moment before replying. 'I suppose there could be. Wouldn't really have a clue. According to what he said, it's in everything. Rocks, sand, clay. Even in plants and animals, he reckoned. It's the concentrated pockets they're after.'

'What about bauxite?'

'Basically, they'll take anything they can get. Claim they're looking for one thing and use that as an excuse to conduct a general survey. Nobody would be any the wiser, especially me. At least that's one area where I have no argument with Tony. We can't go on endlessly ripping the land apart just to exploit the short-term interest. Gone on long enough as it is.'

'He rang today. He's been given an assignment out of Brisbane. Up north.'

'Doing what?'

'Didn't say exactly. Something to do with road-trains. Sounded very pleased about it, anyway.'

'He'll be all right.'

'Nice to hear you expressing some confidence in him for a change.'

Jim pulled a face. 'Now don't start. It's a nice evening, let's not spoil it.'

Rachel took a sip, turned and smiled. 'Just testing.'

Jim took a hefty gulp himself and leaned back. 'You okay?'

He dropped it in as casually as he could, but there was a lot of topspin on it. All the time he was talking to the mining engineer that morning, he found it difficult to concentrate. He had just wanted to get it over with. Rachel monopolised his mind and her image did not rest easily. He couldn't put his finger on it, but something was *definitely* wrong. An extremely subtle shift seemed to have occurred before he saw it coming and it scared the hell out of him. Not since their long-ago row over Dean Coulter had he felt so estranged from her. He'd finally faced the facts while mulling over his paperwork the day before. It was a horrible double-bind. She was giving nothing away and he didn't have the courage to admit he knew something was wrong and attempt to get to the bottom of it. On the other hand . . . His mother's death had been a terrible blow. Perhaps he was reading more into it than was actually there. Perhaps she'd be more like her old self after the Hall of Fame opening. It should be a whale of a time.

'Betsey and I finished all the preserving today . . .' It wasn't any answer. She placed her glass on the table and took a deep breath. 'I'm a bit done in. Time for bed.'

'Yeah,' Jim admitted. 'Bit weary, myself.'

Rachel was already on her feet. She breathed deeply again, let it out, stretched and headed inside. Shaking his head, Jim collected their glasses.

On the landing of the floor below, Jilba's neighbour's door was wide open. He came dancing out as she climbed the stairs, waving an enormous bunch of flowers.

'Came about an hour ago. Gorgeous Puerto Rican boy.' He flapped his stringless wrists. 'Any time, Julio, I said. Any time.'

She dumped her bag inside her door, kicked off her shoes and carried the flowers through to the kitchen. She plucked the little envelope from their midst and opened it. The card said 'Compliments of Coulter Associates'. Jilba turned it over. 'The rushes are excellent,' said the handwriting. 'So far, so good. Well done. Regards – Dean Coulter.' With a secret smile, she dropped the card on the bench, hunted in the cupboard for the old Italian wine carafe she used for a vase, unwrapped the cellophane and began disentangling the stems.

'He's after your ass,' Danny said later.

Jilba grinned and shook her head. 'There's never been a hint of that.'

'Might have to straighten him out, if he keeps it up.'

Jilba put her finger to his lips. 'I'm positive it's not that.'

Danny eyed her sideways. 'Are you disappointed?'

Jilba raised her finger an inch to push in the tip of his nose. 'Don't be mean.'

Their fingers knotted and that was the end of Dean Coulter.

# Twenty-Seven

It was let-your-hair-down week in Longreach for the bicentennial opening of the Stockman's Hall of Fame and Outback Heritage Centre, Queensland's memorial to those explorers, first settlers, cattlemen, sheepmen, drovers, poets and drunkards who pioneered the whole outback way of life.

Longreach was packed to the rafters. Out at the airport, everybody was staring at the sky. There was a loud, communal whoooaahh as two specks suddenly appeared.

'Shit! Look at that!' Billy yelled, earning himself a swift cuff on the ear from his mother.

'Owww!'

'Mind your language,' she hissed.

'Shit. Look at that!' said the kid next door as the parachutes bloomed like flowers in the sky, trailing orange smoke.

There are half a dozen hotels in Longreach and, in every bar, the beer was flowing faster than the Thomson River in flood. In the lounge of the Commercial, Jim and a bunch of local graziers were murdering the new MP.

'He'll do all right, I reckon,' said Jim. 'He understands what comes first.'

A huge, florid cattleman from out along the Barcaldine road scowled. 'As long as he does something about these bloody Abo agitators. Land rights, for God's sake. They'll be wanting to ship us all back to fuckin' England next.'

'The Abos were here first, China, no getting away from that.'

The cattleman went a darker shade of purple. 'Yeah!' he exploded. 'And what the hell did they do with it? Tell me that? Sat on their arses and watched it all go to waste, that's what. We brought them the greatest civilisation in the world and they turned their backs on it. You've heard 'em! All their white-man-properly-different-kind lizard-shit. Now they want two hundred years of hard work handed back on a platter. Over my dead bloody body, mate.'

249

The poor bloke should have been out at the showgrounds for the buckjumping. He'd either shit or go blind.

'Second place,' boomed the PA. 'All the way from Jericho. Let's give a big Longreach hand to . . . Joe Clements.'

A young, redheaded stockman ran a few paces forward from the chutes, removed his hat and turned a slow circle.

'First place, and through to the next round! From Winton . . . Frankie Dawson.'

He appeared from the chutes and ran forward to wave to the spectators: a full-blood Aboriginal stockman, black as night.

Back at the Commercial, Rachel caught Jim's eye and he excused himself. A few of the men waved, keen to catch the eye of the beautiful Mrs Mackay. Rachel summoned up a smile and waved back.

'They're serving lunch now,' she said to Jim. 'These two claim to be starving. I'd like to freshen up a bit first. Won't be long.'

'Okay,' Jim grinned, propelling the boys back through the door. 'Come on, you lot. Let's have some tucker.'

As she unlocked the door and entered their room, Rachel was thankful that Jim had had the foresight to book them into a hotel six months before. It was the nicest room in the whole hotel, with direct access to the verandah. In these last few days of frantic activity, it had been her sanctuary.

She closed the door behind her. She tossed her bag on the bed, slumped into an armchair and kicked off her shoes. Dropping her head back, she took a deep breath and closed her eyes. Ten minutes later, she woke with a start and leapt up. She checked her hair in the mirror, pushing it into place with her fingers, trying to avoid the look of despair in her eyes.

That afternoon, Jim rode with the Winton team in the polocrosse competition. He was loving every minute of Hall of Fame week and he played with a noisy enthusiasm that belied the fact he hadn't done it for a while. Even Rachel, watching from the sidelines, found herself yelling encouragement. When it was over, she took Jack and Billy off to buy them a shandy while they waited for Jim.

At the stalls, still running with perspiration, Jim pulled the saddle off, grabbed a cloth and began to rub down his foaming pony.

'Better luck next time,' said Athol.

Jim straightened, grinned and grabbed his back. 'I'm getting too old for this sort of thing,' he chuckled.

'Oh, I don't know,' said Dud, easing his bum off the wheel-chair. 'Haven't lost your touch, Mackay. Reckon you're good for a few yet.'

Jim cocked an eyebrow at Athol. 'Listen to him, will you? Bloody slave-driver.'

'Keep it up while you can,' Dud cackled. 'That's my motto.'

Jim dropped a hand on Dud's shoulder. He was all skin and bone. 'How about a pony as soon as I get through here?'

'Now there's a game I *really* like,' Dud beamed. 'Better make mine a schooner, though. Feel as old as Captain Cook.'

There was a ball that night in a huge marquee. Queen Elizabeth didn't come, but everyone else was there. From their table, Jim and Rachel watched Jack shyly squiring a local girl around the dance floor. Jim tapped Rachel on the shoulder. Across the other side, Billy was on the floor with one of the tourist girls. They came together and began to bump and grind.

'He dances just like you.'

Jim bumped her with his shoulder. 'Come on. Let's have a fling.'

Before she could argue, he pulled her to her feet and ushered her into the crowd of dancers just as the tune ended and every-one came to a halt and yelled for more. It was 'In the Mood'.

'Perfect,' said Jim, giving her a hug that lifted her off her feet before whirling her away again. Rachel threw back her head and laughed with delight. They turned and turned and turned until she felt quite giddy and eased him down a notch. Jim gazed into her eyes, gave her a cheeky grin and tested her memory.

'It's a nice ball.'

She was quick as a flash. 'Lovely.'

Jim pulled her in even tighter and, cheek to cheek, they slowed the pace, dancing in the past. Then all hell broke loose. Suddenly the tent was filled with wild shouts and cries of alarm. The whole dance floor came to a halt, the band broke off in mid-phrase and everyone surged towards the entrance.

A line of burly graziers' sons stood eyeball to eyeball with a couple of dozen land rights demonstrators. They were wearing T-shirts with all the slogans and brandishing protest signs. Just as Jim got there, they started throwing punches. A savage fist fight erupted between a tall, middle-aged Aboriginal man and one of the young tuxedoed blockaders who was built like a tank. The crowd fanned back as the fight exploded, the two men trading savage, bare-knuckle punches, blow for blow.

251

Jim didn't hesitate. He barged between them, pushed them apart and held them at arm's length.

'Stop that! Cut it out! What the hell do you think this is?'

The two men started swinging either side of him, trying to shove him out of the road and get back at one another. Jim pushed the Aboriginal man hard in the chest, sending him sprawling on his back. Then, with both hands, he grabbed the young buck by the lapels and threw him back into the crowd.

'That's enough!'

The white bloke was already bleeding freely from the nose and happy enough for an excuse to retreat and be comforted by his mates. As he did, the local police sergeant and a couple of rookies came charging through the entrance. The sergeant immediately began shooing the demonstrators out.

'Right, you lot! Outside! Now!'

The protesters glared at him, shuffled a bit, but made no move to comply.

'Outside!' the sergeant repeated angrily, jabbing at the entrance with all the authority he could muster, then glancing at his watch. 'In one minute, or you're all under arrest.'

This time they moved, herding themselves together towards the entrance. As they filed through, one of them began to chant and his lead was quickly taken up by the others.

'Land rights! Land rights! Land rights, now!'

The Aboriginal fighter was still on the floor. He was sitting up now, inspecting the blood on his fingers, gingerly testing a split lip. Jim extended a hand to help him to his feet, but the Aborigine ignored it and stood on his own. Still patting at his mouth, he glared fiercely at Jim. Jim held his eye. A vague sense of recognition dawned. 'Do I know you?'

The Aborigine just continued to stare him down as the police sergeant placed a hand on his shoulder to chuck him out.

'Hang on a minute, sergeant,' Jim requested, turning his attention back to the Aborigine. 'Did you work for me at some time? I recognise you, I'm sure I do.'

The Aborigine stared him down a long time before he spoke. 'You should, Jim.'

From long ago and faraway, recognition came. Jim gaped at the man for several seconds, gathering his wits before he could ask, 'Dougie?'

'What took you so long, Jim? We all look alike? That it? Can't tell one from the other?'

Jesus, they had grown up together. Wild, naked, barefoot, in the days of their Balkenna dreaming.

Jim reached out to place his hands on the shoulders of his boyhood mate, but Dougie brushed them away.

'Times have changed, Jim,' he growled. He turned away and allowed the sergeant to escort him to the entrance. But he stopped before they went through and glanced back. For just a flicker, forty years went up in smoke. Then he turned away again and, with a shove from the sergeant, he was gone. Jim stepped quickly forward to call him back.

'Dougie! Dougie!'

But Dougie didn't turn again as the sergeant hustled him outside and thrust him into the clutch of his now rather forlorn looking fellow demonstrators. There were some curious looks and whispers as Jim turned round and headed back inside, wondering if he should have chased after him, the shock of surprise giving way to a bitter taste of humiliation and loss.

In the hotel dining room the following morning, the Mackays were at their table for breakfast. Rachel had a large glass of tomato juice in front of her and was lacing it with Worcestershire Sauce.

'Here,' she grinned, passing it to Jim. 'That ought to help.'

'I'm never going to drink,' Billy declared, poker-faced.

'You already have,' Jack corrected him.

'Never again,' Billy promised.

They were all taking a bit of a ride on Jim who was feeling dead shady. He'd knocked back a few too many after his confrontation with Dougie the night before. He slowly drained the whole glassful, smacking his lips, and shook his head with mock content.

'Ahhh, better already.'

'Jack's got a girlfriend,' Billy announced, matter-of-fact.

Jack glared at his brother. 'No I haven't. Just someone to dance with.'

'Yeah,' scoffed Billy. 'All night long.'

'And very nice you were together, too,' said Rachel, putting an end to it.

A waitress appeared and doled out a couple of menus. 'You're wanted on the phone, Mr Mackay. You can take it in the lobby, if you like.'

Ten minutes later, their eggs arrived and he still wasn't back.

Rachel found him, slumped in a chair in a small lounge off the main lobby.

'Darling, what is it?'

Jim lifted his head wearily, a look of infinite pain in his eyes. 'Just one damn thing after another. Can't take a trick at the moment.'

'What's wrong? What's happened?'

Jim dropped his head. 'That was Tim.' He broke off and stared blankly into space, lost for words. Rachel gave him time.

'They're dead. The sheep. The new sheep. The whole stinking mob.'

She gasped. 'All three thousand?'

'Every damn one.'

'How?'

'Stupidity,' Jim growled. 'Sheer, blind stupidity. I was stupid to take them on. Stupid bloody things . . .' He shook his head and held it in his hands, frustrated, angry and bilious. 'They're not insured. I was going to fix it up next week, after we got through here. Christ almighty. First mum, now this.'

'Tell me,' Rachel prompted, her hand falling on the back of his neck.

Jim sighed and raised his head. 'Tim blames the wind. Been blowing from the northeast for days. At their backs all the way to the boundary. Stupid damn things didn't find our water.'

'But the bore drain on the run, it always has water, doesn't it?'

'Tim reckons they must have got the scent of the stock route bore on the wind and followed their noses. The fence pulled them up and they just jammed up in the corner, just piled on top of one another. He reckoned he could smell them a mile away.'

Rachel dropped her head on his shoulder and held him tight.

'Been there for days,' Jim whispered.

'I'll go and get the boys.'

'No, hang on. No need for us all to go. You stay and enjoy yourselves.'

Rachel smiled grimly and patted his hand. 'Jack would want to be with you, you know that. Besides, I've had enough of all this, anyway.'

# Twenty-Eight

In the executive apartment of the Coulter Associates building on Madison Avenue, a small, elite crowd was sipping champagne, swapping gossip and monitoring the TV sets provided for the occasion. Dean Coulter found Jilba and squeezed her elbow.

'Where's Danny?'

'Couldn't get away. Said the meeting would go on for hours. Said you'd understand.'

'Only too well,' Coulter smiled. 'Meeting used to be such a nice word, once.'

They touched glasses and took a sip, Coulter eyeing her over the rim. Jilba held his look a moment then dropped her eyes.

'Happy?' he asked quietly.

'Very,' she replied, looking up again.

'You should be,' Coulter smiled. 'God gave you beauty.'

It was casually offered, but it made her heart jump a rope. Colouring, she hid behind her lashes again.

Suddenly, there were a few whistles and someone shouted.

'Here we go . . .'

Jilba immediately pivoted to face the nearest TV. A Jeep ad. And then there she was! Bounding down the steps of a New York brownstone. A real get-up-and-go girl for the eighties, with everything to look forward to and the world at her feet.

Lillian Tompkins bellowed her approval. 'Looks good. Looks good.'

On the screen, Jilba bumps into a mailman at the kerbside. She dazzles him with a smile, pirouettes, and sashays off down the street as every head turns for a second look. She's breathtaking. She passes a building site and the hardhats' wolf whistles trap in their throats. The mailman watches her go, takes off his cap, shakes his head and heaves a long, 'if only' sigh.

'Look your best for the people who count,' suggests the resonant baritone.

Jilba comes straight at the camera, promising you everything. Closer, closer, closer, until her head and shoulders fill the frame and the shot freezes for the ad line: 'Go mad with Opal fever. Light up your life with the new Firestone range from Opal.'

Pop! Pop! Pop! Around the room, the champagne frothed and fizzed into glasses. Jilba was suddenly surrounded by smiling faces, congratulations and kisses. Lillian Tompkins swept across the room to envelope her.

'Come to me, my million-dollar baby . . .'

Laughing with delight, Jilba prised herself loose and drew Lillian's attention to an instant replay flickering into life on the video. Lillian immediately cut the horseplay to concentrate her professional eye. Jilba glanced around the room. Dean Coulter was missing.

In the bedroom next door, Coulter was standing alone, with the lights off, staring out at the skyline, a war going on in his heart. The click of the door took him by surprise. It was Jilba, softly lit by the spill of neon light.

'You didn't see it,' she said.

'I've been watching it all week.'

'What did you think?'

Her eyes were shining in the half-light. Coulter hesitated a moment, then smiled. 'I've already told you.'

Jilba had drunk a little too much Dom Perignon. She felt giddy, flushed with success, all caution gone up in smoke. The offer was there in her eyes, impossible to deny. Coulter braced himself as she glided across the carpet, getting closer and closer.

'You've given me so much,' she whispered. 'You've given me everything. Dreams do come true, don't they?'

'Some dreams.'

'What about you, Dean? What do you dream about?'

Coulter fought himself, to warn her, to arm himself against her.

'Jilba . . .'

But it was too late. She was too close and too beautiful. Too young and headstrong. Too much in love with the possibility. He tried to turn her away, but she slipped between his arms and strained against him, offering her mouth, seeking his.

As her arms snaked round his neck, as Coulter's embargoed hands spread-eagled across her back, as their lips met, he didn't know any more if he was betraying her mother's memory, making love to Rachel through her daughter or simply surrendering to the girl's intoxicating spell, regardless of the consequences. When he pulled his mouth away, there was fright in his eyes.

'Go home . . .'

Jilba stopped, puzzled, then reached for him again. Coulter caught her wrists and forced her back.

'No. Go home. Be a good girl, say goodnight and go home.'

The champagne really had a grip now and tears sprang to Jilba's eyes.

'Why?'

'Because I say so.'

Biting hard, Coulter pushed past her and walked out of the room, leaving Jilba stranded on some giddy sandbank of the soul, her eyes stinging, body aching, head spinning out of control.

Balkenna was burying its dead.

Six gaping pits, the size of small dams, lay in line about thirty yards apart. Two tractors towing tip-trailers were backed up to the monstrous, toppling mountain of fly-blown, maggoty Merinos. Wearing heavy-duty surgical gauze face masks and rubber gloves, Jim and his stockmen were working their way steadily through the carnage. In teams of two, they hauled the carcasses from the pile and heaved them onto the trailers to be trundled to the pits. The sun didn't give a hoot for their troubles and was sucking rivers of sweat out of them all. At the pits, Jim and Tim swung round, backed up, engaged the hydraulics, tipped up and spewed two more loads of woollies onto their dead relatives. They still had about a thousand to go.

Jim's Land Rover and a couple of utes stood some distance away, up wind, in the shade of a small clump of gidgee. As he lowered the trailer back in place to head for another load, Jim glanced into the middle distance and spotted the Ford station wagon pull in. He drove the tractor back to the pile, jumped out, signalled for one of the stockmen to take over and headed for the new arrival.

It was Rachel. She looked terrible.

'What on earth are you doing here? You don't want to see this.'

Rachel looked up at him through the half-open window and

felt a pang of regret she'd come. He looked utterly exhausted.

'I didn't know what to do,' she confessed.

Jim just stared at her, waiting for the rest, too buggered to help her get it out.

'I've just had Ben Molloy on the phone, from Brisbane . . .'

Jim still looked blank.

'Tony's boss,' she reminded him. 'He's been hurt, in a fight.'

He was with her now. 'How bad?'

'He's fractured a couple of ribs and broken his arm.'

Jim raised his hands to heaven in momentary, desperate supplication, then slapped them hard against his thighs.

'For God's sake! What next? Where is he? Brisbane?'

'No, he's way up on Cape York, at the Weipa Aboriginal Reserve. The bauxite company doctor is looking after him.'

'What's he doing there?'

Rachel shook her head and sighed. 'That whole business about road-trains was a fib. They were doing a story on the Reserves. Molloy said they had to be a bit careful.'

Jim stared glumly at the burial work going on in the distance as he took it in. Then he slammed an angry hand on the bonnet.

'It'll be at least ten days before he can travel, unless we hire an air ambulance.'

'What the hell's he doing there? What's he getting mixed up in that for?'

'Why not?' Rachel was defensive. 'I thought that was one of the few things you saw eye to eye on.'

'He can bloody well stay there. Got himself into it, he can bloody well wait to get out. Let the bloody TV mob pay for an ambulance if they want to. Serves him bloody well right.'

'Don't go crook at me,' Rachel snapped. 'It's not my fault. I just thought you should know straightaway, that's all. Sorry I bothered.'

She gunned the motor and crunched into first gear.

'You backed him into the stupid job,' Jim challenged. 'All the bloody way.'

Rachel glared up at him and refused to give ground.

'You wished him good luck, remember? Good luck with no regrets.'

Jim banged the bonnet again in frustration and turned angrily away. 'We'll talk about it tonight.'

Rachel let out the clutch and the vehicle lurched past him,

kicking dust. Jim watched her drive away, half-heartedly raised his hand to beckon her back, then let it drop. Annoyed at himself for losing his temper in front of her, he trudged back to the burial holes, kicking a few clods of dirt out of his path. He caught up with his tractor just as another load slid out of the trailer to cartwheel onto the last lot. He looked down into the confusion of rank wool, mad eyes and piston rod legs, and felt the knot tighten in his stomach. He thumbed at the driver that he was ready to take over.

Rachel felt angry, too. Angry and desolate. She couldn't face going straight back to the house. She left the car in the shade and wandered along the bank of the creek to the rockfall pool. She squatted down with her back to the old river gum that had stood sentinel over the swimming hole in Jim's boyhood, witnessed the splashing shrieks of delight of her own children.

She realised she must have been there for a good half-hour before a flicker of movement on the periphery of her vision disturbed her. It was a frill-neck lizard, meandering its way to sunbake on a flat rock at the water's edge. In Rachel's state of mind, the horny creature stood as a symbol of all she had come to detest about this thankless country. She seized a stick and hurled it as hard as she could. The movement of her arm was enough. As the stick whistled over its back, the lizard scuttled for cover.

Alone again, the world came crashing in on Rachel and she broke. Sobbing uncontrollably, she banged her head repeatedly back against the old gum's trunk and implored the surrounding scrub to throw some light on the dark gathering inside her.

Jilba was sound asleep when the phone rang.

'Hello,' she mumbled. 'Mum!' She was wide awake in a flash. 'What . . .?'

Jilba snapped on the light to check her bedside clock.

'No . . . No. It's all right . . . Don't worry. What's going on? What? I've hardly been here the past few days. Been working really hard. Eating on the run, you know. Just coming back to sleep . . . What? Oh, Mum . . . I said it's all right. Don't worry about it. What's going on?'

Her eyes got wider by the second, as it all came spilling out.

'Faaaaantastic! That's wonderful . . . Really brilliant. Of course . . . Of course. No . . . Not at all. Let's just wait and see. Oh, Mum, of course I am . . . It's great. How's dad?'

Jilba's effervescence dried up as Rachel told her the bad news.

'Oh, poor darling. Give him a big hug and kiss from me, will you? Yes. Okay. 'Bye . . . Yes. Yes. It's great. Lots of love . . . 'Bye.'

Ten minutes later, the phone rang at the Barclays' home in Sydney.

'Jilba, darling!' Jean gushed, with genuine surprise. 'How wonderful to hear you. I'm fine, dear . . . Yes, granddad's fine, too. Playing golf. What? Yes . . . All right, dear. Go ahead, I'm listening . . .'

Jean did feel a little peeved that her carefully-wrought conspiracy had been pre-empted by Rachel taking matters into her own hands. But she had to admit it was good news.

'That's excellent, dear. Excellent. What? . . . No, I know. Well, you weren't exactly looking forward to writing it anyway, were you? No, I understand. Oh, that is good news. Granddad will be pleased as punch. No . . . Not at all. No . . . You're not to worry about a thing, do you hear me? We'll invite ourselves up . . . Yes, granddad, too . . . I promise. We'll look after him. Yes . . . All right. I'll call her this evening. Bless you, darling. It's wonderful news . . . Thank you for calling . . . Yes. 'Bye, precious. 'Bye . . . 'Bye . . .'

Jean wandered back through the house and out onto the verandah to contemplate the harbour waters in the distance. So, Rachel had taken the plunge, organised a solo holiday for herself to spend Christmas in New York with Jilba. A long way off yet, she mused. Time enough for them to arrange their own stay at Balkenna to keep Jim company. She was relieved it was all out in the open. But her relief was tempered by unsettling speculations about her daughter's future beyond New York. What would happen when Rachel came back? Would the break be a temporary healing or a complete cure?

That evening, at Balkenna, Jim and Rachel were sitting in the lounge, doing a lot of staring at the floor. Jim felt like a shag on a rock, devastated by Rachel's hesitant confession of her growing disenchantment with life in the outback, her need to get away from it for a while to find new fuel for her motor. His speculations as to the cause of her moodiness had never gone that far. They had centred on the daily give and take between them and he'd tried to adjust accordingly. To discover that their home had become a prison for her after all these years had devastated him.

The hall door opened and Betsey breezed in, carrying a bowl

of fresh-cut flowers. She stopped as soon as she saw them, read the mood and discreetly tiptoed out again, closing the door behind her. The noise startled Jim out of his morose introspection.

'We could at least have talked about it first,' he muttered. 'Before you made any plans. I could have arranged something . . . For both of us to go . . .'

Rachel raised her eyes and what she saw filled her with guilt. There was no way to tell him she'd felt compelled to plan her escape before discussing it for fear of being dissuaded from taking the step, either by his conviction or her own lack of it. It had been relatively easy to drive back from the creek and pick up the phone. Now she had to pick up the pieces. Her courage had failed her at the last moment. She'd only told him the half of it, said it was a recent problem, assured him a holiday on her own would do the trick. She'd done her best to make him understand she loved him every bit as much as she'd ever done. But how to convince him while explaining that his kingdom was her wasteland, his castle her tomb? In her heart of hearts, she knew she'd failed.

'We both know you don't really like to be away from the place any longer than you have to,' she reminded him quietly. 'You're always anxious to get back. I understand that. I do. I just want some time on my own, that's all. It'll do us both a power of good.'

Jim looked up at her, his eyes full of hurt. 'I'd like to see Jilba too, you know.'

Rachel ducked her head and fiddled with the wedding ring on her finger.

'Of course I do. But you'd be perfectly happy to go for a week, turn round and come right back. I need a *holiday*, a real break, without any pressures . . .'

She couldn't bear it. Taking a deep breath, she pulled herself out of her chair and stepped across to perch on the arm of his and stroke the back of his head.

'Please understand. It's been building up for a while. It's not you. I just need some time off. I'm a city girl, don't forget, born and bred.' She leant down and kissed the top of his head.

'You've lived more than half your life out here,' Jim said. But his opposition was crumbling. He pulled her down into his lap, hugged her to him and kissed her brow. 'Knowing you, if your mind's made up, your mind's made up, and there's bugger all I can do about it.'

Rachel allowed herself a little smile, kissed his cheek and

cradled her head on his shoulder. The hall door opened again and Betsey stuck a cautious head round to check the mood, beaming with delight when she saw Rachel in Jim's lap.

'Dinner's ready,' she called.

Rachel lifted her head. 'Thanks, Betz. We'll be right there.'

Betsey ducked out and Rachel hauled herself up, turned and extended her hands to pull Jim to his feet. They stood together, holding hands and staring into each other's eyes for a moment before Rachel threw her arms round his neck and gave him a long, loving kiss on the mouth. Jim responded, crushing her to him in a hug that got tighter and tighter and tighter.

After dinner Jim called the infirmary up at Weipa. It took a couple of attempts to get through and then he had to wait a good ten minutes for Tony to struggle to the phone, minutes Jim used to bring his fury under control and make sure his voice was free of recrimination when he spoke to his son.

When he hung up, he was smiling. Tony had joked about his plight, wanting his father to have a chuckle at his expense because he couldn't. It hurt too much to laugh. Two white blokes had gone for an Aboriginal youth with a pickaxe handle, claiming he'd stolen some cameras from their car. Tony had rumbled to the rescue. In the circumstances, he reckoned they both got off lightly. The Aborigine had two hairline fractures of the skull and a broken nose. He was insisting his attackers be charged, but everybody knew there was little chance of a result. Tony was being treated as a bit of a dill at the infirmary, but they were looking after him well enough. As soon as he felt his ribs could take the strain, he would catch the first plane back to Brisbane.

There had been genuine warmth in Tony's thanks for his father's call. 'I'm glad we're on the same side, Dad . . . As far as these things go.'

'Yes,' Jim replied. 'Me, too.'

Now, as he rolled himself a smoke and gathered his wits to go and report to Rachel, his eye fell on the crest ring on his finger and he offered a quick, silent prayer that the motto would give him strength to hold together a world that had suddenly fallen apart.

As he leant across to switch off his desk lamp, Jim took the pledge to question her no further. Instead, he would concentrate on making her as happy as possible, as much for Jack and Billy's sake as for their own. He stepped to the door reflecting that, after all, if it came to it, Jack could take over in another six or seven years. With his rapidly maturing abilities and Tim's experience, it would be safe enough to leave him to it and think about buying a place in Brisbane or Sydney for him and Rachel to spend long periods of time. But, as he closed the door behind him, walked a few paces along the verandah and stopped to gaze out at the southern stars, he knew it would break his heart to have to leave.

# Twenty-Nine

Rachel eventually arrived in New York in the second week of November. Already, there were signs that Santa Claus was coming to town to endorse everything money could buy. Even the yellow cab had its own display of Santa stickers, Bethlehem stars and a sign saying 'Happy Holidays'.

The bellboy lugged the last of Rachel's bags into her room, pocketed his tip and left them to it. Mother and daughter stood appraising one another a moment before falling into each other's arms. 'I still wish you'd stay with me,' Jilba protested as they separated. 'I'd be perfectly all right on the couch and I'm sure you'd feel much more at home.'

'This is absolutely fine,' Rachel assured her, glancing approvingly around the room. 'Very cosy. I can come and go as I please and sleep as late as I like without getting in your way. You're not to worry about me, do you hear? I can meet up with you whenever you've got the time, wherever you are.'

Rachel gave her daughter a winning smile and Jilba kissed her cheek and gave her another fond hug. 'Ohhh, it's so good to see you.'

Rachel watched her hurry down the corridor, give a final wave and disappear round the corner. Pleased as punch, she closed the door and hauled the first of her bags onto the bed. The long flight had been pretty exhausting, but now, as she stowed her clothes away, the faintly audible rumble of New York's hustle and bustle gave her a new lease of life and she decided to take a quick walk round the block as soon as she'd unpacked.

Rachel adjusted her coat and scarf against the winter chill and remembered the cab driver's forecast of snow. She set off for the corner, feeling a thrilling sense of foreignness as the cacophony of New York swirled all around her.

Five weeks later, she'd seen every good show and movie in town, found her way to umpteen weird and wonderful locations to meet up with Jilba and felt like a seasoned campaigner in the world's toughest playground.

The Barclays had arrived at Balkenna before Rachel's departure, keeping Jean's promise to provide tender loving care for Jim, Jack and Billy in her absence. They'd been joined for Christmas by Tony and Susan and Athol Ferguson who'd driven down from Winton. Dud's indomitable will had managed to confound all the doctor's expectations. He'd consigned his wheelchair to past history and was now able to hobble about on his 'seventy-sevens', as he called his matching pair of walking sticks. Athol joked to Jim he was totally convinced Dud would outlive them all.

Now, as the whole group sat out on the verandah to knock back a drop before dinner, Tony and Jack took note of Jim's long face.

'Cheer up, Dad.'

Jim dug up a half-hearted grin and set about filling their glasses.

'*So* beautiful,' said Susan to nobody in particular, gazing at the western skyline. 'No wonder the Aborigines worshipped sky spirits.'

Betsey stuck her head through the front door and summoned them all in to dinner. When Susan figured she was out of earshot, she taunted Tony, loud enough for Jim to hear.

'Don't you find it a bit embarrassing. Having an Aboriginal servant?'

In the prickly silence that followed, Tony squirmed in his seat. It was said for effect and she had no right.

'Betsey loves her work here, she loves Balkenna. We all do,' he added meaningfully, glancing at his father. 'She's one of the family.'

But Jim was thousands of miles away. Either he hadn't heard or he didn't give two hoots. As they gathered to head inside, Jim draped his arm across Billy's shoulders and ushered him forward.

'Just think, your mum's walking around in piles of snow . . .'

It *was* snowing in New York. Big cottony flakes were drifting down to layer inches deep on the parked cars and mantle the ungainly iron fire escapes, transforming them into exquisite filigree.

Rachel and her daughter ploughed their way to the entrance of

Jilba's apartment building, wearily negotiated the stairs, tumbled inside and dumped the results of their Christmas shopping spree on the rug. Jilba checked her watch and pulled a face. 'God, look at the time. I'll have to go for my life.'

'Go on then,' Rachel prompted, waving at the door. 'Don't stand around talking about it.'

'Blimey,' Jilba cracked. 'Max better watch out. You'll be wanting to be my agent next.'

'I'll give it some thought.'

Jilba grabbed her bag and headed for the door, giving herself a quick once over in the hall mirror. 'I should be back by seven at the latest. Danny'll be here by then.'

'Don't be late then, please.'

Jilba sighed. 'Oh, Mum. For goodness sake. He thinks you're wonderful.'

'Well, hurry back, anyway,' begged Rachel. 'For the life of me, I don't know what he's talking about half the time.'

Jilba giggled, opened the door and gave her mother a farewell wave. 'See you then.'

' 'Bye, darling.'

Rachel set about clearing away the shopping and tidying the apartment. When she was finished, she fixed herself a cup of coffee and carried it to the couch. She slipped off her shoes and put her feet up. Just as she got comfortable the phone rang.

'Damn,' she muttered, and headed for the bedroom. 'Oh . . . Hello, Danny . . . She just left. Yes, about twenty minutes ago . . . Yes, around seven, she said . . . Fine, Danny. Whenever you like . . . Yes, I'll be here. Fine . . . See you then.'

With a bemused smile, she hung up and shook her head. She liked Danny. She liked his tender protectiveness towards Jilba. But there was anarchy in his eye and it unnerved her, and what she said to Jilba had been only half in jest. She did find the machine-gun delivery and the slang-ridden New York patois almost indecipherable.

As she turned away, her hand snagged a book next to the receiver. It tumbled to the floor and spewed an array of business cards all over the floor. Cursing, she knelt down to repair the damage. Some of them had witty and nonsensical graphics that made her smile. One of them made her blanch. 'The rushes are excellent,' said the vaguely familiar handwriting. 'So far, so good. Well done.'

But it was the signature that made her blood run cold.

'Regards, Dean Coulter.'

Stunned, her mind racing, Rachel sank back on her ankles and stared at the card in disbelief. A couple of minutes passed before she snapped out of it, sufficiently to return the remaining cards to the book and restore it to its place by the phone.

She carried Coulter's card back to the living room, dropped it on the table and continued staring at it as she drank her coffee, becoming more and more agitated. The coffee wasn't strong enough. She poured herself a large brandy, swallowed it on the spot, and poured herself another. She hunched on the edge of the couch and sipped away, almost in a trance. When the glass was empty, she got her bag from the stand in the hall. Even then, she hesitated before opening it. But her fingers had a life of their own. She tore a page from a small memo book. She scribbled down the address of Coulter Associates, folded the paper and hid it deep in her wallet. Done, she carried Coulter's card back to the bedroom and returned it to Jilba's phone book, making sure it was well and truly buried. The whole exercise left her feeling sick with guilt and she hurried back to the kitchen for another brandy.

Up by the main barn, Jim hoisted a cool one, took a long swig and smacked his lips. He was inspecting two fresh dingo pelts, hanging on the fence to dry. The Aboriginal stockman at his side was looking modestly pleased with himself.

'Well done, Davey. I thought we'd never get them.'

'That's a big dog,' said Tim, pointing to the largest pelt. 'Must be a cross.'

'Ran like the wind,' Davey told them quietly.

Tim pushed back a patch of blood-stained hair on the other scalp. 'Good shot, mate. Right behind the ear.'

'She came down looking for him at sundown, she was real toey. I was up-wind, but she must have got a whiff of me. Took a long time to go to him, at any rate.'

Jack shook his head. 'How many calves do you reckon they've taken?'

'About thirty, isn't it?' Jim replied, looking to Tim.

'As far as I can tell,' Tim nodded. 'Weaners and newborn. They've mutilated quite a few more, but they'll live, as long as the bites don't abscess.'

'Why do they do that?' Billy asked him.

'For fun,' Tim spat. 'Just for fun. That's why doggers hate

them so much. A domestic dog won't bite a young thing, human or animal. Not unless it's really cranky. But a dingo will. Go for the kill. Just for the fun of it.'

'They can bring out the worst in men, too,' said Jim. 'Your grandfather kicked some doggers off the place once, when I was about your age. They skinned a dog alive and let it go.'

Billy winced, suitably impressed.

'Not the first time that's happened,' Tim added.

Jim turned back to Davey and slapped him on the back. 'Good on you, mate. They're worth two hundred apiece to me.'

Davey's smile doubled. 'Thanks, boss. Kids have a good Christmas, I reckon.'


As Rachel sat down to supper with Jilba and Danny, she braced herself to make a few tricky enquiries. Danny topped up her glass of wine and she raised it to her daughter.

'Congratulations, darling.'

Jilba raised an eyebrow. 'What have I done now?'

'I seem to see you just about every time I switch on the TV.'

Jilba smiled and raised her own glass to her mother. 'Here's to my mum in the Big Apple.'

Danny clinked Rachel's glass. 'Here's to repeats.'

The joke was lost on Rachel.

'Mediaspeak,' he offered. 'You know, every time Jilba's on air she gets a residual fee. Repeats. The longer the commercial runs, the bigger the bank balance.'

'You mean on top of that enormous fee for the contract?'

'Uh huh.'

Impressed, Rachel grinned and raised her glass again. 'To repeats.'

'I was very lucky. They've been terrific to me.'

'Especially the top brass,' said Danny with a smile.

Rachel looked up in time to see Jilba flush. 'What do you mean?'

'Oh, it's just his fertile imagination. The president of Lillian's company. Danny's convinced he's got a crush on me.'

'More than a crush, if you ask me.'

'Tie a knot in it!'

'Can't help it,' Danny teased. 'I'm a jealous man.'

Jilba pulled a face. 'He's talking through his hat. The man's old enough to be my father. Don't believe a word of it. He just took a particular interest in the promotion, that's all.'

Danny grinned mischievously at Rachel and gave her a wink. 'That's her story and she's sticking to it.'

'I should hope so,' Rachel laughed, keeping her eyes on Danny and her pulse under control. 'What's his name?'

'Coulter, Dean Coulter. Coulter Associates . . .'

Rachel wanted to crawl under the table. Instead, she nodded at Danny's empty plate and asked if he'd like some more. To her relief, he accepted.

'I'll do it,' he offered.

'Stay where you are.'

She grabbed his plate and headed for the kitchen, gulping air as soon as her back was turned.

Rachel took her time. Her blood was racing. The spoon shook in her hand. Her question had been quite deliberate. But still, the very sound of his name had sent her mind reeling. Danny was sharp as a tack. She mustn't give the game away. Or did they know already? She strolled back into the room and set Danny's plate before him.

'There you are.'

'Thanks, that's great.' Danny gave her a winning smile and topped up their glasses.

'Should we book a call?' she asked Jilba. 'For Christmas Day?'

'I already have.'

A silence fell as Danny tucked into his chilli and Jilba fiddled with her glass. She knew the anger she felt towards him at that moment sprang from her own sense of disloyalty. Coulter's rejection of her advances had cut her deep at the time but she hadn't seen the man since and certainly never let on to Danny. Despite the world he operated in, Danny was very much a one-woman man. The sudden introduction of Coulter's name in front of her mother had only managed to revive her guilt.

To Jilba's dismay, her mother picked up the thread of their conversation.

'I presume he's a bachelor then? This Mr Coulter?'

Danny's fork stopped halfway to his mouth. 'Widower,' he replied. 'His wife died years ago. Got a couple of teenage kids. We've been sailing with them a couple of times. He keeps a yacht out at Montauk.'

'Must be fun, sailing.'

'It's wet,' said Danny.

Rachel forced a short laugh and decided enough was enough.

# Thirty

Wielding their prods, the men worked a line of young steers into the race leading to the dip. The bellowing cattle inched forward, humping one another's backs until, pushed by those behind and prodded through the rails on either side, they plunged into the oily waters, came up for air and fought to keep their heads from going under again until they scrambled up the ramp at the far end and emerged in the dripping yard. From there, they were taken two at a time into a small yard to be thrown, branded and cut.

Tim Daley watched over the proceedings with easy authority, moving from one yard to the other, shouting suggestions and advice. He heard his name called above the din.

'We're off, Tim,' Jack yelled. 'See you later.'

Tim gave them a wave as they turned away at a canter. Halfway home, Billy slapped his horse into a gallop and shouted over his shoulder, 'Race you!'

Jack took up the challenge and tore after his younger brother. Heads down over their horses' necks, bums in the air, they streaked across the plain like teenage bats out of hell.

It was a moment Rachel would have loved to see. Despite all her mixed feelings about Balkenna, her pride in her sons' horse-manship would have made her smile. She may have wondered again at the strange cast of genetics that made them so much like their grandfathers; Jack the image of his namesake, Billy showing unmistakable features inherited from her own father. They'd been there for all to see from the first and forced her to double her efforts to play fair and resist making Billy the last-born darling of the tribe and spoiling him rotten. After Jack's peacemaking arrival, she and Jim had decided that three was enough. Billy had knocked them both for a loop.

At that moment, Rachel was being knocked for a bit of a loop by the security staff in the foyer of the Coulter Associates building. She'd been told to take a seat and wait.

271

On the top floor, Coulter's secretary was yawning into the intercom.

'Who? . . . What does she want? . . . Well, didn't you tell her . . . Oh, all right . . . Let her come up, I'll deal with it.'

The speed of the lift was slightly alarming and Rachel heaved a sigh of relief when the doors finally opened. She emerged into the reception area to be met by a steely look.

'Mrs Mackay?'

Rachel nodded. 'I'm sorry to –'

Gina cut her off before she could get going. 'As they told you downstairs, Mrs Mackay, Mr Coulter is not here today. Even if he were, I'm afraid it's quite impossible to just walk in and expect to see him. If you'd like to tell me what it's about and leave your card, perhaps I can get back to you.'

Taken aback, Rachel leapt to her own defence. 'I assure you I don't mean to be a nuisance. It's a private matter. I was hoping to surprise him.'

'I'm afraid that's quite out of the question. If you'd like to leave your number, I'll check with Mr Coulter and let you know.'

'When do you expect him back?' Rachel pressed, getting annoyed.

'I've no idea,' Gina replied blandly.

Clinging to her dignity, Rachel relented and rummaged in her bag for her hotel's card.

'And your business?'

Rachel decided she'd had enough of this. 'Tourist,' she replied, poker-faced.

'Tourist business. Right, Mrs Mackay. I'll pass on your message to Mr Coulter.'

Going down was worse than going up. But when the doors opened and she stepped out, she took an involuntary step back in again. Walking briskly towards her from the main entrance, deep in conversation with two young executives, one on either side of him, was the man she was here to see.

Rachel moved forward then stopped dead in her tracks, panicked by this sudden confrontation in so public an area. Head down, concentrating on the young man on his right, Coulter barely seemed to notice as he side-stepped the figure in front of him. Until he was a couple of paces past her. Then he rocked back on his heels and spun round.

'Hello, Dean.'

Coulter was back to her in a flash, gazing at her in awe. He clutched her shoulders, gazed into her eyes and kissed her cheek. The single word he uttered echoed back twenty years.

'Rachel . . .'

The two young executives shared a look. They were both thinking the same thing: Dean Coulter just dropped the ball.

'See you upstairs, sir.'

He waved them on. 'Catch up with you later.' He turned back to Rachel. 'What a wonderful, wonderful surprise.'

'I'm a bit surprised myself.'

Gina did a double-take ten minutes later when the lift doors opened and her boss emerged with the woman she'd just thrown out. He guided her to his office and ushered her inside. Only then did he acknowledge his secretary, turning to give her a quick smile and raising his hand to a dead halt.

'No calls. I haven't arrived yet, okay? No interruptions.'

Gina nodded, bewildered. As Coulter closed the door, she stared at it in amazement, then concern, wondering if she was in for a carpeting.

Inside, Rachel was at the window, gazing across the Manhattan skyline when she heard the door close. She turned to find Coulter leaning back against it, gazing at her like a man who just woke from the best dream he ever had. Her smile was warm, her eyes full of light.

'How's my favourite Yank?'

Coulter pushed himself away from the door, stepped across and enveloped her in a hug, rolling her from side to side.

'Never better,' he said.


Jim was angry.

'I just don't understand it. It's a bastard of a position to suddenly take at this stage.'

'What reason have they given?' Tim asked quietly.

'Ridiculous,' Jim snarled. 'Kidd at the bank's insisting we absorb the loss of the sheep before we can go ahead. The bastard's put the mockers on it. Sat there, smug as you like, expressing his regrets and whinging about his need to control his outgoings. Absolutely bloody ridiculous.'

'Sounds a bit feeble,' Tim agreed.

'I'm going to fly in and see Will, see what the hell he makes of it. Wouldn't be any of this sort of nonsense if he was still in charge, that's for sure. If it can't be sorted out, they can go to buggery. I'll take our business elsewhere. I'll have a word with Anthony as well. You just press on, old son. I'll let you know tonight.'

Tim gave him a thumbs up and slapped his hat on his head. He stopped at the door and turned back to gee Jim up, but decided against it. He looked fit to kill.


So did Jilba. Her face was white with fury.

'I hate him!' she stormed. 'Toying with me all this time, just to amuse himself, like some glorified peeping Tom . . .'

Her mother's revelations had well and truly pulled the rug out from under her and Jilba felt sick. The memory of her moment with Coulter kept flashing in her mind like a flophouse neon, stirring up shame and resentment, made all the worse by her mother's obvious delight in the unexpected renewal of old acquaintance.

'Darling, he just thought it was best from your point of view, that's all.'

But Jilba was not to be calmed. 'That's rubbish. He could have let me know, right from the start. He could have told me he knew you.'

'He just didn't want you to feel you'd got the job on anything but merit. He decided to keep it to himself, that's all.'

'He could have had the decency to tell me when it was over,' Jilba contested, calming down a notch.

'Well, I think he feels a bit embarrassed about it himself now. He's full of admiration for you. Says you've been a very refreshing change for all concerned. Everyone's delighted with the campaign. He just hopes you won't hold it against him, now that the cat's out of the bag.'

Jilba studied her mother's face a moment, trying to gauge what else might have come out of the bag besides the cat. She appeared to be holding nothing in check. If Coulter kept her secret, maybe she could forgive him the rest.

'He had your best interests at heart,' Rachel confirmed. 'I know he did.'

'At least it explains all those weird looks he used to give me,' Jilba proposed, still far from pleased. 'Danny was right, he was playing games.'

'It doesn't matter now,' said Rachel. 'I think it's very nice of him to invite us. We won't have to bother with all the palaver of cooking Christmas lunch.'

'I was looking forward to it.'

Rachel was sympathetic, but pressed her case. 'He specifically said you must bring Danny, too. If he'd like to come.'

Jilba had simmered down, but her resentment was still bubbling away just below the surface.

'I'll have to think about it.'

Rachel pulled a face.

'I can't help it, Mum,' she flared. 'It just makes me feel angry. Like I've been burgled in my sleep. I don't think Danny'll feel too happy about it either.'

Rachel shrugged into her coat. 'I'll have to fly, darling. Please don't be cross.'

Far from convinced, Jilba gave her a half-hearted little smile.

Rachel held her eyes a moment, ran her fingertips down her daughter's cheek and kissed her goodbye. 'I'll see you tomorrow.'

Jilba saw her out. Then she dumped herself on the couch to mull over all the knotty twists of fate. The phone rang. At first, she declined to answer it. But it went on ringing and she finally dragged herself up.

'Hello.' Her tone was dull, but it changed in a flash. 'Oh . . . Quick! Put it through, please . . .'

She swapped the phone to her good ear.

'Dad! . . . Hi, Dad! . . . Listen, just hang on a minute, will you? Just a sec . . .'

She dropped the phone on the bed and ran to the living room, flung up the window and shivered as the chill blast of winter air hit her. She leant out to scan the street below. Too late. There was no sign of her. She slammed the window shut, crossed her arms and rubbed some warmth back into her shoulders as she hurried back to the phone.

'Dad! . . . Yes . . . Sorry. Mum just left a few minutes ago. I thought I might be able to catch her . . . No . . . She's gone.'

Feet up on his desk, Jim recrossed his legs and wished he'd called a bit sooner.

'How's my girl?'

'Oh, pretty good,' said Jilba. 'Working hard, as usual.'

'All work and no play, eh?' Jim chuckled. 'Have you put a down payment on the Empire State building yet?'

'Not yet, I thought I'd wait a bit longer and buy it outright.'

'That's the spirit,' Jim laughed. 'And how's your mum getting along?'

'She's fine. She bumped into an old friend of yours yesterday.

He's the president of the agency I did some work for. Isn't that weird? I didn't have a clue . . .'

Jim swung his legs off the desk and sat bolt upright in his chair. 'Who's that?'

'Dean Coulter. She said you knew him years ago, in Sydney, I think . . .'

Jim blanched. His throat went tight as a drum.

'Dad? Are you still there?'

Collecting himself, trying to gauge from Jilba's tone what she might know, Jim answered as matter-of-factly as he could.

'Oh, Dean Coulter. Yes, I remember him. How is he?'

'That's where she's gone now. He's taking her out to dinner. And he's invited us all out to his place on Long Island for Christmas.'

She broke off and bit her lip, suddenly sensing her father's isolation. At his end, Jim had the glazed look of a pole-axed steer waiting for the bullet to put it out of its misery.

'Are gran and granddad still there?'

'Yes,' Jim muttered. 'Everyone's here. Tony and Susan. Athol's brought Dud down. He's much better. Getting around on a pair of sticks. Amazing old bugger . . .'

Jilba was relieved. 'Oh, that's good. Give everyone my love.'

'Does he have family?'

'Who?'

'Dean Coulter.'

'Oh. A son and a daughter, David and Joanna. His wife died years ago.'

'That's too bad,' Jim mumbled. 'I'm sorry to hear that. Well, look, ask your mum to give me a call as soon as she can, will you?'

His voice suddenly sounded very husky, had a hollow ring.

'Is everything all right?'

'Yes, mate. We're fine. Just wanted to have a word, you know.'

Jilba smiled, imagining her father in his office, probably with his feet on the desk. But Jim's feet were rooted firmly on the floor and his temples were throbbing as he fought back a flood of jealousy.

'You sound like a lovesick calf,' she teased.

'Am a bit . . .'

'Don't be,' Jilba pleaded. 'She's having a wonderful time. She'll be home soon enough.'

'Yes, I know,' Jim responded, as convincingly as he could. 'Look after her, won't you?'

'Oh, Dad. Don't be silly, of course. It's lovely to hear you.'

'Yeah. You too. Look after yourself as well. It'd be nice to give you a hug.'

'Yes, I know. Lots of love, Dad.'

'Yes,' Jim mumbled. 'Okay, mate. Thanks. Take it easy . . . See you.'

' 'Bye, Dad. Love to everyone. 'Bye.'

She dropped the phone in place and smiled again. Her father was a lovely man. She was a lucky girl.

Jim hung up with much greater reluctance, reluctant to confront the aftermath of their conversation. Through the window, he could see Tony and Susan in the distance, returning from a ride. His eye drifted past them to the horizon beyond as he recoiled from the alarm bells blaring in his head. He clenched his fist and slammed it down on the desk, so hard he had the bruise for a week afterwards.

'Dean bloody Coulter,' he muttered, half under his breath. 'The last bloody person on earth . . .'

Anyone watching might think Dean Coulter had just won the lottery, whether he needed the money or not. His winning smile for the woman across the table said it all.

'Hope you didn't mind my calling so late, I wasn't sure what time I'd get away.'

Rachel reached across and pressed his hand. 'Don't be silly. Of course not. It's a lovely surprise.'

'It sure is,' he beamed.

Rachel held his gaze for a moment, then had to look away. There were too many other things in his eyes, too many questions only temporarily held in check. Questions that she would rather not answer. She concentrated on the menu. 'I haven't eaten a thing since breakfast.'

Coulter took his eyes off her just long enough to beckon the waiter then returned them to drink in her every movement and expression.

It was very late. Jim was in his pyjamas and about to hit the sack when the phone rang. He raced out onto the verandah and along to the office in his bare feet, copping a splinter en route,

277

lunging for the phone in case it cut off. His voice broke as he answered.

'H . . . Hello? Rachel?'

Perched on the edge of her hotel bed, Rachel swallowed hard and got straight to the point.

'Yes, darling. Look, I feel absolutely dreadful. The whole thing's just the most hopeless piece of timing. I was planning to call you tonight, anyway.'

Jim had prepared for this for hours, convinced himself that a good nonchalant performance was the only way to handle it.

'It's all right. Don't worry about it. Just a bit of a surprise, that's all.'

Rachel could just see the expression on his face. Braving it out, playing it down, trying so hard to be blasé. She felt a stab of pain in her heart and resolved to go along with the act. For his sake.

'Well, I feel awful anyway. The whole business is a bit bizarre, to say the least.'

'Jilba got hold of you okay?'

'Yes. She left a message at the hotel. I called her right back to see what you two had talked about.'

Tears welled in her eyes and she fought them back. But she couldn't control the catch in her throat.

'I am sorry, Jim. I should have called you yesterday.'

'It's all right,' Jim lied. 'I understand. How is he?'

'Very well. He looks marvellous.'

She could have bitten her tongue off for that, and quickly shifted the emphasis.

'Sends his warmest, warmest regards to you. Says it would be great to see you, too.'

'Give him mine,' Jim replied flatly. 'Jilba said something about Christmas Day . . .'

At that moment, Rachel could have happily wrung her daughter's neck. But she knew it wasn't Jilba's fault. It wasn't anybody's fault, really, except her own. She'd sought him out.

'He has invited us, yes. But I'm not sure we'll go.'

'But you'll be seeing him again, anyway?'

'Oh, I'm sure we'll have lunch or something,' Rachel hedged, wilting fast.

'Well, say g'day when you do. Is it snowing?'

'Everything's turned to ice. The streets are a bit slushy. How are things there?'

'Hot as hell . . .'

'Jilba said you sounded a bit worried on the phone. Was that just to do with what she told you?'

'No, not at all,' Jim said quickly, on the defensive. 'I've had a bit of trouble with the bank, that's all.'

'What happened?'

'They suddenly turned turtle on the loan for Tim's house. We're still trying to figure out why. Your dad's making some enquiries through his mates in Brisbane.'

'What reason did they give?' Rachel asked, out on a limb.

'The bloody sheep,' Jim growled. 'Reckon I've got to absorb the loss before we can go ahead. It's nonsense and I think Kidd knows it. I may transfer the whole sheebang, if they don't shape up.'

Rachel had already poured her heart down the line. There was not much more she could do except toy, for a fleeting moment, with the idea of telling him she'd return immediately. Instead: 'Is Tim upset?'

'No. You know what he's like. He's more upset for me.'

'Well, tell him I always knew that Kidd was a shit.'

Rachel hardly ever swore. The unexpected ringing in his ear fished a chuckle out of him. 'Will do.'

'Just when you could be getting on with it.'

'Yes,' Jim admitted. 'It's a damn shame. Anyway, like I say, your dad's on the case. He'll get to the bottom of it.'

Jim's carefully cultivated air of nonchalance was failing fast. He felt like a spent balloon. Rachel had her little finger jammed in the corner of her mouth, snipping at a split nail. In the brief silence that followed, she pictured his forlorn and lonely figure, staring out on a starlit night and summoning courage.

'Jim . . . Darling . . . Don't be sad, please. This break is doing me a power of good. I can understand if you feel upset about Dean, but you have no need to be, you know? You're with me every minute.'

'Balkenna isn't the same without you . . .'

Rachel refused to take it up. At this distance, at this time of night, there was no point.

'I'll be home soon, you old rogue. We can set up the tent again, under a big full moon.'

'Don't call me old,' Jim said. But it came out flat as a tack. 'I'll hold you to that . . .'

'You won't have to,' she promised. 'I miss you.'

'Yeah,' he sighed. 'Me, too. All the bloody time.'

'Jim, don't. Please.'

'How's the money holding up?'

'Everything's fine, darling. Don't worry about me so much.'

'Can't help it.'

'Give my love to everyone. Did all the presents arrive?'

'Yeah, they're here. What about ours?'

'They're all safely stored at Jilba's apartment.'

'That's good. Well, I'll speak to you in a couple of days, I guess.'

'Jim.'

'What?'

'I love you.'

'I wish to God you'd come home then.'

'I will. Soon.'

Jim donned his emotional armour for one last chivalrous flourish. 'Say g'day to the Yank. Tell him I said to keep his bloody paws off you.'

It flayed the skin off her own act. Coulter had held her hand all the way back to the hotel and she hadn't resisted the contact, had felt no need to, hadn't wanted to.

'I will,' she promised, with a disastrous attempt at a laugh. ' 'Bye, darling.'

' 'Bye,' Jim whispered.

Rachel blew a kiss in his ear and hung up before he had time to respond. He dropped the phone in place and realised he felt nauseous. He switched on the desk lamp, rummaged in the drawer for a pin and set to work to extract the splinter he'd collected. Done, he padded warily back to the bedroom and parked his bum on the bed. His eyes came to rest on a large, framed photograph on the dresser. He fetched it back to the bed, set it on his lap and studied it intently.

It was a wonderful shot. Taken by a professional newspaper photographer in the early days of their marriage, it captured the full, magical exuberance of the moment. Rachel, ravishingly beautiful and glowing with pride, was dowsing him with a fizzy gusher of champagne as he stood beside her, in full polo rig, his arm round his pony's neck. Happiness radiated from the black and white images.

After a long time, Jim switched off the light. On his back, hands behind his head, he stared at the ceiling and contemplated an unknown world, knowing that sleep was going to be hard to come by.

*   *   *

'What do you think? Perfume?'

'She's only fifteen,' Jilba reminded her. 'I guess she would . . . Better choose something light.'

'Well, come on,' Rachel prompted. 'You're the expert.'

'Maybe some eau de cologne or rosewater,' Jilba said. 'Let's have a look.'

They scrutinised the labels.

Rachel turned and beamed at her daughter. 'I'm so glad you changed your mind, darling.'

There was no way for Jilba to let on to her mother just what it would actually mean to have to look Coulter in the eye again without giving the game away. She'd just have to roll with the flow and lean on Danny. As the saleswoman returned and deposited half a dozen bottles for their inspection, Jilba gave her mother a quick smile of assurance.

'I could tell you really wanted to go. I'd feel a bit of a spoilsport to say no. After all, you *are* on holiday and he *is* an old friend. I guess I'll just have to try and be nice.'

'I'm sure it won't be too difficult,' Rachel said innocently.

Jilba took a deep breath and picked up the nearest bottle.

Her grandfather took a deep breath and picked up his schooner.

'Hopeless!' he pronounced, shaking his head. 'Definitely short of a few quid in the ethics department. Very foolish man. It's bound to get around after my enquiries. You can bet your sweet life on that. Happens all too often, I'm afraid. Blokes like this join the Lodge because they think it'll be good for business. Comes as a bit of a shock to find there's a bit more to it than that . . .' He broke off, lowered his glass and eyed Jim with intent. 'Have you ever thought about my offer?'

'I did give it some thought,' Jim said, taking a swallow. 'Just doesn't seem much point to it out here.'

'There's a point to universal brotherhood,' Anthony insisted. 'Wherever you are, you'd be a part of that. From the bottom to the top.'

Jim gave a noncommittal shrug in reply and Anthony smiled.

'Anyway. You know I'd always be more than happy to propose you. If you ever feel like joining.'

'Thanks,' Jim nodded. 'Perhaps I might. One of these days.'

'As far as this morning goes,' said Anthony, 'you'll be well out of there by my reckoning. Can't have your own bank manager pulling strings behind your back. Just not on. His brother must have really needed that survey. Very badly.'

'Didn't seem that way at the time,' said Jim. 'He just listened to what I had to say and called it a day. Didn't seem all that worried about it.'

'Didn't want to give the game away,' said Anthony. 'He certainly didn't waste any time having a go at his brother and trying to block your loan.' He gave his son-in-law a wicked little smile. 'I'm sure Kidd's head office will be thrilled to bits when they hear he's lost your business.'

'Will is furious,' said Jim. 'You should've heard him. I thought he'd blow a fuse when I told him.'

'Will is a good bloke,' said Anthony, with a smile, raising his glass. 'Few and far between these days, I'm afraid. Here's to him.'

Jim grinned. But his grin faded by the time his glass was back on the table. As the two men lapsed into silence, Anthony was forced to reflect again on the troubles that just kept piling up on his son-in-law's doorstep.

In quick succession, Jim had faced his mother's death, a crippling loss of stock and, above all, the sudden rupture with Rachel. At ten dollars a head, the sheep had come at a good price, but Jim's delay in fixing the insurance meant thirty thousand dollars down the drain. Anthony knew his daughter's disenchantment had opened a wound that refused to stop bleeding, despite everyone's attempt to paint it over and make it seem a momentary hiccup.

Now, this attempted manoeuvre to force him into an extensive mineral survey of Balkenna's acres may yet have wider repercussions. Anthony knew only too well the weight of corporate power that could be brought to bear. Jim had been running the property at maximum carrying capacity for the past five years, using four acres to graze each head of sheep and thirty acres for every head of cattle. To give the land a rest, he really needed to upgrade the ratios to five acres per head of sheep, forty acres per head of cattle. At least the twelve-thousand-acre sheep blocks would get a well-earned rest until he was in a position to restock them. Last year's rainfall had been good, but the struggle for existence ran its never-ending, nerve-wracking course. An ill wind from either side could blow you to bits. Despite the outward trappings of affluence, Balkenna was once again in debt and Anthony knew the various schemes proposed by the devious Mr Kidd were not worth the paper they were written on.

He was always on standby himself to offer bridging loans, but Jim's pride had become more deeply entrenched with each passing year. Athol agreed with him on that score. Jim seemed to have reached a point where he would rather sink than swim on someone else's back. It was as if, having fought and won his battle for Balkenna, discharged all his personal debts and battled to keep the property out of the red, he would feel a shameful sense of failure if he ever had to borrow so much as a red cent from his family or friends again.

If Rachel returned and insisted on making a break, Jim might just be forced to throw in the towel and abandon his dream of passing Balkenna on to another generation of Mackays. Anthony knew his son-in-law too well, had too much admiration for his strength of character, to want to contemplate the consequences – for his daughter, his grandchildren and everyone else. Try as they might, nobody had been able to come up with any obvious solution. Athol seemed to think Jim and Rachel might even end up living separate lives for a few years, until Jim could retire and hand Balkenna safely on to Jack. Knowing the strength of love that still flowed between them, Anthony couldn't see such a move taking place without dire results. Christmas was going to be a bit flat. Untypically, Jim was wearing his heart on his sleeve and its ache was affecting them all.

'Do you fancy another?' Jim offered. 'Or shall we push on?'

'How about you?'

'Call time, I reckon,' Jim smiled.

The two men stepped out into the blinding glare of Eagle Street and headed for the station wagon. As they passed the bank, Jim gave the building a scornful finger. Anthony smiled. But only fleetingly. It was going to take more than gestures to set things to rights.

# Thirty-One

Tony and Susan got the job of decorating the Christmas table and, as everyone took their places, their efforts were heartily congratulated. But they couldn't do anything about the empty place at the end. Nevertheless, anticipation was running high. Jim had insisted this year they would share a traditional meal rather than the usual cold turkey and a bit of lettuce. Charged with Christmas spirit and the glow left over from the excitement of presents around the tree, everyone was nattering away in expectation of the main event.

Elbows on the table, rubbing his palms together in front of him, Jim listened to everyone at once and nobody in particular. His mind was still firmly locked in dialogue with Rachel. Her call had come through just as the household gathered at the tree. It was a bad connection, fraught with static and echo. By the time everyone got on the line to say hello to Rachel and Jilba in turn, there had been neither time nor privacy for any intimate exchange between the two of them. Would she be spending the day with Coulter? That was all he really wanted to know. Rachel had hedged for a bit, then confirmed they had decided to go. There hadn't been a lot to say after that.

Dud tried his luck. He leant over and shoved his cracker under Jim's nose.

'Christ, young Mackay. You look like a sick chook. Here. Wrap your bananas round that and give us a tug.'

Jim snapped out of it. He gave him a fleeting, sheepish grin and the cracker exploded. Dud cackled, shoved the blue paper crown on his head, blew loudly on the plastic whistle, and unfolded his joke.

'What do you get if you cross an elephant with a mouse?'

Nobody had a clue.

'Great big holes in your skirting boards.'

With a big groan, everyone followed Dud's lead, grabbed their own crackers and swapped pulls across the table. Dud's little distraction had done the trick. Jim was forced to put his blues out to pasture and join in the banter, laugh at the jokes that followed.

'Dad!' Tony hushed the rest of them and waited for silence before raising his hands a little in invitation. 'Before we get stuck in, I'd like to ask for a moment's silence. For grandma. I know we're all missing her.'

Everyone bowed their heads for a minute's silence, and the hush took on a life of its own. When it was over, Jim nodded to Tony for the gesture as Betsey appeared through the door bearing a silver oval platter, just big enough for the enormous turkey on top of it. To a chorus of oohs and aahs, she proudly deposited it in front of Jim and hurried out again.

'What a corker!' Athol exclaimed.

'Magnificent,' Anthony concurred.

Betsey reappeared, propelling a traymobile loaded to the hilt with all the rest. She rolled it to a halt by Jim's elbow and impatiently indicated he should get stuck into the carving, waiting to see him begin before scurrying out again as everyone smacked their lips and Tony jumped up to see to it that all glasses were full.

When all was ready, Jim thumped the table a couple of times to quell the hubbub, conjured up a grin, made a show of counting heads, gave Tim a wink and raised his glass.

'Twenty hands, twenty feet, good God, let's eat. Merry Christmas everyone . . .'

Jim's grin was short-lived. As everybody tucked in and the conversation flowed, he retreated further and further into his shell, dredging up his responses more and more grudgingly each time he was called upon to do so. Despite everyone's best efforts to keep up a buoyant party atmosphere, it was painfully obvious he was thousands of miles away.

The object of his longing sat down to Christmas lunch with some trepidation, still vexed that Jilba had been unable to contain her annoyance and exchanged a few heated words with their host shortly after their arrival. Dean, she thought, had handled it with restraint. Danny had leapt in to defuse the situation and the moment had been short-lived. But there had been an undercurrent on Jilba's part. As Coulter's two immaculate Filipinos padded around the table on silent feet to attend to their every need, Rachel dismissed her concern as overreaction.

Jilba, still looking a touch severe, was busy answering the familiar questions from David Coulter about life in outback Queensland. They'd talked about it before and she wished he'd change the subject. She still felt mortified by the flare-up at the door, more for her mother's sake than her own. If Coulter had not received her with such icy civility, it might not have happened at all. She had looked him in the eye and drawn a blank. Now, glancing down the table occasionally to see her mother smiling and giggling at Coulter's side only increased her sense of embarrassment. As one of the Filipino servants refilled her glass, she concentrated on young David Coulter's next question and decided her austere apology would just have to do.

At that moment, Dean Coulter raised his glass.

'To our visitor from far away and long ago,' he toasted. 'A very happy Christmas.'

Rachel held his look for a moment, but it was too intense and she had to look away, a knowing smile tugging at the corners of her mouth.

The moment was not lost on Danny and Jilba saw it, too. She caught her mother's eye just long enough to raise an eyebrow. Caught out, Rachel gave her daughter an embarrassed smile in return, ducked her head and concentrated on her turkey.

Danny took in all three faces and gave way to unbidden feelings of resentment towards the charming, dapper magnate who'd invited him to lunch. The sooner he and Jilba could get away, the better. The man obviously thought he was God's gift to the human race.

The day after Jim's fifty-second birthday, Jean Barclay was happily engaged in the one occupation guaranteed to put her mind at ease. Clippers in hand, she was tending Balkenna's garden and trying not to think.

Rachel's birthday call to Jim had ended in argument. He had angrily told them about the untimely reappearance of Dean Coulter in their lives. It had come as a surprise. Neither she nor Anthony had given him a thought for donkey's years. They had done their best to allay Jim's suspicions and soothe his frustration at Rachel's refusal to set a date for her return. Innocent of the true nature of her daughter's long-ago friendship with the American, she couldn't really understand Jim's dismay.

Despite everybody's efforts, Jim mooched about the place,

hangdog and grumpy. At one point he asked Billy to get his school atlas and, together, they traced the whereabouts of a place called Aspen in Colorado. Rachel had announced her intention of going there to try her hand at skiing.

Jean sauntered across the lawn and dropped to her knees beside the lily pond to begin weeding flagstones. Humming away to herself, totally absorbed, she didn't notice Jim's approach until he was almost on top of her. Sinking back on her ankles, she dabbed at the perspiration on her brow with her forearm and smiled. 'How's my favourite son-in-law?'

Jim grinned and squatted down beside her. 'Your *only* son-in-law has got some fencing to do. I thought Anthony might like to come along.'

'Snoring his head off,' Jean chuckled. 'Still trying to catch up – Christmas, New Year and your birthday. Says he can't take it any more. I think you'd better go on without him.'

'Okay.'

Jim leant forward to give her a quick kiss on the cheek. 'If that wayward daughter of yours should call, tell her your only son-in-law is mending his fences. And would she please hurry up and come home.'

He said it with a grin, but Jean knew better. 'I will,' she promised.


In a New York studio, Jilba Mackay was whirling through her photo-call with studied professionalism. Out of the way, perched on the edge of a high-backed chair, Rachel watched her daughter's performance with admiration, her eardrums split by the disco beat thudding from a speaker just above her head.

Stalking his quarry like a panther hunting its only meal of the day, the photographer kept winding Jilba up until the roll ran out.

'Great! . . . Beautiful, Jilba . . . Let's take a break.'

Jilba paused a moment to get her wind back then threaded through the lights, tripods and cables and flopped down in the chair beside her mother, shooting her legs out in front of her.

'Wonderful, darling, fascinating.'

'Thanks. God, I'm bushed. Still four outfits to go.'

Rachel smiled and checked her watch. 'I'll have to be on my way in a minute, I'm afraid.'

Jilba pulled a face and brushed at a powder smudge on her skirt. 'He's getting to see more of you than I do.'

They'd been through this before.

'You're a busy girl. I made it clear right from the start you were not to worry about me. You know I'm perfectly capable of looking after myself. Dean can spare the time and it's lovely having the company of an old friend to see the sights.'

Jilba continued brushing at the spot on her skirt a moment, making up her mind before turning to look her mother in the eye. To hell with it, she thought. She'd held her curiosity in check too long.

'Just how close a friend was he?'

Rachel held her look and did some quick thinking. The tone of Jilba's probe demanded a straight answer. She looked away, took a deep breath and returned her eyes to her daughter's face.

'As close as a man and woman can be. Once. Just once. Years and years ago, long before you were born.'

'Before you met Dad?'

'I was engaged to a man called David Leslie at the time. Dean came to Sydney on leave from Vietnam and we spent a few days together, that's all.'

Foot in the door, there was no way to stop Jilba now.

'Does Dad know about it?'

'Yes,' Rachel nodded. 'Your father and I have no secrets from one another.' She broke off, grinned, and tried to ease Jilba's intensity. 'He wasn't exactly a virgin himself when we married, you know.'

Jilba didn't give a damn. He was thousands of miles away and her eyes flashed sabres in his defence.

'He's kissed me too, you know.'

It cracked like a whip and Rachel recoiled. She took a moment to respond.

'Yes,' she said quietly. 'Dean told me what happened. When he drove me back on Christmas Day.'

'The bastard!' Jilba snapped, so loud the whole room glanced up to see what was going on. Rachel gave them a flimsy smile and waited for Jilba to simmer down.

'He said you were both a bit tiddly and carried away by the success of your commercial. I certainly don't hold it against him, and I don't see why you should.'

It made sense and Jilba couldn't deny it. Coulter had been chivalrous enough to accept fifty per cent of the blame. He could just as easily have made a case for himself out of her lunge in the wrong direction. Suddenly, now that it was out in the open, her confusion and ambivalence melted away. But her defence of her father didn't.

'Well, anyway . . . All the more reason you shouldn't go to Aspen with him. How the hell's Dad going to feel about that?'

It was Rachel's turn to get angry.

'Now look, Jilba! I really don't see the need to go on with any more of this. There's no reason on earth why Dean shouldn't take me skiing. No reason at all. He's an old friend of your father's as well, don't forget. If it hadn't been for him we might never have been married . . .'

As Jilba's eyes widened, Rachel wished she'd withheld that last remark.

'What do you mean?'

Rachel sighed, checked her watch again and put her arm round Jilba's shoulders to pull her into a quick hug.

'I'll tell you all about it tonight. I must go, darling, or I'll be late. Now please, stop all this worry and suspicion. Just get on with the job.'

'I just can't help wondering how Dad must feel about it,' Jilba insisted. 'The way things are between you . . .'

The previously unspoken observation took Rachel by surprise and she suddenly realised the deeper motivations behind Jilba's concern. She'd been foolish to count on her mother's promise of total confidence. She took her daughter's hands and gazed into her troubled eyes.

'There's nothing wrong between your father and me. Absolutely nothing, do you hear? Between me and Balkenna, well, yes . . . Perhaps. Whatever gran's told you, you've jumped to the wrong conclusion. We can talk about that tonight too, okay?' She leant forward and kissed Jilba's cheek, squeezing her hands even tighter. 'Your father and I love one another, every bit as much as we ever did. Understood? Now, I really *must* go.' She stood and pulled Jilba to her feet for a farewell embrace. 'Thanks for sneaking me in. I enjoyed every minute of it.'

'Jilba!'

The photographer was summoning her back to the rostrum.

# Thirty-Two

Wearing heavy-duty work gloves to protect themselves from the barbs, sweating like hell and shooing flies, Jim and Jack were going hammer and tongs to complete the line of fence they were working on. As Jim applied the cutters, the old rust-encrusted wires twanged apart for Jack to pull back through the line of metal posts before threading in strands from the shiny new rolls and running them back for his father to tie off at the corner post. As soon as the bottom one was in place, Jim attached the strainer and started pumping away to draw the wire to maximum tension.

There was no tension at all as Dean Coulter escorted Rachel through New York's Museum of Modern Art. He knew his stuff and was giving her the lowdown on anything that caught her eye.

'I've got tickets for *Don Giovanni* tonight,' he announced as they paused in front of Warhol's Monroe.

'Oh dear,' said Rachel, turning to face him. 'I'm afraid I can't tonight, Dean. I promised to have dinner with Jilba. I can't let her down, we have some things to talk over.'

Coulter looked momentarily disappointed. Then he shrugged it off. 'No problem. I'll switch them to tomorrow night. You'd like to go, wouldn't you?'

'Love to. But can you do that? Without a lot of bother?'

Coulter gave her a mischievous wink. 'Guile, my dear. Pure guile. And considerable graft.'

Rachel laughed and pecked his cheek. 'You're spoiling me rotten.'

Coulter placed his hands on her shoulders and caressed her with his eyes. 'That's what I'm here for, remember? I said I always would be.'

Rachel remembered. 'You were a generous man then and you're a generous man now.'

'I was a fool, too.'

He tried to say it in jest, make light of the memory, but his voice cracked at the thought of it. Rachel immediately wanted to change the subject, but the catch in his throat hit home. She raised her hand to his cheek.

'Why didn't you ever get in touch? Why didn't you answer Jim's letters?'

It broke the last bank of Coulter's self-control. Here she was, inches away. The memory of her had haunted his own marriage, haunted his life. Up to that moment, he'd studiously observed the protocol of their unexpected reunion all these years later, tried to behave like he was her long-lost brother. Suddenly it was all crumbling at his feet as her eyes bore into him, remembering, demanding an answer.

'I . . . I tried. It was . . .'

He gave up. Words were useless. He tightened his grip on her shoulders and pulled her to him. As a few passers-by turned to smile at their middle-aged canoodling, his arms went round her and he kissed her long and hard, full on the mouth.

Twaaang! The wire couldn't take the strain and snapped. Jim's end recoiled on itself and wrapped his gloved hands in a mesh of knotty barbs. Jack couldn't help laughing at the sight and Jim gave him a wry grin.

'See what I mean?'

'Yeah,' Jack guffawed. 'I get the point.'

Rachel gently prised herself loose and pushed Coulter's arms away. He'd gone white as a sheet, stricken by his loss of control, half expecting her to turn on her heel and hurry away. She did turn away, but only to draw breath. Nevertheless, he could see her back was braced against further invasion. He stood quietly behind her for an eternity before she took a small, involuntary step. He caught her arm and turned her back.

'Rachel, forgive me. Please . . . I lost my head . . .'

He looked so awkward and shame-faced, so abject. She reached out and brushed his cheek with her fingertips, stealing her hand away as she spoke.

'It's all right. Let's just put it down to old time's sake.'

A monstrous junk sculpture came to her rescue. She seized his elbow, turned him round and ushered him towards it.

'What on earth is that supposed to be?'

\*     \*     \*

Jack was leaning on a post taking a breather while his father painstakingly rolled the broken lengths of wire into a neat coil to put away for odd jobs. A wispy flicker on the horizon caught Jack's attention. He shaded his eyes. Suddenly he stiffened.

'Hey, Dad! Look!'

On the horizon, a ragged column of blue smoke was spiralling into the cloudless sky. He didn't need a second look.

'Come on! Quick! That's coming from the house . . .'

They raced for the ute, wrenching off their gloves as they ran. The old banger was long overdue for a service and slow to respond. It took half a dozen turns of the key to spark a start.

Until the silhouette of the house rose above the plain, Jack kept saying it must be one of the outbuildings. Now they could see it all. Balkenna was burning, its northern wing was a wall of roaring flame. Jack was struck dumb. Jim just choked as he floored the accelerator.

'Oh, my God . . .'

He skidded the ute to such a violent halt it tipped and almost rolled before it bounced back on its wheels. Both of them just sat there staring for a moment, too traumatised to make a move.

Every available hose was trained on the main body of the house to fight the flames. Under the frantic direction of Tim Daley, Balkenna's crew had formed a bucket brigade and their gasping, coughing figures emerged from the swirling palls of smoke just long enough to suck a lungful of air before diving back in again.

As Jim threw open his door, Jack grabbed his arm and pointed. A trio stumbled through the front door. They turned and struggled across the verandah to the front steps. At least two of them were struggling. The man in the middle was dragging his feet. Supported by Billy and Davey, the Aboriginal stockman, Anthony Barclay was in a bad way. Jean broke through the door and rushed to help them get him down the steps. As Jim and Jack arrived, they dragged Anthony across the lawn and lay him down beside the lily pond. The shirt had been burned off his body. He was blacker than Davey and covered with livid blisters.

As Jim hesitated beside them, Jean glanced up once. That look said it all: they were trapped in the same unbearable nightmare.

On the beginner's slopes at Aspen, Rachel turned turtle and landed on her backside for the umpteenth time, laughing at her own hopelessness. Laughing with her, Coulter helped her to her feet.

'Lean forward more,' he instructed, bending her into the correct position.

'Oh fine,' Rachel giggled. 'Then I can land on my face.'

'Try one more time.'

She dug in, braced herself and pushed off again, managing to plough a good twenty-five yards this time before her feet went in opposite directions, her arms windmilled and she was down again. Coulter glided in and flopped down in the snow beside her, chuckling with delight. Anyone watching would have guessed they were husband and wife on a second honeymoon or new-found lovers intoxicated by the promise of happiness. As Coulter stood and extended his hand, Rachel scooped a snowball and let him have it. Trying to duck, Coulter lost his own balance and collapsed on top of her. For a second, their faces were inches apart and he had to fight temptation. Rachel rewarded him by swinging her arm round his neck to give him a quick kiss before pushing him off and opting out.

'I think I've tried enough for one morning. I need a drink.'

Coulter didn't particularly relish the idea of having to share her with a bar full of suntans. The pure joy he had experienced being with her the past two wintry days had made him feel like a spring colt, ready to gallop wildly towards any horizon, any possibility. Far from New York, a world away from Balkenna, the closed holiday atmosphere of a luxury hotel and snowy mountains cocooned them from reality. But they'd been out on the slope for nearly four hours and he had to admit he'd had enough himself for a while. He stood again and hauled her up.

'Okay. Let's go back.'

Hearts pounding, lungs tingling from heady draughts of sweet mountain air, they were still brushing away the last clinging snowflakes as they entered the hotel lobby. Coulter put his arm round her to guide her to the stairs. Halfway across, the desk clerk spotted them.

'Mrs Mackay!'

He was waving a message like a hankie. Coulter went to get it. He glanced at the message as he returned to Rachel's side. 'It's from Jilba. Only just missed us.'

On the first floor, Rachel stopped at her door, and flashed him a quick smile. 'Fifteen minutes?'

'Not a second more,' Coulter called as she stepped inside.

Twenty minutes later there was a tap on his door and he opened it to a flood of tears. Panicked, he quickly ushered her inside and sat her down.

'There's been a fire at Balkenna,' she told him, her barely audible whisper hollow with shock. 'My father's in hospital.'

It was a bombshell. 'Is he all right?'

Huge tears were coursing down her cheeks. She clutched his hand fiercely. It was the only lifeline in sight.

'He tried to smother the flames . . . Fell asleep . . . Dropped his cigar . . . Tried to smother the flames before they got a hold . . . Jim had a terrible time getting hold of Jilba . . . Oh, God . . .'

She fell apart at the seams and shivered from head to foot. Coulter wrapped his arms round her, drew her head onto his shoulder and held her tight, waiting for it to pass.

'What about the house?'

Seconds passed before she eased herself away and turned to look at him in utter desperation. She struggled for words, managed one.

'Bad . . .'

She tried to continue, but Coulter saved her the trouble. He laid a hand on her shoulder and swallowed hard. 'I'll get hold of Henry and tell him to get the plane ready.'

Two hours later, they were in the air.

'How's Jim?' he asked, not really wanting to hear.

'He sounded absolutely wretched.'

Coulter already knew the answer to his next question, but he had to ask. 'What did you tell him?'

She glanced up at him, her bewildered eyes begging understanding. 'I told him I was on my way.'

'Of course,' he muttered, turning to stare out of the window again, cursing fire and air and earth and water, fighting to stay on top. Rachel studied his profile a moment, checked her hand as it reached for him and dropped it back in her lap. In the fraught silence that followed, she tipped her head back, closed her eyes and tried desperately hard not to think about anything under the sun. It proved impossible.

The very sun itself seemed to obliterate all she had tried to achieve in balancing her heart and mind for the ordinary difficulties she knew she would have to face when the time came to go home. Now those difficulties would multiply out of all proportion. Despite Jim's obvious dismay, she'd already extended her absence twice over, begging him to understand that she wanted to return in the best possible frame of mind to face up to things. She'd had to fight her longing to see him, her longing to hold him and their sons in her arms. When she called him on his birthday, Jim's jealousy over the man now sitting beside her had flared into uncontrollable anger. He had demanded her immediate return. She refused. He insisted she didn't love him any more, her disenchantment with Balkenna was simply a ruse, an excuse because she couldn't face up to telling him the truth.

She'd waited for him to calm down before she spelled out the real truth of the matter. The simple, unequivocal truth. How much she loved him, how much she feared the slow breakdown of her ability to go on living in the middle of nowhere, in a climate that had sucked the last drop of sufferance from her body. He apologised, then promised they would sort it out, mastered his fears long enough to offer the hope she would enjoy her first go at skiing. But he beseeched her again to set a date for return. Now that date had been set for her.

'Rachel . . .'

Seeing his expression, sensing what was to come, she quickly put her finger to his lips.

'Don't. Please.'

Coulter gently took her finger away and clutched her hand. 'I won't have another chance.'

She couldn't hold his look, dropped her eyes and waited. Coulter twisted in his seat to face her.

'For the second time in my life, I find myself in the position of sending you back to Jim. So, please, let me have my say. There were times . . . After Vietnam . . . I thought of taking a trip to see you both. Whenever it came to it, I always managed to find an excuse. Some real, some I made up. I guess I just knew it would hurt too much. Selfish, perhaps –'

'Dean . . .' Rachel interrupted. But there was no stopping him.

'I took an easier route. Opted for silence. A kind of blind shut-out. I just threw myself into getting the business back on its feet. Then Pop died. My sister took off with her family to California and I found myself staring at the walls every night. Thinking of you . . . What happened between the three of us . . .'

Rachel squeezed his hand. 'What you did, you did for love. If you think I've ever forgotten that, you're wrong. Jim knows it, too. It might be harder for him to admit, but he does know it.'

'That's not strictly true,' Coulter admitted. 'Mostly . . . Loving you, wanting you to be happy. But I used Pop as an excuse as well. The fact that my family owed a debt to Jim's for what his father did. If it hadn't been for that I couldn't . . . wouldn't have gone through with it.'

He paused for Rachel to digest his admission.

'I came to think that might have been a part of it, anyway. I certainly don't love you any the less for it . . .'

Coulter pounced on the phrase. 'Love me?'

Suddenly on thin ice, Rachel chose her words carefully. 'I think you know that. I think this time we've spent together . . . Seeing you again . . .'

Coulter took her hand, brought it to his lips and kissed it.

'You *must* come and see us. Jim would love to see you. After we get this mess sorted out, you *must* come.'

Coulter took the bull by the horns. 'I've got another idea.'

Rachel withdrew her hand and looked away, alarmed by his sudden shift.

'You've told me plain enough what's been going on. It's perfectly clear you've only hung on for his sake. You're only doing this now for the same reason. I think you're just as frightened now of meeting it head on as when you left. Everything, the heat, the dust, the sheer boredom and roughness of the life . . . All the things you find unbearable about it, that you came here to escape from . . .'

'I came here on a holiday, that's all.'

'That's not true and you know it. Don't try to hide from me now. You've told me too much already. You can't take it all back.'

'No,' she admitted reluctantly. 'No, I can't do that. I have found it hard. More than hard. But it's the life I chose, that you helped me choose. I didn't exactly walk in blindfold.'

Coulter saw the opening and cut her off. 'It's Jim who's been wearing the blindfold. Blind to your real needs. For a long, long time.'

'That's not true.'

'Isn't it? You've given him twenty years of your life. His way, year after year after year. Why can't he do the same for you now? Put in a manager, take you away from it? Brisbane? Sydney? Anywhere. Get you out of it?'

'We haven't even discussed it to that point yet. Besides,

there's Jack and Billy. Jack loves the place as much as Jim. If it was that bad, he'd have realised it long ago.'

'Would he?'

Coulter's pressure was relentless. Rachel refused to respond, refused to go on with it.

'Would he?'

She squirmed in her seat and begged indulgence. 'Dean, please . . .'

Coulter gave her a break. He allowed the tension to ease a few degrees before crooking his finger under her chin. 'Listen to me, Rachel.'

She tried to twist her head away, but he insisted she hold his gaze, commanded her attention.

'What I have to say is pretty simple. You do what you have to do. Go back to Jim. Go back to Queensland. I won't argue with that. On one condition. On condition you tell him the truth. The real, hard truth. That you want out, a different life. That you can't resign yourself to wasting away, growing old and grey without all the things that really stimulate you, lift you up. All the things you've loved every minute doing here. All the things you'd like to do before it's too late.'

His mind raced for more, but he drew a blank and he broke off with a hopeless shrug. Rachel gathered her resources. With a quiet, determined tone, she attempted to take control.

'My life *is* there, Dean. With Jim. With the boys and Eliz . . .' She checked herself and faltered, remembering her old ally was no longer there. It unleashed the tears she'd been trying so hard to hold in check. 'Please, Dean. Please, we must stop this.'

Coulter hesitated. Then he took her hands in his. 'Okay, okay. Just promise me this. If it comes to it and you don't want to go on, if Jim refuses to budge, promise me you'll have the courage to walk away. Come back here to America . . . I'll come to Australia. I'll do whatever it takes. Do you understand?'

Rachel took a long time before nodding her head. 'Yes. But I think you've misunderstood me. It's probably my fault. It is all a bit of a jumble, I admit.' She looked him in the eye, imploring him to understand how much she cared for him before continuing. 'I've never stopped loving him, you see.'

Coulter gulped. 'I told you once, long ago. Remember? I said I'd marry you the next day, if you'd have me.'

She couldn't help it. The memory made Rachel smile. 'I think I said I'd go into a convent instead.'

Her smile broke the ice and he grinned. 'And I said I'd come right in after you.' He raised her hand to his lips again, kissed it for old time's sake and glanced at his watch. 'We'll be there in a few minutes.' He suddenly leaned forward and kissed her on the lips. 'I love you, Rachel. I love you as much now as I did then. I'm too old to play the martyr second time round. All I'm asking is that you remember what I've said. Think about it. Remember I'm here. That's all I ask. Will you promise me that?'

The plane suddenly banked steeply. Over Coulter's shoulder, Rachel glimpsed the Manhattan skyline in the distance, the hypodermic shape of the Empire State building puncturing the hazy winter sky. The sight filled her with an irreconcilable sense of loss and her eyes brimmed again as she gave him her hesitant pledge.

'I will . . . I promise.'

# Thirty-Three

Four days later, Rachel emerged from the terminal building at Longreach airport and approached the taxi stand. Stan Petrie saw her coming, ditched his newspaper and dipped his lid.

'G'day, Mrs Mackay. Good to see you back.'

'Hello, Stan,' Rachel smiled. 'Can you take me out to Balkenna?'

'Don't see why not,' Stan grinned, friendly as you like.

'I'm afraid there's a bit of luggage inside.'

'No worries.'

Twenty minutes later, as they cleared the outskirts of town, Rachel glanced at her watch.

'You'll be too late for dinner at the pub. Perhaps you'd like to grab a bite at Balkenna before you head back.'

'Thanks,' he agreed. 'That'd be grouse.'

As she settled down on the front seat beside him, Stan glanced at her and offered his sympathy.

'Rotten bit of luck out your way. Lucky the whole place didn't go up.'

'I'm not looking forward to seeing it,' she admitted.

'They took your dad to Brisbane.'

'Yes, I know. I've seen him.'

'How's he coming along?'

'Slowly. He'll be there for quite a while yet, I'm afraid.'

'As long as he's on the mend, that's the main thing.'

'Yes.' She dropped her head back with a weary sigh.

'You've had quite a trip then.'

'Yes,' said Rachel. 'I'm afraid it's all catching up a bit.'

'Well, you just lie back and take it easy. Have a snooze if you like. We'll have you home in no time.'

He increased his speed to emphasize the point and, as the speedo climbed to seventy, Rachel got comfortable, took his advice and closed her eyes.

'Mmmmmm,' she murmured. 'I think I will . . .'

'That's the ticket.'

Jim and Jack were at the far end of the big barn. Jilba's room had been completely gutted by the fire and they were sorting through what remained of her belongings, discarding items past saving, stacking the rest into cardboard boxes. Jim squatted back on his haunches.

'We'll have to get those boxes up off the floor, mate. Want to see about some boards? Maybe get some of those old bricks up the back, bring some down in the wheelbarrow?'

Jack brushed his hands. 'Okay. What do you want to do next? After we get through with this lot?'

'The harness room, I reckon. Be good to get that out of the way today.' He glanced at his watch and pulled a face. 'If there's time. Otherwise we'll knock it on the head.'

'Okay,' Jack grinned. 'Suits me.' But he stopped at the door. 'Any word on when mum might get here?'

Jim shook his head.

'Not really, mate. I expect she'll give us a call from Brisbane when she gets in. After she's seen your granddad.'

Jack covered up by stomping some ash off the toe of his boot. 'Can't wait to see her.'

Jim's heart went out to him. He grinned and gave him a wink. 'That makes two of us.'

On the Jundah road, Stan Petrie's speedo was sitting on eighty. He sized up an approaching corner, eased back a notch and glanced at the woman beside him. She'd fallen into a sound, blissful sleep. Satisfied, he gave her a little grin and looked back to the road just in time to take the corner. He turned the wheel, leaned into it and panicked. Round the other side, right in the taxi's path, were two full-grown kangaroos, alarmed and starting to move. Stan hit the brakes, fought the wheel and swerved as best he could. But he couldn't avoid the one that hopped right in front of him. It slammed into the grill, upended over the bonnet and smashed through the windscreen. Rachel's eyes flew open as blind Stan lost control and the taxi hurtled off the road into a clump of gidgee. Shattering glass, it ploughed into the thickest tree with a sickening crunch and wrapped round it in a horseshoe of contorted metal, its boot where the front grill used to be. Mercifully, for Stan Petrie and his beautiful passenger death was instantaneous.

* * *

They got through with Jilba's things sooner than expected. Jim and Jack were having a crack at the gear in the harness room when they heard Betsey yelling from the back of the house.

'Mr Mackaaay! Mr Mackaaaay!'

Jim handed the bridle he was holding to Jack, and stuck his head out of the door. Betsey spotted him and mimed a phone to her ear. Jim's heart leapt. He megaphoned his hands and hollered. 'Is it Rachel?'

Betsy shook her head.

'Damn,' he muttered, turning to Jack. 'Thought it might be your mum.'

'Don't worry, I can handle the rest.'

'Okay,' Jim nodded. 'Be as quick as you can.'

Heading for the house, Jim glanced at the stark, burnt-out wing silhouetted against a blaze of glory painted across the western horizon by the setting sun. He shook his head, clicked his tongue and quickened his pace.

As he stepped up to his desk, Jim's eye caught a flicker of movement. A decrepit-looking old crow was perched on the edge of the tank stand just outside. Fascinated by Jim's movements behind the glass, she cocked her head from side to side. Jim drummed his knuckles on the glass but, apart from a quick spread of wings and a half-hearted hop, she refused to budge. Jim pulled a face and picked up the phone.

'Hello . . . Oh, hello, Sergeant. How're things? . . . Fine, thanks. What can I do for you?'

That old black crow was the only witness to the utter destruction of Jim Mackay. She saw him die. Eyes glazed with shock, his face suddenly that of a very old man, Jim slumped into his chair. The buzzing phone fell from his hand and clattered on the desk.

From the kitchen window, Betsey saw him appear at the side of the house and stumble away into open space, walking like a zombie towards the distant sunset. She watched him go for a moment and became alarmed. She quickly wiped her hands on her apron and hurried for the back door to fetch Jack.

Dying on his feet, one foot dragging after the other, Jim continued on his way to nowhere until his path was blocked by the barbed-wire fence a hundred yards from the side of the house. He walked right into it. Without knowing what he was doing, he took hold of the top strand and began pulling at it, rhythmically, harder and harder. He didn't feel a thing as the barbs bit and his hands started to bleed. Staring like a madman into the core of the setting sun, he began calling her name with each pull on the wire.

'Raaaaaaachel! Raaaaaachel! Raaaaaaachel! Raaaaachel!'

Eventually, he let go and fell to his knees, embracing the weather-weary, pale-grey fence post at his side. Tears streaming down his face, his whole body twisted in torment, he wrapped his arms round it, clutched at it with bloody hands, pressed his face against the rough wood. Huge, primeval sobs welled up inside him, suffocating him, strangling his guttural cries.

Harder and harder, he crushed his body against the post, clutched it to him, tighter and tighter. It was Rachel he was holding.

# PART THREE

# Thirty-Four

Somewhere between the undertakers' and Balkenna the screw tightened, the head tore and Jim Mackay lost the thread. In the days following his disappearance, district gossip simply suggested he'd gone mad and gone bush.

He vanished in the late afternoon the day before Rachel's funeral. He'd insisted on driving alone into Longreach to look upon her one last time before the coffin was sealed. The undertaker told the police that Jim sat in the tiny curtained cubicle for nearly two hours before he tapped him on the shoulder and suggested they get on with it. Jim stood up, stared into the open coffin for several minutes, nodded and left without a word.

In the frantic hue and cry that followed, the family delayed Rachel's burial for two days before decency decreed they go ahead without him. Riven with sorrow, the Mackay children, Tim, Betsey, Athol, John Barclay and all their friends from the district buried Rachel beside Jack and Elizabeth Mackay in Longreach cemetery.

Jilba flew in from New York, leaving behind the broken figure of Dean Coulter to take indefinite leave of absence from his business and retire to his Long Island home. Jean Barclay was unable to attend. Within hours of Jean holding her own heartache in check and breaking the news as gently as she could, Anthony Barclay suffered a massive stroke. His survival hung in the balance and she had moved into his hospital room to be in constant attendance. It was left to their son to represent the family.

As the police enquiry widened in the ensuing weeks, two witnesses came forward with vague recollections of seeing Jim's station wagon heading out of Longreach on the Winton road. As he'd also been seen heading home on the Jundah road, the evidence was inconclusive. Violent skid marks were found close to the scene of the accident that had taken Rachel's life. Nobody could be sure. They could have been anybody's.

Tony stayed to help as long as he could before his job demanded his return to Brisbane. Jilba phoned Danny in New York to explain what had happened and asked him to tell Max Gordon to cancel all her work for at least a month. By the time she reluctantly boarded the plane, en route to pick up the pieces of her own working life, her father had still not been found. But the station wagon had.

Stripped of portable parts and wheels, its seatless shell was discovered at the southwestern tip of Lakefield National Park, one hundred and sixty kilometres northwest of Cooktown on Cape York Peninsula. Its petrol tank was bone dry. Had Jim driven it to that point, run out of gas and abandoned it? Or had it been abandoned somewhere else, stolen and driven to this remote place to be plundered? There was no way to tell. As the number plates had been left intact, the police favoured the first hypothesis. Only the unsealed road between Laura and Coen led to the spot. The report forwarded to the Mackays through the Longreach police suggested thieves need not have gone that far. It was more likely Jim had just walked away to God knows where. He was listed officially as a missing person and his likeness circulated to every police station in the land. News broadcasts on Queensland's radio and television stations carried pleas for anyone who believed they had seen him or knew his whereabouts to come forward. Two people did. Both leads proved false.

His disappearance was the more baffling for his stoic performance in the days immediately after Rachel's death. Fighting their own shock and loss, Jack and Tim had gone with him to the mortuary to formally identify her body. He had emerged a ghost of his former self, but somehow managed to hold together and commit himself to supporting his family through the days to come. Later, as the family gathered in mourning, he had remained solid as a rock, comforted and calmed them, gave them strength to confront the tragedy that had engulfed them all.

Then suddenly he was gone.

It was those minutes after the undertaker tapped him on the shoulder that did it. Until that moment, he'd not been able to bring himself to look at her. He'd sat there all that time, summoning the courage to do so. When he did, when the moment was forced upon him, it blew him apart. That moment tore away his last line of defence and propelled him into the gulf. The undertakers had done their best, but the face he looked on was that of some ghastly, dollish caricature. It stared up at him from behind closed, puffily torn eyelids. The muscles around her mouth had contracted and her lips were set in a grotesque grimace that seemed to mock his agonised attempts to find a reason to go on.

Outback of nowhere. Out where the roads dry up and the desert takes over to swallow you body and soul. Out where all the hopes of civilisation burn out in the very furnace that has sustained their existence. Out there, way out there, road-workers battling on the very edge of thirst-crazed endurance erect the signs at the end of the road that indicate what lies beyond. They are diamond-shaped. Canary yellow with black borders. Their message is simple enough. They just say: Nothing.

As Jim Mackay drove away from the undertakers, nothing took over. The prospect of life without her filled his heart and mind with emptiness. He was not unaware of what he was doing. It was just that nothing – family, friends, Balkenna or the future – nothing could give him the will to resist the summons to lose himself in the wilderness, the desire to write his name on a blank wall and let the elements erase it at their pleasure. It is not hard to get lost in Australia.

Once Jim Mackay had been formally declared missing, it didn't take long for the Mackays' misfortune to ring glad tidings in the ears of the predators. Through his brother at the bank, Eddie Kidd quickly learned that Jim's signature was the only one that counted on any dotted line. Nobody had power of attorney to sign in his place. It would be years before he could be assumed dead, whether he was or not.

Kidd couldn't wait to inform his superiors at the Coal, Oil and Land Minerals Exploration Company. Calls were made, doors were opened, men in positions of unlimited power had their palms greased, and nobody cared too much for the fine detail. The less said, the better. Just a nod of the head, the wink of a hyena.

Coalmec was incorporated in Hong Kong. It had so many multinational umbrellas, its true ownership would take more than it was worth to discover, might even do you injury. In the corridors of power, profit was the only criterion. Who owned

309

Coalmec? Nobody gave a hoot. They were quite happy to deal with those put forward as its representatives. Who were the Mackays? Who cared?

Eddie Kidd lied. It wasn't bauxite. It wasn't titanium. The smell of crude oil was in the wind. Coalmec had the satellite photos. All they needed was the right to proceed, to set off a few explosions and check the sound waves, to make a few small-diameter borings and, if they got a clue, sink a wild-cat and pray for black rain.

Within three months of Jim's disappearance, they were ready to go. The Crown leaseholds on the Bindra acres and Big Jack's Whack were revoked, the land resumed and then leased back to Coalmec for exploration. Balkenna was paid a lousy one-third market value by way of compensation. For an original outlay of over half a million dollars, the Mackays received just over one hundred and eighty-three thousand and were forced to stand helplessly by as their boundaries shrunk back to the original fifteen thousand acres.

In the absence of the bed-ridden Anthony Barclay, Athol Ferguson did his level best. But even Athol was out of his depth. Despite his wealth, the influence and skill of his own solicitors, there was nothing he could do without Jim. Being a successful grazier in the Queensland cattle industry was one thing. Going up against big graft that spanned the continental oceans was another matter altogether.

As soon as the first notice of resumption arrived at Balkenna, Tony begged Ben Molloy to help him expose the whole affair. It had taken all Molloy's powers of persuasion to make him realise that it would be all too easy for the mongrels involved to make hay of the bias. Maybe even see to it that Tony lost his job. It left Jim's eldest son in an agony of indecision. Should he abandon his career, his life in Brisbane and return to Balkenna? Throw away all he had worked so hard to achieve and commit himself to a cause he had wholeheartedly rejected in the past?

Tim Daley came to the rescue by insisting that he could manage in a caretaker capacity. He was convinced Jim would either return of his own volition or be found very soon. Tony should stay where he was for the time being and await developments. Jilba seconded Tim's opinion. She ran up huge bills on the phone from New York discussing the situation with Tony, calling Tim and Athol, doing her best at such a distance.

The resumption notices meant further financial loss due to

the sudden unexpected reduction of Balkenna's grazing. Of the twelve hundred head of cattle they were running, seven hundred had to go. Tim and Athol kept the five hundred Herefords, Balkenna's original stock. The Brafords and those Herefords left over went under the hammer in a depressed market at the knock-down price of two hundred dollars a head. There was no time to haggle. There was nowhere to keep them and Athol was already carrying maximum capacity at Glenmore. The loss was over a hundred thousand dollars.

Decisions had to be taken in a hurry. Tim would remain on Balkenna, living at his old place to caretake and tend the remaining stock as best he could. With the utmost reluctance and after some heated argument on his part, Jack was persuaded that the house would have to be closed for the time being. He would go to stay with Athol at Glenmore and Billy would go to live with Tony and continue his schooling in Brisbane. The Piper plane was sold to a local cropduster for cash in hand to cover initial expenses. Betsey would take up a temporary job at a pub in Barcaldine and return immediately in the event of Jim's reappearance. For Jack and Billy, it was like the end of the world. All Billy's boyish exuberance dried up and sank into a vacuum. For Jack, the prospect of Balkenna being on the road to ruin just doubled the ache in his heart for the loss of his mother and the terrible uncertainty hanging over the fate of his father.

Having publicly divorced himself throughout the district from any involvement in his brother's activities, Ralph Kidd nevertheless insisted on clearing all Balkenna's old debts from the proceeds of resumption and forced sale before forwarding the balance to the new bank Jim had chosen. There it would have to sit until the mystery of Jim's whereabouts was resolved. The loss of the sheep, unrecouped equipment loans and an amount to hold on deposit to guarantee Tony's mortgage in Brisbane meant he called in ninety thousand dollars. The numbers were appalling. From a real term value for the land and cattle of over eight hundred thousand dollars, the return was just over two hundred and thirty thousand, a loss of over half a million.

The sting in the tail, the bitter irony of it all, was that district gossip already had it that Coalmec was pissing in the wind. Initial seismic tests brought inconclusive results. The first bores came up empty. The whole show looked more and more like a fiasco. But there was fear in the district nonetheless of the ill winds that had blown Balkenna apart. There but for the grace of God . . . There were plenty of other leaseholds that could be poached. For every individual anticipating the benefits the discovery of oil might bring, there were at least a half a dozen praying for a dry hole.

Once again, on the great rolling swell of the black soil plains, Balkenna homestead stood ghostlike. As Tim returned from driving Betsey to Barcaldine and checked the house over one last time before locking up, bitterness took over. His whole life long he had harboured a strong belief in a God that gave you an even break if you committed yourself to the task body and soul. That belief had been reinforced, time and time again, by the love the Mackays had shown him. Now it had been torn to shreds. If this was their reward, God could go to hell. Anthony Barclay had once told him Masons envisaged God as the Great Architect of the Universe. If that was true, he must be a mongrel of a draughtsman.

His crisis of faith caused him to jump the gun on the clutch and the ute lurched forward and stalled. Cursing it to hell and back, he savagely worked the key in the ignition. The family had instructed him to deal with the immediate cash flow problems by selling off equipment in descending order of importance so that the stock could be maintained. The old banger would be the first to go.

Seven months later, Sergeant Archie Newman of the Longreach police slid open the top drawer of his filing cabinet, wearily extracted a grubby, well-thumbed folder and dumped it on his desk with a sigh. Just routine. Just in case. He'd read the damn thing one too many times already. He didn't have a clue what had happened to Jim Mackay. Nor, it seemed, did anyone else.

# Thirty-Five

The man had only been there a week and he'd had enough of him. Particularly now when the halfwit wanted a drink before he even picked up a broom. The publican came out from behind the bar like a pit bull. Grabbing the bloke by the scruff of the neck and the seat of his filthy pants, he propelled him to the door to chuck him out once and for all. The bloke had the temerity to take a half-blind swing at his head. That was it. The publican hauled back and gave him his best punch, right in the face. Spouting an instant nosebleed, the man went down. The publican had no local reputation for fair play. Underneath the shellac of the genial host lay the heart of a headhunter. As the man made a vain, beetle-like attempt to rise, the publican put the boot in. Stomach and head, as hard as he could.

There were only a couple of other early-morning customers there to see the show. One of them decided it was getting out of hand. He came off his stool like a big bull elephant and smothered the publican's fury in a mighty bear hug.

'Easy, mate. I think you've won.'

The publican tried to shrug him off but he didn't have a hope. The road-train driver slowly relaxed and let him go. The publican dragged the stranger to his feet, out of the door, tripped him up and dumped him in the gutter. He spat a gob on him for good measure and stalked back inside.

The drunk's name was Mac James, if anyone wanted to know. Nobody bothered to ask and anybody who'd known him as Jim Mackay would have been hard-pressed to tell they were one and the same. Gaunt and hollow-eyed, his sunken cheeks betrayed a wretched state of malnutrition. His greasy, knotted hair straggled to his shoulders where it got lost in the sprouting sideburns of a full, matted beard that lipped his chest and hid his face from the world. He'd been more than forty days and nights in the desert. He'd been all the way to oblivion with only the vaguest recollection of the stops along the way. Grog kept at bay the nagging ghost that came to him in semi-sober moments, insisting he had a home to go to and should have reached it long before this.

The struggle to remember who he was and where he came from grew harder by the day, the memory of faces left behind dimmer by the hour.

Two little town kids stared down at him from a distance, wide-eyed and ready to run. Jim focused on them and tried to smile. He couldn't. It hurt. He propped on his elbow and reached out a hand. The kids took to their heels and ran for cover. Jim's arm flopped, his head rolled and he fell back in the gutter as blackness engulfed him.

He awoke to a cacophony. At a shallow ford, assisted by two smart-as-a-lick dogs, the road-train driver had uncoupled his Mack prime mover and stock crate from the single 'dog' trailer and was unloading his cargo of cattle for a drink. Bellowing, kicking, pawing, they clambered out and jostled each other for position at the water's edge. Where on earth was he? What had happened? He didn't have a clue. The driver spotted him and gave a wave as he herded the last of his charges towards the water.

'How's the head?'

Puzzled, Jim gave the merest flutter of his hand in return. 'Who are you?'

'Mick Robertson. I picked you up in Forsayth. You had a bit of strife.'

'What sort of strife?'

'You had a bit of a blue with the bloke that runs the pub there. Things got a bit out of hand so I thought you might like a ride.'

Gingerly, Jim checked the tender spots on his head and struggled to remember. 'Feels like it.'

Mick gave him a sympathetic grin. 'No skin off my nose.'

Jim dispensed with the need for further explanation. He thumbed over his shoulder. 'You got any grog in there?'

Mick noted the plea in the eyes. The symptoms were not unfamiliar. In the humid heat of this wasteland, alkies were two a penny. He fixed Jim with a hard eye and shook his head.

'Not a drop, mate. I stop for mine, or I'd never get anywhere.'

Behind his beard, Jim's Adam's apple went up and down like a yo-yo. He shrugged as if it didn't really matter, but Mick knew better.

'Where are we?'

' 'Bout twenty-five southeast of Einasleigh. Cross the river

314

just down the road a bit. I'm carting this lot to Charters Towers. Taking a bit of a short cut, down past Mount Jordan. Pick up the bitumen north of Lynd station.'

'You going back through town?'

'No, mate. I just told you, been through already.'

Jim suddenly looked anxious and started opening and closing his fists.

'You could walk back if it's that bad,' he suggested.

But Jim was in no condition to take offence. He was too busy wrestling with his thirst. Mick decided he was a bit cuckoo but probably harmless enough.

'Come on,' he prompted. 'At least you can give us a hand to get 'em back on board.'

Hesitantly, shuffling his feet, Jim gave him a rather desperate nod. The fire in his belly and the craving in his blood were spinning his head. Better to do something, anything.

'Yeah, okay.'

They rounded them up and reloaded them, no trouble at all. The cattle had been doing this all the way from Normanton and had long ago given up thoughts of escape. Goaded by Mick's yells and well-timed nips from the dogs, they returned placidly to their cages on wheels. Then Mick backed the mover and crate to the 'dog' and Jim gave him a hand to couple them up. Mick opened the cab door and the dogs leapt into their place behind the sleeping platform. Jim just stood there like a question mark.

'What's it gonna be then?'

Jim struggled to answer, but he didn't know.

'Make up your mind, mate,' Mick insisted. 'Haven't got all day. Got to keep this show on the road.'

Jim tried again, but nothing came.

Mick shrugged, hauled himself into the cab and gunned the motor. 'See ya.'

Jim stood rooted to the spot with the look of a startled animal as the enormous rig slowly ground into motion. At a snail's pace, it inched forward, gathered momentum and lumbered away along the track that would put it back on the unsealed road. Fifty yards on, Mick checked Jim's receding figure in his side mirror. Suddenly it waved and began a shuffling half-run after him. He hit the brakes. Uncertain, chest heaving, trying to catch his breath, Jim hauled himself up into the passenger seat and slammed the door.

'I'll give it a go.'

Mick gave him a wink and eased the clutch again. 'Good on ya.'

For mile upon weary mile, Jim didn't say a word. Hunched well down in his seat, he simply stared out of his window at a passing parade of personal ghosts. He appreciated the casual artistry with which Mick handled the power-house under his control, but had nothing whatsoever to say. Mick glanced at what he could see of his passenger's profile now and then but held his tongue. Until his patience ran out and the need for a yarn took over.

'What's your name?'

The sudden sound of his voice made Jim sit up like a startled rabbit and he shot the driver a quick, furtive glance.

'Mac. Mac James.'

It took a fraction too long to come. As Jim hunched back down and turned his head even further away, Mick gave him a final look, arched his eyebrows, tilted his hat and turned his attention to the road. That was the end of that conversation.

They made the bitumen of the Gregory Developmental Road and did another sixty kilometres before calling it a day where the road crossed Gray Greek, south of Greenvale.

By their camp fire that night, Jim methodically worked the crusts of his bread round his plate, mopping up the last stringy traces of his feed and washed it down with his third mug of tea. The cattle milled about in a rope yard erected in a clump of gidgee. The dogs lay sprawled nearby, trying to sleep with one eye open. Silhouetted against the evening skyline, the road-train loomed over the scene. Apart from a grunt of thanks for his food, Jim hadn't said a word.

'Don't know much, do you, Mac?'

Jim managed a lopsided grin. 'Memory's crook, I'm afraid.'

'Is that because of the grog? Or because you like it that way?'

'Bit of both, I s'pose.'

Too much, too quick. Jim barely managed the reply before turning to stare fixedly into the fire. Mick gave up. He picked up all the eating gear and carried it to the rig. He returned to the fire lugging a battered old guitar case, laid it down and flipped the catches on a worn-out Gibson Hummingbird. He checked the tuning.

'Don't mind, do you?'

'Not at all,' said Jim. 'Go for your life.'

Mick was a diehard Slim Dusty fan. He strummed a few chords, picked the intro of one song, changed his mind and got stuck into 'When the Rain Tumbles Down in July'. He was a strong, plain and simple singer and gave the song a good go.

'Good one that. Slim Dusty, isn't it?'

'Sure is,' Mick smiled and immediately fingered some new chords. 'This one's called "Reedy River". Old Henry Lawson poem. Some bloke in Sydney hung a tune on it. I got it off a record . . .'

As Mick settled himself and closed his eyes, Jim turned back to the fire. The opening chords were slower. Moodier.

> *Ten Miles down Reedy River, one Sunday afternoon,*
> *I rode with Mary Campbell to that broad, bright lagoon.*
> *We left our horses grazing, till shadows climbed the peak,*
> *And strolled beneath the she-oaks on the banks of Rocky Creek.*

Jim swallowed hard. The words immediately flashed him back to Rachel's visit to Glenmore and their first ride together. Down to the creek with her young brother.

> *Then home along the river, that night we rode a race*
> *And the moonlight lent a glory to Mary Campbell's face . . .*

Suddenly, all he could see was Rachel's face in the moonlight. The night of his father's funeral when she turned up out of the blue.

> *I pleaded for my future, all through that moonlight ride,*
> *Until our weary horses drew closer, side by side.*
> *Ten miles from Ryan's Crossing and five below the peak,*
> *I built a little homestead on the banks of Rocky Creek.*
> *I cleared the land and fenced it and ploughed the rich, red loam . . .*

Jack's face swam out of the fire at him and Jim saw them working on a line of fence together, his son sweating with enthusiastic energy, loving every minute of it.

> *And my first crop was golden when I brought my Mary home.*

Rachel again, the day he brought her home after their marriage in Longreach, his mother beaming, Athol Ferguson sporting a grin a mile wide. Still with his eyes clammed shut, Mick didn't see the caged panic spreading across his passenger's face, the agitation of someone on the edge of a fit.

> *Now still down Reedy River, the grassy she-oaks sigh,*
> *The water-holes still mirror the pictures in the sky.*

The words of the song had unleashed an uncontrollable torrent of memories in Jim. His mother and father. Athol Ferguson. Dud Brewley. His sons Tony, Jack and Billy. His daughter Jilba. Beautiful Jilba, so far away . . . So far away . . . He was reeling, losing control.

> *The golden sand is drifting across the rocky bars,*
> *And over all, for ever, go sun and moon and stars.*

Now all he could see was a moment of their last holiday together. The setting of the sun. The rising of the moon. Rachel leaning against him, spellbound by the moment of axis. The echo of her whispered response rang in his ear.
'Beautiful . . .'

> *But of that hut I builded, there are no traces now,*
> *And many rains have levelled the furrows of my plough.*

Eyes closed, singing his heart out, Mick was unaware of Jim struggling to his feet and stealing away into the night. The last two lines of the song drifted after him, mocking his retreat.

> *The glad bright days have vanished for sombre branches*
> *wave*
> *Their wattle blossom golden above my Mary's grave.*

'Arrrrrrgh . . .'
Mick's eyes flew open and the chords died in his hands.
'Arrrrrrgh . . .'
'Jeeeeeesus! What's going on?'
He whacked the guitar back in its case, flipped the catches and peered out into the darkness. The sound of low, guttural

318

sobbing came back at him. More animal than human. He jumped to his feet and took a few steps towards it, trying to define shape beyond the circle of firelight.

'Arrrrrrgh . . .'

That sound was something else again. Mick grabbed his guitar, hurried to the rig and climbed into the cab. He peered through the windscreen, every sense straining to catch the slightest sound or movement. It was hard. The cattle had stirred up and the dogs were yapping. Alone and unknowing, he waited.

'Arrrrrrrgh . . .'

The hair stood up on the back of his neck. There it was again, more gut-wrenching than the last time. It was enough for Mick. He was a big bloke and not easily scared. But that was definitely it. He closed the windows and locked the doors, took down his rifle from its mount above the windscreen and checked the breech. He crawled up into his bunk, laid the rifle by his side and pulled up his blanket. He rolled over to face the windscreen and prepared for a long night.

The following Saturday night, along with his wife and two other couples, he was having a night out under the stars in the beer garden of a Charters Towers pub, celebrating another successful run from Normanton.

'It was bloody spooky, I tell you. I hardly slept a wink.'

His wife pulled a face for the benefit of the others.

'Serves him right. I'm always bloody well telling him not to pick up hitchhikers. 'Specially way out there.'

'He wasn't a hitchhiker,' Mick contradicted her. 'I was trying to help the bloke. He was in a real bad way.'

'Completely off the air by the sound of it.'

'Was there any sign of him in the morning?'

'Not a trace. Didn't look too hard, mind you. Just loaded up and pissed off, fast as I could.'

'You going back to Normanton this week?'

'Yeah.'

'You'll probably pass him on the road.'

Mick leered at his friend and stated his terms. 'He'll eat dust if I do.'

As the others chuckled, Mick's wife tapped her husband's shoulder and drew his attention to the gate.

'There's a bloke over there staring at you.'

Mick turned to find Mac James looking straight at him. He was still dressed in the same worn-out clothes and boots, but he'd made a bit of an effort. His hair was hacked to a manly length and his beard trimmed back. But it only took a skip of his heartbeat for Mick to make the connection.

'Oh, my Christ, that's him!'

Heads turned to check him out. When Jim started straight at them, the men came out of their chairs and braced for trouble while the women prepared for hasty departure. But it was Mick Jim wanted to see. It was as if the others weren't there.

'I went to your depot. They said I'd probably find you here. Just wanted to say thanks. I'm sorry about what happened out there. Been having a bit of a rough time lately and it got the better of me, I'm afraid.' He offered his hand. 'No hard feelings I hope.'

Convinced he could do the bloke if it came to it, Mick gave Jim's hand a shake.

'Okay, Mac. If you say so. No hard feelings.'

Mission accomplished, Jim disintegrated. Suddenly acutely aware of his appearance in the others' eyes, he shuffled with embarrassment and didn't know where to turn next. Neither did Mick. After an awkward silence, Jim just nodded and turned away. Mick caught his arm and turned him back. He fished in his pocket, peeled off a twenty dollar bill and tried to hand it over. Jim immediately pushed it back, but Mick insisted.

'Go on, mate. Take it. It's all right. You helped a bit before we lost each other. Let's call it wages.'

Need overcoming reluctance, Jim accepted the money, shoved it in his pocket, muttered his thanks and hurried away. Mick watched until he disappeared before resuming his seat.

'What do you reckon about that then?'

'Buggered if I know.'

Jim didn't muck about. Pissed as a newt, an unmitigated, staggering disaster to anyone in his path, he headed down the street at closing time, convinced he was walking a dead straight line.

By the time he hit the edge of town, he'd have given his right arm to fire his blood with another whisky. But he had to get away. Charters Towers was too big, his appearance too conspicuous. The compulsion that had driven him for months on end propelled his unsteady, nocturnal flight, drove him beyond the desperate need to fall in a heap and let the world spin out of control. He managed five and a half miles before his body gave out and refused to go a step further. He turned round, back-tracked a little to a culvert he'd just crossed, scrambled off the road and peered in to check it out. Looked dry as a bone. He crawled in and slept for eleven hours.

# Thirty-Six

Fred Paterson yawned, stretched, scratched his shoulders and shouted.

'Gonna be another scorcher!'

He was standing in a small clearing before three aeons-old caves, hidden from the world by rugged bush in a remote stretch of the Seventy Mile Range, southeast of Charters Towers. A rusty, lopsided, much dented Holden ute stood nearby, facing down a barely readable track. Just off it, an old flat-top truck was stashed under a shelter of saplings and bark. A stone fireplace stood in the centre of the clearing and empty oil and kerosene drums were lined up along the rock wall. On the edge of the surrounding scrub, rolls of steel cable and four-ply rope were suspended higgledy-piggledy from the nearest available branches.

Carrying two pressure lamps, Annie Paterson appeared from the smallest cave at the far end. She set them down, grabbed a tin funnel from a niche in the rock above her head, dragged a tin of kero into position and began refilling them.

Fred watched her for a moment, stretched again, shook himself from head to toe and set about gingering the fire to life. Once it caught, he replaced the old stainless steel refrigerator shelves they used for a gridiron and put the billy on to boil.

'Billy's on, love. I'll just go and have a bit of a whack while we wait. How's the egg supply?'

Annie tilted the kero tin back a bit.

'All gone. I put them on the list.'

'Righto,' Fred shrugged. 'Looks like bread and jam then.'

Fred grabbed a pick leaning near the entrance of the centre cave and disappeared into the third. As he got to work, Annie concentrated on the lamps.

The pretty little girl Fred took with him to visit Balkenna in 1953 had grown into a good-looking woman. Though not beautiful in any obvious, classical sense, her heart-shaped face

323

revealed her German ancestry and showed great character, hewn by a hard life. Her nose was slightly askew, the result of a break that had set out of line, and a hairline scar ran across the top of her left eyebrow, tapering off towards the temple. Her eyes were her best feature. Pale, almost ice-blue, they advertised a level-headed, no-nonsense intelligence. They were the eyes of someone who'd seen both sides of life. Her blond hair, bleached even lighter by years of exposure to the sun, was cut short and tapered at the nape of her neck. She stood, picked up the lamps and returned to the cave. Her lanky, small-breasted, narrow-hipped frame, clad in only a loose singlet and cut-offs, moved on bare feet with the grace of an athlete.

Fred Paterson was going hammer and tongs at the back wall. It was already heavily pitted and cracked by months of fruitless gouging. He wiped the sweat from his eyes, lined up another almighty swing, and let it rip. A rock landed on his bare toe. He grimaced and wiggled it in mid-air for a moment before returning to the task.

He was seventy years old, but you'd never know it. A lifetime of prospecting had kept the muscles of his great, lumbering frame strong and supple. Balding at the crown and greying at the temples, he still carried a good head of dark brown hair and the wild and woolly beard he'd sported since his mid-twenties was shot with only a few streaks of silver. The criss-cross of crow's feet at the corners of his still anarchic eyes might give you a clue. But even if you couldn't put the right number of years against his name, you'd certainly want him on side at the first sign of trouble.

He and Annie had been in this ancient place for over a year and he was glad of her company. They had shared many a camp together before, ever since she was a little girl, and his fierce love for her had never wavered, even in the years when they had lost contact altogether.

Fred had only ever truly loved one woman in his life. She had died in his arms giving birth to the woman who, once again, had returned to his side to share his life. It had been months before she began to smile again and he was relieved when she did. He loved his daughter's smile. It was genuinely beautiful. It didn't come easy and it didn't come often, but it came from the heart and filled his own with joy. Though she was occasionally disparaging of his propects for fortune, he knew she had always respected him for what he was, taken for granted his right to choose the way of life that suited him best. It had not made her own any easier.

Fred cleared away the last few pebbles and dirt from the ledge and stared intently at the exposed strata, running his fingertips over its cool flow. He seized the pick again but a loud growl from his stomach suggested a bit of brekkie first wouldn't be such a bad idea.

Jim's breakfast consisted of a bag of peanuts he couldn't remember buying. The road beneath his feet was a minor one and the sun told him he was heading vaguely south. He ate the lot and they churned in his stomach. The salt fanned his raging thirst. No booze out here. Water would have to do. Four miles further on, he crossed another culvert with enough muddy water in a pothole to wet his lips. By mid-morning he'd found a Coca-Cola can. Jim got a stick, rammed it in and methodically worked the sides out again as best he could before shoving it in his pocket to fill at the next water. At the sound of an approaching car, he ducked off the road. It thundered by and disappeared in the direction of the Towers.

Jim made his way back to the road and plodded on. The sun bore down relentlessly, and his mind began to stray. Try as he might, he couldn't stop harking back to the night by the fire with the road-train driver and the song he'd sung. Now, as he strained to stay on an even keel, they came back to taunt him again. Two voices commanded his inner ear. One kept saying go home, go home. The other, more insidious, and still with the upper hand, said there was nothing to go home to.

Jim heard another vehicle coming. The only immediate place to hide was behind some mullock and they were too far away to bother. When a clapped-out old ute chugged into view, he just dropped his eyes, kept walking and didn't look up. Suddenly, there was a shriek of rubber. Jim quickly dodged off the road and looked back. The ute had stopped about a hundred yards on. As he watched, it began to back up towards him. Jim glanced around for somewhere to hide. But he was caught in open space. As the ute drew close, he pulled himself together to deal with the driver as best he could. When the man got out, Jim wished the earth would swallow him whole. Fred Paterson walked a few paces towards him, stopped, and studied him. He couldn't believe his eyes.

'Jim?'

A distant, obscure cousin of a tributary that eventually fed into the Burdekin River far to the east, the creek managed some level of water year round. Nevertheless, her father would come back from the Towers with their four five-gallon plastic tanks full to the brim with town water for drinking.

Breaking through the last line of scrub onto the creek bank, Annie made her way along to her favourite spot, a tiny tumble of waterfall with a shallow rock pool underneath. Dumping the laundry, she gave one of Fred's shirts a good dunking, spread it out on a flat rock and applied a liberal lather of Sunlight. Intent on her task, she worked her way methodically through the pile. She had just about finished when she heard someone coming through the scrub on the far bank. She jumped to her feet, alert and ready, but relaxed at once when an elderly Aboriginal man broke from cover.

'Hello, Tobias. You gave me a bit of a fright.'

'Fred go along town yet?'

'Yes. Left about an hour ago.'

'He remember fetch up baccy?'

Annie laughed. 'Never forgotten yet, has he? No worries.'

Tobias beamed. 'Good fella, Fred.'

'You're not such a bad old bugger yourself. Want to come up for a cuppa?'

Tobias thought about it for a moment. 'Okay.'

On the road to Charters Towers, Fred Paterson was having a dickens of a time getting his friend to join him in the ute. After the initial shock of recognising that his old grubstaker had a few kangaroos running loose in his top paddock, Fred realised there was time enough for questions later. Now all he wanted to do was get him out of the sun. He opened the door but Jim made no move to get in. Fred stepped casually to his side, put a hand on his back and eased him forward.

'Come on, mate. She'll be apples. Can't leave you out here on foot, for Christ's sake.'

Slowly, without a word, Jim shuffled forward and climbed in. Fred slammed the door and hurried round to get behind the wheel. He set the ute in motion before Jim had time to change his mind. His own door was still flapping and he didn't manage to get it shut until they were fifty yards down the road.

Jim had gone through half a bottle of Johnnie Walker he

solicited out of Fred in the Towers by the time they began the long, slow crawl up the excuse for a track that led to the caves.

They arrived as twilight was settling. Annie appeared from her cave and headed over to greet her father, wondering who was with him. Fred leapt out, met her halfway, spun her round and propelled her into the centre cave for a quick confab. He'd managed to wheedle just enough out of Jim to get the drift. They had a problem on their hands. Annie greeted her father's report with wide-eyed astonishment. But by the time they headed outside again, she'd got it under control and set herself to give nothing away.

Uncertain and edgy, Jim had left the ute and was staring back down the track, contemplating flight. He jumped when Fred touched his arm.

'Jim, this is Annie. Knee-high to a grasshopper she was last time you two saw each other.'

Jim turned to face her, but his tongue remained firmly tied and he was glad the sudden flush of shame he felt was hidden by his beard. If she noticed, Annie didn't let on. Her eyes held no questions. Only welcome. She offered her hand and refused to let it drop until Jim brought his own to meet it.

'Hello. 'Fraid I don't remember what he's talking about. Nice to meet you again, anyway. I've heard a lot about you from dad.'

Fred was dead set right about his daughter's smile. It would melt an iceberg at a thousand yards. Fred saw Jim wilt and then relax as his troubled mind surrendered to the prospect of some warm and friendly hospitality with people who would give him time to speak his mind, not give a fig if he didn't. Painstakingly, he groped for a reply.

'I remember. It was a long, long time ago, but I remember. You came to Bal . . . to Bal . . .' It was no go. He couldn't actually say the name. He broke off and turned away, his fists clenching. Annie exchanged a quick look of concern with her father. She placed a hand on Jim's arm. He was forced to look at her.

'You're all right here, Jim. No worries. I'll organise some tucker. You hungry?'

She held his eye, refusing to look away until he answered.

'Yes . . .'

'That's the ticket.'

She let her hand rest on his arm a moment longer. 'Take

about half an hour. Dad, why don't you take him down for a dunk in the creek. There's a clean pair of pants and a couple of shirts on your bunk.'

'Yeah. Good on yer, love. Whatcha reckon, Jim? Fancy a soak?'

Still painfully unsure of himself, Jim reckoned the prospect of a good scrub and change of clothes seemed like the best idea he'd had in years.

The centre cave was the biggest of the three. An old mahogany door, scavenged from the Charters Towers' tip, made do as a table with four neatly chain-sawed stumps for legs. The leftovers had been fashioned into low stools on either side. Against the back wall, a sleeping platform was mounted across a convenient cleft of rock, and an old leather armchair, sprouting several whorls of stuffing, stood nearby. The remains of a once-proud Formica kitchen cabinet housed the Patersons' crockery and cooking utensils and four meat safes stood atop one another, wedged into the cave's only natural annexe.

There was an enormous old Chinese rug spread over the sandy earth. A stack of old fruit crates were stuffed to the gills with newspapers, magazines, books and a well-worn set of *Everyman's Encyclopaedia.* Just inside the entrance, under a crack in the ceiling that provided natural ventilation, a stone fireplace had been carefully designed to take up a minimum of space.

They ate their supper in wary silence in the glow of the pressure lamps. Fred caught Jim staring at the indoor fireplace.

'We cook on that when it's wet. Or if we think there's anyone about.'

The thought startled Jim. He hadn't really considered there might be other people in the vicinity.

'Who?'

'Get the occasional shooter now and then. Never had 'em up to the front door, so to speak. There's an old Aboriginal bloke, Tobias. He lives in a bloody great cave the other side of the mountain. Buggered off from the Reserve years ago. Couldn't stand it, he reckons. Prefers the old way of doing things. Bit of a dingbat, Tobias. Reckons he's looking after the spirits of his ancestors. Yaks with 'em and everything.'

'He's a dear old bloke, really,' said Annie quietly. 'Wouldn't harm a fly.'

Jim had scrubbed himself under the waterfall until it hurt. With a clean shirt on his back, the feel of clean jeans round his loins, the web between his toes already chaffed by the pair of old rubber thongs Fred had produced, his belly full of Annie's rabbit stew and a couple of cans of 4X under his belt, he could hardly believe he'd spent the previous night curled up in a stinking culvert. But there was still much to keep at bay.

'Any luck?' he asked, thumbing over his shoulder in the direction of the work cave.

If Fred's smile was a touch rueful, his words were full of conviction.

'Coming along. There's a mother lode here, Jim, I know it. Sure as God made little apples. Every time we pan the creek there's a result. I *know* we're on the right track in the cave. Positive. Bull's-eye this time, for sure.'

Jim managed to muster a gentle, knowing smile. 'Seems I've heard that one before.'

Not to be put out, Fred chuckled and drummed his fingers on the table a moment. 'Yeah, maybe so. Wait and see, mate. Just you wait and see.'

Jim pitched in to help with the dishes. When it was done, he immediately enquired where he could sleep, feigning exhaustion to escape any further talk. It still hadn't completely dawned on him there'd be no pressure from the Patersons to come up with some answers until he was good and ready. Come up with none, if he preferred.

'See him right, will you, love?' Fred prompted. 'I want to ram that new handle in the pick. Bloody splinters are driving me round the twist.'

She collected a sleeping bag and a couple of old hessian sacks from under Fred's bunk, grabbed one of the lamps, and led him to the work cave. She made an underlay of the hessian sacks, unrolled the sleeping bag, and zipped it open.

'We can fix something up off the floor tomorrow. Hope this'll be all right for tonight.'

'Any snakes?'

'A few, in the scrub. Caught a big black nosing about near the larder last summer.'

Unable to do anything about it, Jim started shaking. Beads of perspiration appeared on his brow.

'Is it bad?'

'A bit,' Jim admitted. 'Not much I can do about it.'

'You can give in, or you can fight. You can win, or you can lose.'

The way she put it to him summed up her whole character. Simple, direct, but spoken with compassion and understanding.

'Hang on a tick.'

She was back in a couple of minutes with the last of the Johnnie Walker. There was just enough left for two or three good swallows. Cringing with embarrassment, Jim tried to deflect her.

'Go on,' Annie insisted. 'Don't be silly. I know the feeling. It'll get you to sleep at least.'

Jim tried to look away but something in her eyes held his. He grasped the bottle and brushed her hand as she pulled it away.

'Thanks . . .'

Annie didn't smile, she just continued gazing at him in the same way a moment longer before turning on her heel.

'Call us in the night, if you need to. Otherwise we'll see you in the morning.'

'I'll be okay.'

But she'd already gone.

He quickly worked the cork, brought the bottle to his lips and allowed all that remained to trickle slowly down his throat. It wasn't much, but it sure beat the hell out of nothing.

He stripped off, carefully folded the clean clothes, tucked them into one of the corn sacks, wriggled into the sleeping bag and zipped it up. He rolled on his side to face the entrance and studied the vista of stars twinkling over the silhouettes of distant ridges. The whisky hit home and produced a mild glow. Perversely, it only heightened his craving for more and produced another attack of the shivers. Fighting the claws in his guts, he curled up in the bag and wrapped his arms round his head to blot out the world. There was nothing he could do, however, to blot out the relentless onslaught of images that crowded his mind.

# Thirty-Seven

Tobias made a visit to the Patersons the day after Jim's arrival. After a hasty introduction and a brief touch of hands, Jim excused himself and withdrew. The Aborigine's mere presence sounded far-off echoes in Jim's heart that he didn't want to hear.

Tobias collected his tobacco and returned the favour with a bag of wild apples. Out of earshot, he offered his own diagnosis. 'That feller lose him dreaming. Him lost. You find him, you reckon?'

'Do our best, mate.' Fred nodded. 'He's still in there somewhere. Just have to let him surface in his own good time.'

Tobias grinned and offered one more piece of advice before threading away through the scrub. 'Make him work. Plenty hard work. Stop him shaking little bit, you bet.'

A week later, Jim was sleeping more easily. Not only had Fred persuaded him to stay for as long as he liked, both he and Annie had stuck to their policy of no questions asked. What little they learned came out gradually.

It hadn't been hard to persuade him to pitch in. He seemed to relish having his hands full. Little telltale signs of improvement soon began to show themselves, like tiny green shoots on a tree presumed dead.

Fred didn't stop for the traditional day of rest. It wasn't through lack of respect. In his own way, he was a religious man. Years of solitary existence in the wilderness had convinced him there was some meaning to it all. He just knew that, along with everything else, God had created gold before he took the day off and Fred went along with that.

As he wielded the pick, Jim shovelled the rubble into plastic buckets, carried them out and added the contents to a pile for later inspection. They'd been at it since early morning and both were covered in sweat that etched channels in the film of dust coating their bodies. Fred downed the pick to knead his weary back. Jim took his chance.

331

'What happened to Annie's husband? Kiwi, wasn't it?'

Fred continued kneading his back a moment and shot a gob out the corner of his mouth. 'Yeah, and a right bastard to boot. Left her black and blue more times than I care to remember.' Fred's expression showed his utter contempt for the man's memory.

'The last time he did her over, the cops took an interest and the bastard shipped out on a freighter from Cairns. Said he'd be back for her, swore all kinds of revenge. Ended up with a knife in his back in Manila. Good bloody riddance as far as I was concerned. Annie didn't exactly weep buckets either . . .' He dropped his hand on Jim's shoulder and turned him towards the daylight. 'Come on, mate. Time for a cuppa.'

As Jim and Annie boiled the billy, Fred poked around in the day's pile of broken rock.

'See what I mean?'

Jim held it up for closer inspection. The sun danced on some unmistakable pinpricks of gold.

'Ridgie-didge, mate,' Fred assured him. 'Genuine article. There's a bank full and more in there somewhere, I promise you.'

Jim smiled and passed the trophy back. 'Here's hoping.'

He drained his mug and reached out to Annie for a refill. The tension in his arm made his hand shake and the mug fell in the dirt. Jim snatched back his hand and buried it in his lap. Fred and Annie exchanged a quick look.

'Think I'll take the rest of the day off. Feel like a bit of a read.'

Fred turned to Annie and thumbed at the mountainside above them. 'Maybe Jim'd like to take a dekko at our back yard.'

Annie cast a glance at Jim, pulled a face and raised her eyebrows to give him a way out if he wanted. But Jim was wise and managed a grin.

'Is that doctor's orders, or does he just want to get rid of us?'

'The latter,' said Fred. 'Like to potter about on my own for a couple of hours without having to bump into your ugly mugs.'

Annie thumped her father on the arm. 'Listen to who's talking, you old bunyip.'

Fred slapped his knee and roared with laughter. To his surprise, Jim found his own face creased with a smile and laughter welling up inside him. It felt good.

Halfway through their climb, he was thinking he'd been mad to agree. The higher they scrambled, the harder it got. They were helping one another, but Annie was doing most of the helping. At one point he put out a hand to pull her up a steep stretch only to lose his feet and send them both for a slide. It was an hour and a half before they stood together on the pinnacle.

'Quite a view,' Jim conceded, his lungs still heaving.

'You should do this every day. Have you back on your feet in no time. Mountains are good for broken hearts.' She felt Jim physically start beside her, and turned. 'I know what I'm talking about, believe me.'

Jim did believe her, but he couldn't respond. He had to look away. Annie gave him a moment. Then she pointed to the far side of the ridge. 'Come and have a look over here.'

She led him to a large flat area of exposed granite, dropped to her knees and began tracing the outlines of some Aboriginal rock carvings with her fingertips.

'Tobias says this was like a church up here. Reckons he never could figure out why we all worship inside buildings. Ring-a-ding-God-boxes, he calls them.'

Jim chuckled and squatted down for a closer look, tracing the outlines with his finger. 'Might have a point there.'

They wandered across the ridge to another of Annie's favourite spots, a tiny natural amphitheatre that commanded a spectacular view of the mountain ridges away towards the west. They sat down and got comfortable with their backs to the rock wall and Annie passed him the old Army water bottle. They'd both worked up a good thirst and half of it was gone before she screwed the cap back on. Drugged by the sun, they sat in silence for a good ten minutes before Annie asked him her first direct question.

'Do your kids know where you are?'

The words tore into Jim like knives. He immediately jumped to his feet and stepped a few paces away to avoid answering.

'Didn't mean to give you a fright. Just curious, that's all.'

Jim heard her. But all he could see was one face dissolving into another. The faces of his children. He had to stop this in its tracks before it got any worse.

'They know I'm all right.'

He had to wait an equal time for her response. It hit home and it hit hard.

'Are you?'

Her tone was matter-of-fact, but there was something

alarmingly finite about her inflection. It seemed to come from a well of awareness outside his understanding. She knew he was lying. He wanted to turn and face her, bluff his way through. But the way her question had been put made that impossible.

'I'm getting there. You and Fred have been good medicine.'

Silence followed. He had to fight even harder against the desire to turn and meet her eyes. He knew there would be wisdom there. Wisdom born of her own struggles. But she might give him a glimpse of the future and he didn't want to know.

'Sorry,' she offered at last. 'I shouldn't have asked.'

'That's okay.'

Another silence followed and when he did finally summon the nerve to turn she was gone. He had to find his way back down to the caves alone.

In the weeks that followed, Annie never once attempted to probe him directly again. But as the three of them went through their daily routines of hard work broken up by moments of spontaneous amusement or plain tomfoolery, Jim found himself opening up more and more. He took Annie's advice and made many solo climbs to the top of the mountain, each time a little quicker than the last. It was a good tonic. He began to feel he was changing and it was definitely a change for the better.

Fred's old flat-top truck had been broken down for months. At the end of November, Jim volunteered to have a go at setting it to rights. It took him two whole weeks, nine to ten hours a day. Bit by bit, section by section, he stripped it down, laid the parts out on an old tarpaulin and spent all his daylight hours and three tins of kero cleaning them up. On Fred's next trip to the Towers he gave him a list of parts and gaskets beyond repair and the electric cable he would need for rewiring. He became totally absorbed in the task, thinking about nothing else from morning till dusk. Fred and Annie more or less gave up on him beyond asking if he wanted another cup of tea.

The slow mechanical transformation somehow mirrored his own. His DTs dried up, and supple strength was returning to his body. Whenever they caught each other's eye, he sensed Annie was silently willing him on to scale the heights and take a fresh look at the world. And some metamorphosis had definitely taken place. He kept catching glimpses of hope on the horizon.

When it was time to give it a go, he summoned Fred and Annie to watch. He hit the starter, the old truck coughed and complained and then she roared into life. Fred smacked the bonnet and whooped.

'You little humdinger!'

Jim was beaming through the windscreen.

'Good on yer, mate. Pearler! You're a bloody genius.'

Annie was standing by the window. 'Well done.'

Jim turned to her and offered thanks. 'You had a hand in this too, you know.'

Annie didn't bother to reply. She just hit him with that smile of hers and it filled him with the first sense of pride he'd felt in a long, long time.

By mid-December Fred and Annie knew they were witness to the birth of a new man. Jim pitched into the work and life of the camp with new zest and a spring in his step.

In their long evenings together he began to describe in detail the downhill slide his life had taken. For the first time since leaving Longreach he found himself able to talk about Rachel's death. The only subject he didn't broach, but which Fred and Annie knew had come to the forefront of his thoughts, was the need to go home and ask forgiveness from the family he had deserted.

On his last trip to the Towers Fred was sorely tempted to make that decision for him by calling Balkenna and suggesting someone come and get him. He'd actually gone into a booth and picked up the phone. But he dropped it back in place. A river makes its own bed. Better to let Jim run his course, find his own way home.

It was Sunday night. Fred had announced he was totally buggered and kicked them out after the evening meal.

Jim had been in Annie's cave in daylight hours, but this was his first night-time visit. The soft, dancing light from the lamp bathed the rock in a rich, warm glow that heightened his awareness of the oddly feminine atmosphere of the place. The walls were covered in photographs clipped from magazines and an assortment of multi-coloured scarves billowed across the low ceiling.

There, against the wall, Annie had positioned her pride and joy, her one true luxury. An old Second World War wooden-framed camp bed, big enough to accommodate a twenty-stone sergeant. Hanging right across the back wall was a large Aboriginal painting Tobias had done for her on a piece of old tarpaulin. Aborigines tend to know a bit more about the night sky than the average white Australian. Tobias's picture depicted the Dreamtime creation of the Southern Cross and its spiral images whirled across the canvas with undeniable power.

Annie was pointing out the various Dreamtime pathways by which the stars had converged to form the best known constellation in the southern hemisphere, the pride of the Australian national flag. An uncertain silence fell. Jim rubbed his knees and made a move to stand up.

'Well, we better get some shuteye too . . .'

Annie caught his arm. 'When are you going home?'

She caught him completely unawares and Jim immediately dropped his eyes. Several seconds passed before he could muster a reply.

'I don't really know. Soon.'

It wasn't easy and she knew it. But she pressed him. 'How soon?'

She immediately regretted it. Several shadows flickered across his face, his eyes glazed and his mouth pulled into a hard, tight line.

'Doesn't matter. Forget it.'

Jim studied the floor for a moment, then shook himself out of it. 'No, it's all right. I've been asking myself the same question.'

'That's why I asked.'

'It's hard to know. I'm not really sure how to tackle it. I walked out on them, don't forget. They might prefer to leave it that way.'

She looked him right in the eye. 'The longer you leave it, the harder it'll be.'

Jim held her look. There was no point in avoiding it. She was right again and he knew it. 'At least I'm thinking about it. If it hadn't been for you . . . I owe you a lot, Annie. And Fred.'

Annie smiled and patted his hand. 'That's all right. We've been in debt to you for years.'

Jim chuckled. 'You've got an answer for everything.'

He leaned forward and gave her a token kiss on the cheek. 'Thanks anyway.'

'My pleasure. Our pleasure.'

But it really was her particular pleasure. At first her care for him had been purely and simply humanitarian, born of the knowledge that this shambling wreck who'd shown up on her doorstep had, in better days, repeatedly financed her father's schemes, often enough against his better judgement. But Jim's gradual metamorphosis had tugged her own feelings in an unexpected direction. As the man her father had so often described with genuine affection and respect emerged from his burnt-out shell, the harder it became for her to deny that her feelings were no longer simply a ministry of mercy.

After years of indifference to just about any man except her own father, Annie found herself in the strange position of being forced to admit she'd taken a shine. And the more she got to know him, the more it shone. At first it had been limited to the daytime, but lately she'd been dreaming about him as well. Impossible dreams. Jim's heart may have healed considerably, but she had absolutely no illusions about where it lay. It was buried in a grave far to the west. A grave he had yet to see. Perhaps when he did, when he was forced to confront the reality again, things would be different. There was no way to tell.

Nor, until that moment, had there been any way to tell him what he'd done for her in return. She eased herself off the bed, knelt in front of him and casually reached up to take his head between her hands.

'You've worked some wonders of your own . . .'

She leant forward and gave him a kiss on the mouth. Jim tensed and turned his face away. But slowly, gently, Annie pulled him back. She kissed his brow, ran her lips down his cheek, found his mouth again and fluttered her lips across it. Jim's tension just melted away. All the pain and heartache came welling up and took flight. Impulsively, he clutched her to him, opened his mouth to hers and drowned his sorrows in their kiss.

Just as suddenly, he came to. He pushed her back, held her at arm's length and stared at her with something close to horror. Annie reached out to soothe his agitation but Jim lurched to his feet in such panic he sent her sprawling. She tried to grab him but he turned away and, without looking back, ran out into the night.

'Jim . . .'

It was no use, he'd gone. Annie sat up and stared at the entrance, praying he'd reappear. Minutes passed before she drew her knees up, wrapped her arms round her legs and tried to rock away a rush of regret. Eventually, she hauled herself onto the bed without bothering to undress.

She awoke with a start from a dream she couldn't remember.

Just one image, a big black catfish trapped in a shallow pool underneath a broken bridge, its shiny back breaking the surface of the water as it thrashed about. She checked her watch. It was already way past nine. She'd slept much longer than usual.

She stepped from the cave and blinked in the bright sunlight for a moment, waiting for her eyes to adjust, before she stretched and opened herself up to the warmth of another cloudless day. She caught a flicker of movement at the side of the track.

'He's gone.'

Annie stiffened. 'What do you mean?'

'Just what I bloody well said. Gone. Buggered off. I just bumped into Tobias down the track. He was up on the top ridge at sparrow fart this morning and spotted him way down at the far end. Thought he might have just gone for a walk. There's no bloody sign of him anywhere.'

Annie stepped quickly to her father's side and stuck out her hand. 'Give me the key for the ute. Quick!'

'What the hell's going on here?'

'Just give me the key. I'll tell you later.'

'What's wrong with right now?'

Annie boiled over. 'Look, it's my car, for Christ's sake. Give me the bloody key!'

Nonplussed, Fred pulled a face, fished in his pocket and handed it over. 'I was just gonna go myself . . .'

'Leave it to me,' said Annie.

She ran to the ute, jumped in and tore away, bumping and grinding down the track. Fred watched her out of sight, turning over a couple of scenarios that sprang irresistibly to mind. He picked up a gibber and hurled it angrily away at nothing in particular.

Annie stamped on the brakes when she hit the road. Which way? The answer took her flat out in the direction of the Towers, praying intuition hadn't failed her.

When she got to the outskirts of the town she was figuring maybe it had. Unless he'd managed to hitch a lift, she should have caught up with him miles back. She brought the ute to a shuddering halt outside the first pub she could see.

She had no luck in the first two, but she found him in the third. The morning boozers brightened up a lot when she stepped through the door. All except one, and Annie crumpled when she saw him. Sitting at a small table in the darkest corner, he was already a hunched and pickled mess. She let go of the door and it closed behind her with a loud, pneumatic hiss.

Jim still hadn't seen her. He probably couldn't see more than three feet in front of his face anyway. All eyes on her, Annie weaved through the tables, and slipped into the chair beside him. Jim looked up, toppled over with the effort and fell against her. She whispered in his ear.

'I'm so sorry, Jim . . . I can't tell you.'

Wobbling, he pulled away to look at her. He gave her a bleary nod of recognition and dismissed her with his hand as if it didn't matter a bit.

The barman eyed them with weary distaste. He was a short ginger-bearded tub of lard with only one good eye. The other one was full of milky cataract. Annie stared him down until he turned away and began racking some clean glasses.

Four o'clock that afternoon, Jim was sitting on the narrow ledge directly under the waterfall down on the creek below the caves. Eyes closed, his face upturned to the cold, clear flow, he was willing the water to wash away his shame. Annie was sitting in the shallow pool in front of him, still adding up the damage she'd done.

Fred was watching from the bank, half bemused, half worried sick. Since Jim had been sober enough to understand what was being said to him, Fred had made light of the whole thing and restricted himself to a few mild digs. Now, another one sprang to mind.

'This is what they mean by stone cold sober . . .'

It did the trick, it made Jim smile to himself. Fred eyed his daughter with a look that said she still had some explaining to do.

'I'll head on up and put the billy on.'

Annie gave nothing away. 'We'll be up soon.'

When he'd gone, Jim finally conquered his shame enough to stick his head out of the tumbling water. He quickly looked away again but she summoned his eyes back to her face.

'Jim, I'm sorry. Don't know what got into me.'

Jim just stared back, unblinking and apparently emotionless. But the water had washed away most of the booze. He was sobering fast and seeing her in a very different light. He eased himself off the ledge into the pool in front of her.

'Me too, Annie. More than I can say.'

She tried to smile. But all she managed was a nervous flutter at the corners of her mouth.

'I . . . I, uh . . . Look, Annie, it's just that . . .'

Annie pressed her finger to his lips to save him the trouble. She didn't particularly relish the idea of hearing what might have followed anyway.

'There's no need to explain. I understand. It was my fault, not yours. You got shickered, now you're sober.' She managed to smile this time. 'I hope.'

That evening, Fred and Annie made sure Jim had a bellyful of food and got him to bed good and early. Fred stayed with him to yarn for a while and, at the first sign of drowsiness, took his leave. But Jim had something to get off his chest.

'I'm afraid the larder tin's light a few dollars . . .'

Fred gave him a grin and chuckled. 'Yeah, I know. Doesn't matter, mate. It's your dough anyway.'

Knees drawn up, arms round her legs, Annie was sitting by the fire staring at its dying embers when her father plonked down beside her.

'How is he?'

'Out for the count.'

Fred picked abstractedly at a callus on his hand and silently contemplated the glowing coals himself for a while, getting a line on his thoughts. Then he reached over and patted his daughter's arm.

'Sorry I got after you, love. I'm a bit blinkered these days. Got a bit of a one-track mind. I think I know how you feel. Put the rest out to pasture and he's a good man, real good. Time'll do the trick, I reckon.'

Annie gave her father a grateful look and shrugged. 'It's okay. It was my fault anyway.'

'Oh, I dunno,' said Fred. 'Might have done him a favour in the long run. He'll come through, I betcha.' He put his arm round her and gave her a kiss on the cheek. 'Don't go blaming yourself, that's all.'

With a pale, grateful smile, Annie hugged him back. 'Thanks, Dad.'

# Thirty-Eight

Jim stirred at first light. He was up on top of the mountain in time to see the sun soar into view. As its pale rays raced across the distant ridges and dissolved the bush shadows below him, he asked God to spare him.

His religion was close to Fred's. Simply ground into him by years of living on the land and dealing with the seesaw odds on offer. Tommy Douglas once told him 'Hughie' was in everything, animate and inanimate. Years later, when his mother set him an essay on the subject, he went through five pages of his exercise book in an attempt to square Tommy's Aboriginal ideas with what they told him on the family's occasional visits to church in Longreach. He was pleased with his effort. Elizabeth gave him eight out of ten for subject matter, five out of ten for neatness.

Years later, when his own children wanted to know what was what, he summed it up in a phrase or two. Tony's fevered intellect pounced. At dinner the following night, with all the solemn gravity his fifteen years could muster, he announced that, having duly consulted the theology and philosophy sections of his encyclopaedia, he'd come to the conclusion his old man was a pagan.

Now, as Jim watched the sun come up, offering silent prayers for Rachel's soul and his own deliverance, that phrase or two came back to him. Alone on a ridge in the middle of nowhere, surrounded on all sides by seamless bush, he spoke it loud and clear, willing his prayers to travel as far as the eye could see.

'God is alive and well and living in everything. We are everything, all the time, everywhere . . .'

When he began his scrambling descent to the caves, hoping to have the billy on by the time Fred and Annie woke up, every stick and stone seemed urgently to confirm his sudden conviction that the time had come. He must and would go home.

341

He made it in good time. He had the billy boiling when Fred and Annie finally appeared. Breakfast passed without reference to the previous day's events. Only when it was over did Jim broach the subject himself.

'I want to thank you both, for yesterday. I felt like a real dingo going to sleep last night. It won't happen again, I can promise you that.'

'No harm done,' said Fred. 'Don't worry about it.'

'Well, thanks anyway. I think some good may have come of it.'

'What's that then?'

'Reckon it's time to make a push for home.'

'When?'

'Couple of days maybe.'

Fred glanced at Annie but she didn't bat an eyelid. His old heart went out to her nevertheless. He spoke for them both.

'Well, that's good news and bad. Good for you, bad for us. Sort of got used to having you around. Have to put up a vacancy sign.'

Jim laughed and looked at Annie. 'I'll miss you both, too, don't worry. Very much.'

Annie couldn't cope. She gathered their plates and mugs and disappeared into the cave. Fred watched her go. Then he turned back to Jim with a knowing eye.

'She'll miss you the most, mate. Go easy on her.'

Jim dropped his eyes for a moment, then raised them to his old friend's weather-beaten face. 'She's a good girl, Fred. Don't think I don't know it.'

Fred patted Jim's shoulder and slapped his hat on his head. 'Well, I'm off.'

'Where to?'

'Ravenswood. There's a bloke there with a couple of old generators going cheap. Reckon I might need one up here when I hit that vein. Whack a pneumatic on that back wall. Bastard's wearing me to a frazzle.'

'*When* you hit the vein?' said Jim, with a smile. 'Not *if*?'

Fred gave him a cheeky nod of confirmation. 'No *if* about it, mate. Just a matter of time.'

'I'll come too, if you like,' Jim offered. 'Check them over for you.'

'No, it's okay. Clive's an old mate. He wouldn't flog me a bodgie job.'

Jim spent the entire morning in the work cave, going as hard

342

as he could to sweat the last traces of booze out of his system. After lunch, he went straight back to the rock face and got stuck in again. He'd been at it for an hour when Annie strolled in. He downed the pick for a welcome breather. All through lunch he'd felt awkward. He kept their conversation well away from anything to do with each other. Still feeling the same awkwardness, he flicked the sweat off his brow and waited for her to speak. He needn't have worried. Annie was right on the edge of her own feelings and not about to linger.

'I'm just going down to the creek to wash a few things.'

'Okay, I'll stick on here.'

For a long time after she headed out, Jim simply stared at the entrance. Until he left, he would have to handle her with care. He wouldn't hurt her for all the tea in China. Only when she reappeared for a moment, on the far side of the clearing, did he seize the pick, take a deep breath and resume his fight with the rock face.


Annie felt jaded. She couldn't get Jim out of her mind. A couple of times she sensed he was in the scrub, coming down to join her. She put it down to wishful thinking. Now, apart from the crescendo of insects, all was still. She made a neat pile of the wet clothes on the scrubbing rock, stood up and stripped off.

Her sixth sense hadn't deceived her. From the opposite bank, a pair of mean eyes were watching her at work. Now, as she stood naked to the sun for a moment and began to move round to the pool, those eyes glittered with lust.

Annie eased herself into the pool and lay back in the shallow water. It barely covered her body. She closed her eyes and lost herself, tried to shut down her thoughts altogether. She concentrated on the dance of light behind her lids.

She'd only taken a couple of steps towards her clothes when a gruff voice spoke behind her.

'What's the rush?'

Annie froze. She quickly covered herself with her hands, spun round and blanched with fright. A prematurely-balding, brawny man in his mid-twenties was on the opposite bank and his Remington .22 was pointing straight at her. Lips peeled back, he jumped easily across and came towards her. The bulge in his pants left Annie in no doubt. She spun again and made a move for her clothes, but the sound of the bolt working the rifle's breech made her freeze and her legs began to shake.

'That's it, beautiful. Like I said, what's the rush?'

Without turning round, Annie made a desperate attempt to get him to talk. 'What are you doing here?'

'What's it to you?'

'Just wondered.'

'Shooting 'roos. Haven't seen one all day.' He poked Annie hard in the buttock with the rifle and laughed. 'Too busy lookin' at you, sweetheart.' Perversely, he had a nice, light laugh.

'My father, up the hill . . . He'll hear me if I yell . . .'

In the silence that followed, she had to fight the urge to turn. Suddenly, she felt the muzzle of the rifle right behind her ear and his voice dropped to a hoarse, excited whisper.

'Get down!'

Annie made no move to comply and he jabbed her skull so hard it made her ear ring.

'Get down, I said! Now!'

Slowly, still trying to cover herself, Annie sank to her knees and dropped her head. The shooter stuck the rifle under her chin and forced her head back up. She closed her eyes and refused to look at him. This time, he jabbed her hard in the throat and it made her choke with fright.

'Open your fuckin' eyes. I've got something to show you.'

He made her watch. He unbuckled his pants and let them fall. He pulled off his briefs.

'On your back.'

Annie flinched and then relaxed. It was time to take a gamble.

'Okay,' she said. 'Okay.' She looked up at him with an expression of sweet surrender, and pleaded for mercy. 'Just don't hurt me. Please. Please just let me go when you've finished.'

The shooter smirked. 'Anything you say, sweetheart.'

In the instant he eased the pressure of the muzzle on her neck, Annie made her move. She twisted sideways, grabbed the barrel with both hands, wrenched it back over her shoulder and let go an ear-splitting scream as the rifle went off.

Jim froze in mid-swing. In seconds flat, he was charging down through the scrub like a mad bull.

The shooter dropped his rifle and went after Annie with his fists. He grabbed her hair, pulled her head back and gave her a savage, hooking punch on the temple. Annie toppled on her side and clawed at the ground in a desperate attempt to crawl out of reach. The shooter stomped on her hand, tugged her back and punched her again. Near senseless, Annie made another attempt to scramble away but he jumped on her back and heaved on her shoulder to roll her over. Suddenly he heard Jim tearing through the scrub towards them. He dived off Annie and grabbed his rifle just as Jim broke cover.

'Back off!'

Jim stopped dead in his tracks. Keeping the rifle trained, the shooter sneered. He nodded in Annie's direction. 'Want to try for some yourself?'

Helpless, Jim could only stand and stare. He glanced at Annie and took an involuntary step towards her. The shooter checked him.

'Don't move, arsehole, or I'll blow your fuckin' head off.'

Jim turned back to him, his eyes filling with contempt. 'You lay another hand on her and I'll kill you, you rotten mongrel.'

The shooter spread his legs and braced himself.

'Have a go if you like.'

As the two men locked eyes, each waiting for the other to make a move, Annie shook the fuzziness out of her head and began inching towards the shooter's back on her hands and knees. He was so intent on Jim he didn't notice. But Jim did.

'You yellow-bellied creep. Without that Remington you're nothing.'

Anger clouded the shooter's eyes. 'Real smart arse, aren't you, shitface.' He brought the rifle to his shoulder and took aim at Jim's right knee. 'That's gonna cost you a leg.'

Annie was close enough now. She lunged forward and swung her arm up between the shooter's spreadeagled legs and got hold of his balls. He yelped with pain and fright and the rifle went off. But Jim dodged as Annie struck. The bullet whistled off the rocks behind him.

Doubled over, the shooter panicked. He clubbed at Annie with the rifle then brought it to bear on Jim again. But Annie jumped on his back, snaked her arm round his throat and pulled his hair as hard as she could. Quickfire, the shooter sank his elbow into her side. He shook her off and she fell to her hands and knees gulping air. But the shooter's time was up. Jim barrelled into him with the fury of a force-ten gale.

The rifle went flying as the two men tumbled to the ground, thrashing, kicking and clawing at each other. The shooter was a mean and dirty fighter and his young man's strength took Jim by surprise. He opened his mouth over the fleshy part of Jim's shoulder and sank his teeth in up to the gums. Jim clutched at it in agony and the shooter wriggled out from under him and lunged for the rifle. Annie beat him to it but he grabbed it before she could do anything.

Blood oozing from his shoulder, Jim grabbed a river rock the size of his fist. The shooter wrenched the rifle away from Annie, spun round and shot from the hip. In the millisecond before the pin hit the cap, Annie whacked the barrel and the bullet seared across Jim's forearm without breaking the skin. It felt like a scald. White-hot pain exploded behind Jim's eyes and rocked him back to his heels. He shook his head, sucked air through clenched teeth, lunged forward and slammed the stone against the shooter's temple. There was a horrible crunching sound. As the shooter went down, blood gushed from his ear. He writhed in the dirt like a fish on a river bank, his facial muscles twitching out of control. Suddenly, his legs pistoned, locked stiff as ramrods, and he began to quiver violently from head to foot. Blood flooded from his ear and nose. Slowly, too slowly for the two of them watching, his body sagged and lay still.

Jim dropped to his knees, tore open the shooter's shirt and began frantically to pump his heart. He pumped hard and harder and harder until Annie's hand pulled gently at his shoulder.

'It's no go, Jim. He's had it.'

Jim fell back on his ankles and stared at the shooter in disbelief. Just a few minutes ago he'd been happily picking away at the back wall of the work cave, contemplating the best way to go about contacting the family he'd deserted, wondering if he should telephone or just walk in out of the blue and hope for the best.

Now, at a bat of an eyelid, he was plunged back into chaos. It wasn't the first time he'd killed a man. But in Vietnam none of them had ever looked quite as dead as this. Annie left her hand on his shoulder for a moment, then withdrew it, and walked back to the scrubbing rock to pull on her clothes. As the possible consequences chased each other through Jim's mind, he buried his face in his hands. When he took them away, the sight before him made him gag and gulp for air. Jim got up, retrieved the man's pants, and set about pulling them back on the inert form. He worked fast, desperate to restore some semblance of normality, as if he could bring the shooter back to life.

Annie watched in silence. She couldn't help him. She couldn't have laid a finger on the man at that moment if you'd paid her. Jim did up the shooter's belt. He stood up and turned to Annie. They simply locked eyes in silent recognition of what they had done. A shadow fell across their lives. Slowly, helplessly, they came together in a long, tight embrace, each trying to soothe the other's shock and distress.

'What are we going to do?' she whispered.

Jim glanced down at the shooter's body. Already, regiments of ants were streaming all over him and a couple of blow-flies were busily exploring his gaping mouth.

'We'll have to report it.'

Annie's eyes filled with tears. 'Oh, Jesus. I can't believe it. I just can't believe it . . .'

Jim placed his hands on her shoulders and waited for it to pass. 'Help me get him up on my shoulder. I'll carry him up to the caves.'

'We should leave him here, if we're going to report it.'

Fighting his own agitation, Jim kept his voice calm. 'It'll be at least four hours, maybe five, before the police can get here. He'll be eaten alive by then. There's some bloody huge goannas in the scrub here. You know that as well as I do. They'll be out here ripping at him the minute our backs are turned.'

Annie pulled out from under his hands and turned to glance at the corpse herself. 'We could bring a tarp down. We could cover him up. Weight it down . . .'

But Jim's mind was made up. 'No, Annie. I'll take him up.'

He stepped back to the shooter, hauled him into a sitting position and, with a fireman's lift, got him up onto his left shoulder. The drag and pressure immediately doubled the pain from the bite on his shoulder. He staggered a couple of steps, adjusting the dead weight to ease it. Then, without another word, he humped the load into the scrub and onto the path leading up to the caves.

Annie hurried after him. Shoving the laundry under one arm, she used her free hand to steady Jim's progress, recoiling every time she was forced to touch the dead man's sulky flesh.

When they got to the clearing, Jim made a beeline for the ute. He worked the bolts on the tailgate, let it drop, heaved the body over the end and clambered up to drag it all the way in. He jumped down, closed the tailgate, climbed into the cab, slammed the door and turned the key.

347

'What are you doing?'

'Nothing. I'm just going to move it into some shade.'

As he climbed out of the cab, his legs turned to jelly and he could hardly lift his feet. Annie took his arm, ushered him into her cave and made him lie down.

'I'll get the medicine tin.'

Outside, her eye fell on the ute. Tobias might show up any minute to see what all the shooting was about. She grabbed a couple of corn sacks and spread them over the body. There was a big coil of four-ply rope hanging nearby and she dragged it down and flung it on top of the sacks. Five minutes later she had the body well hidden under a pile of firewood and half a dozen empty kero tins. Then she returned to the centre cave to collect the old biscuit tin that housed their medical supplies.

The bite on Jim's shoulder was already inflamed and discoloured by bruising. As soon as the first antiseptic evaporated, she poured on another dose, soaked a piece of gauze and taped it in position. Then, squeezing what remained of a tube of burn ointment, she rubbed the lot onto the scald on his forearm. A puffy red welt was coming up along the line of her cheekbone. With care, Jim coated her bruises with a thick film of the cream. Luckily, the skin wasn't broken. They ministered to each other in total silence. They were too numb to think, let alone talk. But when it was over, there was no getting away from the dead man in the back of the ute.

'We may as well just drive in with him in the back,' said Jim. 'It was an accident, self-defence. The police are only going to want to see where it happened.'

'What if they don't believe us?'

It hit him like a hammer. It hadn't crossed his mind for a second.

'Of course they'll believe us. Look at the wounds we've got.'

'Not bullet wounds.'

Jim held up his arm. 'What about this?'

'Lots of things could have done that, the gridiron, the billy, anything. It's not like either of us has got a hole in us. I know the cops, Jim. They're not always that interested in the obvious. They could just as easily think we got hurt by that bastard trying to defend himself.'

'But that's nonsense.'

'Only you and I know that,' Annie reminded him. 'They're not going to get any statement out of him. Once they come up here and see what we're up to they could make all kinds of assumptions.'

Jim balled his fist. 'For God's sake, Annie, don't make it worse than it is. Of course we've got to report it. I know it's going to blow the lid for Fred, but what else can we do?'

But she'd sown a seed of doubt. And Annie seized on it. She didn't give a damn about the man lying in the back of the ute. As far as she was concerned he'd got what was coming to him. She saw no reason why her life and Jim's and, most of all, her father's should be wrecked as a result.

'We can think about it.'

'What are you suggesting?' he asked quietly.

'Nothing right at this minute, but let's not rush off half-cocked. I agree with you in principle. We should report it. But we owe it to ourselves, and to dad, to have a damn good think about it first.'

Jim continued to stare out at the ute and didn't reply. A plan was already forming in Annie's mind but she knew she was going to have to play Jim very, very carefully indeed.

She figured Tobias would have put in an appearance by now if he was going to. He'd either gone walkabout or simply put the shots down to another one of the shooters they'd all heard in the area from time to time. The echoes would have been more distorted on his side of the mountain. They would have seemed much further away.

Jim wished he could just wake up and dismiss the whole thing as a bad dream. Annie's words had hit home. Fred and Annie had pulled him out of the fire. They had given him a new lease of life, made him face up to himself and the responsibilities he'd walked out on. Now their lives could be torn apart by what he'd done.

He hadn't meant to kill the bastard, but the bastard had certainly meant to kill him. What if the police did question it? Even if they didn't, he could be charged with manslaughter, maybe even go to prison.

Annie was the only witness and she was right. What was Jim doing here anyway, holed up in a cave in the Thirty Mile Range hundreds of miles from home? The shooter probably came from the Towers. He probably had family there. Friends would leap to his defence against the loony prospectors with something to hide.

Annie took his hand. 'He must have left a car down the bottom somewhere . . . Let's go and see if we can find it.'

'What's the point?'

Annie kept her tone calm and deliberate. 'Come on. At least we'll know where it is. We can talk about it on the way.'

Jim shuffled his feet. His confusion was making him angry.

Before he could answer, she turned on her heel and headed for the track.

They found the shooter's car way down at the far end, hidden between two crops of granite overgrown with blackberry bushes. An old Peugot station wagon, hand-sprayed lime green with yellow roof and rims. Its windows were plastered with flashy decals from tourist spots up and down the Sunshine Coast and a couple of idiotic slogans. One said 'You Bumpa My Car, I Smasha Your Face'. All the doors were locked. Jim cursed their lack of foresight in not having checked the dead man's pockets for the keys.

The track was already strewn with late afternoon shadows. Rabbits flashed their white tails as they fled from their approach. A third of the way up, a lithe, grey kangaroo bounded across the track in front of them.

'The one that got away,' Annie muttered.

'What?'

'The one that got away,' she repeated. 'That's what he was doing. Shooting 'roos.'

'Oh.'

Jim could hardly speak. The pain in his shoulder was coursing up his neck and he had a violent headache. He was sick in his heart and wracked with black doubt. But by the time they hit the top and walked into the clearing, Annie's powers of persuasion had done the trick and Jim had agreed, though with the utmost reluctance. If he hadn't owed them so much, he wouldn't have even considered it. If it went wrong, they'd be a damn sight worse off than they were already.

He jumped across the creek and headed for the spot where Annie reckoned the shooter had been hiding to spy on her. He found the footprints and flayed at them with a corn sack, obliterating them in a whirl of dirt, twigs and leaves. He followed them back to the scene of the fight. It wasn't hard to get rid of them. The shooter's hiking boots had deep ripple soles and the furrows they left quickly filled and disappeared into the scrub floor. It was one of the few times in his life Jim thanked the heavens above for the lack of recent rain.

At the scene of the fight he wrapped the corn sack round his hand and propped the Remington rifle against a tree. He found the stone he'd used to club the man, washed it carefully in the creek and hurled it as far as he could into the deepest pool. He used a shovel to scoop up the bloodstained earth from where the shooter's head had come to rest, and tossed it into the creek.

The flush of colour was gone in a moment. He found a few more blood spots leading to the path and did the same. Then, methodically, hypnotically, he set about obliterating all traces of the shooter's footprints on that side of the creek. He deliberately left as many prints of his own and Annie's as possible and walked all over the areas he'd cleared when he'd finished. He found the spot where the bullet had richocheted off the rocks and used another stone to pound and scar it beyond recognition. He meticulously checked over everything, retrieved the shovel, used the sack to pick up the rifle, and headed for the caves. All the way up the path he kept his eyes glued to the ground. He carefully scooped up a few blood spots he found and shovelled them into the scrub.

Numbed, unusually chilled in the early dusk, he joined Annie at the fire. He held the shovel in the flames to burn off any blood that might have got into the metal. Done, he flopped on his back, aching with exhaustion. Annie leaned over and placed a mug by his hand.

'There's some tea . . .'

Neither of them slept a wink all night. At the first glimmer of murky morning light they set off to carry out Annie's plan.

An hour later, Jim brought the shooter's Peugeot to a halt at an S-bend on the side of a hill with an almost sheer two hundred foot drop.

The shooter was belted into the passenger seat beside him and his rifle was on the back seat. Jim had cleaned it thoroughly to wipe out any trace of Annie's fingerprints and then pressed the shooter's clammy hands all over it.

Fifty yards behind, Annie rolled the ute to a stop, pulled on the handbrake and left the engine running. Jim quickly checked the road in both directions. Nothing coming.

He reversed into the middle of the road until the wagon was forty-five degrees to the edge and left it ticking over. He leapt out, dragged the shooter behind the wheel and buckled him up. He grabbed a torn cotton shirt and rubbed down the wheel, the gearshift, the door handles, anything and everything he'd touched. He grabbed the shooter's hands and forced them onto the wheel. Rigor mortis made it hard going but he managed to press the man's fingerprints onto the surfaces. Then, he wrapped his hand in the shirt, released the handbrake and slammed the door. It was one slam too many.

High up on the hill at their backs, a lone bushwalker was camping in the open. Curled up in his sleeping bag, he'd already drowsily dismissed the sound of engines running and drifted back to sleep without bothering to check. But that last slam stirred him up. Annoyed, he sat up to check the road below.

Jim and Annie were behind the station wagon, shoving it towards the edge as fast as they could. They had to be sure it had enough momentum to carry once the front wheels were over. It did. It sailed into space, cartwheeled to the very bottom of the drop and landed on its roof, smashed to smithereens, its front wheels sheered off and bouncing away into the bush.

The bushwalker smiled to himself. Probably ditching an old banger to claim the insurance. He'd done the same thing himself. He was on the point of giving them a yell and a thumbs up but he changed his mind.

Jim and Annie didn't wait another second. They raced back and jumped into the ute. Annie hung a U-ey and they tore away as fast as the old banger would go.

Something about the way they ran and then the U-turn itself wiped the smile off the bushwalker's face. He lunged for his backpack. He just managed to train his binoculars on the back of the ute before it disappeared. He mouthed the number plate to himself and kept repeating it over and over until he'd made a note of it.

Four miles on, Jim and Annie had still passed nothing going in the opposite direction. Jim glanced through the rear window to check the long straight section of road they'd covered.

'Nothing in sight.'

They exchanged a look. Annie took a deep breath and allowed herself a big sigh of relief. Jim saved his for when they made it to the turn-off, hit the end of the track and disappeared from view into the scrub. They still hadn't seen or passed another vehicle.

When they came to a halt at the top of the track, they just sat in the cab and stared across the clearing at the caves, too wound-up and exhausted to make a move. After a long time, they swapped a look, and Jim slipped his arm round her shoulders.

'You all right?'

Annie dipped her head to let it rest on his shoulder for a moment. 'Fine. What about you?'

Jim took a couple of deep breaths and tried to steady his nerves. His heart was going nineteen to the dozen and his stomach was clenched by cramp.

'Mad as a hatter.'

When Fred's old flat-top laboured into view at four o'clock that afternoon, Jim and Annie strolled towards it as casually as possible. A small, scarred and battered ex-Army generator was roped on the back and Fred jumped down from the cab grinning from ear to ear. It froze to his face when he saw his daughter.

'Christ, love! What happened to you?'

Annie shrugged, gave him a grin to make light of it, waved her hand dismissively and spun him the yarn they had ready.

'I took Jim over the other side yesterday to show him the balancing rock and bloody well fell off. Whacked myself on that shelf underneath.'

He put his finger to her chin and turned her head away for a closer look. 'Jesus, you didn't half do yourself. Is it hurting?'

'Not so much today. Jim's been layering it with arnica for me.'

Fred turned to give Jim a nod. 'Good on yer.'

'I see you bought it.'

Jim was wearing a long-sleeved khaki twill shirt in expectation of Fred's any-time arrival. The cuffs flapped open at his wrists but he had it done up in front except for the top button and he'd turned the collar up. It hid his wounds from view, but it didn't go unnoticed.

'He's given me the loan of it for a while.' He nodded at Jim's shirt and gave him a cheeky grin. 'Having a day off, are we?'

Jim smiled back and played along. 'Yeah, figured I'd had enough of slave wages for a while.'

Fred laughed and thumbed the generator. 'Give you a dollar to help me get this lot off.'

'You're on.'

Fred slapped him on the back. 'That's the ticket. By the way, I've got some news for you. Good news I reckon, if you like the sound of it.'

353

Jim slung a look at Annie and waited. Fred began undoing the ropes.

'Clive's brother's a plane mechanic at the Towers. You know, just light aircraft stuff. Does a lot of work for the Aero Club. He's off to Brisbane tomorrow to deliver some rich bugger's Piper that broke down on a trip up here. He was out at Clive's place this morning. I told him I knew a bloke who might like to hitch a ride and he said sure thing. Seemed a good idea at the time, dunno how you feel about it. I figured it'd give you the chance to see Tony, and have a yak.'

Jim didn't risk looking at Annie again. He just accepted on the spot. 'That's terrific, mate. You're dead right. Tony's a good place to start.'

'Probably the hardest, too, I reckon,' said Fred.

Jim dropped his eyes and nodded. 'No two ways about that. Just have to hope for the best.'

Fred slapped his hands together. 'Right then. That's settled. We'll run you in first thing. He wants to be away by nine. Come on, let's haul this nutcracker off before I run out of juice.'

Their last meal together that night was a nightmare. Fred kept up a stream of chat and didn't seem to notice the long silences in between. As it was Jim's last night, he stayed up way past his usual bedtime backtracking over the time they'd spent together, teasing Jim about the legless wreck he'd been on arrival. When Fred finally yawned loudly and announced he was for bed, Jim accompanied him into the cave, bid him a fond goodnight and returned to the fire.

He found Annie sitting on her big old bed in the cave.

'I feel like I'm leaving you in the lurch.'

Annie took his hand. She looked up at him with love in her eyes. 'You'll be well away. If the cops should come sniffing around up here for any reason it just leaves me to play dumb and dad won't know what the hell they're on about. I'll be all right. You're not to worry about me. Just get on with things. I'll be keeping my fingers crossed and . . .' She dropped her eyes and rubbed his hand affectionately. 'And I hope you know I'll be thinking of you. That I'll miss you.'

Jim slowly pulled his hand away and lifted it to brush his knuckles tenderly down her cheek. 'I'll write to you.'

'Better not.'

'But . . .'

'Just keep your eye on the papers. You can bet your sweet life there'll be something if they think there's anything fishy.'

They fell silent then. Finally Jim stood up. She raised her eyes to his. He reached down and took her hands.

'Whatever happens, I want you to know how much I appreciate what you've done for me. God knows how I'd have ended up. If things work out at Balkenna, it'll be you and Fred that made it possible. You're a wonderful woman, Annie. You said so many things at just the right time I . . . Well . . . I just want you to know I won't forget. Ever.'

Annie squeezed his hands and tried to smile. It flickered for a moment and was gone.

'My pleasure.'

She let go of his hands and watched him disappear through the entrance. She undressed, climbed into bed and lay listening to the cries and croaks of the bush by night.

Sleep was painfully slow in coming. It wasn't just the traumatic events of the previous forty-eight hours. She was swamped by a terrible wave of sadness. The only decent man she'd come across in years was going to walk out of her life in the morning and there wasn't a damn thing she could do about it.

Their goodbye was brief. Fred was already in the ute, gunning the motor. Annie declined to accompany them. Fred drummed his fingers impatiently on the steering wheel and watched his old friend give his daughter a long hug and a kiss goodbye. As he set the ute in motion down the track, Jim stuck his head out of the window and looked back. Annie's façade crumbled and she suddenly looked small and frightened. Jim just managed to shout one last farewell before she was lost from view.

'I'll miss you . . .'

Fred chatted all the way into the Towers. Jim held his breath as they approached the fatal S-bend and slowed. It was all he could do not to ask him to pull over so he could jump out and take a look.

At the airport, Fred fished in his pocket and shoved a wad of rock lobsters into Jim's hand.

'There's four hundred nicker there, mate. From Annie and me . . .' He checked himself and grinned. 'Well, from Annie, truth be known. I'm still running on your dough. She wanted you to have it. Didn't fancy the idea of you having to ask Tony for a loan the minute you showed your face.'

Jim immediately passed it back. But Fred was adamant.

'She wanted you to have it, mate. Don't bloody argue. You can send it back to her when you get yourself sorted out, okay?' He grabbed Jim in a long, back-slapping bear hug. 'You look after yourself, you hear? And let us know . . .'

'I will,' Jim promised. 'You know what I owe you.'

Fred stepped back. 'Likewise, mate. We'll settle up some-day. Go on, jump to, or the bugger'll take off without you.'

Half an hour later, Jim was eight thousand feet above the Seventy Mile Range with his forehead pressed to the window glass. From behind the controls, Andy Roberts shot him a glance.

'Looking for something in particular?'

Jim pulled his face away from the glass, grinned and made a joke of it.

'Thought I saw paradise.'

'Didn't we all,' the pilot chuckled. 'I caught a glimpse up in Cairns a couple of weeks ago. Five seven, dark red hair, built like a dream. Only trouble was the bloke with her was six seven, red-faced and built like a lorry. Paradise lost, you might say.'

Jim laughed and turned back to the ranges below. He knew all about paradise lost. It was coming out the other end of the maze that concerned him now. He wished he could make out the spot where, at that very moment, Annie was shading her eyes, gazing up at the tiny plane and wishing him God speed.

# Thirty-Nine

In the back yard of a house in the Brisbane suburb of St Lucia a rowdy Saturday afternoon barbecue was in full swing. Tony and Susan Mackay were putting on their end-of-year Christmas bash. A trestle table offered a big choice of salads and two of Tony's mates in charge of the barbie were shelling out the steaks, chops, sausages and prawns. Everyone was talking at the same time and shuffling their feet to a steady throb of R & B coming from a couple of speakers on the back verandah.

Sitting on the back steps, tapping along to the Little River Band going full bore either side of him, Billy Mackay was murdering a can of 4X. Tony tipped him a wink.

'Go easy, little brother. Don't want a cot-case on my hands.'

'Lay off,' Billy protested. 'This is the only can I've had.'

Tony grabbed his arm and pulled him to his feet. 'Glad to hear it. Go and give Susan a hand to dish out the salad, will you?'

'What for?'

'Because I asked you to.'

Billy pulled a face. 'Bloody hell . . .'

'And lay off the language,' Tony called after him.

Without looking back, Billy stuck up a finger.

Tony chuckled. He was heading for the barbie when a latecomer appeared through the back door.

'Paul! Good on you, mate. Thought you weren't gonna show.'

'G'day, Tone. Got tired of bloody waiting around. Sand-mining scandals . . .' He drew his finger across his throat. 'I've had 'em up to here.'

Tony chuckled and pointed him in the right direction. 'Grab yourself a beer.'

'Yeah. Thanks, mate.' Paul headed for the grog in the garage. 'Oh, by the way. There's a bloke out front wants to see you.'

'Who's that, mate?'

'Search me, didn't say.'

The front door was wide open but there was nobody in sight.

357

Tony stepped out onto the front verandah. The man was standing at the far end, apparently studying the house next door.

'Yeah, what can I do for you?'

The man turned.

Tony slumped against the door frame with shock. 'I don't believe it!'

Jim strode down the verandah and stuck out his hand. He'd shaved his beard off for the occasion. He looked a bit raw and there was a nick on his chin.

'Hello, son. Having a bit of a shindig . . .'

Tony shook hands. But it was purely a reflex action. He pushed past his father and took a few steps down the verandah, stopped to collect himself and turned back. The initial shock had passed.

'Yeah. Christmas party.'

'Susan here?'

His son just stood there glaring at him in disbelief. When he finally answered, his tone was hard and tight.

'Jesus. What a turn up. Yeah, she's here. She lives here. We were married last month.'

Jim didn't know what to say. Then he grinned. 'Congratulations. Bit on the young side though, aren't you?'

Tony's expression didn't falter. 'We don't think so. Anyway, she's up the duff.'

Jim digested the news a moment. Then his smile spread and he stepped forward. 'That's great, Tony. Really great.'

But Tony ducked the embrace.

Jim swallowed hard. 'I knew you two would tie the knot some day.' Then, as if to remind Tony who he was: 'Your mother did too.'

It didn't work.

'Yeah, I know. Pity you weren't around. We could have sent you an invitation.'

Jim took another involuntary step towards him, but Tony stepped back. Jim turned away.

'Look, Tony. I know we've got a lot to talk about . . . A hell of a lot.'

'You can say that again,' Tony snapped.

Jim turned back to him, a desperate appeal in his eyes. 'Let's just take it easy, can we? One step at a time. Your mother would have been very happy about it. You getting married. Having a baby. And I am too.'

Tony glared, but his father's face was suddenly so haunted, he was forced to lower his guard. He didn't really know what to do, but gestured towards the door.

'You want to come in? Billy's out the back.'

That threw Jim for a loop. He stiffened, glanced nervously at the door and shook his head. 'Not now. Don't want to spoil your party.'

Tony didn't press it. His flash of compassion had quickly drowned in another wave of resentment. 'Come back tonight then. This'll be over about six, or seven.'

Jim shook his head again, and attempted to assert himself. 'I'd rather come tomorrow, if that's all right. You'll be a bit worn out tonight, I expect. Will Billy still be here tomorrow?'

'Yeah, he'll be here. But we've all been asked out to lunch. You'll have to come around five or something, unless you want to come in the morning. Have you got a place to stay?'

'Yes,' Jim nodded. 'Don't worry about it.' He stepped forward and placed a hand on Tony's shoulder. 'Five will be fine. Say hello to Susan for me, and Billy . . .' He turned away and headed for the front steps. 'I'll see you then.'

Tony suddenly felt like a lousy cow. 'You can say hello now, if you want to. I'll go and get them . . .'

But it was too late.

'Tomorrow. I'll see you tomorrow.' Jim turned on his heel, strode down the path and out through the gate. Tony watched him disappear up the street and shook his head.

It was hard to believe. His clothes were new. He looked lean and fit, almost as if he'd never been away.

The following evening, Susan broke the uneasy silence.

'I'm sorry we were a bit late. Hope you weren't waiting too long.'

Jim had got there punctually at five and had had to wait half an hour before they turned up. But he let her off the hook.

'Not too long. Where's Billy?'

'Gone to visit a friend. He'll be back later. We haven't told him yet. Tony thought you should talk first.' She turned to him for help. 'Didn't you?'

Tony's reply was resolutely hostile. 'I want to know where the hell you've been, for a start. The police'd probably like to know, too. They've been looking for you for months.'

Jim fidgeted for a minute before he answered. 'Up north,

359

mostly. All over the place. Nowhere in particular.'

'Oh, great. That's a great way to start. Real mine of information.'

Jim bowed his head and stared at the floor. Susan caught Tony's eye and shook her head to call him off. Jim's voice was just above a whisper when he spoke again.

'I don't expect you to forgive me, Tony. I can only ask you to try and understand. I just couldn't bear the thought of going back to Balkenna that day . . . With your mother gone. I don't really know what happened. I just couldn't do it, that's all. Go for me all you want, if it makes you feel any better. It certainly won't make me feel any worse than I do already. I just lost my wheels, that's all. Fred Paterson found me eventually. I'd probably still be out there somewhere but for him . . . And his girl, Annie. I was dead to the world when they took me in.'

There was no trace of self-pity. Just a simple statement of the facts. In the unhappy silence that followed, Tony recoiled from the images that sprang to mind of the road his father had taken. He felt a rush of empathy but he was unable to give it a voice. Irrespective of his motives or his state of mind, his father had walked out and brought untold havoc and misery into their lives.

'Would you like a cup of tea?' Susan asked quietly.

Jim looked up at her and nodded. 'I would, yes. Thanks . . . That'd be good . . .'

She gave him a sympathetic nod, and retreated to the sanctuary of the kitchen.

Jim lifted his eyes back to Tony and decided to get on with it. He hadn't really expected to get very far with him anyway. He didn't blame him. There were a lot of other things he was anxious to know about.

'How come Billy's here?'

Tony suddenly realised that, apart from anything else, his father didn't have a clue what had happened in his absence. He was in for a few shocks. Better go easy and not hit him with everything at once.

'We just thought he should come and stay with me for a bit. He's been going to the school down the road. Doing quite well.'

'And Jack? Is he at home?'

There was no way of avoiding this one. Tony's grumpy reply didn't attempt to disguise his anger. 'Following in your footsteps, you might say . . .'

'What do you mean?'

'What I said. After you pissed off he went up to stay with Athol. They had a row and he took off.'

'What about? What did they row about?'

Tony curled his lip. 'What would you think?'

'About me?'

'Wasn't about the price of Vegemite.'

'Do you know where he is?'

'Yeah . . . Well, I know where he was a couple of months ago. Last time I saw him . . .' He broke off, wondering how best to finish the story.

'Well?' Jim demanded. 'Where is he?'

'Got a job on a property up near Hughenden. He got into a bit of strife and I had to go up and help sort it out. Bail him out, if you really want to know. He was up for D and D.'

'D and D?'

'Drunk and disorderly and . . . well . . . you may as well know, aggravated assault. He beat the shit out of some middle-aged bloke he reckoned tried to touch him up in the pub. Really did him over, took everything out on him. Maybe the bloke did try and muck about with him, I don't know. He certainly paid for it if he did. Me too. He was bound over and I had to divvy up the bloody fine. His boss chipped in with the court costs.'

Jim fought to hold them back, but his eyes brimmed with tears and he quickly buried his face in his hands. Tony's anger wilted on the spot. He dropped an unsteady hand on his father's heaving shoulder. Susan appeared in the door with a tray of tea and biscuits. Tony shook his head and she quickly backed out again.

'Let's go out in the back yard,' he suggested. 'It's a bit stuffy in here.'

Half an hour later, Jim knew it all.

'It's been a bloody nightmare. An absolute bloody nightmare. I mean, have you got any idea? Have you got any idea what you dumped us all in? Mum's death hit us pretty hard too, you know.'

Still reeling from the sorry facts and figures, face to face with the wreckage he'd left in his wake, Jim sank onto the garden bench. Tony gave him a moment to collect himself. Then he walked over and sat down beside him. For a long time they sat in silence, until Jim could summon himself back from the brink.

'I'm here to make amends, Tony. If I can.'

'You'll have a harder time with Jilba. And Jack.'

'I can only try. God knows I'm sorry enough. I don't really have any excuses. I know how you must feel, all of you. I said I don't expect forgiveness. I just hope we can reach an understanding, that's all.'

'Do you want to call Jilba?'

Jim shook his head. 'Don't think I could face it at the moment.'

'I don't mean right this bloody minute. After dinner, maybe.'

'I hadn't planned on staying for dinner.'

'Well, you better. Susan went to a lot of trouble this morning. Lasagne . . .' He reached over and patted his father's knees. 'You like lasagne, don't you?'

Jim offered an edgy smile.

'And you'll give Jilba a ring, okay? She deserves to know as soon as possible. She's been a bloody trojan through all this, much to my amazement. I was gonna call her this morning, but it should come from you.'

Jim's smile grew a bit wider. 'Just need to catch my wind a bit. How is she?'

'Same as usual, gadding about all over the place. Rome, Tokyo, you name it. Earning a bloody fortune. That Danny Serrano bloke's trying to waltz her up the aisle as well but she's holding fire at the moment. Keeps ringing me up to bash my ear about married life. What the hell can I tell her? Bed of roses one minute, bed of nails the next.'

Jim smiled properly this time and, despite everything, Tony was very pleased to see it.

'That bloke from New York you and mum used to know was out here. Round about June I think it was. He went all the way up to Longreach to visit mum's grave.'

Jim's smile vanished. 'Dean Coulter?'

'Yeah. He was staying at the bloody Sheraton. I had a couple of drinks with him after he came back. Nice bloke. It was nice of him to go all that way. To pay his respects . . .'

Mortified by the thought that Coulter had been at Rachel's graveside before him, Jim's voice dropped to a whisper. 'Yes . . . It was . . .'

Tony was sorry he'd brought it up. He flung his arm round his father's shoulders and gave him a quick squeeze.

'Hey now, come on. Don't get down in the dumps again. I know all about it. Jilba told me. He couldn't have been nicer. He was really worried about you. Said if there was anything he could do, anything at all, just to give him a call.'

Jim tried to put Dean Coulter to the back of his mind. He studied the ground and tapped his fingertips. He felt trapped, caught between two worlds of problems no man could ever solve.

'You all right? You've gone as white as a sheet.'

Jim rubbed his knees, took a deep breath. 'Yeah, I'm okay. Just a bit much to take in all at once.'

Susan came to the back door and gave them a shout. 'Tony, do you two gentlemen want a drink before dinner?'

Tony gave her a wave. 'Okay, we'll be in in a minute.'

She waved back and returned inside. Jim gave Tony a fatherly smile. 'She looks well, mate.'

'Bearing up,' Tony grinned. 'There's a way to go yet. She'll be okay. She's as strong as an ox.'

'Didn't expect to be a grandfather quite so soon. It's the best bit of news I could have come home to.'

Tony held his father's eyes. He still had mixed feelings about his sudden reappearance and they were confused by a flood of memories. Only his mother had ever understood his wish for a different kind of life. Her sudden death had left him high and dry.

Tony had called his father every name under the sun for his vanishing act and continued to do so through all the harrowing months that followed. Now he was sitting right beside him, and it was almost as if he'd never been away, almost as if his mother might appear at any moment too. There was no denying the genuine delight that lay behind his father's simple words. Whatever the gulf between them, he was his father. Even when they'd been most fiercely at loggerheads over his rejection of Balkenna, he'd always held a basic respect for Jim. That respect had vanished when he did.

'I'm glad to hear it. We're going to need all the babysitters we can get.'

'Daaaaaad!'

Billy Mackay hurtled down the back steps, jumped the last four and came racing towards them. No recriminations here, he was just thrilled to bits. Jim jumped up, opened his arms and Billy bounded into them, hugging his father for all he was worth. It was so pure, so joyful, so artless, Tony got a lump in his throat you could choke on. He eased himself off the bench and patted his father's shoulder. 'See you inside.'

Holding Billy off the ground, rolling this wriggling ball of arms and legs from side to side, Jim gave his eldest son a nod in return.

# Forty

It was Christmas Day four days later. Jim was sitting with his other son in the cab of a Dodge pick-up truck on the southern bank of a branch of the Flinders River, just north of Hughenden. Jack made Tony's welcome seem mild by comparison. He listened to his father's weary explanation with an air of bored indifference. He didn't look at him once. Now, as he dried up, Jim studied his son for any sign of give.

'That's all there is. There's nothing more to tell. I'm sorry, Jack, I couldn't be sorrier. Whatever the reasons, I was wrong, and if you think I haven't learnt that the hard way, you're very much mistaken.'

It was late afternoon. Jack just continued staring at the river gum shadows fanning across the muddy surface flowing by below. When it came, his reply was icy cold.

'Forget it.'

'Not much chance of that,' Jim muttered.

'That's your problem.'

For a split second, Jim bridled at his impudence and he nearly cuffed him. He waited for it to pass.

'It's our problem, mate. You're my son.'

'Pity you didn't think of that before you pissed off.' He wasn't giving an inch.

Jim took a deep breath and said it again. 'Your mother was my whole life, Jack. It just fell apart and I couldn't put it back together, for a long, long time.'

'You been to her grave?'

It was so sudden, so perfunctory, it completely took the wind out of Jim's sails.

His visit to Rachel's grave the day of his return had torn him apart, yet, in a peculiar way, it completed the catharsis that had begun with the words of a song unwittingly sung to him by a total stranger at Gray Creek, south of Greenvale.

He had hesitated at the cemetery's iron gate, wondering if he had the strength to go through with it. Weaving through the headstones, terrified of coming to the place. Seeing her name. The shrivelling, suffocating heat of the mid-afternoon sun as he stood stock still and read the inscription Jilba had chosen on behalf of the family that ended with a quotation from Wordsworth: 'There Hath Passed Away a Glory From the Earth.' Squatting, then sitting by her grave, his tears had slowly subsided till he felt at peace.

As he had taken his leave, a brief breeze scudded across the cemetery and swayed the little cluster of wild flowers growing on one side of her headstone. As if she were waving him good-bye. He'd closed the gate behind him knowing she had given him a new lease of life.

'Well?' Jack demanded.

'Yes. I did. Before I went back to the house.'

'Not before time.'

Again, Jim had to fight a desire to thump him. Instead, he agreed. 'You're right. Not before time. There's a lot of things I have to put right. That's why I'm here.'

'You shouldn't have bothered,' Jack snapped. 'I'm fine.'

Another silence fell. Jack continued staring through the windscreen, adamantly refusing to give his father his attention. Jim waited, he gave him a chance, but nothing came. It was time to stop beating about the bush.

'I'm going home. Back to Balkenna.'

Jack just snorted. 'Too late, Dad.'

'I'll need all the help I can get.'

Jack snorted again. 'You should have thought of that before you left. I'm on contract to Mr Carter.'

'I'll speak to him,' Jim offered, keeping his tone conciliatory. 'I'm sure he'll understand.'

'He paid my costs when I had to go to court. I'm paying him back out of my wages.' For the first time since they'd pulled up, Jack turned and looked his father in the eye, as if he didn't want to miss the shock value of the punchline. 'I was up for aggravated assault.' He was disappointed with the result.

'Yes,' Jim acknowledged quietly. 'I know. Tony told me all about it. I'll pay off what you owe.'

'Rather do it myself.' But Jack's glare dimmed a bit and there was a slight quaver in his voice. Jim sensed a chink in his son's hard hide and held his tongue. Jack turned back to the river again. 'When are you going back?'

Jim dropped his hand on Jack's shoulder, and gave it a squeeze. 'Not until you come too.'

Jack flinched, pulled away and immediately turned the key in the ignition. He wrenched it into reverse and dropped the handbrake.

'I've got to get the truck back now, okay?'

Jim leaned across and switched it off. 'I want you to come home with me, Jack.'

Angrily, Jack pulled his father's hand away. 'What the hell for? So I can sit around wondering if you've done another bunk every time you're half an hour late or something? Tim's there. Work it out with him.'

'I already have.'

Jack's curiosity got the better of him. 'What did he say?'

'Not a lot. You know what he's like. Looked like a stunned mullet when I knocked on his door. He's done a helluva job in the circumstances, that's for sure. If anyone was going to read me the riot act about the place, it should've been him. But he didn't. Just started bashing my ear about what needed to be done.'

Jack couldn't help it. The picture made him laugh. He quickly choked it off, but the damage was done. Jim jumped in to the thaw.

'He'd like you to come and give us a hand too.'

Jack started her up again, looked over his shoulder and began to back away from the river. 'I'll have to think about it. Right now I've got to get the truck back.'

'Fine,' Jim agreed. 'I'll come back with you and have a word with Mr Carter.'

Jack stamped on the brake so hard he nearly threw their necks out.

'You weren't listening. I said I'd have to think about it.'

Jim raised his hands in surrender. 'Okay, okay, okay. Drop me back at the hotel then.'

Jack hit the accelerator, backed up some more, wrenched the truck through a grinding turn and bucked away across the trackless stretch of country that would bring them to the road into Hughenden. He thrashed through the gears like a rally driver. Jim didn't mind a bit. He smiled quietly to himself and figured he'd made some good solid progress.

Three days later he wasn't so sure. Jim had spent a sleepless night, tormented by a plague of warring voices. Now, as he groggily came to, they came back to bombard him again.

Jilba's tongue-lashing was still ringing in his ears. After the first shock and relief of hearing his voice, she chastised him royally for the pain he'd caused them. She sounded so cold and disaffected, he put Tony on the line to finish explaining where he'd been and why.

He went out onto the front verandah to wait until it was over. When Tony finally joined him, there wasn't much comfort in his assurance that she was as stunned as he had been and she'd come round in time. In fact, she called back an hour and a half later with a half-hearted apology.

The following day brought a confrontation with Sergeant Archie Newman when he reported to the police station as soon as his plane landed in Longreach. Archie didn't take too kindly to his explanation. Nevertheless, he was forced to accept it. He advised Jim he would take the necessary steps to have him removed from the missing persons list. But his cranky recital of all the trouble and paperwork they'd been put through left Jim in no doubt about his feelings and only increased the sense of shame he took with him to the interview and carried away on the long walk to the cemetery.

At dinner time both the previous evenings he'd called Jack at the Carter place only to suffer further rebuffs. He rolled out of bed thinking there was nothing for it but to go out there and take him on face to face again. It was a double-edged sword. He couldn't go home without him. Yet, if Jack persisted, he would have to or his tentative plans for Balkenna would suffer the consequences.

Still mulling it over, he applied a liberal lather of shaving soap and began scraping at his stubble, wondering if he should let his beard grow back to save the trouble. By the last couple of scrapes down his neck, he decided he didn't mind the ritual so much after all and it was good to see what he actually looked like for a change. Suddenly, he had the weird sensation that the eyes in the mirror were not his own. All he could see was the shooter writhing on the ground. He recoiled from the image but it wouldn't let go. He saw the man's quivering reach its peak in that last long horrendous shudder as the life ran out of him. The spasm was so violent he could hardly breathe. Gripping the basin fiercely, he braced himself and waited for the shakes to subside. Then he staggered to the bed.

Tony Mackay yawned and scratched his head as he headed

down the front path in his dressing-gown to check the letter box. There were four letters. He wandered back to the house shuffling them for inspection. One caught his eye in particular and, as he mounted the front steps, he ripped it open and scanned the contents. They stopped him in mid-stride. Susan was dressed for work and downing her second cup of tea when he came in and offered the letter in amazement.

'You're not going to believe this. Dad's paying off our mortgage. He says it's a wedding present.'

Thunderstruck, Susan just gaped at him and slowly took the letter. When she'd read it, she looked back up and shook her head. Then she beamed with delight, looked down and patted her belly. 'You hear that, junior? Your grandfather's a weird and wonderful man.'

Jim figured a good breakfast might help. All through the meal, he pondered the best way to get Jack on side. When he finished, he decided to go straight on out to the Carter place.

He walked across the yard at the back of the hotel and climbed into one of Balkenna's few remaining assets, the Ford station wagon. Tim's meticulous account of items sold and sums received to keep the wolf from the door had made pretty depressing reading and, on the long drive to Hughenden, Jim's head teemed with all the financial complexities of any attempt to salvage Balkenna from the ashes.

A visit to his new bank manager to arrange Tony's mortgage had left him in no doubt whatsoever on that score. In the first place, it had been acutely embarrassing. Word of his return had spread through the town like wildfire and, as soon as he announced himself, the bank's employees all turned out to stare at him. After half an hour in the manager's office he felt only marginally more at ease.

Wally Jenkins turned out to be as Will Mackenzie had promised. One of his kind. He went over the figures with the utmost courtesy. Which was just as well. They were bad enough on their own. Any attitude on top would have been intolerable. Jenkins seemed to recognise immediately that Jim had taken the damage squarely on his own shoulders and was not about to lay blame at anyone else's door. The proceeds of resumption and forced sale that Ralph Kidd had forwarded to Jim's account would cover Tony's mortgage. With interest accrued in his long absence, he had just over two hundred and fifty thousand dollars. A big pile to most people, chicken-feed to a grazier with the problems he faced.

The grim mathematics rose up to mock him again as he slammed the car door and produced another flutter of nerves. He gripped the wheel, breathed evenly and concentrated on the immediate task ahead. He was about to hit the road when the back door opened and something thudded onto the back seat. Startled, he turned in time to see his son toss a rucksack in beside the canvas bag. Jack plonked into the passenger seat and slammed the door. He didn't even look at Jim.

'Let's go.'

'I was just on my way out to see you.'

'So I've saved you a trip. Let's go, for Christ's sake.'

'Home?'

Jack pulled a face. 'Where else? That's what you want, isn't it?'

'Too right.'

'Well, get on with it.'

With a surge of relief, Jim studied his son's truculent profile for a minute, then he squeezed his shoulder and left his hand there.

'Good on you, mate. I'll have to go and get my things and settle up. Do you want to come in?'

But Jack was a long way from letting bygones be bygones. He rolled down the window, stuck his arm out and drummed his fingers on the roof.

'I'll wait here.'

'What about Mr Carter?'

'What about him? He said it's all right and I said you'd send him the money. So you better.'

'Of course I will. We can stick a cheque in the post before we leave.'

'Whatever you like. Just as long as he gets it.'

Jim squeezed his shoulder again. 'Sit tight. I'll be as quick as I can.'

He walked casually across the yard and into the hotel. As soon as the door closed behind him, he went like a rocket, terrified he might return to find Jack vanished as suddenly as he'd appeared. In five minutes flat, he jumbled his gear into his suitcase, paid the bill, and breathed a big sigh of relief when he hurried into the yard again to find Jack as he had left him.

Half an hour later, they left the bitumen southwest of

Hughenden for the long, hot, dusty drive on the unsealed road to Winton. Except for his grumbled thanks when Jim sent Carter's cheque down the chute, Jack remained mean, moody and silent. Jim didn't press it. He was just glad to have him beside him.

A little over two hours later, as they left the outskirts of Corfield behind, Jim cautiously floated his next move.

'I want to call into Glenmore and see Athol on the way through.'

'Whatever you like,' said Jack.

Jim paused diplomatically before continuing. 'Tony told me about your row with him. It'd be good to straighten things out.'

'Makes no difference to me. I'll wait in the car.'

'I'm sure he'd like to see you, no matter what happened.'

Jack didn't bother to reply. Jim was about to prompt him again but thought better of it and let it rest.

As it turned out, they drove all the way to Glenmore only to discover Athol was in Winton for a stockyard sale. When they got to Winton Jack insisted he'd wait in the pub.

Jim's reunion with Athol Ferguson was fraught. Initially stunned by the tap on the shoulder, Athol responded in a friendly enough manner. But he made no attempt to hide his low opinion of Jim's behaviour. He went to great pains to explain the exact nature of his row with Jack and left Jim in no doubt as to who he felt was really to blame.

'I understand how you must have felt, Jim. Of course I do. You disappointed me, that's all.'

That cut. All Jim had to offer was his repentance. 'I'm over the hump, Athol, and I'm ready to knuckle down. There's a lot of work to do . . .'

'No doubt about that. I did what I could at the time but it was a bit out of my league and I had enough problems of my own at Glenmore.'

'Yes, I know,' said Jim. 'Tony gave me the drum on the whole business. I'm thankful for all the support you gave them.'

'Didn't amount to much in the long run.'

As they listened to the quick-fire calls of the auctioneer and watched the sale of a yard full of heifers, Jim tentatively outlined his scheme for regaining the leases filched in his absence.

'Maybe you should just hang onto what you've got and be thankful for that,' Athol suggested, with unusual prudence.

But Jim shook his head. He wouldn't rest until he'd dealt with all the consequences of his actions. To restore Balkenna to its pre-resumption holding would also, hopefully, restore his family's trust. Athol nodded and then, to Jim's dismay, he excused himself from further talk. Jim was just going to ask him back to the pub for a drink with Jack in an attempt to heal the rift.

'It is good to see you, Jim. I mean that. This scheme of yours sounds a bit hare-brained to me but if you still have your old determination I'm sure you'll pull it off. Let's hope so, anyway. I'm afraid I'm not in a position to involve myself in Balkenna as I did before.'

Jim's face went white. 'I wouldn't dream of asking you,' he countered stiffly. 'My debt to you was paid a long, long time ago, with interest. I certainly wouldn't want to be in that position again. Not that I wasn't grateful. You know I was. Or you ought to. As far as I'm concerned the best part of all that was our friendship. I always thought you felt that too . . .'

Athol immediately regretted his remark. He was, he decided, getting old and the heat was killing him. But he was not above an apology when it was due.

'Sorry. Thoughtless. I'm getting a bit long in the tooth for sudden surprises. You're a turn-up for the books, Jim. Don't hold it against me.'

Jim was only too happy to brush it aside.

Athol glanced at his watch. 'Look, Jim, I'll have to go. I'm late already.'

Jim offered his hand. 'Go for your life. I'll call you in a couple of days.'

As Athol shook hands, he gave Jim a long, hard look that eventually softened into a slight smile.

'It is good to see you, Jim. In spite of everything. Sorry if I was a bit rough earlier on. Bit slow off the mark these days. I certainly didn't expect to bump into you here, that's for sure.'

Jim was slow to release his grip. 'No. I understand. I'm very glad we did.'

Jim watched him go with mixed feelings. Suddenly, Athol stopped. 'Look, Jim. Just quickly . . . This scheme of yours . . . I've got around four hundred head of second-stringers to offload. If it's any help I could let you have them. Buy now, pay later. When you get yourself sorted out. Give it some thought . . .'

Jim was completely taken aback. Athol acknowledged his surprise with a quick smile and hurried away through the crowd before he could reply. Jim watched him go the second time with no mixed feelings at all.

But the warm glow of friendship he carried back to the pub didn't last long. Jack was perched on a stool at the bar, toying with an empty glass. He watched his father's approach in the mirror behind the bar without turning.

'My shout.'

'No thanks.' Jack turned and gave his father a quick up-and-down. 'Well?'

'Whenever you're ready,' Jim muttered.

Jack dumped his glass, swung off the stool and headed for the door.

# Forty-One

The house loomed ghost-like in the twilight, its burnt-out wing bearing mute testimony to catastrophe.

Jack jumped out, grabbed his bags and headed inside. Jim sat in the car, draped his arms across the wheel and dropped his chin on them to gaze at the house for a while. He felt like he'd been gone for years and years, rather than just a matter of months. One by one, he pictured those with whom he'd shared this lost kingdom on the western plains before they left it for ever.

There was still an aching sadness in his heart. They all passed before him. His grandparents, his father, his mother, Rachel . . . Rachel. He could actually whisper her name without the numbing pain that had so many times trapped it in his throat. He'd made a strange discovery at Rachel's graveside. He could communicate with her. Not in some nutty spiritualist sense but simply by stilling his heart and mind to hear intuitively what she would say to him. He knew that, for the rest of his days, whenever doubt arose or trouble clouded his love, he could turn to her for solace, wisdom and guidance.

He found Jack standing in the middle of the haunted lounge. Tim had uncovered the couch and a couple of chairs but the rest of the furniture was still shrouded under sheets and blankets.

'What do we do now?'

'Jack, I've got to ask you to put everything aside for a while.'

'I'm listening,' Jack responded curtly.

'Yes . . . This is pretty complicated. I can sketch it out for you on paper later, if you like. But we've got to talk about it first.'

Jack swung his legs over the arm of a chair, settled himself and glared at this father. 'Okay, okay, I'm listening.'

Jim took a deep breath.

'As you know, the Coalmec people drew a blank after getting

their hands on Bindra and Big Jack's Whack. Serves the bastards right, as far as I'm concerned. The main thing is they've quit their pitch and put the leases up for sale. They're gunning for top dollar – thirty dollars an acre. That's a total of just over a million dollars . . .'

Jack's eyes widened slightly but otherwise his expression remained ungiving.

'Now, I've had a long talk to Wally Jenkins. He's our new bank manager. Very nice bloke. More like Will Mackenzie than that other bastard. He's got his ear to the ground and he reckons they'd accept twenty-five dollars an acre cash down. That's eight hundred and seventy five thousand.'

'How much have you got?'

'Just under two hundred and fifty.'

'Well, that's the end of that then, isn't it?'

'No,' said Jim. 'That's not the end of it at all. That's nothing like the end of it. I've spent a lifetime building up this holding and I'll be damned if I'm going to let it slip away in the pockets of a bunch of mongrels who only wanted to rip its guts out . . .'

'You already have.'

It was one thrust too many.

'That's enough of that, Jack. Put the bloody lid on it and listen!'

Jack swung his legs off the arm and straightened. For a second Jim thought he was going to get up and walk out. But he relaxed again and leaned back in his chair.

'Yeah, okay,' he replied sulkily. 'They've got the leases and you've got no dough.'

'We've still got five hundred head of prime beef running here, don't forget. And Athol, God bless him . . . He's just offered me four hundred head of second-grade stock he wants off Glenmore. Buy now, pay later. Knowing him, they'll be rock bottom price. Really swing the odds in our favour.'

Jack was listening a bit more intently now, curious to get the drift of what his father was on about. 'We can't bring them here. Five hundred's all we can handle anyway on what we've got left.'

'I'm not going to bring them here. I'm going to ship them to Townsville.'

Jack's curiosity was roused. This time his question dried on his lips.

'I spent a lot of time in bars up north, Jack. A damn sight

more than I should have. But it wasn't a total waste. I got to hear a few things . . . Even managed to remember them,' he added with a crooked grin. 'There's a Malaysian outfit in Townsville who pay top dollar for liveweight stock on the doorstep. They have their own Muslim slaughtering set-up in Malaya. Halal slaughtering they call it. They drain all the blood out of the carcass before they skin it. There are places that do it here, under licence. But it's expensive. Every carcass has to have a government stamp before it can leave the country. This mob prefer to ship 'em on the hoof. That way they avoid the local slaughter levy.'

'Why don't you just sell them locally?'

'Tim tells me prices are way down at the moment. We'd be lucky to get sixty cents on the dollar and I can't afford to hang about waiting for them to go up again. Not if we're to get first shot at those leases.'

'Is anyone else after them?'

'Not at the moment. But who knows?'

'What about the transport costs?'

'Even with the transport costs, we're still in front.'

Jack was silent for a moment. Then he shook his head. 'Seems like a bit of a long shot to me.'

'Not as long as it looks. There's plenty of risk, I don't deny that. It puts it right on the line. But it's the best shot we've got as far as I can see.'

'What about Tim? What does he think?'

'Keen as mustard. Offered to put his life savings into the pot. I told him I'd wait and see how things went.'

Jack had always respected Tim's opinion, ever since he was a little boy. He took his time. But once his mind was made up, he could be as stubborn as a mule.

'How would you ship them?'

'By rail. Be around four dollars a head cheaper than road-trains and we can send the lot in one shipment. We need to get them there lickety-split to keep their condition. If we can keep 'em around the three hundred kilo a head mark they should fetch about a hundred and seventy-five thousand. Athol's lot won't be in such good nick. I reckon around a hundred and twenty thousand for them, if we're lucky. With a hundred and fifty thousand from my account we'll be over the halfway mark the bank needs for down payment – if Jenkins is right about them knocking the lot down at twenty-five an acre. He'll come in with the rest on a fifteen-year mortgage.'

Jack was struggling a bit. 'I don't see the point in getting the land back if we've got nothing left to run on it.'

'Land's land, Jack. We can always build the herd up again, take another crack at some sheep. Fifteen years is a long time, mate. Once we've got the land back we've got security. Jenkins is a country bloke, born and raised up at Richmond. Not only that but he came across as pretty shrewd to me. He's not going to stick himself out on a limb for nothing. He reckons the man on the land's taking enough of a battering as it is.'

Jack pondered the floor and struggled with the warring voices in his heart. Just being back in the house had taken the edge off months of bitterness borne of his forced exile. He knew his father didn't really have to go through all this. He could just go ahead and do it anyway. It was his way of trying to make it up. Balkenna's survival was his own. Jack had decided to return as much for his love of the place as to go along with his father. It felt like Jim was asking him to make the decision and it was too much to ask.

'How much would the transport costs be?' he asked hesitantly.

'About fourteen and a half, fifteen thousand. That's the rail side. Then there'll be trucking costs to get them to the railway yards. I thought we could use the Winton road-train mob for that. And there'll be yarding costs at the other end. But if we time it right we should be able to keep them to a minimum. With our fares and keep . . . Let's say a round figure of twenty grand. It'll be tight, mate. Tight as hell. We'll be into Athol for eighty-eight grand. I know he probably won't be in a rush for it but it would be right to divvy up. Say a third of it straightaway. We'll be scrimping, that's for sure, and we'll have to keep a bloody tight rein on it. Maybe we could dip into some of Tim's dough, if we have to. But I'd rather not if we can avoid it. That's his nest-egg. The plans your granny and I had for him are well and truly up in smoke now.'

'Yeah,' Jack nodded. 'I know what you mean.'

He withdrew into himself again and left his father on a knife-edge. There wasn't much point to any of it if Jack didn't want to know. Tony certainly didn't and Billy seemed to have taken to city life under his big brother's roof, even if he had talked nonstop about Balkenna in their short time together.

'I do understand how you feel, Jack,' he offered quietly. 'But I need your help. If you can't go along just for me, then do it for Balkenna. This was your mother's home too, don't forget . . .'

The look Jack gave him cut him dead. 'I'm hardly likely to forget that.'

'No, of course not. That was a silly thing to say. I'm just trying to make the point that it's your future we're talking about here as much as mine. I just meant I owe it to your mum, to all of you, to try and make amends for what's happened. To set something up for the future. I'm not pretending it'll be a piece of cake. Far from it. But it'll be a hell of a go.'

To his dismay, Jack just stood up and headed for the door. 'I've got to take a leak.'

He was out of the door and gone, leaving Jim to twiddle his thumbs and wait. It was a long wait. He couldn't sit still any longer. He got up and started wandering around the room, tugging at the covers. After an eternity, Jack strolled in and leaned against the mantelpiece.

'Well?'

Jack gave him a long, lofty look, before he ever so slightly nodded his head. 'Sounds all right.'

'Good on you, son.'

Jack didn't respond to Jim's embrace but he didn't pull away either. Jim didn't push it and quickly let him go.

Jack looked at his father. 'I know where we might be able to get a few more.'

'Cattle?'

'Up the other side of Hughenden. Along the eastern side of Porcupine Creek, where the national park is. There's a whole bunch of unbranded strays there.'

'How do you know?'

'Mr Carter used to go and flush a few out a few years ago but he gave it away. It's a bugger of a place to get in and out of. Reckoned it was more trouble than it was worth. There's still a lot there from what I heard.'

'Who owns them?'

'Nobody. They're strays, unbranded. Some old bloke was droving them into Hughenden on the stock route about thirty years ago. He had a heart attack and they all just pissed off along the Flinders. It was years before anyone knew where they'd got to.'

'How many are there now?'

'Nobody knows for sure. Could be two or three hundred, maybe more. Mr Carter says they're strung out in little bunches all along the creek. They don't bother crossing over and don't go too far east. There's no more water until you hit the Flinders again and that's over thirty kilometres.'

'Scrubbers.'

'Yeah. But the ones he used to get weren't in bad nick. I know he used to get a price for them.'

Jim sat back. Carter was probably right, more trouble than it was worth. But every extra head was worth something. And it was Jack's idea. If he was right and they were in reasonable nick then they'd cover their transport and make a few dollars on top.

'Just thought I'd mention it. Mr Carter'd probably let us have some horses.'

'How's it going?'

They both jumped as Tim appeared in the door carrying an enormous box of groceries.

'Christ, mate, you gave me a start there.'

Tim shoved out his hand to Jack. 'G'day, champ. Good to see you.'

Jack jumped up to shake hands. 'G'day, Tim. Yeah, it's good to be back. Haven't had a chance to look around yet. Dad says you've been doing a fantastic job.'

Tim's natural reticence took a back seat. He puffed his fingernails and rubbed his heart. 'Yeah, I think so too.'

Jack's laugh was music to his father's ears. Jim was still trying to digest his son's wild proposal. The last thing in the world he wanted to do now was put a damper on Jack's enthusiasm. To hell with it, he decided. The ins and outs would have to come later. He gave him a wink.

'Let's give it a go.'

For the first time since their reunion, Jack smiled. 'Might be worth a crack.'

Jim turned out three plates of eggs, tomatoes and chips. But during the course of the meal the gaps in conversation grew longer.

For his part, Tim was just damn glad to have them home. The intervening months had been a lonely, nerve-wracking time for him, as Balkenna disintegrated day by day, despite everything he did to stay on top of things. He'd actually reached the point of exhaustion when Jim turned up. It had come as a very welcome surprise. His faith was restored on the spot. He favoured Jim's Townsville scheme but he wasn't so sure about rooting strays out of Porcupine Creek. Having never seen the place, he could only go by Jack's description and it didn't sound too inviting. But as Jim had asked him to stay behind and oversee the road-train loading, he could only wish them luck.

Watching Tim out of the corner of his eye, Jim gave thanks again for the wisdom of his father's choice when adding to Balkenna's personnel so long ago. He was a gem of a bloke, solid as a rock.

Jack was watching his father, wondering what was really going on in his mind. All along he had a vague sense of something unspoken. Perhaps it was just being back in the house, particularly in the room his mother had devoted so much time to. Despite the animosity he felt over his father's desertion, he did realise it must be very, very painful for him to be surrounded by so many reminders of her. He himself had come across a shopping list of his mother's while putting the groceries away in the larder when his father was telling Tim about Porcupine Creek. The sight of the familiar handwriting had made him cry, and he was thankful they weren't around to see it.

Jack and Tim got stuck into the cleaning up while Jim went off to organise beds for the night. He paused at the door of the master bedroom to take a deep breath before flinging it open. He knew Jilba had seen to the task of packing and storing her mother's clothes but he still wasn't quite sure if he could handle it. He entered slowly. Like a magnet, his eye was drawn to his favourite photograph on the dresser. There she was . . . Glowing with pride and dousing him in champagne. The minute he saw it he knew everything would be all right. He made up the bed and returned to the lounge room.

Tim had a couple of things he wanted to take care of at his place first thing in the morning. He bid them a warm goodnight and took his leave. Arm over his shoulders, Jim walked him to the door and waved him off. He watched until the tail-lights were cat's eyes in the night, smiling to himself as he remembered Tim going crook at the ute, calling it the most cantankerous bloody piece of machinery in the history of internal combustion. But he'd been forced to hang onto it. It was the only vehicle left for carting wire and humping feed.

Jack was bushed. Jim felt a flutter of disappointment. He'd hoped their conversation would go on well into the night. But he figured Jack probably needed some time on his own to come to terms with coming home.

'Okay, mate. Know how you feel. It's been quite a day. I'm pretty bushed myself.'

He grabbed his son in a quick hug and stepped back, not waiting for any response. Jack just managed to give him a pat on the back before he did and it made Jim wish he'd waited.

'I think I'll give your grandma a call before I turn in. Want to talk to her?'

Jack shook his head. 'Give her my love. Better tell her I'm already out of it. Don't want to hurt her feelings. Just don't feel up to it right now.' He gave his father a small, shy smile and headed for the door. 'See you in the morning.'

Jim's call to Sydney sent his newly-won confidence into freefall. John Barclay was polite enough. But when Jean came on the line she was withering. She answered his questions, insisted Anthony couldn't come to the phone, managed hollow noises about his safe return, and cut him off short with the excuse of a bad line.

Sleep came for Jim only when he persuaded himself he should have written first. The phone had been too sudden. Everything would be all right when he could get down to Sydney to see them.

# Forty-Two

Four weeks later, Jim was so stiff and sore it was all he could do
to stay in the saddle. It had been a long, long time since he'd
done such hard riding. But he was enjoying himself, and was
running in high gear. Up ahead of him were twenty-seven head,
in surprisingly good condition. Wild they might be, but in the
heat of the noonday sun they were offering little resistance to
being driven back along the creek. The three Stoker dogs were
doing a top job keeping them in check on the outside flank.

Les and Reg Stoker, seventy-two and seventy. What a pair
they were. Bachelor brothers straight out of Speewa, that
mythological home of heroic deeds, tall tales and true. Legends
in the Hughenden district for their horse-breaking skills, Les
and Reg now ran a small trucking company and bred cattle dogs
in their semi-retirement. Geoff Carter had recommended the
Stokers as the ideal pair and so it had turned out.

They set up at the northern end of a twenty-kilometre stretch
above the gorge, at a spot where the track leading out to the
Kennedy road actually crossed the creek. The Stokers knew the
area well, they'd ridden over every square inch of it in their
younger days catching brumbies, either for breaking themselves or for selling unbroken to the buckjumping circuits.
Each day they slapped Balkenna's brand onto the previous
day's haul and trucked them into the Hughenden railway yards,
a round trip of about a hundred and eighty kilometres. A hundred and thirty-three so far, much to everyone's satisfaction.

Jim shooed some flies and stood in the stirrups to give his
raw bum a breather. Just as he eased it down again, an enormous old-man goanna, seven foot if he was an inch, sat up with
a start right in front of the leading bullock. It rose on its hind
legs, hissed a warning and scuttled out of the road. The bullock
jumped with fright, bellowed, pigrooted, veered away from the
others and broke into a run. In a flash, three more broke away
and tore after him before the dogs moved in. Jim yelled at the

dogs to keep them bunched and set off after the breakaways. They quickly slowed to a lope and he rode out on a wide arc to head them off and turn them back. They dodged and twisted a couple of times but he managed to swing them to the others and, once they saw them, they more or less headed back of their own accord.

Just as they got back, Jim's horse stumbled badly and sent him cart-wheeling into the dirt. The horse regained its footing, walked a little way off and stood waiting, the saddle skewwhiff down its side. Jim took his time to sit up. His palms had taken the full brunt and they were badly grazed. He brushed the bits of grit away, spat on them and worked them together to clean off the dirt, until his spit ran dry. They weren't too bad, but it was going to make it a bugger to hold the reins. Oh well. He glanced around for his hat, to be confronted by the goanna, poised motionless about twenty feet away and giving him a very beady eye. Jim showed the lizard his bloody hands.

'Now look what you've gone and done.'

The goanna blinked a couple of times, rose on its hind legs and waddled off as if it couldn't give a damn. Jim chuckled, got up, dusted himself off, retrieved his hat, and gathered his horse. As he pulled himself into the saddle and called the dogs to get them moving again, he realised he'd been lucky. He could easily have broken an arm or a leg, or both. The 'roo shooter appeared in his mind's eye, bucking on the ground. Jim shook his head to chase his ghost away and set off after the cattle.

He wondered if Fred and Annie had got his letter yet. He'd spent a long time over it the night before leaving Balkenna. All through telling them about the reunion with his family, their plans and the adventure he and Jack were setting out on the following day, he forcibly repressed all thoughts of the nightmare ending to his spell in the Thirty Mile Range. He prayed Annie was all right.

Jack wasn't having much luck, but he was having the time of his life. So far, the day had only produced five head, one of them a cow in pretty ordinary condition. He might try the western side of the creek in the morning, just to see. They only had two days left, so anything was worth a shot. For the first time since his mother's death and his father's disappearance he felt the future had some promise. There was still a lingering sense of estrangement from his father but the gulf was narrowing all the time. He had made an effort to put himself in his father's place and wonder what he might have done. Deep down, he was sure he would never have acted the same way. But who could tell? Coming up to his eighteenth birthday, he still had a lot to learn about what made people tick.

It took his father a whole day on the phone to track down the Hashim Brothers Export Company but, when he did, they couldn't have been more co-operative. They said yes to the deal in principle on the spot, the price to depend on weight at time of arrival. They advised a date when their ship would be ready to take the consignment, and had a covering letter of agreement to Balkenna within a week. Arranging the road-trains to get the stock to the railway yards had been a piece of cake. At this very moment Tim and the extra hands would be mustering Balkenna's cattle and bringing them into the holding yards. Bill Tulley would be doing the same at Glenmore. Jim had taken it all as an extremely good omen for this search for strays and Jack was feeling more than a little relieved by the success they'd had so far. To go to all this trouble for ten or twenty head would have definitely taken the edge off.

Above all, this was the life. Beyond any shadow of a doubt he knew it was what he was cut out for. Despite its pitfalls, dangers and heartbreak, the land always paid you back. Big cities made him choke. Even a place the size of Longreach made Jack claustrophobic after a while. He knew there was a solitary streak in his nature that was at home in the vast, mythic landscape of Queensland, a wilderness twice the size of Texas and five times bigger than the British Isles.

That night, as the four men sat yarning round the campfire, he studied his father and had to admit how alike they were. He knew that, despite his faults, he loved him for what he was, a man of the land. A man for whom no other way of life was possible, who had bred in him the sense of responsibility you needed to give back what you got.

'I had these two dogs for sale once,' said Reg. 'A bloke comes to have a look. Checks 'em over pretty thoroughly so I figure he knows what he's on about. Then he says he wants to see 'em run. So we go down the paddock and I send 'em after a few steers I kept for training. I knew which dog'd get there first and it did, a good twenty yards ahead. Bugger me if he doesn't buy the other one. Reckoned the first one ran for speed but the other one ran for his character . . .'

Jim threw back his head and roared with laughter. Jack got busy with another cup of tea.

'They still raising goats for export down your way?' asked Les.

'Oh yes,' said Jim. 'Big business.'

'Funny thing that,' said Les. 'I can eat just about anything you put in front of me. Shoved snake meat down me gullet more than once. But I couldn't come at goat meat if you paid me.'

'Or dog,' Reg added.

'Or dog,' Les confirmed.

'Nothing wrong with a bit of goat,' said Jack.

'Why can't you eat it?' Jim asked.

'Dunno really,' said Les. 'They were all over the place when we was kids. Our uncle used to keep them. For milk and that, not meat. Just sort of got to like 'em, I suppose. Like dogs. The people from the Hall of Fame came up to see what we had left of his gear for their exhibits. Gave 'em a couple of sets of harness, stuff like that.'

'Goats were the backbone of Longreach in the old days,' Jim recalled. 'My grandfather used to say you couldn't move in the town sometimes. There'd be teams of six or eight all over the place, hauling wood, water, everything. They even used to have goat races, he said, and everybody'd punt their last razoo.'

Without another word, Reg Stoker threw back his head and started singing:

> Come all you lads of the droving days, you gentlemen unafraid;
> I'll tell you of the strangest trip that ever a drover made.
> For we rolled our swags and packed our bags and, taking our lives in hand,
> Oh, we started away with a thousand goats on the Billygoat Overland.
> There wasn't a fence that'd hold the mob, to keep 'em from their desires;
> They skipped along the top of the post and cakewalked on the wires;
> And whenever the lanes were bare of grass and the paddocks were nice and green,
> Oh, the goats they travelled outside the lanes, and we rode in between.

> *The squatters started to drive them back, but that was no good
> at all;*
> *The horses ran for the lick of their lives from scent that was
> like a wall.*
> *And never a dog had pluck enough in front of the mob to stand*
> *And face the charge of a thousand goats on the Billygoat
> Overland.*
> *We found we were hundreds over strength when we started to
> count the mob:*
> *And they put us in jail for a crowd of thieves that travelled to
> steal and rob.*
> *For every goat between here and Bourke that scented our spicy
> band*
> *Had left his home and his friends to join the Billygoat
> Overland.*

Jim and Jack laughed.

'Banjo Paterson wrote that. The words anyway. Takes all
sorts . . .'

Jim blanched momentarily at the name Paterson, but kept
smiling.

As the Stokers headed off to sleep, Jim caught Jack watching
them go.

'They don't make them like that any more,' he whispered.

The last two days Jim and Jack went at it from sun-up until well
past sundown. Their efforts were rewarded by another fifty
head, all bar three of them in reasonable condition. Early the following morning the Stokers set off to truck the last of the haul
into Hughenden and take their cattle dogs home. It was left to
Jim and Jack to break camp. Long shadows were falling across
the site by the time the Stokers returned. They made a thorough
check to see nothing had been overlooked and headed for the
trucks. Before climbing in, Jack turned for a last look back at the
scene of their endeavours. Jim slung an arm round his shoulders.

'We did well here, mate.'

Jack gave him a playful thump on the arm. 'You found more
than I did.'

'Wouldn't have found any but for you. Come on, better not
keep them waiting.'

As he watched his father trudge over to Reg's truck and haul
himself in, Jack suddenly noticed how much his mother's death

and its aftermath had aged him. He'd been far too preoccupied with his own hurt feelings really to notice before. As Les slowly eased the truck away, Jack glanced back one last time at their camp site and offered silent thanks. It had bridged the gulf.

By eight o'clock that night they finished unloading the trucks at the Stokers' farm just east of Hughenden and the brothers insisted the Mackays stay on for a few beers.

It was one thirty in the morning when Jim reluctantly suggested they should make a push back to the motel.

'You know where we are,' said Les. 'Just give us a shout if there's anything we can do.'

'I'd like to come back and get some dogs off you in a few months. When we get Balkenna stocked again. They're really good workers, really know their stuff.'

Les shoved out his hand. 'Be our guest. We'll pick you out a couple of bottlers.'

Jim and Jack finally made it to the station wagon and headed for the motel on the outskirts of Hughenden.

'Jesus, that was great,' said Jack, as they pulled out. 'I could listen to them for hours.'

'For sure,' Jim agreed. 'Blokes like them are national treasures, I reckon.'

'They reminded me of "Duke" Tritton, the man who wrote that *Time Means Tucker* book you gave me.'

'Yeah,' Jim nodded. 'Know what you mean. Different trades but same kind of bushmen. Few enough left now, I'm afraid.'

Jack lapsed into silence. If they did come back for some dogs, he'd have to shell out for a cassette recorder and get a few of the Stokers' stories and songs on tape. He'd never really had a hobby but he could see one on the horizon.

They had time to kill the next day. The train from Winton wasn't due until five. They had breakfast in the café of a service station and went straight to the railway yards to check on the haul of strays with Balkenna's freshly scorched brand on their hides. Jim was glad that a good part of the cattle's long journey to Townsville would be made at night. It would reduce stress on the stock and help them weather the change from the arid outback air to the steaming humidity they'd get on the coast.

Jack felt a real puff of pride when the huge diesels towed the long line of cattle trucks into the Hughenden depot. There they were. The wild eyes, sweating flanks and switching tails of

Balkenna's future. His pride doubled when the shunting was over and the trucks containing his strays were coupled on. When the diesels chugged and took the strain and the last trucks carrying their hard-won extras passed by, Jack yahooed at the top of his lungs.

They were on the road themselves soon afterwards and quickly caught up with the train where the railway ran parallel to the Flinders Highway. As the Ford drew level with the locomotives, Jack honked the horn like crazy and waved his hat. One of the drivers gave him the thumbs up.

'Must think we're a couple of lunatics,' Jim observed dryly, tipping his hat over his eyes and settling back for the drive to Pentland where they planned to break their journey.

In their motel room that night, Jim was sitting at the table jotting down some notes as Jack climbed into bed.

'What are you doing?'

'Just looking at some figures on the new lot.'

'How's it look?'

'Pretty damn good. I reckon a hundred and eighty of them could pull around a hundred and fifty each. The other thirty, well, maybe a hundred each, if we're lucky. Take off the transport and the Stokers and we should be twenty-six grand in front . . .' He broke off, raised his eyes and gave his son a big wink. 'Well done, mate.'

'That much?'

'Maybe I'm being a bit optimistic. But even if it turns out to be half that, it's been well worth it as far as I'm concerned. On top of everything else, I had a bloody good time.'

'Yeah,' Jack yawned. 'Me too.'

As he switched off the light and punched his pillow to get comfortable, Jim felt like a whole man again. He drifted off to sleep with a big grin on his face.

But in the dead of night, he met the 'roo shooter again. Only this time the last act was different. He swung round to find Annie and saw that the shallow rock pool had become a deep, savage whirlpool, surrounded on all sides by black, slimy rocks. Annie was in it, struggling desperately against the water. The only lifeline was the shooter's rifle. He scooped it up, ran to the edge, kneeled down and frantically held it out to her. Her fingertips brushed it but couldn't get a grip. There was panic in her eyes. Round she came again. Still, she couldn't grab hold. He inched forward on his knees, braced himself and stretched as far as he could to catch her the next time. But the rocks were too greasy. He was slipping, slipping. A great gurgling roar filled his ears.

His eyes flew open. He lurched up and banged his head hard against the shelf over the bed.

From across the room Jack made a sleepy enquiry. 'You all right, Dad?'

'Yes, mate. I'm fine. Just bumped my head, that's all.'

# Forty-Three

Leaning on the rails of the Townsville holding yards, Jack was well pleased with the sight in front of him. All eleven hundred and fifteen head had made the journey safely and were now milling about, jostling one another at the water troughs and piles of feed, bellowing just for the hell of it. On the far side, his father was deep in conversation with the yard boss. As he watched, the two men came to an agreement, nodded in time, and shook hands.

'Okay, Dad?'

'Couldn't be better,' Jim said. 'Top notch bloke. No problems there. The feed'll be in by mid-afternoon and they'll check the water twice a day.'

'What about the vet?'

'Thought I'd go down to the Hashims' office right now and sort it out. You want to come along?'

Jack hesitated and glanced in the direction of the wide blue Pacific.

'I thought I'd take a squint at the harbour.'

'Fine. Come on, I'll drop you off.'

Townsville was now the largest tropical city in Australia. But still, every street and every familiar building brought back memories of thirty-six years ago. The bedlam of the meatworks, the good times shared with Tony Halpin. His bout of the seafaring life aboard the *Kingfisher* under Captain Barry Baldman. His spartan room in the boarding house with its close-knit community of wharfies and meatworkers. Balmy tropical weekends ogling the girls on Pallarenda Beach and passionate teenage embraces with Marjorie on those same sands at night. He wondered if he'd recognise her if he bumped into her. Or she him. Probably not. Married with kids of her own, more than likely.

As they pulled up on the Strand overlooking the long arm of the Bulk Sugar Terminal jutting out from Magazine Island,

Jack jabbed his finger at the docks in front of them.

'Is this where you used to sail from?'

'Over on south side. We can go and take a look this arvo, if you like.'

Jack jumped out, slammed the door and leant in through the window. 'Okay. Where should I meet you?'

'Think you can find your way back to the hotel okay?'

Jack pulled a face.

'Okay, okay. Just checking.' He fished in his pocket and forked out a twenty dollar note. 'You're on. Twelve thirty. Here, just in case you decide to buy a yacht.'

It had only just gone nine thirty so he had plenty of time. Jack decided to head north and check out the fort on Kissing Point. There was a good breeze fluffing in off the bay and he felt on top of the world.

He arrived in the dining room of Lowth's Hotel a quarter of an hour early and ordered a beer. He took a long pull as soon as it arrived and settled back to study the other diners. His attention was quickly drawn to three men at the table nearest him who had ordered two double whiskies and a tall glass of lemonade. The lemonade was for the suave, brilliantined, immaculately suited, Chinese gentleman. The whiskies were for his companions, two well-built white Australians wearing shiny lightweight business suits.

As the Chinese sipped his lemonade, he glanced up and caught Jack staring at them. Holding Jack's eye, he slowly lowered the glass to the table and lifted an eyebrow. The Australian with his back to Jack swivelled round. He had a mean face, a boxer's nose and eyes like a front-row forward packing down for a five-yard scrum. There was no mistaking the message. Mind your own fuckin' business. Jack swallowed and quickly looked away.

His father still hadn't appeared by a quarter to one. Jack was halfway through a T-bone when he saw Jim come through the door. One look was enough. He in no way resembled the man he'd left on the seafront. All the colour had drained from his face.

'Hey, you all right?'

He said it a little too loudly and the three men at the next table looked up as Jim slumped into his chair and rubbed his hand across his face.

'Dad, for Christ's sake. What's the matter? Do you need a doctor?'

Jim shook his head. He cleared his throat and slowly brought his eyes up to meet his son's. He didn't want to tell him, but he had to.

'The deal's off, Jack.' He clicked his fingers. 'Just like that.'

It was Jack's turn to go pale. He fell back in his chair and stared at his father in disbelief. 'What do you mean off?'

Jim dropped his eyes.

'What do you mean the deal's off?' Jack demanded. Louder this time, oblivious to anybody listening.

Jim gestured to Jack to keep it down. 'The wharfies went on strike at midnight last night,' he said. 'It seems they could be out for days. The Hashims must sail by Friday at the latest. Something to do with a cargo in Penang. If we can't load in time, it's no go. They'll sail empty.'

'The bastards,' Jack growled.

'It's not their fault,' Jim said. 'The wharfies are refusing to handle any cargo, including livestock. We're buggered if they don't go back in time. The Hashims know the ropes here. They don't think there's a chance. They've cancelled the veterinary inspection.'

Jack slapped the table with his palm. 'Shit! What a bunch of bastards!'

Several heads turned. The Chinese pursed his lips to restrain a tight little smile.

'Can't we load them ourselves? Hire some blokes to give us a hand?'

Jim shook his head. 'Not a chance. They'd be blacklegs. It'd be like starting a war.'

Jack stretched across the table and grabbed his father's arm. 'Do you want something to eat?'

Jim shook his head. 'No thanks, mate. I couldn't eat a thing.' He braced himself against the table and pushed himself to his feet.

'Where are you going?'

'You stay here, finish your lunch. I'm going down to the docks to see if I can have a word with the local union rep.'

'I'll come too.'

'No, better I go on my own. Better I talk to him one to one, if I can get to him.' He stretched over and patted Jack's shoulder. 'Just sit tight for me here and keep your fingers crossed. Maybe there's a way round this. Okay?'

Jack gave him the most encouraging smile he could muster. 'All right, if you think that's best.'

Jack felt like crying. He just couldn't believe it. After a time, he tried to finish his steak. But he was no longer hungry. After the first mouthful, he pushed the plate aside. He swallowed the rest of his beer in one gulp, propped his chin in his hand and stared at the weave in the tablecloth. He didn't notice the two burly Australians leave the dining room.

'May I?'

Startled, Jack looked up. The Chinese man was gripping the back of his father's chair and smiling. Jack waved his hand. 'Help yourself.'

To his surprise, the man pulled the chair out and sat down. 'Perhaps I can be of assistance.'

Jack was in no mood for strangers and simply looked away without bothering to reply. The man waited a moment. Then he leant forward and offered his hand. 'Pi Kok.'

'Well, how do you do,' Jack sneered. He shoved the man's hand aside. 'Now why don't you just piss off and mind your own business.'

But Kok slowly pulled out his wallet, extracted a business card, clicked his pen and scrawled on the back.

'I'm at the Breakwater, Room 101.'

He stood up, tucked in the chair and placed the card on the table in front of Jack. Mildly curious, Jack picked it up. Kok gave him the merest inclination of his head and a wispy little smile. 'I shall expect you.'

He turned and left the dining room. Jack checked the card over again, shoved it in his pocket and signalled the waiter for another beer.

Jim tried the handle but it was locked. He rang the bell and waited. He had to repeat the process four times before the door opened a crack and a troubled young face appeared.

'I'd like to speak to Mr Kelly.'

'He's not seeing anyone at the moment. He's busy.'

'Yes, I know,' said Jim. 'I'm sure he is. I only need a few minutes.'

'You a reporter?'

'No, mate. Far from it. Just tell him I wouldn't bother him if it wasn't important, will you?'

The young man eyed him suspiciously. Jim shifted his weight.

'Hang on.'

The door slammed in his face and he heard an extra bolt shoot home. He waited and waited. He was reaching for the bell again when the door finally opened and the young man beckoned him in. There were at least a dozen men in the room, and they were all busy on the phone, scanning newspapers or hunching over mounds of paperwork on the desks.

'He's in there.' The young man thumbed at the door on the far side. Jim quickly crossed the room and knocked.

'Yeah?'

As well as the man behind the desk, there were four others lounging around wherever they could fit. The man at the desk beckoned him forward and offered his hand without rising. 'Kevin Kelly. What can I do for you?'

His manner was friendly but with a tough, no-nonsense air. Well-sprung biceps strained the arms of his short-sleeved shirt and his eyes shone with the clear certainty of a kid who got through night school. He was around Jim's age, he'd obviously been at the union game for years and no one'd better forget it. Jim released his hand.

'Jim Mackay. I've come about the strike . . .'

'Hasn't everyone?' one of the other men interjected.

'Hang on, Ed. Give him a go.' He turned back to Jim and hurried him up. 'What about the strike?'

Jim took a deep breath. 'I've just brought in eleven hundred and fifteen head of cattle . . .'

'That your mob in the holding yards?'

'Yes. Some of them have come all the way from Longreach.'

'You've got a deal with the Hashim Brothers.'

A bit taken aback, Jim nodded. 'So you know my problem.'

Kelly's reply was to the point. 'We know everything about these docks, Mr Mackay. What's on them, where it's come from and where it's going. That's what I'm here for. I presume you want to know the chances of us going back in time to save your arse?'

Jim could only nod.

'None and Buckley's, I'm afraid,' said Kelly. 'McKinley's down there in Brisbane thinking he can flatten us. Hasn't really left us any choice. Unless he swallows our claim, he'll choke on it.'

Kelly's explanation was immediately backed up by a chorus of support.

'I'm sorry. It doesn't give me any pleasure to have to tell you that, believe me. It's just the way it is. We could be out another week, another month. Six months, if we have to. We've had it.' He drew his finger across his throat. 'Up to here.'

Jim tried again. 'I know you have a grievance. I understand your right to take whatever action you see fit. I'm not here to argue the politics of it, one way or the other. I had a union ticket myself once when I was a younger bloke.'

'Yeah?' Kelly enquired. 'What union was that?'

Jim thought he'd made a good point and doubled it. 'I was in two, actually. The meatworkers' here in Townsville for a time and the miners' in Isa. I understand what's involved. I just thought that, as this is a local issue, you might be able to make an allowance. It's not like a bunch of containers I'm talking about. I've got over a thousand cattle, on the hoof. I've got everything riding on them being loaded. I'm pleading a personal case, that's all . . .'

Kelly bridled. 'So am I, Mr Mackay. So am I.'

Jim was fighting to keep his mounting desperation under control. 'Those cattle are everything I've got, everything my family's got. The future of my property. I can't just hold them here, waiting on you. I've got a contract to fulfil and I can't afford to lose it. If the Hashims' ship sails empty, we're buggered.'

Kelly's eyes scanned his comrades. He leant forward and doodled on the pad in front of him, deep in thought. For a moment, Jim thought he'd made his point. But when Kelly sat back and looked up again, his face was like a brick wall.

'Maybe you had a couple of tickets when it suited you, Mr Mackay. But, contrary to what you say, I don't think you understand what's involved at all. Our jobs, Mr Mackay, are everything *we've* got, everything *our* families have got, everything *our* properties have got . . .'

One of the other men butted in. 'How big's your fuckin' property anyway?'

Without thinking, Jim rattled off the figure. 'Fifteen thousand acres at the moment.'

'You fuckin' graziers are all the same. You've got your feet on too much fuckin' ground and your head in the fuckin' clouds. I'm fighting for a fuckin' semi with a bastard of a fuckin' mortgage and a garden too fuckin' small to swing a fuckin' cat! Who the fuck do you think you are to come in here and put the hard word on us?'

Jim turned on him. The wharfie took one look at his boiling eyes and started thinking about backing off.

'I said I know how you feel,' said Jim through his teeth. 'I'm *not* here to talk politics or tell you how to run your union, or anything else. I'm asking for help, that's all. If you want a contribution to union funds from the proceeds, just tell me how much. I *am* talking about everything I've got. You can't black every attempt at free enterprise with the same brush. I'm here as an individual, just as you are –'

'Mr Mackay,' Kelly interrupted. 'There's nothing we can do. Unless McKinley comes to his senses we expect to be out for quite a while. I'm sorry about your beef and that's a fact. There's a lot of other produce that'll probably go to rot before this is over. It's a shame, but it's the name of the game.'

An hour later, Jack stood to one side as his father knocked at the door of Room 101 at the Sheraton – Breakwater Hotel. It was opened almost immediately by Pi Kok himself, in shirt sleeves now but still dapper, not a shiny hair out of place. He smiled at Jack over Jim's shoulder and made room for them to enter.

Jim got straight to the point. 'Jack tells me you say you can help us.'

'Indeed,' Kok responded, sitting down to face them and crossing his legs. 'I believe I could be of assistance.'

'Are you in the cattle business?'

'I dabble. I own a small farm. Nothing like the acreage you are used to. A mere five hundred, near Cromarty.'

Jim didn't like the look of the man at all. 'So? How can you help?'

Kok shifted a couple of times to settle himself. 'You have an agreement with the Hashim brothers, I believe.'

'That's right.'

'But now, with this unfortunate situation on the docks, they've cancelled your veterinary inspection.'

'How do you know that?' Jim asked.

Kok raised his knee slightly, released the tension in the crease of his pants, dropped it back and glanced at Jack.

'I'm afraid I couldn't help but overhear your conversation in the dining room at Lowth's. You were both a little, shall we say, over-excited? And the Hashims and myself are no strangers to one another.'

'What do you mean?' asked Jack.

Kok gave him a courteous smile, like you smile at a puppy who just wet the rug. 'Let's just say I have some influence there.'

'What sort of influence?'

Kok's eyes narrowed slightly as he focused on Jim again and he was deliberately slow to answer.

'Business . . .'

'That may be,' said Jim. 'But my problem isn't the Hashims, it's the wharfies' strike.'

Kok's look was piercing. 'Your problem, Mr Mackay, is survival. Let us not beat about the bush.'

Jim suddenly felt out of his depth. 'I'm listening.'

Kok strained the silence that followed to the absolute limit before he went on.

'My partners and I would be interested in taking your cattle off your hands . . . At the right price.'

'How much?'

'The Hashims inform me they were prepared to offer three hundred thousand dollars.'

'I was hoping for three twenty-five.'

'Ah, yes,' Kok acknowledged. 'Unfortunately what we hope for and what we get in this world are not always one and the same. As I'm sure you'll agree.'

'I was still hoping for three two five.'

'The Hashims' price, of course, was dependent on successful veterinary inspection.'

'There wouldn't have been any problems there. I can vouch for that.'

'It would, of course, depend on who made the inspection.'

'What do you mean? Inspection's the same for everybody.'

'True, true.' Kok waved his beautiful hands. 'But, as I'm sure you're well aware, costs are high and competition fierce. Export charges, slaughter levies, they all take their toll.'

'That's why I brought them to the Hashims in the first place, to avoid slaughter levies and all the rest. These cattle are to be slaughtered in Malaya.'

'Regrettably,' Kok observed, 'that would no longer seem to be the case.'

'Perhaps,' Jim conceded.

Kok glanced at Jack and then returned his gaze to Jim. His eyes glittered in the dusty afternoon light. 'Perhaps your son would like to be excused from the rest of our negotiations.'

Jack bridled.

Kok hadn't taken his eyes off Jim. When he failed to intercede, he simply arched an eyebrow which said he should have.

'Jack's fine,' said Jim. 'This concerns him as much as me. Whatever you have to say, you can say to both of us. We were talking about a price.'

Kok leant forward and dropped his voice to a whisper. 'As you wish, Mr Mackay. But bear this in mind. What passes between us is just that, between us. Any disclosure beyond this room will incur penalties.'

Jack blanched and glanced at his father.

'Is that a fact,' Jim muttered tersely, standing up. 'Come on, Jack. We seem to be wasting our time here.'

But Jack refused to budge. He was more than curious now. He was fascinated. 'I want to hear what he's got to say. What's the point of coming otherwise?'

Jim's anger flashed. 'Come on, Jack. Now!'

'Please, Dad. Let's just hear what he's got to offer. What's wrong with that?'

Jim was about to grab him by the arm and drag him out of there but Kok intervened.

'Gentlemen, gentlemen. Please. I have no wish to cause a family dispute. My choice of words was perhaps a little unfortunate. It's just that, our discussions must of necessity remain . . . confidential.' He touched Jim lightly on the arm. 'Please, Mr Mackay. No offence. Please, sit down.'

Jim was still looking at Jack, willing him to get up so they could clear out. But Jack remained in his chair.

'I just want to hear what he's got to say.'

Angry, Jim resumed his seat. As Kok sat down again, Jim gave him a look he hoped would leave him in no doubt about his feelings.

'Righto. Get on with it. What's your price?'

Kok smiled again. 'My Australian associates and I are, like the Hashims, in the fortunate position of being able to arrange veterinary inspection . . . And more besides. Ritual slaughter free of levies and shipment free of export charges.'

'That's impossible,' Jim snapped. 'Every carcass requires a government stamp before it can go anywhere.'

Kok opened his hands. 'A stamp is a stamp, Mr Mackay. A stencil on fat. It's of little consequence.'

'So let me get this straight. You want to buy my cattle,

slaughter 'em illegally and ship 'em out of the country illegally, is that it?'

'I prefer to use the word unencumbered.'

Jack was stupefied, but what the hell? It was a way out as far as he could see. Kok bought the cattle, who cared what he did with them? It wasn't their problem. Balkenna was their problem. He couldn't contain himself any longer.

'How much?' he blurted. 'What'll you pay us?'

Kok turned his bland smile on him for a moment, but it faded as he turned back to Jim and his eyes narrowed again to cut him down to size.

'Sixty cents on the dollar. One hundred and eighty thousand. Cash.'

Jim laughed in his face. 'You're well and truly up yourself there, my friend. No way. And that goes for the lot of it.' He leapt out of his chair, towered over Kok and raised a finger inches from his face. 'You can stick it.'

Jack leapt up too, but for a different reason. 'Dad, for Christ's sake! What are you doing? Think about it a minute! Isn't it better to lose a bit than lose the lot? We don't *have* to get both leases back. We could get one of them for that. Think about it!'

Jim wheeled on him. 'I'm not doing this, mate, and that's for sure. Not in a million years. Come on. We're wasting our time here.' He strode across the room, yanked open the door, and held it back.

'Dad, think about it, won't you?' Jack pleaded.

For the first time since their reunion, Jim was forced to pull rank. 'I said it's time to go, Jack. Now. Come on!'

And he turned on his heel and disappeared into the corridor. Jack slumped for a moment, then hauled himself out of his chair and slouched past Kok. He couldn't look at him. He could only mumble, 'Thanks for talking to us.'

Kok placed a hand on Jack's arm and blocked his passage to the door. He waited for Jack to look him in the eye and then he chuckled. 'Perhaps your father is a little old-fashioned.'

Jack made no reply. He just stared at him a moment and left the room. When he stepped into the corridor his father was nowhere in sight and he hurried to catch up.

They left the hotel in silence. But as soon as they were back in their own room at Lowth's, Jack wanted to argue the point.

'What difference does it make?'

'There's nothing more to discuss, Jack. And that's final.'

Frustrated, bewildered, Jack walked to the window and stared out. 'Well, what the hell *are* you going to do? Tell me that.'

'You're going to hold the fort here,' Jim announced. 'Keep an eye on the stock and make sure the yard people do their job properly until I get back.'

Jack wheeled to face him. 'Back from where?'

'Brisbane. First flight I can get on.'

'For what?' Jack demanded.

'To see McKinley and explain the situation. Maybe there's a way out of this mess, maybe we can still get the stock loaded in time.'

'What if he's not there? How do you know he'll see you?'

'I'm going to call his office right now and make an appointment. Your grandfather knows him. He'll see me.'

# Forty-Four

Three o'clock sharp the following day, Jim strode through the door of the Department of Trade and Industry in Brisbane. The receptionist directed him to McKinley's office where he ran head on into a brick wall.

'I'm sorry, Mr Mackay. Mr McKinley was called away to Sydney early this morning on urgent business. I've had to cancel all his appointments for today. He asked me to extend his apologies . . .'

Jim boiled over on the spot. 'Why on earth didn't you let me know, for God's sake?'

'I'm afraid I didn't know where to contact you. You said you were calling from Townsville and would be in Brisbane for the day . . .'

'But you yourself confirmed my appointment.'

'I'm sorry, Mr Mackay, but there's nothing I can do.' She opened an appointments book and looked up. 'Would you like me to pencil you in for his return?'

'When will that be?'

'The day after tomorrow.'

Jim clenched his fists. 'No. That's no good to me at all. I don't have that much time. Where can I contact him in Sydney?'

'You can't,' she replied, stony-faced. 'He's fully engaged with meetings and a conference. I have strict instructions not to disturb him except on government business.'

'Can't I reach him by phone?'

'I'm afraid not.' To put an end to the matter, she scanned the appointments book. 'He could see you at eleven thirty, if that's convenient.'

'No, that's not convenient, damn it. It can't wait.'

'As you wish.'

Jim stared at her in disbelief. He opened his mouth to try again, thought better of it, turned on his heel and marched out of the office. The secretary watched his departure with raised eyebrows, tutted her distaste and returned to her paperwork.

In the lobby, he called Jack at Lowth's. The operator told him Jack was out and Jim figured he was probably still at the yards. He got through to reception and dictated a message, asked for it to be read back, hung up and rushed into the street to hail the first taxi he could see.

Anthony Barclay clasped the late-night brandy his son had poured him and shuffled across the rug to ease himself into his favourite armchair. His right leg dragged with difficulty across the pile and his right arm hung uselessly at his side. From her chair, Jean watched his awkward passage with the same concern that had coaxed him back to consciousness in the Brisbane hospital, and nurtured his long, painful convalescence. Restoring his speech alone had taken months. Now, apart from the paralysis, he was something like his old self. Satisfied he was comfortably settled, Jean took her glass from her son and took a sip of his brandy.

'Everything all right, John? At the office?'

John Barclay gave her a bright smile and saluted his father with his glass. 'Good as gold, Mum. I had a good teacher, don't forget.'

Anthony rode the compliment. 'Keep them guessing. That's the way. Right up to the dotted line.'

'We do our best,' John chuckled.

The front doorbell chimed in the hall. Jean glanced at the clock on the mantelpiece. 'Who on earth?'

'I'll get it,' John said.

'Who is it, dear?' Jean enquired as John stepped back into the lounge. Her eyes widened as Jim appeared behind him. Anthony looked up and his jaw dropped.

'I don't believe it . . .'

With a warm smile, Jim strode across the room, leant down and, before she had time to recover, gave Jean a kiss on the cheek.

'Hello, Jean. How are you?'

She just looked up at him in stunned amazement. Jim turned to his father-in-law.

'Hello, Anthony. Good to see you looking so well.'

Anthony gave him a curt nod. 'Jim . . .'

Jim offered his hand. To his dismay, Anthony ignored it for a moment before raising his good left hand for the merest touch. Everybody suddenly looked extremely uncomfortable.

'I have to go, I'm afraid,' said John. 'I said I'd pick Kay up at ten. Sorry I can't stay, Jim. Have to try and catch up with you tomorrow. How long are you down for?'

'That depends,' Jim replied, gripping his hand tightly before releasing it. 'Good to see you, John. Everything going all right, I hope?'

'Yes, can't complain. You know . . .'

'I'm glad.'

A more awkward silence followed his departure. Jim waited until they heard the front door close.

'He looks fit,' he said.

All Anthony's reserve went out of the window. With a speed that defied his disabilities, he rose from his chair, braced himself against it and let go with both barrels.

'You've got a hell of a hide, Jim. You just walk in here out of nowhere. No phone call, no warning, no nothing. Just damn well walk in as if nothing in between had ever happened.'

'I know I've got a lot of explaining to do. Believe me, I do. And I will. All of it, as best I can. But not now, not tonight. I didn't want to trouble you at all . . . I've been tramping from one end of Sydney to the other all day trying to see Ian McKinley.'

Anthony didn't bat an eyelid.

'I need your help, Anthony. It's desperately urgent. I'll explain what I can as we go along and you'll see why I just can't go into all of what's happened right at this moment.' He shot Jean a look. 'Please, I must ask you . . . Just bear with me . . .'

'I understand just one thing, Jim,' Anthony fumed. 'Your bloody cheek! You come barging in here, unannounced, in the middle of the night . . . And you have the audacity to tell us you've no time for explanations! Damn you, man. Just who the hell do you think you are?'

Jean stood up and moved quickly to her husband's side.

'You could have given us *some* warning, Jim. I'm afraid we're getting a bit old for sudden shocks. You know Anthony isn't well.'

Jim raised a hand, and acknowledged his mistake. 'Jean, I'm sorry. Of course, you're right. I should have called first. I just didn't stop to think.' He locked eyes with Anthony again before continuing. 'I meant no disrespect. Please, Anthony, just hear me out?'

Anthony continued to glare at him. He kept Jim on a tight-rope for a good few seconds before easing himself back into his chair. 'Make it quick.'

Tears welled in Jean's eyes and she hurried out. 'I'll make some coffee.'

'Thanks, Jean,' Jim called after her. His eye fell on John's unfinished brandy. He wouldn't have minded one of those either. But there didn't seem to be any on offer.

Jean sank into a chair and cradled her head in her hands on the kitchen table. The kettle had long since boiled and switched itself off by the time she stood up and dabbed her eyes dry. She heaved a long sigh and set about preparing a tray. But she didn't have time to finish it. Suddenly angry voices broke from the lounge.

'No, damn it! I've no intention of speaking to McKinley, or anyone else. Not through the firm, not through the Lodge! You got yourself into another mess, you can damn well get yourself out of it.'

'Anthony, for God's sake!' Jim cried. 'It's Jack as well. Be reasonable!'

'Don't you dare say that to me! Don't you dare talk to me about being reasonable! You disappear without a trace, leave our daughter's children – our grandchildren – and everyone else in the lurch . . . Leave us all in a misery of uncertainty . . . Trample over our lives just to indulge your own selfish feelings. You had all the love and support in the world from us! Now you have the unbelievable gall to come waltzing in here demanding more! Well, *you can go to hell!*'

He looked as if he might actually strike out. Jean flung her arm round him to restrain him. She turned her pleading eyes on Jim and begged him to go.

'Please, Jim. Perhaps you should call us tomorrow. Anthony is not well. You know that as well as I do. I just can't allow him to be upset like this.'

Jim was sinking fast. He just didn't know what to say. When Anthony suddenly doubled up and started coughing he took a couple of involuntary steps in retreat. Jean helped Anthony back into his chair and began massaging his back. When she turned back to Jim her voice was hard.

'No more, do you hear? I won't stand for it.'

Jim didn't know how to stop. 'Jean, please . . .'

'No more!' she screamed. 'I will not listen to another word. For God's sake, leave us alone!'

'Jean . . .'

'You wretched man! You've had our blood! What more do you want?'

Jim rocked back on his heels. There was nothing more to say after that. Staring at them with a mixture of disbelief, frustration and defeat, he retreated to the door.

'I'm sorry,' he whispered. 'Truly, I'm so sorry . . .'

Anthony and Jean still clutched each other long after they heard the front door close quietly behind him.

Jim made his way down the hill in a daze, shame and guilt fogging his brain. The fairground play of the harbourside lights sparkling on the water seemed to mock his every step. As he turned the corner at the bottom of the hill and made his way onto Old South Head Road he wondered what was he going to do.

His day-long search for McKinley had been met by bureaucratic resistance at every turn. His father-in-law had represented his last, desperate hope. What now? There was obviously nothing more to be achieved in Sydney. Go back to Brisbane? Try to see McKinley there? No point. Time had run out. He would have to go back to Townsville and find another buyer. Wear all the charges he'd tried to avoid and sell direct to an abattoir. Either to one of the legitimate Halal outfits or maybe even the very place where he'd slaved his guts out as a washer all those years ago.

He didn't see the taxi until the violent shriek of brakes. It ended up broadside on just inches away from him and the driver stuck his head out of the window to hurl abuse at him in his native Greek, rounding off with a few well-chosen expletives from his adopted tongue. Jim asked him if he wanted a fare.

When he finally let himself into a motel room at the airport, he was so physically and mentally exhausted it was all he could do to undress before climbing into bed. He was asleep the minute his head hit the pillow.

When he awoke the following morning he checked his watch and found he'd been out for ten and a half hours.

At the booking counter he got another slap in the face. No direct flight to Townsville. He would have to change planes in Brisbane. The first available seat was on a four-thirty flight that afternoon. If he was lucky, he might make the last Townsville connection. If not . . . He didn't have any choice. He took the seat and made his way to the restaurant. He bought a copy of the

*Sydney Morning Herald*, more to distract himself than to catch up on the news.

It was twelve thirty when he finished eating, a good time to call Jack. He'd probably be back at Lowth's for some lunch himself. He found a phone at the end of a long row in a corner. It was reasonably quiet. When he came away from it, he looked like a fighter that had taken just one too many blows to the head. In hushed tones, the hotel manager had taken his call and informed him that his son was in Townsville hospital after being involved in an accident off the premises. He gave him the number and Jim's second call confirmed it. Yes, Jack Mackay had been hospitalised. Yes, he'd been involved in an accident. Yes, he had sustained serious head injuries and would have to be detained. Yes, they looked forward to his attendance as soon as possible.

Jim thrust his way through the milling passengers. Sunlight blinded him as he stepped out of the terminal building and the heat was suffocating. He scanned the plaza for a hiding place.

The hours that followed were the longest of his life. He missed the Townsville connection, was forced to spend the night in another motel near Brisbane airport and did not arrive at the hospital until early afternoon the following day.

A sister conducted him down a narrow corridor and ushered him into the consultant's office. The doctor rose to greet him.

'Why can't I see him?' Jim demanded. 'The sister won't let me into his room. What the hell's going on?'

The doctor studied him sympathetically for a moment and offered a small smile of encouragement. 'I'll take you in myself in a few minutes, Mr Mackay. There are some things we should talk about –'

'What happened to him?' Jim interrupted.

'We believe he was beaten up. He was found in your car, out near the cemetery. Just off the road leading to the caravan park. A man staying there noticed the car with the driver's door open. When he went to have a look he found your son unconscious on the back seat. The police are holding your car at the station. They'd like to have a word with you as soon as possible. I understand you were in Brisbane –'

'What do you mean beaten up? By who?'

'I'm afraid, at this stage, the police have no idea. That's why they'd like to see you.'

'How is he?'

The consultant raised a hand. 'Please, Mr Mackay, I understand your anxiety. The situation is this. Your son was not just beaten up in the usual way. He was literally punched unconscious. He was still that way five hours after admission. Fortunately, he's come out of it and as far as we can tell there's no sign of brain damage or haemorrhaging. He's out of the coma but still suffering severe concussion. I doubt that he knows where he is or what's happened at this stage. In a way, that's a good thing.'

'Why? Why on earth is that a good thing?'

'Because we're having to keep him in a fixed position on his right side.'

Jim was frightened now.

'Please. Let me explain first and then ask as many questions as you like. He suffered damage to his right eye. The retina is detached . . .'

Jim slumped back in his chair and buried his face in his hands.

'Mr Mackay . . .'

His hands shook like leaves as he dropped them in his lap. It was an effort to raise his head.

'I'm sorry. It's distressing news, I know. But, on the plus side, it's not as bad as it could be.' He stood up and directed Jim's attention to a diagram on the wall. 'It might be easier if I point out exactly what's happened.'

Jim swivelled in his chair. There was a large diagram of the human eye on the wall.

'There are two things in his favour. The macula, here, has not come away. The detachment is confined to the peripheral retina which is this area here. We call this a "positive scotoma". The plus there is that we can tell exactly where the fluid lies and position his head accordingly. That prevents any more peeling of the retina itself and safeguards the macula.'

'What happens if the macula gets damaged?' Jim asked quietly. 'Comes away . . .'

'Full vision would be permanently impaired. How much would depend on the degree of macula detachment. That's the worst that could happen. But I must stress that has not happened in your son's case. It's the periphery of the retina that's detached . . . Here . . . On the right-hand side of his eye. That is why we have to keep him on his right side, until the specialist sees him.'

'When will that be?'

'That's what I want to discuss with you. Please, sit down.'

He gave Jim a friendly smile as he resumed his seat.

'My name's Bower, by the way. Richard Bower. I'm the ophthalmic consultant here and I can tell you that the chances of your son recovering full vision in the eye are quite good. But the operation must be done as soon as possible. To be perfectly frank, my experience in this area is pretty limited. I've already contacted an associate of mine, Alan Reeves. Funnily enough he's based in Mackay, so perhaps we can take that as a good omen . . .'

It was all Jim could do to take in the information.

'He specialises in retina operations and I can guarantee his skill. Absolutely first rate. He's expensive, but I presume you have normal cover.'

Jim shook his head. 'I'm afraid it's probably lapsed. I've been away. But go on. Whatever it costs, I'll pay. What are the chances, really?'

'Just what I said, quite good. In Alan's hands, very good. I can only stress that speed is of the essence. If you wish, he can fly up immediately. Hopefully, your son's concussion will recover considerably in the next ten or twelve hours. All being well, we should be able to operate tomorrow afternoon. All I need is your permission to proceed.'

'Do whatever you think best. Permission, money, anything . . .' His voice cracked. 'Just don't let him go blind. For God's sake, don't let him go blind . . .'

Bower stepped round his desk and dropped a hand on Jim's shoulder. 'I assure you he'll be in good hands.'

Bower hadn't prepared Jim for the shock of actually seeing Jack. He was strapped in position, braced along his back by a barricade of pillows. His exposed left shoulder and the arm lying outside the sheet were covered in violent mustard and purple bruises. He was sound asleep. Jim squatted by the bed and gazed at all he could see of his son's face below the bandage covering his head. He had to strangle a cry of pain. The tears trickled down his cheek as he lightly touched Jack's hand with his fingertips.

When Jim was ready, Bower supported him out of the room and back along the corridor to the door of his office.

'You all right?'

Jim took a couple of huge deep breaths. 'Yes,' he mumbled. 'The bruises . . .'

'Whoever did him over certainly didn't pull their punches. Now look. I want you to get some rest too. Are you still at Lowth's?'

Jim nodded.

'Fine. Call in and see the police on your way back. Sergeant Stewart's the man to see. Get that out of the way, go back to the hotel and take it easy. I'll give you a call later this afternoon once I know which flight we can get Alan on and the theatre times tomorrow. Okay? Keep your spirits up and get some rest. We'll need you in top form when he's coming round.'

Jim offered his hand with genuine appreciation. 'Thanks very much, doctor. You've been very considerate. There is one thing I have to take care of. Perhaps it would be best if I called you . . .'

'Fine. Give me a call around six thirty. I'll be free again then and I'll let you know what we've lined up.'

Jim had to beat off a wave of uneasiness as he entered the police station. He had to find out what they knew about Jack, but fronting the police was something he didn't relish in the slightest. Fortunately for him, Sergeant Stewart put his obvious nervousness down to strain.

He told Jim little more than he already knew. They had no idea who the culprit or culprits might have been and were hoping he might give them a clue or two to open a line of enquiry. Jack had been found at seven a.m. the previous morning with fifteen dollars in his pocket, his driver's licence and the hotel keyring in the glove box. Stewart pressed Jim to rack his brains for anyone that might have wanted to harm his son. When Jim shook his head and said there was nobody he could think of, Sergeant Stewart shrugged.

'Well, we'll continue to look into it, of course. We've questioned everyone staying at the caravan park except for two cars that left around the same time. We checked the register. They were both retired couples on touring holidays. Drew a blank with the rest, I'm afraid. Nobody seems to have seen or heard a thing. The doc told me about his eye. What do they reckon his chances are now?'

'Have to wait for the specialist.'

'You staying on at Lowth's?'

'Yes.'

'Righto. I'll be in touch if we come up with anything. Give us a shout if you think of anything yourself.'

Jim left the station none the wiser.

Only when he arrived at the railway yards did he start to make sense of things. Two of the yards were jammed with Merinos. The others were empty. He leapt from the Ford and charged into the yard boss's office.

'Don't do your block at me, mate,' the yard boss hollered. He opened a drawer of his desk, dug out some papers and flung them down for Jim to see. 'There's the yard bill, loading receipt, tally. The lot. Signed and paid for.'

'But he didn't have that much money on him,' Jim protested.

'He did when he paid off this lot, mate. How the hell was I supposed to know? He had all the papers. Said you'd been called away on urgent business and left him to take care of it all. They were hauled out of here late the following afternoon.'

'Which afternoon?'

Getting crankier by the minute, the yard boss drummed his finger on the loading receipt. 'There's the date. Right in front of you. Day before yesterday.'

'Where?' Jim demanded. 'Where were they taken?'

The yard boss drummed his finger on the spot. 'Rockhampton, according to this.'

'Bastards,' Jim spat, half under his breath.

The yard boss thought it was meant for him. He stood up and strode out of the door. 'Bugger you, mate. I've got work to do.'

Jim thought about calling him back, but there was no point. The damage was done. It was obvious the man had acted in good faith. He studied the papers in his hand, dropped them on the desk and returned to the station wagon. He glanced at his watch as he got behind the wheel. There was just enough of the business day left to try the first thing that sprang to mind. He drove straight to the Hashim Brothers Export Company on Palmer Street.

The local Townsville girl who worked the desk was busily typing away and getting to grips with a new piece of gum. When the door banged against the wall, she nearly jumped out of her skin.

'Jeez, Mr Mackay, you might've knocked.'

'The Hashims here?' Jim demanded, thumbing at the inner door.

'No,' she answered shakily. 'They're away, I'm afraid. Both of them.'

'Away where?' Jim demanded. Before she could reply, he flung open the inner door to double-check.

'They're not here, Mr Mackay, honest.'

'Where are they?'

'In Kuala Lumpur. Both of them, on business. Honest.'

Jim strode back, leant across the desk and gave her a withering look. 'You telling me the truth?'

She was nearly sliding off her chair. 'They're both in Kuala Lumpur. Honest . . .'

'For how long?'

'They never said. They just said keep an eye on things till they got back.'

'You better be telling the truth, young lady, or you're in big trouble.'

She plucked the gum out of her mouth in case she swallowed it in fright, and waved her other hand to fend him off. 'It is . . . It is . . . Cross my heart.'

'You know a man called Kok? Pi Kok?'

She shook her head.

'He knows the Hashims. You must have heard his name.'

'No, I haven't. Honest. I'd tell you if I had. Why wouldn't I?'

'Who knows?'

As Jim stood there glaring at her, she toyed with the idea of making a dash for the door. She decided she'd never make it.

'If I find out you've been lying, I'll be back. Just remember that.'

He turned on his heel and stormed out, slamming the door behind him. The secretary moved fast. She flicked the safety catch on the lock and leaned heavily against the door.

On his way back to the hotel, Jim racked his brains to try and remember the name of the place Kok said he had a farm. But it wouldn't come. As he entered the lobby, he went straight to the front desk and bought a tourist map of north Queensland.

On the way to his room, he detoured via the bar and downed a double Scotch on the rocks to take the edge off. It was just generating a bit of heat as he let himself in, tore off his coat and tie and spread the map across the bed. He got down on his knees, pinpointed the Townsville area and scanned the surrounding districts, squinting hard to read the finer print. After five minutes his fingernail ran across it.

'Cromarty. That's it . . .'

He dumped the map and checked his watch. Still fifteen minutes to go before he could call Bower at the hospital. He flopped on his back on the bed, stuck his hands behind his head and replayed the day's events on the ceiling, trying to fill in the gaps. Kok was at the centre of it, he was sure of that. But how?

413

Had Jack gone back to him the minute his back was turned and agreed to the bastard's offer? No, he couldn't have ... He wouldn't ... Had Kok found out Jim was out of town and approached Jack again? Maybe upped the price a few thousand? Or worse, threatened him with violence if he didn't play ball? He broke off his speculations, called the Sheraton – Breakwater and asked for Room 101. A thick German accent answered. His name was Kapp, not Kok. He knew nobody by that name. He was trying to be helpful and, Jim figured, probably telling the truth. So he called the hotel back immediately and asked for Kok by name. After a wait, he was informed that Kok had checked out three days previously. The day after he left for Brisbane.

Richard Bower informed him Jack was comfortable, but still very groggy and only waking for brief moments. He advised against another visit that night. Reeves was expected at noon. He would have to make his own examination. All being well, Jack would be under the anaesthetic by five p.m. He knew it was hard, but Bower begged Jim to try not to worry too much and to get a good night's sleep.

No sooner was Bower off the line than Jim was back to the switchboard to dictate Balkenna's number on the off-chance that Tim might be there. He let it ring a good thirty times before hanging up. After a moment's thought, he got a sheet of hotel paper and wrote Tim a quick letter. Without going into detail, he simply advised him there'd been a bit of a hiccup. They were sorting it out but it would delay their return. He asked Tim to phone him at Lowth's whenever he could and to keep trying until he managed to catch him.

He shoved the letter in the hotel's post box on his way to the dining room. He wasn't the least big hungry but he figured he ought to force himself to keep his strength up. He managed a bowl of pea soup.

What in the name of God had happened? Pi Kok's presence still loomed largest in his reckoning and he knew he would have to find him. The bill of sale Jack showed to the yard boss must have been genuine or he wouldn't have acted on it. But who the hell was J. P. Davis? How had Jack been forced into it? And where was the money? The police said they'd found nothing in the car and neither had he. No copies of receipts, nothing.

Jack ... Balkenna ... Anthony and Jean ... He had an overwhelming desire to call Tony, or Jilba. He fought against it. It wasn't fair. Better wait till he knew the result of the operation.

Despite his best efforts to keep Bower's reassurance in mind, the thought of it filled him with dread. If all their efforts resulted in Jack's being blind, he knew he'd never find the strength to face it. He felt condemned for the deadly secret he shared with only one other person on earth.

He was being punished for his weakness and lack of responsibility towards his family following Rachel's death. Rachel . . . Rachel . . . Her presence suddenly filled the room. Her scent flooded his nostrils. He saw her so perfectly, so clearly, he crossed his arms, hugged his own shoulders as if he was holding her and begged her forgiveness for what he'd brought upon their son.

He left the hotel and set off on a long, dogged walk to try and tire himself out. He had to sleep. He had to be in the best possible shape for Jack's ordeal the next day. But it was hopeless. The further he walked, the more his mind churned. He gave up, returned to the hotel, bought a bottle of Scotch and carried it up to his room. He took a few hefty swigs, undressed and got into bed. When the whisky began to work, he took some more and put the bottle on the bedside table. There was a book lying there. Gideon's Bible, brand new and unread. As the whisky swaddled his senses, he lay back, opened the book at random and read the first verse his eye fell on. It was Isaiah twenty-six, twenty. When he got to the next verse, it chilled his blood: For behold, the Lord cometh out of his place to punish the inhabitants of the earth for their iniquity: the earth also shall disclose her blood, and shall no more cover her slain. He slammed the book shut in dismay, dropped it back in the cupboard, groped for the bottle and methodically drank himself into oblivion.

# Forty-Five

A different duty sister greeted him on Jack's wing. With a smile, thank God. Jack had slept well and they were satisfied his concussion had recovered to a point where they need no longer be concerned about his fitness for the operation later in the day.

Jim eased himself into the room and quietly called his name. 'Jack . . .'

Jack raised his battered left arm and reached out towards the sound. 'Dad.'

Jim pulled up a chair and held his son's hand tightly in his with all the love and tenderness he could will into them.

'How's it going, old mate? They tell me you had a comfortable night.'

Jack's grip was vice-like in reply. 'Do you know what happened?'

'Yes,' Jim whispered. 'I've been to the yards.'

'Have you got the car?'

'Yes. The police gave it back to me yesterday.'

Jack squeezed his hand even tighter and anxiously moistened his lips. 'Did you . . . Did you find the bag? . . . With the money?'

'No, mate. You'll have to tell me about that later. When you're better.'

'What about the police? Maybe they've got it.'

'No. There was nothing in the car.'

Jack's top lip fluttered. He ran his tongue over it again as Jim struggled for words.

'I'm sorry, Dad . . .'

'Shssssssh,' said Jim. 'Don't work yourself up. What's done is done. It's you I'm concerned about, nothing else.'

'I shouldn't have done it. I know I shouldn't have . . .'

'Shssssssh . . . Shssssssh.'

'I've got to have an operation . . .'

Wishing to God he could see the whole of his son's face, that they could actually look at one another, Jim fought to keep his voice calm and matter-of-fact.

'Yes, later on this afternoon. It'll be all right.'

'Something's happened to my eye.'

'It's just a little thing, mate. You've got a cut. They've just got to fix it up, that's all. Won't take long and you'll be as good as new.'

Jack tugged at his father's hands. 'Is that the truth?'

'Absolutely. It's just a little thing. They'll give you an anaesthetic and fix it up in no time. I promise.'

Jack lapsed into silence for a moment. 'I'm a bit scared . . . I can't help it . . .'

Jim took one of his hands away and gently stroked his son's shoulder with his fingertips, tracing a delicate line between the two worst bruises there.

'I know, I know. Hospitals and dentists have pretty much the same effect on everybody. It's nothing to be ashamed of. This time tomorrow it'll all be over and done with and you'll be wondering what the hell you were so worried about.'

Jack's mouth pulled into a grim smile. 'I hope so . . .'

Another silence followed as Jim groped for what to say next. Jack grabbed his hand again.

'I'm sorry, Dad. I really blew it . . .'

'I said we don't have to talk about that now.'

'You've got to know what happened.'

At that moment, the door opened and a spritely young red-headed nurse came breezing it, walked straight over and gave Jack a pat on the bum.

'How's our hero getting along?'

'As well as can be expected, I think,' Jim answered for him, with a brief smile.

'That's the ticket! Can't wait to see him with the bandages off. The girls in casualty reckon he's the best-looking bloke we've had in here since Jack Thompson fell off his horse.'

Jack's mouth creased into a real smile this time and he wiggled his toes in embarrassment.

'Can't wait to see you either,' he said.

'It'll be love at first sight,' she promised, giving his pillows a quick professional once-over. 'Right. That ought to do you for a while. Don't go 'way now . . .' She gave Jim a conspirator's wink and hurried out.

'Looks like you've won a few hearts around the place.'

'She's a real hard case that one,' said Jack. 'They've all been great. I've been such a stupid pig . . .'

'Now calm down, calm down. We can talk about it later. Easy does it, okay?'

'I went back to Mr Kok. I know I shouldn't have, but I did.'

Jim fought to keep his tone free of recrimination. 'Why? Why on earth did you do that?'

Jack's mouth drew into a hard, tight line. 'For you . . . For Balkenna. I just thought you'd be wasting your time in Brizzie. I thought we were going to lose everything and it just didn't seem right if there was a way out. It didn't seem to matter to me what Kok did with the stock. We'd have the money, that's all . . .'

'All right. I can accept that. I may not necessarily agree with it. You know I don't. But I understand.'

'I told Kok I'd sell him the lot if he upped the price to two hundred thousand. He was all over me like a rash. Couldn't have been nicer. He asked me what you'd think about it and I said you'd probably agree it was better to have something in the long run. I told him it was my decision and I'd face up to you about it when you came back . . .' He suddenly pulled his hand away and groped for his father's face. 'I'm sorry, Dad . . .'

Jim pressed Jack's hand against his face for a moment before drawing it away and gently pushing it back to the bed.

'It's all right, mate. You know I think you were wrong to do it. I'm not going to kid you about that. But I know you thought you were doing the best thing.'

'Kok told me what a courageous decision it was and all that kind of stuff. How much you'd appreciate it when you had the cash in hand. Said I didn't have to worry about a thing, he'd take care of it all. Said the stock would actually be bought by a man called Davis. He turned out to be one of the blokes with Kok that day at Lowth's. He gave me the money to pay all the yard expenses and everything. The Davis bloke came to Kok's hotel room and we did the bill of sale.'

'All on the day I went to Brisbane?'

'Yeah. Same day. The deal was all done in Kok's room. He got onto someone in the railways the minute I said yes in the morning. It was all arranged by the time Davis got there. All I was supposed to do was stick with Kok the next afternoon while the stock was being trucked at the yards and wait for Davis's call . . .'

He broke off, wetting his lips nervously before continuing. Jim squeezed his hand again.

419

'You don't have to tell me this now if you don't want to. It can wait.'

'No . . . It's all right . . . I mean it all would have been all right except for the bloke that clobbered me. It was nothing to do with Kok or Davis . . . Or his mate. They all kept their word.'

Stunned, puzzled, Jim leant closer. 'Go on.'

'Well, I did like Kok said. I went back to Lowth's for the night and booked a wake-up call for five in the morning.'

'Why so early?'

'That was what Kok had arranged. I had to meet Davis and his partner out at the caravan park at half past five to collect the money. They had to leave early so's they'd make it to Rockhampton in time to be there when the stock arrived.'

'Were they actually staying there? In a caravan?'

'Yeah. A real flash one, with a big Toyota Landcruiser. I told you Davis was a real bad-looking bugger. But he wasn't like that at all. He was really nice and friendly. They had the money waiting for me.'

'Who was the other man? His partner?'

'I don't know his name. He was the other bloke who was with Kok at Lowth's.'

'Go on. What happened then?'

'They had the money for me . . . In a big shoulder bag . . . You know, like an airline bag. They had the blinds down and we sat at the table in the caravan and counted it together. It was all there, two hundred thousand in hundreds and fifties. It looked amazing . . .'

He faltered again. He seemed to be struggling to recall what happened next. Jim gave him a moment and then prompted gently. 'Then what?'

'We'd just got the money back in the bag when there was a knock on the door. It was an old bloke, grey-haired. He wanted to know how much longer they'd be. I thought it was a bit weird, but I had the money and that was all I cared about. I knew it was all there and I just wanted to clear out.'

'Where was Kok through all this?'

'I don't know. At his hotel, I suppose. They didn't say and I didn't ask.'

'So you just said goodbye and they let you go?'

'Yeah. I said I hoped they'd have a good trip and the stock'd be all right after the journey and that was it. I just got in the car to go straight back to Lowth's.'

'What time was that?'

'I don't know. About six fifteen or something like that. I didn't look. All I wanted to do was get the money back to our room. I was just going to open the bag and tip it all out on the bed when you came back. I figured when you saw it all, you wouldn't mind so much . . .'

As Jack gathered himself to continue, his bottom lip trembled and he pulled his hand away from Jim's.

'Everything was fine. There wasn't another soul on the road. But then . . . near the cemetery . . . I saw this bloke lying by the side of the road . . . Like he'd been knocked down, or collapsed or something. He was lying face down and didn't move until I was almost up to him. Then he just sort of crawled onto the road and waved his arm a bit, like he needed help. I asked him what was wrong. I didn't get out, I just hung out the window. He reckoned he thought he'd had a heart attack and could I take him to the hospital.'

'What did he look like?'

'I can hardly remember. He was well built, I know that. Probably about thirty or something . . .'

'Had you seen him before? Anywhere?'

'Not that I can remember. I didn't know what to do. I didn't want to leave him lying there but I didn't want to get out of the car either. I had the bag on the floor in front. I just told him to hang on and I'd get an ambulance. Then he just jumped up and went for me . . . Like a shot. I didn't even have time to pull my head in the window. He grabbed my shirt and started punching me. Next thing I remember was hearing voices . . . Here I suppose. Miles away . . . I kept blacking out and hearing them again when I woke up . . .'

Grim-faced, Jim reached up and traced his fingertips along Jack's shoulder. Jack was blind to the obvious. It would only make his guilt that much harder to bear. Or perhaps that wasn't it. Perhaps it just hadn't crossed his mind. But it was certainly crossing Jim's. Kok at his hotel and his partners still at the caravan park. Proper bill of sale and payment in cash. Another bastard to get the money back and nobody's any the wiser. That was the way it had happened. He didn't doubt it for a minute.

'Did he steal the car?' Jack asked.

'Yes,' Jim lied. He'd heard enough. All that mattered now was keeping Jack on an even keel. There was no point adding insult to injury. If Jack really hadn't figured it out yet, it was just as well. 'The police found it at the railway station. I guess when he found the money he dumped the car and jumped on the first train to Bullamakanka.'

'Is that what the police think?'

'No, mate. They just think it was some big bodgie out for a joy-ride. They don't know about the money. Only you and I know that. And Pi Kok and his mates. Anyway, enough's enough for now. I'm glad you told me. Let's just forget about it.'

'But you should tell the police about the money . . .'

'I will, I will. All in good time. As soon as you're on the mend, okay?'

'But you should tell them right away.'

Jim reached up, gently pulled Jack's hand away from his head and pressed it back on the bed, guarding it with his own.

'Now, come on, you. You promised me not to get yourself in a knot. You've got it off your chest. Just let me handle it from here, okay?'

Jack fell silent again then slowly turned his hand to grip Jim's again.

'I am sorry, Dad.'

Alan Reeves was a bit of a fright. A pale, thin, bird-like creature with eyes on stalks. His hand felt like a woman's. It was small and narrow with long pianist's fingers.

'And how's young Jack? I'm the doctor who's going to fix you up a bit later on.'

Jack raised his hand off the bed and Reeves gave it a shake, withdrawing his own immediately and flipping it a couple of times for Jim's benefit. 'Fit enough by the feel of that . . .'

Bower gave Jim a wink.

'Now, your dad's going to have to make himself scarce for a while. We've got to check you over, make sure you've got your head screwed on straight.'

Jack smiled and groped in mid-air for his father. Jim grabbed his hand and gave it a squeeze.

'Take it easy now, son. Stop thinking about all that other stuff and just concentrate on the job in hand, okay?'

'Okay, Dad. Thanks. Will you come back? When they're through?'

'No, mate. I'm off to Woop Woop. Of course I'll be back, you mug.'

'We'll be about an hour,' Bower advised. 'I've told sister you can wait in my office if you like. She might even trot you out a cup of tea.'

As Jim closed the door behind him he looked back to see the skeletal figure of Alan Reeves already bent over his son, gently peeling the piece of tape holding the head bandage in place. He clicked the door shut quietly and wandered down the corridor, hoping that Bower was right about his friend.

At twenty to eight that night, he could have kissed him.

'It went very well. He's fit and strong, I don't expect any complications. Richard will see to the removal of the dressing. Normally it would come off in a couple of days but we'll give him an extra twenty-four hours just to be on the safe side. He'll let me know how it looks.'

Jim immediately seized Reeves by his scrawny shoulders. 'God bless you. I can't thank you enough.'

Reeves smiled and waited for Jim to release him. 'That's what we're here for, Mr Mackay. I'm glad it went so well. For both of you.'

'Three days seems awful quick. Do you have to keep him in a dark room, or what?'

'Oh no. Obviously, we avoid harsh light for a while.'

'You mean he'll be able to see straightaway?'

'Oh yes. The nerves and muscles will take a while to warm up, but he'll be able to see as soon as the dressing comes off.'

Jim glanced at Bower, as his grin spread. 'Thanks, mate. You know what it means to me . . .'

Before Bower could answer, Reeves excused himself and took his leave.

Jim shook his head in deep but bemused appreciation. 'Looks like he couldn't blow out a candle.'

'I should have warned you. People are a bit taken aback the first time they meet him,' Bower agreed, with a smile. 'But the man's a magician. I've watched him operate right inside the eye. He's got the hands of St Paul.'

'He'll do me,' said Jim. And the grin on his face stretched so far you could hang your washing out to dry.

Back in his room, he collapsed on a chair and allowed the delicious waves of relief to roll over him. The rest of it was trouble, but he was ready for it now.

# Forty-Six

The man at the Cromarty Ampol Station sneered.

'Pi Kok? You a friend of his?'

'Just want to have a word with him, that's all. I hear he's got some stock for sale.'

'Call him a farmer? Wouldn't know a shit from apple butter, if you ask me. That joint of his is more like a glorified weekender. Snooty bastard, too, like all your fuckin' Chows.'

'Yeah, well you're right there,' said Jim. 'Still like to have a word with the cunt. How do I get there?'

Twenty minutes later, Jim hit the brakes on a side road and peered through the windscreen. The house was just as the garage man had described it. Halfway up a small hill and partly hidden by a windbreak of pine trees. He spotted the entrance a little further on, dropped into gear, turned in and roared up the drive, spitting gravel.

He came to a skidding halt, leapt out, bounded up the front steps, rang the bell and started pounding on the door. Nothing happened. He could hear the bell ringing inside, but nobody came. He made his way along the verandah, peering in the windows. The curtains were almost drawn and it was impossible to see anything beyond the interior lace. He dropped off the end of the verandah and headed round the back, double-checking each window as he passed.

There was a long line of outbuildings at the back of the house. In the middle, parking space housed two Holden sedans and a Mercedes 500 SEL saloon. And there was something else. Mounted on the roof, a satellite dish glistened in the afternoon sun. The back door was locked tight. Without further hesitation, Jim stood back, gave himself leg room and swung his boot at the lock. It took a while, but he could feel it going. With one almighty last kick the door flew open. Jim stepped in and stopped dead. The man with a mean face and a boxer's nose was holding a pistol right in his face. It only took him a split second to recognise Jack's description of J. P. Davis.

'That's gonna cost you, sport.'

'Where's Kok?' Jim demanded, standing his ground.

Davis decided to settle on the spot. 'Be a good boy now. Do what you're told. Shift your arse in here or I'll fuckin' well blow it off.'

Jim thought about diving back out of the door but the odds were well against him. He did as he was told.

'Where's the boss?'

'In here.'

Jim hesitated. Davis raised his arm at full stretch and aimed the pistol straight at his head.

'Now, arsehole. Move it!'

'Friendly sort of bloke, aren't you?' said Jim.

Davis shoved him into the room. It was all designer farmhouse chic. The kind of luxury that costs top dollar yet looks like shit. Standing with his back to an open fireplace, Pi Kok greeted Jim's entrance with bland indifference.

'Mr Mackay, we meet again.'

'Where's my money?'

'Where are your manners, Mr Mackay? What did you use, a sledge-hammer?'

'My money, Kok. Two hundred thousand dollars.'

'Paid in full, Mr Mackay. I suggest you consult your son.' He snapped his fingers at the man in the chair. 'Show Mr Mackay the receipt.'

'Don't bother,' Jim stalled. 'I know you paid him, but he didn't get very far with it, did he? Before you beat him to a pulp and took it back.'

Kok raised his hands to heaven. 'Mr Mackay, please. I have absolutely no idea what you're talking about. My associates paid your son the full price agreed between us. Whatever happened after that is nothing to do with me. Why should I be so foolish? The price was a good one. Naturally, I understand you may harbour some ill feeling towards me for accommodating your son's wishes behind your back, but I must point out he *is* of an age to think and make decisions for himself.'

'Don't give me that shit,' Jim spat. 'You're in it up to your eyeballs. You, the Hashims, and these two galahs.'

Davis made a move to belt him, but Kok raised a hand.

'You are mistaken, Mr Mackay. It is not the custom of Muslims and Chinese to consort on business matters in my country. Except for cosmetic accommodations.'

'You're Malaysian too.'

'I am,' Kok confirmed. 'Malay of Chinese extraction and if you will allow me a small boast, extremely proud of my ancestors' achievements, and the contribution they have made to Malaysian prosperity. Now, if I may have your assurance of no further assault on my property or any more wild claims as to this business of your son, you are free to leave.'

Jim glared back at him then made a show of relenting, as if he took Kok at his word. Inside, he charged his batteries and braced himself for action.

'My son was beaten senseless. Seriously injured. He had to have an operation to save an eye –'

'I'm sorry to hear that,' Kok interrupted. 'Such a nice young man, so outgoing. Such a, shall we say, get up and go attitude.'

'Cut it out, Kok. You're wasting your breath.'

'As you wish,' Kok smiled. He looked at Davis and tossed his head at the door.

But Jim didn't budge. 'I'll tell you something, Kok. Beyond any shadow of a doubt, you're the smarmiest, most conceited, yellow-bellied, lying son-of-a-bitch I've ever come across in my life.'

It did the trick. Kok snapped. He leapt across the floor and gave Jim a slap across the face.

'And you hit like a woman.'

Livid with rage, the struts of his self-esteem blown away, Kok stepped back and stabbed angrily at Davis to get the man out of his sight. As Jim had hoped, Davis moved in to prod him in the ribs with the pistol.

'Out.'

Jim took him completely by surprise. He dropped into a crouch and slammed his elbow up into the man's crutch. Davis gasped with shock, doubled over from the pain that surged into his stomach and retched. Before Kok and the other man had time to move, Jim knotted his fists together and gave Davis an uppercut that snapped his head back like a puppet. As he buckled, Jim wrenched the pistol from his hand and had it staring at Pi Kok before he knew what had happened. It took 2.05 seconds. Which was slow, but he was out of practice. The Vietnam war ended nearly twenty years ago.

'Now, you mongrel. Where's my money?'

The other man was half out of his chair.

'That's far enough, ratbag. Don't even blink.'

The man eased himself back into the chair and Jim stepped behind it to cover the back of his head and Kok at the same time.

'Take off your clothes. Both of you. And do it bloody slowly, I warn you. You're vermin, Kok. Just give me an excuse and I'll be happy to oblige. You first, Kok.'

'May I ask why?'

'Just do it.'

Flabbergasted, Kok slowly unbuttoned his shirt. It landed in a pretty heap of expensive silk on the floor. As he pulled his singlet over his head, Jim had to give him credit. Stunned he may have been, but he was showing no fear. The man in the chair, on the other hand, was shaking like a leaf. Suddenly, with a low groan, Davis stirred on the floor. Jim stepped back and kicked him in the head to put him out of his misery. When Kok had removed his pants, shoes and socks, Jim kicked the clothes to the other side of the room. Then he ordered the other man to get up and stand beside him.

'Slow, remember. Nice and slow . . .'

Jim figured he was probably carrying a pistol as well. But when he tested the discarded clothes with his foot he couldn't feel another weapon.

'Really, Mr Mackay. Is this absolutely necessary?'

'You bet your life,' Jim snapped. 'I've still got my boy's score to settle with you.'

'Your son decided for himself what was best in your mutual interests. A wise decision in my estimation. My associates and I . . . how do you say? . . . lent over backwards to accommodate him. Rather successfully, I might add.'

'Is that a fact.'

'Yes, it it. He knew you stood to lose everything and I think he may have considered your attitude, shall we say, a little old-fashioned.'

'You!' Jim snapped at the other man. 'Strip him off and then I want him outside. One stupid move and your little fat friend here's got a hole in his head. Go!'

The man's hands were shaking so badly it took him an age to strip Davis's clothes and start dragging him to the door. The peculiar procession made its way along the hall, out through the splintered back door and across the yard to the out-buildings. Fifteen minutes later, inside the smallest of the

428

barns, Pi Kok was on his knees following Jim's instructions, tying the last knot. Davis and his offsider were spreadeagled face down on the floor, strung up by their wrists and ankles to the towing frame of a Ferguson tractor. The ropes were biting into their flesh all right and he gave each one a savage yank to make sure the knots were secure. Davis was still half out of it, but the other man yelped and hissed through gritted teeth.

'You'll pay for this, mate.'

'Is that a fact, mate? How would you like a thump in the ear as well?'

The threat was enough.

Back in the house, in front of the fireplace, Kok crossed his arms, hugged himself and shivered.

'Perhaps you might allow me my shirt. I feel a chill . . .'

'In this heat?'

'In this atmosphere.'

'Where's my money?'

'That is a matter you must take up with your son . . .'

'Okay, Kok,' said Jim, fishing in his pocket. 'Have it your own way.' He pulled out a scrap of paper. 'Get on the phone. Townsville police. Here's the number. Tell them we're having a party.'

Kok took the paper from Jim's hand and studied it a moment. Then, taunting Jim with his eyes, he slowly scrunched it into a little ball and dropped it at his feet. 'That won't be necessary.'

The explosion sounded off the walls and filled the room with the stench of cordite. Kok jumped with fright as the floorboards ruptured a hair's breadth from his foot.

'Do it!' Jim shouted, 'or so help me the next one will take some of your toes with it.'

'Are you mad?'

'Yeah,' Jim shouted, closing on him. 'Mad as a cut snake. Here, this is for my boy.' He gave Kok half a dozen hard rapid-fire slaps across the face. The desire to hit him with the pistol as well was overwhelming and he quickly stepped back again to get a grip on his rage. Kok's eyes narrowed.

'That was a mistake, Mr Mackay.'

'I'll tell you the only mistake I made,' Jim fumed. 'I should have gone straight to the authorities the minute I left your bloody room at the Breakwater.'

'You're a fool, Mr Mackay, and I don't, as they say, suffer

429

fools gladly.' Ignoring the pistol in Jim's hands, he took a step closer. 'Go ahead! Call the police! And here's something to think about while you wait. You have a beautiful daughter, I believe.'

Jim's spine turned to ice. 'What's that supposed to mean?'

'Just what I said,' Kok snarled. 'You have a beautiful daughter. Her beauty is, shall we say, her fortune, is it not? I'm sure you wouldn't want it damaged in any way.'

'My daughter has nothing to do with it.'

'Ah,' Kok gloated. 'I see you're surprised. Who do you think you're talking to? Some second-hand cow dealer? Is that what you think? Your miserable cattle mean nothing to me.' He snapped his fingers. 'A footnote to a busy week. Would you like to know where your daughter is right at this moment?'

'I know where she is,' Jim replied sullenly.

'And where's that?'

'That's my business.'

'It's also my business. New York? Is that what you think?'

Chalk-white, Jim raised the pistol again but Kok just dismissed it with a twisted little smile and Jim let his arm drop.

'You can't be sure, can you, Mr Mackay? Well, let me tell you, just so you know, as they say. At the moment your beautiful daughter is being photographed in London for one of those stupid magazines bored women must read from cover to cover before they know what to wear. From there she will fly to Sao Paulo, to model clothes in a fashion show for some fool who wishes to hang his garments on the wives of Brazilian army officers. Like leeches on the terminally ill. Ah, but I see I have upset you. Perhaps if you will excuse me.'

Eyes dancing, he dismissed Jim, retrieved his clothes and began dressing. Jim watched him with helpless fascination. A taipan had come out of the toy box. As Kok retrieved his shoes, Jim braced himself, raised the pistol and worked the breech. The dull, metallic click made Kok look up.

'What's to stop me?'

'Two people, Mr Mackay. You and me. Hurt me and someone you love gets hurt. Your daughter? Your son in Brisbane? Your son here? Who can say? Kill me and you forfeit your own life. I can assure you of that. Where? When? How?' He shrugged. 'A decision for those who honour me. A week? A month? A year? Who knows? Revenge is sweetest when least expected, as I'm sure you'll agree.' He pulled his second shoe over his toes, stood up and wriggled his foot.

430

Jim wasn't intimidated by the threat to himself, but the threat to his children filled him with dread. He leapt forward, shoved Kok back into the armchair and held the pistol inches from his face.

'If you so much as harm one hair of my girl's head, if you or any of your friends ever come near one of my sons again, I swear to God I'll kill you. And that's a promise.'

But it was an empty one. Kok simply brushed the pistol aside.

'Let's be clear about this, absolutely clear. One word, just one word to the police, the port authorities or anyone else, and your daughter's face will be cut beyond repair.'

'You wouldn't dare . . .'

'It never ceases to amaze me what some people will do for really quite small amounts of money. Knives, unfortunate accidents with phials of acid – the possibilities are endless.'

'God in heaven,' Jim protested. 'What kind of man are you?'

'My own,' Kok snapped. 'Now, I really must relieve my friends of their discomfort, so I suggest you be on your way. They may not take such a lenient view. Our business is over. Your son gambled on your behalf. He lost, and so have you. I suggest you accept that as, shall we say, a fact of life. Barring further melodramatics on your part, I shall personally consider the matter closed. I strongly recommend you do the same. Life is, as they say, a learning of lessons. I trust you have learnt yours.'

Never in his life had Jim felt so humiliated. 'Those cattle represented just about everything I've got . . .'

'You may leave the pistol on the desk,' said Kok.

Jim didn't bother with the desk. He just dropped the pistol at his feet.

'Just tell me one thing. Why didn't you tell me all this straight up? When your offsider brought me in here?'

Kok smiled. 'I'm always fascinated to see just how far a man will go. You must forgive me. A weakness of mine. I find people to be at their most receptive when they reach a point of questioning their own morality. It is also prudent to entertain some caution when a man takes leave of his senses with a gun in his hand. Besides, believe it or not, I gave strict instructions your son was not to be subjected to unnecessary violence. I rather admired the directness and determination of his approach to me. My instructions were quite explicit. Unfortunately, my associate failed to pass them on with sufficient emphasis. Let's hope you have taught him a lesson. You've got five minutes to get off my property.'

'You might be able to big-note yourself now. But you'll get yours. Maybe not from me, but you'll get it. All rotten apples fall eventually. Someday, somewhere. London to a brick on that.'

The anger that flashed in Kok's eyes was reward of a sort. He was at the window as Jim drove away.

He drove back to Townsville at a snail's pace. Kok had it all covered. Jim had his own good reason to avoid the police. He was lying in a gully off the road to Charters Towers.

As he crossed the bridge over Ross River, he glanced at his watch. It had already gone five thirty. Jack wouldn't wait.

He sat up the moment the door opened and immediately wanted to know what was going on. It used up the last reserves of Jim's will to duck his son's questions as casually as possible, reassuring him the police were doing all they could, they'd agreed with Jim that, for the sake of their enquiry, the story would be kept out of the papers as long as possible. Then, talking about anything else under the sun he could think of, he stayed for an hour and a half, fed Jack his supper, told him to keep his pecker up and promised to return in the morning.

As he made his way across the parking area to the station wagon, he realised he couldn't keep it up too long. Another forty-eight hours and Jack's dressing would come off. If all was well, they would at least be able to look at one another. Even so, he figured he'd better wait a couple of days more before explaining things. It was going to knock Jack for six, no two ways about that. Coming to terms with his debacle was going to be a very painful process indeed.

He tossed his coat on the chair, tugged off his tie, and looked for the bottle of Scotch. He did a quick count of what he had left in cash. Jack's medical bills and their extended stay in Townsville would take a big bite out of the little he had left in the bank. Another wave of hopelessness rolled in, and he shook his head, flipping over the plastic pockets of his wallet until he came to Rachel's photograph. He had taken it himself on their tenth wedding anniversary. Radiant happiness shone in her eyes for the man behind the camera. He stared and stared at it, tracing the outline of her features with his fingernail.

'Well, my love,' he muttered. 'We've really dumped ourselves in it this time . . .'

He flipped past a photo of Tony, Jack and Billy, taken one year at the Starlight Stampede in Longreach, and came to his favourite shot of Jilba, a stunning black and white portrait taken by Avedon, who Tony reckoned was a pretty famous photographer. And the penny dropped.

He clicked his fingers and rabbited in his coat for his phone book. He found her number, recited it to the switchboard and held his breath. He let it ring and ring before he hung up, empty. He wished to God he had her agent's number. But Rachel had kept that in her book and it was in the desk at Balkenna. If only Tim would call, he could ask him to look it up.

He started taking off his shoes and socks, and had another flash of inspiration. He grabbed his wallet, carefully slid Jilba's photo out of the plastic holder and flipped it over. There it was. This time his call was answered by a machine. Still, it was better than nothing. He recorded his message, stressing the urgency she return his call as soon as possible. He repeated the hotel number twice over to make sure. When he hung up, he crossed his fingers over the phone for luck.

He got back on the phone and called Brisbane. He just wanted to hear their voices.

Susan gave him a lot of excited details about the baby's first major check-up, every square inch of the scan. All was well. Tony, as expected, proved trickier to handle. With his journalist's ear to the ground, he immediately asked if the Townsville dock strike had created any problems. Jim surprised himself with the casual aplomb with which he managed to duck the issue. Yes, it had stymied their original plan but they'd managed to find a buyer for the domestic market. It would mean a bit of a loss but, in the circumstances, they'd have to wear it. No, he couldn't have a word with him, Jack was out on the town. From that point he simply bombarded Tony with questions until Billy grabbed the phone and started shouting down the line. As he hung up, Billy asked in a sad little voice when he'd be going back to Balkenna. Jim promised faithfully they would all have a long talk about that very soon.

The phone jangled at ten to eight the following morning. His greeting was answered by a brisk but friendly American woman informing him she was returning his call to the Max Gordon Agency in New York City. Unfortunately, Mr Gordon was in

433

Los Angeles on business. Could she be of assistance? Even before he finished his explanation, the woman cut in to tell him the worst. Jilba was also out of town, in London on a photographic assignment. She would not be back for some time. She was going on to Brazil direct from London. Was there anything she could do? She could provide a number in London, if that would help. She told him to have a nice day. Dazed, Jim hung up, rolled back on the bed, stared at the ceiling and came to terms with the fact that Pi Kok wasn't bluffing. It was not the way to start a nice day at all.

There was a knock at the door. Jim's heart skipped a beat. The knock was repeated.

'Open up, Mr Mackay. It's Sergeant Stewart.'

The sergeant all but tied Jim up in knots. Though he had nothing further on Jack's assailant, he had established some other facts. He now knew about the dock strike, Jim's confrontation with the local secretary of the Australian Waterside Workers' Federation, the subsequent sale of the cattle to a Mr Davis and their shipment by rail to Rockhampton. Could any of these issues relate to his son's assault? Was Jack, for instance, in possession of any substantial amount of money at the time?

Ducking and weaving, Jim managed to brazen it out. No, he was absolutely sure neither the wharfies nor the buyers of his stock could be implicated in any way at all. His discussions with Kevin Kelly had been disappointing, but understandable in the circumstances. The purchase of his cattle had been made by bank cheque and that was safely on its way to his station manager in Longreach. Then, as a capper, he made a show of taking Stewart into his confidence. His son had a bit of a short fuse. He'd been in trouble before in a hotel brawl that got a little, well, out of hand. In Hughenden. There'd been a fine for aggravated assault. Jack was admitting nothing of the sort, but perhaps his injuries had resulted from some dispute or challenge match in his father's absence. If that was the case, Jack had obviously bitten off more than he could chew.

It did the trick. Stewart started looking at his watch. The minute he was gone, Jim took a couple of shots of Scotch to oil his jangling nerves.

At four thirty the following afternoon he was dealing with another rush of nerves as he waited in Bower's office for the removal of Jack's dressing. When Bower finally breezed in, gave him a thumbs up and declared the operation a complete success,

Jim forgave the worm of the world for everything, and thanked Bower from the bottom of his heart.

The fluorescent lights had been switched off and the room was lit only by what late afternoon sunlight managed to filter through the closed venetian blinds. But it was enough. Jack's bruised face burst into a huge cheeky grin as Jim let himself in and hurried to embrace him. Jack gave as good as he got.

'Christ! What a shiner!'

'Yeah, I know. The sister gave me a squiz at myself in a mirror. My kisser's really gone to the pack, hasn't it?'

'That's for sure,' Jim chuckled. 'That's for sure. You'll get over it. How'd the redhead react?'

'Said she couldn't tell,' Jack smiled. 'Have to give me another once-over when the bruises are gone. Put me on a promise . . .'

Back at Lowth's, he was getting stuck into his rhubarb and custard when he got a phone call. It was Tim.

After swearing him to utter secrecy, particularly as far as the rest of the family were concerned, Jim told him all that had happened since their arrival in Townsville. Tim heard him out in silence. When it was over, his immediate reaction was so typical, it made Jim smile.

'Well, you can have what I've got saved, Jim. You know that. As long as we keep the place on the go, that's all that matters to me. I can get it out of the bank tomorrow, if it'll help.'

Jim had to clear a catch in his throat before he spoke.

'Bless you, Tim. You're a bottler. But no, mate. Hang on to it for the moment. I've been kicking another scheme around in my skull all day. Still not too sure what I really think about it. But there's one thing you can do for me, first thing in the morning, if you can.'

'Sure. What is it?'

'It'll mean a trip into Longreach.'

'No worries. What is it?'

'My passport. You'll find it in the bottom right-hand drawer of my desk in the office. It's inside one of those cardboard wallet things. The green one, I think. Can you send it to me here at Lowth's? Better make it special delivery.'

There was no response and Jim suddenly thought they'd been cut off.

'Hello? Tim? You there? Hello?'

'Yeah,' came the subdued reply at last. 'Jim . . . You're not gonna do a disappearing act on us again, are you?'

'Not a chance, mate,' Jim chuckled. 'No worries on that score. It's up and at 'em as far as I'm concerned. I'll be buggered if I'm going to let these mongrels put us out of the race. Not a bit of it. I'm feeling pretty bushed, with Jack and everything. But I am thinking about something and, if I decide to give it a go, I'll have to make a quick trip, that's all.'

'Where to?'

'China.'

'Dinkum?' Tim asked incredulously.

'No, mate. Pulling your leg. Just do it for me, will you? Try and be on the doorstep when the post office opens up, if you can. That way I should get it the day after tomorrow.'

'Well, tell me where you're heading for, for Christ's sake.'

'I want to have a real good hard think about it first, Tim. Give us another call around this time tomorrow night, will you? I'll tell you then, if I've decided to give it a go.'

'Okay, Jim. Whatever you say. She'll be first down the chute, don't worry. I was gonna tell you to give Jack a thick ear for me, but I guess he's got one already.'

'Just about the only thing he hasn't got. Thick head covers the lot, I reckon.'

'Okay. Well, tell him he's got a kick in the bum coming from me for being such a nong.'

'That won't do any good either, mate. He's too busy kicking himself to notice. I'll let him know how you feel, anyway.'

'Better not, just tell him I'm glad he's out the other side of it okay.'

'Will do.'

'Okay, Jim.'

'Tim. I know all this is going to knock you for a loop the minute you put the phone down. The whole thing's a bastard, no getting around that. But keep your pecker up, mate. Where there's a will, and all that. Now that Jack's in the clear, I'm going to bust a gut to find it. Okay?'

'Just don't do anything I wouldn't do,' Tim admonished dryly.

'That's a promise.'

They'd been talking for an hour and his rhubarb had long since returned to the kitchen. But Jim felt like a bit of company and so he adjourned to the bar for a few snorts and what turned out to be a long nag with an English tour guide having a night off. He was from a place called Ripon and Jim had to concentrate hard on his broad North Yorkshire accent.

By the time he returned to his room, he was feeling a lot more relaxed. He sat down with pen and paper to have that real good hard think he'd promised himself. He filled twelve pages with endless permutations. He became so totally absorbed he'd been at it for nearly an hour and a half when a long satisfying yawn told him it was time to hit the sack.

Three days later he was contemplating the far horizons of the wide blue Pacific Ocean from thirty-five thousand feet. This was the way that Rachel went. The mosaic of coral shell fanning the edge of the world must have taken her breath away. Jim held her in his mind's eye and wondered if, in some mysterious way, she had planted the seed of the idea for this journey, involving, as it must, the final laying to rest of the one real grievance that had ever come between them.

# Forty-Seven

Dean Coulter got up, stepped to the window of his office and contemplated the familiar view of Madison Avenue. He knew this was no easier for the Queensland bushman seated at his desk than it was for himself. Jim's call from Townsville had been a bolt from the blue. He knew he must have agonised long and hard before he picked up the phone. The hesitancy in his voice told him that. He returned to his desk, gave Jim a brief smile and sat down.

'How did he take it? Jack?'

'Not too good,' Jim admitted. 'I eased him into it as best I could. But he knows he's been taken for the biggest ride of his life. There wasn't much I could do on that score. He was still pretty down in the dumps when I left. It would have been good if I could have brought him along to take his mind off it. But he's in good hands at the hospital. Lots of attention. One of the nurses has taken a shine to him.'

'How did he handle the police?'

'All right. But I knew he was a bundle of nerves. They didn't seem to notice. Past caring, I think, to tell you the truth. We had plenty of time to rehearse.'

Coulter reflected for a moment.

'Well, I'm sure you made the right decision. These people generally mean what they say. We had a guy here just a couple of weeks ago. A Wall Street broker. Got tangled up somehow with one of the mobs in Atlantic City. They poured petrol over his wife and kids and burnt his house to the ground. Up in New Bedford. Poor guy shot himself in his office a couple of days later.'

'I just hadn't come face to face with it on that level before. The minute I knew he wasn't pulling the wool about Jilba, that was it. There was no way to get back after that.'

'Damn shame she's out of town,' said Coulter. 'She'll raise the roof.'

'Yeah. It's a bugger. Still, can't be helped. Have to make up for it next time round. How is she? Do you see much of her?'

'Yes, quite a bit. I put up some money for her boyfriend, Danny Serrano, to get his new management agency off the ground. The money's ridiculous. Paid me back in six months. Interest, everything. Made me pull my head in I can tell you. I kind of thought I'd be lucky to see a penny . . .' He broke off.

'Tony told me he's been after Jilba to marry him.'

'Yes,' Coulter smiled. 'I think that's about the only thing he can't swing at the moment. A very independent young lady.'

'Is he around?'

'No, he's in London with her. Said he had some business. Probably set up a couple of meetings so he could keep an eye on her.'

'What do you think of him? Apart from the business side?'

'Didn't take to him at first. A bit off the wall for my taste. But that was just me feeling my age, I guess. I've grown to like him. He's got a good heart.'

'I've worried about her.'

'I keep an eye on her too, Jim, don't forget.'

Jim looked away. 'Yeah. I know. I've appreciated it.'

Coulter studied him with intensely mixed feelings until Jim's eyes met his again. When they did, he had to look away himself.

'So you need just under half a million for the bank to play ball?'

'I'm afraid so,' Jim admitted.

'What's that make the total purchase price?'

'Around the eight seventy-five mark.'

'Plus interest.'

'Plus interest, yeah. I can swing a fifteen-year spread on that. It'd be tight as a fish's bum to start with. First few seasons . . .' Jim held his fingers up and crossed them. 'But, if they went well, we'd be home and hosed.'

'Have you talked to Jack?'

'Yeah, of course. He's got no illusions. It'll be like it was for me twenty years ago. Starting from scratch, in hock up to my eyeballs. The only thing I can say is it's a bloody good way to learn.'

'Do you think he'll stick it out? They are a different generation, Jim. Not necessarily the worse for it. But when they've had it on a plate growing up, it's hard to take a cut. David was mad keen to come into the business, start at the bottom. But he'd only experienced it at my level and I think it came as one hell of a shock. He's still hanging in there, but I worry about him.'

Jim nodded. 'I know what you mean. The only thing I can say for sure is Jack loves the land, and the life. Only time will tell, I suppose.'

Coulter stood up and padded back to the window, deep in thought. Jim stared at his back with mounting unease. Maybe he shouldn't have come. It was asking a lot, far more than the money involved. Despite the subterfuge he'd found so hard to stomach, this man had already done him the biggest favour of his life, long, long ago. If nothing else, Rachel had drummed that into him. He didn't doubt how much it must have hurt. He was on the point of taking it all back when Coulter turned.

'Well, Aussie, if I'm about to go into the Queensland cattle business, I better get myself a head start. Once you've got the leases back, the quickest way to turn a buck would be to stock the place to capacity, am I right?'

'Too right,' Jim confirmed, putting his reticence aside. 'They're a bugger to deal with, but I'd turn half of it over to sheep to begin with, for the first few years. You get a quicker turnover. There's a lot less fluctuation in the wool market. I'm a cattle man at heart, but it would be stupid to ignore it. Camp on the bugger's doorstep if we have to,' he chuckled. 'I know Tim would.'

'By a billabong, I suppose.'

'Yeah. Bit of luck they'll find it this time. Look, Dean, I wouldn't ask . . . I wouldn't have come, believe me, if Tony hadn't told me about the chat you had in Brisbane. Now . . . Well, I know we all say things on occasions like that, and we mean them at the time. But . . . Well, if the whole thing's a pain in the arse, just say so, will you? Enough has happened between us without overloading the cart –'

Coulter raised a hand and cut him off. 'Hold on, hold on. We're talking about a whole new ball game for me. Light years away from all this,' he added, with a wave at corporate America. 'I don't need to make any more money, but I don't like to lose any, either. Wherever else I may fall down, I do good business. I've had to. I'm planning to toss it in fairly soon and take a ride on the slow train. But even if he hangs in there, David won't be ready for this seat for years. I've got four vice-presidents here, all falling over themselves to help me retire. But I'm hard to toss. I just want to know I have a very clear picture of what's involved. What's bubbling under the surface. Is there anything else I should know about? Hidden costs, other debts or obligations. Anything that might throw a spanner in the works?'

In the split second that followed, Jim took one of the biggest gambles of his life.

'There is something. Whether it's right to let you in on it or not, I don't know. You'll have to keep it under your hat.'

Intrigued, Coulter leant back in his chair, and waited. Jim weathered a flutter of nerves, took a deep breath and put his hands on the desk. It took him twenty minutes. Coulter heard him out in silence. The drunken despair he knew all about. But when Jim got to the Thirty Mile Range, his season in the wilderness, he was starting to flounder, and when he got to the violent climax, he was stunned.

'Jesus! You have been in the wars, haven't you?'

'Haven't been able to take a trick in the last couple of years,' Jim admitted grimly. 'That's why I'm betting it's got to be time for a change.'

'What about the other two? Fred and Annie? Where are they now?'

'Still there, as far as I know.'

'And there hasn't been a word since?'

'Not a squeak. I asked Tim the other night if there were any letters for me from Charters Towers. I'll have to get Annie on one side . . . I was planning to look in on them on the way home from Townsville.'

'She must be quite a woman.'

'She's nobody's fool, that's for sure. I owe her a great deal. She was the one who pulled me through, really. And she had a job on convincing me. If I hadn't owed her so much, and Fred, in his way, I wouldn't have even considered it. As far as any deal between us, well, if it were to blow up, it's just me that's involved. Tim and Jack would still be there to run Balkenna.'

'That would have happened by now.'

'God knows. I suppose so. But it's still there, ticking away in the background. Funny thing is I feel so bad about it. You'd think after all the poor bastards we killed in 'Nam . . . And all for nothing.'

'All for nothing,' Coulter concurred. 'We handled a

promotion campaign for the veterans here. Gratis. Really racked me up I can tell you. When you see what some of them have got to live with . . . Everything lost and nothing gained.'

The two men lapsed into silence for a moment as their memories blundered over the ashes of their dead youth. Coulter shook his head, released a sigh and broke the spell.

'I can hardly say I'm *glad* you told me, Jim. But I appreciate it. Thanks.'

'Only fair in the circumstances,' said Jim. 'Good reason for you to give it a miss, if you want to.'

Coulter picked up a pencil. 'Okay, here's what we'll do. I don't see any point in making it harder than we have to. I've already got some money in Australia – we had an associate company there for years, in Melbourne. Just a small outfit. They hit a rough spot and we bought them out. Six or seven years ago. I paid off the old management and put in some young blood, all Melbourne people. They offered me a two point two million profit to take a walk a couple of years ago, and I took it. I'll have to get onto my man in Melbourne for the finer points, but here's what I say we do. I'll buy in for the price of the leases. Flat ten per cent interest over whatever term you need. That way your bankers can get you restocked immediately and my money will be happier. How does that sound?'

Like the kiss of life. The giddy waves surged and Jim slumped back in his chair, too rapt to respond. Coulter gave him room.

'You look done in, Aussie,' he observed quietly.

Jim looked up and nodded. 'I am a bit. Longest flight I've ever made . . .' He paused, gathering strength. 'That's more than I could have possibly hoped for. I'll pay you back, Dean. Every cent.'

'Cross that bridge when we come to it.'

Another silence took root and grew. Jim contemplated his hands in his lap. The sudden release of pressure left him strangely listless. It was nothing to do with jet lag. There was more than an imported Italian desk between himself and the man who'd just thrown him a lifeline. He knew her image had hung in Coulter's mind throughout their conversation, just as much as it had in his. The room had been full of her from the moment Coulter's secretary ushered him in and the two of them shook hands – with a touch of reserve on both sides. As he looked back up and saw the expression on Coulter's face, she could no longer be denied. He took the plunge.

'You know how much Rachel would appreciate what you're doing. For Jack, as much as me . . .'

Coulter flinched and dropped his eyes. It took a while before he could look up again. He stared at Jim like a blind man.

'You're out on your feet. You'll keel over if you don't get some sleep. We've got an apartment here, on the second floor. I want you to go down there and sack out. Sleep as long as you like. I'll have to get onto Griffiths in Melbourne and figure out how we go about this. I've got to take the guy's advice, that's what I pay him for.'

Jim just nodded.

As Coulter's secretary accompanied him down in the lift, unlocked the apartment and ushered him in, Jim went along with her in a sort of trance.

She hesitated at the door. 'I was very sorry to hear about your wife. She was a real lady . . .'

'Thank you,' said Jim. 'That's kind.'

The apartment had the look of an expensive hotel suite. When Jim saw the bed, it was all he could do to pull off his coat and tie.

A distant hammer finally dragged him back to consciousness. It took a moment to remember where he was. The hammer was Coulter knocking on the door.

'How's the patient?'

'A bit rickety,' Jim smiled. 'I must have blacked out the minute my head hit the pillow.'

'Five and a half hours.'

'Good Lord.'

'Are you awake?'

'I hope so.'

'I'd hate this to go to waste. Sit down.'

Jim plonked down in the nearest chair.

'I got onto Chris Griffiths. Caught him at a weak moment. He'd just backed three winners in a row. He was about ready to take over running the planet.'

'Good on him,' Jim laughed.

'He tells me he can get out of BHP and have the money in your account within ten days.'

Jim could hardly believe it. Not only did he have the loan but, despite everything that lay like a minefield between them,

Coulter kept it all on a courteous, businesslike basis, defusing the awful sensation of cap-in-hand that had stalked him earlier in the day. If Rachel *had* planted the seed, the fruit had bloomed. He stretched forward and stuck out his hand. 'Bless you, mate. I don't know quite what to say. Grateful seems a bit short of the mark.'

Coulter shook his hand warmly in reply. 'No worries, cobber. It's not just for you and Jack. And Rachel. Pop always wanted to do something for your father in his lifetime, for pulling him out of that shitfight in New Guinea. It hurt him when your old man didn't answer his letters. I guess he understood why when he found out, but it hurt him all the same. I guess I'm just trying to get even.'

'That may be, Dean. But it's a hell of a lot more besides, as far as I'm concerned.'

'Let's just say it's for old times' sake then,' Coulter grinned.

Seeing the sheer relief was making Jim a bit shaky, Coulter got up and dropped a hand on his shoulder.

'You sure you want to go straight back tomorrow? You don't want to stay a couple of days now that this is out of the way?'

'I'd like to, but I promised Jack I'd make it a round trip. He'll be bursting his boiler to know the result.'

'Why not give him a call?'

'This is one thing,' Jim smiled, 'I've got to tell him face to face. I wouldn't miss that for all the tea in China.'

'Okay. I've got about another hour's worth upstairs. Why don't you take a shower, get yourself together and then we can go get some dinner.'

Coulter opened the door.

'Dean. Thanks again, from all of us.'

Coulter smiled and gave him a wink. 'No worries, right?'

Jim stared at the door long and hard, savouring the full significance of his long, weary, desperate journey. He wandered back to the bedroom, picked up his coat, took out his wallet, brought her image to his lips and gave it a kiss.

'For old times' sake,' he whispered.

Coulter took him to a Vietnamese restaurant called Indo-Chine. As they picked their way through a succession of spicy delicacies, they stuck to basics, the big picture of Coulter's business empire and the practicalities of running an outback property such as Balkenna. But, by the time the waiter arrived with coffee and brandy, they had both temporarily run out of things to say and Jim was far, far away in his thoughts. Coulter helped himself to sugar.

'You still with us?'

Jim started and came back to earth with a chuckle. 'It's funny. I was just thinking, this is the first time I've ever eaten Vietnamese food.'

'You're kidding!'

'No, I'm not. I avoided it like the plague in 'Nam. Only ate our grub. Too scared of the bugs, I guess.'

'Me, I lapped it up. Love the stuff. I've spent a fortune in this place.'

'Well,' Jim admitted with a grin. 'I can see why. There's not enough Rs in grouse, as we say.'

Coulter laughed with pleasure.

Jim laughed too, but it didn't last. Coulter waved goodbye to somebody leaving another table. When his eyes returned to Jim's there was a mutual flash of recognition that another presence could no longer be denied, though they'd tried.

'Did you bring Rachel here?' Jim asked quietly.

'Yes,' said Coulter, sadly. 'Several times.'

'I'll bet she enjoyed it.'

'Yes,' he admitted. 'She did.'

That was as far as they got. It was up to Jim, and he knew it.

'She was excited about you meeting up again,' he confessed. 'It was good to know you were keeping an eye on her . . .'

The candid acceptance was not lost on Coulter, and he responded in kind, though his smile was taut and haunted.

'I didn't get a lot of work done in those weeks, I must admit. Needless to say, I didn't regret it for a minute.' He looked Jim right in the eye and owned up to the full strength of his feelings. 'I didn't want her to leave, Jim.'

Jim held his look a long time before he answered. 'No. I figured as much. It took me a long time to realise she was fed up with life at Balkenna. And then it was too late. What about Rachel? Did she want to stay?'

Coulter had to look at his lap.

'I begged her to,' he said quietly. 'I can't deny that. I loved her, Jim, I think you know that. I couldn't bear the thought of losing her again . . . Not to you or anyone else . . .'

'What did she say?' he asked. He didn't want to know. But he had to.

Coulter just shook his head. 'Lots of things . . .'

'I need to know, Dean.'

Coulter looked back up, his eyes full of anguish. 'Torn. Not between you and me. Torn between her love for you and her need to get away from Balkenna. I think she'd kept it from you for years. There was no question she loved you, Jim. More than me. Though I know she loved me, too, in her way.'

It was Jim's turn to look to his lap.

'If nothing else, I think I managed to persuade her to bring it out in the open with you. I'm not going to pretend I wouldn't have been more than happy to play second-best if things hadn't worked out between you. No point denying that.'

Jim digested Coulter's frank admission for a moment, fighting a lightning flash of resentment. When it passed, he looked up, and made his peace.

'That would have been fair enough. After all, you brought us together in the first place. I just didn't really have any idea *how* unhappy she was. It broke my heart when I found out.'

'Who told you? Jilba?'

'No, her mother. When I had to call her about the . . . about the accident. Jilba had known about it, too, evidently. But Rachel swore them all to secrecy.'

It was that word, 'accident'. Neither man knew how to continue and they lapsed into silence. When Coulter broke it, it came from the depths of his heart.

'She loved you, Jim. Beyond any shadow of a doubt. She just felt life was slipping away from her and there were a lot of things she wanted to do. She may have swept it all under the carpet again, gone back and never said a word. I don't know . . .' He reached across the table and covered Jim's hand with his own. 'That's her secret now. Let's just leave it at that.'

Jim turned his hand and gripped Coulter's with the ferocity of friendship. 'One thing I know for sure. She'd be very happy to see us here together. Yeah, you're right. Let's just leave it at that.'

Coulter tapped his glass, and his eyes clouded. 'To Rachel.'

'To Rachel,' Jim responded and drained his glass.

Jim was wide awake by six and decided to have a quick squint at a bit of New York before the morning rush hour took over. The security man let him out and he set off on a slow walkabout, just following his nose, enjoying the sights and sounds of the big

447

mean city rumbling into the life of a new day. The spring in his step told him just how much of a burden had been lifted from his shoulders. He felt distinctly lightheaded.

He eventually came across a delicatessen already humming and half full of early-birds. He found an empty stool at the far end of the counter and stalled a couple of times while he read the menu on the wall.

When the deli man returned for the third time, he played safe.

'Give us a toasted bacon, lettuce and tomato sandwich, please. Brown bread. And a drop of coffee, no milk.'

'Mayo?'

'Come again?'

'Mayonnaise?'

'Oh . . . Yes, why not? Just a bit.'

The deli man smirked. 'BLT rye down, easy mayo, coffee nude.' Deadpan, he turned back to Jim and ran a rheumy eye over his bushman's threads. 'Australia?'

'Yeah, mate. Queensland.'

'Didn't think you was from Brooklyn,' he cracked, turning away immediately to slice a two-foot long salami at the speed of light.

Jim couldn't believe the thing when it arrived. He gave some serious thought to sending out for a fork-lift truck. But he ate the lot, and washed it down with some of the best coffee he reckoned he'd ever tasted.

He had another hour with Coulter in his office, during which they telexed his account number to Melbourne. At Coulter's insistence, they also sent a long telex to Wally Jenkins at the bank in Longreach, instructing him to make an immediate offer to purchase both the Coalmec leases outright. Promptly at eleven, Coulter offered his hand and pointed at the long, black limo waiting at the curb.

'Sorry I can't come out with you, Jim. Antonio will get you there in good time.'

Jim took his hand and held it for a long time. 'Thanks again, Dean. For everything.'

'You'll let me know . . .'

'Of course,' Jim promised. 'And don't forget what I said about coming to have a look at your investment, okay? Soon as you can.'

'It's a deal,' Coulter smiled. 'Say hello to Tony for me, will you? And Jack, of course. I'll look forward to meeting him.'

'Will do. God bless you, mate. I'll never forget this.'

'You better not, Aussie,' Coulter cracked. 'Or I'll have to send some of *my* mob after you.'

Jim laughed, gave his hand a final shake, picked up his suitcase and headed for the limo. Coulter watched through the smoky glass. The chauffeur took over Jim's suitcase and opened the rear door. He crouched, ducked his head, eased in and froze.

'G'day, Dad.' Jilba greeted him with misty eyes and open arms.

Stunned, Jim ducked right out again and spun round. He could only just make him out, grinning behind the glass. With a casual salute, he disappeared. Jim climbed back into the limo, sat back and stared at his daughter, completely at a loss for words. The mistiness in Jilba's eyes gave way to two large tears that rolled down her cheeks as she opened her arms.

'Hi . . .'

Jim fell. He clung to her for all he was worth, rocking her gently in his arms, as the chauffeur slowly pulled away.

There was so much to say and so little time to say it. Her first shock was how much he had aged. She hadn't seen him since her grandmother's funeral. Now she could see the full toll her mother's death had taken. It was written all over his face.

'Forgive me,' Jim asked gently. 'For all the trouble . . .'

Jilba simply grabbed him back and buried her face on his shoulder. He held her tight, his heart soaring.

'I thought you were supposed to be on your way to Brazil.'

'I am,' she snuffled. 'On my way to Brazil, I mean. Dean called me the minute you left his office yesterday. I flew back on Concorde this morning.'

'So,' Jim chuckled. 'That's another one I owe him.'

'I guess,' she replied, sitting back, affectionately straightening his tie and brushing at the tear stains on his lapel. 'My flight's at two, so I'll be able to see you off for a change.'

As Antonio crossed the Bridge, Jim took Jilba's hand in his and told her all that had happened since he spoke to her on the phone at Tony's house in Brisbane. They reached the Kennedy exit by the time he finished. He didn't leave anything out till he got to his showdown with Pi Kok. He made no mention of the threats he'd made, particularly about her.

'Did you believe him?' she pressed. 'Did you believe he

really didn't know what had happened to Jack after the money was handed over?'

'I had no option. It was just supposition. There was nothing I could give the police. He had Jack's receipt and there was no way to link them to the rest of it, really. Maybe it *was* just some ratbag out to steal the car. I don't know. Got a nice big handshake on top, that's for sure. The police haven't got a clue.'

'Is Jack really all right? You're not holding anything back?'

Jim patted her knee reassuringly. 'Absolutely not. The operation was a complete success. He's a bit black and blue, but he'll be all right. I promise. Especially when I give him the news. He'll be as happy as Larry, I reckon.'

'Well, you tell him his sister said he's a chump . . . And then give him a big hug and a kiss, will you?'

'I will,' Jim promised. 'In that order.'

They had time for just one drink. Jilba bought him *Newsweek* and the *New Yorker* and bustled him into the nearest bar. All the time they talked, Jim saw Pi Kok's evil grin in the bottom of his glass. He had to fight to keep the worry out of his voice. When they called his flight and Jilba reluctantly said they better make a move, Jim filled with fatherly concern.

'I hear this bloke Serrano reckons he might be my son-in-law.'

Jilba tossed her head and giggled with delight. 'You should see the expression on your face.'

'That doesn't answer my question.'

'Might,' she beamed. 'That's the big word at the moment.'

'Well, just count me in if you do, will you? Don't do it when I'm not looking. I've already missed Tony's.'

'Well, who's fault was that?'

'Yeah, I know. But just keep it in mind, will you? Please?'

'Do you want him to come and ask for my hand?'

'I'm not *that* old-fashioned,' Jim chuckled ruefully. 'But come to think of it, now that you mention it . . .'

Jilba pulled him to his feet and gave him a kiss. 'I'll bear it in mind. Come on.'

At the gate, Jilba embraced him fiercely. Their time had been unbearably brief.

'I'll be back in New York in about ten days,' she said. 'Will you call me? When you're back at Balkenna?'

Holding her hands, Jim stepped back to look at her, suddenly haunted by the traces of Rachel indelibly etched into her own special looks.

'Can I take it I'm forgiven then? For deserting the ship?'

'Forgiven,' she said. 'I was pretty cranky, mind you.'

Suddenly, in a terrible rush, everything caught up and Jim's eyes brimmed. 'I just couldn't bear the thought of her not being there. I know it was wrong . . . But I just couldn't face it . . .'

'Oh, Dad, it's all right. It's all right. We've all had to handle it in our own way. I understand, we all do. It just took a little while, that's all. Please don't be sad.' She gave him a long kiss on the cheek and stepped back with a bright gee-up smile. 'Go on, you better make a run for it before I start howling.'

Jim leaned forward and returned her kiss. 'I love you, girl. Very much. Look after yourself . . .'

'You too,' she said, as he turned away.

Jim looked back once, to catch her eye and wave. It gave his old heart a kick to realise the stunningly beautiful woman waving back was his daughter. Puffed with pride, he joined the queue in the tunnel and thanked his lucky stars.

# Forty-Eight

As Jim and Jack left the outskirts of Townsville and took the road to Charters Towers, they were both sweating from the humidity and hot sun streaming into the station wagon.

'How're you feeling? All right?'

'Like a galah,' Jack mumbled, behind his sunglasses.

'No, you dingbat. I mean how are you feeling? You've been on your back for two weeks.'

'Yeah,' Jack assured him, 'I'm all right. Just feel like the biggest galah in the whole of Queensland.'

Jim couldn't help a little smile. 'Now, come on. We all get taken for a ride somewhere along the line. Stop kicking yourself so hard.'

'I can't help thinking about it, Dad.'

'That was a bit of a right royal send-off you got this morning. That little redhead seemed sad to see you go.'

'Deirdre.'

'What's her name?'

'Deirdre O'Connell.'

'Hungarian, is she?'

'Ha, ha. Very funny.'

'Well, she seemed like a good sort.'

'I'm glad,' Jack announced. 'I've invited her out to Balkenna for her holidays. Hope you don't mind.'

Jim had to glance out of his window to hide a grin a mile wide. 'Not a bit, son. It'll be nice to have the chance to repay all her kindness.'

Their eyes met, and Jim's were dancing with innuendo. Jack gave his father a thump on the arm and looked away, blushing beetroot.

'Just leave off.'

Jim chuckled as Jack stretched out, put his head back and closed his eyes. 'You sure you're all right?'

'Yeah. Shouldn't have had so much beer with lunch.'

'That's okay. Have a snooze. I'll give you a shout when we get there.'

Ten minutes later he was snoring his head off and Jim gave his mind to the road ahead.

Coalmec had accepted Jenkins' offer on Jim's behalf after only twenty-four hours' consideration and all the paperwork was drawn up awaiting his signature. Coulter's life-saving cheque was already on deposit and, as far as Jim was concerned, the western skyline in the distance promised a new lease on life. His gamble had paid off, but in the most extraordinary and unexpected way. The one cloud on the horizon hung over this visit to Fred and Annie.

He could see her now, sticking her face through the waterfall the day she brought him back from his bender. He could see her little, perplexed smile, he could hear the sadness in her voice as she told him she was sorry for letting her heart run away with her head. Looking back now, he realised how much her feelings must have been hurt by the dogged way he shied away from any physical contact with her that night and in the days that followed. He didn't doubt she understood the reason, but it must have cut her nonetheless. It had come as a shock to realise the long weeks of her care and consideration were motivated by something more than common humanity. He was looking forward to seeing her, quite apart from the secret they shared. And Fred, too.

His visits to his old Townsville haunts over the past few days had left him with plenty to think about. He was astonished to find his old lodging was still a boarding house.

Marjorie was a washout. The old florist's shop turned out to be a travel agent. His visit to the meatworks was more successful. Presenting himself to the front office as what he was – a grazier from Longreach, interested in looking over the works – they gave him the conducted tour. The whole layout had changed. All except the knocking box. The sickly-sweet stench got to him just as it had in his first few days there and, as he stood and watched the rowdy boisterousness of the blokes on the line, he could see himself and Tony Halpin ribbing each other shitless as they turned their hoses on the bloody carcasses.

Jim adjusted his hat and glanced at Jack. He was still fast asleep, his chin on his chest. He was going to have a crick in his neck when he woke up. Jim smiled to himself and slowed down passing through Mingela. Out the other side, he accelerated back to seventy, glanced at Jack again and let his mind wander.

He could see Annie's lovely, warm smile at the window of the truck, the day it roared back to life. He wondered if old Tobias was still around. Suddenly, the wheels came off. The shooter leapt into the mirage in his mind. Whack! The sound of the stone splintering his skull rang in his ear! The car swerved violently as Jim reeled from the shock and there was a screech of rubber as he fought the spinning wheel. Jack sat up with a start.

'What was that?'

'It's okay. Just drifted away there for a minute.'

Jim was sweating too much, gripping the wheel too tight. His knuckles were white. Alarmed, Jack put his hand on his shoulder.

'Are you all right? Do you feel sick or something?'

Jim struggled for breath. 'No, no. I'm all right. Just delayed reaction, I guess. Everything caught up in a bit of a rush.'

'You want me to take over?'

'You feel up to it?'

'Yeah, sure. Pull over.'

Glad of the offer, Jim brought the Ford to a halt and slid across the seat. As they pulled away, Jack shot him a look.

'Better?'

'Yeah.'

'What was it?'

'Oh . . . Just all of it really. Everything we've been through in the past few weeks. Hasn't exactly been a picnic.'

'No, I know,' Jack said, ruefully. 'But we're in the clear now, eh? First thing I want to do when we get home is write to Mr Coulter. Just to thank him myself.'

'He'd appreciate that.'

'Why don't you have a snooze yourself?'

'I'm okay, mate. We'll be in the Towers soon anyway. I'll have to direct you from there.'

'Is it far?'

'No,' Jim chuckled, recognising his impatience. 'We'll be home soon enough, mate. Keep your shirt on.'

Jack shot him a look and grinned. 'Can't wait.'

'Yeah, I know. But I have to do this. It wouldn't be right to be so close and not look in on them. Not after all they did for me.'

'Yeah,' Jack nodded, and he settled down to the job of getting them there.

The other side of Charters Towers on the road running southeast of the Seventy Mile Range, Jack put his foot down. When they came to the fatal S-bend Jim sat up with stiff, studied nonchalance and gave it a once-over. He could still feel the hair on his neck standing on end long after they'd left it behind.

They almost missed the turn-off to the caves because Jim didn't recognise it. In place of the familiar, anonymous track, a much wider dirt road snaked away into the scrub. It was clearly marked by two bold white posts. With a mixture of curiosity and rising alarm, he gave Jack the word, noting as they got into the scrub that the track had come in for some heavy use of late. When they began the climb up the mountain it looked more like a forestry road than anything he remembered.

'You sure this is right?' Jack asked, noting his father's look.

'Yeah, keep going. This is the place, all right.'

When they turned the corner at the top, Jim couldn't believe his eyes. The caves no longer existed. In their place was a huge shell-shaped cavern, like a giant had taken a bite out of the mountain. Two heavy-duty generators were parked nearby and four men he'd never seen before were going hammer and tongs with pneumatic drills on the concave rock face. A caterpillar-tracked excavator and a heavyweight Leyland tip-truck stood poised for action and, nestling on the edge of the scrub, two mobile homes were parked end to end. One had a simple black and white sign over the door: Bush Girl Mining Company Limited. A man stood in the door, his fists on his hips, staring intently at the new arrivals.

'What's all this about then?' asked Jack.

'Buggered if I know,' said Jim, absolutely flummoxed. 'Hang on a minute . . .'

Jack watched him speak to the man in the door who immediately beckoned him inside. The excavator moved in to scoop up the shattered rock, swung about and dumped it into the waiting truck. When Jim reappeared there was a big, excited, happy grin on his face.

'Bull's-eye!' he announced. 'Would you believe it? The old bugger finally cracked it! Come on, turn round, quick! Back to the Towers!'

'You mean he found gold?'

'He didn't find spaghetti bolognese.'

'How much?'

'I don't know. Bloke refused point blank to say. We have to see Fred. God! He must be tickled pink.'

After a couple of enquiries they finally found their way to a handsome two-storeyed Edwardian house on the edge of town. Half an hour later, after a noisy reunion in which Jack couldn't help but notice the special delight with which Annie Paterson greeted his father's appearance, Fred Paterson sat back in his chair and pronounced judgement.

'God almighty! What a saga!'

'You can say that again.'

'All behind you now, mate,' Fred chuckled, geeing him up. 'Sounds like you're gonna be as flat out as a one-armed bill-poster in a high wind. May as well put it all out of your mind now.'

Jack laughed, and nodded. 'Yeah, I guess.'

'So, Mackay,' Fred observed. 'You're in hock up to your eye-balls again. Guess I won't be able to put the bite on you for a while.'

' 'Fraid not,' Jim grinned. 'Anyway, enough of us. Tell us what's happened. When did you hit it?'

'About a week or two after you left. Remember that little generator I borrowed?'

'Yeah.'

'I should have borrowed the little bastard long before that. It did the bloody trick. A month's hard yakker in a couple of days. And there she was . . .' He broke off and glanced at Annie. A secret little smile was playing on her lips.

'Well, go on, for Christ's sake,' Jim prompted.

'Gold, you nong. What else?'

'What sort of grade?'

'Not bad,' Fred shrugged. 'Maybe not as good as I'd hoped, but not bad. We're making a bob or two. Enough to keep the show going and buy us a feed.'

'That's great!'

Munching his sandwich, Jack saw Annie glance at his father then quickly look down and start fiddling with the folds of her skirt. He thought she looked embarrassed.

'We've managed to put a few bucks aside for you, of course,' Fred added.

'For what?'

'Against your stake, you dimwit. Wages, if you like. Christ!

This blue you've been through's left you short a sheet of bark, hasn't it? Where's your brains?'

'That wasn't work,' Jim laughed. 'Recuperation, more like it.' He glanced at Annie. 'Tender love and care.'

Jack noted what a nice smile Annie had.

'You worked very hard,' she said. 'Earned every penny as far as I'm concerned,' she added, with an emphasis only Jim understood.

'Get the book for me, will you, love?' said Fred. 'Have to have a dekko. I can't remember offhand. It's in the office.'

'The office?' Jim teased him. 'Three-piece suit next, I suppose.'

'Watch it, Mackay. I'm a bit cranky about all this living in town lark. More for Annie's sake than mine.'

Annie reappeared carrying a large, cloth-bound ledger and dumped it nonchalantly in Fred's lap.

'Thanks, love.'

Again Jack noticed there was something funny about the way his father and Annie looked at each other. Jim still had his eyes on her as Fred found what he was looking for.

'Right. Here we are. Bank of Queensland. We opened a little account in your name . . .' He didn't notice Jim wasn't listening as he ran his finger down to the bottom of the column. 'Let's see, according to this it stands at one million, two hundred and seventy-one thousand, one hundred and sixty-five dollars and thirty-two cents . . .'

Jack had a lump of ham sandwich halfway down his throat and he nearly choked to death on the spot.

'Ease up, mate. You'll swallow your tongue in a minute.'

'Did you hear what dad said?' Annie asked quietly, still smiling.

Jim came out of his trance and turned to Fred. 'Sorry, mate. Miles away.'

Jack finally managed to get it all the way down and he leapt up in a frenzy, knocking his empty plate for six.

'For Christ's sake, Dad! He just said you've got over a million bloody dollars in the bank.'

Jim couldn't take it in. He fixed Fred with a perplexed look. 'What's he talking about?'

Fred threw back his head and roared with laughter. 'Got ya, Mackay! King hit!'

Annie's smile was a mile wide now and Jack was absolutely beside himself. But Jim was still bewildered.

'What's the joke?'

'No joke, you dingbat!' Fred shouted. 'I wouldn't joke about a thing like that. It's the drum. I know you walked in here in hock up to your eyeballs. But you're actually a ridgie-didge bloody millionaire! On paper, at least. The dough won't start coming through for a bit.'

'Yaaaaaaahoo! Jack exploded, pogoing up and down like a kangaroo at a high fence. He lunged over, dragged his father to his feet and spun him round.

'Say something, for God's sake . . .'

But Jim was struck dumb. Absolutely pole-axed. He simply stared at Fred in disbelief. Annie jumped up, wrapped father and son in her arms and gave Jim a quick kiss on the cheek.

'It's true, Jim. We've taken out over five million's worth so far. It's the biggest private strike for donkey's years. We spend more time with the accountants than we do at the mine these days.'

'Yeah,' said Fred, scowling. 'Doing something about that, I am.'

'But . . .' Jim stuttered. 'I don't understand . . .'

'Strewth, Mackay! You're as silly as a square wheel. Quarter share stake, remember? That was the deal, right from the start. With your old man and then you. The thirty-two cents is your wages, by the way.'

'You're serious,' Jim mumbled, incredulous.

'Give him a belt in the ear will you, Annie. Wake the poor bastard up.'

Grinning with delight, Annie brought her lips close to Jim's ear and yelled, 'It's truuuuuuue!'

Jim jumped, and Fred stood up to offer his hand.

'Thanks, partner. Thanks for keeping the faith so long. That goes for your old man, too.'

Jim's eyes began to dance as the truth of it finally hit home and his face lit up like a Christmas tree. He let go of Fred's hand, grabbed him in a bear hug, lifted him off the floor and started spinning his great bulk around as if he was nothing more than a sack of cotton wool.

'You bloody old pirate,' he yelled. 'Do you realise what you've done?'

Fred pulled a face. 'Put me down, for God's sake. I'm scared of heights.'

Jack let go another yahoo! at the top of his lungs.

'Fair go, young feller. You'll shatter me crystals.'

But Jim refused to let go. Jack grabbed Annie, whirled her round and gave her a big soggy kiss on the cheek.

Much to Fred's relief, Jim finally dropped him back on his feet. Fred stood back with a knowing smirk.

'Told you, Mackay . . .'

'You did, indeed,' Jim grinned. 'Bull's-eye, you said. For sure . . .'

'Bloody oath. Only you thought I was on to a run of fool's, didn't you?'

'Not completely,' Jim hedged.

'Get out of here!'

'Well, maybe I had a *few* doubts.'

'Shame on you, Mackay! Shame! The assayers' office is going bananas. If the grade holds up they're estimating somewhere between ten and fifteen million smackers. We're all gonna be so filthy, stinking rich we'll have to shower ten times a day!'

Half an hour later, round a table in the lounge of Fred's favourite pub, they were toasting each other's luck to kingdom come and back and all the gods in between. Jim failed to notice it was the same room in which he'd ended up obliterated the weekend he fled from the caves. But Annie remembered only too well. She slipped her arm through his and gave it a squeeze.

Jim gave her a quick peck on the cheek. 'God, this is something, I tell you.'

'We thought you might be pleased,' she grinned.

For a split second as he looked into her eyes, the light dimmed and he raised his eyebrows a notch.

Annie quickly shook her head. She held his eye a moment, then looked away.

'Do you remember that table in the corner?'

Jim stared at it for a moment, as his memory changed gear. 'Vaguely. There was someone who looked a bit like Florence Nightingale . . .'

'In shorts! You've got to be joking.'

'I remember her voice as much as anything,' Jim recalled, turning back to her. 'And all the good things she told me. I've heard it many times since.'

Annie squeezed his arm again and then withdrew her own. 'I'm glad.'

'Dad! Fred reckons he's got a rock as big as his fist up at the house. Want to go and have a look?'

'Not right this minute,' Jim stalled, tapping his glass.

Fred jumped up. 'Come on, young feller. Get that under your belt and I'll show you something you'll never forget.' He gave Jim a wink as Jack gulped his beer. 'You'll have a case of "the fever" on your hands here if you don't watch out.'

Jim saluted with his glass. 'Well, at least I know where to find the doctor.'

When the door swung shut behind them, he turned back to Annie and dropped his voice to a whisper. 'Has anything happened?'

She kept her voice low. 'They found the wreck. It was reported in the local papers as an accident. His name was Murphy. He lived with his mother, here, in the Towers. She was quoted as saying what a wonderful son he was and that sort of stuff. There was a small obituary a few days later . . .' She broke off and bit her lip. 'It said he was well liked by those who knew him. A respected member of the community. He was in the local rifle club, evidently. He'd won some cups . . .'

'Nothing else?'

'No, not a word.'

Jim squeezed her hand and breathed a sigh of relief. 'Pray God that's the end of it then.'

'I think it's going to be all right now,' she assured him. 'The police let a local wrecker do it over for parts.'

'You mean it's still there?'

'What's left of it. Dad got out one day to have a look, of course. Told me all about it.'

'Who found it?'

'That I don't know. It just said "found" in the papers. I haven't discussed it with a soul.'

Jim held her hand a moment longer. Then Annie withdrew. She straightened her back to break the spell and took a long drink from her glass. 'Haven't really had time to think about it. The thrill of the strike was enormous.'

'I'll bet,' Jim grinned.

'I thought dad would blow a gasket. Not so much for the money, more because his hunch proved right. A lot of people around here were starting to look at him as if he was a bit troppo. Now they're all lining up to piss in his pocket.'

'Yeah,' Jim laughed. 'I can just imagine.'

'He hates all that side of it. I do all the books, but he's the one who has to negotiate with everyone. Everybody's got his hand out.'

'He seems in pretty good form.'

'Oh, he's all right. Talks them all blind if he has to. But he's got itchy feet already, wants to go bush again. Some place up in the Gulf Country that he worked years ago. Probably one of the times he ran out of cash and headed for your place. Now he's got the dough behind him he reckons he could do it over properly.'

'Getting a bit long in the tooth, isn't he?'

'Yes. But he'll go barmy if he has to sit around the house all day. Keeps running out to the mine on the smallest excuse. Of course, he thinks he'll live for ever, but . . .'

'Who'd run the show here?'

'We've got two offers for the mine already. But he wants to hang onto it, at least until this vein runs its course. We're looking for some management people to run it full-time. He's talked to three outfits so far but he reckoned none of them cut the mustard. There's another crowd coming up from Brisbane next week. They sound a bit more promising. If it all works out okay, I'll take a back seat too. Let them get on with it.'

'What will you do?' Jim asked quietly.

'Don't really know, to tell you the truth. Go overseas, maybe. See a few places. My mother came from Germany.'

'Yes, I know,' said Jim. 'I've never forgotten the night Fred told us about her. I remember how gently he spoke about her. It stuck in my mind because he was always such a roaring bull most of the time.'

'Oh, I don't know, Jim. I just thought maybe I'd take a trip, try and find out something about her. She was born at a place called Kassel. Maybe I've got some relatives over there I don't know about. Just a thought. Haven't got the foggiest, really. It's very weird suddenly to be in a position where money's no object. I'm not at all sure what to do with a big pile of dough.'

'Just think,' said Jim. 'I went all the way to America and back to borrow money I didn't know I already had.'

'If you hadn't, you wouldn't know what a good friend you've got there, would you?' Annie observed.

'Absolutely not. That was the best part of it, really. As far as Rachel's concerned . . .'

Jim toyed with his glass for a moment, but then decided against it.

'Maybe I can explain it to you someday. Not now. It just helped me come to terms with an awful lot of guilt I've been carrying around. How the life at Balkenna had been getting her down. I had no idea just how much.'

'And did he? This bloke in New York?'

Jim simply nodded and took a swig of his beer. In her wisdom, Annie didn't press it.

'I should imagine he's going to keel over when he finds out you can pay him back almost immediately.'

'He might even be a bit cheesed off about it. He sold off a whole block of investments he had in Melbourne to raise the loan.'

'Maybe he won't want it back. He might want to stay on as your partner for a while.'

'Might do,' Jim grinned. 'It's going to knock him for a loop whichever way he looks at it.'

'If these Brisbane people turn out to be the bee's knees, I should think you'll be able to pay him back in six months or so.'

'I'll buy the best bloody cattle I can lay my hands on,' said Jim. 'I was thinking of turning half of Balkenna over to sheep again. Wasn't looking forward to it one bit. I won't have to worry about that now. Jack's got a bee in his bonnet about trying some Santa Gertrudis on the place, besides our usual Herefords. I could let him have his head on that one. See how he gets on. I'm not sure they'd go so well on Balkenna. But I could be wide of the mark . . .' He broke off, grinned like a Cheshire cat at the thought and nodded at Annie's glass. 'Give him a go, I reckon. Do you want another beer?'

Annie shook her head.

'I was thinking we'd probably press on to Pentland this evening but, in the circumstances, I don't think Jack'll moan about it.'

'I should hope not,' Annie replied. 'Dad would be mortified if you didn't stay for one night, at least. I know he'll want to talk about your father. He's been getting quite maudlin about it with me. Once the full impact of the strike sank in. Said he would have loved to have seen the expression on his face. Just like he did on yours today. So you *must* stay.'

Jim grinned, moved round the table and made a show of

offering his arm. 'May I see you home, Miss Paterson?'

'You may, sir,' Annie replied.

It was a big night. Fred insisted on buying just about every 'special dish' on the Chinese menu and laid in enough beer to last till dawn. Jack was as mesmerised by Fred as his father had been in his youth and he kept pestering him for more and more about the old days. He realised the man was a walking encyclopaedia of bush lore and saw him as another likely candidate for his research, especially when Fred told him he had a few old mining songs from the days of the great Queensland rushes written down somewhere and he might be able to remember the tunes once he had the words in front of him.

Annie's happiness was subdued by moments of introspection as she recognised the continuing strength of her feelings for this man she had helped pull back from the brink. In the full flush of his excitement, full of visions of a brilliantly rosy future rebuilding Balkenna with Jack at his side, all that she loved about Jim shone through and lit up the space between them. Whenever their eyes met, she saw Jim held her in very special regard. But she knew it was more to do with the Florence Nightingale he joked about than anything else.

Everyone slept late and woke up with hangovers. Jack made a joke of it by downing a can of 4X for breakfast and ribbing the rest of them for quitting while they were ahead.

By eleven they were in the Ford and ready to go.

'It's fantastic, mate,' said Jim. 'Absolutely bloody fantastic.'

'It's your dough,' said Fred. 'Your mate in New York'll be a bit relieved too, I imagine.'

'He's a very rich man.'

'Aren't we all?' Fred cackled.

'I guess we are,' said Jim with a grin.

'Had his reasons, I expect.'

'It's a bloody miracle, that's what it is,' said Jack.

Fred scowled, mock hurt. 'No, mate. The miracle was the stuff being there in the first place.' He tapped his nose and winked. 'The rest was this and hard yakker.'

'All right,' said Jim, chuckling. 'You're a miracle yourself. Okay?'

'Strewth, Mackay! Fair crack of the whip. It's just mathematics, mate. Your old man struck the deal and stuck to it, through thick and thin. I know you only forked out for his sake in the beginning. But I think we came to our own understanding, didn't we?'

His hand on the wheel, Jim was staring at the crest ring on his finger as Fred spoke, pictures of his father riding through the back pages of his mind.

'Once I got to know you,' he said.

'Hope you're not sorry.'

Jim looked back at him and replied deadpan. 'Yeah, mate. Deep regrets about the whole thing.'

'That's the spirit.' As he studied Jim's face, Fred's grin faded slowly and his eyes took on a faraway look. 'Wherever he is now, I just hope your old man's heard the news. He was the best mate I ever had, Jim. I want you to know that.'

Jim shoved his hand out of the window to shake goodbye. 'I'm glad. I know how happy he'd be. For all of us.'

Fred simply nodded in reply and stood back as Jim turned the key. At the far window, Annie nodded past Jack at his father.

'Look after him.'

'For sure,' said Jack.

Annie leant in and gave Jim a quick kiss goodbye. 'Let us know how it's going, won't you?'

'Of course,' Jim promised.

Their eyes locked in recognition of the secret they shared.

'Safe journey.'

'See you,' Jim nodded, one last time.

As they pulled away, waving like mad, Fred and Annie waited until the car turned the corner at the bottom of the street. Annie lowered her hand slowly, and bit her lip. Fred put his arm round her, and held her.

'Don't be hard on yourself, love.'

Annie glanced into his face, gave him a sad little smile and patted his arm. 'Can't help it, I'm afraid.'

# Forty-Nine

'Well, I'll be blowed . . .'

Tim Daley was dumbfounded. He already believed Dean Coulter's investment was a gift from God; he had humbly taken back all his doubts about divine benevolence and fair go for the deserving. As the Mackays swapped a smile at the expression on his face, Tim snapped out of it, rocked forward and slapped his knee.

'I hear there's a couple of Barnaby Joker's stock for sale at Augathella. Maybe we should get right down there and take a look.'

'Sounds good to me,' said Jim.

'You little beauty!' said Jack, leaping to his feet.

Jim hauled himself up and grabbed Tim by the shoulders. 'But before we do a thing, old son, thank you. From me and all the family. None of this would have been possible if you hadn't hung on for us.'

'That's okay, Jim,' he replied. 'I had a few doubts along the way, I don't mind telling you. But I s'pose I kind of thought things'd have to pan out somewhere along the line. I mean, think of it! We'll be back to normal in no time with this lot.'

'That's for sure,' said Jim. 'As far as I'm concerned, tomorrow won't be soon enough.'

'Give us a break,' Tim laughed. 'How about the end of the week?'

And so began four months that passed in a blur of activity for all three of them.

Jim's first call was to Dean Coulter. His news was met by total silence for a moment, then a sustained burst of delighted if ironical laughter. As Annie had prophesied, he told Jim there was not much point in pulling out now. Jim told him about Jack wanting to try some Santa Gertrudis stock on the place and Coulter suggested the bulk of his investment be used for that; he'd be Jack's silent partner in the venture. So they struck a new deal for repayment of his loan plus interest in three years with an additional five-year seven per cent profit share if the Gertrudis herd proved successful.

Jim's call to Jilba was long, loving and left her fresh out of Kleenex. Her trip to Brazil had been one thing after another. She could laugh about it now, but it was hell at the time. Thrilled to bits by her father's sudden and wonderful change of fortune, she simply gave notice that, if she ever did decide to get married, she expected the biggest shindig Balkenna had ever hosted in its history.

The day after their return, Jim drove to Longreach for a long meeting with Wally Jenkins at the bank, to sign the contracts for the leases and discuss Balkenna's immediate spending power. A quick call to Charters Towers confirmed Jim's new financial status and Jenkins happily underwrote an open-ended policy for Balkenna's immediate revival. Jim left the office on cloud nine. He bought some flowers and went straight to spend some time at Rachel's grave.

A week later, he and Jack were in Augathella inspecting two direct descendants of the pedigree bull that had sired Balkenna's top-quality Hereford bloodlines when Jim was his son's age. Jack followed every minute step of his father's examination of the two eighteen-month-old bulls to make sure he fully understood the reasons for his final choice. In honour of the man who made it all possible they named him Frederick Joker the First and arranged with a local trucker for his immediate transportation to his new home.

They stopped off in Barcaldine on the way through. When Jim stuck his head through the door of the hotel kitchen, Betsey Johnson didn't know where to put the kingsized dish of baked potatoes she'd just pulled from the oven. As Jim stepped in with Jack close behind him, she shoved it right back in again, wiped her hands on her apron and marched into Jim's embrace with tears in her eyes. Jack planted a big kiss on her cheek and pre-empted his father by immediately demanding to know how soon she could come home.

Three weeks later, she was back in the house she had kept for years and ruling her three male charges with a rod of iron. To celebrate her return, Jim put in a new stove, fridge and washing machine and bought a new Hoover. He also bought her a special orthopaedic bed to ease the sciatica that troubled her from time to time.

Annie Paterson phoned Jim a few days after their return. Fred was satisfied with the Brisbane consortium and was already planning his escape to the Gulf Country. Her own plans were still indefinite.

From that point on, they went on a spending spree to re-equip and restock Balkenna. The first item of business was a brand new Holden utility for Tim so he could finally kiss the old banger goodbye. Through the stock and station agents in Longreach, Jim made a string of purchases that saw the property grazing a thousand head of the best Herefords money could buy, much to his and Frederick the First's satisfaction.

Jim set aside the ten thousand acres of Big Jack's Whack for his son's Gertrudis experiment and it wasn't'too long before that slice of the property began to be referred to by one and all as the Jack-Jack. Three hundred heifers and a bull set them back close to two hundred thousand dollars; the bull alone cost forty-five thousand. Originally bred in Texas through the cross-breeding of Brahman and Shorthorn cattle, Santa Gertrudis are a deep cherry red in colour and perform well in arid conditions. To make a point of Jack's new responsibility, Jim bought the stock in his son's name. And crossed his fingers.

Next on Jim's agenda was the demolition of the burnt-out wing of the house. The painful memories locked in its charred shell were out of keeping with Balkenna's new spirit of optimism. He got hold of some builders from Longreach and they finished the job in three weeks flat. There was no point in thinking about replacing it. They had more than enough room as it was.

At the Mackays' insistence, Tim came to live at Balkenna and took over the attic rooms. His old place was turned over to the new stockmen Jim hired to help with the day-to-day running of their rejuvenated acres. The Sugden brothers were of the same Yirandhali Aboriginal descent as Tommy and Dougie Douglas. At thirty-eight, Rex was the elder and a confirmed bachelor in the Tim Daley mould. Stewie had just turned thirty. He and his wife, Clare, had a four-year-old tearaway called Bobby.

They were recommended to Jim by Athol Ferguson, whose personal satisfaction with his old protégé's change of fortune and Balkenna's resurrection put paid to any lingering doubts. One of the earliest pleasures for Jim, above and beyond the thrill of seeing Balkenna's rebirth, was the first visit of his old friend and the indomitable Dud Brewley. It gave him the opportunity to hand Athol a cheque for forty-five thousand dollars, half the money owed for the Glenmore stock they took to Townsville. It was a big weekend for all concerned. Jack, particularly, recognized in Dud someone he'd always taken a bit for granted in the past, another pioneer he had to get a wealth of stories out of before it was too late.

Jim spent another packet doing up Tim's place before the Sugdens moved in, adding a proper laundry at the back, installing a brand new kitchen and painting the place from top to bottom, inside and out. Clare Sugden showed her appreciation by baking them the biggest and best fruit cake any of them had eaten. It was accompanied by a page of drawings of some of the fruit by young Bobby. Jim stuck it up above his desk in the office.

Once all the new stock was settled, Jim took a week off to visit the rest of his family in Brisbane and discuss Billy's future with Tony. They were days of sweet and sour. Jim had a devil of a time persuading Tony that what had happened in Townsville had to be kept in the family at all costs. Tony argued vehemently that placing the information in the public arena would immediately scratch any threats Pi Kok had made. Their debate was long and heated and only finally decided in Jim's favour by Susan's intervention. Now that everything had changed for the family, she saw no reason to make waves and told Tony to pull his head in and forget it. She was blooming with health, heavy with Jim's first grandchild and her strength of conviction was impressive. Tony capitulated with good grace. But it hurt like hell to see such a heady by-line sink without trace.

Their decision over Billy was taken out of their hands by the boy himself. His academic ability kept him consistently in the top half-dozen of his class with seemingly little effort and he had his own view of the future. He wanted to do medicine, with the long-term aim of getting a pilot's licence and joining the Flying Surgeon Service. The first of its kind anywhere in the world, it had begun in Longreach in 1959 and was still based at Longreach Hospital. That way, he told his father quietly, he could have the best of both worlds, living at Balkenna and doing a job that meant something. It set Jim back on his heels a bit, but he could see Billy had given the matter a lot of thought. So it was decided he should stay on with Tony and Susan. If he eventually qualified for university, Jim promised to set him up in digs of his own. It was a relief for Billy. He'd been worried sick his father would be hurt if he didn't want to join forces full-time with Jack on Balkenna.

Jim and Jack came away from a sleepless weekend with the Stokers with four Blues and two Speckled Reds. From Reg, Jack learnt that all cattle dogs, whether they were known as Australian, Queensland or just plain old Blue Heelers, descended originally from blue smooth-haired collies imported from Scotland around 1840 by a man called Hall who owned a property at Muswellbrook in New South Wales. They proved to be good workers but had a tendency to bark a lot and run to the head of the mob if they got over-excited. Hall's solution was to cross them with Australia's wild dog, the dingo, whose silent stealth was legendary. They became known as Hall's Heelers and remained the leading cattle working dogs until the 1870s when other people began to cross Hall's breed with black and tan kelpies, resulting in the Blues and Speckled Reds whose love of their work and silent tenacity soon stabilised the breed. The instinctive talents of Jim's purchases had, as promised, been put to the test and fine-tuned by Reg and Les.

Just as important for Jack, he had two ninety-minute tapes in his bag, chock-a-block with yarns and songs. The Stokers had taken unmerciful piss out of each other and they provided Jack and his father with a lot of good laughs on the long drive home.

The next item on Jim's shopping list was another plane. When he told Jack and Tim he was thinking of buying a second-hand Piper from a man in Longreach, they wondered about the wisdom of not investing in a new machine. But Jim had another scheme up his sleeve. What they really needed was a helicopter and he intended to learn to fly one and get a licence as soon as he had time. Jack immediately told him to count him in. Tim, who always figured the back of a horse was far enough off the ground and learnt to fly only out of necessity, acquiesced with a smile.

In quiet moments, Jim found himself reflecting time and again on the re-emergence of his father's spiritual presence on Balkenna. The revival was all due to the friendship struck with Fred Paterson and the support he gave him all those long, long years ago.

Alone in the library one evening, Jim hauled down the family Bible. His eye lingered on the familiar crest, motto and family tree, remembering the good times he had shared with his father between his bouts of illness. Glancing back and forth between the ring on his finger and the crest on the page, he became curious to know more of their historical origins. He found a piece of tracing paper and made a careful copy of the crest and motto. He owed Tony a letter anyway. He enclosed the tracing and asked him to see if he could come up with anything in his spare time.

Three weeks later he received a fat envelope from a Brisbane genealogist called Wooton. As a boy, Jim learnt from his mother that Balkenna was the name of a tiny place in Ayrshire, Scotland. Now he knew what it meant. It comprised two Gaelic words – *Baile* which applied to any permanent human settlement such as a village, hamlet, home or farm, and *Ken* which generally meant a headland or point.

The rest of Wooton's six pages provided him with a general history of the Clan Mackay from 1415 to the present day.

The symbolism of the hand in the crest, Wooton advised, was twofold. To the ancient Gaels, the hand represented family. So it meant not only defence of their territory with a strong, individual hand, but also that the whole family, or clan, was united in defence of themselves and their traditional lands. The Gaelic line at the bottom of Jim's family tree, *Bratach bhan mhic Aoidh*, meant 'The White Banner of the Mackays'.

That night, he sat down to share the information with Jack and they spent a couple of hours taking it all in and checking names, places and battles in the encyclopaedia.

When Deirdre O'Connell duly turned up, Jim didn't see a lot of his son the next couple of weeks. Jack took her all over the district to show her the sights. He took her for long rides on Balkenna and they were gone so long, it took Jim back to his youthful days by the rock pool with Anna Henderson.

It was obvious to anybody watching they had taken a shine to one another and Jim was happy that something so good had come out of his son's disaster. When Jack got back home from putting her on the plane to Townsville, Jim took one look at his face and knew his son had fallen in love.

Jack didn't deny it. Deirdre felt the same, and was going to see about a transfer to Longreach Hospital. Jim went to bed that night feeling on top of the world.

The weekend after her return to Townsville, Jack turned out for the local polocrosse team against a team from Winton at the

Longreach showgrounds. It was close, but Jack's second goal clinched a win for the home side. As it flew through the sticks, Dud waved his crutch like a nullah-nullah.

'You little ripper! That oughta nail the buggers.' He turned to Jim and unpeeled his gums. 'Reminds me of a young bloke I saw ride in Sydney once.'

'Me, too,' Jim laughed. 'A bit. But I think this bloke's got the edge.'

'Chip off the old block,' said Athol, patting Jim on the back.

As Jim watched his son canter across the arena, his expression changed to one of momentary, wistful sadness. Athol and Tim had already begun threading their way through the crowd, but Dud caught his look.

'Come on, you miserable streak. I know what you're thinking. She'd be jumping up and down like a blue-arsed fly.'

Jim acknowledged the old-timer with a rueful smile. 'Not just Rachel. I can't help thinking sometimes how sad it is that my old man never lived to see any of them, to see Jack ride like that.'

'Maybe he did,' said Dud, rolling his eyes to the wide blue yonder. 'Sort of hope so in a way. Be up there myself before too much longer.'

'Not a chance,' Jim chuckled. 'We all know you're determined to outlive the lot of us.'

'Who told you?'

'Saint Peter.'

'Oh, bugger it. I told the silly old coot not to give the game away.'

Dud turned and propelled himself away on his sticks at alarming speed. Jim had to hurry to catch up.

That night, Jim shouted them all dinner. They were still at it well past closing time.

It was one of those starry outback nights you have to see to believe. With Jack and Tim lost in their own musings, Jim drove out along the Jundah road towards the skyline. There was so much to be thankful for.

Sunday morning, Jim spent a couple of hours in his office, throwing away a lot of deadwood, reorganising his filing system and clearing his desk. Tim, as was his habit of late, had taken himself off to Longreach for morning service at St Andrews, something he'd begun a couple of weeks after their return from Fred and Annie. He'd come in for some ribbing on the subject from Jack and, to a lesser degree, from Betsey. But Jim had quickly had a quiet word with them to put the lid on it. Jack got the message. Betsey simply shrugged and muttered something about mumbo-jumbo. For his part, Jim admired the quiet unaffected way Tim accepted the obligation to pay homage in the traditional way and was grateful for the peace of mind it brought him.

He wandered through to the kitchen to see how Betsey was getting on with the roast. She immediately shooed him right back out again. He loved to tease her and she gave as good as she got. The only thing he found disconcerting since her return was the way she sometimes spoke of Rachel and his mother as if they were simply off in another part of the house, and would be back in a minute.

That night, the ABC moved into the state news on the TV with a run-down of the latest political and economic shenanigans down in Brisbane. Jack was half out of his chair to switch it off when his hand froze.

'Police in Charters Towers have arrested the 38-year-old daughter of Mr Fred Paterson whose discovery of the local Bush Girl gold mine seven months ago made him a multi-millionaire overnight. Miss Annie Paterson has been arraigned to appear on murder charges in connection with the death of Charters Towers resident Mr Geoff Murphy, whose body was found in the wreckage of his car in December last year . . .'

Jim's can of Castlemaine clattered to the floor and spilled foam. Jack's jaw dropped in disbelief as a photograph of Annie appeared.

'Today's formal charges have sent shock waves through the Charters Towers community. A police spokesman confirmed that Mr Paterson, believed to be prospecting in an isolated area of the Gulf Country, was not being sought in connection with the matter. They are, however, seeking another man in connection with the charges brought against Miss Paterson. And now, here's Greg with the weather . . .'

As the weatherman appeared on the screen, Jim jumped up and thumbed the off button. White as a sheet, he braced himself against the set and tried to gather his fractured wits. Tim finally found his tongue.

'Good God . . .'

Jim hung his head in his hands. Jack shot Tim a frantic look, but neither of them knew what to do.

'I'm jinxed, just bloody well jinxed . . . Just when everything was looking so good . . .'

Tim dropped a hand on his shoulder. 'Come on, Jim. It's a shock. But it's not your fault.'

Jim shook his head violently in his hands and spun out of range, knocking Jack back on his bum. Tim tried to hang on, but Jim shrugged him off and headed for the door.

'I need some air . . .'

Jack made to follow, but Tim restrained him as his father disappeared into the darkness.

'Hang on, mate. Let him go.'

Jack braced himself against the mantelpiece and stared into the empty fire grate to hide the tears welling in his eyes.

Under a blazing night sky, Jim wandered far away from the house. Ruby, one of the new bitches from the Stokers, came running up to join him. He slumped, buried his hands in his pockets, turned on his heel and headed down the track, going nowhere. He kept going for another half-mile before he came to a familiar clump of boulders that had been there since the world began and sat down for a breather.

As Ruby sat beside him and leant against his leg, Jim stared at the black horizon with a mixture of confusion and mounting anger. Sensing his distress, Ruby pressed even harder against his leg and muttered a low, troubled whine. Jim reached down and gave her a pat.

'Well, Ruby,' he muttered. 'What am I going to do now, eh? Just tell me that . . .'

Ruby simply looked up at him, licked her lips and whined.

'What in God's name am I going to do?'

# PART FOUR

# Fifty

By five p.m. the following afternoon he'd done it. He was sitting in the interview room of Charters Towers Police Station, totally knackered. He'd got no sleep the night before. It took him till dawn to tell Jack and Tim the truth. At his insistence, they'd put him on a chartered Cessna out of Longreach first thing in the morning.

On the other side of the table, the homicide detective in charge of the case finished checking over the signed statement Jim had made within an hour of his arrival. He'd been called back to have it read to him again to see if there was anything he wished to add. When he shook his head, the detective set it to one side and folded his hands.

'Thank you again for coming forward, Mr Mackay.'

'What happens now?'

'We'll hold you here overnight. There'll be a formal charge hearing tomorrow.'

Jim nodded hopelessly and hung his head. 'I asked my family to organise a solicitor . . .'

'Name's Phillips. Good bloke. He's already been in touch with us.'

'Will I be able to see him alone?'

'Goes without saying.'

'I'm sorry,' Jim mumbled. 'I haven't got a clue about all this. Will Miss Paterson be released now? In view of what I've told you?'

'That's up to the Director of Prosecutions.'

'Could I see her?'

'I'm afraid not.'

Jim couldn't think of anything else to say.

He was placed in a different cell this time. When the door banged shut and the key rattled in the lock, Jim stared at his sleeping cellmate, then lay down on the opposite bunk. His body craved sleep but his mind was seething with a million questions as he closed his eyes and tried to remember if he *had* left any vital information out of his statement. The man's snoring cut through with nagging regularity, disrupting any hope of coherence. He'd got no further twenty minutes later when the sergeant reappeared, unlocked the door, and waved him out.

Andrew Phillips was a flashy dresser, with a mouth full of dazzling teeth.

'Sorry I wasn't here sooner,' he apologised, motioning Jim to take a seat. 'I was in court all day. By the time I spoke to your son, you'd already made your statement.'

'That's all right,' said Jim. 'I'm just glad they managed to get hold of you.'

'Yes, well, I just wish you'd spoken to me before you came in here.'

'My immediate concern was for Annie Paterson.'

'I can understand that, Mr Mackay. But it would have been best for us to consult before you signed it. Rather lets the cat out of the bag.'

'I just wanted her out as soon as possible.'

'Yes. Well, we'll just have to make the best of it.'

'What's going to happen to her?' Jim persisted. He seemed to Phillips to be oblivious to his own situation.

'I've been onto the Prosecutor's office. I expect they'll release her, once your statement has hit all the right desks. She's still liable to other charges, but they're bailable.'

'What charges?'

'Improperly interfering with a dead body, unlawful destruction of a motor vehicle.'

'Is someone representing her?'

'Yes. A Brisbane firm.'

'Could they make those charges stick?'

'That would largely depend on the outcome of your trial. As your only friendly witness, she'll take a hammering in court. No doubt about that.'

'Why?' Jim was perplexed. 'Why should she take a hammering? It's true what I told them, every word of it.'

Phillips studied him long and hard before replying.

'Because they'll be doing their level best to convict you, that's why.'

Simple as that. Jim accepted Phillips' flat statement with a dull nod.

'Now, I had a long talk with your son on the phone this afternoon. And with Mr Daley. I've also just seen Miss Paterson, so I have a pretty good idea –'

'How is she?'

'She seemed quite calm. Painted me a clear picture of the time you spent with her and her father. I'd say she's as worried about you as you are about her, which leads me inevitably to ask you this. What was the exact nature of your relationship?'

Jim frowned and didn't reply.

Phillips softened his tone and leaned across the table. 'Look, Mr Mackay . . .'

'Jim.'

'Jim. The quickest way we can get on is for you to be absolutely one hundred per cent on the level with me. She was very distressed on your behalf, spoke of you with considerable affection. I can only assume the two of you were having an affair.'

Jim stared at him numbly, then looked away and shook his head. 'I'm very fond of her, and I know she's fond of me. She and her father were very good to me at a difficult time in my life. But there was never any physical relationship between Annie and me. None whatsoever. Apart from anything else, I'd only recently lost my wife. Annie was well aware of that . . .'

'Yes,' Phillips acknowledged. 'Your son told me all about it. I'm sorry. It sounds like you had a pretty rough trot there for a while.'

'I didn't handle it very well,' Jim admitted. 'But I assure you, we were friends. That was as far as it went. And that's the truth.'

Phillips gave him another appraisal. Then he smiled his blinding smile. 'Just testing the water. She told me the same thing. I accept that's the truth of it. But the opposition will do their best to say otherwise. You can bet your sweet life on that.'

'Well, it's just not true,' Jim repeated.

Phillips' smile was a shade weary this time. He wrenched a legal pad from his briefcase, dug for his pen and went to work. 'Righto. We've got a bit to get through here.'

'Do my best.'

'You'll have to engage a barrister for your trial and I'd like to recommend Digby Willis.'

'Is he good?'

'About the best there is for a case like this. Charges, of course, but from what your son tells me, that's not the problem.'

He paused to pull out his copy of Jim's statement. 'This is.'

Jim stared at the document and waited for Phillips to continue.

'Is that all right with you, then? We brief Willis?'

'I'm in your hands now. Whatever you think's best.'

'Good. That's settled then. As soon as I've got my side of things sorted out, I'll arrange for him to see you. You'll like him. Now, they've advised me you'll be formally charged tomorrow morning. It's a straightforward procedure, a formality. Don't let it get you tied up in knots. I'll be with you, of course.'

'What will I be charged with?'

Phillips studied him for a moment. 'They're going for murder, I'm afraid.'

Everything stopped. The clock stopped ticking, the tap stopped dripping, the world stopped turning.

'God almighty,' said Jim. 'I thought it would just be manslaughter.'

'So did I,' Phillips went on. 'When I first read your statement. Unfortunately, it seems Miss Paterson leant over backwards to cover for you after her arrest. She refused point blank to identify you. They knew all along there was another man involved.'

'How?'

'The two of you were seen pushing the car off the road.'

'But there was nobody around.'

'Not that you were aware of, obviously. But there was someone, a bush-walker. Out camping. When the papers reported it as an accident and he realised there had been a man inside, he informed the police. He'd made a note of the number of Miss Paterson's utility. Inaccurately, as it turned out. That's why it took the police so long to trace it to her.'

Jim stared at the table in front of him and shook his head in disbelief. 'But it's still only manslaughter, surely?'

'As I understand it, yes. But any corroboration she offers now will conflict with some of her earlier statements. The police seem to have convinced the Prosecutor's office that Murphy came to grief because the two of you caught him sniffing round the mine.'

'That's absolute rubbish,' Jim protested. 'The bastard would have raped her if I hadn't turned up.'

'I believe you. They don't. Even though you have come forward and taken full responsibility, they still think it's murder.'

'But Annie can back me up now.'

'I'll certainly get an affidavit from her,' said Phillips. 'But it doesn't alter the present situation. They wouldn't go for murder if they didn't think they could get a result.'

Jim's head was spinning. 'What sort of sentence will I get?' he asked, almost inaudibly.

'They *have* to get a conviction first,' Phillips reminded him gently. 'They have to prove you intended to kill Murphy, or do him grievous bodily harm.'

'If they did?' Jim pressed.

Phillips tried to hold his eye, but the man looked so wretched he had to look down at his pad to reply. 'It's mandatory. Hard labour for life. In normal circumstances you'd be entitled to parole after twelve to fifteen years . . .'

Jim blanched, slumped and buried his face in his hands.

Phillips tried to soften the blow. 'I'm sorry, Jim. There's no easy way round this. Obviously, it's my job to inform you of the possibilities.'

Jim took a deep breath, steadied his jangling nerves, raised his head and nodded. Phillips attempted a cheering smile in return but it didn't work.

Jim braced himself. 'What does grievous bodily harm mean exactly? In a situation like that? You know I didn't intend to kill him.'

'Bodily injury of such a nature as to endanger or be likely to endanger life.'

Another small hope dashed. 'Well, that sums it up, doesn't it?'

Phillips raised a hand. 'Just a minute, just a minute. Please. Let me explain and then we can discuss it.'

Jim was doing his best, but his nerves were burning up and he was finding it impossible to quell the trembling in his legs under the table. He folded his arms, gripped them tightly and nodded. 'Go on.'

'The prosecution will certainly try to make it apply in your case. They'll have to. But you must keep in mind at all times that the onus is on *them* to prove it.'

'Beyond reasonable doubt.'

'Exactly,' Phillips smiled. 'Never forget that. Now, our defence, of course, will be self-defence on your part. Both of yourself and Miss Paterson. And, there again, the onus is on the Crown to prove that you *didn't* act in self-defence.'

'How do they define self-defence?'

'Broadly speaking, we will argue that Miss Paterson and you were subjected to an unprovoked assault of such violence as to place you in reasonable fear of your own lives or grievous bodily harm. In such a situation, it is lawful for you to respond with whatever force you felt necessary to defend her and yourself. If the plea were accepted and the opposition couldn't prove otherwise, you'd be entitled to a verdict of not guilty and complete acquittal.'

'What are the chances?'

Phillips pondered the papers in front of him for a long time before he replied.

'There's no point in beating about the bush, Jim. They're not great. It would have been even money if you'd come forward at the time. They'll have a field day with what you did, and Miss Paterson, if they go for her. Her team will have to try and make a case for coercion on your part, even though she assured me it was the other way round.'

'I'll admit to that, if it'll help her.'

'You've admitted to enough already. Let's cross that bridge when we come to it. First things first, and that's tomorrow's hearing. I'll apply for bail, of course.'

'Not much chance of that, is there?'

'Hard to say until I have another word with the Crown's mob,' said Phillips. 'It's possible they may not object. Bit late in the day, but you have come forward voluntarily and . . .' He shuffled Jim's statement back to the top of his papers and frowned. 'Virtually handed them their case on a platter. They may feel inclined to be charitable, top of the scale bail and an offer to surrender your passport might swing it. Have to wait and see.'

'Is there any point?'

'You wouldn't have to stay on remand. That's the point. Unless you want to, of course. Otherwise you could go home and get on with your life.'

'What happens if I stay on remand? Would that do me any good? In the eyes of the court, I mean.'

'Not a scrap.' Phillips shrugged and began collecting his papers together. 'I can only repeat what I said before. At this moment in time, your position is not particularly good.'

Jim could no longer contain his anger. He slapped the table in front of him. 'But it *was* an accident. I didn't mean to kill the bastard! I had to do something, for God's sake!'

Phillips eyed him sympathetically and nodded. 'I realise that and, as I've said, we'll plead accordingly. The fly in the ointment is your failure to report it, the steps you took to disguise what happened . . .'

Jim slumped back in silence for a moment as Phillips stuffed his papers into his briefcase.

'Where will I be tried?' he asked finally.

'Townsville Supreme Court.'

Another kick in the teeth. As he shook his head in dismay at the fatal role the city continued to play in his life, Pi Kok's mocking laugh rang in his mind.

'In view of the circumstances, with your statement and everything, I should imagine they'll try and slot it in as soon as possible. Six weeks, or thereabouts.'

Phillips stood up, picked up his briefcase and gave Jim a long, penetrating look.

'That's it for the moment, Jim. I know it's hard, but try and keep your chin up. Bear our plea in mind. Remember you *are* presumed innocent until proved otherwise, so don't let 'em rattle you.'

'He just came out of nowhere,' Jim mumbled hollowly.

'Trouble generally does,' said Andrew Phillips.

The door opened again and the sergeant appeared to take Jim back to the cell.

As the door swung shut, Jim's cellmate studied him with hard black cockatoo eyes.

'How ya goin', mate? Orright?'

'Been better.'

'Yeah, know what ya mean . . .'

At that moment, there was a racket in the corridor and the constable appeared with a trolley. Corn-beef salad and tinned peaches smothered in lumpy yellow custard.

'Whatcha in for, anyway?'

'Had some trouble with a car.'

'Yeah? What? Ya thieved one?'

'Something like that. How about you?'

'Assault,' the little bloke announced, with obvious satisfaction. 'Did over a tax inspector. Galah walked into me house like he owned the joint and started wanting to know how many fuckin' smokes I get through in a day. Told him to piss off out of it and mind his own fuckin' business. Bastard just stood there screaming "I've got a right, I've got a right." So I said so have I and let him fuckin' have it.'

Jim couldn't help but laugh.

After their trays had been taken away, Jim lay down again and said goodnight. The little bloke told him to go right ahead, but he kept talking anyway. He was still at it when Jim's exhaustion finally overcame his troubled mind.

'See, the way I look at it, it's not a battle between good and evil. Like, how good's good and how good's evil? I mean, it's just a matter of how you tilt your hat, isn't it? Like your odds with your bookie. I knew this bookie, 'bout as good an evil bastard as you're ever likely to meet . . .'

It was all lost on Jim. He'd gone.

The next morning Andrew Phillips' application for bail was denied after objections from the police. Jim was charged with murder and remanded in custody to appear before the Supreme Court, Townsville, in seven weeks' time. Phillips did his best to bolster his confidence before he was led away, but it had little effect. His life was in ruins.

# Fifty-One

Townsville's Supreme Court is housed in a modern brick building on Walker Street. The courtroom itself is panelled in wood. Prussian blue wall-to-wall carpeting on the floor creates an imposing atmosphere.

The court is entered through two glass doors at the back. Above, there is a recessed public gallery of twenty-seven seats, reached via an outside corridor on the floor above. Immediately to the right on ground level are half a dozen more public seats. Beyond them, a door leads to the cells. On the other side is the jury box, two rows of six seats facing squarely across the court to the opposite wall. Beyond that again, and just behind the witness box, another door leads to the jury room. To the left of the entrance doors, there's another block of twenty-four public seats which end at the dock. The dock itself is roughly in the shape of a horseshoe and unusually open. It faces diagonally across the front of the jury box towards the witness box in the top right-hand corner of the court. The bar table for the prosecution and defence counsels stretches in front of and parallel to the dock so that it too faces the witness box. The judge's bench is raised and stretches across the head of the court. In front of it, on floor level, a smaller bench seats the judge's associate, and the court reporters. Immediately to the left, facing squarely across the court, is a small desk where the bailiff sits.

On the opening day of Jim's trial, the air-conditioning was working flat out. The case had been headlines for weeks, guaranteeing early morning queues for the limited public seating. Now, the lucky ones were eagerly anticipating the blood sport to come and fanning themselves furiously with whatever they could get their hands on as they watched the last-minute preparations.

Crown prosecutor Michael Lewis and his clerk were busily sorting their papers into piles. At the other end, Andrew

Phillips was huddled in conference with the portly figure of Digby Willis. As crumpled in appearance as Phillips was flamboyant, Willis looked more like an absent-minded antiquarian than the renowned barrister he was. As he listened to his instructing solicitor, his eyelids drooped every time he nodded agreement. In contrast to the orderliness at the other end of the table, the paperwork before him was stacked in one, chaotic-looking bundle.

The court reporters were busily checking their machines, watched by two poker-faced police officers.

The Mackay family had managed to reserve aisle seats in the first two rows of public seating closest to the dock. Jilba and Tony in front, Jack and Billy behind them. That way they were all guaranteed a full view of their father and he had only to glance to his right to see them.

Having just flown in from San Francisco the previous afternoon, all Jilba wanted to do was hide. Fidgeting beside her, Tony was worried sick. At the end of July, he was able to bring his father at least one bit of good news. His grandson had tipped the scales at just over eight pounds and they called him Angus after his great-great-grandfather. The grim surroundings made Jim's teary-eyed inspection of the first photographs heart-rending to watch and those tears came back to Tony now as he visualised his father waiting to make his reluctant entrance on this terrible stage.

Billy Mackay was scared stiff and unable to hide it. Beside him, Jack was studying the Crown prosecutor and his clerk with undisguised disdain. As far as he was concerned, the whole thing was a ridiculous sham, and the blame lay squarely at Michael Lewis's door. His father had been forced to retaliate against a man who was threatening to shoot him. What could be simpler? Okay, the man had died and that was regrettable. But no excuse to stick his dad in gaol and drag him through this farce. He just couldn't understand why they refused to accept the facts. Okay, it had been wrong for him and Annie to try and cover it up. But they'd done it for Fred's sake, not their own. They'd owned up now and told the truth. That should be enough.

At that moment, Jim was sitting in the holding cells, reading Dud Brewley's letter for the umpteenth time. The poor old bloke had taken a nasty tumble at Glenmore, severely aggravating his chronic hip and making it impossible to be anywhere but flat on his back until it eased. Otherwise, he would be there in person. He'd already made one long journey to Townsville, with Athol Ferguson on one of the two visits he'd made to Jim in prison.

Jim folded the letter and tucked it into the inside pocket of his coat. There were five others there. From Susan, Betsey, Clare Sugden, Dean Coulter and, most especially, a brief note from Anthony Barclay on behalf of himself and Jean. Though somewhat formally expressed, it was obviously heartfelt and certainly better than nothing.

He let the flap of his coat fall, leant back and studied the portrait of Her Majesty the Queen, hanging on the wall at the far end of the corridor, just visible through the bars of his cell. He had gone to war in defence of her realm. Now she was the enemy. Her representatives were about to do their level best to lock him up for good. He shook his head to clear the air and thought about Balkenna. A smile tugged at his lips as he remembered Jack's last visit. Balkenna Dean the First, the prize Santa Gertrudis bull named in honour of its American benefactor, had broken out of the Jack-Jack and had its way with at least twenty, maybe more, of Jim's brown-eyed pedigree Herefords. Like it or not, there were going to be some new crossbreeds on the property.

Jim was interrupted by the appearance of his accompanying prison officer. All was ready. Any minute now. Butterflies immediately took flight in Jim's stomach and he swallowed hard to drown them. The prison officer said something as he unlocked the door, but Jim didn't take it in. All he could think about was the sight of his family, waiting in the arena just down the corridor. Jilba's distress the previous afternoon had been pretty harrowing. He would give anything for them not to have to go through this.

When the prison officer opened the door, it squeaked. Jim allowed himself one quick scan of their faces. His family tried as hard as they could to radiate confidence. But it was agony for them all. Once he was seated in the dock, he couldn't see them without turning his head and looking past the prison officer sitting beside him. But he could feel their eyes on him.

On the other side of town, three other people dear to his heart noted the time and lapsed into uneasy silence as they huddled over the kitchen table in the big old house Fred Paterson had managed to rent for a month. Fred had got back to

Charters Towers from the Gulf Country just four days after Annie's arrest. The house had been his idea so that the Mackay family could stay there as well. It meant roughing it a bit and sharing bedrooms, but everybody agreed it was much better to be under one roof.

As Annie came in to join Athol, Tim and her father, all four of them eyed one another in mute recognition of the ordeal they knew was about to begin. They were all due to be called as witnesses and were forbidden to attend the trial until they had given their evidence and been excused by the judge.

'Oh, yea! Oh, yea!'

The muttering that rippled through the court on Jim's appearance dried up as the bailiff called them to order. Along with everybody else, Jim stood up as the judge appeared in his blood-red robes and took up his position on the bench. There was more commotion as everybody resumed their seats. The judge waited for it to pass before nodding at the bailiff.

'The defendant will rise and face the bench.'

It echoed inside Jim's skull like it came through miles of concrete pipe. He took a deep, deep breath, stood up and looked the judge in the eye. This was it. The judge studied him impassively for a moment and then directed the Crown prosecutor to proceed with the indictment.

Michael Lewis spoke in clear, incisive tones that carried easily to all corners of the court. When he was through, Jim was called upon to plead. He took another deep breath, held himself erect, kept his eyes on the judge and, as Digby Willis had instructed, answered with firm, straightforward conviction.

'Not guilty.'

The judge's associate made a note of his plea. The bailiff told him to sit down again and the judge called for jury selection to begin. The prison officer immediately shifted his bum, stretched his legs as far as he could and got comfortable. Obviously a seasoned campaigner, Jim thought.

Andrew Phillips had told him jury selection would take up a good part, perhaps all, of the morning's session. Jim could feel an electric charge radiating from his family but he figured it was not an appropriate time to turn and look at them. Instead, he concentrated on his defending counsel's challenge of the first juror. A skinny housewife with a lisp, she stood in front of the witness box with a look of sheer unmitigated terror, as if she was on trial herself. She made way for a man who turned out to be a chicken farmer who was immediately challenged by Lewis.

As the process continued, Jim watched with sickening fascination one minute, an eerie sense of detachment the next. Willis and Lewis were challenging the credentials and good sense of these people to decide his fate while, at the same time, trying to probe their likely vulnerabilities to the art of persuasion. Phillips had told him that if a full jury was not empanelled on the first run through, both prosecution and defence had a further fourteen standbys and challenges without cause. It was going to be a long, drawn-out business.

He focused on the Crown prosecutor, sizing him up for the showdown to come. Willis had made very sure Jim harboured no illusions about the formidable talents Lewis would bring to bear, describing him as a skilful courtroom tactician.

A good man, well-liked and respected in coastal Queensland, Michael Lewis was also widely rumoured to have political ambitions. There was no mileage in coming out on the losing end of a case that had already made headlines all round Australia. As Jim watched Lewis's clinical dissection of one juror after another, the accuracy of Willis's estimation became all too apparent.

Willis scared him. Over the course of their meetings to prepare his defence, Jim had become more and more disconcerted by the man's air of bumbling other-worldliness, as if it was beneath him to concentrate on any one thing at a time. Most disconcerting of all, he never in any way attempted to hide his view that they had a tough fight on their hands.

But Phillips kept reassuring him and Jim had persevered with his solicitor's choice of barrister despite his doubts. Watching him now, Willis appeared to be holding his end up. But, to Jim's eye, there was still no sign of genius. Nor did any appear by the end of the morning's session when a jury of six men and six women was finally empanelled and the judge adjourned the proceedings ten minutes early for lunch.

When the court reconvened and the judge returned, Jim was startled by his appearance. As was apparently his habit, he had dispensed with his wig for the remainder of the trial. It was much more unsettling to see an ordinary everyday face looming over the bench, minus the familiar headgear. He was a slightly built man with short jet-black hair. His name was Heywood and, according to Phillips, he ran a tight court. Once again he waited for complete and utter silence before asking Michael Lewis to open for the Crown.

For the next hour, Lewis used all his charm and guile to sell the jury the case for the prosecution. Contrary to the defence's plea and the claims they would no doubt hear from his learned friend, the prosecution would prove beyond any shadow of a doubt that murder had resulted from a firm intention to cause grievous bodily harm. As witnesses would later testify, the hapless victim, Geoffrey Murphy, was a man of good reputation. He had no criminal record and was well-liked by those who knew him.

Lewis asked for Jim's statement to be read to the court and entered it as Exhibit A. Then he tore it to shreds. He called it a pack of lies, concocted by the accused in collusion with the woman involved who was, herself, on bail facing charges in connection with Murphy's death. The real clue to the matter lay in the action taken by the accused and Miss Annie Paterson following Murphy's murder. The lengths they went to to fake a road accident in an attempt to make their victim's death appear accidental.

According to the defendant, their intention was to safeguard the whereabouts of the mine they worked with the woman's father, to protect it from scrutiny by the outside world at all costs. It was the only part of Jim's statement, Lewis insisted, that came near to the truth. It gave a clue to the real motive for murdering Murphy who had, obviously, inadvertently stumbled on their mine and been killed to keep it secret. History had shown the fabulous wealth they were prepared to kill for to protect, and Lewis quoted the figures. He had no need to remind the jury of the truth of I Timothy, chapter six, verse ten, but he did anyway. 'For the love of money is the root of all evil; which while some coveted after, they have erred from the faith, and pierced themselves through with many sorrows.'

A simple substitution of the word 'law' for 'faith', Lewis suggested, might persuade the jury that the accused must now endure those many sorrows. He was so persuasive, he even had Jim spellbound.

Lewis spelt out the chain of misfortune which had led Jim to take up residence with the Patersons, beginning with his mysterious disappearance following the death of his wife. He had deserted his family, leaving them to suffer months of agonising uncertainty as to his fate. As a result, he had lost a major part of his Longreach property and faced financial ruin upon his return, a loss later averted in the sort of way most people could only ever dream about.

In the months of his absence, his family had been forced to formally declare him a missing person and considerable sums of public resources had gone into attempts by the Queensland police to trace his whereabouts. Regrettably, Lewis knew of no offer by the accused to make compensation for the trouble he'd caused, though one might have expected his new-found wealth might have inspired some contribution to any number of worthy charitable organisations aided and supported by the state's police force.

Then, to the dismay of the defence, Lewis went on to describe a matter which had come to light in February of that year following an assault on the defendant's son in Townsville by an unknown assailant. During the course of their investigation into the incident, it had been brought to the attention of the police that the defendant had attempted to circumvent a strike on the Townsville docks at the time. He had done so in the hope of being able to proceed with a shipment of a large consignment of cattle to Malaysia. Lewis described Jim's offer of a contribution to union funds as nothing more than an outright attempt to bribe the local branch of the Australian Waterside Workers' Federation, and he was bound to suggest the jury might well draw the same conclusion.

By the time he was through, the court was left with the distinct impression that the defendant, James Mackay, was a greedy self-serving debauchee who would stop at nothing to feather his own nest.

Then Digby Willis rose. Congratulating the Crown prosecutor on his Biblical erudition, he was sure Lewis also recalled John, chapter eight, verse thirty-two.

'And ye shall know the truth . . . And the truth shall make thee free.'

Even Lewis was unable to swallow a small smile.

Willis took up the rest of the afternoon. Contrary to the prosecution's intemperate attempts at character assassination, he promised the jury would come to understand that Jim's actions following Mr Murphy's unfortunate demise were anything but self-serving and were in fact motivated by the much loftier, some might think quixotic, ideals of deep concern and loyalty towards those he considered primarily responsible for salvaging him from a long period of wayward alcoholism induced by the tragic and premature death of his beloved wife.

His first instinct had been to report Murphy's death to the authorities immediately. Only when it was pointed out to him what that would mean in terms of attracting widespread unwelcome attention to the location of his friends' strike did he agree to go along with an attempt to fake a road accident. Mr Paterson was a prospector of considerable reputation who believed he was close to the find of his life. Subsequent events bore witness to the accuracy of his intuition. Once known, his reputation would have inevitably attracted other prospectors to the location, exposing them to the threat of professional claim-jumpers and a rush of gold-mad amateurs seeking easy money.

To rebut the prosecution's attempt to blacken the defendant's character, he promised to call witnesses of impeccable probity who would testify to the very opposite.

The jury would come to recognise the fundamental honesty and goodness of the man in the dock, a man totally and utterly incapable of premeditated murder. The man's death was of his own making, spelt out in Jim's *voluntary* statement describing the events leading up to it. The defendant had acted purely and simply in self-defence, of himself and Miss Paterson. Unarmed, they had been threatened and then fired upon by an armed man in such a way as to place them in fear of their own lives.

Willis wound up the afternoon session by asking for Jim's statement to be read to the jury again, slowly and clearly, in order that they might judge for themselves its open frankness without prejudice.

As the prison officer led him from the dock, Jim gave his family a brave smile, and they did their best to respond. But there was no hiding it. Willis had turned in a good, measured performance. But so had Lewis. And the jury looked like they believed him.

# Fifty-Two

The second morning opened with Michael Lewis calling Detective-Sergeant Charles Allen. Once he had taken the oath, Lewis quickly identified him to the jury as the homicide detective from Charters Towers who had led police enquiries. Allen was well used to court procedure and the jury was fascinated as Lewis led him slowly and methodically through his testimony.

Constantly referring to his notes, he began with the unexpected evidence from an independent witness that led the police to revise their earlier verdict that Murphy had died in a road accident. That witness, who lived in Mount Coolon, had not read a newspaper report of the accident until after the deceased's burial, necessitating exhumation. The witness had initially presumed that what he saw was the disposal of an older model car, perhaps to claim insurance. Only after reading the newspaper report did he realise there had been a man inside when the vehicle was pushed off the road.

Detailed microscopic examination of the dead man's skull fracture revealed minute traces of soil and leaf uncommon to the immediate vicinity of the wrecked car. Following the successful tracing of another vehicle reported by the witness, a warrant had been obtained to conduct a forensic examination of the location now known as the Bush Girl Mine.

Despite the fact intensive mining had drastically altered its topography a bloodstain the size of a pinprick on the wooden handle of a shovel proved to have come from the deceased, Geoffrey Murphy, as did other traces of blood found impregnated in rust on the carrying tray of the Holden utility traced to Miss Annie Paterson. Under interrogation, she admitted faking a road accident but had refused point blank to identify a man reported by the witness as being her accomplice in pushing Murphy's car off the road. Following further interrogation, Miss Paterson was charged with murder, a charge later dropped when the defendant came forward, identified himself and admitted responsibility for Murphy's death.

However, the defendant's statement contradicted in several instances earlier statements made by Miss Paterson, and his claim of self-defence of both her and himself proved unacceptable, leading to a charge of murder for which the defendant was now on trial.

Digby Willis began his cross-examination by informing Allen that, in view of his client's own statement, it was not his intention to dispute the main details concerning the police investigation, the forensic evidence produced by the autopsy or subsequent discoveries at the Bush Girl Mine. What he did dispute, and would continue to dispute, was the prosecution challenge to the defendant's claim of self-defence against an unprovoked assault of such violence as to place him in reasonable fear of his own life and that of Miss Paterson.

Allen suggested that people with nothing to hide would not in normal circumstances go to such extraordinary lengths to dispose of the body.

Reminding him that he was in the box to answer questions, not to make suggestions, Willis was bound to wonder whether or not both the initial post-mortem and subsequent autopsy revealed other injuries sustained by the deceased after his car had plunged off the road.

Allen nodded. The victim had sustained multiple injuries. But there was no doubt whatsoever in the pathologists' minds that skull fracture and brain haemorrhage had led to and been the principal cause of Murphy's death. That fracture had resulted from a ferocious blow to the side of the head with a hard, blunt object.

Willis asked if those same pathology reports indicated instantaneous death, or as near as you can get to it.

Allen claimed he was not in a position to know.

Willis found that hard to believe and pressed him on the point.

Allen admitted they indicated almost instantaneous death, the victim probably never knew what hit him.

Willis had just one more question, or, to put it more correctly, request. Would the witness be good enough to assure the jury once more that the defendant, James Mackay, had come forward of his own free will and made a voluntary statement admitting his responsibility. Allen turned to face the jury and agreed that it was so.

No further questions.

There was a pause while Lewis handed over the signed affidavit of the next witness. Lewis asked for it to be read to the court and entered it into evidence as Exhibit B. He then asked the bailiff to call Rodney Clark. At last Jim got a good look at the agent of his downfall. He didn't look like much.

Clutching a folder, Lewis strode to his side and gave him a friendly smile.

'Mr Clark . . .' He opened the folder, took out a ten-by-eight, black and white photograph of Geoff Murphy posing beside his Peugeot station wagon and handed it to Clark. 'Is this the vehicle you saw being pushed off the road?'

'Yes.'

'You're quite sure?'

'Positive.'

'Just answer yes or no, please.'

'Yes.'

Lewis retrieved the photograph and handed it to the jury foreman, for their inspection. When they had finished, Lewis asked for it to be entered as Exhibit C.

'Now, Mr Clark. You have said you saw that vehicle being pushed off the road by a man and a woman who then ran to another vehicle, described by you as a Holden utility in poor condition. Is that correct?'

'Yes.'

'And after that Holden utility made a U-turn on the road and drove away, you made a note of the registration number which you were able to see quite clearly through binoculars.'

'Yes.'

'Thank you, Mr Clark. No further questions at the moment.'

Willis rose slowly and approached the witness with a pensive, slightly perplexed look on his face. He leant against the witness box, drummed his fingers on its top rail a moment and studied Clark as an owl might a dormouse. Clark shifted his seat and braced himself for a grilling. But Willis appeared to change his mind, crossed to the bench, asked for the photograph and studied it intently as he slowly returned. Clark licked his lips.

'Mr Clark. You have positively identified this vehicle as the one you saw being pushed off the road on the morning in question.'

'Yes,' said Clark, almost inaudibly.

'Speak up, please, Mr Clark,' said the judge.

'Yes,' Clark repeated, a little louder.

'Beyond a shadow of a doubt?'

'Yes.'

Willis knotted his eyebrows. 'Tell me, Mr Clark. How many such vehicles would you say there are in the state of Queensland?'

Before he could reply, the Crown prosecutor intervened. 'Objection, Your Honour. The question is purely speculative and I fail to see its relevance.'

'I'll rephrase, Your Honour,' said Willis, pre-empting a ruling. Lewis sat down and Willis turned back to Rodney Clark.

'Have you ever seen a vehicle like this one before, Mr Clark?'

'Not painted like that one.'

Willis studied him wearily for a moment, as if the man was an out and out moron. 'I was referring to the make and model, Mr Clark. A Peugeot 403 station wagon.'

'Yes.'

'Yes, what?'

'I've seen one before.'

'Where, exactly?'

'All over the place.'

'So you have seen a great many such vehicles?'

'Who hasn't?'

'Just answer the question, please, Mr Clark.'

'Yes,' Clark snapped, losing his grip. 'Of course I have.'

'And yet you're absolutely certain, beyond any shadow of a doubt, that this is the one you saw that morning?'

Lewis leapt to his feet again. 'Objection! Your Honour, I fail to see the relevance of this line of questioning. The defendant's own statement refers to the vehicle, by make, model and colour.'

'Your Honour,' Willis replied. 'As we can all plainly see, the photograph entered as Exhibit C is in black and white, leaving the question of colour to the imagination.'

'I still object, Your Honour,' said Lewis. 'Irrespective of this particular photograph, the colour combination of the vehicle was highly unusual and not to the maker's specifications, thereby making identification by the witness that much simpler.'

'What a shame the deceased didn't leave us a colour photograph to place in evidence, Your Honour,' said Willis. 'Then we could also have seen the colour of the rifle so provocatively displayed.'

Lewis let his exasperation show. 'Your Honour . . .'

But Judge Heywood raised his hand to call a halt to any further argument. 'Objection overruled, Mr Lewis. Proceed, please, Mr Willis.'

As Lewis paraded his irritation, Willis gave the judge a courteous nod and returned to the witness box.

'I must ask you again, Mr Clark. Are you absolutely sure that the vehicle in the photograph is the one you saw being pushed off the road?'

'Yes,' Clark confirmed. But then, he hedged his bet. 'I'm ninety-nine per cent sure, anyway.'

Willis gave him a winning smile. 'That leaves us with a clear one per cent of doubt in your mind.'

'Not really,' Clark stammered, trying to recover. 'Just a figure of speech, you know.'

'One thing I do know, Mr Clark. A one per cent swing can unseat a government and change the course of history.'

Rod Clark was out of his depth. Willis turned, pondered a moment for the jury's benefit, then turned back to him.

'Now, Mr Clark. About this business of the number plate . . .'

He let the phrase hang and Clark couldn't help himself. He had to blunder into the hole.

'What about it?'

'Is it not true,' Willis was smiling now, 'that the registration number you wrote down and subsequently handed to the police proved to be that of another vehicle altogether? Belonging to a schoolteacher by the name of Hilary Joyner?'

'That was because of the dirt.'

'Ahhh, yes. The dirt. The dirt confused you, is that correct?'

'Sort of.'

'Yes or no, Mr Clark. Did the dirt confuse you or not?'

'Yes,' Clark gulped. 'Sort of . . .'

Willis gave him another winning smile.

'It made the double eight look like a double six. You know that already.'

'Thank you, Mr Clark. I just wanted the jury to be quite clear on the matter. In fact, you got the number wrong, even though we have heard you had binoculars trained on the number plate of the vehicle you described leaving the scene.'

'I didn't get it wrong,' Clark snapped, losing control again. 'I just didn't get it quite right.'

Even Judge Heywood couldn't hide a quick smile as titters ran round the public galleries.

'Exactly,' Willis confirmed. 'You just didn't get it quite right. Thank you, Mr Clark, that will be all. No further questions, Your Honour.'

Willis immediately spun away and headed for the bar table. His departure was so sudden, Clark involuntarily raised his hand, as if to summon him back.

'Does the Crown have any more questions for this witness?'

Lewis hesitated a moment, then rose to reply. 'No, Your Honour.'

'Thank you, Mr Lewis,' the Judge responded, with just a hint of relief. 'The witness is excused.'

Clark shot him a beseeching look. But Judge Heywood was busily jotting some notes on his pad and Clark stepped down blushing beetroot.

It had been a wily display. Lewis had been quite right, of course. In view of Jim's own statement, it didn't make much difference one way or the other. But it was obvious the jury felt some confusion over the issue. A few of them eyed Clark's departing back with rising scepticism. More importantly, perhaps, several others were watching as Willis fumbled through the untidy pile of papers in front of him, presumably seeing him in a new light as well.

It was five to one and, without further ado, the judge finished his note-taking and adjourned for lunch.

When the afternoon session opened, Michael Lewis lost no time calling four witnesses in quick succession.

The first was a man named Bostock, a lifelong friend of Murphy's. Done up like a sore toe for the occasion in his best suit and tie, he testified he and Murphy had gone to school together and known one another ever since. He left the jury in no doubt he'd lost the best friend he'd ever had, or was ever likely to have. He described Murphy as a generous, warm-hearted, fun-loving human being. Among many other acts of kindness, he had once lent him the money to put a down payment on a car. When Lewis asked him specifically if, to the best of his knowledge, Murphy had ever displayed violent or sadistic tendencies towards women, Bostock said no way in the world.

Cross-examining, Digby Willis managed to get him to agree

that, if challenged to a fight, Murphy wouldn't hesitate. He was, perhaps, a bit of a loner at heart with a thing about guns. But the prosecution team had primed him well and Bostock stoutly resisted all further attempts by Willis to bring his dead friend down a notch or two.

Willis had a bit more success with the next witness. But, to Jim's eye, it was doubtful if the jury warmed to his relentless badgering of an apparently innocent and, in the circumstances, sadly bewildered young woman. Barbara Porter had been Murphy's girlfriend for just over a year prior to his death. Softly spoken and quite good-looking, she seemed incompatible with Jim's memory of the slavering rapist who'd tried to kill him.

Barbara spoke of Geoff Murphy in glowing terms. She had hoped to marry him. She found it totally incomprehensible that anyone could believe him capable of rape or threatening to shoot someone. The gentle consideration with which Lewis took her through her testimony made a good impression on the jury. But it also lulled her into a false sense of security.

Despite some strenuous objections by Lewis, Willis managed to get some reluctant admissions out of her. She had at times been a bit put off by Murphy's fondness for his guns, but more because he often left her to her own devices on those weekends he went off shooting in the bush. She had no illusions about which way the wind would blow if it came down to a choice between her or his shooting trips, either alone or with some of his mates. But it hadn't worried her all that much. He was one of the boys and she accepted that.

Willis switched his sights to their sexual relationship. She admitted Murphy had not been her first lover, she'd had other boyfriends before taking up with him. Willis suggested she would, therefore, be able to assist the court in assessing Murphy's sexual appetites. There were audible sniggers in the public galleries when she confirmed that 'Geoff liked to do it'. And if, Willis wondered, for some reason she didn't feel like it at the time? She snookered him on that one. She never had. She liked to do it too.

The next witness for the Crown was another of Murphy's mates, a regular companion on shooting trips who testified to his friend's compassion towards animals only wounded by a first or second shot and the speed with which Murphy would move to give them the *coup de grâce*.

On that note, Judge Heywood suggested the jury might like a cup of tea and announced a twenty-minute recess.

Elizabeth Murphy was a small-boned woman in her late fifties, all the battles of a lifetime on the breadline written across her pinched and bitter face. She marched up to the witness box with purpose and took the oath in a way that left the court in no doubt she would, indeed, be telling the truth.

Under Lewis's guidance, she recalled her only child's life from infancy to death. Describing her husband's desertion shortly after her son's fifth birthday, she agreed with Lewis that life had been far from easy for the two of them. But they coped and, apart from normal everyday boyish pranks and minor felonies, her son had never been any trouble. Anticipating Willis, Lewis asked her if, under the circumstances, she might have been guilty of over-protectiveness in the years of his adolescence. It was possible. But then, to his relief, she qualified her answer by pointing out that it only applied as far as the Church was concerned. She had done her level best to protect his soul by insisting on regular attendance at Mass.

When Willis finally attempted some gentle cross-examination, she met the merest inference with the utmost contempt. Willis was forced to raise an issue presumably known to the Crown and, for obvious reasons, left firmly locked in the cupboard. Did she recall an occasion in her son's sixteenth year when, in her absence at work, he borrowed a friend's rifle and deliberately and methodically shot out every window of their home, causing extensive damage in the process?

Lewis's mouth drew into a grim line.

Mrs Murphy immediately sought Judge Heywood's advice as to whether she had to answer. When he informed her the court must hear all the facts, no matter how painful, she acknowledged the incident in a way she hoped would diminish its significance. Her son had been deeply upset at the time, filled with remorse afterwards, and did penance by replacing all the broken glass himself and raising the money doing odd jobs outside school hours. Willis asked her to tell the court what had precipitated his action. Painfully, she explained that her son's sweetheart at the time had passed him over for one of his classmates, a boy a year older than himself. She broke down in tears, sobbing over and over again that she had lost the best son a mother could ever hope to have.

Her distress stilled the court. Willis decided any further cross-examination would do more harm than good. He thanked her quietly for her assistance and returned to the bar table.

As Mrs Murphy left the box, Andrew Phillips noticed several of the jurors were staring with obvious distaste at the dock behind him. He turned to see Jim's head hanging so low, his chin was on his chest. Their look said that a man with nothing to hide would not be afraid to hold his head high and look his accuser in the eye.

Jim stared doggedly at the carpet under his feet as the prison officer led him out. Reading the despair in his shoulders, his children watched him leave the court in agony.

In the afternoon, Digby Willis set out to redress the balance. He called Athol Ferguson, Tim Daley, Fred Paterson and Dave Reynolds. Jim's former commanding officer in Vietnam had been tracked down by Andrew Phillips' office through the Returned Services League. Now the successful owner of a string of garden centres throughout southeast Queensland, Reynolds had willingly made himself available to testify on Jim's behalf.

Describing the years of their association, Athol's weighty and dignified testimonial to the fine qualities that had attracted him to Jim in the first place and led to their later collaboration in the Balkenna Pastoral Company carried the ring of prophecy. Athol was here to warn each and every one of them that a terrible injustice could be done in this room if they did not heed his every word. He went on to describe their friendship as one of the great and enduring joys of his life. In no way whatsoever could he entertain the prosecution's claims, and he stressed, time and again, his unflinching belief in the truth of Jim's statement in every detail.

The only small hiccup occurred during cross-examination when Lewis forced him, under oath, to admit that his first reaction to Jim's desertion of his family following his wife's death had been one of incomprehension and dismay. But, despite Lewis's attempt to deflect him, Athol went on to record his admiration for the way in which Jim had subsequently sorted his life out and bent over backwards to make up for any distress he'd caused his family. Lewis gave up after that.

Tim's testimony moved Jilba to tears. Rising heroically to the occasion, he overcame a lifetime's reticence and poured his heart out in defence of the man who was, to all intents and purposes, his brother. Moving tributes to Jim's loyal, trustworthy, compassionate humanity tumbled out with such raw, naked feeling, it was impossible to doubt a word he said. Above all, he stressed the generosity of spirit with which two generations of Mackays had made him one of their family, a family that loved and cared for him like a son.

Riding Tim for all he was worth, Digby Willis orchestrated his testimony beautifully and brought it to a resonant climax when Tim finished by saying it was impossible to work hand in glove with a man through umpteen years in the Queensland outback without getting to know him inside and out. He knew, the way he knew Christ died on the Cross for us all, that Jim Mackay was incapable of murder. What happened could only have been an accident. There was no getting away from it, and there was no getting around it.

Lewis did his best to take some of the shine off, but he soon gave it away as a lost cause. The man was a rock.

When Tim left the witness box and headed for his seat, Jack had to sit on his hands to suppress an irresistible urge to applaud him all the way. Come hell or high water, the rest of life would be richer for the memory of Tim's day in court.

Fred Paterson didn't fare so well. He was still cranky about his poor showing over the dinner table that night. Everyone did their best to buck him up, but Fred was inconsolable.

He started all right. Willis conducted him through the years of his association with Jack Mackay Snr and his son. He made no bones about it. But for their financial support, nobody would have ever heard of the Bush Girl Mine. He handled the details of Jim's breakdown, and the time he spent in the care of himself and his daughter with skill and wit, choosing his words with care and peppering them with a few ripe observations that went down well all round.

It was when Lewis got stuck into him that he dropped his bundle. He managed to restrain himself for most of the prosecutor's cross-examination. But Lewis just kept at him, challenging time and again his claim that his daughter and Jim had left him in the dark about Murphy's death and the means

504

they chose to dispose of his body. So much so that Judge Heywood upheld an objection from Willis that the witness was not on trial and no charges were pending against him in connection with the case before the court.

Lewis changed his tune then, and set out to impress on the jury the idea that a man who enjoyed such a lifestyle as the witness would not be particularly inclined to respect the truth in the sense they would themselves, indeed might be counted upon to distort it to defend a mate threatened with imprisonment.

He bombarded Fred with a flurry of deliberately disjointed questions and the more he asked, the more he was able to get Fred to contradict himself. Tugging at his beard, Fred stood for it up to the point where Lewis turned his back on him and addressed the jury directly, suggesting that the witness's idea of the truth, and that of men like him, such as the man in the dock, was based on expediency and self-preservation, motivated by flagrant defiance of civilised values and the rule of law. That did it. Fred pounded the top of the witness box and did his block.

'Listen, fancy pants. Back there I swore to tell the truth and that's what I've done! If you can't hear it, you better get your bloody ears checked!'

His outburst brought a swift reprimand from the bench. Any more of the same and the witness might well find himself in contempt. Lewis quit while he was ahead. When the judge excused him, Fred lumbered back to his seat unable to hide his fury.

Dave Reynolds had gone to seed a bit in the long years since Vietnam and carried a fair-sized beer belly into the witness box. But his wartime memory of Sergeant Jim Mackay was clear as a bell and he paid fitting tribute to a brother-in-arms.

He made much of Jim's devotion to duty and the high regard in which he'd been held by those serving under him. In particular, he stressed his own gratitude for the way Jim had seen to the needs of new arrivals faced with going into action for the first time. In his opinion, Jim had played no small part in the mercifully low casualty figures sustained by those men during their tour of duty.

It was approaching four thirty by the time Willis thanked Reynolds for his testimony and deferred to Lewis. Judge Heywood suggested that, in view of the time, the Crown prosecutor might prefer to save his cross-examination for the following morning. To the puzzlement of Andrew Phillips and the more suspicious concern of Digby Willis, Lewis announced that would not be necessary. He had no wish to cross-examine the witness and was happy to allow his testimony to stand. On that note, Judge Heywood brought the day's proceedings to a close.

# Fifty-Three

The sound of his own name sent a shiver down Jim's spine. When the prison officer stood up to let him out of the dock, Jim moved slowly, allowing himself time for eye contact with each member of his family and the three men who had stood up and done their best on his behalf. All of them promised light on the horizon. But they all knew, only too well, that that day might prove to be very far away . . .

Once in the box, he managed to state his name and take the oath without his voice betraying the mayhem in his head. As Lewis came with slow determination from the bar table, Jim braced himself.

'Mr Mackay, I'd like you to cast your mind back to the sequence of events leading to Mr Murphy's death, as described by you in your statement to the Charters Towers police on the twenty-eighth of June this year.'

As Jim collected his thoughts, Lewis turned away and moved towards the jury, making sure they took note of his good grace in allowing the defendant plenty of time. Then he wheeled on him.

'Is there anything, anything at all, you wish to add to that statement?'

'No,' Jim answered firmly. 'I've told the truth about what happened. There's nothing . . .'

Lewis immediately raised his hand. 'Please, Mr Mackay, just answer yes or no.'

'No,' Jim repeated.

'So you stand by every word of that statement as it's been read before this court?'

'Yes.'

'Thank you. Now . . . The better part of yesterday afternoon's sitting was taken up by those witnesses called upon by my learned friend to testify to your background, your previous good character and your position of prominence as a grazier in the Longreach district.'

Lewis paused, as if inviting Jim to comment. But Jim didn't rise to the bait and Lewis was forced to continue. 'We also heard testimony regarding the tragic circumstances of your wife's death and the effect it had upon your mental and physical wellbeing.'

Again, Jim didn't respond.

'We also heard from your former commanding officer that you served your country with distinction in Vietnam.'

Jim just stared at him, waiting. After holding his eye a moment, Lewis turned his back and continued speaking directly to the jury. 'The one thing we didn't hear, of course, was in exactly what capacity you served your country.' He spun back, and demanded an answer. 'Did we?'

'I'm not quite sure what you mean.'

Lewis flapped his arms in an exaggerated gesture of exasperation. 'On the contrary, Mr Mackay. I'm sure you know exactly what I mean.'

'I was in the Army,' Jim replied, still not sure what he was driving at.

Lewis strode over to the bar table, accepted a document from his clerk with a flourish, studied it for a beat, handed it back and returned to Jim.

'The Army is a big place, Mr Mackay. I'd prefer to be more specific. In fact, you served in the SAS, did you not?'

Jim glanced quickly at Digby Willis. His nod said answer the question.

'Yes.'

'And your rank, as we have heard, was sergeant. Is that correct?'

'Yes.'

'And, as a sergeant, you were also an SAS Instructor?'

'Yes.'

'And, as an Instructor, you were responsible for training SAS recruits?'

'No,' Jim corrected. 'Not recruits. Trained servicemen arriving in Vietnam for their first tour of duty.'

'Oh, very well,' Lewis shrugged. 'Let's call them raw recruits to the theatre of war.'

'In that way they were,' Jim agreed. 'Yes.'

'And you trained them to kill, is that correct?'

'Objection!' Willis protested. 'Your Honour, all military instruction involves training men to kill the enemy in one way or another. It is a regrettable consequence of human conflict. The question is misleading . . .'

'The question is relevant to the case before the court, Your Honour,' Lewis countered. 'As I intend to show.'

Judge Heywood considered a moment, looking back and forth between the two counsels before settling his gaze on Willis.

'I take your point, Mr Willis, but I'll allow the question. Objection overruled.'

'I put it to you again, Mr Mackay. You trained men to kill. Is that correct?'

Fighting to keep his tone flat and even, Jim nodded. 'Among other things. SAS personnel were instructed in many diff –'

Lewis promptly cut him off. 'Just answer yes or no, thank you. In fact, you were a skilled instructor in the art of unarmed combat, were you not? Those techniques used to kill an enemy in situations that, for any number of reasons, might preclude the use of weapons.'

Jim could see where he was heading now. But he didn't know what the hell to say.

'Answer the question, Mr Mackay,' Lewis demanded. 'Did you or did you not teach the ways and means of killing a man without the use of weapons?'

Jim glanced at his legal team for guidance, but Willis and Phillips were looking at each other and they didn't look good. He returned his gaze to Lewis, still unable to muster an answer. The prosecutor raised his voice.

'Answer the question!'

'Yes,' said Jim, under his breath.

'Could you speak up, please. The jury must hear your response.'

Jim looked at the jury. They were craning forward, concentrating hard.

'Yes,' he told them, as simply as he could. 'It was part of the training.'

He returned his eyes to the Prosecutor. It had been a long time coming, but it suddenly dawned on Jim that the man really and truly did believe he was guilty of murder.

Lewis milked the pause, like he expected Jim to break down and confess.

'Thank you, Mr Mackay. It's my understanding that some of these techniques are extremely subtle and require a knowledge of human anatomy beyond the understanding of the average person. Is that correct?'

It was so cheap, Jim had the urge simply to get up and walk out. Once he got back under control, he decided the only way to handle Lewis was to give him as little as possible.

'Yes.'

'Are there many ways of killing a man in such a situation?'

'No.'

'How many?'

'Three or four.'

'One of them, I presume, would be strangulation?'

'Yes.'

'How many men have your strangled, Mr Mackay?'

Willis finally blew a fuse. He objected in the strongest possible terms that the Crown was trying to use a man's honourable service of his country in time of war to bloody his reputation in time of peace. To his dismay, Judge Heywood overruled, agreeing with Lewis that the specialised nature of Jim's service did bear some relevance to the case before them.

'Again, Mr Mackay. What methods of strangulation did you teach?'

'By hand, by forearm and by wire,' Jim answered matter-of-factly, as if he were reading from an Army annual.

'What about breaking a man's neck? How would you go about that?'

'There's a way of twisting his head and jerking it back.'

'Resulting in death?'

'Yes.'

'I believe,' said Lewis, 'there are some what we may loosely term "karate chops". Am I right?'

'Yes.'

'And there are also certain points on the body which, through the application of pressure, can immobilise and kill. Is that correct?'

'Yes.'

'Would you agree that an essential part of training men in these techniques involved teaching them to know their own strength?'

'Yes.'

'How much time would you have devoted to teaching the men under your instruction on that point? About the hairline between life and death?'

'I'd like to point out that all the training involved teaching methods of survival.'

'Survival of the fittest?'

'Yes.'

'May we presume, therefore, that you proved to be the fitter of the two of you when you crushed Mr Murphy's skull with a rock?'

'Objection!' Willis was on his feet and fuming. 'Your Honour, the deceased was half the defendant's age and armed with a rifle at the time.'

'I don't dispute the age difference, Your Honour,' said Lewis. 'Whether or not the victim was armed at the time, we have only the defendant's word. And I don't believe him.'

Judge Heywood sympathised with Willis this time and sustained his objection. He suggested to Lewis that the jury must have a pretty good impression of the defendant's military background by now, and perhaps there were some other points he wished to make. Lewis deferred, turned and eyed the jury meaningfully, as if to emphasise he had touched on not only the raw nerve of the defendant, but also the case for the defence. When he turned back to Jim, he threw out a direct challenge.

'I put it to you, Mr Mackay, that restraint was the furthest thing from your mind when you killed Geoffrey Murphy and that it was your firm intention to do so.'

'That's not true.'

'That by accidentally stumbling on the activities of the Patersons and yourself he became a victim of greed.'

'That's not true, either.'

'That the road accident you faked in conspiracy with Miss Paterson was not just for the reason offered in your statement. It was to disguise a deliberate act of murder and, hopefully, avoid its discovery and the inevitable consequence of prosecution.'

Jim had already endured two days of this. He was six inches from the end of his tether and he didn't care any more who knew it.

'You're entitled to your opinion, but it's a load of bloody rubbish!'

Lewis eyed him for a moment, turned his back, stepped up to the jury box and studied the jurors for several seconds before replying.

'I think we'll leave that to these good people to decide, Mr Mackay.'

With that, he returned to the bar table.

Willis and Phillips had expected him to subject Jim to intensive line-by-line grilling on his statement in the hope of tricking him into conflicting answers. As Judge Heywood looked enquiringly in their direction, the defence team held a quick, whispered conference before Willis got up.

'Thank you, Your Honour. Just a couple of questions.' He rose purposefully and approached Jim with an expression of sublime assurance.

'Mr Mackay, you are aware that you are under oath?'

'Yes.'

'And I presume you fully accept your responsibility to that oath before God?'

'I do.'

'Then I have just one further question. Is your account of the circumstances leading up to, and culminating in, the death of Geoffrey Murphy true in each and every detail?'

'Yes. It is.'

Willis turned and looked at the jury like they were long-lost friends and relations.

'My learned friend is right. Ultimately it is up to you good people to decide whether or not the defendant is telling the truth. I can only suggest that the sincerity and the strength of conviction behind the answers you have just heard will enable you to come to the right decision at the proper time.' He turned back to Jim and nodded warmly. 'Thank you, Mr Mackay. That will be all.'

Jim made his way back to the dock with all the dignity he could muster. Again, the telegraph messages from the eyes of his family and friends attempted to lift his spirits as he took his place. But, from the low buzz running round the public galleries and the look on the faces of most of the jurors, there was no doubt Lewis's heavy emphasis on Jim's SAS experience had sown further seeds of doubt and thrown his claim of self-defence into freefall.

There was a short lull in the proceedings as Lewis conferred with his clerk and Judge Heywood took the opportunity to scribble some notes. When he finished, he asked the Crown prosecutor if he wished to call another witness. Lewis rose and explained he was aware that the Crown's next witness was also due to be called for the defence. He was happy to defer if they wished to call their witness at this stage, providing they had no objection to immediate cross-examination to save the witness being recalled.

Willis and Phillips did some quick arithmetic. It was six of one, half a dozen of the other. If Annie Paterson performed well, she could go a long way towards unseating the picture Lewis had painted of Jim as a trained killer. On the other hand, once Lewis got stuck into her, she could just as easily be torn to pieces. Willis decided to risk it. As he rose to address the bench, Lewis exchanged a look with his clerk.

'The defence has no objection to immediate cross-examination,' said Willis. 'Though I must point out that, in all probability, it may be delayed by the luncheon recess. Otherwise, we are happy to accept the Crown's proposal, Your Honour.'

'Mr Lewis?' Judge Heywood double-checked.

'We are prepared to cross-examine at the appropriate time, Your Honour. Whenever the defence has finished with the witness, before or after lunch.'

Judge Heywood studied the clock on the wall.

'In that case, Mr Willis, although it is slightly earlier than the usual time, I suggest we take a fifteen-minute recess to allow the jury to refresh themselves before we proceed.'

'As you wish, Your Honour,' Willis deferred graciously. He was actually glad of the time. It would allow him precious extra minutes to consult with Phillips and have a quick word with Annie. It would also allow the jury to have a good natter over a cup of tea and, perhaps, return to the court in a mellower frame of mind than they appeared to be at that moment. As they rose for Judge Heywood's departure, their eyes were riveted on his client. The details of Jim's Army background had done a great deal of damage.

Following the recess, Judge Heywood waited for total silence before asking the defence to proceed. Willis rose and called Annie Paterson. A murmur ran round the court as the bailiff leant into his intercom to summon her from the witness rooms.

Jim focused on the doors. This was his first sight of her since February. The gap was only six months but it seemed more like six years.

Suddenly, there she was, just outside the glass doors. That first glimpse of her cancelled out any lingering regret he felt for allowing her to persuade him to keep Fred's secret after Murphy's death. If he had to reap the whirlwind for that action, so be it.

A mix of feelings rose in him as he watched her push through the doors and head for the front of the court. Looking straight ahead, purpose in every step, she carried an aura of calm and certainty.

The closer she got, the more Jim was startled by his reaction to seeing her again. She didn't look at him as she approached, nor as she passed the dock, and he had an overwhelming desire to reach out and touch her. And something else. Something he realised in no way betrayed or violated his memory of Rachel. A sudden recognition that he loved her, pure and simple. Up to that moment, he'd only ever allowed himself to think of Annie as his Florence Nightingale. Now he could admit it. He loved her. What a turn up for the books. What an illumination to have sitting in the dock of Townsville's Supreme Court, charged with murder.

The bailiff approached Annie to administer the oath. Before repeating the first line after him, she raised her eyes and found Jim. She didn't let go till she'd sworn to tell the truth, the whole truth and nothing but the truth, so help her God. Jim was so surprised by the strength of feeling surging through him, his smile broke out in response, oblivious to time, place or what the hell the jury might think.

Jilba leaned close to whisper in Tony's ear. Startled, he eyed her for a moment, then fixed his attention on his father, seeking confirmation. Jilba shifted hers to Annie. In the brief few days they'd spent together, she had taken a liking to her, beyond the deep affection she felt for all Annie and Fred had done for her father. Now she agonised for her.

For his part, Tony was distinctly unsettled. He couldn't help feeling a flash of indignation at what looked like the betrayal of his mother's memory.

The low hubbub in the public galleries subsided as Digby Willis hauled himself to his feet. His strategy was simple. Annie was her own best defence. He wanted to give the jury time to study her in repose for a while as they listened to her words. To that end, he positioned himself on the far side of the box so the jury had an unrestricted view of her.

'Miss Paterson, I have here your sworn affidavit testifying to the circumstances surrounding the death of Geoffrey Murphy. Would you just confirm for the jury that it is, indeed, your affidavit, signed by your own hand.'

Annie accepted it from him, scanned it, and handed it back. 'Yes. It is.'

'Thank you,' Willis responded, turning to the judge. 'Your

Honour, I ask for Miss Paterson's affidavit to be read to the court.'

The associate read it in a loud flat monotone. It was a blow-by-blow account of Murphy's assault on her and the fight that followed, true in every detail. But only she and Jim knew that and, as he listened to it, Jim watched the jury closely. Their reactions varied, particularly during the description of Murphy's attempt to rape her and the physical punishment he dealt out when she resisted. At that point, gender took over. The women looked at Annie with a degree of sympathy, the men kept their eyes firmly fixed on the associate, though a couple of them did glance at her once or twice, only to look away again as the affidavit reached the point of Jim's appearance and Annie's own part in the fight that followed.

Through it all, Annie kept her eyes on the area of carpet between the witness box and the bar table, reliving every moment. When it came to the instant of death, she closed her eyes as if to blot out the sight and bowed her head in remorse. But, by that time, the jury were hanging on the associate's every word and, to Jim's eye, none of them really seemed to notice how she felt.

Willis thanked the associate and asked him to enter Annie's affidavit in evidence as Exhibit D. Then he turned and studied Annie compassionately, making sure she was composed and ready to proceed.

'I'm sure we all appreciate how harrowing it must be for you to have to go over and over the events of that day, not only in your heart and mind, but particularly in the circumstances of public scrutiny.'

Annie simply nodded and waited for him to continue.

'Nevertheless, a man is on trial here for a crime carrying a maximum penalty of life imprisonment and I'm sure you accept your responsibility, under oath, to help us all, particularly the jury, to arrive at the truth of the matter.' There was no question in his voice, but he paused and waited for Annie to respond. When she did, her voice carried clearly across the court.

'Yes, I do. I am here to tell the truth.'

'Thank you,' said Willis turning to direct his next remark to the jury. 'I, for one, have absolutely no doubt of that.'

For the next hour, Willis took her back over her affidavit, concentrating on every nuance, particularly what it felt like for a woman to be threatened with imminent rape. He made her rehearse the sequence of the fight like a slow-motion replay, plumbing her memory for exactly how she felt at each stage of it, what it felt like to have the fear of rape turn to fear for her very life.

His job was made easier by the fact they weren't shadow-boxing around the truth but simply dealing with facts in which Willis himself believed. When it came to the faking of the road accident, he highlighted Annie's admission that it had been her idea. She hammered home the point that she had to work hard at talking Jim into it, that he argued against it, insisting they should report Murphy's death immediately.

Through it all, Willis never left his position on the top side of the witness box, allowing the jury their unrestricted view of Annie. It also allowed him to keep a wary eye on them and orchestrate her responses. By the time it was over, he was reasonably pleased. For the major part, they had given her fairly fixed concentration and seemed to have become increasingly engaged by her directness and, at times, her obvious distress. As he padded back to the bar table to resume his seat with a distinct air of case proven, Andrew Phillips glanced at him admiringly. He'd timed it to the letter. It was three minutes to one and the Crown prosecutor's cross-examination would, indeed, be stalled by lunch.

As the prison officer led him back into the dock for the afternoon session, Jim still felt quite buoyed up by Willis's delicate handling of Annie, believing in his heart that it could only have made a good overall impression on the jury. When they filed back into the jury box, their faces confirmed it.

But his anxiety came back as he watched her enter the court and walk to the witness box. Jim had no illusions Lewis would do his level best to undermine her. He hoped he would do so with courtesy. But the way the Crown prosecutor stood up at the bar table, adjusted his robes with a flourish, made his way to Annie's side and gave her a professional smile only increased Jim's anxiety. Lewis seemed well and truly primed, perfectly sure of himself, still riding a wave after his damaging confrontation with Jim himself.

'There are just one or two matters I'd like to clarify, Miss Paterson,' Lewis opened, turning on the charm. 'I'll try to be as brief as possible.'

Visibly relieved, Annie settled herself, relaxed a notch and gave him her full attention. Lewis had played the moment well. Not only had his apparent consideration registered on the jury, but he had her just the way he wanted her.

'This morning we heard the details of your sworn affidavit concerning the circumstances surrounding Geoffrey Murphy's death.' He paused, turned away and studied the jury, to make sure they were recalling the details they'd heard. 'And, I must say, it corroborated the defendant's story in a most persuasive and orderly fashion.'

'Objection!' Willis was on his feet. 'The prosecuting counsel's deliberate use of the word "story" implies a fiction where none exists.'

'The defence appears overly sensitive to me, Your Honour.'

'Nevertheless,' Judge Heywood replied, 'I'll sustain the objection. Please refer to the defendant's statement as such.'

'As you wish, Your Honour,' said Lewis, more pleased by Willis's reaction than irritated by the Judge's ruling.

'Would you agree with that, Miss Paterson?' he pressed.

'With what?' Annie parried, on guard.

'That your affidavit corroborates the defendant's statement in a most persuasive and orderly fashion?'

'I don't know,' Annie answered. 'I wasn't in court to hear the defendant's statement.' She had, of course seen Andrew Phillips' copy of it, but why give the bugger an inch.

'You're avoiding the question, Miss Paterson,' Lewis insisted, realising he had a tussle on his hands.

'Objection!'

'Sustained.'

'I've told the truth,' Annie stated flatly. 'And I've never known the defendant to lie.'

Lewis turned away, faced the jury and paused. You could hear a pin drop.

'That being the case,' he said finally, 'there is one aspect of your affidavit which I believe must bear closer scrutiny.'

When the Prosecutor turned back to her, his expression made Annie blink. All pretence was over now and there was sulphur in his eyes.

'I mean, of course, the exact nature of your relationship with the accused.'

Annie just couldn't help herself. Her eyes flew to Jim in the dock. Her action was not lost on the jury.

'How do you mean?'

'You have claimed, using a rather worn phrase, that you and the defendant were "just good friends" at the time the incident before this court took place.'

'That's right.'

'Do you still maintain this to be the case?'

'Yes.'

'If I were to put it to you, Miss Paterson, that just prior to Mr Murphy's death, you were seen in a public bar in Charters Towers hugging and caressing the defendant in a most uninhibited manner, you would still maintain this to be the case?'

It hit her then. On her arrival that day, she had accidentally gone into the wrong witness room and been redirected. There was a man waiting in the first room and she'd been racking her brains to try and remember where she'd seen him before. Now, his pudgy, wall-eyed, ginger-bearded face swam before her eyes. Of course! He was the barman who'd looked on with such evident disapproval as she struggled to get Jim out of the bar. Obviously, Lewis could call him to testify to that fact. She knew she was taking far too long to reply.

'Well, Miss Paterson?' Lewis demanded curtly. 'Do you maintain that to be the case or not?'

Still the right words wouldn't come. Annie fought to maintain her poise. Caught off guard, Willis and Phillips couldn't see the thrust of Lewis's questioning. What the hell was he on about? Jim knew. He didn't know about the barman, but he knew about the public bar in Charters Towers only too well. Lewis let her wriggle on the line for as long as he could get away with it, then he pressed her again.

'The court is waiting for your answer.'

'He was sick,' Annie whispered.

'Could you speak up, please, Miss Paterson,' said Judge Heywood.

'He was sick,' Annie repeated, directly to the judge, glad of the chance to look away from Lewis. 'I was simply trying to help him.'

'So you agree that the incident took place?'

'Yes.'

'Thank you,' Lewis smiled, turning to eye the jury knowingly, emphasising his next point. 'That saves me the trouble of calling a witness to the business.'

When he turned back to her, Annie had the same flash Jim had had earlier. The man really did believe they were guilty. Guilty as hell.

'So, the defendant was sick and you were only trying to help. Is that correct?'

'Yes.'

'By sick, you mean dead drunk, don't you?'

'Objection!' Willis shouted, jumping to his feet.

'Overruled,' Judge Heywood responded, quick as a flash. He was curious to know the answer himself.

'Thank you, Your Honour.' The prosecutor eyed Annie long and hard to let her know she was well and truly on the hook.

'The defendant had gone on a bender, as they say. Hadn't he?'

'He'd been drinking, yes.'

'Would it be fair to say he'd been drinking heavily?'

'I suppose so.'

'Let's leave supposition aside, Miss Paterson. Yes or no?'

'Yes.'

'Thank you. Now, let me get this clear. For several weeks prior to this occasion, the two of you had been living an adventurous, one might even say romantic life together in isolated bushland. Is that correct?'

'Mr Mackay was staying with my father and myself.'

'Living in caves, I believe?'

'Yes. We were living at my father's prospecting site.'

Lewis spun away and directed his next question directly to the jury.

'Would you not agree such a life-style might lead some people to the less charitable conviction that you were, perhaps, living like animals?'

Willis wouldn't stand for that and roared his objection. Judge Heywood considered for a moment and then overruled. 'It is not unreasonable to assume that people living a more routine lifestyle might place such a reading on it, Mr Willis, justified or not. I'll allow the question.'

'Is that the case?'

'Is what the case?' Annie challenged, her temper rising.

'That you were living together in a romantic adventurous way?'

'You just said we were living like animals,' Annie snapped. 'Which case do you want?'

Lewis's eyes glinted with satisfaction. He'd got to her, no doubt about that.

'Just answer the question, please.'

'We were living there, with my father. You know that already.'

As if he regretted having to force the issue, Lewis suddenly turned on all his charm again, and lowered his tone.

'I'm sorry, I have no wish to cause you undue distress. I'm sure you understand it is necessary for the court to understand the exact nature of the relationship between yourself and the defendant.'

Annie held her tongue.

'Now,' Lewis continued smoothly, waving his arm in the direction of the jury. 'Perhaps, for the benefit of the court, you could explain exactly what it was that caused the defendant to leave this idyllic situation, travel all the way to Charters Towers and go on a drinking spree from which you were forced to rescue him?'

'He was upset at the time. He wouldn't have done it otherwise.'

Annie couldn't help glancing at Jim. He was sitting stock still in the dock, looking absolutely wretched. There was no way she could come clean. It would only plunge them deeper into the pit. Behind him, his family and friends were watching her with wide eyes, hanging on her answer.

Jim was rapidly losing control. That Annie had to be subjected to this was bad enough. But the constant inference behind Lewis's tone was making him bloody angry.

Lewis stood to one side, allowing the jury a good view of the interplay between Annie and Jim. Now, he moved back to block her view.

'I ask you again, Miss Paterson. Why was the defendant so upset that he left you and your father, his good friends, by all accounts to go on a drinking spree in Charters Towers?'

Annie's brave façade wilted. She looked into her lap and there was a catch in her throat as she replied. 'I . . . I told you. He was . . . He was just upset, that's all.'

Lewis spun away with exaggerated annoyance and raised his eyebrows to the jury. Getting full mileage, he adjusted his robes, shook his head in dismay and spun back to face her, his eyes boring into her, his voice terse.

'Is it not the case, Miss Paterson, that the defendant left your father's prospecting site, arrived in Charters Towers and went on a drinking spree in order to drown his sorrows and blot out the consequences of a lovers' quarrel between the two of you?'

'No,' Annie whispered.

'Speak up, please.'

'No.'

'I remind you that you are under oath and subject to the usual penalties for perjury. And I ask you again, it is not true that you and the defendant, James Mackay, were lovers?'

'No, I said,' Annie cried. 'No! No! No!'

'Then why,' Lewis asked smugly, 'does the question distress you so much?'

Jim snapped. He leapt to his feet and shouted at Lewis's back. 'Leave her alone, for God's sake! It's got nothing to do with her! I'm the one that's on trial here! Leave her alone!'

A thrill ran round the public galleries. As the prison officer tried to pull Jim back down, Digby Willis buried his face in his hands. Andrew Phillips leant back in his chair, sucked air through clenched teeth and raised beseeching eyes to the ceiling. Behind the dock, Jim's family and friends were struck dumb. He'd completely blown it. Tears welling in her eyes, Jilba clutched at Tony's arm. Tony leant forward and, in as loud a whisper as he could get away with, begged his father to sit down. Willis was gesturing at Jim to sit down. Annie, too, was frantically trying to catch his eye. Through it all, Judge Heywood studied Jim as he might an earwig in his soup.

But Jim wouldn't quit. The more the prison officer tugged at his coat, the harder he tried to brush him off. Pounding on the dock rail in front of him, he began shouting directly at the judge.

'Why does she have to be subjected to this? Why do you allow it? The man tried to rape her, for God's sake! Under a gun! Isn't that enough for her to have been through without this?'

The bailiff rushed to the prison officer's aid and demanded Jim resume his seat. But Jim was unleashed.

'You've got no right to allow this man to hound her! No right at all!'

As the two policemen at the back of the court began a slow prowl forward, Judge Heywood stood up and thumped the bench with a force that shook the court like a gun going off.

'Silence!'

As the pandemonium subsided, Jim was left stranded on his feet, suddenly painfully aware of the furore he'd caused. As he gripped the dock rail for support and slowly sank into his seat, Judge Heywood remained on his feet, glaring at him. When total silence finally descended, he gathered his red robes and sat down himself, still furious.

'Any more outbursts like that, Mr Willis, and these proceedings will continue in your client's absence.'

Willis stood up with a small, messy bow. 'I apologise for my client's behaviour and beg the court's indulgence. I can only point out that he is under enormous strain in this matter. May I request a short recess?'

Not in the least pacified by the defence counsel's apology, Judge Heywood turned immediately to Lewis. 'If you concur, Mr Lewis, I am inclined to grant Mr Willis's request upon completion of your questioning of this witness.'

'As you wish, Your Honour.' It didn't matter to Michael Lewis one way or the other. The violent outburst he'd just inadvertently managed to provoke was a gift from heaven, the best result he could possibly have hoped for. From the moment Jim started yelling at him, he'd been the only person to keep one eye on the jury and he liked what he saw. The sight of this supposedly quiet, unassuming, mild-mannered grazier pounding the dock with clenched fist and spewing his anger at the court had just about won him the case.

He turned back to Annie, primed himself to pick up the thread. But there was no need. The expression on her face said it all. Horrified by the implications of Jim's outburst, Annie couldn't take her eyes off him. It was perfectly obvious to anybody watching that she'd do anything for him. With a slow, dramatic turn of his head, Lewis followed the line of her gaze to the man in the dock. He didn't need to utter another word. He just stood there, looking back and forth between the two of them for the jury's benefit, as the look they shared bore silent witness not only to the truth of his claim about their relationship, but also to their complicity in murder. With perfect timing, he waited until the absolute limit, then turned respectfully to the bench and gave Judge Heywood a small, deferential bow.

'No further questions, Your Honour.'

Judge Heywood didn't even bother to check if counsel wished to recall her at a later stage. He simply stood Annie down and announced a fifteen-minute recess.

As the jurors began to file out, they glanced back repeatedly to check on the two of them until the bailiff tapped Annie on the arm, broke the spell and indicated she should step down.

Sometimes, when all looks lost, the truth is your only hope. When the court reconvened, Willis rose and asked the bailiff to recall Annie Paterson. This time, under strict instruction, Jim kept his eyes firmly fixed on the top of the rail in front of him and didn't look in Annie's direction.

As gently as he could, Willis persuaded her to admit the depth of her feelings for the defendant at the time of Murphy's death, and led her into the further admission that her feelings had not been reciprocated. She agreed that sudden awareness of her feelings had driven Jim to Charters Towers to find solace in drink. Her own action in going to seek him out was driven by remorse for having, she believed, intruded on the sorrow of his recent bereavement, and plunged him into a relapse from which she and her father had struggled to wean him in order to restore a sense of balance, dignity and purpose to his life.

Annie was doing her level best to make up some lost ground. But it was obvious from the majority of the jurors' faces that they were more inclined to believe she was simply acting on an overwhelming desire to protect her lover at all costs. That became clear to Annie herself when Willis asked her to face the jury directly to answer his last question.

'And, finally, I ask you again, Miss Paterson. Are the details of your sworn affidavit and testimony, as presented under oath before this court today, unquestionably true in each and every regard?'

Annie turned and scanned all twelve faces before summoning every ounce of conviction she could muster.

'Yes. They are.'

To her dismay, several of the jurors responded with total disbelief. Willis had done the best he could but, as he sat down, he knew it wasn't enough.

With that, Annie was excused. As she left the witness box, she looked anywhere but at Jim. Fred had kept a seat for her beside him, but she ignored it. She headed straight for the back of the court and squeezed herself in behind the half-dozen public seats just inside the entrance doors, working her way right into the corner to be out of the jury's line of sight. Once there, she braced her back against the wall to weather a terrible fit of the shakes.

Judge Heywood finished scribbling some notes, pushed his pad to one side, checked the clock and cleared his throat.

'Members of the jury, ladies and gentlemen. I am advised you have now heard all the statements, affidavits and witness testimony, on behalf of both the prosecution and the defence. In the normal course of events, we would move immediately into the period of summing-up for both sides in this case. However, as it is already after four, I have decided to adjourn the court for what little time remains this afternoon in order that summations may begin tomorrow morning. Mr Lewis will speak first for the prosecution. In the meantime, I must stress upon you your solemn obligation to refrain from discussing any aspects of the case or the evidence you have heard beyond the jurisdiction of the court. I suggest you all take the opportunity to have a good rest and refresh your minds for the difficult and conscientous task ahead of you. Court is adjourned until ten o'clock tomorrow morning.'

As the prison officer gripped his arm, Jim turned to confront his family and friends. Despite the best of intentions, none of them could convey anything other than the destitution of their spirits. There was just no denying the damage he'd done. He shook his head quickly to convey regret for his behaviour and offered no resistance as the prison officer propelled him, with more than his usual firmness, towards the door to the cells.

On the way, he caught a fleeting glimpse of Annie as she hurried through the entrance doors. He would have given anything for just a few seconds of conversation to bolster her spirits. He stopped at the door to the cells and glanced back at the now isolated group of family, friends and defence team, all of whom had followed his passage with fear in their hearts. They all knew he was going to lose. Years of life with his family were about to be chopped off at the roots. Given his age and the mental and physical side effects, it was possible he might never make it out of gaol alive.

After he disappeared from view, silence lay like a shroud on the little group. Billy Mackay was shaking and Jilba hugged him tight, barely able to control her own trembling. Jack was first to head away, walking towards the entrance with his hands in his pockets, his head sunk. Tim hurried after him. Athol and Fred followed, side by side, mute and empty. As Jilba edged Billy after them, Willis and Phillips returned to the bar table to collect their papers and Tony decided to have a quick word. But one look at Digby Willis's face changed his mind. Now was definitely not the time. On top of everything else, the Crown prosecutor was still in discussion with his clerk at the other end of the table. They both looked like they had just found the only diamond in the rough.

# Fifty-Four

The public galleries were buzzing like a hive. The trial was the talk of the town and those early enough to get a seat were feeling pleased with themselves. This was the Last Act, this was their chance to see a big rich bastard bite the dust. It promised to be a good day out.

Huddled in the seats behind the dock, the Mackays blanched when Jim was led in. He looked ill. All the colour drained from his face, his shoulders stooped, his gait shambling. He'd only managed a couple of fitful hours' sleep all night.

As he entered the dock, it was all he could do to raise his eyes to his family and friends.

As he settled into his seat and the prison officer shifted his own chair a bit closer than usual, Jim realised something that was already causing his supporters increasing concern. In contrast to the purposeful presence of Lewis and his clerk behind a mountain of paperwork, the defence end of the bar table was empty.

By five to ten, when the jury began to file in, Jim's nervousness rose to outright alarm and he craned past the prison officer to scan the friendly faces for a clue. All they could do was shrug. Tony and Athol eased out of their seats and hurried outside to see where they had got to. At two minutes to ten, they returned to their places shaking their heads. The bailiff hurried to the judge's chambers. But he reappeared on the stroke of ten and called the court to order. Judge Heywood had obviously decided to proceed, irrespective of the defence counsel's absence. When his red-robed figure appeared, Jim's heart went through the floor. What in God's name were Willis and Phillips doing to him? The jury couldn't help but smell rats deserting a sinking ship.

Judge Heywood immediately asked Jim point blank why they were not in attendance. Jim could only mutter an apology. Perhaps their car . . .

'As Mr Lewis is scheduled to begin summing up for the Crown anyway, I intend to let him proceed. I can only hope that, in due course, certainly by the time his own summation is due, Mr Willis will have honoured us with his presence. Mr Lewis.'

Tickled pink, Michael Lewis strode to the jury box and scanned the juror's faces as if welcoming guests to a party.

'Ladies and gentlemen, my task, I believe, is a simple one. The facts of this case speak for themselves . . .'

That was as far as he got. All eyes suddenly shifted to the back of the court as Digby Willis waddled breathlessly into view with Andrew Phillips a short step behind. They hurried to their positions at the bar table and Phillips sat down immediately, trying to make himself as small as possible. Willis remained on his feet.

'My apologies to the court, Your Honour. Our arrival was delayed by a matter of the utmost importance. If I may approach the bench . . .'

Judge Heywood's sympathies lay with the Crown prosecutor.

'I am quite happy to hear what Mr Willis has to say at a later stage, Mr Lewis. If you wish to proceed . . .'

Lewis figured it was better to cut his losses. The jury would only be wondering about it anyway.

'Thank you, Your Honour, I would prefer to recommence when the court is settled.'

With that, he returned to the bar table, tossed his papers down in front of him and sat down, leaving the jury in no doubt how he felt.

As Willis hurried to the bench for a whispered conference, Lewis displayed a complete lack of concern. But as it went on and on, concern took over. Judge Heywood's expression changed from annoyance to puzzled curiosity and, finally, to grave consideration. He summoned Lewis to join them.

The prosecutor couldn't wait. When he got there, he didn't like what he heard one bit. He suddenly seemed not so sure of himself. Jim glanced quickly at his family. As he returned to the bar table, Willis looked Jim right in the eye and smiled. They were on the edge of their seats as Judge Heywood cleared his throat and swivelled in his chair to address the jury.

'Ladies and gentlemen, the defence has requested a delay in summing-up in order to present some new evidence which, I am informed, only came to light at a late hour this morning. It is my belief that this evidence is of sufficient importance to warrant such procedure and I have, therefore, with the prosecution's agreement, granted Mr Willis's application.'

In the dock, Jim's imagination was going a mile a minute. Behind him, his supporters were breathless.

'Please proceed, Mr Willis.'

Willis held a whispered discussion with Phillips and jotted some notes before hauling himself slowly to his feet.

'Thank you, Your Honour. The defence calls Tobias Wilson.'

Fred and Annie turned to one another in astonishment. They pivoted, rising half out of their seats for a view of the entrance doors. In the dock, Jim could hardly believe his ears. When Tobias appeared, he could hardly believe his eyes either. His rag-bag bush garb had been replaced by a dark blue lightweight business suit, pale blue shirt, dark red tie and shiny black riding boots. Where on earth had he sprung from?

A ripple of excitement ran through the public galleries as Tobias headed up the court. Regal, calmly determined, he eased his wiry old frame into the witness box. He remained on his feet after taking the oath.

'You may sit down, Mr Wilson,' Judge Heywood directed.

'Rather stand, Judge,' Tobias replied soberly.

'The court would rather you sat down, Mr Wilson. If you don't mind.'

'Okay, Judge,' Tobias responded amiably, scoring a quick smile of thanks from the judge. Back straight, hands resting on his lap, Tobias settled himself in perfect stillness and fixed his eyes on one of the small windows in the opposite wall. Judge Heywood continued to appraise him for a moment before raising his eyebrows and getting down to business.

'Mr Willis.'

Willis approached the witness box with measured steps. The man's appearance at his office at nine that morning had unleashed a flurry of activity just short of a panic. Time for discussion had been painfully brief and they'd been forced to continue it in the car en route to the court.

As Willis paused at the witness box and studied the notes in his hand, Annie started to shake and Fred slipped his arm round her shoulders to calm her. Behind them, Jack had an irresistible urge to lean forward and ask what it was all about. But he kept his place, his eyes on Tobias. Jilba, Tony, the whole clan held their breath.

'Mr Wilson, you have come forward at this late stage in the belief that you can shed some light on the proceedings before this court. Is that correct?'

'Yeah.'

'Thank you.' He meant it. 'May I just ask why you didn't come forward earlier?'

'Been bush. Didn't know about trial till day before yesterday.'

'Thank you. Now . . .' Willis turned to the jury as a doctor might a patient. 'Ladies and gentlemen, before Mr Wilson presents his testimony, it is important you should know something of his background and his knowledge of the defendant.' He turned back to Tobias. 'Mr Wilson, am I correct in saying that you are an Elder of your tribe?'

'Yeah.'

'And, as an Elder, you would be considered an authority on tribal law and mythology?'

'Yeah.'

'You would be consulted on those subjects by younger adults?'

'Yeah. Little bit, now. More on the Reserve.'

'That being the Palm Island Reserve.'

'Yeah.'

'Where you were also a councillor, I believe.'

'Yeah.'

'You left Palm Island several years ago to live alone in the bush near Charters Towers.'

'Yeah.'

'Why did you choose to do that?'

'Palm Island bad place. All time trouble. Wanted to be close up alongside old places my people.'

'I see. And the place where you eventually made your permanent camp was, I believe, close to the area now known as the Bush Girl Mine, owned by Mr Fred Paterson and his daughter.'

'Close up, little bit. Yeah.'

'How close?'

'Other side mountain.'

'How far away, approximately? How long would it take you to walk from your camp to theirs?'

'Forty minutes, hour, maybe. Depend how fast walkin'.'

A few chuckles fell out of the public galleries and Willis smiled.

'I see. And during the course of their prospecting, you got to know Mr Paterson and his daughter quite well?'

'Yeah.'

'And after he came to stay at the Patersons' camp, you got to know the defendant, James Mackay?'

'Little bit. Not too good.'

'But you did talk with him on several occasions.'

'Talk sometime. Yeah.'

'Thank you, Mr Wilson. Now, in your own words, please tell the court exactly why you have come forward at this time. I believe what you have to tell us is of vital importance to evidence already presented in this case, so take your time.'

Tobias nodded and, as Willis stood to one side, he turned his liquid brown eyes to the jury. They were already hanging on his every word. He slowly scanned each face, making a quick note of those chipped and chaffed by generations of Queensland racism. With a couple of exceptions, he figured he might get a reasonably fair hearing. He glanced at Jim in the dock, raised his hand in a simple gesture of acknowledgement and turned back to the jury.

'I seen fight between Jim Mackay 'n' other fella . . .'

A huge wave of relief rolled over Jim, his family and friends. Their spirits soared. Jim strained for a quick view of Annie and, in the brief moment their eyes met, a surge of hope passed between them.

'Like say,' Tobias continued. 'That day, I come along see Fred. Come along from my place. Round mountain. Walk through bush above creek. Look down, seen Annie, swimmin'. Swimmin' 'n' washin' herself. Look away quick, 'cause private. Private time, Annie. Then hear this fella call her. This fella come from bush other side creek. Annie all naked, got no clothes. This fella poke her backside with rifle. This fella put rifle up alongside her head, make her kneel down. I get big fright for Annie. Look like properly bad fella. Stick rifle here, up under Annie's chin, make her watch. Make her watch him drop pants. Show himself. Show Annie hard pene. Then he pushed her, try make her lie down. Annie push rifle away 'n' it go off. Annie yell out, scream out, real loud. Fella drop rifle 'n' grab her hair. Hit her. Hit her real hard up alongside head. Annie try get away, try crawl away. But fella drag her back, hit her again. Hit her on head. Annie look bad hurt, but she try crawl away again. This fella sit on her then. Sit on her back, try to make her roll over.

'All same time, Jim Mackay come plenty quick. Come

runnin' from caves, seen what fella doin'. Jim Mackay real angry, don't know what to do, start yellin'. This fella take real good aim, get set shoot him. But Annie get up behind him, punch him. Punch him hard up between legs. Fella get big hurt, big fright, 'n' rifle go off. Fella try hit Annie with rifle little bit, then aim up on Jim Mackay again.

'Annie jump on his back, hold on real tight. Start pullin' his hair. Fella shake her off pretty quick, but Jim Mackay up alongside him then, run into him. Fella fall over, drop rifle. Jim Mackay fall down all the same 'n' they start have big fight. Bad fight. This fella bite Jim Mackay. Bit his shoulder. Hurt him, hurt him real bad. Make him let go 'n' fella go for rifle again. Annie, too. Get it off her and aim up on Jim Mackay again. Aim up close, real close, can't miss. All same time he fire, Annie hit rifle. Jim Mackay real lucky. Bullet just nick him. Look like nick on his arm. Annie jump in, hang on real hard 'n' they have big push 'n' shove. Jim Mackay get up alongside him again. Hit him. Hit him up alongside head with stone, make him stop. Fella fall down quick, get real bad shakes. Head bleedin' pretty bad. Jim Mackay kneel down plenty quick, try 'n' help fella. Try make him come back. No good. Annie pull Jim Mackay away, 'cause fella dead.'

Tobias finished so abruptly, he left the court in mid-air. There wasn't a flicker of movement anywhere. The stark and simple power of his account had carried them all to the south-west, to the banks of a nameless back water in the Seventy Mile Range and it was going to take them a minute or two to get back.

Digby Willis was the first to come up for air.

'Thank you, Mr Wilson,' he said, as quietly as he could so as not to break the spell.

'That's all I seen.'

'What did you do then?'

'Went back along my camp real quick. Like Annie. Like Fred. Jim Mackay seem all right fella, too. But white-fella trouble. They figure it out, I reckon. Later time, friend come along see me. I tell him 'n' he say forget about, too.'

'But now, after all, you have decided to come forward and tell us what you saw.'

'Yeah,' Tobias nodded, looking directly at the jury. 'Aboriginal friend come along see me, day before yesterday. Tell me Jim Mackay go gaol for murder. Feel real bad, 'cause not his fault. Jim Mackay not start fight, only helping Annie. That fella properly bad bloke. Go for her, hurt her real bad. Want sex. Try to force her. Annie not want to. Get big fight 'n' try get away. Jim Mackay come along help her. Have to fight, fight real hard. Other fella young, strong bloke. Try shoot him. Jim Mackay have to hit him with stone, see. Make him stop. No way, murder. Jim Mackay only helpin' Annie. Fight for life.'

'Thank you, Mr Wilson,' Willis nodded graciously. 'That's exactly what the defendant has claimed throughout the trial.'

'Don't wonder,' Tobias shrugged. 'True.'

'Mr Wilson,' said the judge. 'This friend of yours, this Aboriginal friend who came to find you the day before yesterday. Was this the same man who visited you the day of the incident, following the events you described?'

'Yeah. Dougie tell him come look for me.'

'Who?'

Tobias pointed to the back of the court. 'Him. Up there. Dougie Douglas.'

As the whole court followed the direction of his finger, Jim came halfway out of his chair. There he was. Dougie, standing just inside the doors, leaning back against the wood panelling. Jim swallowed hard.

'Thank you, Mr Wilson,' Willis said.

Jim's attention remained fixed on Dougie. Dougie Douglas. A lifetime ago, they'd run wild together, ridden together, on the forgotten fields of Balkenna. Forged their childhood under Balkenna's boundless skies. Now, in the fleeting moment their eyes met, they acknowledged it all. Acknowledged what Dougie had so vehemently denied at the bicentennial ball at Longreach. Dougie raised his hand in a quick, simple gesture, nodded and returned his eyes to Tobias. That was all. As Jim dropped back into his seat, he started to shake.

Tobias was still staring hypnotically at the jury, as if silently contesting any doubts about his testimony. Several of the jurors returned his gaze, others contemplated Jim and the rest stared at Annie who was gazing at Tobias with dewy eyes.

Beside her, Fred looked as if he'd like to buy his old cobber fifty schooners in a row just to wet his lips. The Mackays didn't know where to look. Jilba slipped her hand in Billy's and gripped it tight. Providing Tobias could stand up to Michael Lewis, the odds had taken a huge turn for the better. Billy squeezed her hand in return, but he wasn't so sure.

'Mr Lewis?'

Michael Lewis approached the witness box with a swagger, as if to demonstrate the witness wasn't worth two bob and he was here to mop up a mess. But the way Tobias looked at him unsettled Lewis even before he began. He was looking for a direct challenge in the Aboriginal's eyes. Instead, they seemed perfectly empty.

'Mr Wilson, we have heard that you lived for some considerable time in the vicinity of the Paterson's prospecting site.'

'There first,' Tobias qualified, scoring a couple of knowing chuckles from the public galleries.

'Oh. Very well. You were there first.'

'Yeah.'

'Pity you didn't find the gold then, isn't it?'

'Not hunt gold, mate,' Tobias responded charitably. 'Look after Aboriginal place.'

'Oh, I see! By that, I take it you mean some sort of sacred place. A religious place of some kind.'

'Place belong my people,' Tobias replied. 'Dreaming place belong my people.'

'And in the course of this you became friendly with Mr Paterson and his daughter after they set up their own camp.'

'Fred Paterson good bloke. Like Annie plenty, too. She real good person. Understand problems we Aborigines got.'

'What about the defendant? Did you become friendly with him, too?'

'Jim Mackay come along one day. Live up alongside Fred 'n' Annie. Don't know him too good. Seem all right. Pretty soon, all gone anyway. Mine come, make big mess, big noise. I go along, too. Go along other camp, different place.'

'Did you ever help one another?'

'How you mean?'

'Well, for instance, did the Patersons ever give you things. Like tools, clothes, food, perhaps?'

'Baccy.'

'Pardon?'

'Baccy. Fred fetch me up baccy sometime.'

'Tobacco.'

'Yeah.'

'I see. Did he give you the tobacco, or did you pay for it?'

Tobias studied Lewis with a twinkle in his eye. He'd seen blokes like Lewis before. He'd seen them come and he'd seen them go.

'Fred fetch me up baccy, I fetch him up apples, blackberries.'

'I see. So it was a sort of trade.'

'Yeah.'

'What about food? Did the Patersons give you food?'

'Don't ask white-fella tucker. Don't need it.'

As more amusement rippled from the public galleries, Lewis tugged at his robes and turned to face the jury.

'Nevertheless, Mr Wilson, I put it to you that Mr Paterson and his daughter were good to you. Through them you maintained contact with the outside world. Tenuous contact, perhaps, but contact nontheless. You knew they were there. In befriending you, they had, as a matter of course, demonstrated a willingness to help you should the need arise. That's the truth of it, isn't it?'

'Said already. Live on own again now. No Fred, no Annie, no Jim Mackay. So what?'

This time, to Lewis's rising exasperation, a couple of loud guffaws echoed through the court.

'I'll tell you what, Mr Wilson. Irrespective of where you happen·to live at the present time, you have only come forward in this matter because of the Patersons' past kindness to you. You would do, or say, anything to help them, or any friend of theirs such as the defendant, because your first allegience is to your friends rather than the law of the land. Isn't it?'

'Which law talkin' about? Aboriginal law, or white-fella law?'

'Don't try and evade the issue, Mr Wilson,' Lewis shouted, losing his temper. 'You know exactly what I'm talking about. You have paraded in here with a cock-and-bull story in return for past favours.' Lewis spun away and gestured to the jury. 'In an attempt to disrupt these proceedings and divert the attention of these good people away from the cold hard truth . . .' he whipped back on Tobias, getting angrier by the second, 'you have tried to impress this court with a pack of lies, no doubt carefully orchestrated by the defence in a desperate last-ditch attempt . . .'

'Objection,' Willis called laconically, as a matter of course.

'Sustained,' Judge Heywood agreed, glaring at Lewis. 'The witness is under oath, Mr Lewis. I'm sure the jury is adequately aware that both the defence and the prosecution discuss the presentation of testimony with their prospective witnesses.' He leant over the bench and instructed the court reporters to delete the offending remarks.

It was the first real slap on the wrist for the Crown prosecutor in the whole course of the trial and Lewis was furious with himself.

'That is the fact of the matter, isn't it, Mr Wilson? You have come before this court for one reason and one reason only, in the hope of being able to help get some old friends out of trouble?'

Tobias didn't even bother to respond. He just looked at Lewis like he was the biggest nitwit on earth.

'Well?' Lewis demanded, his temper rising again.

Tobias just continued staring at him.

'As the bench has pointed out, Mr Wilson, you are under oath. We are dealing with the truth here.'

Still, Tobias stared him down.

'Answer the question!' Lewis demanded, hanging onto his temper by a whisker.

Slowly, majestically, ignoring two hundred years of white rule in Australia, Tobias stood up, raised his right hand, spreadeagled it palm down across his chest and made his own kind of pledge.

'Belong Biri people,' he announced. 'Don't tell lies. Lies big waste of time. Truth other way. You try tell lie now, waste court's time. True, what I seen. You don't understand, too bad. You worried, not me.' With that, he turned to the judge. 'Sorry, Judge.' He was apologising for standing up in court. But it didn't come across that way. It came across as an apology for Lewis's dismal lack of comprehension.

Lewis had run out of steam and it showed. He did his best to keep up appearances for the jury's benefit.

'Your Honour, I am afraid there is confusion on the witness's part between the requirements under oath of due process and those laws with which he is possibly more familiar. On that basis, there seems little point in attempting further cross-examination.' With that, he strode back to the bar table with as much dignity as he could muster, sat down and began leafing through his papers as if he didn't have a worry in the world. It was a pretty good effort. But it didn't cut the mustard.

For the first time, Tobias turned and held Jim's eye, just for a moment. Jim made no attempt to disguise his nod of thanks or the little, triumphant smile that accompanied it.

Jim felt a twinge of disappointment when he was led back into court for the afternoon session and Tobias and Dougie were nowhere to be seen. But he couldn't complain. They had given him a straw to grasp. How strong it was remained to be seen. Tobias had sworn on the Bible all right, no trouble at all. But this wasn't Heaven. This was Queensland.

Lewis had gathered his wits during the luncheon recess. Even Digby Willis had to admit to himself his address to the jury that afternoon was pretty nigh faultless. Meticulously, he took the jury back over the minutest details of all they had heard and seen. Over and over he reminded the jury of those witnesses who had testified to the victim's good character. Young Geoff Murphy had never been charged with any criminal offence, violent or passive. By way of contrast, he begged them to recall the defendant's explosive temper. He lingered mischievously over Jim's SAS record, implying that a man who had killed night after night in the horrific intimacy of hand-to-hand combat would, by his very experience, have less compunction than most in battering to death an intruder whose appearance threatened a vast fortune in gold, running into millions of dollars.

Which led him into the main strength of his argument. The deliberate attempt to have the world believe Mr Murphy died in a road accident many miles away from all the defendant sought to protect. Such was his own admission and the admission of the leading witness for the defence. Because of their own stake in the prospecting venture, they stood to lose heavily if news of their find reached the outside world and alerted hordes of other prospectors to the area. They were about to become rich beyond their wildest dreams and had absolutely no intention of allowing an outsider to threaten their good fortune. Innocent people just did not go to such lengths to conceal an accidental death. The obvious, decent, law-abiding course of action would have been to notify the authorities immediately and show due remorse for what had happened. Instead, the defendant, in conspiracy with Miss Paterson, had chosen to do exactly the opposite because he knew a claim of self-defence against unprovoked attack would not stand up to the investigation that would automatically follow. But for the observations of the witness, Rodney Clark, he would, in all probability, have got away with it.

When it came to the testimony of Mr Tobias Wilson, Lewis was remorseless. No doubt, Mr Wilson's surprise appearance was governed by the best of intentions. But those good intentions were directed solely and exclusively towards doing whatever he could to help people who had befriended him, provided him with a link to the outside world and leant over backwards to make him aware they did not harbour the attitudes he had come to fear from whites. Lewis assured the jury he could show them heaps of records of other trials where the testimony of Aboriginal witnesses had been proved, time and time again, to be motivated by a fierce allegiance to the family, or anyone considered to be part of that family. He had no argument with such allegiance in principle. It was a worthy and honourable attitude for which Aboriginal people were respected. But he did take issue when it provoked a sadly misguided attempt to shield people Mr Wilson may have come to think of as family.

The defence claim that Mr Wilson had only come forward on the very morning of his testimony had to be taken at face value. Perhaps Mr Wilson possessed an exceptionally good memory. But, to his mind, the vivid details of his testimony suggested a lot of rehearsal. He was happy to leave the jury to make up their own minds on that score. He, for one, was absolutely sure they would come to the right decision. Both the course of justice and the memory of Geoffrey Murphy would be served by their finding the defendant, James Mackay, guilty of murder.

There was a terrible stillness in the court as the jurors' eyes followed Lewis's return to the bar table. He had held them in the palm of his hand.

Digby Willis pulled out all the stops he could. He high-lighted the dubious side of Murphy's character that emerged in cross-examination, stressing his love of guns, his attitude towards women, the fact that even his closest friends considered him something of a loner, too quick to take offence. He poured scorn on what he was bound to call an extremely distasteful attempt by the prosecution to use a man's honourable wartime service to imply it made him a cold-blooded killer for the rest of his life. If that were true, he suggested, the entire continent of Australia was crawling with potential murderers just waiting for the slightest provocation to reawaken skills which most of them wished to God they'd never had to learn in the first place.

Willis openly admitted that the decision by his client and Miss Paterson to try and direct attention away from her father's mine by removing Murphy's body from the scene and attempting to fake a road accident was not just wrong, it was criminal. But what was the defendant's response to Miss Paterson's arrest? He might well have presumed that she would refuse to divulge his identity and gone about his business as if nothing had happened, hoping no blame would find its way to his door. Instead, he had come forward immediately to make a full and voluntary statement of his responsibility, detailing the circumstances of Mr Murphy's death. The jury had now heard independent corroboration of those circumstances. To ignore it on the flimsy grounds presented by the prosecution would place them in grave peril of being responsible for a tragic miscarriage of justice and the sentencing of an innocent man to a long term of imprisonment which, given his age, might well prove to be the term of his natural life.

Willis came last to Tobias's sudden appearance. His good conscience would not be denied by fear of white authority and rules of law which, rightly or wrongly, generations of his people had come to fear and mistrust. He could just as easily have rejected the appeal to come forward and justified his refusal on any number of grounds. But good conscience dictated otherwise. Good conscience would not allow that an innocent man be judged guilty of a crime for which he was not responsible. So, Mr Wilson had come forward and, Willis suggested, his good citizenship and faith in a system he perhaps found wanting at times could only be honoured in turn by allowing him to return to his chosen way of life, secure in the knowledge that justice had been done and was due the respect it deserved.

The jury gave him a good, hard hearing. It looked like they wanted to believe him, but were hamstrung by the nagging seeds of doubt so eloquently planted by the prosecutor. Willis returned to the bar table sensing that the odds were no better than fifty-fifty. Still, fifty-fifty at least put them back in the running.

Judge Heywood's summary was brief and free of bias. At least until he came to Tobias's testimony. Then, to Willis's consternation, he seemed ever so slightly to take sides with the prosecution. He suggested the jury must take special note of the late appearance of a witness whose testimony so thoroughly corroborated the defendant's statement and Miss Paterson's affidavit. To Willis, that was fair enough. You could look at it either way. But, choosing his words very carefully, the judge went on to wonder why, with all the media attention that had been focused on the case, the witness had not been approached by his friends to come forward at an earlier time. The manner of his appearance in court had been undeniably dramatic. However, he begged to remind the jury that, though it may appear so at times, the court was not a theatre. He reminded them that Queensland's Criminal Code did not allow for a majority verdict. They must reach a unanimous decision. On that note, he instructed them to retire.

As Willis and Phillips had expected and advised Jim, every single one of them glanced at him at least once as they filed out of the box. Following his defence team's instructions as best he could, Jim never flinched, attempting to convey not only total belief in his own innocence, but also his faith in their abilities to judge him accordingly. Inside, it was different. It was only by superhuman effort that he managed to hold himself together for the sake of his family and friends. The tremors running through him seemed to be pulling in every direction at once. The harder he tried to stop them, the stronger they got. The show was over. His hour had come.

It was twenty past twelve when the jury retired. They could have been back before lunch, but they weren't. Nor immediately after it. As the afternoon wore on, Andrew Phillips made repeated trips from the witness room where the Mackays had gathered to Jim's cell to keep him abreast of developments. At a quarter to four, Judge Heywood sent the bailiff to the jury room to find out how things were going. He was advised they were still considering. At four fifteen, he sent the bailiff back, again with the same result. They were no closer to unanimous decision and Judge Heywood had no alternative other than to reconvene the court just long enough to tell the jury he must, therefore, send them to a hotel for the weekend.

Jim was not required to attend. When Phillips brought him the news, he relived a sensation harking all the way back to his teenage years when Tommy Douglas helped him into the saddle for his first attempt at breaking a horse. He just didn't know how the hell he was going to ride it.

# Fifty-Five

Eight exhausted and extremely nervous people took their usual places in the front rows behind the dock at nine forty the following Monday morning. Annie glanced at the clock over the jury box, sat down and immediately wished she was somewhere else.

Apart from Jack's visit to Deirdre O'Connell on Saturday afternoon and Tim's trip to a local church on Sunday morning, they'd all spent the entire weekend in the house, wandering aimlessly from room to room. With conversation more or less restricted to pass the salt, the place had the atmosphere of a religious community.

The hours had been doubly difficult for her. These were the children of the man she loved. They'd sat there like everybody else and watched her spill it out in open court for all the world to hear, in a desperate attempt to save him from the chaos. She was the agent of his downfall. It was all her fault, and Tony for one made it plain as day. He didn't say it. He didn't have to. He never said a word to her.

Jack was kinder. Jilba, too. All Billy's thoughts were for his father. Jilba tried to buck him up by playing endless hands of gin rummy. Annie smiled inwardly as she remembered that, at the last count, Jilba owed her little brother something in the vicinity of three hundred bucks.

Fred shifted restlessly in the seat beside her and Annie felt a surge of love for her father. For most of the weekend he'd done his best to keep up a brave front. But it had taken a nose-dive Sunday afternoon when Andrew Phillips telephoned to inform them the jury had reached a verdict. At the close of play on Friday, he and Willis, so as not to raise false hopes, had rated Jim's chances at fifty-fifty. Knowing that the jury had finally tipped the scales one way or the other knocked the stuffing out of all of them. From that point, Fred took a back seat and allowed Athol to take over. He'd always been there as something

539

of a grandfather figure to Jim's children and that night they leant on him as never before.

Jim felt sick. After four hours' sleep, he'd woken up just after five thirty that morning with a sharp pain in his chest every time he tried to take a deep breath. He'd been tempted to ask to see the prison doctor before being transferred to court. But if he kept his breathing shallow, it only hurt him every now and then. Not a lot of point doing anything about it until he knew his fate. But the pain had got worse. At first it was only the left hand side of his chest. Now, he was feeling it shoot on up into his shoulder as well.

Apart from Andrew Phillips, he'd not been allowed visitors over the weekend. He didn't resent it all that much. They'd all visited him in his mind. Time and again, he sensed Rachel's spirit at his side. The strange calm he felt now, as he waited for the knock on the door, came from her.

And Balkenna . . . These last hours he'd been back there time and time again, seen its beloved landscape with the pristine clarity of a December daybreak, allowed a flood of memories to wash over him. It was there. Its future was secure. If it came to it, Jack would have to take up the reins as he himself had been forced to do all those long years ago.

But he wouldn't have to start from scratch. He'd have the support, guidance and encouragement of a man who'd given his life to the place. Balkenna and the family owed Tim more than they could ever repay.

Jilba, Tony and Billy would be able to follow their chosen stars knowing that, should the need ever arise, Balkenna was there for them as well.

Billy, in particular. He realised that, over the years, he'd been guilty of neglecting him a bit. Last born, he'd always been the darling of the family. But Jim recognised he'd not given him quite the same amount of time and input he'd given the others. There was not much he could do about it now.

'Time to go.'

Jim hadn't noticed the prison officer's approach, and the sound of his voice made him start. The surge of pain seemed to fan out through his whole chest this time, and into his shoulder and the left-hand side of his neck as well. He had to brace himself against the wall and hold his breath.

'Just a bit short of breath,' he muttered, scared of taking any more air into his lungs than he had to.

His appearance shattered his family and friends. He looked ten times worse than he had at the end of the previous week. He seemed to be having difficulty keeping his balance as the prison officer led him to the dock. Athol managed to pat Tony on the knee to reassure him. Inwardly, he thought his old friend looked as if he might collapse at any moment.

The prison officer allowed Jim to pause at the entrance to the dock. He acknowledged with a quick nod the sympathetic looks of those present, and managed a little tight-lipped smile when Fred attempted to take the sting out by giving him a wink and thumbs up. Never in his life had he so achingly longed to embrace his children. The prison officer touched his arm to indicate that he was to move on. Jim eased into the dock, sat down and fixed his eyes on the empty jury box, visualising the twelve absent faces now so familiar to him.

The bailiff didn't really need to call for order. The minute he stood up, silence fell like a guillotine. Nevertheless, he had to go through the motions and, as his first 'Oh, yea' rang out, Jim had an overwhelming desire to take a couple of deep breaths to steady his nerves. Instead, he gripped his thighs and dug his fingers in as hard as he could.

Judge Heywood had his wig on. He took his place on the bench and shuffled his papers with an impassiveness that would have done justice to some of the Buddha statues Jim'd seen in Vietnam. A quick glance at Lewis and Willis to ensure they were ready for the verdict, then he turned and gave the bailiff a nod. The bailiff rose from his desk, crossed the court and disappeared through the door leading to the jury room.

Phillips had told Jim what to expect, but when the door opened again a few seconds later and the bailiff led the jury in, he watched the procession with the same heart-stopping terror as he would seeing a bushfire leap out of control. Not one of them looked in his direction. One by one, they lined up in front of the jury box, the foreman last of all in order to be closest to the bench. Without exception, they either stared at the carpet or fixed their eyes firmly on Judge Heywood.

When the Bailiff indicated that Jim should stand, a few of them finally glanced in his direction, only to look away again just as quickly.

Judge Heywood waited until the bailiff had returned to his desk before he glanced at Jim himself. Then he leant forward and directed the associate to proceed. As the associate cleared his throat, Jim's family and friends clutched at one another and held their breath.

'Members of the jury, are you agreed upon your verdict?'

'We are.'

'Members of the jury, how do you find the accused, James Mackay? Guilty or not guilty of murder?'

'Not guilty,' the Foreman announced. His tone said he was damn glad it was all over and done with.

The air split with wild cries that nothing could contain. There was a whoop from Jack and a blood-curdling 'You little ripper!' from Fred Paterson. Judge Heywood scowled and the bailiff called for silence. Jim was gripping the dock rail for all he was worth. His gasp of relief had sent white-hot pain searing across his chest. But he managed to glance quickly at his family and friends and saw eight pairs of the shiniest eyes he'd ever seen beaming back at him.

'So say your foreman, so say you all?'

The jury's reply was met by a wail of pain. In the public gallery at the back of the court, the diminutive tearful figure of Mrs Murphy was on her feet, stabbing an accusing finger straight at Jim and screaming her lungs out.

'Shame! Shame! That man killed my son! That man and his harlot murdered my boy! You ought to be ashamed of yourselves. All of you! My boy never did no harm to anyone! That man's a murderer, but none of you care. None of you . . .!'

The bailiff was out of his chair in a flash and hurrying up the court, gesturing furiously at her to sit down and be quiet. But Mrs Murphy was unhinged by grief, raining terrible curses down on Jim, the court and everyone connected with it, till two police officers dragged her out, kicking and screaming. Even then, her protests could be heard echoing down the corridor outside, gradually receding as she was ushered away.

As the hubbub in the court gradually subsided, the fire in Jim's chest flared and he had to brace the full weight of his body against the dock rail to keep from keeling over.

Looking slightly dazed, Judge Heywood waited for silence. He gave the bailiff a nod of thanks as he returned to his desk, and glanced at Mrs Murphy's empty seat to reassure himself his troubles were over before he returned to the formalities of the court. He thanked the jury for their service and discharged them. As they filed out, Jim silently thanked each and every one of them from the bottom of his heart. Judge Heywood paused briefly after the door had closed behind them, then directed his attention to Jim. His expression gave no clue as to what he personally thought of the verdict.

'James Mackay, you have been tried and found not guilty of murder. You are, therefore, fully acquitted of the charge brought against you by the Crown and hereby discharged.'

That was it. The final, formal pronouncement. It was over. He'd won. He risked enough air to make his voice carry to the bench.

'Thank you.'

When the judge's red robes finally disappeared from view, Jim turned to his family and friends. Amid the babble boiling over in the public galleries, they sat transfixed, silently returning his gaze, savouring the sweet freedom in the air between them. He was free. Free to walk out of the door. Free to go home.

The spell held them all for several seconds before Jim eased himself out of the dock and they leapt from their seats. He gave them all as good as he got. Ignoring the shooting pain, Jim embraced each and every one of them long and hard.

When it came to Annie, their eyes said it all. Their long, secret nightmare was over. No matter how long the memory took to fade, Geoff Murphy was no longer a threat to their liberty. But when Jim gathered her into his arms, Annie held back. Given Jim's recognition of how he really felt about her, that troubled him. But it was neither the time nor the place to dwell on it.

His barrister and solicitor accepted his thanks with warmth and good grace. In a lifetime of hits and misses, Digby Willis had seen it all before, but he well understood the Mackays were ecstatic, and they promised to meet at Willis's office around six that evening so he could take them out for a beer.

As it turned out, Jim was unable to keep the appointment.

They lingered for a while before slowly making their way out of the court building. When they stepped into the balmy, tropical air, Fred celebrated by grabbing Jim and lifting him off the ground for a couple of royal pirouettes. The smiles died on their faces when Fred finally bounced him back on his feet. Jim tried to steady himself, but this time the pain refused to go away. It just got stronger and stronger until he couldn't bear to breathe at all and he dropped to his knees. He fell forward on his hands, propped like a dog on all fours for a moment, then collapsed on his side.

It wasn't a heart attack. Just after two that afternoon, following cardiography, X-rays and blood tests at Townsville Hospital, their worst fear was laid to rest, though there was still cause for alarm. It was viral pneumonia. The doctors informed them that painkillers would help to ease his breathing and antibiotics were at work on the infection. Barring unforeseen complications, Jim would be back on his feet after a couple of weeks in hospital. But he'd have to take it easy for at least another month after that, and lay off the fags.

An hour and a half later, they were allowed to crowd into his room. Any attempt at conversation hurt like hell. But he raised his hand to let them know he was coping and glad to see them. Thereafter, he was happy to lie back and listen.

Just after four, they were all startled when the door opened a crack and a female voice announced it was well and truly time they all shot through. Deirdre O'Connell had just come on duty. She gave them all a cheeky grin, stepped straight over to Jim and gave him a big kiss on the forehead, while she sorted out his pillows. Jim grinned, Jack fell in love all over again and Fred went strewth.

'Christ, Mackay, if that's what goes on in here, I can't wait to get crook myself.'

# Fifty-Six

The following afternoon, Jim was sitting up. Billy gave him a graphic account of the debauch he considered his father had been fortunate enough to miss the night before. It hurt too much to join in the general laughter that punctuated Billy's description but, by the time it was over, Jim had a grin from ear to ear. When the merriment subsided, he got down to business.

'Look, I just want you all to know that what we've been through is history as far as I'm concerned. Well and truly. I don't want any of us to dwell on it. Let's just get stuck into the future. I want you to all go home and get on with it. There's no point hanging about here. I'll be all right. Quite looking forward to the rest, to tell you the truth. I'll make my own way home when I'm better.'

Fred and Annie insisted they would stay on in Townsville and keep him company until he was discharged. But Jim was absolutely adamant about the others and they finally gave him the nod.

Jack and Tim promised to get back to Balkenna immediately, to relieve the pressure on Betsey and the Sugdens and see to it that all was in order for his homecoming. Tony couldn't wait to get back to his family anyway and Jim had little trouble getting Billy to admit he was just as keen to get back to Brisbane and catch up. Knowing how much his father was longing to see his grandson, Tony promised that he and Susan would organise a trip to Balkenna as soon as possible, even if it meant just flying up for a weekend. Provided the old bugger was well enough to make the journey, Athol promised to bring Dud to Balkenna for a visit as soon as Jim was firing on all cylinders.

'Tell him the Royal Suite will be ready and waiting . . .'

Jilba decided she could use some rest and recuperation herself before returning to America.

'I'll go back with Jack and Tim. Charge my batteries and wait for you. Then I can spend a few days making damn sure

545

you keep your promise not to overdo it the minute you get there. All right?'

Jim crossed his heart. 'Good as gold, I promise.'

The only thing that worried Jim was Annie. She didn't contribute much to the flow of conversation and, at times, seemed to tune out altogether. He'd sensed the same reserve in the quick embrace she'd given him on arrival. Acquittal having automatically lifted the injunction he'd placed on telling her the way he felt about her, he was disturbed that she appeared intent on keeping her distance. He didn't doubt she was happy for him. Not for a minute. But with a strange air of detachment. What they needed was some time together on their own.

They got their chance the following afternoon. Fred spent the day shuttling the others to Garbutt Airport to catch their planes. That out of the way, he decided to get on the trail of Dougie and Tobias and dropped Annie off at the hospital.

At first, their conversation focused on the trial. They still had two misdemeanour charges each hanging over their heads.

'Andrew says he doesn't want to get their backs up, especially Lewis. It all boils down to him, evidently, in the long run. If they decide to go ahead, he'd have to handle it.'

'Just have to hope his nose isn't too far out of joint then, I guess,' said Jim.

As they gradually began to talk of other things, Jim struggled to find a way of telling her how he felt. But the right moment never came, the right words eluded him.

To his relief, she became visibly more relaxed towards the end of her visit. When she said she hoped his family bore her no grudges, Jim thought he'd diagnosed the probable cause of much of her reticence. Perhaps she thought they'd pressed him for details of what really went on between them at the caves. No doubt she'd been feeling unsure of herself in their presence ever since being forced to own up to her feelings about him in open court.

'I think *I'm* the only person entitled to bear a grudge around here,' he teased her.

Annie smiled. But he hadn't really answered her question.

When visiting time was up, Annie took her leave with a quick kiss that implied nothing more. But Jim felt its haste was more for her sake than his and held her hand for an extra moment which he hoped might give her the first inkling of his recent acceptance of something deeper.

After another night's blissful sleep, Jim awoke to discover the pain in his lungs had receded, allowing him to breathe normally. Luxuriating in the early morning care and attention of the nursing staff, he had to admit that another ten days of this wouldn't be hard to take at all. He was anxious to get home, but the rest was long overdue.

Shortly after breakfast, there was a tap on the door and a familiar face appeared.

'Turning the place into a family concern, are we?'

' 'Fraid so,' Jim grinned. 'How are you?'

'Could be worse, I suppose.' Richard Bower shrugged. 'Just had a couple of weeks off. Seemed to go by faster than Phar Lap and here I am back with the panic buttons. Got an op in half an hour, so I've got to go. Just wanted to see how you're getting along. They tell me you're on the mend.'

'Seem to be.'

'That's good. I'll try and get back for a yarn in the next couple of days.'

'I'd like that.'

Within a few seconds of his departure, Bower's head reappeared around the door. 'Congratulations on the result, by the way.'

'Thanks.'

'Gave me a bit of a shock, I can tell you,' Bower admitted. 'But I knew all along they were barking up the wrong tree.'

'Thanks,' Jim smiled. 'So did I.'

Still smiling, Jim elbowed his pillow and lay back. Bower's visit had made a good start to the day.

That afternoon, Fred had news.

'Dougie Douglas is in Brizzie, apparently. Doing something or other for the Aboriginal and Islander Council.'

'What about Tobias?'

'Buggered straight off back to the bush. From what they tell me, he's just moved deeper into the Range, that's all. Think I've got a fair line on it. I'll see if I can dig him out as soon as I get back to the Towers. I owe him for Annie, too, don't forget.'

Jim caught a funny look in Annie's eye and had the fleeting sensation they were keeping something from him.

'I splashed out this morning,' she said. 'Don't know what got into me. Just felt like celebrating, I suppose.'

'What did you buy?' Jim asked quickly, hoping it wasn't a ticket to Europe.

'A Range Rover. It's outside.'

'That's great! You've more than earned it.'

'It was worth it just to see the look on the bloke's face when he came back from checking up on the cheque,' said Fred. 'I think he thought we didn't have two bob between us.'

'I was thinking maybe I could drive you home in it, if you like. Be a good way of getting some miles on the clock. Give me a chance to see Balkenna . . .'

In her uncertainty, Annie was scared she'd backed him into a corner and that he wouldn't know what to say. She immediately offered a way out.

'Just a thought. It'd mean a slow trip, of course. I can understand if you'd rather jump on a plane the minute you're out of here . . .'

Watching the slow grin spread across Jim's face, Fred got the picture they were both too blind to see. It was going to take time and it was going to take work. But with a bit of luck, they'd get there in the end.

'You're on,' said Jim. And that was that. 'Look,' he went on, 'I'm not sure how either of you might feel about this, but I was wondering if we should ask Phillips to approach Murphy's mother. You know, see if we can't do the right thing, financially, whatever . . .'

Fred shot a glance at Annie, shrugged and rubbed his hand over his face.

'I already did that, mate. I wasn't going to tell you about it until you got out of here. I thought a visit from me might be better than from either of you or the legal eagles, but she sent me packing, I'm afraid. Well and truly. I still had "shame" and "blood money" ringing in my ears for half an hour afterwards. Maybe I shouldn't have gone, I dunno. The minute she realised who I was, that was it. The riot act and the bum's rush. Might be worth having another crack but I don't think so somehow. Can't blame her, I suppose.'

'No,' said Jim quietly. 'Probably do the same thing myself if I was in her shoes. Maybe it wasn't such a great idea after all. But thanks. Thanks for giving it a try. I'd like to do something . . .'

'Yeah,' said Fred. 'I know what you mean.'

Andrew Phillips turned up right at the end of visiting hours. One look told them he was the bearer of glad tidings and he wasted no time passing them on.

'They're dropping the other charges, against both of you.'

The news flung Jim and Annie together in a hug, and Fred expressed his own satisfaction by giving Phillips a thump on the back that nearly knocked him off his feet.

'It was Lewis's decision. I've just come from his office. He still believes the two of you did the wrong thing, mind you, and I don't think it was an easy decision for him. But he just said that, when it came right down to it, your acquittal made it all rather academic. To be perfectly honest, I thought he'd have a go.'

'I'll go and see him first thing tomorrow morning,' Annie volunteered. 'Promise him we're not sticking pins in his effigy.'

'He's still licking his wounds a bit,' Phillips warned. 'Go easy on the salt.' He stood up, fished in his coat pocket and passed a piece of paper to Jim. 'Before I forget, here's Dave Reynolds' address.'

'You leaving now?'

'Yes. Might as well get back tonight.'

'Go tomorrow,' said Annie. 'Have some dinner with us.'

'Thanks all the same, Miss Paterson,' Phillips smiled. 'I don't think I've got over the last one yet.'

'Billy told me all about it,' Jim chuckled, as they shook hands for the last time. 'Sounded like a good rort. Andrew . . . There aren't really words, you know?'

'Hope you still feel the same when you get your bill.'

'Thanks, mate. Thanks for everything. There were a couple of times in that bloody gaol when just having to talk to you saved me from going under altogether.'

'My pleasure,' Phillips smiled. As he turned away, he gave Fred and Annie a quick wink. 'I trust you'll be keeping on the straight and narrow once you're out of here?'

'No worries,' Annie promised. 'Safe journey.'


Jim began his eighth day in hospital feeling fit as a fiddle, but still weak at the knees. Barring any relapse, they said they'd be happy to let him leave after a final once-over on Friday afternoon. When Annie turned up, he couldn't wait to pass on the good news.

'I was thinking, if you were ready and waiting, we could push off straight from here.'

To his surprise, she balked at the idea. 'I'd rather not, Jim.

549

Dad's planning to head for the Towers sometime on Saturday himself. He'd be a bit upset if you didn't take the chance to spend a few hours with him, you know that.'

It wouldn't make that much difference. Irrespective of when they set out, he was greatly looking forward to the hours they would have alone together, watching the outback unfold as they headed ever westward. Once and for all, they would be leaving behind the grim shadow that had hung over their lives, and the embargo he'd placed on his heart.

And if he managed to find the right words, the slow dawning he hoped for in Annie's heart might break somewhere along the way.

After lunch, Deirdre brought him a copy of the *Courier Mail* and suggested a little exercise wouldn't go amiss.

Jim made his way out onto the verandah and plonked himself down in a cane armchair. He dropped his head back and breathed deeply, feeling his lungs were healing.

He shaded his eyes and studied the wide arc of Cleveland Bay in the distance. A fishing trawler chugged into view and he followed its progress for a while. That might be Barry Baldman out there. Or Barry Baldman's son. The thought crossed his mind that it was little wonder Jesus chose fisherman to accompany him on his dangerous journey. With the possible exception of miners, he could think of no other working men who so consistently put their lives on the line.

When the glare began to strain his eyes, he eased back in the chair, pulled the *Courier Mail* from his pocket and flipped it open. His eye fell on a boxed item at the bottom of the front page and his jaw dropped.

KUALA LUMPUR, Tues. – John Percival Davis, a 38-year-old Australian businessman from Rockhampton, Queensland, was arrested here today and charged with the murder of Mr Pi Kok, the 49-year-old Malaysian found shot dead in the grounds of his Penang home yesterday.

Following the arrest, police confirmed they were investigating allegations that several of Pi Kok's international group of companies were a front for a wide range of criminal activities, including large-scale traffic in heroin.

Pi Kok is known to have spent various periods of time

in Australia over the past five years. He had a home near Townsville in Queensland. He also had homes in the United States and Holland.

Davis, said to be a long-term associate of Kok's, was arrested at Kuala Lumpur's Subang International Airport as he attempted to board a plane for Manila. A police spokesman said further charges were expected to be brought against Davis for narcotics-related offences.

Under Malaysia's strict anti-drugs laws, anyone convicted of trafficking in heroin faces a mandatory death sentence.

Jim dropped the paper in his lap. He lay back and contemplated the rafters. All through the trial he'd half expected to look up one day and see Pi Kok's bland smile mocking him from one of the public galleries. Little wonder he hadn't. Jim couldn't help a grim smile as he remembered Pi Kok's observation that 'revenge is sweetest when least expected'. He would have to keep a close eye on the papers over the next few days.

He couldn't wait to see the look on Jack's face. It would make a strange homecoming gift to his son. He, after all, had suffered most at the bastards' hands.

Fred and Annie laid on a feast the following Friday night to celebrate his successful discharge from hospital. There had been just one further press report to add to the story. As anticipated, the Malaysian authorities had charged Davis with large-scale heroin smuggling offences. He'd applied to the Malaysian courts to be allowed Australian legal representation in addition to his Malaysian lawyers. His application had been granted, but the report inferred it was likely to have little bearing on the eventual outcome.

Picking at the last of his lobster, Jim had to admit it was a bit of a worry. Any investigation of Davis's Australian affairs might dredge up a copy of the bill of sale for the cattle, with Jack's name on it.

'Maybe I should see the Townsville police on our way out in the morning . . .'

Fred squelched the idea on the spot. 'There's no point, mate. You've had more than enough to do with the cops lately as it is.'

Annie agreed. 'I should think it's pretty unlikely people like that would keep any incriminating paperwork, anyway.'

'Yeah. Fat chance,' said Fred.

Inwardly, the thought still troubled him. But Fred put it out of his mind when, with uncharacteristic seriousness, he suggested they brace themselves for an important announcement. The two of them fell mute. His knotty old hands clenched tightly on the table in front of him, Fred kept up his serious expression for a second before shrugging if off with a grin. Then, to Annie's delight, he told them his prospecting days were over.

'It was the trip up the Gulf persuaded me. Dunno whether it was because we'd just cracked it or because I'm just too bloody long in the tooth, but it wasn't the same somehow. Heart wasn't really in it. The heat got to me, the flies got to me and the bloody mossies up there are murder. I didn't get any sleep and just felt bloody tired all day.'

'You're not going to like this,' said Annie. 'But I was sort of hoping you'd have a bugger of a time.'

Fred gave Jim a knowing wink. 'That's what I like. Loyalty in the family.' But he took her hand and patted it with tremendous affection. 'Truth is, you were right, love. After the strike. You were right. Should have quit while I was champ.'

'Well, I'm not sorry if that's all it took to persuade you,' Annie smiled. 'I'm just really pleased, you know? It's about time.'

'Yes,' said Jim. 'You've earned it, mate. Put your feet up and take it easy. I won't hesitate when the time comes, I can tell you.'

'Oh yeah,' said Fred. 'We'll have to remind him of that when he's a hundred and one and still dodging cow-pats on Balkenna.'

'Maybe we should stay a couple of days at your place on our way through the Towers,' said Jim. 'It'd give me a chance to go with your dad and find Tobias. I've got to let him know what it meant to . . .'

Annie shot a quick glance at Fred and shook her head. 'I don't think that's such a good idea. You're supposed to take it easy for another month, don't forget. That doesn't mean crawling around in the bush.'

'No bloody way,' said Fred. 'Leave it to me, mate.'

'You can't keep Jilba hanging about. Or Jack, for that matter.'

After a moment's hesitation, Jim bowed to their advice. 'Yes. You're right. I'll catch up with him later.'

Annie headed for the kitchen and the two men lapsed into silence for a moment. Fred studied the scars on the table, then raised his eyes and fixed Jim with a look he would remember for the rest of his life.

'You know what I think, don't you?'

'About what?'

'You and Annie.'

Jim held his eye for a long time before replying. 'Yes.'

'Good.'

# Fifty-Seven

Jim was still thinking about the look in old Fred's eye as he and Annie hit the last stretch of the Landsborough Highway and the outskirts of Longreach swam into view on the horizon ahead of them.

'Is that it?'

Jim nodded. 'Queen City of the west. Just plain old "town" to me.'

'Have to try and see the Hall of Fame while I'm here.'

'We can go tomorrow, if you like.'

'Better wait and see,' said Annie. 'I'm sure Jilba and Jack will have something to say about that.'

She said it lightly enough, but it was another hint of her underlying nervousness about coming face to face with his family on their home turf. There had been a few others along the way and they'd made him pull his head in. In a strange way, her uneasiness was infectious. He too was starting to feel anxious about how Jilba and Jack would react to Annie's actual presence at Balkenna. If they had given it any thought at all, the possibility of a new woman in his life must have seemed pretty remote in faraway Townsville. It might be another matter altogether when Annie walked through the door and his feelings for her were held up to scrutiny.

The nearest he'd come to letting Annie know openly how he felt was during dinner in Hughenden the night before. With all the nonchalance he could muster, he'd asked her if she could ever imagine herself living in the outback. Annie held his eye for a split second, then looked away and told him she would probably find it hard not to be within striking distance of the sea. But, basically, if she was happy, she could live anywhere.

Annie adjusted her visor against the fierce late afternoon sun and studied the approaching outlines of Jim's home town. She was thinking about that fragment of dinner conversation as well. Behind Jim's studied nonchalance, she sensed what he was asking. By the time they got to Hughenden, she knew just about all there was to know about him. He'd taken her way back to his childhood and youth, and filled her head with images of a magic kingdom seen through the eyes of a child and those of a young man who grew up too soon.

In turn, Jim pressed her for her own memories of migrations from camp to camp as her father followed the gleam in his eye. He made her relive her life for him up to the time of her own marriage. It had all somehow led to that apparently offhand question over dinner, a question that made her heart soar with renewed hope. But it also stoked the fear that had slowly built up ever since her father wished them good luck and sent them on their way. She was actually scared stiff of Balkenna. She was scared of the ghost of Rachel Mackay.

Jim sat up and snapped his fingers.

'What?'

'Got it! Just thought of what I could do for Dougie Douglas. Been trying to think of something ever since the trial. It just came to me then.'

Jim paused.

'What have you got in mind?'

'Dougie's Yirandhali, and Betsey. The Sugdens, too, come to think of it. They were the local tribe, ruled the roost around here for God knows how long before we all marched in and took over. Dougie took me to this place once, when we were kids. In secret. Said Tommy'd skin him alive if he found out. It was a mystery to me, I'd never been there before. It's right on the creek. Lovely spot, actually. I was thinking I could give it to him, that piece of land. Whatever it takes to set up some kind of centre there. A sort of Yirandhali cultural place. Some sort of Aboriginal Hall of Fame. Not just a museum though, something active. A study centre for Yirandhali ways, or something. Aboriginal ways in general, maybe. Don't know, really. Have to track the bugger down and sound him out, see what he thinks.'

'Do you think you could actually bear to part with a piece of Balkenna?'

'For something like that I could,' Jim chuckled.

'Sounds good to me.'

'Soon find out. Have to locate him first.'

'You never know,' Annie smiled. 'Maybe he'll turn up. It's his home town, too, isn't it?'

'I doubt it,' said Jim. 'Not exactly a hotbed of Aboriginal politics around here.'

As they pulled into Longreach, Jim got her to slow to a crawl and turned their passage through town into a sort of pilgrimage, pointing out various buildings and businesses that had been there for as long as he could remember. By the time they reached the Jundah road, he was grinning like an urchin.

'You should see your face. Anyone would think we'd just been through Heaven.'

'Not yet,' Jim replied, deadpan. 'But we'll get to it in a while.'

Jim kept up a running commentary on the district all the way to Balkenna's front gate.

He jumped out, opened the gate, bowed low and waved Annie through with a flourish. He was about to shove the bolt home when the westering sun suddenly reflected off the ring on his finger. Etched in the flare, the engraved crest seemed to leap up at him. When he raised his eyes again and looked across the top rail of the gate, he suddenly felt as if he hadn't lived his adult life at all. It was all just a figment of his imagination. For a few fleeting seconds, Jim was nine years old again, waiting with bated breath for the father he'd never known. He glanced down the road, half expecting to see Dougie ride up on his pony. It was as if the spirit of his father had been waiting for him and deliberately angled the ring at the furnace in the sky to remind him of all it stood for. All that had been lost and won. All those who had come and gone through that very same gateway. Jim braced against the gatepost, waiting for the giddy wave to pass and roll on down the road before bolting the gate. Annie put it down to Rachel. The last three miles passed in a state of hushed expectancy.

When the house came into view, Annie slowed to a snail's pace. Fighting the catch in his throat, he spoke its name, almost by way of formal introduction.

'Balkenna . . .'

'Thought it might be. I have been here before, you know.'

'But you said you can't remember.'

'I can't. But, between you and dad, I've heard enough to make me think I can.'

'What do you think?'

'I see what you mean now.'

'About what?'

'Heaven being a bit further down the road.'

'Yep. This is it. No sign of Saint Peter though. Wonder where everybody is. You can generally hear a car half a mile down the track.'

Jim jumped out, stood back and studied the house for a moment, drinking it in, imagining himself already inside. Annie slipped her arm through his.

'I imagined this moment so many times.'

Annie gave his arm a squeeze. 'Is it as good as you thought?'

'Every bit,' Jim confessed. 'Even better with you here.'

Annie's heart skipped a beat. There was no mistaking it. He meant to let her know. It confirmed what she had suddenly sensed in Hughenden the night before.

'Thanks.'

Annie shied away from him and continued gazing at the house, reminding herself of its occupants. Despite the joy she hardly dared feel, there was no knowing what lay in store.

Jim tapped her shoulder and pointed to the eastern skyline. There, high in the darkening haze, a lone wedge-tailed eagle was spiralling slowly earthwards on its own homeward journey.

'They can be a pest,' he muttered, 'but I always loved them when I was a kid. Used to follow them for miles. Tommy Douglas used to tease the hell out of me about it sometimes. Reckoned I must have been an eagle-totem Aborigine in a previous life.'

'A good omen then,' Annie smiled. 'Spotting one the minute you're home.'

'Someone to welcome us, at least,' Jim chuckled. 'Come on, let's go and see where everybody got to.'

As he ushered her up the steps and through the front door, Annie fought another terrible rush of nerves. She knew that, somewhere inside, she was bound to see Rachel Mackay staring out at her from some photograph or other. Not only might she challenge her right to be at Balkenna at all, but her father had often described Rachel as the most beautiful woman he'd ever seen.

Jim gave a shout, but nobody answered and he led Annie straight down the hall and into the living room. The lamp on the table by the fireplace was burning, but there was no sign of life.

'Looks like everyone's done a bunk,' he observed ruefully. 'Grab a seat. I'll just check the kitchen.' He bounded up the steps, flung open the door and peered in. 'Bloody hell . . .'

When he turned back, Annie was holding a piece of paper up to the light. 'What's that?'

'A note,' Annie chuckled, holding it out. 'Here, you'd better read it.'

> 'Dear Dad & Annie – G'day! Sorry about this. Jilba and Betsey should be back soon. They've gone over to the Sugdens'. Bobby's pony threw him or something. Me and Tim are out in the barn. Balkenna Dean's crook and we had to bring him in. Can't leave him at the moment. Stick your head in as soon as you get back. Welcome home by the way – Jack.'

Eyes twinkling, Jim looked up at Annie, pulled a face and shook his head.

'How do you like that? A bloody bull's more important than his old man.'

The day was fading fast as they left the back of the house and headed for the outbuildings and Annie glanced at the riot of gold erupting across the western skyline.

'I see what you mean about the sunsets out here.'

'Wait till you see a good one.'

Annie was still smiling when they reached the side door of the main barn. He stuck his head in and yelled at the top of his lungs. 'Hey, Jack! You in here?' This time he got an answer, echoing back with equal gusto.

'Yeah, Dad. In here! Come and have a look.'

'What's happened to the lights?'

'The vet said to keep them off!' Jack yelled. 'We've got a lamp! Tim's here . . .'

Jim shook his head for Annie's benefit, took her hand and led her in. They groped their way down the short, panelled corridor just inside, turned into the main body of the barn and –

Shazzam! They were blinded by the light. Every bulb in the place switched on at once as the ever-ready, ever-faithful Longreach dance band struck up the slowest rendition of 'For He's a Jolly Good Fellow' they'd ever played in their lives. And there they all were. Singing their hearts out. From far and wide, from halfway round the world, they'd come to bring Jim Mackay home. As their voices soared, Jim spun, absolutely flabbergasted, to Annie.

Eyes dancing with mischief, she hit him with that smile of

hers, gave him a wink and a quick kiss on the cheek. 'Let me be the first . . .'

Jim gave her a hug and scanned the sea of faces, getting more dumbfounded by the second. There was Dougie Douglas, right there! Standing with the Sugdens and . . . Good Lord! Tobias! There, grouped together, was his family. Jack acting as conductor for the song with Deirdre O'Connell grinning cheekily at his side. Jilba looked absolutely stunning. Billy had a grin so wide he could hardly sing. Tony and Susan, holding his grandson up to see the show. Tim looked like he'd just won the lottery. Betsey was beside him, looking like a mother-hen who'd just found a long-lost chick. And Dud! There was Dud, leering at him from his wheelchair. Athol stood behind him, eyes dancing in the light. There was Fred, looking a bit frazzled, his beard yo-yoing as he sang. Must have caught a plane from Charters Towers. Fred was flanked either side by the men who'd got him off. Digby Willis, giving forth like an opera singer. Andrew Phillips, miming.

As Jim's eyes swivelled from face to face, he realised most of his neighbours from adjoining properties and business friends from Longreach were there too. There was Wally Jenkins from the bank. Jim's grin nearly fell off his face when he recognised the bloke saluting him with a foaming schooner at Jenkins' side. Dave Reynolds had already made one trip to testify on his behalf. Now he'd made another to welcome his old sergeant home from the wars. And there were the Stoker brothers, done up in their best duds for the occasion, rocking on their boot heels as they sang. Two of the pedigree Heelers they'd sold him were sitting at their feet, licking their lips and slobbering all over the place.

When his eyes fell on the next face, Jim just couldn't believe it. Laughing as he sang, Dean Coulter gave him a big Pacific wink. And, Jim figured, the strong-faced olive-skinned elegantly dressed young man at his side could only be Danny Serrano.

A huge length of canvas was slung across the width of the barn, saying 'Welcome Home' in letters six feet high. And, in the midst of it all, Balkenna Dean The First eyed him balefully through the rails of an improvised pen erected especially for the occasion. The magnificent Santa Gertrudis bull looked as if he couldn't give a tinker's cuss about all the hullabaloo and would much rather be on the job.

When the song came to its shattering climax and the band broke off, Jack filled his lungs and let go a 'Hip hip . . .!'

The floor shook as the assembled voices responded.

'Hooraaaaaay!'

The second time, it seemed to Jim the whole building shifted on its foundations, and the third time round convinced him they had actually raised the roof. It all broke up in a sustained round of applause, drumming boot heels, whistles, and laughter. Before he could even begin to recover, they surged forward and enveloped him in a welter of kisses, hugs, handshakes, pats on the back and good-natured thumps on the arm, all of which let him know they weren't just there for the hell of it.

Jim hugged his family to him, one at a time and then in one great, mauling clutch. Susan passed their baby son to Tony. Glowing with pride, he formally introduced Angus to his grandfather and bundled him into Jim's eager arms. He cradled his grandson and stared down at the tiny face, lost in adoration. Eventually, he kissed him gently on the brow and tickled his cheek.

'Hello, young Angus.'

A gurgle made him chuckle. But it suddenly turned into a wail of protest and Jim quickly handed him back to Susan.

'Guess he knows a gaolbird when he sees one.'

'Too much excitement,' Susan giggled. 'That's all.'

Jim embraced them both for a second and gave her a kiss. 'Bless you, Susan. You've done us proud.'

Jim's unbridled joy was reward enough for Tony, but when his father turned and gave him a hug as well, its warmth buried a lifetime of old hatchets.

'Thanks a lot,' Jim grinned as Jack shoved in, cocking an ear. 'What the hell did you do with all the cars?'

'Whacked 'em all over to the Sugdens,' Jack chuckled. 'Been running a bloody shuttle service all afternoon. Jilba handled the airport. Did you really get a surprise, or did you think something was going on?'

'Didn't have a clue,' Jim smiled, giving him a thump on the arm. 'Caught me with my pants down, well and truly.'

'Well, you'd better pull them up and start circulating, before everyone gets so newted they can't remember who you are.'

Dean Coulter was hanging back a bit.

'G'day, Yank. Fancy finding you here.'

'Howdy, Aussie,' Coulter laughed, opening his arms. 'Thought I'd better check up on my investment.'

'Good on you,' said Jim, slapping his back, pleased as punch.

'Brought this guy along for the ride. Jim Mackay, Danny Serrano.'

'Thought it might be,' said Jim, offering his hand. 'Good to meet you at last, Danny. Welcome to Balkenna.'

'Thanks,' said Danny. 'Nice to be here. How's it going?'

'On the grass at the moment,' Jim confessed, waving at the mob. 'Never expected anything like this.'

'Don't wonder,' Danny grinned, wondering what on earth he meant by 'on the grass'. 'It's been like the CIA around here.'

Jilba pushed through the crowd to join them, crossing her fingers. Danny suddenly looked a bit embarrassed and shuffled his feet. It was the first time Jilba had ever seen him look even remotely self-conscious and she cracked up as she snuggled into her father's shoulder.

'Are you thrilled?'

'What do you think? Can't believe it. Buggered if I know how you managed it.'

'It was Jack's idea. We started organising it the minute you packed us off home. Annie had strict instructions not to let you go anywhere near any of the bedrooms. They look like stock camps. Bedrolls all over the place . . . Come on, you'd better circulate.'

Jim gave Danny a nod. 'See you in a while.'

Danny decided now was as good a time as any. 'Sure, talk to you later, if that's all right?'

A quick glance at Jilba was all Jim needed. 'Do I know what it's about?'

'Probably,' Danny smiled.

'There's no dowry, you know . . .'

That earned him a wallop on the arm from his daughter. 'You've got a cheek.'

'Two of them,' Jim puffed. 'Kiss on each, please.'

At that moment, something barrelled into the back of his legs and nearly knocked him for six.

'What about a word for the lowly, Mackay?' Dud cackled. 'Or has it all gone to your head?'

Jim spun round, dropped to his haunches and embraced his wizened old friend, wheelchair and all.

'G'day, you old bugger.'

'Watch your language,' said Dud, shooing him off. 'And mind me bloody spokes. They cost a bomb.'

'Just like those nags you used to make me groom a hundred times a day, eh?'

'Nags! Nags, he calls them! Best horseflesh he ever had his mitts on! Anyway, you got off light, mate. Bloke before you did a hundred and fifty.'

'So *that's* why he quit,' said Athol.

'What would you know about it, Ferguson?' Dud snorted. 'All you ever did was sit on your bloody verandah reading the paper all day.'

'How would you like me to wheel you in with that bull over there?'

Dud eyed Balkenna Dean for a moment and pulled a face. 'See what I have to put up with? Can't bloody beat me at cards, so he wants to get me gored to death.' He leered back up at Athol again and waved him on. 'To the kegs, driver. To the kegs . . .'

'Take it easy.'

'I'll be back,' Dud threatened. 'Still want to know why they didn't throw you in the bloody slammer where you belong.'

As Jim watched them go, shaking his head, Dean Coulter gave him a nudge. 'Jack wants you.'

He was standing with the Sugdens, Dougie and Tobias. Jim hurried over to join them, rehearsing his thanks as he went. He gave Clare a kiss, lifted young Bobby off the floor, set him back on his feet and turned to Tobias.

'You know what I owe you, mate.'

Tobias gave his hand a shake. 'That's okay, Jim. Little bit help, maybe.'

'More than a little,' Jim corrected. 'Wouldn't be here but for you. And you, Dougie,' he added, turning to him. He seemed a bit standoffish. Uncomfortable, perhaps, in this white-fella shindig. But his handshake was strong and friendly.

'Good to see you home, Jim. Sort of homecoming for me, too.'

'I'm glad.' Jim's eyes were stinging. 'Hope you'll always feel that way. Got something important I'd like to talk to you about later, when things have quietened down a bit. So don't bugger off on me, all right? Please?'

'I'll be around a couple of days.'

'Great. Let's get together tomorrow.'

'Okay.'

Jim was about to move on to the next group of well-wishers

when there was a fanfare from the band and Jack directed everyone's attention to a row of trestle tables along the back wall of the barn. A hush descended as Betsey stepped forward and, with Billy's help, began peeling the sheets away one by one, revealing a spread fit for a king. When the last sheet came away she smiled.

'Thought you might be hungry.'

'Tucker's been a bit scarce,' Jim grinned. 'Where should I start?'

'Wherever you like. This lot's just for you. Everyone else is eating over at the house.'

Jim cracked up and heaved her off the ground, much to her delight. She made a great show of struggling to free herself, frantically waving everyone forward to get stuck in.

Jim spent a few minutes with Tim, catching up on the state of the property, before he caught up with Dave Reynolds. They were on their way back for a second helping of Betsey's pie, when Tony came up and grabbed his arm.

'Got a couple of late arrivals. Want to come and say hello?'

'Sure . . .'

Jim shoved his plate on the table and followed his son's weaving passage through the crowd. As they broke through the last line of smiling faces, Tony stepped aside and Jim's eyes fell on Anthony and Jean Barclay. They were standing just inside the door, looking a bit unsure of themselves. Jim stopped dead in his tracks and spun to Tony.

Tony simply nodded and hoped for the best. He needn't have worried. His father threw a grateful arm round his shoulders and propelled him forward. Still uncertain of its reception, Anthony slowly offered his good left hand.

'Hello, Jim.'

That was as far as he got. Ignoring his hand, Jim just clutched the two of them into a long, tight, silent embrace. Jean began to cry quietly and Tony wrapped his arms round all three to cement the bond. It was some time before Anthony found his tongue again.

'We . . . I feel we owe you an apology . . .'

Jim let go. 'Nonsense. I'm just thrilled to bits you're here, that's all.' He stepped aside and waved them in. 'Come in, come in. Come and have some of Betsey's wonderful grub.'

Once they were past him, Jim grabbed Tony's arm and whispered in his ear. 'Thanks, mate. With all my heart. You couldn't have done me a bigger favour.'

'Seemed right they should be here.'

'Absolutely,' Jim confirmed, his eyes glistening. 'Good on you.'

Across a sea of heads, Jilba, Jack and Billy had been watching the reunion. Relieved by what they saw, they made their own way to the food tables and the whole family happily teamed up to see to the Barclays' needs. Despite assurances, Anthony and Jean had insisted on staying at a hotel in Longreach and making their own way out by taxi.

Jim scanned heads for Annie and spotted her talking to Fred and Tobias at the far end of the room. He caught her eye and beckoned her over. When she quickly shook her head and looked away, he realised it had been a stupid thing to do and instantly regretted it. It was definitely *not* the moment to introduce her to Rachel's parents.

The band's first couple of brackets had provided a good background throb, but failed to spring any dancers. As they struck up again, Jilba decided to give them a hand. Next thing Jim knew, his daughter was whirling him round in an ever-increasing circle as the guests rippled back and egged them on. She didn't keep it up for too long. She wound them down to a gentle shuffle and waved the other couples into action behind his back.

After the second number, a swinging happy-go-lucky version of 'Blue Skies', Jilba retired her father to the sidelines. Jim made his way over to Jack who was checking to see that Balkenna Dean was still coping all right in his role of mascot for the evening. Jim reached in and patted the bull's shoulder.

'Hello, you big larrikin. I hear you've been having a fling with some of my Herefords.'

'Can't get enough,' Jack grinned.

'I should hope not, considering what he cost.'

'He'll make it back, don't worry,' Jack promised. 'Hundred times over.'

His son's boast had been offered nonchalantly enough. But Jim delighted in the unabashed stockman's pride behind it.

'I'm sure he will,' he agreed, giving the bull another rub. 'Won't you, you old rogue? Just stick to your own girls in future, that's all.' He withdrew his hand and gave Jack a wink. 'He's a beauty all right, mate. No doubt about it.'

Billy went by clutching three snowy schooners.

'They all for you?' Jim enquired laconically.

'Me and Mr Coulter and Mr Serrano,' Billy replied without

stopping, trying not to spill a drop. But his father stuck a foot out and he had to stop.

'Watch out!'

'What's it like being back at school?'

'Okay. What's it like being out of gaol?'

'Okay,' Jim chuckled, sending him on his way. 'Go on, you cheeky bugger, before you drop the lot.'

Jilba draped her arm over her father's shoulder. 'I take it you two have been talking shop.'

'Just for a minute,' Jim admitted, tipping Jack the wink. 'I still can't quite believe all this, you know? Especially after the past few weeks.'

'Well,' Jack shrugged. 'You told us not to dwell on it.'

'Can't argue with that. Thanks, mate. Jilba tells me it was all your idea.'

'Just solid teamwork.'

'Took a bit of doing,' Jilba admitted happily. 'But we had a right old time, I can tell you. Fred and Annie had the hardest part, keeping you in the dark.'

Where was she? He couldn't spot her. He craned on tiptoe to check further afield, but he still couldn't see her.

'I was just talking to her,' said Jilba. 'She's gone out for a breath of fresh air.'

'Oh, good,' said Jim, dropping back on his heels, oblivious to the fact that his daughter could read his mind. Jilba and Jack exchanged a look.

'Why don't you go and see if you can find her?' Jilba suggested.

'She'll be right,' said Jim, still oblivious, gazing about as if he didn't have a care in the world. 'Be back in a minute . . .'

Suppressing outright laughter this time, Jilba and Jack exchanged another look.

'Why don't you just go and see, anyway,' Jack prompted.

'Yes, go on,' Jilba seconded, giving her father a push in the right direction.

Suddenly realising he'd been caught out, Jim couldn't look at either of them and settled for his boots.

'She'll be right,' he repeated sheepishly.

'Oh, go on, for God's sake,' said Jilba, giving him another push. 'It's all right, you know?'

Tongue-tied, Jim raised his eyes and looked from his daughter to his son. They understood.

'It is. It's all right.'

Even so, Jim hesitated, still unsure. When he did manage to speak, his voice was low, and nearly broke. 'What about . . . Tony? And . . . And . . . Billy? How do they feel, do you know?'

'Tone's got his back up a bit,' Jilba admitted. 'But he knows you've got your own life to live, just as he has. He'll come round. Don't worry about it.'

'And Billy?'

'I don't think he knows quite what to think at the moment. One way or the other.'

Still, Jim hesitated. So Jilba gave him another push, firmer this time. 'Just go on, will you? Please? Just go and see she's all right.'

It did the trick. With a wonderful feeling of relief, Jim accepted their blessings. Wordlessly, he reached out and drew the two of them into a grateful embrace. As the three of them locked together, Jilba and Jack hung on tight.

'Just remember that we love you,' Jilba whispered. 'That we want you to be happy.'

'Yeah, Dad,' Jack muttered, running out of breath in the crush. 'We understand, we do . . .'

Jim stood back, gazed at them for a moment, and began making his way towards the door, interrupted en route by several friends and neighbours who had not yet had the chance to shake his hand.

He found Annie sitting on top of the gate leading to the paddock on the western side of the barn. He paused to watch her for a moment before approaching. Elbows on her knees, chin resting in her hands, she was totally absorbed in the last traces of the sun's passage below the skyline. It had been gone for quite a while, but the horizon was still lit by a hazy pale lemon fan which was slowly dissolving through successive layers of lilac, lavender and violet into the dark indigo of a night already alive with stars.

'Hope it lived up to its reputation.'

He gave her a fright. As he crossed his arms on the top rail, Annie turned and smiled.

'Must be wonderful having a show like that every night.'

'Except in a drought. All seems a bit of a mockery then.'

Jim dropped his arms over the rail, craned forward and turned his head just enough to see her face. Her beautiful pale-blue eyes were mottled by the distant light. They were the eyes of a woman wise to the ways of the bush. Receptive to the primitive pageantry of its seasons, resolved to its struggles. Conscious of its treasures, alert to its dangers. Eager for its joys, accepting of its sorrows.

The soft, peaceful afterglow spilling across her face reminded him of the lantern light in her cave so far away, so long ago. He thought of the moment in court when he suddenly recognised he loved her. But, even in the intimate beauty of the moment, he could still sense her reserve.

'They'll be even more spectacular soon,' he said. 'In the spring, when the rains come. You get to see the sun go down behind rolling thunderheads, walls of sheet lightning. It's something to see.'

Annie turned to him, and searched his eyes, plumbing the depths of his soul. Jim had seen that look before. On top of the mountain at the caves. The first time she took him up there. The day she called his bluff. When it came, it was as telling as her look.

'You must be missing Rachel tonight.'

Jim held her eye for a long time, then turned his face to the receding light. Slowly he shook his head. And he told her the truth.

'No, because she's here, always will be. That part of her that loved us all, loved it here in the beginning. She was weary of it by the end, I know that now. Came to terms with that in America. Not us. Just weary of the way of life, the isolation. Balkenna. I just regret I was blind to it for so long. She's left us a lot to remember. It was a good love, kind and gentle, something to cherish. It will always be here . . .'

As he broke off, Annie studied his profile. He was, she realised, no longer a man of constant sorrow. There was no trace of the pain she'd seen so often and wondered if she might see again once he was home. He was a little road-weary, perhaps. But he was looking at the future with an open heart. The direct simplicity of his quietly spoken words summed up all that she loved about him, all the fine qualities she saw slowly emerge from his torment. What he'd said had come straight from his bushman's heart and unchained her own. She had no quarrel with the ghost of Rachel Mackay. Simple, loving acceptance was the answer. Acceptance of Rachel's life at Balkenna and her abiding presence in the memories of Jim and the children she had borne him. In their brief conversation inside, she had a funny feeling Jilba had been trying to tell her pretty much the same thing. She gazed at him a moment longer, then slipped her arm round him and brushed her cheek against his shoulder.

Jim put his arm round her, pulled her closer and rested his head on top of hers. They stood that way for some time before Annie spoke again.

'I'd like to be here . . . in the spring . . . when the rains come . . .'

Jim hugged her to him, even tighter, and kissed her tenderly on the brow.

'I was hoping you would.'

# A selection of bestsellers from Headline

**FICTION**

| | | |
|---|---|---|
| THE EIGHT | Katherine Neville | £4.50 □ |
| THE POTTER'S FIELD | Ellis Peters | £5.99 □ |
| MIDNIGHT | Dean R Koontz | £4.50 □ |
| LAMPLIGHT ON THE THAMES | Pamela Evans | £3.99 □ |
| THE HOUSE OF SECRETS | Unity Hall | £4.50 □ |

**NON-FICTION**

| | | |
|---|---|---|
| TOSCANINI'S FUMBLE | Harold L Klawans | £3.50 □ |
| GOOD HOUSEKEEPING EATING FOR A HEALTHY SKIN | Alix Kirsta | £4.99 □ |

**SCIENCE FICTION AND FANTASY**

| | | |
|---|---|---|
| THE RAINBOW SWORD | Adrienne Martine-Barnes | £2.99 □ |
| THE DRACULA CAPER Time Wars VIII | Simon Hawke | £2.99 □ |
| MORNING OF CREATION The Destiny Makers 2 | Mike Shupp | £3.99 □ |
| SWORD AND SORCERESS 5 | Marion Zimmer Bradley | £3.99 □ |

*All Headline books are available at your local bookshop or newsagent, or can be ordered direct from the publisher. Just tick the titles you want and fill in the form below. Prices and availability subject to change without notice.*

Headline Book Publishing PLC, Cash Sales Department, PO Box 11, Falmouth, Cornwall, TR10 9EN, England.

Please enclose a cheque or postal order to the value of the cover price and allow the following for postage and packing:

UK: 60p for the first book, 25p for the second book and 15p for each additional book ordered up to a maximum charge of £1.90

BFPO: 60p for the first book, 25p for the second book and 15p per copy for the next seven books, thereafter 9p per book

OVERSEAS & EIRE: £1.25 for the first book, 75p for the second book and 28p for each subsequent book.

Name ......................................................................................

Address ..................................................................................

..............................................................................................

..............................................................................................